THE HAZARDS
OF GOOD FORTUNE

Seth Greenland

THE HAZARDS
OF GOOD FORTUNE

Europa
editions

Europa Editions
214 West 29th Street
New York, N.Y. 10001
www.europaeditions.com
info@europaeditions.com

Library of Congress Cataloging in Publication Data is available
ISBN 978-1-60945-462-3

Greenland, Seth
The Hazards of Good Fortune

Book design by Emanuele Ragnisco
www.mekkanografici.com

Cover photos © tedmochen/Pixabay and StockSnap/Pixabay

Cover treatment by Emanuele Ragnisco from photographs
by tedmochen/Pixabay and StockSnap/Pixabay

Prepress by Grafica Punto Print – Rome

Printed in the USA

CONTENTS

To Susan, Allegra, Gabe, and Drew.

PART I

"Now there arose up a new king
over Egypt, which knew not Joseph."
—EXODUS 1:8

CHAPTER ONE

From his customary sideline seat at the center of the brightly lit basketball court, Harold Jay Gladstone surveyed his kingdom. He was trim and good-looking with an open face and outstanding posture. His brown eyes might have been a little too closely set; his prominent nose revealed a slight bump. Dark, wavy hair was thinning at the crown. But the white teeth were straight in his wide mouth and the warm confidence with which he displayed them put those who observed him at ease. They recognized a serious and gracious man, one born to take care of his responsibilities. He wore a gray chalk stripe suit, a pale pink shirt with a tasteful silk tie. The silver buckle of his alligator belt was discreetly engraved with the initials *HJG*. His wingtips were well worn but agreeably polished. Other than a wedding band, his only jewelry was a simple gold watch, a gift from his parents, decades earlier on his twenty-first birthday. That was the year he jettisoned "Harold," the name he had been known by since boyhood, and declared himself Jay Gladstone. Jauntier, more heedless, "Jay" hinted at soaring possibilities in a way the more earthbound Harold never would. Now in his fifties, he was a picture of understated elegance, nothing too new and flash, or too old and rumpled, at once approachable but slightly remote.

He faced both benches and the chattering broadcasters, in plain view, front, side, and back, of the eighteen thousand-strong crowd, no one paying attention, much less deference, to him. He didn't sit courtside because he wanted anyone's attention. He sat there because he had loved basketball since he was a child.

And because he owned the team.

It was a frigid Wednesday night at Sanitary Solutions Arena in Newark, New Jersey, and his players were battling for a spot in the NBA playoffs. With two minutes left in the fourth quarter, the game was tied 96-96. The Celtics had just knotted the score on a jump shot by Rajon Rondo and Alvin "Church" Scott, the coach of the home team, had called a timeout. There was a palpable buzz tonight because the franchise was currently battling for the eighth and final playoff seed in the Eastern Conference.

The players ambled toward their benches and crossed paths with the Lycra-sheathed cheerleaders strutting toward center court. Hip-hop blasted over the P.A. system and the nubile young women—white, black, Hispanic, Asian, every racial permutation one could reasonably expect to find in the Tri-State Area in 2012—began their gyrations. The squad was there because research had shown fans liked cheerleaders. They were good for business.

To own a professional sports team was a privilege of the fabulously wealthy. But ownership wasn't all victories, fawning media coverage, and locker room championship celebrations where excited players sprayed champagne, dousing each other and their ecstatic overlords. The possibility of thorny headaches abounded. The press could decimate you and once they established an owner's tabloid identity—egotistical moneybags was the preferred caricature—it was hard to shake. Then there were the decisions that had to be made involving the commitment of hundreds of millions in salary to players with balky joints, or a tendency to consume too many cheeseburgers during the offseason, or personal lives that distracted from professional responsibilities. To lure these players, luxurious pleasure domes had to be constructed at even greater cost. While Jay watched the cheerleaders throw a petite red-head into the air where she executed a triple somersault before landing in a net of arms, his mind was on real estate.

Everyone hated Sanitary Solutions Arena. Built with public funds at the dawn of the Reagan Era, the concrete edifice was outdated almost as soon as the contractors finished their work. Concession areas too small, hallways too narrow, and the cramped squalor of the restrooms suggested the need for vaccinations before entering. The roof leaked. The acoustics were dreadful. The too-small size of the skyboxes made it difficult to entice free-spending corporate clients who could max out their platinum cards at a safe remove from actual fans. Naming rights had been sold by the State of New Jersey to the giant waste management company whose role as a near-constant defendant in a series of environmental litigations had earned them the nickname Sanitary Pollutions. Yes, the Rolling Stones had performed there. U2 and a reconstituted version of The Who had all blasted through. One year Bruce Springsteen played so many dates he might as well have moved in. Still, Sanitary Solutions Arena was a dump, a poor relation of the shiny new sports and entertainment palaces in cities like Phoenix, Atlanta, and Dallas.

Despite all of this, it was with a sense of optimism that Jay turned to the goateed African-American seated on his right, Mayor Major House of Newark, and in a voice mellifluous and full of casual assurance said, "We're going to win this game, Major." Recently he had learned that the politician's mother had named him Major so people would address her son with respect and Jay always made a point of using it.

"Always been a positive thinker," the mayor replied, a grin spread across his broad face. In a charcoal gray off-the-rack suit, white shirt, and striped tie, House looked like a school superintendent, his occupation until a few years earlier, when politics presented itself as a viable alternative.

"Do you think the game's going into overtime?" asked Nicole Gladstone, Jay's second wife, seated on his other side.

"I have no idea. Why?"

"Because I want to order another glass of wine." One of the attempts at upgrading the amenities at the current arena—with its rudimentary design and great swaths of exposed concrete it exuded all the charm of an apartment block in Bucharest—was VIP courtside service. Fans could order sushi, nachos, and beer or wine from waitresses sporting formfitting team gear while they watched the action unfold. "Will you order me another, or do you want me to do it?" A tincture of hostility betrayed Nicole's attempt at sober composure. She believed Jay kept too close an eye on her alcohol consumption.

Nicole was in her late thirties and through a religious devotion to daily yoga, the right genes, and a diet free of fat and sugar (copious intake of white wine excepted) had retained the beauty of her youth. She wore an olive-green silk bomber jacket, slim black pants, and stiletto heels. Expertly cut, subtly colored blonde hair pulled into a chignon. Golden hazel eyes delicately shadowed, and cheekbones that could slice a pineapple. There was an air of mischief around Nicole, a feeling that you never knew quite what to expect, but it had been a while since her husband found this quality charming and he suspected more wine would only heighten it. She had already consumed several glasses, and he worried about her volubility on the ride home to Bedford in the far reaches of Westchester County. A little too much to drink and his otherwise amiable wife might take offense at an innocent comment or become argumentative over a remark she would ordinarily let pass. He knew it was useless to point out there was no alcohol served after the third quarter. She would remind him that he was the owner and if he wanted to procure an additional dose of chardonnay it could be arranged.

"I'll take care of it," he said.

While pretending to look for a member of the wait staff, Jay glanced across the court at D'Angelo Maxwell, the team's star player. Everyone, the fans, the media, his mother, called Maxwell "Dag." Built for headlines, the handle was quick, terse, and contained a hint of lethality. Like Michael or Magic, it was all that was needed to convey his mastery of basketball skills, the self-confidence he exuded, the cultivated detachment that suggested—even when the television cameras were trained on him and millions watched—he was balling alone in his driveway.

When Jay purchased the team, he hired Church Scott as the coach and general manager and challenged him to win a championship. Then he opened his checkbook. Scott proceeded to rebuild the team, and his splashiest acquisition was Dag Maxwell. Although Jay loved attending the games—the improvisational genius of professional basketball, its hypnotic combination of speed, potency, and an aesthetically charged physicality so pure it had the power to alter the psychological state of those who witnessed it, was a quality absent in his own life—to the owner's displeasure, the team had fallen considerably short of expectations.

Jay noticed Nicole staring intently at the bench where Church Scott kneeled in front of his players, pointing at a clipboard. His three nattily attired assistants (the league mandated business attire for the coaching staff) stood at a respectful distance. The twelve-man squad consisted of ten African-Americans, a Frenchman of Senegalese extraction, and a 7'1" Lithuanian tank. But it was the charismatic Dag who held the world's attention.

"Are you going to get me the wine?" Nicole asked.

There were no waitresses in the immediate area, so to forestall his wife wandering off in search of it, Jay told her he would go to the concession stand. It was a stalling maneuver. And he liked to mingle with the fans, not so much to glean what they were thinking about the team but, rather, to imply that he was one of them. He prided himself on doing it without a single body man, much less the herd-of-bison security detail that routinely surrounded men of his importance when they ventured out in public. The vox populi, even when slightly discordant, was music to his democratic (small d) consciousness.

When Jay rose from his seat, his regal bearing conveyed above average physical stature, although he measured slightly less than six feet, the exact height he had reached as a sixteen-year-old. Mayor House was surprised to see him get up and reminded his host there were only three minutes left in the game.

"I'll hustle," Jay said and started walking.

A fan called out, "Yo, Mr. Gladstone!" The owner smiled in the direction of the voice and gave a slight nod. Someone yelled, "Mayor Major!" and House waved and smiled. The politician was popular here, and Jay liked to think at least some of that popularity reflected on the team owner. Another fan yelled, "Go, Jay!" and Jay turned toward that person, touched two fingers to his forehead, and pointed in a jaunty half-salute. He didn't mind the familiarity. If the paying public wanted to be on a first name basis with him, that was all right. These interactions enabled Jay to tell himself that rather than being another inaccessible magnate separated from the masses by a vast fortune, he possessed the common touch. He might not show up at the games in the man-of-the-people fashion of owners who wore jeans and T-shirts while they capered around the sidelines like Ritalin-deprived teenagers, but the fans seemed to like him just the same.

"YOU SUCK, GLADSTONE!"

The voice was froggy, basso, and it cut through the arena hum, this malediction, rendered in fluent Jersey.

Jay had the presence of mind to call out, "Thank you, sir!" and this engendered laughter from the surrounding seats. He was satisfied with how he handled the catcall. Knew it wouldn't escalate. Interchanges like this between owners and fans were simply an outgrowth of the egalitarian age so Jay let it slide off his well-tailored back as he headed up a short row of steps which led to a tunnel that would bring him to the lower level concourse. He calculated the time it would take to do his errand and quickened his pace.

Because the game was tied and there were only a couple of minutes left on the clock, no fans wanted to abandon their seats, so the hall was mostly deserted. A janitor tied off a plastic garbage bag, a soda vendor thumbed through a thick wad of bills. Neither noticed Jay as he passed. He would buy a bottle of water for his wife and tell her the concession stand had run out of wine.

Jay pondered how the culture had descended to where a fan at a professional sporting event believed that it was socially acceptable to yell insults at the team owner. It reflected the coarseness that seemed to metastasize every day, manifesting as road rage, feverish Internet comment threads, and the turbocharged political discourse that rendered all opponents as mortal enemies, developments Jay found deplorable. He made every effort in his conduct to be nonadversarial.

The sight of three black teenagers headed toward him interrupted these ruminations. Jay's first thought was: What are these kids doing on this level? Access was allowed only to those seated in the arena's lower bowl, the most expensive seats in the house, so Jay assumed these boys had snuck down. But he quickly upbraided himself for this reaction. One of them might have been the son of a season ticket holder. Or perhaps they were successful rappers and had purchased the tickets themselves. Jay didn't know much about pop culture but was aware that young entertainers could be economic juggernauts. The three boys were dressed nearly identically in baggy jeans that hung low revealing what appeared to be acres of boxer shorts, oversized flannel shirts, and spanking new white high-top sneakers accented in various tropical colors. The kid in the middle was Jay's size, and two glowering beanpoles flanked him. He realized the beanpoles were twins. All of them wore baseball caps turned sideways. The cap belonging to the one in the middle bore a Lakers logo. The twins were Knick fans, apparently.

"Yo, Jewstone," the one wearing the Lakers cap said. "Wassup?"

The three stared at him.

Had Jay heard this correctly? *Jewstone?* Had it suddenly become acceptable to hurl an ethnic slur at a complete stranger during a public encounter? Yes, anti-Semitism was on the rise around the world, there had been tension between blacks and Jews, and as evinced by the fan that yelled You suck, the public sphere was an indecorous place, but *Jewstone?* This was an affront that beggared the imagination. So unexpected, so . . . so crude and frontal and . . . ugly! Jay could not ignore this the way he had ignored the hostile fan. He wanted to drag the kid by the band of his low-slung boxer shorts to the nearest Holocaust museum and school him about the deportations, the camps, the chimneys spewing human ash, but that was not practical. Should he summon security and get him ejected from the building? Calling for aid would show weakness. Offer a stern rebuke to his rudeness and continue toward the concession stand? They would laugh at him. How did they even know he was Jewish? It wasn't as if they had seen the annual check he wrote to the Anti-Defamation League. Jay felt his neck muscles constrict. Adrenalin rousted his heart causing it to leap and buck. Was he about to be mugged? This could not be happening on the lower concourse of his team's arena. The Beanpole on the left angled his head as if to say, *You gonna talk?* The other Beanpole nudged Lakers Cap and whispered something in his ear.

"Gladstone!" Lakers Cap declared. "Mr. *Gladstone!* Dang!" He laughed at the faux pas, if indeed it were a faux pas, as if he, the Beanpoles, and Jay were playing the dozens backstage at the BET Awards.

"Dang!" the twin on the left echoed.

"What do you want?" Jay said.

"You gonna re-sign Dag?"

"We'll see," Jay replied and pushed past them toward the concession stand.

"Yo, Gladstone!" It was Lakers Cap again.

The kid left out the Mister, but at least he had called him Gladstone this time. After a split-second internal debate about whether he should ignore him anyway, Jay turned around.

"Stick a fork in that nigga. He done!" More laughter and the trio moved toward the tunnel that would take them into the arena. Jay shook his head. It was impossible to fathom why black people would refer to each other using that word. It would be like Jews calling each other "kike." Certain African-Americans could talk all they wanted about reclaiming the slur, repurposing it, snatching it from the hands of the bigots and performing the same sleight of hand gays and lesbians had done with "queer" but Jay believed their reasoning to be specious. Rap moguls, bejeweled pop culture titans who pumped their product into millions of ears, tossed *nigga* back and forth like it was a beach ball. Jay couldn't understand it. But as a white man, he was prohibited from having an opinion on the subject. As a white man, it wasn't his word to parse, much less throw around. To weigh in on the subject was paternalistic, so mind your own. If he said anything about race, some right-minded person was going to label him a racist. The whole business was a proverbial "third rail" that Jay did not want to touch.

The crew was totting up the receipts at the concession

stand. Jay ordered a bottle of water, paid for it with cash, and dispensed smiles and thank-yous to the two women and one man working there. The women were black, the man Latino. They knew who he was, had seen him in Sanitary Solutions Arena many times, and the respect with which they responded to the boss's presence returned Jay's world to its former equilibrium. He knew what the concession workers thought of the word nigga.

Did the kid mean to say Jewstone? Whether or not it was purposeful was immaterial, Jay concluded, since that was likely how those three referred to him in private. The deterioration in relations between blacks and Jews troubled him, and it was a matter to which he had devoted considerable thought. Jews came to America more or less willingly (insofar as people *willingly* flee pogroms)—Africans did not. Jay knew black people had a right to be angry, but resented being the target of this enmity.

"They were out of wine?" Nicole was not happy when her husband handed her the water bottle.

"That won't happen in the new arena," the mayor said and winked at Jay, who gave him a genial slap on the back.

Nicole unscrewed the bottle cap and took a long pull from the water.

"What took so long?"

"Some fans wanted to talk to me." Why tell his wife what had happened? Nicole occasionally accused him of sensing anti-Semitism where, in her—admittedly gentile—view, it didn't exist, and he was not primed for that kind of conversation.

There were seventeen seconds left in the game with the score still tied at 96 when Jay settled into his seat. Church Scott was standing in front of the bench, his face impassive as he watched the point guard, Drew Hill, dribble across midcourt and throw a bounce pass to Dag on the left side where the Celtics' Kevin Garnett guarded him. Dag began to back Garnett down. A notoriously grinding defender, Garnett leaned on Dag in an attempt to arrest his progress. Dag swiped the hand away and thrust his backside into Garnett. Drew Hill was open at the top of the key, but Dag ignored him. The seven-foot center, Odell Tracy, came over to set a pick and Dag waved him off. He and Garnett banged against each other like a pair of Brahma bulls, muscles taut, eyes blazing. Rivulets of sweat streamed off of the two antagonists as they vied for advantage. The crowd held its collective breath, willing their hero to perform a feat that would briefly enable them to rise above their colorless lives, uninspiring jobs, overdue bills, the east coast winter weather, everything they yearned to transcend, and summon the bliss that victory can release. The loud report of the leather basketball—*thunk thunk thunk thunk thunk*—as it repeatedly struck the hardwood floor reverberated through the hushed arena.

Entirely in his element, Dag was ready to display his essential, ineffable, what-made-him-a-superstar *Dag-ness*. Fifteen feet from the basket with his back still toward Garnett, he dipped his shoulder to the right, getting the big man to bite on the fake, then deftly spun to his left and falling backward hoisted a fadeaway over the defender's outstretched arm. The ball sailed through the air with perfect backspin, tracing an exquisite parabola against the sea of spectators gaping in anticipation, and fell into the net as eighteen thousand voices erupted in a chorus of joy and deliverance.

"Bang bang, motherfucker!" Dag roared, his trademarked phrase (TM: BangBangMotherfucker, 2011), uttered whenever he drilled a shot at a crucial moment. The bench players jumped to their feet, clapping and cheering. Church Scott frantically gesticulated for his team to get back and play defense. Dag shimmied his hips then cocked his hands like six-shooters and fired into the air before jamming them into imaginary holsters.

As Nicole screamed *YEEEAAHHH* with an exuberance that surprised her husband, Kevin Garnett coolly retrieved the ball, stepped behind the baseline and winged a pass to Paul Pierce at half court. Pierce took two dribbles and, before the nearest defender could close him out, launched a three-point shot from the right side which rippled the net to eviscerate Dag and his teammates—so recently exulting—who suddenly looked as if all of their blood had been drained. One second left, 99-98, Celtics.

The home team did not score again.

When the final buzzer sounded, scattered boos rained down. There weren't many but enough to indicate that more than a few fans were disappointed in how the team had performed. As the arena emptied, a lone voice yelled, "Trade Dag!"

Jay placed his hand on the mayor's shoulder. "I wish I could've arranged for a win."

Despite the loss, House was sanguine. "Heck of a game," he declared. Then: "I look around this place, and I think how much better the team is gonna play when their home reflects their talent."

Jay shrugged like a man who was accustomed to overcoming insurmountable obstacles. The Mayor wanted a new arena for his city and all of the ancillary economic development that would follow. But he had the usual and seemingly intractable urban manager's dilemma of union contracts, pension obligations, and a shrinking tax base. Inconveniently, the price tag for these life-giving structures had risen to stratospheric heights, so funds of this scale could not be obtained from the hemorrhaging coffers of Newark. This is where Jay Gladstone came in. If Jay achieved the arena deal, New Jersey would hail him as a patron saint, and it would cement his position as a key player in the world of professional sports ownership, something that had great resonance for him as a lifelong fan. He reveled in his role as the potential savior of a fallen city.

"It's going to be the most impressive arena in the league," Jay told the mayor.

Oblivious to the business being discussed, Nicole joined the conversation and said, "Dag was fantastic." Despite having attended countless games with her husband, she remained blind to certain basketball nuances such as the one that indicated Dag was supposed to be guarding Paul Pierce at the end of the game.

"That was some shot he hit with Garnett draped on him," Jay said. Nicole liked Dag personally, always chatted with him when she attended team functions, and Jay saw no advantage in pointing out that his blown defensive assignment had cost their team the win.

Mayor House thanked Jay for the ticket, turned to Nicole, and pecked her on the cheek. Apparently unsatisfied with this, Nicole wrapped her arms around him and pulled him close in a way that, to her husband, seemed overly friendly. Jay could see the mayor's spine straighten. When she released him, House looked at Jay with an awkward grin and walked off to greet a prospective campaign donor on the other side of the court. Nicole air-kissed women but any silverback male found himself enveloped in her embrace. Jay had spoken about it to her, but she dismissed his concerns as generational. Tonight, he chose to say nothing.

An hour later, the two of them lay next to each other in bed, Jay on his side facing Nicole who was on her back, eyes closed, a biography of Spinoza resting open on her chest. He wore pajamas and she a camisole, yoga pants, and an eye mask. After a "rocky patch" in the marriage he believed to have been caused by too much business travel, the couple had been getting along better lately. Professional basketball was a hobby for Jay, a diversion. He was the co-chairman of the Gladstone Group, the family-held real estate company founded by his father and uncle. Recently, he had started a massive construction project in South Africa. Nicole accompanied him once but had declined to go back. Although she kept busy with charity work and her horses, Jay believed his absences had worn on her. She was distant when he returned, and even if he had been away less than a week, it took them several days to get back on an even keel.

It was just after midnight, and he had the stirrings of an erection. It had been weeks since they had had sex and it was his firm belief that a healthy sex life was an important component of marriage, a philosophy that occasionally necessitated having sex when sleep might have been more desirable. He removed the Spinoza biography, placed it on the nightstand, and pressed himself against his wife's hip. She murmured something he could not make out. Choosing to interpret this as encouragement, he slid his hand over her breast. When this did not produce the hoped-for reaction, he slipped his hand beneath the camisole and gently rubbed her nipple with his thumb and forefinger. She swatted his hand away and rolled on her side with her back to him.

"Tomorrow," she mumbled. Her voice had a raspy quality that was magnified by fatigue. She adjusted her pillow.

Because his attempt to make love had a desultory aspect, it was without much disappointment that Jay retreated, rolling on to his left side, his back to her. In this position—back-to-back—he thought about his relative lack of ardor. His wife was still a lovely woman, her body youthful and fit. Her intelligence restless and undiminished. When they had first met the sex was seismic and revelatory. So, what was it that made this night's attempt feel perfunctory? Jay had the usual worries of a man who ran a multi-billion-dollar empire, but he had become an expert at managing the stress commensurate with that level of responsibility. If the real estate market cratered and the value of the Gladstone family holdings dipped by a hundred million dollars no one would miss a meal. He worried about his health but, physically, he felt hale and strong. He had thrown himself into the basketball team's business with a fervor that seemed to surprise his wife, whose own life lacked a similar passion. Nicole had worked as a model and then in government but left the workforce when she married Jay. A year ago, she informed him she wanted to resume a more active professional life (a small Kabbalah-themed jewelry business— available in Barney's, Bonwit Teller, and I. Magnin—had briefly occupied her), but as far as Jay could tell this meant having a lot of lunches with friends to talk about her options. As he considered whether his reaction to Nicole's full-body embrace of Major House reflected anything other than a projection of the dissatisfaction he had been feeling, Jay decided he needed to engage her in some way that would reflect enthusiasm for the marriage. But what to do? Buy her another home? They already owned five (Bedford, East Hampton, Manhattan, Aspen, London, St. Kitts). Perhaps a work of art would charm her, a painting or sculpture? But Nicole was not materialistic, and while she would appreciate the quality, it would not move her. What then? She was a woman who sought to devour life, who craved exhilaration. What fresh thrills could he provide? He began to enumerate a list of possibilities but caught himself. Was that his role, he wondered, to create endless diversions? There was too much else that required his attention.

CHAPTER TWO

The ragged quilt of dirty snow that covered the ground in front of the red-brick apartment building was considerably enlivened by the presence of a naked man doing push-ups on a patch of frozen grass. It was just after seven o'clock the following morning.

The man was wiry and young, and his muscles flexed as he lowered his torso then pushed hard and straightened his arms. Jagged noises emerged from his throat. It was impossible to tell if he was counting since the guttural sounds were indecipherable. After a series of push-ups and accompanying grunts, the man bounded to his feet and, pink soles flashing, dashed into the apartment building past a startled woman who was emerging through the glass doors carrying a 2' x 2' cardboard box. The woman blinked as if to make sure what she had seen was not an apparition, delicately placed the box on the ground, reached for her cell phone, called the police, and reported what she had just witnessed. Then she picked the box up, walked a hundred yards away from the building, and waited.

Less than a minute later she watched as the man materialized on a second-floor balcony where he climbed on to the metal railing and, hands on hips and still resplendently exposed, surveyed his domain. On the short side, he looked to be about a hundred and forty pounds without an ounce of fat. Unkempt hair clung to his head in uneven clumps. His penis was flaccid and unexceptional. A tattoo on his arm displayed two crossed M16 rifles cradling a skull crowned by the words *U.S. Army*. His eyes were hectic, and he did not appear to be taking in the tableau in front of him, a row of identical apartment houses known as Gladstone Village, constructed in the 1960s, or the bystanders gaping at him. The marble stillness of his pose was compromised by the twitching of his left eye.

A staccato *SQUAWK!SCREE!SQUAWK!* emerged from his throat, bizarre and otherworldly, and like a superhero, arms spread wide and chest thrust out, he leaped to the ground where he landed on his feet, thighs flexed, knees absorbing the impact, and sprinted back to the spot where he had been doing push-ups. Then he threw himself face down on the ground and resumed his routine.

The woman—her name was Gloria Alvarez—had lived in the building for nearly ten years. She was a school teacher in Harlem, and this guy's shenanigans were going to make her miss the train. The cardboard box in her arms was the prototype of a device through which her students would be able to view a solar eclipse the following week.

It wasn't the first time she had observed this man acting strangely. A few weeks ago, he was muttering to himself at the mailboxes in the lobby. In the basement laundry room, she encountered him wearing boxer shorts and staring at the window of a dryer that was not running. She had seen him around before that but hadn't noticed anything unusual about his behavior. Maybe something had happened to him. She knew a sweet guy in the Queens neighborhood where she grew up who killed a neighbor's dog because he said it was talking to him. Sometimes people bug out. It was a fact of life.

Gloria Alvarez lived with her husband and daughter, a fifth-grader. Her daughter's bus had taken her to school half an hour earlier, so the little girl had missed the freak show this morning—thank you, Jesus! But what if the naked guy started making a habit of parading around like this? Gloria was not inclined to put anyone in the crosshairs of the system, but this naked *cabron* appeared to be in serious need of professional help. She figured the authorities would send the appropriate representatives who would take him to a safe environment and get him sorted out.

A maintenance worker named Gustavo Solis was at a bachelor party the previous evening and as a result of too many beers had overslept. It was a Thursday, the day he checked all of the interior lights in the public spaces of the apartment complex and replaced any bulbs that might have burned out. He clutched a large black coffee as he emerged from his truck and blearily made his way toward Building #1. This was when he noticed the naked man doing pushups. Gustavo was about the same age as the naked man and had seen him around the complex fully clothed, skateboarding with the teenagers, singing to no one in particular but not causing any problems. This clothing-optional look was new. Gustavo looked around for the security guard who was meant to be patrolling but didn't see him. He didn't want to deal with this nonsense. His head was pounding from last night's revels—the coffee had barely started to work—but he was the only official representative of Gladstone Village who seemed to be around, and he felt some responsibility to hold the fort until help arrived.

Gustavo called out to get his attention, but the man continued the up and down of his push-ups. The intense physical exercise was causing his sternum to expand and contract and from a distance of fifty feet Gustavo could see clouds of breath visible in the cold air. Cautiously he moved closer. Then the man jumped to his feet and whirled on Gustavo. Assuming a martial arts stance, Gustavo prayed the man would not charge him. He did not want to wrestle anyone who was naked. Gustavo was relieved when the man turned and sprinted into the building.

"He's gonna jump off the balcony," a woman's voice said.

Gustavo turned to see Gloria Alvarez standing a safe distance away. "I called the police a minute ago." He knew her from around, but they had never spoken. Keeping the box balanced between her elbows, she offered that trans-ethnic New York, palms-up, *aayyywhaddyagonnado?* Gustavo tried to smile, but his head hurt. He wished he had stayed in bed. A birdlike sound emanating from Building #1 drew his attention. When he looked toward the source, he saw the naked man standing on the second-floor balcony.

A pot-bellied, fiftyish white man and his sallow adult son emerged from a van with a faded *McCain/Palin* sticker on the rear bumper next to one that read *Obummer*. They were carrying a tarpaulin and several cans of paint toward the building when they observed what was going on and froze in their tracks. The sight of public nakedness was transfixing. The combination of aggression and vulnerability a human in this state manifests will exert a hypnotic pull. So, they stared. The man, again perched on the railing, pirouetted as if on an exercise bar. Rather than beholding his cold-shrunk maleness, the onlookers were now treated to an unobstructed view of his backside.

Two hours earlier, in a small apartment in Port Chester, Russell Plesko was avoiding a fight with his wife, Crystal. The previous night they argued about who was doing more for their young family, comprised of the two of them and their baby daughter. Russell had been watching one of the local professional basketball teams lose to the Celtics. After a trying day at work, he didn't want to deal with Crystal. It was the usual beef couples at that stage of life get into, hardworking people who labor long hours, don't get enough sleep, and can never seem to attend to all their mundane obligations. Russell had spent a fitful night on the living room couch where he got no more than two hours of solid rest. Lately, he and Crystal had been scrapping like weasels, and he was beginning to wonder whether their union was built to last. For the past hour, he had been thinking about checking into a motel to teach his wife a lesson. Let Crystal try to raise their daughter on her own, see how she liked that. She had called him lazy. Lazy! Russell Plesko lettered in two sports at Port Chester High School, spent summers as a teenager working in his uncle's landscaping business with a crew of Central American immigrants, earned his associate's degree in criminal justice at Westchester Community College, and became a police officer at twenty-five. Now, at twenty-seven, he was poised for his first promotion. Lazy? Officer Russell Plesko did not think so.

When Crystal entered their small kitchen that morning, Russell didn't glance up from his bowl of cereal. He kissed his daughter and left without saying goodbye to his wife. The desk sergeant told him it looked like he hadn't slept. Russell prided himself on his professionalism. However volubly he might behave at home, at work he was known for his unflappable demeanor. Was the rough night that visible? Now the cold snap was aggravating an old sports injury, one he had strategically chosen not to reveal when he filled out the forms for his job application to the White Plains Police Department. He carried prescription painkillers for when this happened, and although he had popped one twenty minutes earlier, the pain had worsened. Driving his patrol car west on Post Road when the call came over the radio—unidentified black male, approximately thirty years old, acting erratically inside and in front of Building #1 at Gladstone Village—Officer Plesko was in no mood.

It would strike an ordinary person as odd, the idea that anyone could forget they had taken off all their clothes on a frigid March morning in suburban New York, but John Eagle was not an ordinary person and had forgotten his nakedness. He had been born in a small Ohio town and enlisted in the Army after high school where he had been a tenacious defensive back on the football team and sung baritone in the choir. Following two tours in Iraq, during which he saw extensive combat in the Anbar Province and reached the rank of corporal, he received an honorable discharge and made his way to New York to pursue a career as a recording artist. After his time in Iraq, John Eagle was proud to live in a country where the various ethnic groups were not constantly tearing at each other's throats.

In New York City, he worked as a security guard, a restaurant deliveryman, and a telemarketer. Luck in relationships was spotty. His love of individual women was intense but the ability to focus less so. A souvenir of this tendency two different tattoos rendered on opposite sides of his neck in cursive lettering: *Vanessa* on one, *Donelle* on the other. Each had temporarily been the love of his life.

Although his psychological condition had begun to deteriorate almost from the day of his discharge, he was able to continue to make music with a secondhand laptop he had purchased on Craigslist. A series of rhythm and blues tracks on his SoundCloud page featured an acceptable (if not professional quality) voice warbling over generic music. Flanking these links were inspirational slogans like "Built to Win" and "Never Gonna Give Up My Dream." John Eagle randomly contacted strangers on social media and sent them links to his music accompanied by notes like "Hope you enjoy it!" His psychiatrist at the Veterans Affairs Hospital was treating him for bipolar disorder and had recently prescribed both antidepressant and antipsychotic drugs.

That the metal railing on which his feet rested was cold enough to freeze skin tissue did not register with John Eagle. Nor did the sun, breaking through the clouds now. He could not taste the sourness the drugs caused in his saliva, or smell the exhaust from a passing bus. He could not hear the traffic on Melville Road or the faraway voice of Gustavo Solis calling for him to climb down and put some clothes on. What he did hear or, more accurately, *thought* he heard, was a distant whooshing sound, threatening and mobile, careening around, first coming from here where it grew loud and more insistent and then from there, quiet and sinister, now inside of his head, inescapable. This sound evoked his time in the desert. The relentless wind that churned sand and debris, getting into his mouth and nostrils, coating his skin. He could handle it with his buddies, but you didn't want that wind to kick up if you were alone. Safety in numbers. It was drilled into each recruit, never be caught solo. Every soldier had your back. They headed out in pods of twos or threes or fours. No one wanted to be alone in the desert. Between the wind and the locals— *and, damn, those folks always looked angry about something—* he didn't want to think about it.

The drugs prescribed for him by the doctors at the Veterans Affairs hospital were powerful juju. John Eagle had vowed to stop taking them but they helped him forget that he couldn't hold a job or stay in a relationship, that he'd been making music for nearly three years and wasn't getting any closer to achieving his elusive dream of a recording career, and that his future appeared as a dreary, decades-long stretch of frustration and disappointment. He wanted to cut a swath through life, for the world to take notice. Maybe he'd get a peacock tattoo across his back. There was a guy in Iraq who had one, all blue, green, yellow, and colors he couldn't begin to name. And those oval markings that look like eyes. A feathered fan of colored eyes inked into his back staring out at people. That was some awesomely freaky shit! He'd get it done today.

John Eagle tensed his calf muscles.

Oh, sweet mother of Christ, Russell Plesko thought as he trudged across the caked snow toward Building #1 in Gladstone

Village. The mope is naked. Buck fucking naked. The dispatcher had failed to mention that little detail. At the moment, the guy was balancing on a second-floor balcony railing, treating the frigid suburban morning to a moon shot. At least he wasn't a jumper. If the man were suicidal he'd be on a higher floor, so that was positive. Russell reached for the radio mic attached to his coat and requested immediate backup. The dispatcher informed him another cruiser was less than three minutes away. Russell signed off and turned his attention to the immediate surroundings. In training, he had learned that a police officer is always onstage. There was a middle-aged Latina watching, and a maintenance worker—Latino, too, from the look of him—and two white workmen probably here to paint an apartment. The citizens all had their eyes locked on him, every one of them. He noticed the male Latino had taken out a smartphone and was recording the scene. Should he ask him to stop? Civilians were doing a lot of that lately. Why was he worried? He'd dealt with far scarier perpetrators than this one.

In a voice meant to convey authority Russell called out, "Anyone know this gentleman's name?"

"He lives in the building," the Latina answered.

The painters gazed at Russell with bovine indifference.

The maintenance worker who was shooting with his phone shrugged and said, "I've seen him around."

None of this was helpful.

"Sir," Russell called to the man on the balcony. "I'm respectfully inviting you to get down from there and put some clothes on." The choice of words was not improvisatory. Police all over America were being trained in nonconfrontational tactics, to get what they want through the use of unthreatening language. *Respectfully*, an adjective meant to defuse, *Invite* a verb of surpassing friendliness. In theory, far superior to the more traditional *Get your ass down*.

The man did not respond and remained immobile. A flock of pigeons fluttered across Russell's line of vision. After a brief pause, he employed the same words and, unsurprisingly, achieved identical results. Polite language usually didn't work, but Russell was doing his job by the book, and he could now check that item off the list.

In his training, the young officer had been taught to think about outcomes. Don't just act but consider the consequence of each action. What were the possible outcomes this morning? Best case, the man stayed where he was and with more forceful words Russell might convince him to abandon his perch. Then he could book him for causing a public nuisance and get on with his day. Worst case, the guy slipped and broke his neck, an unfortunate result for all concerned. Cops saw things they couldn't forget, and Russell didn't need to see this guy land on his head. He was already having a bad day. Reflexively, he tugged on his duty belt, weighed down with a police issue Glock 9mm revolver, handcuffs, summons pad, Taser, baton, flashlight, portable radio, and pepper spray. The pain in his knee had sharpened. He was tired. Russell volunteered as a coach for a youth league basketball team and worried he wouldn't feel well enough to show up at practice that afternoon.

Watching the man on the balcony, his nakedness an ongoing affront to propriety and worldly order, Russell questioned why he hadn't called in sick today. Then he remembered: his wife. He had left the apartment like it was on fire.

More than anything Russell wished this winter nudist was not a black man. In Florida, less than two weeks earlier some shit-for-brains Neighborhood Watch knucklehead had shot an African-American teenager named Trayvon Martin, and the whole country was going berserk. The president himself had weighed in. Gasbags on cable TV were calling for a National Conversation On Race, whatever that was. Russell was no racist. Growing up, he had played sports with black kids. Was as friendly with them as you could be in a high school where whites mostly sat at one set of lunchroom tables and blacks at another. Nothing resembling genuine racism disturbed his conscience unless the feeling that after this recent Florida calamity he needed to be more sensitive when dealing with black people was an even more subtle form of it.

Russell needed to establish communication, get a bead on the exact level of psycho he was dealing with this morning. No-clothes-in-March was an indicator, but there were gradations. Was he intoxicated? Certifiable? It was unlikely that he was a health nut, but Russell had seen a YouTube video about the Polar Bear Club in Brooklyn, those extreme fitness enthusiasts who every New Year's Day jumped into the Atlantic Ocean. So, you never knew. In the time that it took to formulate a direct order something happened that caught the cop off guard. The man dipped his knees like an Olympic diver then flung himself into the morning air, his spine arched, toes over his head, and executed a reverse somersault before landing on his feet in the snow.

Oh, Jeez, Russell thought. He's an acrobat! Then: Where's my backup? They were supposed to be three minutes from here. He looked around. No sign of them. The situation felt more volatile than it had a few seconds earlier. Everyone watching, waiting to see how this representative of government authority would handle the situation, what he, Russell Plesko, the man in whom these powers were vested, would do. The aerialist wheeled, spotted him and blinked as if awakening from a trance. He began moving toward Russell.

The expression on the man's face was tough to interpret. His eyes were opened wide, his lips parted—Was that a sardonic grin or a pained grimace?—to reveal teeth whose even brightness stood in sharp contrast to the rest of his physical and psychological dishevelment. It was hard to tell if he was angry or confused but what played on his features seemed like a rendering of the disturbing images that Russell imagined must be unspooling in his fevered brain. Russell had undergone training in dealing with the mentally ill, and the one fact he knew was that their behavior could be dangerously unpredictable. If it was impossible to pinpoint what was going on in the man's head, it no longer mattered now that this vessel of anarchy was bearing down on him.

The man was seventy-five feet away when Russell shouted for him to halt. He kept coming, lurching over snow and frozen grass. Russell was conscious of the ache in his knee. The swift assessment of whether one man can physically overpower another now occurred in Russell's mind. Even with his knee acting up he could win a fight but he didn't want to start grappling and have the man reach for his gun. Things could get out of hand quickly. Colleagues on the force had informed him that weird bursts of strength had been known to accompany people in the throes of psychotic episodes and Russell didn't want to find out whether or not these reports were apocryphal.

The man was thirty feet away and despite his uneven gait seemed to be gaining speed. Russell again shouted for him to halt but the man relentlessly advanced. Nothing prepares a police officer for the sensation that accompanies being charged by a deranged naked man, Russell thought as he reached for the Taser hanging on his duty belt, and yanked the device out of its holster. At the same moment, a twinge in his aching knee caused it to buckle. When he threw his arm up to regain his balance and keep from tumbling to the ground, the Taser flew out of his hand and arced through the cold air before landing in the snow somewhere behind him. The man was fifteen feet away and hurtling toward Russell, arms beating like a raptor's wings and—*SHHKREEEEEE!!! SHHKREEEE!!!*—emitting unearthly sounds. Panicked, Russell spotted the Taser and mapped its location relative to his own and the velocity of the incoming force and wondered whether he could reach it in time to save himself from the havoc headed his way.

The bullet caught John Eagle directly in the chest and arrested his forward progress. A look of confusion blotted his features. He collapsed facedown, and the gray snow ran red.

CHAPTER THREE

The late winter weather had warmed, and most of the snow covering the riding trails in Bedford had melted so Jay, in a state of semi-wakefulness, decided he would take one of his horses out before going to the office. The bedroom windows betrayed no hint of dawn when he slipped quietly from between Egyptian cotton sheets, trying to not wake Nicole, tiptoed into his walk-in closet (they each had their own), and pulled on a pair of worn Levis and a heavy sweater. His boots were downstairs in the mudroom just off the kitchen.

Peasants had raised Harold Jay Gladstone to be an aristocrat. Jay's Bronx born father had learned to ride in Van Cortlandt Park when other boys were playing stoop ball and the elder Gladstone believed these equestrian endeavors were one of the key factors that enabled him to rise above his Walton Avenue origins. This he wanted to pass along to his children. When Jay was ten years old his mother, a woman who in her Brooklyn girlhood had aspired to a more sophisticated life, took him to a local stable where she arranged for riding lessons. Child Jay wanted to learn to ride western-style in the fashion of the cowboys he'd seen in the movies, but his mother had presciently insisted he learn to ride in the English manner. Although he never entered competitions (too stuffy), Jay cantered, galloped, and jumped with the natural ability of a peer of the realm riding to hounds. "You're turning our boy into a Cossack!" his father jokingly exclaimed in a fake

Yiddish accent to his mother whenever the two of them were on their way to a Saturday lesson, but the elder Gladstone secretly relished the potent image of a young Jew astride a horse. Jay didn't know this at the time but his father's father, born in Russia at the end of the 19th century, remembered being driven from his shtetl in the Pale of Settlement by mounted Cossacks who gave no mercy to the villagers they cruelly herded down the muddy street. To be the Jew on the horse rather than the Jew running from the horsemen was nothing less than the miraculous promise of America.

The grand, perfectly maintained house, constructed in the 1920s, was stone and shingle but through the tender ministrations of a celebrity architect (who never did private residences), impeccably updated. When Jay stepped through the French doors to the veranda that overlooked the grounds, the sun was just breaking over the tree line in the distance, painting the sky in pastel streaks of salmon and pink. His boots were knee-high. He wore a field jacket and held a mug of coffee in his hand. A diaphanous mist hung over the rolling property and the sunlight at this early hour caused it to glow, lending the entire place an enchanted quality, an effect Jay never failed to appreciate. He took a sip of the strong coffee and surveyed the lawns, the tennis court, the pool and pool house (converted to a guest cottage), the stables, the twenty-acre meadow that would soon burst with wildflowers, and the woods—elms, maples, birches—that ringed it all. His love for the land was profound, and he felt deeply rooted here, inviolable. He inhaled the crisp, loamy air. The morning was splendid; the coffee warmed his stomach, and—

"Are you going riding?" Nicole was standing in the doorway, wearing faded jeans, scuffed cowboy boots, and a sweater. Her voice was sleepy, and he could tell that she was making an effort to sound agreeable. When Jay told her yes, he was, she asked if he wanted company. Although he had been looking forward to a solitary canter through the woods, that particular pleasure would have to wait.

A short while later they were ambling on a bridle path astride a pair of Arabians that appeared hewn from marble, Nicole in front on Sugarplum, Jay behind riding Mingus. The stable hand had not yet arrived for work, and the couple had saddled and bridled the animals themselves. They rode quietly. Only the soft percussion of the horses' hooves on the trail broke the sylvan hush. Jay had wanted to think about the coming day—he was scheduled to appear before the Department of City Planning later in the week to speak in favor of a colossal mixed-use project he intended to build in Brooklyn (public opposition was vigorous and well-organized) and needed to draft remarks—but the sight of his wife's gently swaying form several yards ahead turned his thoughts inevitably in her direction and how she came to occupy that saddle on this morning.

Before Nicole, he had been married to Jude Feldman, of Woodmere, Long Island, daughter of a periodontist. The marriage lasted a decade and produced one daughter, Aviva Golda (after Jude's grandmother). At an East Hampton fundraiser for Hillary Clinton's first presidential campaign, Mort Zuckerman introduced Nicole McGrory to his newly single friend Jay Gladstone. Vivacious where his ex-wife was dour, adventurous where Jude was tentative, and unburdened by Jude's constant thoughts of the Jews and their lachrymose history, Nicole had an appetite for food, art, travel, horses, anything that might allow her to live her life to its furthest extreme. In her twenties, she had bungee jumped from a bridge. She wanted to try skydiving. There was something wild about Nicole and sometimes Jay wondered if that's why he fell for her.

The daughter of a Pan Am pilot and a former stewardess, Nicole was ten when her mother and father divorced. There were an older brother and younger sister, but she was not close to them or her parents. Her family name was Pflueger, and growing up in Richmond, Virginia she was known as Nickie Pflueger. A cheerleader in high school, and an A student, she graduated from the University of Virginia with a degree in political science. She married her college boyfriend, but the marriage was volatile and only lasted a year. His one enduring gift was his surname: McGrory, which she happily adopted. On a visit to New York, she was approached by a representative of the Wilhelmina Agency and paid off her college loans modeling. Nicole found the fashion world predictably vapid and, frustrated by her colleagues' obsessing over diets and relationships when she was more intrigued by trade policy with Japan, eventually got in touch with her college economics professor, now an advisor to the speaker of the House of Representatives. Through his connections, she obtained a staff position on the House Select Committee on Ethics just as the investigation into the Clinton scandals was winding down. Doing research, writing position papers, providing background to journalists, she thrived. If politics is "show business for ugly people," the physical plainness of its practitioners functioned as a black velvet pillow from which Nicole beamed with gemlike brilliance. Her combination of beauty and smarts caught people off guard. She quickly became a fixture on the D.C. social scene and was a sought-after guest at gatherings of every political stripe. Her co-workers marveled at her ability to appear, sparkling, in press coverage of the Gridiron Club Dinner, the White House Correspondents' Dinner, or, memorably, the Second Inaugural Ball of George W. Bush, which she attended as the date of a Republican Congressman from Georgia. Ultimately, she found the culture of Washington too stultifying and it was while in the early stages of casting about for the next thing that she attended the Long Island party where she met Jay Gladstone.

As a Jewish man, north of fifty, marrying a glamorous, considerably younger gentile, it did not escape Jay that he was personifying a longstanding cultural cliché, but this did not trouble him. His child was Jewish-identified so he had done his part in maintaining the tradition and he was hardly rabbinic. Nicole was witty and spontaneous. Through her work in government, she was friendly with Tony Blair and when she heard Jay admired him, she arranged drinks at the former prime minister's hotel in New York that turned into a weekend at Jay's East Hampton home and an ongoing friendship. Whenever they were together, Jay always felt like Nicole was on the verge of making something better happen.

But he was in no rush to marry again, so a year passed before he asked her to sign a prenuptial agreement. She was in her middle thirties with no significant savings, divorced, without close family relationships, and looking for a soft landing, so she readily agreed. They were married in a small ceremony on the beach in St. Kitts.

Jay had been traveling for work, and Nicole was bored with the round of yoga classes, lunches with girlfriends, gallery visits, and fundraisers that constituted her daily life. The previous summer they had flown to Ascot for the races—Jay was thinking about getting into the thoroughbred game—and with friends had chartered a yacht in the Caribbean over the holidays, but these trips felt obligatory. He had begun to harbor an inchoate malaise but was not sure if it was a function of his age—the previous week his physician described his prostate as "boggy" and performed a biopsy (results inconclusive, a wait-and-see approach)—or of something amiss in the marriage. Disinclined to blame others for his displeasure, Jay wanted to be certain of its origin before establishing a new course. Until recently, he knew he did not want to go through another divorce, but he had become less sure of this. The flush of infatuation had resolved into the familiar, and although his wife was no less captivating, the amount of attention she devoted to him had ebbed. When they drove together, she sat next to him transfixed by the latest app on her phone. In conversation, she often seemed preoccupied. These thoughts were on his mind when he stepped on to the veranda that morning, and he hoped to consider them on his ride. But it was hard to think about anything that involved his wife objectively when she was bouncing along in the saddle directly in front of him.

The bridle path led through a sycamore grove and Jay could hear the chirping of birds in the branches. He grew calm as he imagined the green buds that would appear in the next few weeks. Spring was his favorite time of year. The pink and white dogwoods were a sign of universal beneficence. As he pictured their riotous blossoming, Nicole said:

"I want to have a baby."

"Excuse me?" He wasn't sure he had heard correctly.

She gently pulled Sugarplum's reins and turned to face her husband. Jay's horse halted. "I said I want to have a baby."

"This is new," and not a conversation in which he wanted to engage. It then occurred to him that here was the opportunity to make the grand gesture he had been searching for while lying in bed last night. If they were drifting apart, what better way to bridge the divide before it ruptured into a chasm? Babies were glue; the means by which many battling spouses repaired nearly sundered marriages. As providers of shared experience, children were more reliable than mountains and rivers. They were Experience with a capital "E" painted in colors that were ever shifting and lifelong. But if babies represented all this, then why did Jay feel his entire body contracting?

"When I married you I didn't know I wanted to be a mother, but things change, don't they? I'm nearly forty and I'm not ready to put my ovaries on the shelf."

"I have a child. One is plenty, believe me."

"Maybe you'll like being a parent more this time. You're older, wiser, better looking."

"Nicole, this was settled. I don't want to relitigate it."

One of the clauses in the prenup spelled out that they had mutually agreed not to have children together. Jay was not a man who believed he needed to litter the earth with offspring. He had texted Aviva yesterday—he tried to keep in touch, despite her lack of interest—and had not heard back. This was typical. His relationship with his only child brought him little satisfaction, and he did not want to roll the genetic dice again.

"I know, I know," she said. "But that was a long time ago, and I thought we might revisit it."

The quaver in her voice, and the vulnerability it implied, told him his wife was willing to ignore the blunt nature of their exchange to advance her point. Jay had anticipated this discussion. Over the course of the past year, he noticed that whenever they were around young children, Nicole displayed an interest new to her. Where she had disregarded their presence before, now she crouched or got on the floor to play with them. That and what he interpreted as a morbid interest in the rapid approach of her fortieth birthday, along with jokingly referring to her shriveling ovaries, were clues that led him to believe something significant was brewing. Jay knew this to be a sensitive area with many women whose ability to bear children was waning and tried to soften his tone.

"We both went into this marriage with our eyes open."

"People change," she said.

"Look, I'm sorry you feel this way because, well, it's going to make things—" He stopped himself. There was no point completing this thought because it would lead to a ratcheting up of tension and all he wanted was an agreeable hour on his horse.

"Make them what?"

"You know I like to do anything I can for you, right?"

"Mostly, yes."

"Fair enough. Almost anything. But, look—we agreed, and I'm not going to change my mind."

"I'll convert. I'll become a Jew. We can raise another Jew together."

"Nicole, come on. Be serious"

"I'm dead serious."

"It isn't about religion. You can convert if you'd like. If that's your path, by all means, follow it. But this was decided before we got married and I'm not going to entertain the question."

"You won't even think about it?"

"I thought about it before we got married, and if you had insisted on it then—" his voice trailed off.

"What? You wouldn't have married me?"

"I'd like to continue riding." Jay slapped the horse's haunch, and Mingus moved up the path.

"Would you have married me?" The rewording rendered the question a demand.

He was past her now. Jay began to trot and then canter. A full day at work lay ahead of him and as far as he was concerned this conversation had ended five years ago. What did she mean by offering to convert? That felt glib to him, a gambit rather than a sincere declaration of anything other than a desire to get him to procreate. But if Nicole were Jewish, would he be more inclined to have another child? He dismissed the thought. Jay was not that retrograde.

In the distance, he heard her voice as if emanating from the very woods that surrounded him. "You should think about it, Jay. You really should think about it." He wasn't sure what that meant. Then: "I'm going to ride another trail."

Jay raised his hand over his head and waved but did not turn around.

Since Nicole had come to the marriage with little other than her looks and intelligence, theirs was not a blending of economic equals, and because, as Karl Marx put it in another context, everything is ultimately about who controls the means of production, her power was solely of the soft variety. In other words, she would not come out of a divorce with a dime more than had been contractually agreed to. Having a child might alter those prospects. Although Jay was not a lawyer, he knew that introducing children into a divorce was a wild card. Custody battles could be brutish and long. He had friends whose ex-wives used their children to vitiate "ironclad" prenups with outlandish requests for child support. Jay knew a six-year-old girl with a court mandated five-thousand-dollar-a-month clothing allowance. Often enough those conflicts found their way into a media ravenous for them. The damage two otherwise civilized people could inflict on one another in family court was grotesque.

And the words Nicole had called out to him when they parted: *You really should think about it.* He was not sure how to interpret that sentence. Was she saying that he should think about it because she believed it was the right course for the two of them as a couple, or were her words a veiled threat? How serious was she? Was this a whim that would pass in the manner of others (following a holiday in the Burgundy region of France, Nicole briefly intended to acquire a vineyard) or was this something that a recalcitrant husband could not wait out?

Nicole was absent when Jay came downstairs from his shower dressed for the office. As he was preparing a bowl of oatmeal, he returned a call from the president of Tate College, his daughter's school. A biologist by training whose name was Winslow Chapin, the president told him that the college was going to try something new this year and have a parent speak at commencement. He wanted to know if, as a prominent entrepreneur and a member of the Tate College board of trustees, Jay would be willing to be the first one to do it.

"You can put a benevolent face on capitalism," the president said. "It would be a fresh perspective for our students. Meryl Streep is going to deliver the commencement address."

Jay was flattered. He often spoke to business groups and was occasionally quoted in the media, but had never been asked to speak at a college graduation. He realized the invitation was a precursor to being asked to make another large gift to the college but that was fair, and he admired Meryl Streep. When he hung up his mood was considerably improved.

CHAPTER FOUR

S eated in the back of a chauffeur driven town car en route from her home in Larchmont to her White Plains office, Westchester County District Attorney Christine Lupo felt a low-grade anxiety. Her son was waiting to hear from the five colleges he had applied to and later in the day she wanted to attend her high school freshman daughter's volleyball game. To make her schedule work, she would have to move a meeting with a family court judge, which she had already rescheduled twice. Then there were the usual indictments, plea allocutions, grand jury subpoenas, sentencing recommendations, court pleadings, and scheduling orders she had to deal with every day. Her driver/bodyguard was Sean Purcell, a thirty-seven-year-old father of three. His base salary was eighty thousand dollars, and with the overtime he earned driving his ambitious boss to her constant public appearances, he nearly doubled it.

Christine listened through earbuds to the lush tones of Verdi's *La Traviata*. The lofty peaks and bottomless valleys of the music, the plangent intonations of the singers, the world apart they evoked served as a distraction from her troubles. Sometimes she played it on the car's sound system. Earbuds signaled Sean to be quiet.

As the car sped north, she noticed the bareness of the trees silhouetted against the sky and hoped it would be an early spring this year. Christine had just turned forty-eight and her winter had not been easy. Getting older was not a big issue for her, and she had learned to cope with the mudslide of work that landed on her desk each day, but there was a vexing problem in her personal life. She suspected her husband of infidelity. They had been attending couples therapy for the last six months, did exercises that involved looking into one another's eyes, went on therapist-mandated "date nights," and this was the result. At least she thought it was.

The office of District Attorney of Westchester County was not traditionally a launching pad for political careers, but Christine Marie Lupo intended to change that narrative. She had served as the DA for the past four years and was running for reelection against an opponent with so little chance she might as well have been unopposed. One of five kids raised by a Stella D'Oro factory foreman and a housewife in the Arthur Avenue neighborhood of the Bronx, valedictorian at Our Lady of Perpetual Sorrow, Notre Dame on a full scholarship (History, BA), and Fordham Law School. Although she could have gone to work for a Wall Street firm, Christine didn't feel she would be in her element there as a working class Catholic girl, what with all the expensive, well-bred legal talent prowling the halls in tailored wardrobes and hundred dollar haircuts. Instead, she took a job as an assistant DA in the Westchester office, married an Italian-American businessman, and had a son and daughter in quick succession. Reliable and ambitious, and possessed of an offhand attractiveness, neither her wedding ring nor the small gold cross worn around her neck deterred the occasional colleague from testing how seriously the young prosecutor took her marital vows (the answer: extremely). After nearly a decade as an increasingly hardworking assistant DA, she became a judge. Four years later no one was surprised to learn she intended to run for district attorney. She locked up the usual rogues' gallery of domestic abusers, rapists, and killers, and her dynamic personality, form-fitting wardrobe, and impressive verbal skills made her a live wire on local television news. It was an open secret that her chocolate-brown eyes were trained on the state capitol.

Her current office was located just off the Bronx River Parkway in an eighteen-story eyesore on Martin Luther King Jr. Boulevard that loomed in solitary ugliness, the only tall building in an otherwise undistinguished area. Sean pointed the car into the lot across the street and parked in her reserved space. Before getting out, she inspected her look in a hand mirror with the dark-eyed gaze of a warrior queen. Auburn hair styled fashionably short. Coral lipstick applied to full lips. The flawless skin beneath a subtle application of rouge. She ran a red fingernail beneath her lower lip, smoothing an imperfection in her makeup like a sculptor working a piece of clay. Christine Lupo appreciated the value of optics, particularly for women. She understood that a woman in public life was at a disadvantage and often had to pay attention to details a man could ignore. In college, she had studied Hatshepsut and Eleanor of Aquitaine, but her role model, about whom she wrote an undergraduate thesis, was Boadicea, the British queen who led an uprising against the Roman Empire. Boadicea gave no quarter.

Sean held the door open for the DA. He was six three, two twenty, a former football star at Roosevelt High in Yonkers. As much as she may have identified with Queen Boadicea, Sean's impressive physicality was a comfort.

"Slay the dragons, Chief," Sean said, as he did every morning.

The figure she cut in her knee-length navy wool overcoat with the cinched belt as the wind mussed her hair was not arrived at by accident. She had analyzed her appearance as if it were a legal issue. It wasn't that she was beautiful, exactly, although she carried herself that way. But she was striking and potent, and wanted your vote.

Every week Christine led a meeting where the assistant

DAs who headed bureaus joined her in the conference room around an oblong table, with their boss at the head, and described what they believed to be their most vital cases. She listened purposefully as the chiefs of Financial Crimes, Sex Crimes, Homicide, Rackets, Criminal Courts, Narcotics and Firearms, Career Criminals, Bias, Arson, and Vehicular Crimes made their presentations. Her staff gave concise accounts of how their cases were progressing (Christine calculating which ones were likeliest to land her on television) while she sipped coffee and jotted notes.

Today's meeting had been going on for nearly an hour when she looked up and asked, "Is it a winner?" The question was directed at Vere Olmstead, a fortyish black female assistant DA who headed the Sex Crimes unit. The case in question involved a male history teacher at a private school in the town of Rye who allegedly had a sexual relationship with a sophomore, also male. The ADA told her the minor's parents wanted to bring the hammer down on the teacher, but the accused maintained his innocence and had the aggressive backing of his union. Christine was eager to prosecute a case like this, but it was not a subject she wanted to talk about on television. She told the ADA to bring it to a grand jury.

The next hour featured a massive stock fraud in Elmsford, a heroin ring in New Rochelle, and an orthodontist suspected of fondling an unconscious patient in Ardsley. None of the cases she heard about made her want to contact Public Relations and set up a press conference. When she brought the meeting to a close, Christine returned to her office and gave an interview to a newspaper reporter who was doing a story on a recent increase in domestic violence cases and wanted to know what the District Attorney's office was doing about it. ("We're prosecuting it, that's what we're doing!")

Despite the busy morning, Christine's thoughts kept boomeranging back toward her husband. When they had married, she was already considering a political career, and her choice of spouse reflected her ambition. Dominic Lupo was low-key, industrious, and wanted children. His import-export business was growing, and she had believed him to be just the right helpmate for an ambitious wife. She had locked up hundreds of criminals. Her record in office was spotless. Only an unforeseen event could get in the way of the ascent she had adroitly plotted, and now it looked like that might be what was happening. Christine had made discreet inquiries and last week took the bold step of hiring a cybersecurity expert to hack Dominic Lupo's phone in hopes of catching him in the act. She had expected to hear from the investigator by now.

Just before lunch, she looked up from the trial transcript she was notating and saw her secretary standing on the well-worn rug in front of her desk. Kelly was always starving herself on a trendy diet, and Christine had given up trying to discern whether the perpetually pained expression on her subordinate's face was dismay or hunger. Where was the operative from Kronos Cyber Security? Surely, he would provide more impactful information than her secretary. This assessment proved wildly inaccurate because when the DA asked Kelly what she wanted the young woman took a deep breath and informed her boss that a Caucasian police officer had just shot and killed a naked black man.

THE ACE, W.A.C.E. AM
NEW YORK SPORTS TALK RADIO
WITH SAL D'AMICO AND THE SPORTSCHICK

SAL: You're listening to the ACE, W.A.C.E., with Sal and the Sportschick. We're talking D'Angelo Maxwell. You're on the air.
CALLER #1: Yo, Sal, Mikey from Bayside, longtime listener, first-time caller.

SAL: *Hey, Mikey, how you doing?*

CALLER #1: *Bayside, represent!*

SAL: *We all love Bayside. What's your question?*

CALLER #1: *My question is I think Dag is, like, the most overpaid guy in the league.*

SAL: *Not a question. Sportschick, you agree? Is Dag Maxwell the most overpaid? I mean, they're all overpaid.*

SPORTSCHICK: *The market determines their value, Sal.*

SAL: *I respect you, Sportschick, but you don't know what you're talking about. What kind of message do these player salaries send to kids?*

SPORTSCHICK: *What're you, a socialist?*

CALLER #1: *Trade his lazy ass.*

SPORTSCHICK: *He puts up big numbers, Mikey.*

CALLER #1: *He's a lazy overpaid bum. I'm not saying he doesn't have a lot of inborn talent, but he's a thug.*

SPORTSCHICK: *Why is he a thug, Mikey? Because he has a lot of tattoos?*

CALLER #1: *Have you watched him play? Guy's a knucklehead!*

SAL: *Thanks for calling, Mikey. Tito from Staten Island, you're on the air.*

CALLER #2: *Hey, I've been on hold for an hour.*

SAL: *What's up, Tito?*

CALLER #2: *The team don't make the playoffs, they got to trade Dag while he still has value.*

SPORTSCHICK: *Dag Maxwell on the block, Tito? In the NBA, you need a superstar to win.*

CALLER #2: *You see him showboating last night? He hits that last shot, then instead of getting back on D he's firing pretend guns in the air like it's a riot.*

SAL: *I don't like the violent imagery. What's the fascination with guns?*

SPORTSCHICK: *Come on, Sal. Sanitary Solutions is like the Roman coliseum. He's a gladiator playing to the gallery.*

CALLER #2: *Guy has good instincts, but he doesn't think. I'm saying Dag should be in the circus, not the NBA, and he should take Gladstone with him.*

SAL: *You don't like Prince Jay?*

CALLER #2: *He trades away half the team to get Maxwell, and the guy's an idiot. Gladstone knows nothing about basketball. He should stick to polo.*

SAL: *Prince Jay plays polo?*

CALLER #2: *If he doesn't he should. It's what rich guys do. Meanwhile, have you seen that reality show Dag's wife is on?*

SAL: *Hoop Ladies! That show's a piece of crap, but my wife's seen every episode.*

SPORTSCHICK: *How's that relevant, Tito?*

CALLER #2: *I'll tell you how. Guy marries a gold digger; the man has no judgment. None!*

SPORTSCHICK: *Lotta hostility toward women today, Sal.*

SAL: *Next caller, you're on the ACE with Sal and the Sportschick.*

CALLER #3: *Yeah, this is Antoine from Brooklyn.*

SAL: *What's up, Antoine?*

CALLER #3: *My question for you two is why do you use your show as a consistent platform for casual racism?*

SAL: *What does that have to do with D'Angelo Maxwell?*

CALLER #3: *Every time a white caller wants to disparage him you hear words like "lazy" or "inborn" or "thug" which are all dog whistles that say shiftless N-word. These dudes would be dropping N-bombs on the show if you let 'em.*

SAL: *Whoa, whoa, whoa, let me stop you right there, pal. I am not a racist.*

SPORTSCHICK: *I can vouch for Sal, Antoine. He hates everyone.*

Chapter Five

When Jay stepped out of his front door, he saw a Ukrainian-American man leaning against a late-model Toyota Camry, sipping take-out coffee as he scanned *The Real Deal*, the New York real estate industry bible. In his late twenties, Boris Reznikov was a junior executive at the Gladstone Group and Jay's distant cousin. Tall and lanky, he wore a fashionable suit, wool scarf wrapped around his neck. With the mop of dark hair rising from his forehead and round, horn-rimmed glasses, he resembled a young Trotsky.

"When are we going to move the business to the Bahamas?" Boris asked. This was a running joke between the two of them. "I'm freezing my ass off." Boris sniffled. Every year he had a mild cold from November until May.

"You should get a place there," Jay said. "They need lazy Russians."

Boris was not lazy, or Russian, although Jay used "Russian" to tease him. He had been employed by his cousin since graduating from Hunter College as a business major, worked part-time while he earned an MBA from Columbia, and purchased a condo in Stamford, Connecticut, so that he could commute to the city each day with Jay.

"I'm thinking about it," Boris said, a memory of Queens Boulevard in his voice.

Nicole appeared, returning from the stable. While Boris greeted her familiarly, she and Jay barely acknowledged one another. Jay would have liked to share the invitation he'd just received to speak at Aviva's commencement, to have let his wife know he would be on the platform in a cap and gown with Meryl Streep (whom Nicole loved) but the disconnect he was feeling from her stopped him from acting on the impulse. As Boris backed an imposing Mercedes sedan out of the garage, Jay watched her walk into the house. He appreciated that Boris never asked questions about Nicole. He climbed into the passenger seat and picked up the three newspapers Boris had laid out for him.

"Tough game last night," Boris said. "I lost a hundred bucks on your guys."

"Don't talk to me about gambling," Jay replied, settling in for the ride to the city as Boris tuned the radio to the all-news station. "I don't want to get subpoenaed and have to testify that my cousin who works for me bets on games."

Although the younger man drove, he was not technically a chauffeur. Jay was grooming Boris for an upper-echelon position in the organization. For this reason, he periodically offered to hire a driver, but Boris demurred. In his view, driving Jay was an opportunity.

When they merged into highway traffic ten minutes later, Boris asked if Jay was ready for the City Planning Commission hearing.

"Not yet."

Although Jay did not look up from the article he was reading in the *Financial Times*, he knew that Boris was not happy. The company had proposed to erect what would be the tallest building in Brooklyn, and it was to be the first project where Jay had agreed to have Boris at his side from filing the permits to cutting the ribbon.

"I realize how full your plate is," Boris said.

"In more ways than you know," Jay said, still not looking up.

"You want me to draft remarks for you to deliver at the hearing?"

"I like your initiative, but I'll handle it."

Boris had a great deal riding on Jay dazzling the Planning Commission. If everything went as planned, by the time they were done Boris would be a force to be reckoned with, both in the company and in the Hobbesian world of New York real estate. This was a far cry from his origins. He was the American-born son of a Soviet émigré named Marat Reznikov, part of the first trickle of Jews allowed to leave the workers' paradise at the dawn of detente. In New York, the Gladstone family hired the new arrival as a rent collector, a tough role that required the kind of person attuned to the possibility of violence. Boris's father was that kind of person. He cultivated the right contacts, branched out, and eventually bought a Brooklyn nightclub that catered to other Eastern Europeans from which he ran various highly successful illegal businesses. Marat, though intelligent, was a brute. Boris was different. A reader of books, a chess player, he lacked his father's taste for pillage. The elder Reznikov recognized this and wanted his son to make a legitimate living, so he called Jay Gladstone, who gave Boris a job. The young Ukrainian-American made the most of his opportunity. He studied the real estate industry, was familiar with its history, players, trends. Jay liked that Boris drove a Toyota when he could have purchased something flashier.

The car radio reported that a police officer in White Plains had shot and killed a tenant at Gladstone Village, a complex of apartments built in 1964, and still in the portfolio of the Gladstone Group. The circumstances of the shooting were hazy. The relevant details were that the shooter was white, the victim black and, in a strange twist, naked.

How does a cop shoot a naked black man? Jay wondered. Especially in the current environment. The Westchester County District Attorney's office was investigating the incident and the district attorney, Christine Lupo, was expected to announce whether she would seek an indictment of the officer, some poor bastard named Russell Plesko, as soon as the following week.

Jay said, "I wish it hadn't happened at one of our buildings. That's not something you want associated with the family name."

"It's awful," Boris agreed. "But it won't affect the property value."

Jay was not thinking about the fiscal ramifications. It was his perception that these heartbreaking situations unfolded predictably. There would be a certain degree of clucking on the part of the authorities, and then the DA would soberly announce that the use of lethal force was justified. The anger he felt at the uneven application of justice in America led him to make generous donations to organizations that fought to rectify the problem.

Jay asked Boris if he thought the cop would be indicted.

"I hope not."

"Really? Why?"

"Cops do what they do so people like us can sleep at night," Boris said. "That guy who got killed could've shot the cop."

"He was naked," Jay pointed out. "He had no weapon."

"The guy could've grabbed the cop's gun."

"The police have an obligation to prevent tragedies, Boris, not to abet them."

"I'm not saying he deserved it but, man, would you take off all your clothes and run at a cop?" The question was rhetorical. "No, you wouldn't. Because you're a responsible citizen who knows what a privilege it is to live in the greatest nation in the world. I feel sorry for the dead guy but, c'mon, what did he think would happen?"

Growing up with a Ukrainian mother and stepfather in Queens had left Boris with a dim view of humanity. Surviving hundreds of years as Jews in Eastern Europe had embedded in the family DNA a predilection to assume that the least happy conclusion of any situation was the one that would unfailingly occur. In Kiev, Boris's stepfather was an engineer. In America, he drove a taxi until a bad back forced him to retire. His mother worked as a bookkeeper. As immigrant Jews, it was their belief that in their new country the government would protect them and police, as representatives of the state, were always afforded the benefit of the doubt (unlike in Ukraine). The family thinking: If citizens attack police, the social order will fragment, and anti-Jewish violence invariably breaks out. It didn't matter to them that this rarely occurred in America. Anyone who reads history knew what could happen wherever Jews were in the minority. Boris's perspective was not quite as provincial as that of his parents, but he nonetheless considered Jay's views slightly naïve. To this end, he was the owner of two handguns.

They were driving on the Hutchinson River Parkway past Saxon Woods, a public golf course Jay and his friends frequented when they were in high school. It had been a long time since he had teed off on one of those fairways. It would've been enjoyable to play a round in the spring weather but he needed to get on the phone with Church Scott to discuss Dag Maxwell's future, prepare for the appearance in front of the Planning Commission, and there was an important meeting scheduled with an official from the union that represented workers in residential buildings. It was a contract year and negotiations had ground to a halt.

Jay pulled out his phone and checked his email. There were the usual updates from the organizations on whose boards he served, an inquiry from his alma mater about whether he would be willing to fund a new building at the business school in exchange for having it named after him, and a message from someone at the accounting firm employed by the Gladstone Group. This last email contained an attachment consisting of financial documents pertaining to family interests in the gaming industry. A cursory glance at the data led him to wonder if a particular Gladstone Group executive was diverting large sums of money into a personal account. Jay's first thought was that it could not possibly be the case since the colleague in question was his cousin Franklin, the other co-chairman of the company.

CHAPTER SIX

I n Alpine, New Jersey, across the Hudson River from Manhattan and north on Route 9, was an eleven thousand square foot stone mansion of recent vintage with twenty-two rooms, a five-car garage, a swimming pool, and a guesthouse. The trees were striplings and the property, purchased by its current owner for slightly north of twenty million dollars, was less than five years old. A tall hedge surrounded the four-acre spread. Security cameras swept the perimeter. Wrought iron gates obscured a circular driveway where a late-model SUV, a Maybach, and a custom-built McLaren preened. This showplace was the home of basketball superstar D'Angelo Maxwell, who could be found in the sunny kitchen talking to his agent, an Armani-suited, athletic-looking young black man with a diamond in his left ear. Dressed in a T-shirt and sweats, Dag leaned against the marble counter, frustration creasing his handsome face.

"You're thirty-two years old, Dag," Jamal Jones said. "Late middle age in basketball years."

"I know how old I am, Jamal. It's not a secret," Dag said. His chef, an older black man with Chinese characters tattooed on both forearms, stood at the kitchen island and chopped fruit for a smoothie. Dag reminded him to soak the almonds before grinding them.

"But you deserve respect," Jamal said, looking up at his client.

At six foot eight and two hundred and thirty-five pounds,

D'Angelo Maxwell dwarfed his agent. His upper torso carved from granite. Arms and neck festooned with tattoos, headband crowning short hair. The highest paid player on his team, he was on the final lap of a four-year deal paying him twenty-two million dollars annually. The numbers he produced—23 points, 6 rebounds, and 3.2 assists a game—were solid, enough to maintain his position in the league elite, but not stellar. He was a perennial All-Star who had never reached the finals or been named first team All-NBA, the highest achievement of every universally acknowledged wealth-generating, sneaker-automobile-energy-drink-endorsing superstar.

The rap on Dag was that, while his skills were unassailable, he was one of those players who did not make his teammates better, had never, after over a decade in the league, advanced to the conference finals, much less won a championship, so was he really worth a huge investment this late in his career? A team could bank on promise, but observers who closely followed the league believed that Dag was, simply put, not "a winner." Not a loser, to be sure. His previous team always won a lot of regular season games, but without playoff success that was an increasingly hollow accomplishment. There was a litany of great players who had retired without having managed to win an NBA title, and a growing consensus had emerged among league executives that Dag was destined to join their melancholy ranks.

Dag heard the talk. Although he had spent only one year at the University of Kentucky before jumping to the pros, he understood the business well enough to know another franchise was unlikely to sign him at his current rate. But it was his firm belief that his aging body, for all of its infirmities—the creaky knees that required icing during time-outs, the sore feet plunged into an ice bath after each game, the lower back that required electric stimulation and the daily ministrations of a masseur—was capable of earning one more epic payday.

"It's why I came out to the crib to talk to you in person," Jamal said.

Jamal was not an exceptionally gifted basketball player but he had played at the University of Maryland where he had earned a business degree, worked two years for a famous sneaker company, and then parlayed his relationships with the more talented guys he had played with—he met Dag on the tournament circuit when they were teenagers—into his position at the forefront of the sports agent ranks.

"You got good news?"

"I think it's good news."

"That Chevy deal we talked about?"

Product endorsements were worth additional millions but, more importantly, conveyed status. They were essential building blocks of a player's "brand." World-class athletes hustled cars and soft drinks. An invitation to be the face of an insurance company that pitched its product to every family in America was ideal. Dag's most recent endorsement had been for Odor-Eaters, a shoe insert. This gig did not please him despite the munificent amount he was paid for three hours of work. He longed to be among the elite pitchmen; they were endorsing pickup trucks and energy drinks, not Odor-Eaters.

"I'm still trying to make Chevy happen," Jamal said. "Big ticket stuff takes time."

Dag sucked in his cheeks. "You gonna tell me?" In the pause that followed this question, they heard the hum of a television from another room. Dag looked toward the offending sound and yelled, "TURN DOWN THE TV!" before bringing his attention back to the agent.

"I talked to Church yesterday," Jamal said.

As the coach and general manager of the team, Church Scott was the man responsible for not only guiding the players on the court every night but determining which ones were worth what amount of money.

"What did he say?"

There began a discordant roar of what sounded uncannily like a pneumatic drill run through an amplifier. Dag looked over at his chef standing at the blender. The chef smiled apologetically. The racket made it too loud to talk. After what seemed an eternity the chef turned the machine off and poured the contents into a pint glass which he handed to Dag who immediately placed it on the counter.

"Yo, man," he said to the chef, "Would you mind giving us a little privacy?" The chef nodded and departed.

"I want you to hear me out before you respond," Jamal said.

"What the fuck did he say?"

"He wants to win a title, Dag."

"We all want to win a title."

"The man needs flexibility under the salary cap."

"I want the max deal allowable under the union agreement, Jamal. Five years, a hundred and twenty-five million."

As loud as the kitchen had been, that's how quiet it was now. The only sound was coming from one of the several large screen televisions in the house which members of Dag's entourage were still watching. No one had lowered the volume.

Dag shouted, "I SAID TURN DOWN THE DAMN TV!"

He stared at the smaller man, waiting. The offending noise abated slightly.

"Then let me cut to the chase," Jamal said, delaying the inevitable.

"Damn, man, spit it out."

The agent stroked his smooth chin as if considering the most delicate way to impart his information. He bit his lip, rubbed his nose. These delaying tactics were too much for Dag. "Come on, Jamal!"

"Ain't gonna be no max deal," the agent blurted.

"Church said that?"

"Basically."

"How much did he offer?"

"Four years guaranteed, and at your age that's amazing."

"For how much?"

"Ten million a year," like it was the greatest news imaginable.

"He can't be serious."

"You're coming off a torn ACL; you turn thirty-three this summer—come on, Dag, forty million guaranteed?" The part of his job that entailed begging spoiled athletes to accept a paltry forty million dollars for their services was not something Jamal enjoyed.

"That's bullshit."

"You're still a superstar."

"Does Gladstone know about this? Did he sign off?"

"Church is the general manager, man. You know that. He's got final word."

With supreme effort, Dag reined himself in. Pro ball was a business, and he was a businessman. Couldn't keep popping off if he intended to flourish as an entrepreneur when he retired. Some former players died indigent; others got invited to play golf with the President of the United States because they had parlayed their basketball talents into commercial success and were now tycoons. He knew which one he would be.

"I had dinner with Gladstone before I signed with the team and the man looked me in the eye and said he wanted me here for life." The respect in Dag's voice when he invoked the owner's name was unmistakable. Dag admired his business acumen and intended to emulate it when he retired, in what he hoped was the distant future. It was inconceivable to him that Jay Gladstone would not do what Dag believed to be the right thing. "For life, Jamal. The man said he wants me here for life!"

"He probably does," Jamal agreed. "At four and ten."

"Gladstone can't know what's up with Church."

"I don't negotiate with Gladstone. I negotiate with Church, and he's authorized to speak for Gladstone."

Dag thought about this. He took a sip of his smoothie. "If they ain't gonna give me a max, I want a trade."

Jamal did not immediately respond, but from the look on his face, Dag knew whatever came next would be less than optimal.

"I made a few calls around the league," Jamal said. "Everybody got much respect for your game, Dag. Much respect. But ain't no one signing Dag Maxwell to a max deal."

Jamal's declaration hung in the air. Dag cracked his knuckles. He took another sip of the drink, placed the glass back on the counter.

"Who put you in that Maybach?"

"Dag, I appreciate that you let me represent you."

"Then talk to Church again."

The view through the kitchen window from where Jamal stood was of the meticulously landscaped backyard. The pool was still covered, but in a few weeks the tarpaulin would be rolled back, and sunlight would sparkle off the ultramarine water. Jamal thought about all he had set up on Dag's behalf, the charitable endeavors like the D'Angelo Maxwell Foundation and the D'Angelo Maxwell Summer Basketball Jam, the business ventures they were involved in—the clothing line (*DagWear*) and their nascent video game company (*DagTronics*)—everything big and small he had attended to for his illustrious client, and wondered why, for some people, there could never be enough.

"It won't help," the agent said.

There was something about the finality with which his representative uttered these words that made Dag hesitate. The player lapsed into a silence that lasted for thirty seconds during which the sound of the TV continued to bleed into the kitchen. Without another word to Jamal, he stomped off in the direction of the noise.

On the sofa in front of a large screen television, Dag's younger brother Trey held a bong between his knees. He glanced up as his older sibling appeared.

"Yo, Dag," he said, by way of greeting. "Jamal still here?"

"We're *workin'*," Dag said, extra mustard on the verb.

Trey was in his late twenties, six foot five and sturdily built, with an elaborate neck tattoo of a cross, a souvenir from his brief embrace of Jesus. When Dag signed as a free agent, he negotiated an invitation for his younger brother, who had played a year of Division I college ball at Tennessee State, to try out for the team. Trey was on the roster through the pre-season but was cut loose before the first game of the regular season. Now he served as his brother's lieutenant. Anything Dag needed, breakfast cooked, dry cleaning dropped off, gassing up Dag's custom-built McLaren, Trey handled it promptly unless he was high in which case it took a little longer. Lately, he was stoned every day, and Dag had meant to talk to him about it. Two young black men flanked Trey. Babatunde (formerly Stephen) Worrell, a diminutive bodybuilder in shorts, and a tight T-shirt who rechristened himself after becoming obsessed with the Civil War in high school and determining Stephen was a slave name, and Lourawls Poe, an ex-shot putter from the University of Texas clad in a DagWear hoodie. They were life-long friends of Dag's. The coffee table in front of them was strewn with video game cartridges, several empty pizza boxes, and a forest of soda cans. In the middle of the mess lay a copy of *The Classic Slave Narratives* by Henry Louis Gates, Jr. A male Rhodesian ridgeback snored near a Nerf hoop that had been set up for the visits of Dag's six-year-old son.

The crew was watching *Hoop Ladies*, a reality show about the antics of a group of current and former NBA wives. One of the hoop ladies caught Dag's attention. This was Brittany Maxwell, his almost ex-spouse (the couple had separated just before the current NBA season began and had filed for divorce in January). She was in a clothing store listening to an agitated white woman ranting about a perceived slight from some "bitch" of their acquaintance, presumably another cast member. Brittany was nodding her head and repeating, "Totally, right." Both women sheathed in outfits that accented butts and breasts. Bling bedecked their fingers and wrists. Dag scowled at the sixty-inch screen, his candy-wrapped ex, the gold-plated post-divorce lifestyle the legal system provided, and thought of the ocean of alimony that was going to be required to keep the whole catastrophe afloat.

What made it particularly unbearable was that he was still attracted to Brittany, still a little in love. She was fine-looking, smart, and a good mother. Right now, he wished he had not been a serial adulterer, or at least had not been a serial adulterer that got caught. When Brittany discovered the cell phone snapshots of his impressive harem—a seemingly endless display of female pulchritude—and threw him out of their Bel Air home (like many NBA stars, Dag maintained a house in Los Angeles), there was no defense.

"I told you to turn off the damn TV," Dag said. "Why are you watching this shit?"

"It's hilarious, man," Lourawls said. "It's more like a satire of the lifestyle than a reflection of it. But I guess it's kind of a reflection, too."

Unamused, Dag asked, "What's in that bong?"

"Some dank," Lourawls grinned.

"Brittany's got it going on," Babatunde said.

"Shut the fuck up," Dag said.

He grabbed the remote control from the coffee table and changed the channel to a cable news show. A female newscaster of indeterminate ethnicity was reporting about the police shooting that had occurred in White Plains.

"Ain't no way that cop does time," Trey said.

"The guy was naked," Lourawls said.

The annoyance on Dag's face downshifted to endurance.

"Police do whatever they want to a black man," Dag said. The crew stared at their benefactor. "I catch any of y'all watching that show my wife's on, Ima throw your ass outta the house. Y'all need to get up on the news."

To punctuate his point, he flung the remote control against the TV screen. It bounced off and rolled on to the shag rug. This caused the slumbering dog to stir. The animal lifted his massive head. Dag glowered at his crew. Any notion Trey, Babatunde, and Lourawls had that Dag might have discharged his anger by flinging the remote control was now abandoned.

"When was the last time Biggie got a walk?" Dag asked. "Damn dog can't walk himself, right, Trey?"

"Naw, man," Trey said. "Biggie ain't learned that trick." Lourawls stifled a laugh. Dag glared in his direction. Trey turned to Babatunde. "Walk the dog, man."

"I walked him last time," the beleaguered subordinate said. "It's Lou's turn."

The fiery coals in Dag's eye sockets scorched Babatunde, whose brawny physique seemed to melt beneath the withering blast. There was a chain of command from Dag to Trey, then south toward the other two, neither of whom had any clout, and Babatunde had violated it.

"You above walking Biggie?" Dag said to Babatunde. "You too important now? You too essential to the way things run up in here to get your ass off the couch and do your damn job?"

"Why you so salty?" Babatunde said.

"What the fuck you just say?" Dag inquired.

"I ain't say nothing."

"Do your job with some dignity," Dag said.

After another pause that was too long for Dag's liking, Babatunde rose from the couch and skulked out of the room. Before working for Dag, Babatunde had been a personal trainer. Now his only client was Biggie.

"Where are you going?" Dag demanded.

"Dog needs his leash," Babatunde replied. "He's dangerous."

Dignity was vital to Dag. He admired it in others and tried to manifest it himself. An important component of a dignified bearing, in his view, was how you did your job. Whether it was as an NBA star or as someone who walked the dog of an NBA star, you discharged professional tasks in a dignified way. Today's brief exposure to *Hoop Ladies* had compounded the irritation he already felt because he believed it was undignified of Brittany, as the soon-to-be-ex-wife of D'Angelo Maxwell, to display herself in such a degrading context. Why did people watch those shows if not to see brassy, uncouth women bite, scratch, and tear each other's weaves out? Dag might have screamed Bang bang, Motherfucker, inarguably a vulgarity, at top volume whenever he scaled new heights on a basketball court, but that was always in the heat of a game, under the bright lights. Anyway, he was a basketball star and that, as far as he was concerned, made it not only excusable but inspiring. Now Babatunde, who Dag's business manager was paying god-knows-what to hang around, smoke weed, and read paperbacks about black history, was balking at handling his obligations. It was a challenge, Dag reflected, to maintain his dignity in an environment where the workforce was too high to walk the dog.

Who had saddled him with these fools, and why was he obligated to look after them? He was tired of loyalty, the unwritten code that someone like him who, by dint of hard work, divinely bestowed talent, and, yes, perhaps a little bit of luck, was somehow responsible for providing in perpetuity for this collection of sybaritic parasites. When it came to someone like his revered mother, he was thrilled to spoil her. She had worked three jobs, kept him off the streets, been his biggest booster, and never asked for anything. If the Baptists anointed saints, Kimberly Maxwell would have been one. She lived to witness her son's success before diabetes caused her premature death two years ago. But these jokers, and everyone else he ever knew who always seemed to have a hand out when he approached, took mooching to dizzying heights. And Dag was an easy touch. Checks to this group, that organization, piles of money into the riskiest, craziest business ventures of friends and extended family and where had it gotten him? He had earned well over a hundred million dollars in his career and had already burned through a hefty portion of it. He wished he could talk the situation over with one of his guys, bat it around, examine it from various angles, but that was impossible. Jamal was sympathetic, but couldn't empathize with what Dag was going through as an aging professional athlete. The entire state of affairs infuriated him, and to expend the energy it took to hide how he felt was exhausting.

Babatunde reappeared with a dog leash in his hand. Dag regarded the man as if he'd like to extract his molars with kitchen tongs.

"Why you throwin' shade?" Babatunde asked. "I got it."

Dag stalked out of the room.

In the kitchen, Jamal drank a glass of water. He knew that his conversation with Dag was not over, that he would have to listen to more complaining before he could leave.

"Can you believe what I gotta put up with?" Dag said as he re-entered the kitchen. He took a deep breath and collected himself. He looked at the prominent tattoo on his right bicep: *the 5th*. The ink was a reference to Houston's Fifth Ward, the combat zone of a neighborhood where Dag grew up. Through his talents, he had burst from its rickety streets, but he never pretended he was anything other than a kid from the Fifth. For him, the tattoo was a touchstone, a visit home. He rubbed it with his palm.

"I'm paying my brother and them guys to watch TV. I bought houses for two of my sisters. I lost track of how many

millions I gave Brittany so she can live like a damn queen and
raise our kids with all the shit I never had. I pay my bills. I take
care of my family. I'm a responsible motherfucker, Jamal."
"You're a good man."
"And I'm a good father."
"True that."
"My father, man, whatever he did, I did the opposite."
"Your kids love you."
"Responsibility costs."
"Indeed, Dag. Indeed. Wise words."
"Which is why you gonna get me a max deal."
A strong belief in God allowed Jamal to cope with his great-
est challenges, and in Dag's absence, the agent had prayed that
the player would absorb the words of wisdom he had
attempted to impart. Jamal groaned.
"I told you, I can't snap my fingers and make that happen."
Dag turned the dominant force of his personality toward
the backyard, where a flock of starlings had alighted on the
lawn. The player watched as they hopped along the grass
searching for food.
Jamal knew ornithology was not Dag's thing, and as the gap
in their conversation lengthened he worried what his friend
might be thinking. Being yelled at was easier than being
ignored. Dag kept staring at the birds. What was Jamal supposed to say? He tried this:
"I wish I could."
Dag bowed his head for a moment. There was no point in
yelling at Jamal.
"Explain to me how we're supposed to elevate my brand
because I don't see how we do that if I'm not playing on a max
deal."
"That's our challenge."
"And you're sure you can't get that contract?"
"I tried, man. I told you."

"Then you're fired," Dag said.

"I'm fired?" Jamal laughed.

"Why you laughing? Ain't nothing funny."

Jamal angled his head, tried to plumb Dag's thinking.

"For real?"

"Most definitely."

This particular exchange had occurred several times before, ending with Dag giving his agent a fist bump and saying, "I'm just playing." But if it was a joke, he was taking it further than he had in the past. When Dag broke eye contact and looked away, Jamal realized he meant it.

"That ain't right."

"You disappointed me."

"We boys!"

Occasionally Dag's shots misfired, and the team lost, but reality off the court nearly always bent to his expectations. The news Jamal delivered? It did not compute with Dag's all-conquering outlook. Someone had to pay.

"We ain't boys," Dag said. "You bush league, man. Rinky-dink."

"You don't mean that."

"Get your ass outta my house."

"C'mon, D'Angelo—"

"I'm done with you, man."

Once more, Jamal thought about making a case to Dag, but he would not debase himself. He was aware of the value Dag placed on comportment. He was not going to point out everything they had accomplished, all of the money they had made together. When the agent turned toward his biggest client, now former client, he humbly lowered his eyes.

"Thank you for letting me represent you," Jamal said.

"I gotta get mine," Dag explained.

Jamal left and Dag was alone in the kitchen. He thought about joining the entourage in the TV room. Maybe smoking a little weed and playing NBA 2K would get his mind off the situation. But he quickly dismissed the thought when he realized hanging out with Trey, Babatunde, and Lourawls would only remind him of his obligations. His obligations! Damn, he spent a lot of money. And his earning window, if Jamal's report was anywhere near correct, appeared to be closing. Best-case scenario he could play another five or six years. Then what? He saw the kinds of penny-ante products ex-players were asked to endorse. Stain removers and cockroach traps. The big payday? Forget that. You grabbed the main chance by the neck, and if you still had game, you wrung every dollar out of it. He knew he was worth a max deal and he suspected the owner agreed with him.

Owner. Dag didn't like that word. In the sphere of American race relations, its connotations were unavoidable. During union negotiations with the league, there was always one player that would refer to the NBA as a "plantation," but Dag refused to countenance that interpretation. No one got millions of dollars to endorse sneakers on any plantation he knew. Still, it chafed him that the ownership class appeared to be a photographic negative of the league itself. He was aware that it was beyond his ability to alleviate centuries of systematized inequality single-handedly. But getting a max deal from Jay Gladstone was something else. That he could do.

CHAPTER SEVEN

I n the winter of 1911, a young Russian immigrant named Yacov Glatstein arrived in London with a few coins in his tattered pocket. With the stroke of an official's pen, he became Jacob Gladstone. Soon he discovered that to be a Jew in England was not something to which a sensible person would aspire and a year later sailed for America, bearing only the clothes he wore and his shiny new name. In New York, the industrious greenhorn found work with a cousin who was a plumber on the Lower East Side. He married a young factory worker named Ida Abramovitch, fathered two sons and a daughter, and less than a decade later had his own successful plumbing business with other workmen in his employ and jobs in all five boroughs. When the exultant racket of the 1920s flung the entire city skyward and all new construction required sinks, tubs, toilets, showers, pipes, and drains, Jacob was ready. In the years after World War II, Gladstone Plumbing was one of the most successful outfits in the city, designing and fitting the innards of addresses where the brash century's Anglo-Saxon elite turned the taps with unsoiled fingers.

Jacob's sons, Bernard (who acquired the nickname Bingo as a student at James Monroe High School) and Jerome (always called Jerry), enlisted in the armed forces, served, respectively, in Europe and the Pacific, and, upon their discharges, followed their father into the business where they contributed to its continued growth. Bingo married Helen and begat Jay and Beatrice. Jerry's contribution to the legacy consisted of his wife, the former Estelle Schatz, and their children, Franklin and Deborah (now married to a radiologist and living in Chicago).

Bingo and Jerry worked like camels, pooled their money, and bought their first apartment building in the Bronx in the late fifties. In the sixties, they started developing real estate— the brothers had a preternatural ability to intuit what marginal neighborhoods would cycle back from the near-doom of white flight to the advent of gentrification—and a decade later were among the wealthiest real estate families in New York City.

More than merely capitalists, the Gladstones were civic-minded boosters lavishly donating to public projects around the city, a fountain at Lincoln Center, a copse of birch trees in Central Park, grace notes that belied their aggressive business practices. In the dire, arson-scarred 1970s, the Gladstones were among the real estate dynasties that, by agreeing to pay six hundred million dollars in property taxes a year ahead of time, helped save the metropolis from—FORD TO CITY: DROP DEAD screamed the infamous *Daily News* headline— bankruptcy. In Queens, Brooklyn, and the Bronx, Gladstone Properties built middle-class housing under the Mitchell-Lama plan. They were not known for their aesthetic aspirations: "Whatever its blocky design and red-brick facades might lack in poetry," a prominent architecture critic wrote, "the Gladstone brothers more than compensate for in welcome efficiency." Years later, the *Wall Street Journal* quoted Bingo: "We gave the people what they wanted at a price they could afford. We took them out of public housing, out of ghettos. And I put our name on it. Our first big project, my brother wanted to call it Windsor Court. I said, 'What are we, English?'"

Jay idolized his late father, but where Bingo blustered, his son was smooth. Bingo ordered, Jay cajoled. The Bronx and World War II formed Bingo, who never lost his New York accent. Jay was a creature of Westchester County and the Ivy

League, and when he spoke, it was impossible to discern his birthplace. He could raise his voice but preferred to whisper. And where Bingo was intuitive, a believer in gut instincts, Jay preferred to talk things over. Of all the highly competent, well-remunerated people who worked for the Gladstone Group, the one whose guidance Jay consistently sought was his sister Beatrice, known to everyone as Bebe.

If you were to ask Jay what Bebe's finest qualities were, he would say her keenness of insight and her loyalty. What Jay could not say, because it would reflect a degree of psychological insight he did not possess, was that Bebe, while capable, assertive, and accomplished, was also skillful enough to let her older brother shine.

"This isn't going to fly," she said. Her voice was like the lower register of an oboe, clear and penetrating.

Jay was seated on a sofa in his sister's large office on the 44th floor of the steel and glass tower on Park Avenue just north of Grand Central Station built by their father and uncle in the 1980s. She was opposite him in a pearl gray chair. The siblings usually checked in with each other in person several times throughout the day. Bebe had redone the space in the mid-century modern style popularized by a current television drama. Several framed and matted photographs of Palm Springs, California, taken by Julius Shulman, were arranged on one wall. The wall opposite featured a geometric painting by Piet Mondrian, one of two recently purchased by Bebe in an auction at Sotheby's (the other hung in her East 73rd Street duplex). On the teardrop shaped coffee table, a small Henry Moore sculpture commanded attention. Three years younger than Jay, Bebe's attractive face was tanned from a recent European ski vacation. Through diet and thrice-weekly work-outs with a trainer, she retained a youthful physique. Her hair was dyed honey blonde and fell loosely to the shoulders of her cream-colored pullover. She wore matching wool drill trousers, ankle high black boots of the softest leather. Her jewelry—earrings, a bracelet—was straightforward and stylish. There was a folder on her lap and she had just finished scanning the contents.

"What do I tell Franklin?" Jay asked although he knew the answer.

"He needs to present more thorough documentation."

"You don't think he could be stealing?"

"I hope not," Bebe said. A graduate of Smith, she served on the boards of several cultural institutions (generously funded by the Gladstone Family Foundation, of which she was the president), where she was known for her ability to understand spreadsheets and budgets.

"Do you want me to talk to him with you?"

"He'll think we're ganging up and then he'll tell Ari and Ezra to join the meeting."

"We don't want the twins," Bebe said.

They no longer bothered to roll their eyes when either invoked the names of Franklin's twin sons. Because the young men were Gladstones, Jay and Bebe tolerated their presence in the family business, but Ari and Ezra did not yet warrant respect. It was unspoken between Jay and Bebe that neither believed this was a remote possibility. The mention of his young cousins sent Jay's mind reeling back to the previous evening and the malevolent twins he encountered on the deserted concourse of the arena. He wondered if their appearance portended some incipient nastiness—their materialization seemingly out of nowhere had been strange—but quickly dismissed the idea. He considered relating what had happened to Bebe but repressed any further thought on the subject. Instead, he told her about the invitation he had received from the president of Tate College.

His sister was impressed. "And what are you going to tell the graduates?"

"I'm going to talk about the joys of working with relatives."
Bebe's laugh filled the room.

The last Gladstone project built in New York City was a
residential rental building on the Upper West Side of Manhattan
nearly ten years earlier, while Bingo and Jerry were still nominally running the business. It was a reliable moneymaker for
the family, but like much of what Jay's father and uncle had
done, architecturally undistinguished. Jay wanted to leave his
mark on the portfolio and his imprint on the metropolis, so he
was in the process of arranging to purchase the city land on
which a Brooklyn branch library currently stood. On that par-
cel, he intended to build the tallest structure in Brooklyn, one
that would redraw the skyline, now a feast of rectilinear
tedium. To that end, he had retained the world-renowned
architect Renzo Piano, and his design for the Sapphire was, in
Jay's view, nothing short of a tone poem composed of steel
and glass. The gently curving structure—to Jay it suggested
the hip of a female athlete, forceful, tensile, a hint of motion—
didn't contain a single straight line and rose to just over a
thousand feet, nearly doubling the height of Brooklyn's next
tallest building. The Sapphire would be to the Brooklyn skyline what the Empire State Building has been to Manhattan's;
the signature, the flourish. When illuminated, it would blaze
like a monumental gemstone. Let the other developers erect
their boring modernist boxes. Jay would bring the soul. As for
the library that he planned to demolish, he intended to
replace it with a more modest, mostly subterranean, state-of-
the-art version.

Sipping a double espresso, Jay stood in his large office
admiring Renzo Piano's scale model. Rendered in paper, wood,
and titanium, the Brancusi-like sweep had been difficult to
fabricate. Three feet tall, it rested on a table surrounded by a
mock-up of the projected landscaping. On the wall behind the

model hung the architectural drawings. Jay had thought the plans would only be there temporarily, but it had been over a year since he had pinned them up. In the many fights with local groups who viewed the project with everything from suspicion to outright contempt, gazing at them on his office wall every day was a constant reminder to remain steadfast. Jay's vision would be forty-two stories when complete. The plan he intended to submit to the city was for a building of only forty stories, the zoning limit for the area. He did not want to apply for a waiver and was willing to gamble that the city did not want to spend years in expensive litigation over an edifice that would be the envy of the world.

Jay finished the espresso and placed the cup on the coffee table next to a transparent case that held a scuffed baseball. He opened the case, removed the ball, and felt the rough red stitching with his fingers. It was a souvenir from his Little League team in 1967, when he was twelve. They were called the Gas House Gang, after the mighty St. Louis Cardinal teams of the 1940s, and Bingo was the coach. The players had all signed the ball, their decades-old signatures now faded. For years Bingo had kept the memento on his desk. It was a talisman, an object of connection, and although Jay was not superstitious, he would occasionally touch it for luck.

While some builders slap their names in huge gold letters on everything, trumpeting their importance directly into the world's collective ear, Jay preferred to operate in a less brazen mode and this was reflected in his office décor. Thick solid mahogany moldings, raised paneled walls, and fluted pilasters with a hand-rubbed "French polish" finish. The Carpathian walnut burled desk. The leather and antique brass nail head Chesterfield couch and matching overstuffed guest chairs. The sculptural bronze and smoked glass coffee table that lay on the antique hand-dyed Indian print rug.

The traditional design of the office contrasted with Renzo

Piano's thrilling display, and Jay applauded the difference. The tedious boxes that currently comprised the Brooklyn skyline would, in their aggressive tepidness, serve as a neutral background against which Jay's dynamic slash of steel and glass would instantly draw the eye. The bold strokes of this building might not have been in keeping with his more low-key modus operandi, but he had his reasons for undertaking something so striking. The Sapphire would be the first New York City project he was going to build out of Bingo's long shadow, and, if it went well, it might also be his last.

Like many individuals of his great station, Jay saw a larger role for himself in the world than that afforded him by the real estate business and professional sports. Civic life had long drawn his interest, and he had donated bountiful sums of money to the Democratic Party. Particularly unstinting when Barack Obama ran for president in 2008, he developed a friendly relationship with the magnetic senator, even playing golf with him on Martha's Vineyard two years earlier in a foursome that included the U.S. Trade Representative, and former NBA great Charles Barkley. Through appropriate channels Jay conveyed that, in the event of Obama's re-election, he would like to be appointed the ambassador to Germany. Until his dying day, his father refused to contribute a dime to the German economy. When his friends purchased Mercedes, Bingo stuck resolutely to Cadillacs. He could never forgive. Jay's ambassadorship would be Bingo's revenge. To this end, he had been meeting with a German language tutor. Recently, he had stood in front of his bathroom mirror and intoned: *Als Botschafter, begrube ich Sie auf die US-Botschaft un jetzt bitte kussen sie meinen Judischen kiester.* Which translated to: As the ambassador, I welcome you to the American embassy, and now you may kiss my Jewish ass.

That morning Jay went over cash flow reports. He met with

the chief investment officer about a deal they were considering to build a mixed use high rise in Boston. The property manager briefed him on the situation with the union leader he was to meet with later in the day. When that meeting ended, Jay thought he might walk down the hall and talk to his cousin Franklin. He preferred to deal with things obliquely, and because he was not sure how obliquely he could accuse someone of embezzlement, he continued to put it off.

At lunchtime, Jay met with his trainer, a young Israeli woman, at the executive gym two floors below his office. It was a well-designed space equipped with state-of-the-art strength training equipment, cardio machines, and ceiling-mounted television monitors always tuned to news or financial channels. He stretched and lifted, grunting and sweating through his routine. Several other Gladstone Group executives were exercising, engrossed by whatever played in their headphones. Gym etiquette required that they not address the boss unless he spoke to them first. On this day, Jay was not interested in conversation. He finished the workout, toweled off, and thanked his trainer.

In the sauna, his thoughts jumped from Franklin to Nicole and her declaration about having a baby, to the Sapphire and the pride he would feel upon its completion, to his basketball team and what he would do if they failed to qualify for the playoffs. Losing was not in his nature. He ate a tuna sandwich at his desk as he drafted a letter to the NBA commissioner regarding the possibility of shortening the season. There had been too many injuries recently, and Jay believed fewer games would result in less wear and tear on his guys. It was important to him that he be perceived by the players in the league as one of their advocates.

When he left the office at the end of the day, he still had not spoken with Franklin.

Jay and Boris sipped club sodas with lemon and bitters in the bar of the 21 Club. It was late afternoon, and they were talking about the Sapphire. Three Chinese businessmen sat at a corner table conversing in Mandarin. Jay was a popular figure in the building industry, as well regarded by the unions as anyone in his position could be. For this reason, he was asked from time to time by his colleagues to engage in back-channel communications during contentious negotiations.

A white man in his forties arrived at the table. The dark suit he wore could barely contain his impressive musculature. A thick head of hair was moussed and he wore an ID bracelet. Boris stood to shake his hand. Jay remained seated. The man shook Jay's hand first, and Jay introduced Boris.

Gus Breeze registered the name Reznikov. "Any relation?"

"His son," Boris said.

Breeze shrugged. Marat Reznikov had been the subject of an article in *New York* several years earlier. It had been years since Jay had spent time with him but he enjoyed seeing the reaction his name produced. To invoke it casually was not to overtly threaten, merely to inform. But the leader of the Service Employees International Union did not seem worried.

A waiter appeared, and Breeze ordered a beer.

The union contract was up, and it appeared that a labor action was imminent. If there were a strike, Jay knew it would inconvenience thousands of his tenants. Breeze told Jay that if all the union demands were not met, a strike would be unavoidable.

The beer arrived and when the waiter tried to pour it into a glass Breeze waved him away and performed the task himself. He took a sip, then put the glass down on the table. Instead of speaking, he exhaled slowly through his lips like a tire losing air.

"You're a man with a lot of weight on your shoulders," Jay remarked.

"I can handle it," Breeze said. "I wish I had better news for you." He spoke in the sandpapery tones of someone who has seen too many gangster movies where the tougher the tough guy is the more quietly he speaks. "But it is what it is." *It is what it is.* A phrase Jay found annoying, what a dullard remarked when he couldn't think of anything else. "And listen, Jay, I don't have to tell you what a huge inconvenience this is going to be for your tenants. I did a little research and found out how many rental units your family controls. That's a lot of pissed off customers." Breeze took another sip of his beer. Over the rim of his glass, he looked at Boris in a way that let him know he was not afraid of Marat Reznikov. Boris said nothing, only returned Breeze's gaze.

"It would be extremely inconvenient for them," Jay said.

"We all want to avoid that," Breeze gangster-whispered.

Jay smiled in a way to suggest he was taking the labor leader into his confidence. It was painless, disarming. Had he not been born into a successful business this smile would have helped him build one.

"Here's the thing," Jay said, placidly. The union leader tilted his head back and jutted his smooth chin. Jay looked directly into his dark, slightly bloodshot eyes. "I hired a private investigator and a forensic accountant. I didn't tell any of my associates, so you don't have to worry about that."

Breeze tried to hide his astonishment at this news, but a quiver of the left eyelid was his tell. "You got to the books?" Jay nodded. "How'd you get to the books?" He asked as if he were inquiring about directions to 34th Street, no big deal.

"Come on, Gus," Jay said. "Who do you think you're dealing with? The house you purchased in Southampton last year with money siphoned from the pension fund, the one on Swallow Lane with the four bedrooms a block from the beach that the union owns but only you and your family seem to use? It could be a problem with your membership, not to mention the attorney general of New York. The same goes for the condo in the Virgin Islands. You needed both? Maybe your union might have overlooked one vacation home, but two?"

This information was all imparted in the friendliest, most confiding way.

"It's not what it looks like."

"Listen, Gus, it pains me to say this, but I'm—I think disappointed would be the word. Yes, I'm disappointed. How long have we known each other?" Breeze did not answer, nor did Jay expect him to. "Over a decade. We've been honest with each other, forthright. But after we offer your union a fair deal, one that I believe to be generous, you put me in a position where I have to hire a private investigator."

At this point in the conversation, Gus Breeze resembled a flounder pulled from Sheepshead Bay lying in a dinghy, mouth open, lips moving barely perceptibly.

Jay continued, "This reputable man who I have no reason to distrust comes to me with certain information and then you and I have to talk about these problems you've created for yourself that in other circumstances would not be any of my business. You think I enjoy squeezing you? I don't enjoy it at all. I don't want to dig around in your personal affairs like this, believe me. Everyone knows I like to operate on the up and up. What you've done might have passed in 1962, but it doesn't fly for a union leader in 2012. So, I'd like to get these negotiations wrapped up."

Breeze mumbled something about how unions operate, but the confidence to press the point had abandoned him.

"Think about what you want to do, Gus."

Jay paid the bill, and he and Boris walked out. It had been a strange day. Nicole had implicitly threatened their marriage, Franklin appeared to be siphoning funds from the company, and this union ballbreaker thought he could press an advantage. Perhaps if Jay were more swaggering, more puffed up and bullying, he would never be challenged. But that was not remotely his style. When would people learn that no one was going to beat Jay Gladstone?

Chapter Eight

The same morning Jay began to suspect his cousin Franklin was looting the family till, his daughter Aviva careened down a tree-lined path that ran along the north side of the main quadrangle of Tate College astride a fat-wheeled bicycle with old-fashioned upright handlebars. Fierce brown eyes, full lips lightly glossed, and a nose in no way too big but one a less confident person might have considered having bobbed, arranged in a pretty face. Wavy chestnut hair cascaded to the middle of her back from beneath an emerald green knit hat. Bright sunlight illuminated five gold studs piercing her left ear.

The campus was located in Schuylkill, a quaint town in the Hudson River Valley. Founded in the 19th century as a Christian seminary, it had become a model of progressive education that attracted the kind of student who formulated her own interdisciplinary major and aspired to found a nonprofit, be an artist, or create an app designed to end world hunger. Individualism was extolled, conformity abhorred. Aviva fit right in. Born with a right leg that was ¾ of an inch shorter than the left, Aviva had worn a lift in her shoe since childhood. The sense of apartness this caused waxed and waned, but she always felt different.

Laboring over a paper on Djuna Barnes for her Gender Theory class deep into the night, she had overslept and was late for rehearsal. The next day she was leaving on a free trip to Israel provided by an organization whose mission was to expose young Diaspora Jews to the prodigious history and manifold delights of the Jewish state, and still hadn't gone over the packing checklist. Like her father, Aviva had too much to do.

The March wind gusting off the river reddened her pale cheeks as she vigorously pedaled, wool scarf fluttering over her nylon backpack, unbuttoned pea coat flapping like a pirate flag over a sweater and ripped jeans. She rang the bell on her bike and weaved past two boys ambling down the path holding hands. When Aviva flew by them, one shouted a greeting. Aviva acknowledged her friend with a wave and nearly lost control of the bike. She quickly righted herself and sped toward the theater.

Aviva's phone rang. Continuing to pedal, she reached into her pocket and extracted it. Her father.

"What's up?"

"I'm just calling to tell you to have fun in Israel and stay out of trouble."

"Why would I get into trouble?" Guarded, wary of aggression.

"Aviva—" She could hear him sigh. This strained back-and-forth was the pattern of their interactions. "It's an expression."

"Okay. I won't. Anything else?"

"Your mother told me she's going to be out of town on Passover so I'd like it if you came to the Seder at our house this year. Nicole's pulling out all the stops."

Aviva said she would think about it.

Her parents divorced when she was fourteen, and until Aviva went to college, she shuttled between their two households. In the wake of the split, when Jay's ex-wife wanted to move from the Bedford home to the city, he agreed to spend weekdays in Manhattan as well so his daughter's life would be less disrupted.

In the manner of guilt-ridden parents of means, her father

plied her with gifts, trips, a horse (Aviva: Can I sell him and give the money to charity?)—but his attention had no discernible effect. To his sensitive daughter, Jay was a series of large gestures and loud sounds. He was obsessed with his work, which did not interest her, and sports, which she viewed as a waste of time. When Aviva was in fourth grade, he insisted she play basketball in the local recreational league and he coached the team. Although the lift in her sneaker allowed her to run comfortably, she would pretend to limp just to get her father to remove her from the game. On the rides home, he would give her pointers and Aviva would either ignore him or say, "Leave me alone, I'm a cripple." If the price of his attention was going to be the development of athletic skills, she wasn't interested.

Aviva had a complicated relationship with her infirmity. Although her parents assured her it meant nothing, for Aviva, it had been a humiliating flaw. As a small child, she attended a school where the social-emotional learning component did little to stop playground taunts. She was angry about what nature had wrought and often expressed that anger, indirectly, at her parents. The weakness it represented to her was anathema. But it made her strongly identify with marginality, economic, racial, or gendered. Alienated from her circumstances, these were her people. The children with cleft palates in magazine advertisements, indigenous tribes whose forest redoubts were being despoiled by the ravages of capitalism, street beggars in India, they all tore at her. In their dire need for protection, they were the opposite of Jay Gladstone, who towered over her world like a forbidding peak. She allowed that missing ¾ of an inch to define her, as what she deemed to be her father's perfection came to represent Aviva's view of him.

When she was still living at home, they would often talk about politics.

A typical exchange:

"All property is theft."

"Feel free to donate everything you're going to inherit."

"Watch me. I will."

"And then you can live in a hovel somewhere."

"That's my plan anyway."

"How are you going to earn money for rent?"

"By helping people."

"That's admirable, Aviva."

"The differently abled are just as capable of contributing to society as any other group. No one is going to push us aside."

Jay viewed his daughter's handicap differently. You overcame obstacles. A person moved forward, a view inculcated in Jay by his father.

"Your grandfather was born on March 4th," he said. "March f-o-r-t-h. It was his motto."

"I don't believe in mottos."

Another exchange:

"The rents in your buildings are crazy, where are the poor people supposed to live?"

"There's housing for people in all income brackets."

"What about the homeless, where should they go?"

"There are shelters."

"You should build homes for them."

"I'm not the government."

"The government is an occupying force."

"Why don't you run for office and change things?"

"Because the whole system is corrupt."

Although Aviva considered herself to be the polar opposite of her father, when it came to will she was his mirror image. Her bat mitzvah project entailed calling every one of her parents' hopelessly bourgeois friends to request they donate one old coat, then asking those people to each call five friends and implore them to do the same. By the time she finished pestering, one thousand two hundred and fifty-three homeless people had winter coats. The bitter February afternoon Aviva spotted a man panhandling in a Comme des Garçons was one of the happiest moments of her life.

"I don't see why I can't play Field Marshall Cinque," Aviva said.

"For real?" Imani asked. "You can't play Cinque because he was a black man." She was a rangy black woman. In the winter uniform of jeans and a hoodie, she had smooth, light skin and smelled pleasingly of coconut oil. Her curly hair had blonde tips and was tied back with a strip of kente cloth, a gift from Aviva when they started sleeping together in October.

"Why can't I play the dude?" Noah asked. "At least I'm black."

Half black, half Jewish, and gay, Noah Booker (uniform: jeans and hoodie) was a slim six foot two with a long, thin face. Short dreadlocks peeked from a do-rag.

"Semi-black," Imani teased.

"Said the soul sister," Noah responded.

"The white girl playing the black dude is more provocative," Axel said. Imagine the face of a Leni Riefenstahl subject upholstered with a scrubby growth of beard, dirty blond hair gathered in a short ponytail. Six feet tall and broad-shouldered, he wore a pullover sweatshirt, cargo pants, and canvas shoes. Although no longer enrolled in the college, he had become their de facto director.

In the otherwise empty rehearsal space in the basement of the theater arts building, the four of them sat on folding chairs arranged around a table. Scripts covered in markings next to Styrofoam cups of cold coffee. On the walls, rows of framed posters of student performances going back to the 1960s, Stoppard, Chekhov, Shepard.

"Don't we want to mess with people's preconceptions?" Aviva said. She knew the status conferred by society on people like the Gladstones had the reverse effect in her current environment where both her "whiteness" and her family's wealth left her at a constant disadvantage, but still felt bound to advocate for her position.

"Absolutely," Imani said. "We do. But those are some weird racial politics."

Aviva's self-designed major was Form and Mechanism of Political Art, and for her senior project, her intention was to create an original theater piece. A fruitless week of staring at a computer screen led her to ask Imani and Noah to collaborate. To help facilitate their conversations, they invited Axel, who lived in the same off-campus house as Noah, to join them. The show they devised told the story of the Symbionese Liberation Army, a ragtag group of bumbling revolutionaries—deadly and incompetent in equal measure—that exploded into international prominence in the 1970s with the kidnapping of the newspaper heiress Patricia Hearst.

Working title: *Patty Revolution*.

Performances set for early May, just before graduation. The show revolved around the connection between Patty Hearst and Field Marshall Cinque, the ex-convict who was the leader of the SLA.

"What white folks need to understand (it sounded like *unnastan*)," Imani began, her oval face arranged in a parody of pedantry, "is that black people gotta play black people." She scrunched her features, and Aviva tried not to laugh. Imani liked to experiment with dialect and knew how to be funny about it.

"You gonna get all black up in here?" Aviva said, her sassiness intended as a meta-take on "sassiness," rather than the thing itself.

"You're damn right Ima get all black," Imani said. The chaffing dynamic was a familiar one, and there was no resentment in her voice. She pushed up the sleeves of her hoodie. "Can't no white girl play a black man. That shit is blackface."

"Tell it, girl," Noah said, ironically.

"It's a lot of appropriation, for sure," Axel said to Aviva. "Maybe she's right."

"Maybe?" Imani said.

Axel said he needed to think about it.

"It's not blackface if I'm doing it as me," Aviva said. "I would be a white woman playing a black man. Tell me how that's any different than a black actor playing some Greek like Oedipus."

"Oedipus is a fictional character created by Sophocles to illuminate a universal truth," Noah offered, flexing his theater history.

"It's cool how you memorized that," Axel said. Noah did not appreciate being patronized and flipped his pen at Axel, who snatched it out of the air.

Ignoring the male dominance game, Imani said, "Cinque was a for real black man."

"Race blind casting only goes one way?" Aviva said.

"Until there's full equality for black people, yeah, that's right," Imani said and crossed her arms. "Give it up, baby. I'm not going on that free trip to Israel 'cause I'm not Jewish and you're not gonna be Cinque."

"I'm not sure those two things are equivalent," Aviva said and looked at Axel to see if he agreed. In the eyes of his peers, he was uniquely qualified to adjudicate disputes like this one because his revolutionary bona fides put him on a different moral plane. The son of radical European academics (his father an authority on the Spanish Civil War, his mother a Marxist economist), Axel had moved to America as a six-year-old when they accepted teaching appointments at the University of Wisconsin. In political matters, he exuded more gravitas than the typical Tate student and was usually treated by his friends as something of an oracle.

"It's like when we liberated the pigs," Axel said.

Two years earlier, he had dropped out of college and traveled to Oregon to join a renegade environmentalist collective. Their most successful action, according to Axel, was the freeing of two thousand pigs from a pig farm.

"We've heard the pig farm story, like, a hundred times," Noah said.

"Because pigs are a useful metaphor for a lot of things, which you would know if you read George Orwell," Axel said, as Noah buried his head in his hands.

"I read *Animal Farm* in middle school," Noah said to his palms.

"The pigs didn't care what color we were," Axel said, "because it wasn't relevant. Here, it's relevant."

Imani nodded, deferring to his perspective.

"I'm glad we've established that pigs aren't racist," Aviva said. "But I'm not sure what it has to do with—"

"Imani is right," Axel concluded. "You can't be a black man."

Aviva understood that arguments about race between people of different races rarely ended well (and given that Imani was currently her girlfriend, this one was particularly fraught), so it was time to retreat. She agreed to be Patty Hearst, and Imani would play Field Marshall Cinque. They spent the next hour working on the kidnapping scene. Over and over Imani and Noah burst through an imaginary door and confronted Aviva as Patty. They played with the idea of violence, miming it without touching one another. There was a slapstick chase. There was improvisation. Aviva experimented with her reactions. She screamed. Laughed. Sang a lullaby while Imani pretended to blindfold her. Noah danced into the room. Imani used her script as a megaphone. Noah and Imani picked up Aviva's legs, and Aviva wheelbarrowed around the table on her hands. The games exhilarated all of them, Aviva most of all. Her family's wealth was an unwanted carapace, a boundary separating her from others. Only in abandon did it dissolve.

Axel videotaped the rehearsal with his phone, and the performers watched themselves, pulsing from exertion. Noah suggested adding another piece of business to the scene. Axel liked the idea and offered an adjustment. Aviva felt Imani's hand on her shoulder. She looked over and saw the smile on Imani's face as the antics of the group animated the small screen. Here she was with her three peers from the far, and to Aviva more meaningful, side of the social scale, and she felt like one of them. Not entirely, of course, because some gorges could never be fully bridged, but their connection was close enough.

"You shouldn't go to Israel," Axel said to Aviva. "Your presence there is an endorsement of the government's policies." She sat on a mattress on the floor of his small, bare-walled room. They were drinking herbal tea from cracked cups. The rehearsal had ended an hour earlier, and they had gone back to the ramshackle off-campus house he shared with Noah and several other Tate undergraduates. Axel sat cross-legged on the scuffed floor with a copy of the script. Next to him was a ratty bookshelf choked with paperbacks—novels, history, politics. There was no other furniture in the room, which felt not unlike the cell of a bookish monk. They had been working on the script, trying to incorporate the best of the improvisational material, and Axel's comment was a non-sequitur. "I wasn't going to say anything because I want to respect your agency, but if you go you're endorsing the policies of the Israeli government."

"Okay, so to follow your logic, no one should have visited America during the Iraq war?"

"That would've been cool," he said.

"They have an oppressive government in Sudan, but you never talk about that," she said. "Or Zimbabwe, or—"

Cutting her off, Axel said, "Those are Africans subjugating Africans. Sucks, but not my fight."

"Why isn't that your fight?"

She waited for his answer.

During freshman year, Aviva and Axel had slept together several times, but now they were more like siblings. She held him in high regard, as much because of his biography as his intelligence. His family had been living in Wisconsin less than six months when Axel's father died of a heart attack at forty-four. Rather than return to Europe, his mother elected to remain in America. He was raised on a diet of Karl Marx and John Lennon, and as a child accompanied his surviving parent to conferences in places like Cuba, where he learned how to roll a cigar from a man who fought in the revolution, and Algeria where a former member of the PLO taught him to shoot a semiautomatic rifle. So he claimed. It was impossible to verify any of his stories, but he told them with conviction. When Axel was eighteen, he matriculated at Tate College on a full scholarship. That much was true.

Despite having read more widely than most of his classmates, and having had a far wider range of experience (again: he claimed), whether from boredom, delayed onset of mourning his father, or just the belief that radicals did not need college degrees—no one could say—he stopped attending classes. By the end of second semester sophomore year, Axel had flunked out. He rode a bus to Sacramento and spent time as a migrant laborer (once more: he claimed), following the harvest from California, to Oregon where he hooked up with a group of animal rights activists with whom he may or may not have participated in the pig liberation about which he was so fond of talking. He filled several journals (Aviva had seen them) with handwritten observations because one day the world would be interested in how he had spent his early years. Eventually, he wandered back to the upstate town of Schuylkill in an old pickup truck he swore he won in a card game.

"Why isn't it your fight?" she repeated.

"Do me a favor and read this." Axel pulled a paperback from the shelf and tossed it to Aviva. *The Wretched of the Earth* by Frantz Fanon. The cover was beat-up, several pages folded back. She flipped through it and noticed the heavy underlining and extensive marginalia. "It tells you everything you need to know."

"Is this as dense as that Edward Said book you lent me?"

"*The Orientalists?* Yeah, kinda."

"I only got through half of that."

"These aren't novels, Aviva. They're not meant to entertain you."

Earlier in their friendship, because of her background, which stood in such sharp contrast to Axel's, Aviva felt that she was constantly in danger of failing some unspoken test. But her confidence had grown since freshman year. She accepted that he did not want to answer the question she posed.

"Let's get back to the script," she said.

"So, you're gonna go legitimize the Zionists?"

For all of his intellectual curiosity, Axel's politics did not allow for complexity. Unlike him, Aviva knew when to stop arguing.

"We need to finish up here," she said. "I still have to pack for the trip."

CHAPTER NINE

J ohn Eagle had been dead for one day. Angry community
groups, the police union, and the media expected face
time with the district attorney. Christine Lupo intended to
hold all of them off until her plan crystallized. No one running
for office in the current racial climate could afford to impro-
vise, and she was intent on gaming out all possibilities to avoid
mistakes.

While she sat at her desk in the early morning quiet cogi-
tating on this, the report from Kronos Cyber Security arrived
in her email. It revealed a series of calls her husband made to
a young woman, and further research showed visits to a "love
nest" in Battery Park City, several of which had taken place on
days he had told his wife he was out of town on business.
Although the tangible evidence only confirmed what Christine
had suspected, the news hit like a death in the family. She may
have prepared for the impact, but the reality was brutal. A
wave of grief flushed through her. She was insensate, conscious
only of pure emotion. This brief fugue eventually subsided
and, although she was not religious, she crossed herself
because this is what her parents did when something terrible
happened. From her purse, she removed an iPod, cued *La
Boheme*, placed it in the dock on the credenza behind her
desk, and let Puccini's music coax her down from the ceiling.

She considered taking the rest of the day off but that would
be to give in, and she had not ascended to her current station
by capitulating to personal feelings. She regarded the framed

picture of their children on her desk. What was she going to tell them? That their father had cheated on her? Her daughter was a sensitive kid, her son prone to sullenness. Neither would take it well.

Briefly, she wept but chose to believe her reaction had more to do with her husband's stupidity than sorrow that her marriage was about to end. When was the last time they had shared a confidence? They slept with their bodies as far away from each other as possible. Who knew when they last had sex? She did not have the self-abnegation gene that would allow her to overlook his behavior in the interest of her political career. Divorced politicians were as common as pigeons so what was one more? She might even gain the support of women who would find inspiration in her resilience. A red anger lit her. The Lupos were going to a restaurant this evening for their weekly "date night." Now, she was looking forward to it.

Ibrahim Muhammad had called the office multiple times since yesterday and had identified himself as the imam at the mosque attended by the shooting victim. He was demanding a meeting with the district attorney to discuss the case. She tried to concentrate on the Puccini playing softly in the background.

Uscio nel mezzo, altro a sinistra.

"He insists on meeting with you," her assistant informed her. She was standing in front of her boss's desk, prepared to flinch. Kelly preferred not to talk to the DA when opera was playing in the office because she knew it was often palliative and she was reluctant to interrupt treatment.

"What did you tell him?"

"He's coming in at noon?" Kelly said, her voice rising at the end of the sentence.

"Are you asking me? Is that a question?"

"No," Kelly said. "He's coming in at noon. Today."

"Why did you set that meeting without discussing it with me?"

"You told me to take more initiative if I want to get promoted."

"This is not what I meant, Kelly," Christine said with less than infinite patience. "I was thinking more along the lines of you getting my case files better organized without my having to remind you."

"I'm sorry," Kelly said. "What do you want me to do?"

What indeed? In a situation like this, it was standard for someone from the DA's office to meet with religious leaders. But she had no idea who Imam Ibrahim Muhammad was. Were he a prominent cleric, that would be a different order of business. But she had never heard of him. Why should she take time out of her packed schedule to meet with some obscure holy man?

"You don't hand out meetings with the district attorney like they're after dinner mints," Christine admonished her assistant. "Tell him he's welcome to meet with one of the assistant DAs."

Kelly said she would take care of it. Then she informed her boss that her 8:30 meeting was waiting in the conference room.

"How long have they been sitting there?"

"Fifteen minutes."

As Christine walked briskly past her subordinate, she vowed that when she ascended to the office of governor, Kelly would not accompany her to Albany.

The White Plains Police Benevolent Association represented all police officers below the rank of chief employed by the City of White Plains. Their elected leader was a forty-two-year old pit bull of a Sergeant named Brian O'Rourke. He wore his uniform with a sidearm in a holster on his hip. A full head of jet-black hair slicked straight back and small, ratlike eyes that said I take shit from no one. This morning O'Rourke and three uniformed associates were seated in the DA's conference room across the table from Christine. O'Rourke's multiethnic coalition of fellow officers, Irish-American, Asian-American, and African-American, were all roughly their leader's age. Christine's second-in-command—Lou Pagano, an ADA for nearly a decade—sat to her right, scribbling notes on a yellow legal pad. He was in his late thirties, but sunken eyes and a harried look made him appear older.

"What you need to understand, Ms. Lupo," O'Rourke said, his voice raspy and insinuating, "is that Officer Plesko acted according to police procedure and to even think about convening a grand jury to hear evidence would be a slap in the face not just to the officer but to the entire department."

Christine suspected he used the prefix Ms. because it was required. And so he put a little spin on it, one that said I'm calling you *Ms. Lupo* but I won't pretend it's not some brainless, politically correct nonsense. As if the societal changes wrought by the 1960s had never happened. She had known men like O'Rourke her entire life, attended the same Catholic schools, saw them at mass on Christmas and Easter. Pugnacious, traditionbound, and often bigoted, changing times had forced them to submerge that third quality in the interest of career advancement. She couldn't stand him. He and his wingmen had been hammering her for nearly an hour, O'Rourke doing most of the heavy hitting. He talked in the manner of her soon-to-be-ex-husband, forcefully and with great certitude. He interrupted and harangued. Typical alpha male.

The meeting had begun pleasantly enough—greetings, handshakes, how do you like your coffee? But as soon as the district attorney had introduced the topic of the grand jury, the mood darkened. No one had touched the assortment of pastries displayed on the table.

"I understand your feelings, Sergeant O'Rourke," the DA said, "but I don't see that I have a choice."

"Don't have a choice?" O'Rourke spitting words like pellets. "All due respect, you're the DA, and you can do whatever the hell you want."

Christine took a deep breath and waited. What troubled her about the tenor of this meeting was that she was known as indisputably pro-police. Did she have to explain the particular nature of the current situation again? She wanted to ask the African-American officer to enlighten O'Rourke. Wanted to say, Don't you know this case is racially charged? Are you not aware of what just happened down in Florida with that Trayvon Martin kid? Do you have any idea what it's going to look like if we bypass the grand jury system? She glanced at the black cop, a thickset man with a mustache and soft brown eyes. His face was impassive. No help would come from that pension-protecting corner.

"A citizen was killed by a police officer," the DA said to O'Rourke as if she was explaining the whys and wherefores to a golden retriever. "The grand jury's job is to hear the evidence. If the officer is blameless, there won't be an indictment but to not let the system function is a dereliction of duty on the part of my office." She took a sip of her cold coffee. It was time to bring this confab to a close. "So, thank you, gentlemen for coming in."

"Whoa, whoa, whoa," O'Rourke said and held up his hand. "Not so fast."

"You've been here nearly an hour," Lou Pagano interjected.

"Am I talking to you?" O'Rourke said. This was a standard bullyboy tactic. O'Rourke trafficked in intimidation. But Pagano was the son of a New York City transit cop and had spent his entire career around police officers. He wasn't intimidated and was careful not to react. He looked at his boss. The DA met her colleague's gaze and indicated she would take care of it.

"What you need to understand, Sergeant O'Rourke—"

"Excuse me, *Ms.* Lupo, but what *you* need to understand," the cop interrupted, his voice rising, "again, all due respect, is that anything can happen in a grand jury room, and we all know anything can happen at a trial, am I right?" Here he turned to his fellow officers for confirmation and together they sagely nodded. "When a prosecutor can't convict a wife-killing scumbag just because he was on a television show, we all know the system is broken. Let's not mince words."

"No," the DA said, patience vanishing. "Let's not. You listen to me. I have been courteously hearing you out, and for the last twenty minutes, you've been saying the same thing ten different ways. I've got another meeting waiting. A meeting that's at least as important as this one, all due respect." She wielded all due respect the way he employed Ms., like a weapon. "So, let's see if we can—"

O'Rourke interjected, "Ms. Lupo—"

Again with the *Ms.*

"Excuse me," she barked. Christine Lupo had had it. O'Rourke's eyebrows rose, and his head rolled back as if from the physical force of her will. Having gotten his attention, she proceeded in a more measured tone. "I understand that Russell Plesko seems to be a first-rate officer and appreciate the support he's getting from the union. I commend that. Now, I'm aware of your concerns regarding the legal system and will take them under advisement. Mr. Pagano is the number two person in this office, and he will interview Officer Plesko himself." Pagano puffed up at this and looked at O'Rourke, who did not meet his gaze.

The DA continued, "He'll talk to all the witnesses and report to me. At that point, having done due diligence, I'll decide how to proceed."

O'Rourke said, "Mind if I ask you a question, Ms. Lupo?"

If this guy says *Ms* one more time, she thought, and said, "Fine. Then we need to wrap up."

"Is this gonna be your last government job?"

"How is my employment situation relevant to the conversation?"

"Just that people talk, and I've heard things. There's chatter you want to be governor."

This was true, but if O'Rourke was hinting at some below the radar quid pro quo, he was an even bigger jackass than she suspected. Here was Pagano, and O'Rourke's water carriers. Did he think she was going to engage in this kind of negotiation with an audience?

"I appreciate your interest in my career, but I'm not getting into hypotheticals."

"Union support still matters."

She knew she should end this right now but wanted to see whether O'Rourke would hang himself. "What are you saying?"

"Nothing. I'm not a quid pro quo guy." He said the words. She was surprised he knew what they meant. "But you should do the right thing."

"Are you done, Sergeant?"

"Russell Plesko gets indicted," O'Rourke said, "and what kind of message does that send to the young people who might want to join the police? Their government doesn't stand behind them?" He pushed away from the table indicating the show was over. "That's gonna be on you."

Christine stood up, and Lou Pagano followed suit. The cops rose. O'Rourke stared down at the DA. He was over six feet tall, but the five foot six DA regarded him the way an ax-wielding lumberjack looks at a tree.

"Thanks for coming in," she said.

There was requisite handshaking, except for Lou Pagano who made a point of snubbing O'Rourke, and then Christine and her deputy left the room.

The pair walked past a row of desks staffed by department secretaries stationed in front of offices manned by their ADA bosses. When they were out of earshot, the District Attorney of Westchester County turned to Lou Pagano and as twelve years of parochial school indoctrination burst its tightly bound ropes, demurely said, "Fuck that Irish cocksucker." She laughed loudly then caught herself and looked around to make sure no one had overheard.

Back at her desk, the DA tried to medicate herself with more Puccini but found she could not concentrate. The daunting prospect of having to tell the children their parents were splitting up, the logistical nightmare of divorce, that overbearing cop who had hardly bothered to dress up his threats, all of it was upsetting. She needed a cigarette. Christine had quit smoking during the nineties, so this was more of a surprise than the revelations about her husband. Walking down the hall where the ADAs worked, she stepped into Vere Olmstead's office.

The head of Sex Crimes wore a navy pantsuit, starched white blouse, and pumps. Hair straightened and styled conservatively, a small gold hoop in each ear. She looked up from a brief she was marking up and smiled at her boss, white teeth in sharp contrast to her dark skin. Olmstead had quit smoking, too, but her professional duties and the nature of the defendants in her purview caused the occasional relapse. The DA asked if she could bum a smoke. To her surprise, Olmstead volunteered to join her. Christine was not the kind of executive who took breaks with her subordinates but, in her current state, she welcomed it.

The women stood to the side of the building, Olmstead lighting two cigarettes. She handed one to her boss and said, "My mom called this morning."

The DA liked Olmstead. Her parents were originally from Antigua, and she had grown up in Ossining. She was hardworking and levelheaded. Already serving in a supervisory capacity, her future was promising.

Christine took a deep drag of the cigarette. "How's your mom?"

"She wanted me to ask you a question."

"You can tell her you're a valuable member of the team."

Olmstead smiled. "Thanks, but that's not what she wanted to know." The DA took another long drag. It tasted better than she remembered. "Mom wanted to know when you think you're going to convene a grand jury on the John Eagle shooting."

It was one of those transitional winter-to-spring days when the warming temperatures, the sun's rays, the pleasant smells, all feel like a reward for surviving another northeastern winter. To be outside, to relax, to partake in this annual seasonal rite. Was it too much to ask for a few uncomplicated minutes? That was all the district attorney had wanted, nothing more than a low-key interlude with a trusted colleague, perhaps some small talk about each other's children, or where to travel over summer vacation. Instead, a significant breach of protocol. ADAs, as a rule, did not attempt to divine their boss's intentions. They followed orders. Christine tried not to think about skin color, but she had the fleeting thought that if Vere Olmstead had been white, she would not have asked this question. Then, she chastised herself for thinking that. Why wouldn't a white ADA have questioned her? Still, she felt sandbagged.

"Tell your mother that the process will take its course." Christine's manner indicated that the matter was now closed. The query notched her anxiety level up. She had just received actual confirmation of her husband's behavior, and the emotional fallout would be long and painful. There was a political campaign to think about. The arrival of a racially explosive situation smack in the middle of these already challenging circumstances was not welcome.

"I'm not going to leak it," Olmstead said.

"You worry about Sex Crimes, all right?"

Her words came out more curtly than intended but the DA did not care. Pressure from below was unacceptable. She pressed the cigarette to her lips and inhaled deeply once more, letting the smoke fill her lungs, before exhaling through her nose. Then she dropped it half-smoked and ground it out with her shoe. The DA told Olmstead she wanted to take a walk and stretch her legs, but the real reason was that she didn't want to ride up in the elevator together and risk further conversation on the subject of John Eagle.

CHAPTER TEN

T he moneyed murmur in the elegant Stanford White dining room of the Paladin Club obscured the confidential nature of the lunch conversation that was taking place at a corner table between Jay Gladstone and D'Angelo Maxwell, who had dressed for the occasion in a suit so impeccably tailored it looked as if it could be removed only by molting.

When Jay became a team owner, he learned that fraternization with players was, for the most part, minimal. Although he occasionally allowed himself the indulgence of flying on the team plane, he didn't socialize with the players unless it was a team-sponsored event, and was careful not to foist his presence upon them in unwelcome ways. Unlike many extremely wealthy individuals, Jay had a well-developed sense of how others viewed him, and he was intent on not being perceived as someone who was only in the room because he had the most money.

He had been dreading this lunch. When D'Angelo called and asked for a meeting, the club was Jay's tactical choice. It was an environment in which he felt exceedingly comfortable. His father had been a member and had brought him to family events here, and now he was an officer.

To preserve his current waistline, Jay had ordered a Kobe beef hamburger without a bun. He sliced into the meat as he talked.

"We try to keep all of our assets in the best shape possible," he was saying. "So, when we want to sell, should we ever want to sell, we're not scrambling. It's the same with horses. I treat them well because I'm a humane person, but they're assets." Jay stuck a forkful of the beef into his mouth and chewed. He looked forward to the lunch ending.

"Did you inherit all that real estate from your daddy?" Dag asked, cutting a piece of the asparagus next to his sea bass.

"A lot of it. But since I've been in charge, our company has developed several properties here in America, and we're doing a major project in South Africa now."

Jay was proud of his work in Africa and did not mind sharing the information with people of all races. He was familiar with the history of grandstanding white people trying to save Africa for their own reasons and was careful to not be perceived as one of them.

"I did a bunch of clinics in Africa last year," Dag said. "With my foundation."

"We're developing an entire town, a small eco-friendly city actually, and if it goes well, if it's replicable, we believe it will intrigue other developing nations."

Dag took a sip of water and licked his lips.

"What do you get out of it?"

"Financially? Not much." Jay chose not to elaborate. He was aware that good intentions were often regarded with suspicion and didn't want to come off like another white intruder. "But it gets me away from my desk."

The conversation had meandered for half an hour, and Dag was not pursuing any discernible line of inquiry. Jay expected that he wanted to talk about the contract and wished he would bring it up so they could be done with it.

"My money guy has me in a bunch of real estate investments," Dag said, impaling a piece of sea bass and placing it in his mouth.

"What kind?" Jay asked, to keep the conversational ball in

the air. Jay was thinking about his daughter, who was now in Israel. He had texted her and had not heard back.

"I'm not sure to tell you the truth. Shopping centers, condos, some golf resort down in Nicaragua—"

"A golf resort in Nicaragua?" Jay repeated, making sure he had heard correctly, as a vision of a Sandinista soldier teeing off burbled up. "Do you want me to vet any of them for you?"

"You don't have to do that. But, listen, Mr. Gladstone, there's something I want to talk to you about."

At last, Jay thought, they were going to get down to business. But then a middle-aged white man in a Brooks Brothers suit approached their table. His short hair and his smile were equally crinkly. Jay made as if to stand.

"Don't get up," the visitor said, a trace of Canarsie in his accent. "I wanted to come over and see if I could get Mr. Maxwell to sign with the Knicks."

"Chuck, I believe that's called tampering," Jay said.

"I'm not an owner," he said. "I can't tamper." The friendly man chuckled and looked at Dag, who nodded uneasily.

Jay said, "Dag, have you met Senator Schumer?"

"No, I haven't," Dag said and extended his hand, which the politician clasped and shook.

"The Knicks could use you," Senator Charles Schumer (D—NY) informed him, placing his other hand over the one that was already holding Dag's.

"I have a contract with Mr. Gladstone's team," Dag said, pulling his hand away as Senator Schumer reluctantly released his grip. "You understand."

"But you're a free agent once the season's over, am I right?"

Dag's eyes darted around the room. He was the only black man there who was not pushing a cart or carrying a tray. Although D'Angelo Maxwell was a man of many accomplishments on and off the basketball court, it concerned him that in this context he might be unfairly viewed as just another

African-American jock surrounded by two far more influential men of European descent whose ingrained sense of dispensation, and the gilded environment in which it was being exercised, rendered him a prop in the conversation. He wasn't sure if Senator Schumer was serious or not but wanted to know why Jay didn't just shut down the whole line of questioning. The way the politician beamed in Dag's direction made him uneasy.

Then Senator Schumer turned his ingratiating attention to Jay. "Are you coming to the dinner for President Obama at the Waldorf?"

"I'll be there if I'm in town," Jay said. "The company bought a table, but I've been doing more traveling than Marco Polo."

"Did you ever play that game in a swimming pool when you were a kid?" Senator Schumer asked Dag. "I say Marco; you say Polo."

"They didn't have that game in my neighborhood," Dag said.

"Hey, I grew up in Brooklyn," Schumer answered. "Before it was fancy."

"You O.G.," Dag said, trying to get into the jocular spirit.

"Have you met the President, Mr. Maxwell?"

Mr. Maxwell? Dag liked that. "Not yet."

"Bring this man to the dinner, Jay," Senator Schumer said. "I'm sure the president would enjoy meeting him. He's a big basketball fan." Then, to Dag: "Get your owner to take you."

Your *owner*. That word again, with all of its antediluvian implications. Never mind that it was not the liberal speaker's intention. Dag was already on edge. He didn't like sitting across from this boundlessly privileged white man, born rich, who never had to contend with anything resembling the trials of Houston's 5th Ward in order to ask that he be paid what he believed himself to be worth for his talent and prodigious labor. He resented the whole dance and was trying to tamp down these restive feelings. He had an agent, so these kinds of conversations should be unnecessary.

But he didn't have an agent. Why had he fired Jamal?

To the senator's suggestion, Dag said, "We'll see about that."

"And if you come to the Obama dinner," Senator Schumer said, "I promise not to talk about the Knicks."

Jay and Dag both feigned laughter, Jay's the mirth of satisfaction, Dag's the heh-heh of social obligation.

"You're one of the great players of your generation," Schumer gushed to Dag.

"And he's all ours," Jay said.

Dag seemed gratified by the owner's declaration, knew it would give him leverage. Schumer gave Jay's shoulder a friendly pat before strolling back to his table. Dag wondered why the encounter with the senator had made him uncomfortable.

"Knick fans are crazy," Dag said.

"They never lose hope," Jay said.

And then Dag wondered why he had said Knick fans *are* crazy when with his boys he would have said Knick fans *be* crazy. Why was he kowtowing to Jay Gladstone?

"But I appreciated the respect," Dag said. He took another sip of water, swallowed, and rolled his neck. A loud crack ensued. "Mr. Gladstone, I think the Knicks would pay me."

"Lots of teams would pay you, Dag. I hope you re-sign with us."

"Yeah, well. I want to."

This news delighted Jay. He waited for Dag to say what was on his mind. He knew enough to never negotiate against himself. But Dag did not elaborate on his declaration.

"How's your fish?"

"Tasty."

Jay noticed Dag was massaging his neck, which seemed to be causing him discomfort. Did the player have an injury he

had not disclosed? It was bad enough that he was already playing on a surgically reconstructed knee. Now Dag shifted his
shoulder, so a joint in his back audibly cracked. His body,
imposing in so many ways, had a lot of mileage on it.

"My agent told me he had a conversation with Church
about a new deal."

"I heard something about that."

Dag outlined the parameters of the offer Jamal had relayed.
"My agent said that's your opinion, too. No max deal."

Jay measured his words. "You're a great player, Dag, certainly one of the best in the league." Dag agreed. They could
have been discussing an element on the periodic table. "And as
you know, we're trying to build a contender."

"I'm all about winning."

"We love that about you," Jay said. "The basketball minds
in the organization, Church and his guys in the front office,
they've made a determination. If that's how he wants to allo-
cate the funds allowable under the salary cap, then my job is to
support him."

"Yeah, well, we know who the best player on the team is,"
Dag said, with the supreme confidence that comes with having
been a star when he was ten years old, and in high school
where he was the best player in Texas, and as an all-American
during his one college season, and for most of his career in the
pros. "And when you look around the league, I don't care what
team, the best player gets a max."

"That's not true. Teams get stuck with bad deals, declining
productivity puts them in situations where they're overpaying.
But let's not wander into the weeds here. This is between your
agent and Church."

"I fired my agent," Dag said. "I'm negotiating."

The rashness this decision indicated caused Jay to pause. It
was unheard of for a player of Dag's caliber to enter into a high
stakes negotiation without representation.

"Listen, Dag. Since you've been on the team, we've gotten to know each other a little bit, and at this point, well, I don't think it's too much of a leap to say that I consider you a friend."

"We're buddies," Dag said, in a faintly derisive tone that Jay chose to ignore.

"I know this is a business and you're going to do whatever it is you have to do for you and your family. I respect that. But negotiating a deal like this without an agent—" Jay did not have to finish the thought, but could not help himself. "You might want to rethink that plan."

"Like you said, I gotta do what I gotta do."

Dag seemed entirely rational. Church had told Jay that the appetite around the league for lavishing a huge contract on him was not there which meant that they could call his bluff. But Jay was genuinely fond of Dag and wanted to keep him on the roster with no hard feelings.

"Why don't you hire a new agent?"

Dag appeared to ponder that possibility. There was a proliferation of cutthroat agents, shrewd operators who could obtain close to max deals for players who were not necessarily worth the investment. But if he wanted to do that he wouldn't have asked to meet for lunch. Dag was a talented offensive machine who fans forked over hundreds of dollars per ticket to see work his mojo live. And the television networks? The checks they wrote for the rights to broadcast the games had ballooned to the billions since the time he had entered the league. Sure, everyone in the NBA was a world-class player, but it was the superstars who drove the money wagon, and Dag was still undeniably a superstar. That he had seen his last gargantuan payday was, to him, beyond comprehension.

"You know we're one game out of the playoffs right now," Dag pointed out.

"Yes, I follow the team," Jay said, an attempt at humor. He hoped it hadn't veered into condescension.

"And you want to make the playoffs, right?"

The expression on Jay's face slid from genial concern past barely concealed surprise and arrived at mild distress.

"We count on you to play your best every night," Jay said. "Especially in a contract year."

"Dag always delivers."

At this juncture, Jay could have just nodded his assent. He could have corroborated Dag's self-assessment quickly enough. Could have said Let me think about it. He did not do any of these things. Instead, he drilled down:

"To your point, we committed the maximum salary allowed to you. You're our guy, and if the season were to end today, we wouldn't be in the playoffs. Sorry to put it quite so bluntly, but you brought it up."

This lightning bolt of a reality check hurled from the summit of Mount Gladstone stunned Dag. Its implication—if you were as good as you claim, no one would be wondering if the team was going to qualify for the playoffs—was, at the very least, insulting. It was also, in Dag's estimation, rude, insolent, and, on the most basic level, emasculating (its undeniable accuracy immaterial). To Dag, who made his living asserting his potency, his physical superiority, and his iron determination over other athletic marvels, this was enraging. His right bicep, the one with 5th tattooed on it, twitched beneath the wool sleeve of his suit jacket.

"So, you're telling me what?"

"You really should hire a new agent," Jay said. "I'm not going to negotiate. I have too much respect for you."

Dag underwent a brief impulse of wanting to upend the table and drive his fist into the owner's face as payback for having dared violate the unspoken pact that prohibited anything but happy talk when discussing the career of a superstar of Dag's magnitude with the actual superstar, but the august surroundings and the high stakes of the conversation had an inhibiting effect. Also, Dag *had* brought it up, so the athlete only smoldered. He recognized how undignified an outburst would have appeared to the other diners, not to mention the Internet clickbait that would have resulted—DAG DECKS OWNER IN DINING ROOM DUSTUP—and remained immobile, though no less infuriated. Then he upped the ante:

"How many black faces do you see here besides the waiter or the dude who handed me a towel in the washroom?"

"We have black members."

Dag didn't have the patience for an extended back-and-forth. They were playing on Jay's home court, the owner had all the advantages. He needed to knock Jay off his game, gain some kind of competitive advantage. Dag probed: "Would you pay me if I was white?"

It was as if he had tossed a grenade. Jay absorbed the scabrous question. The only perceptible sound was the voice in his head telling him he had treated this man seated across the table from him with nothing but respect for nearly four years, had not tried to be pals in the manner of some owners. He had expressed his appreciation of everything Dag contributed to whatever success the team had known. He was bewildered that Dag would invoke race as a factor when owners paid nearly all of the top-tier salaries to black players. But wait. Was that a wry glimmer in Dag's eye?

"Are you joking?"

"What do you think?" If this question was meant tongue in cheek, Jay couldn't tell.

"Are you accusing me of being racist?"

"I didn't accuse you," Dag said. "I floated it." He seemed to enjoy making the boss squirm.

Jay sipped ice water from the glass in front of him, felt the coolness on his fingers, in his throat. Tight-lipped, he stared at Dag. "When my father was in high school in the 1930s he fought for racial equality. That's the kind of stock I come from.

I was the Anti-Defamation League man of the year. And that's an organization that doesn't just fight hatred against Jews, either. They fight all kinds of prejudice, including prejudice against black people. You think my attitude to your contract negotiations comes from a position of race? Don't be ridiculous. Race has nothing to do with it."

Dag absorbed Jay's lecture. He waited until he was certain his host had finished. Then said:

"I was playing with you."

This brought Jay up short. Had he completely misread Dag's intent? *Was* he actually joking? He failed to see the humor in the topic.

"But here's the truth," Dag continued, "Race always has *something* to do with it."

"Come on, Dag. You're better than that."

Jay was surprised to find his own emotions riled after the implied accusation of racism, and briefly considered sharing with the player his lifelong fascination, appreciation, nothing short of love for black culture, *blackness*, as if that somehow inoculated him against Dag's egregious suggestion. But then he would have been the one being ridiculous.

"You should think about it, Mr. Gladstone."

"You know I'm not a racist," Jay said. "You can recite all the theories about how everyone is at least a little bit racist, and I won't argue that it isn't on some level true. And by the way, I wouldn't exclude you from this. And if you thought about it, you probably wouldn't exclude yourself."

Jay waited to see how Dag would react to the last statement. Although he appeared unconvinced, he was still listening.

"But in my behavior, both in business and in my private life," Jay continued, "I scrupulously, and I mean *scrupulously*, avoid the slightest hint of ever basing any of my thinking on someone else's race."

"I'm no racist," Dag said.

"Well, neither am I." Jay was surprised to find his throat had again gone dry. Once more, he reached for his water glass. He took another sip, straining the ice with his teeth. He wondered if Dag had exposed something that festered within him. Was it possible he harbored attitudes that were on some level racist? He held the notion up to the light, scrutinized it from every conceivable angle. He dismissed the idea. "Now that we've got that cleared up, I'll tell you two things. The first is that I'll talk to Church and, while I can't promise he'll change his mind, I'll get him to give the situation another look."

"I appreciate that."

"The second thing is that I'd like you to come as my guest to the Obama dinner."

This was the sign that Jay viewed Dag as a social equal to the extent that he was welcome at his table for the presidential event. No other player on the team would be attending. Dag nodded, considering the proposal. He did not appear awed by the opportunity to meet the first black president.

"Church and his wife are coming as our guests."

Dag was intrigued by the information that Church Scott, a man he esteemed, a coach who had won an NBA championship in his previous job, would attend.

"Do you know Steve Ballmer?" Jay asked. Dag did not know Steve Ballmer. "He runs a little company called Microsoft, and he loves basketball."

"I know them," Dag said.

"He'll be there, too. It wouldn't hurt to know a guy like Steve."

They passed the remainder of the meal in an exchange of irrelevancies marked by the low-grade dyspepsia Jay suffered from having been put in such a discomfiting position and Dag's veiled pleasure at having effectively toyed with what he perceived to be the owner's self-regard. Dag accepted the invitation to the Obama dinner as a show of good faith.

"One more thing," Jay said. "I know I'm a little formal around the team, but you've been playing with us for four seasons, you're the main guy, I think you and I have a terrific relationship."

"I think we do, too."

"Well, I want you to call me Jay."

"Okay, Jay," Dag said, with a trace of amusement. He knew certain owners demanded that everyone address them as "Mr." and others were all "Call-me-Bill-or-Bob-or-Stan." He always felt strange calling Jay "Mr. Gladstone."

The check came. Dag chatted with the manager at the front of the room while Jay, in his capacity as a club officer, briefly spoke with a couple of diners about the dues assessment levied on each member for capital improvements. He hoped to be the club president when the incumbent's term was up and asked for their votes.

The club manager was a slender Frenchman with a fastidious air about him named Jean-Pierre. He produced a small camera and asked Dag if it was all right to take a picture with him. A waiter was pressed into service as a photographer and as Dag posed he watched Jay engage in tableside banter with the other members and marveled at how at home he seemed. Maybe Dag would ask Jay about becoming a member. Not that he wanted to be one. But he'd like to see how Jay would react to the possibility.

"Mr. Gladstone, it is such a pleasure to see Mr. Maxwell at the club," Jean-Pierre said when Jay joined them. "Mr. Maxwell, I hope to see you again. You are my favorite player."

Dag beamed and thanked the club manager.

"I didn't pay you to say that, did I?" Jay asked.

"You did not pay me, Mr. Gladstone," Jean-Pierre said with a laugh.

The player and the owner parted with a handshake in front of the club.

"We're kings, you and me," Jay said.

"I appreciate that."

"Never forget how lucky we are."

From his great height, Dag gazed directly into Jay's eyes. He placed a large hand on the smaller man's shoulder. "We're real, you and me," Dag said, situating Jay in their shared moral universe, one in which both were virtuous actors. "We do what's right."

Jay nodded. That was his north star. But he wasn't sure if Dag meant it.

Trey answered his brother's texted order and produced the McLaren two minutes later, freshly washed, waxed, and with a brimming tank. To Dag's relief, the car did not reek of weed. He climbed behind the wheel and pointed in the direction of the team's practice facility in New Jersey. On the ride through the Holland Tunnel Dag thought about what he had said at the club. He didn't believe the man was an actual racist, any more than anyone in his position was an actual racist. But Dag was an intuitive enough negotiator to understand the value of destabilizing one's counterpart. If he could get the owner to consider the slightest possibility that his thinking could be racially motivated, it might cause enough of a fissure to enable Dag to slip through and collect the riches he believed were due him. Who cared if he used gamesmanship to achieve his ends. If he could get Jay to bite on the fake, well, isn't that what players of Dag's caliber did? And Jay Gladstone probably *was* a little bit racist. Wasn't everyone? Jay had said so himself.

When the car emerged from the darkness of the tunnel, Dag squinted in the light and reached into the glove compartment for his sunglasses. Nestled next to them was a handgun. What was it doing there?

"You got a permit for this?" Trey laughed, which Dag did not appreciate. "Dang, Trey, some cop stops you cause you're a black man driving a McLaren, they gonna find this mother-fucker, haul your ass to jail, and then it's *my* name in the papers."

"How am I supposed to protect you?"

"I didn't say don't have a piece, just get a damn license."

Frustrated with the way his day was going, Dag slipped the sunglasses on. He needed to think about how he was going to hoist his team on his back and haul them into the playoffs and didn't have time to worry about his brother's poor judgment.

When Dag's phone began to vibrate in his pocket his mood was so foul he nearly chose not to see who it was, but curiosity got the better of him. He looked at the screen and saw the phone number of his Los Angeles home. Why was his wife calling him? Probably to discuss some minor detail of the divorce. They had already settled all the larger ones. Dag did not particularly want to speak with Brittany but a sense of duty impelled him to press the icon that would initiate the conver-sation. When he said, "What's up?" and heard the voice of his oldest child, six-year-old D'Angelo Jr., Dag's attitude immedi-ately improved. But his son sounded miserable.

CHAPTER ELEVEN

The ring of cigar smoke hung over the ship-sized desk like a billboard advertising the prosperity and influence of the hefty man from whose mouth it had disgorged. The office was capacious, the walls adorned with an impressive display of sports memorabilia: framed uniforms belonging to New York baseball legends Mickey Mantle (#7), Willie Mays (#24), and as if that wasn't enough to humble every male who stood on the carpet, there was the jersey Jackie Robinson (#42) wore during the 1955 season. Accompanying the baseball troika was a Giants jersey worn by Y.A. Tittle (#14) and a white Jets jersey that had belonged to Joe Namath (#12). Representing the Rangers was the jersey of the player who led them to their first Stanley Cup in forty years, Mark Messier (#11). There was a Plexiglas-encased basketball used in the NBA Finals signed by Wilt Chamberlain. A vintage pinball machine with a Yankees theme was mounted on a short plinth and lit as if it were the Magna Carta. The décor reflected the taste of Jay's cousin Franklin Gladstone, the fifty-five-year-old mogul currently blowing smoke rings from the Havana grasped in his meaty paw.

Jay stood in front of Franklin's desk, a folder in his hand, watching as Franklin shifted in his chair. He could tell Franklin was struggling to present a serene exterior and the breeziness implied by smoke rings was feigned. Through the cigar smoke, Jay could discern the sharp scent of his cousin's cologne. He was still smarting from his lunch with Dag and would rather have delayed talking to Franklin, but the forensic accountant had informed him that his cousin had once again moved funds in an unauthorized manner and so a confrontation was no longer avoidable.

"You're going to have me audited?"

"I didn't say that. Come on, Franklin."

"That's what you're implying."

"The financial reports you provided are cursory," Jay said, waving the cigar smoke away. He dropped the folder on the desk where it landed next to a framed family photograph of Franklin, his wife Marcy, and their three children, taken on a yacht somewhere in the Mediterranean. Gazing directly at Franklin, Jay placed his forefinger on the folder. "You can't expect me to accept these."

Franklin tapped the end of his cigar on the rim of an ashtray commemorating one of George Foreman's heavyweight title bouts. He appeared to consider what Jay had just told him. Franklin Gladstone's parents named him for Franklin Delano Roosevelt, who deftly exercised authority with a patrician ease the namesake's mother and father hoped their son might learn to emulate. These hopes had not borne fruit. Since he was a kid, Franklin had been burly. Now his bulk had swelled, and his cardiologist wanted him to lose forty pounds. All of it was sheathed in a conservative gray suit custom-tailored for Franklin in London from enough material to craft a pup tent. A violet shirt with starched white cuffs and collar, and a yellow patterned tie, all accented by a pair of cuff links fashioned from tiny crossed hockey sticks rendered in forty karat gold. His fingernails were manicured and buffed to a pearly sheen, and when he ran them through his thick, curly hair, they looked like tiny fish darting beneath the surface of a stream. Placing his hands on his lap, he twisted his thick gold wedding band.

"You asked to see the reports," Franklin said. "Those are the reports."

"And I didn't say I was going to have you audited. Give me a break, all right? I don't want to do that."

Franklin was two years younger than Jay. Their fathers had passed them the keys to the kingdom—the millions had multiplied to billions—and decreed their progeny be co-heads of what was no longer simply a real estate company called Gladstone Properties but rather, the Gladstone Group. Not satisfied with having built one of the most prominent real estate organizations in New York, the founders had diversified. As the boisterous 1980s shifted into overdrive, the elder Gladstones bought and sold companies in oil, shipping, and fast food. When the wheeling and dealing slowed down, the businesses they found most conducive to continued growth and minimal headaches, after real estate: hotels and gaming.

The fathers had been famously close, celebrating Thanksgiving every year at Jerry's house, and Passover at Bingo's; even vacationing together, sailing off the Maine coast, Colorado for skiing, grand tours of Europe, all with their families in tow. Jay and Franklin bonded as kids, more siblings than cousins, with Jay in the dominant role. When the boys' families socialized, the two threw a baseball around, or played penny-ante poker, or shared purloined copies of *Playboy*. Summers, they attended the same sports camp in the Berkshires where counselors organized sons of Brookline, West Orange, and Great Neck into "tribes" of Iroquois, Apaches, and Mohicans. But when Jay went off to the University of Pennsylvania, the relationship shifted. He had been the superior athlete, had performed better in school, had a college girlfriend who looked like a movie star, and Franklin—who eventually escaped to Arizona State University—grew tired of dwelling in the shadow of his more athletic, taller, and better-looking cousin.

Franklin passed his college years in a haze of beer and marijuana. He stayed away from home for extended periods of time, often traveling during school vacations to the beaches of Florida, Mexico, and the Caribbean. Reports of his cousin reached him: Jay made dean's list, spent his junior year at Oxford, got accepted to the MBA program at Wharton—but the two rarely saw one another and when they did the easy rapport of their boyhood was gone. Franklin recognized that Jay would shine in any circumstance, but it was his unspoken fear that in the eyes of the world he was not his cousin's equal. There were those that would not be bothered by this, would accept their good fortune and play a lot of golf. Franklin Gladstone was not one of them. When Jay was assigned to work on the development of a high-status property, Franklin viewed it as a personal slight. If someone in the organization did not show him the respect he believed was his due, Franklin would try to have that person reassigned or fired. This behavior did not go over well with Jerry and Bingo, who reminded him that they were a family business, one that treated non-family members like family. Employees of the firm preferred to work with Jay, who by the time he was thirty was developing real estate projects of his own and not paying much attention to his cousin.

Two princes of such different dispositions could not hold sway over the Gladstone realm together, and their prescient fathers determined that, in the service of family peace, they would divide the responsibilities. It was with this in mind that Jay and Bebe were tasked with managing the real estate empire—the family developed and owned projects in New York, Philadelphia, San Francisco, Los Angeles, and Seattle—and Franklin was to supervise the hotels and gaming.

The Gladstones owned the Omniverse Hotel and Casino in Las Vegas, but the majority of their gaming interests were in Hong Kong, Singapore, and Macao. Because of this geography, it was a challenge for Jay to stay abreast of what Franklin was doing. The incriminating email that caught his attention several days earlier (sent by an employee in the Hong Kong office) reported a twenty-million-dollar loan Franklin had taken from their gambling operation, something he was required to report to his partners. No family member was allowed to use any of the businesses as a personal piggy bank. All employees of the Gladstone Group were required to sign a morals clause, and this included Jay and Franklin. In their case, a violation would result in removal from the board of directors and cessation of day-to-day involvement in the business. Jay didn't need to remind Franklin of this.

What made Jay a virtuoso was his awareness of when to dominate overtly and when to cloak his intentions in bluff geniality. To relieve the tension, he asked, "How was Macao?" Franklin had overseen construction on a state-of-the-art casino, cantilevered over the South China Sea.

"Ahead of schedule," Franklin said. He relit his cigar with a lighter camouflaged as a baseball, the flame reflected on the face of the chunky watch he wore. "I was on New York time the whole two days I was there. The new jet makes it a breeze." The family had recently upgraded to the latest model Gulfstream 6, which Jay refused to fly on for ecological reasons. "Hey, tough loss against the Celtics."

"Heartbreaking," Jay agreed.

"They need a shake-up."

"I'm meeting the coach to talk about the draft this afternoon," Jay said.

"You gonna fire him if they miss the playoffs?"

"I'll owe him eight million to not coach if I do."

Like many American men, Jay and Franklin were most comfortable together when talking about sports. Wins and losses, records set and broken, who was the best of all time at what exalted skill formed a buoyant language that obscured the abyss between them.

"Licensed robbery," Franklin said.

Jay thought once more about mentioning the loan but decided against it. He did not want to reveal the depths of his suspicions. "If you don't mind, I'd like to see a more detailed report by next week, okay?"

"It's like you don't trust me."

"Come on, Franklin. It's called discharging fiduciary responsibility."

"I'm just saying." Franklin looked directly at Jay and made a point of holding his gaze. "We're like Mantle and Maris, aren't we?"

"In what way?"

"We're both power hitters," Franklin said. "But we're on the same team and our team is winning."

"Did you not hear what I said?"

"I'm flying down to Austin this afternoon. I'll deal with it when I get back."

This answer did not satisfy Jay, but he was not going to press further right now. Franklin was on notice. If the surreptitious loan went unremarked in the next report, Jay would consult his lawyer.

"What are you doing in Texas?"

"I'm meeting with the governor down there to talk about the casino business," he said in the voice of Cary Grant. A tic of Franklin's that got on Jay's nerves was his tendency to slip into dated celebrity impressions. In the persona of the star of *North By Northwest*, he continued, "It's a swell business but the old chap doesn't like it and I'm going to change his mind."

This tendency of Franklin's—he also did mediocre versions of actors like James Cagney, Tony Curtis, and Bing Crosby—had a long history. After graduating from college, he moved to Los Angeles for a year to pursue a career as an impressionist. At open mic nights, he would enthusiastically perform his act, but interest in his repertoire of characters—which by then had grown to include Burt Lancaster, Kirk Douglas, and Bette Davis, among other equally anachronistic points of reference (one historically-inclined heckler had shouted a request for Fiorello La Guardia)—was as limited as his skill set, so he returned to New York and his sinecure in the family business. Franklin's lifelong interest in mimicry suggested to Jay that he lacked something essential, that his core was a ball of string whose threads were always threatening to unravel.

"Are you going to be back for Passover?"

"I w-w-w-wouldn't miss it," Jimmy Stewart stuttered.

The ritual of celebrating holidays together had survived the deaths of Bingo (2009), and Jerry (2004), thus Jay had inherited Passover. As often happens with the passing of the older generation, family traditions that had been in place for decades started to fray, and the gatherings had begun to feel increasingly obligatory.

"Then I'll see you at the Seder," Jay said.

As he turned to go, Franklin stopped him.

"One other thing."

Jay tried to hide his impatience. "Yes?"

"I've been studying with the rabbi at our shul. I don't like his politics around Israel, they're a little too liberal, but he's the genuine article. Anyway, I wanted to ask you if it was all right if I lead the service this year. I know you don't take it that seriously."

Jay was not a godly man. His parents were revolving door Jews, in at Rosh Hashanah, out at Yom Kippur, and he had inherited their secularism. Still, it was not easy for him to control the degree to which this request annoyed him. The family always celebrated Passover at Bingo's house, and that tradition had passed to Jay.

"First, I do take it seriously, and since it's at our house, I'm going to lead the service. But if you want to flip Passover and Thanksgiving next year, we can discuss it."

Franklin nodded, concealing his resentment as efficiently as Jay had hidden his pique.

When Jay left the office, Franklin exhaled, a long airstream of relief. Who does that prick think he is, to come in here like some puffed up dictator and make demands? Does he think I'm one of those pituitary cases he overpays to play for him on that pathetic excuse of a basketball team?

Franklin swung around and gazed out the window. The vista took in Park Avenue up to Harlem and beyond—its median bursting with the yellows and reds of spring annuals— the greensward of Central Park to the west, and to the north the steel necklace of the George Washington Bridge. In the other direction, he could see the gray ribbon of the East River, and beyond that the apartments, warehouses, and cemeteries of Queens all the way to the airports and Jamaica Bay. Whenever Franklin felt diminished, mishandled, or not accorded the respect he believed he deserved, he liked to lean back in his ergonomic desk chair and spot the individual build-ings that comprised the nucleus of the family portfolio and think yes, yes, yes, I am a Gladstone.

But when Franklin really wanted to feel like a god, he would stand on the roof of the building and take in the three-hundred-and-sixty-degree view. There he imagined himself as an heir to Howard Roark, the main character of his favorite novel, *The Fountainhead* (he had listened to the audiobook five times), only with higher status because he owned considerably more property than Howard Roark, a lowly architect when you got down to it. Franklin hired and fired the Howard Roarks of the world. Grabbing his phone, he called his sons Ari and Ezra and summoned them to the roof.

The April afternoon had warmed, and the sun hit Franklin's ruddy face. When Bingo and Jerry divided the business and

Franklin ascended to the leadership of the half bequeathed him, he had ordered the construction of an observation deck. From this aerie, he could make out the family holdings not just in the tonier uptown precincts, but also downtown and in Brooklyn. There were Gladstone apartment houses on the west side and the east side, both luxury buildings and structures that, in Manhattan, passed for affordable, and office buildings all over town with Fortune 500 companies as tenants. Together these holdings were as impressive a portfolio of real estate as any currently held in private hands. And then there were the less prestigious properties in Queens and Westchester, which he only thought about when there were problems. Like this week, when a police officer in White Plains had killed someone at one of their apartment houses. Franklin wasn't going to worry about that unless it became a Gladstone issue and he couldn't imagine how that could ever come to pass.

Since the family's New York real estate portfolio was Jay's responsibility, none of these impressive edifices could provide him with the electric charge he got from his successes in the glittery world of hotels and gaming. The casino in Las Vegas and the expansion of the family footprint to Singapore, Hong Kong, and Macao, these were his alone. And now he intended to move into a new area. Franklin had a dream, and that dream was to be the owner of a professional sports franchise. That his cousin Jay had managed to purchase an NBA team magnified his already finely-honed sense of grievance. For all of Franklin's wealth, he was still capable of feeling diminished, and that was the role Jay had assumed in Franklin's life: Diminisher-in-Chief. It wasn't anything Jay did on purpose, but lately, his very existence riled his younger cousin. Jay had overshadowed Franklin in youth, been a better athlete, gone to a more prestigious college, and grabbed the glittering prize— presidency of the Gladstone real estate division.

As if all of that wasn't bad enough, Jay had, with his fortune, made a bold and risky bet on the performance of gold in the commodity markets and Franklin, who secretly harbored a nagging belief in Jay's superiority, had followed his shrewd cousin's lead. Jay rode gold like a dazzling rocket, and when he liquidated his position, he poured eye-popping eight-figure profits into NBA ownership. Franklin, thinking Jay had bailed too soon, held his gold position, suffered through the precipitous crash of the gold market in 2011 that knocked his holdings down forty percent in value, and was still waiting for the recovery. This meant Jay was now significantly wealthier than Franklin, another blow to his delicate spirit.

And then there was the matter of the social realm where Jay was a sought-after member of boards and private clubs, and now had a stunningly sexy, much younger wife. These baubles had eluded Franklin, and after years of enduring this condition, he developed a degree of umbrage at the way things had turned out.

In the past decade, Franklin put together a group of investors and attempted to purchase the National Football League's Indianapolis Colts. He withdrew his NFL bid after the league commissioner informed him that he didn't have the requisite votes on the ownership committee to be approved. (Translation: We don't want someone like you in our club.) When his attempt to become an NFL owner did not succeed, he divested himself of partners—Franklin Gladstone could not comprehend that he was the problem—and tried to buy the Los Angeles Dodgers. He blew the Dodger deal when his nerve failed him once the price climbed to two billion. These disappointments only heightened his need to own a pro team.

"Dad!"

Franklin turned around to see his identical twin sons, Ari and Ezra. It was Ezra who had spoken. Sometimes their voices were the only way Franklin could tell them apart, Ezra's a slightly lower register. It was easier when they played high school hockey. Ezra was #14, and Ari was #22. Franklin wished they still wore numbered jerseys. Broad-shouldered, pumped up from the gym—the kind of physique that too much beer will quickly swell to fat—and a couple of inches taller than their father, they inhabited their tailored suits like beachwear. Ari and Ezra were so relaxed, everything they wore seemed like beachwear. They had attended the University of Miami together and exuded the country club casualness of men who had accomplished a great deal and were now savoring life, despite having accomplished nothing other than being born Gladstones. Their thick dark hair was gelled, and both sported a three-day stubble. Designer sunglasses raked their full faces. They could have been vacationing hit men from the Mossad.

"What are we doing on the roof?" Ezra asked.

"My father used to bring me up here when he wanted to talk privately."

"You told us that, like, a million times," Ari said.

Franklin did not appreciate his son's tone. "What, am I interrupting something?"

"No, no," Ezra said. "Take it easy."

One way he was able to tell his boys apart was that Ari got lippy. Ezra never did. Sometimes he wanted to smack his son—Jerry Gladstone had belted Franklin a couple of times, always with an open hand, never a closed fist, and he didn't suffer for it—but he could never bring himself to strike his wisenheimer son.

"I ask you to come up, you come up," Franklin said. "And if I want to talk about Grandpa, who busted his ass for this family, you two are damn well gonna listen."

Ari hadn't meant to set his father off. "We're listening," he said. Ezra chimed in with the information that they had been on the Internet checking out potential development opportunities in Jersey City.

"You're supposed to be researching gaming regulations in Texas," Franklin said.

"We're doing that, too," Ari said.

"So, what's with Jersey City?" Franklin was already off message. Could these two not just follow orders?

"We want to develop," Ezra said. "Be like Grandpa and Uncle Bingo."

"Ch-ching!" Ari said.

"I want to talk to you guys about something else." They looked at him like a pair of spaniels waiting for their bowls to be filled. "What's your favorite sport?"

Together, they said, "Football."

"After football."

Together again: "Cross-training."

"Cross-training?" their father said. "What?"

"Totally," Ari said. "It rocks."

"What about hockey?" their father asked.

"We love hockey," Ari said.

"Cross-training's not even a sport," Franklin said, shaking his head. Sometimes he wondered if his sons had what it took to succeed. "All right. Listen. I'm thinking about making a play for the Buffalo franchise in the National Hockey League."

The mouths of the twins gaped open at the same time. When they spoke, it was to express amazement and delight. They could barely tolerate the awesomeness this heralded.

"I think we can get it for around half a billion," Franklin told them.

"Chump change," Ari said as if he were used to hearing these amounts every day. But he was not, the boys rarely granted access to the big-time dealing in which their father and Jay engaged.

"And if we get it," Franklin said, "I want to move it to Miami."

The news had traveled from great to greatest. The twins

loved Miami. White sand beaches, sweet cigarette boats, tight bikinis stretched over the comeliest of female bodies! The flames gathering behind their eyes were about to morph into full-fledged conflagrations when Ari said, "Dad, wait." He was still trying to get back on his father's good side after pissing him off earlier. "I totally love the idea, but there's, like, no hockey tradition down there. It's hella Latinos. They're into soccer and boxing, right? Hockey not so much."

"Cause they don't know it yet!" Ezra said. "Dude, they got a hockey team in Phoenix, and that place is all cactus and Mexicans."

"That's racist," Ari said, not that he cared. He did, however, have a vague perception that invoking an ethnic group in a general way had become unacceptable—even though he had done exactly that a moment earlier when commenting on the demographics of Miami.

"How is that racist?" his less sensitive sibling asked. "There's hella Mexicans in Arizona. It's a fact."

"Never mind about Arizona," Franklin said, ending the argument. "Ezra's right. Someone's gonna bring hockey to South Beach—it might as well be us."

Us? Did he say us? Was this going to be their project? All thoughts of properties in Jersey City were instantly forgotten.

"Does Jay know?" Ezra asked.

"This has nothing to do with him." Franklin's sons exchanged a conspiratorial glance. Something forbidden was happening, and they were thrilled at what appeared to be their inclusion. "There are other potential buyers, and our best chance of success is an all-cash bid."

The boys were not certain how to process this information. Although both boasted the title of vice-president, neither was privy to the inner workings of any aspect of the business. They had no real idea how much cash their father was able to access.

"Dope," Ezra said. Ari nodded.

Given their limited understanding, it most definitely sounded dope.

"If I buy the team, the three of us are going to run it."

When Ezra heard this, his knees wobbled.

Ari let out a whoop, then: "Holy shit!"

"Now, listen. Jay? I don't want him to get wind of this."

Together, Ari and Ezra asked, "Why?"

"Trust me; I just don't. The guy runs his basketball team, does he discuss it with us? No, he does not. Makes all kinds of decisions, doesn't come into my office and ask my opinion. I'm not saying he should. That team is his business. This one? Ours!"

Franklin had never felt so convinced of his ability to escape his cousin's shadow. Now he gazed past the twins to the city, spread out before them like a glorious banquet. He and his boys were going to grab their plates and claim a place at the table. And if the table they wound up at happened to be in Miami, at least it wasn't Buffalo.

"Let Jay find out when he sees it on ESPN," Franklin said. Ari and Ezra looked at one another and nodded. They could do that. "Don't tell Bebe, don't tell Boris. Don't mention it to anyone."

"We won't," Ari assured him.

Franklin extended his right hand, the light glinting off the diamond on his pinkie like a celestial benediction, and both sons, as they had done many times since they were boys, placed theirs on top of his. "Are you guys with me?"

Oh, they were. They certainly were.

Franklin teed them up: "We are—"

"The Gladstones!" the three men shouted, and threw their arms jubilantly in the air. A flock of seagulls wheeled below them. A cumulonimbus cloud scudded overhead propelled by the gusty spring wind. The observation platform, bathed in sunlight seconds ago, was in shadow.

"Can we get off the roof now?" Ari asked, shivering. "I'm freezing my cojones off."

"Cojones, bro!" Ezra shouted. "You're gonna kill it in Miami."

The twins slapped palms as their father cradled a make-believe machine gun and in the Cuban-accented voice of Al Pacino as Scarface hollered, "Jay, say hello to my little friend." Then Franklin sprayed Manhattan with bullets from his imaginary Uzi before realizing that if he wanted his sons to respect him the way he respected his father, perhaps waving an imaginary machine gun around the rooftop was not the best way to do it. He immediately ceased the pantomime, thumped his sons on their backs, and reminded them that the most important thing was family.

CHAPTER TWELVE

I t was late afternoon and as Jay's legs pumped on the elliptical machine in the executive gym, he could not stop thinking about the lunch with Dag. His trainer had left five minutes earlier and he was alone. A cable news financial show flickered on the television monitor above him, but he ignored it as his mind ranged back to his youth. How could anyone, much less one of his players, insinuate that his attitudes about race were in any way questionable? When it came to the position occupied by "people of color" (a label he believed would eventually be as out of date as "colored," but nonetheless employed because if others accepted it who was he to rock the boat?) in America, Jay held that no white person was more sensitive, kindhearted, and benevolent than he.

Witness:

The summer Louis Armstrong's horn sounded its last blue note and the south tower of the World Trade Center pierced the clouds above Manhattan to become the tallest building on the planet, sixteen-year-old Harold Jay Gladstone got dunked on at a basketball camp in the Catskill Mountains. It was 1971 and to the greater world what happened on that sweltering afternoon had no larger meaning, but Jay learned a painful lesson that remained with him for the rest of his life: However much an individual might believe himself to be at the zenith of his power, capability, and influence, he is always one small slip away from ruin.

A skinny white kid from the broad-lawned New York

suburbs, land of golf and tennis, dry martinis, private swimming pools, European vacations, elite colleges, and psychoanalysis, Jay was devoted to all things "Negro," a label still acceptable then. Understand: He wasn't a clown about it. He had too much deeply held respect to approach the subject from that angle. Jay didn't dress black and didn't make the embarrassing mistake of so many white boys that tried to mimic the speech, the walk, the innumerable signifiers of blackness, but was entranced by the remarkable culture conjured by African-Americans in all its rowdy proliferation.

On a typical Saturday, he rode his ten-speed bicycle from his home in Scarsdale—a town where the minority population consisted of a three-foot-tall ceramic lawn jockey standing sentinel in front of a neighbor's center hall Colonial—to the nearby and far more diverse city of White Plains where he bought a ticket at the Palace Theater on Main Street to absorb the lessons of *Shaft*, get a slice and a soda at Nicky's Pizzeria, purchase the Black Panther Party newspaper from an intimidating street vendor, and then pedal back to his family's five-bedroom house, where he slouched on his bed beneath a five-foot-high poster of Jimi Hendrix immolating a Fender Stratocaster, and eagerly devoured the fevered accounts of violent inner city life. Three years earlier he'd been the only kid in his eighth-grade class to read Eldridge Cleaver's memoir.

"You should look at this," Jay said to Claudie one day after school, offering her his worn copy of *Soul On Ice*. They were standing outside his bedroom door and he had to raise his voice to be heard over the whirr of the Electrolux vacuum cleaner. A black woman from Georgia, Claudie had been working for the Gladstones for as long as Jay could remember. Ancient and blue haired, she fixed him with a quizzical stare. Jay offered her the book but she shook her head. The boy was puzzled. The possibility that the housekeeper might be perplexed by the son of her wealthy employers purveying the literature of revolution while she tried to clean the upstairs hallway eluded him completely.

The stultifying traditions that surrounded him, the world of his parents and grandparents, the round of brain-numbing Seders, High Holy Days services that droned on for hours, and bar mitzvahs where his schoolmates in madras jackets, pressed slacks, and loafers (boys), paisley or polka dot dresses and Courreges boots (girls), awkwardly Watusied around the dance floor to anemic bands that played deracinated versions of current AM radio hits, held none of the outlaw brio he craved. That resided in Harlem, a place known to Jay only through the finger-snapping novels of Chester Himes, an author to whom he had been alerted by a sympathetic librarian.

What Jay lived for—more than his tattered Chester Himes paperbacks, *Soul Train*, and seeing the Supremes in the flesh on a family trip to Expo 67 in Montreal—was basketball, specifically the New York Knicks. A year earlier they had won their first NBA title and the liquid way the team played the game, the seamless passing, cutting, and shooting in which they engaged with the heedless swing of the jazz cats his father savored, was the Platonic ideal of what sport was meant to represent. It would not be an exaggeration to say Jay Gladstone worshipped them. On winter nights, he reverently listened to Marv Albert's Brighton Beach boom on WNBC emanating from the transistor radio nestled next to his pillow intoning names of deities like Frazier, Bradley, and Reed, and he would envision himself on the court at Madison Square Garden running with his heroes. "Gladstone from the corner . . . " he imagined the famous sportscaster declaim. Then: "Yes!"

The previous April he had taken the Metro-North train into the city, devoured a sub at Blimpie for dinner, and furtively purchased a ticket from a scalper outside the Garden, where he attended game seven of the Eastern Conference semifinal

playoff series when the Knicks squared off against Earl
Monroe and the Baltimore Bullets. From his perch in the nosebleed seats young Jay hollered himself hoarse, throat in tatters
as he willed the Knicks to victory and a place in the NBA
Finals. The transformation he underwent that night, the sense
of abandonment, of release, of beatitude was no less profound
for him than what the Baal Shem Tov, about whom he had
learned in Sunday school, experienced during his mystic
visions three centuries earlier in the forests of Poland.

A shard of history and it belonged to him.

And Jay played the game, oh, how he played the game. It
wasn't that he was particularly talented, although he harbored
a fantasy that he could achieve a certain level of competence,
but his devotion to improvement knew no bounds. There was
a backboard mounted on the garage, and it was there that Jay
worked on his skills in the morning, after school, and on weekends. His sister rebounded the ball and passed it to him so he
could shoot without breaking his rhythm. Days were measured
in jump shots, layups, and free throws, dribbling drills where
the ball went behind his back and through his legs, all of which
were put to use in an endless round of playground pickup
games.

Jay started playing organized ball in the fourth grade,
played on the freshman team, and then on the junior varsity. In
the autumn of 1971 the varsity squad loomed. While not quite
elite, he was talented, and scrappy enough to play at the next
level so his ascension to the empyrean realm—letter jackets,
cheerleaders, and the approbation of the entire community
that crammed into the gym on game days (his adolescent mind
swam at the richness of this vision)—was a near given.

For a year, desperate to improve his jumping ability, Jay had
been plodding around with weights laced to his ankles.

"Watch this," Jay commanded his sister one humid afternoon when the two of them were in the driveway of their large,

Tudor-style home. They were playing with a basketball made from rubber. Gym shorts and gray T-shirts soaked with perspiration. The gardener had been there in the morning and the air was awash with the sweet smell of freshly cut grass. Jay turned on a nearby hose and wet the ball. Then he stretched his fingers over the rubber surface and palmed it. Bebe's eyes widened. She asked how he did it. This was not a skill typically found in the repertoire of an average-sized suburban teenager. To his sibling it seemed like magic. Jay couldn't palm a regulation leather ball, but if the ball was rubber, and it was wet, he could now get it to stay on his hand—secret knowledge gleaned after a recent rainfall when he astonished himself by picking it up off the ground without putting his hand under it. It felt supernatural.

Humid air filled his lungs as he inhaled deeply and focused his eyes on the rim looming ten feet over the asphalt. Five running steps and he leapt toward the basket, elevated, and—was his entire wrist over the rim?—threw down a one-handed dunk. Bebe screamed. They slapped moist palms.

Jay grinned and with practiced aplomb said, "Damn right."

Bebe asked if that was the first time he had ever dunked it.

"Been practicing. Last week I did it with a baseball. Then yesterday I dunked a cantaloupe."

She wondered, "Does Mom know you were playing with fruit?"

Their mother, raised by European immigrants, had a phobia about wasting food.

"I ate it."

Jay Gladstone was still fifteen (his birthday was in early August). A scrawny kid, short for a basketball player, and he had dunked. It didn't matter that the ball was rubber, not the regulation leather, or that he had slicked it down so the surface would stick to his hand. He *dunked* the ball. The long months of tramping around with weights strapped to his lower extremities had worked. Jay had transformed himself into that most lofty category of basketball players, a category rarely breached by white people—he was a *leaper*. There were stories he heard of New York City playground legends like Herman "The Helicopter" Knowings and Earl Manigault, men that could pluck a silver dollar from the top of a backboard. He did not expect to achieve those dizzying heights, had no hope that he would ever tomahawk (two-handed) dunk, the ultimate agreed-upon sign of basketball machismo. But he swelled with a pride he had not felt since he flawlessly read from the Torah on the day of his bar mitzvah.

When it was time to get a summer job after his sophomore year in high school, Jay was adamant that he didn't want to commute into the city to work at Gladstone Properties. His father, to his surprise, took this in stride. "As long as you earn some money," he said, "you can dig ditches." Bingo Gladstone was gregarious, the kind of man who would strike up conversations with strangers, and one morning when he and Jay stood in line at Bagel Haven to pick up lox and a dozen onion bialys for Sunday brunch he said to the owner, "Hey, my number one needs a summer job. You think he'd be a good bagel maker?" For three dollars and twenty-five cents an hour Jay was enlisted to show up at Bagel Haven before dawn five days a week and assist in baking the cornucopia of bagels, bialys, and twists offered at the shop. He didn't mind the work. After studying as hard as he did during the school year it was a welcome relief to do something less intellectually taxing, even if he had to be awake before the birds began to chirp. And he earned enough money that by the end of August he was able to pay his own way to Walt Frazier's basketball camp. Jay esteemed the entire New York Knicks roster but Walt "Clyde" Frazier was his personal idol. Consummate smooth operator, sine qua non of gliding, sliding precision, a sinuous and mellow tenor saxophone solo sprung to vivid life, Clyde Frazier was the athletic godhead to which Jay prostrated.

It was there at the camp that he found himself on an outdoor court surrounded by over a hundred teenaged boys (and Clyde, for god sakes! Clyde was watching!), crouched at the top of the key, guarding the best player on the opposing squad, with five seconds left in the championship game and his team up by one point.

Dave Bailey was a seventeen-year-old black kid, six foot three and explosive. He was a star at Mount Vernon High School, and the buzz in the camp was that at least three Division I college programs were recruiting him. Jay had switched on to Bailey because the teammate who was guarding him had been flattened by a pick. Dave Bailey sized Jay up as if he were eyeing a succulent morsel and faked left. When Jay didn't go for it, Bailey drove right with Jay stuck to his hip. Then the taller player bounded toward the basket. As he reared his arm to dunk, Jay, suffused with pride in having altered the ability of his body to perform feats heretofore impossible, secure in the belief that he could against all expectations stymie his high-flying opponent, and pulsing with adrenaline, leaped and extended his arm to block the shot. He met the ball five inches over the rim—higher than he had ever jumped, he was airborne!—where the force of Bailey's arm rocketed Jay's hand into the iron. The ball went through the rim and the screams emitted by the crowd, the festive sideline dancing to celebrate the burn inflicted, the mayhem unleashed by Bailey's ability to rule, all combined to make Jay ignore the throbbing in his hand where X-rays would later reveal a hairline fracture.

Dave Bailey? That kid looked as if he had dropped a quarter in the soda machine and a can of Coke appeared. What were you expecting? his eyes seemed to say. The impassive reaction to his splendid feat reflected a self-assurance the white suburban victim could only begin to imagine.

When Jay retreated to the nearby woods to escape the consoling words of his teammates, all of whom secretly thrilled it hadn't happened to them, he tried to believe the tears he could no longer hold back were from the pain he felt and not the humiliation.

"Good try, son," Clyde had said to him.

Clyde had said! In a voice like velvet! To him!

But despite this personal interaction with his hero, the hidden meaning of Good try's pat on the back was the inescapable punch in the nose of You failed.

Jay was devastated. He managed to choke out a response but the scrambled manner in which the words tumbled off his tongue led the Knick divinity to nod and smile sympathetically before turning his attention to another camper. Jay never forgot that when he tried to talk to Clyde Frazier he had sounded like an idiot. That night he lay awake in his bunk endlessly replaying what had happened and concluded consciously what he had been unwilling to admit. He had no business being on the court with a player as talented as Dave Bailey, and his entire infatuation with black culture struck him for the first time as a little silly. Black culture had dunked on him and Jay realized he would have to evolve into a better version of what he already was, and not try to be something else.

When he climbed off the elliptical machine after forty-five minutes, twilight inked Manhattan and Bebe was riding a stationary bicycle. He hadn't noticed her arrival. They greeted each other and Jay asked if she had plans this evening.

"Big date," she said. "It's why I'm in the gym."

"Who with?"

She told Jay that it was someone she met at a benefit, the first deputy director of the International Monetary Fund. As it happened, Jay was acquainted with him.

"We had an interesting conversation about Africa," he said. "Don't embarrass the family."

Bebe smiled and increased the resistance on the bike. She had been married and divorced twice—once to a bankruptcy lawyer and once to a political consultant active in Democratic politics—and had no children. Her marriages had foundered because Bebe Gladstone was accustomed to getting her way. The only man she would defer to was her brother. Being single did not concern her, and she viewed dating like a sport, something to do in order to keep in shape.

"Did you talk to Franklin?"

"I did," Jay said.

"And?"

He paused before answering and Bebe's expression darkened. "He was puffing on one of his cigars and he blew a lot of smoke."

"Franklin's the king of the metaphor," Bebe said, pumping away on the stationary bike.

"All I can say is I hope there's nothing to it."

"But you think there might be."

"He's complicated. I'll leave it at that."

"Unsatisfying."

"All will be revealed."

In the locker room Jay grabbed a clean towel from a freshly laundered and folded stack. The thought loop in his head rewound and he wondered whether he should have told the Dave Bailey story to Dag. It would have been a sign of humility. Boris was changing into workout clothes and they coordinated a time for the drive back to Westchester. While he was showering, it occurred to him that if he told Dag what had happened in the summer of 1971, the player might think that everything Jay had done in the world of basketball since then was built on revenge. You never knew how someone would react. Better to not have mentioned it.

Traffic was light when Boris steered the Mercedes over the Third Avenue Bridge and on to the Major Deegan Expressway. Jay had been looking for ways to further empower his young cousin—he had begun to view Boris as something of a surrogate son—and on the ride back to Bedford considered sharing his concerns about Franklin. But to communicate his suspicions might poison Boris's opinion and Jay, being a fair-minded man, did not want to risk that in the event they proved unfounded. He still wanted to believe that Franklin, while problematic, was not that devious.

CHAPTER THIRTEEN

I n the six months since they had entered the socially sanctioned, sadomasochistic rite known as marriage counseling, Christine Lupo and her husband Dominic had gone on over ten "dates" with each other. It was their therapist's idea and intended to reignite the absent spark in their nearly twenty-year relationship. These evenings invariably began in fragile stasis, as if both wife and husband were wary of doing or saying the wrong thing, but by the time they had consumed cocktails and a bottle of Pino Grigio, embers flickered, and they usually managed a moment or two of intimacy. This had not happened tonight.

They were at Castaldi's, a red sauce Italian restaurant in Harrison. Christine ordered the veal marsala. She consumed her usual vodka martini with an olive and a twist and was nursing a second glass of wine. The place was half full, local couples, soft conversations. The Lupos had been there for over an hour, and the district attorney had not yet broached the subject of her husband's transgressions. It would be easy to describe this behavior as sadistic, but sadism was not her motivation. As he droned on about his week, what was new at the office, an upcoming business trip to Europe intended to explore the possibility of importing a particular cheese he had recently discovered at a food convention he had allegedly attended the previous week, she tried to observe him with the objectivity of an anthropologist.

In his late forties with a lean face, Dominic Lupo's features had improved with age. His long nose was straight, and his lips curled slightly upward, so his resting expression appeared to be a smile. His hair was streaked with gray and had begun to recede, but that only seemed to heighten the acuity in his dark, lying eyes, the ones that concealed a sordid, hidden life that was about to be his undoing. Thrice weekly workouts at a Manhattan gym—she wondered if that was where he met the whore with whom he was betraying their marital vows—enabled him to retain his youthful physique. The tailored jacket he wore hung loosely over an open-collared oxford shirt that left the soft declivity in his neck just above his breastbone exposed. He gestured with his fingers as he spoke, pianist's fingers. That Dominic played some piano and could sing a little—Did he sing to the tramp? Lying in bed after the two of them had sex, did the cheating sonofabitch sing?—were qualities that Christine was drawn to when they first met. She remembered the long-ago night when, after several glasses of wine, he had sung an Abba song to her, "Dancing Queen," made up lyrics for the one he wanted to impress—*See that girl, watch that scene, her name's Christine, she's my dancing queen.* The thought that her husband might have been serenading another woman was making Christine nauseous.

He wore a diamond-encrusted gold wedding band, and she looked at it as he twirled the remains of his linguine al vongole. The man I've spent most of my adult life with, she thought as the veal marsala repeated and she covered her mouth, is blathering as if this were just another evening out; as if the two of us will have one like it next week and the week after. As if we'll finish dinner, have coffee, drive home, go to bed, then wake up and repeat the whole charade. How was it that I missed this sadly predictable midlife meltdown of my husband's? And why did I decide to confront him in a restaurant where I feel myself becoming ill? Yes, of course, the kids, the kids, always the kids, who do not need to overhear our marriage fragment while they try to do their homework. But I can't possibly drag this out any longer, let it go on another day, wake up next to him and pretend I have no idea what he has done to me, to our children, to our lives.

Her husband's lips were moving but, for the last minute, Christine had not heard a word. Now she focused her attention on what he was saying.

"This cheese we're going to import is like no artisanal cheese I've ever tasted." Cheese! Their world was ending, and Dominic was yammering about cheese! "A cross between Reggiano and manchego, pungent but not too, and the cheese maker creates this earthy flavor with only six months of aging." He stabbed a clam and stuck it in his mouth.

"Pungent but not too?" She said this in a way designed to see if he was paying attention to her. The remark meant to be banal.

"Exactly," he said, and confirmed her suspicion.

The waiter appeared at the table, and Christine requested a club soda. She indicated that he should clear her plate, but Dominic asked for more of the restaurant's "delicious rustic bread" so he could dip it in the broth which, he always told her, everyone knew was the best part of the meal. The waiter, an elfin man in his seventies with a crooner's head of dyed black hair, smiled wearily and retreated to the kitchen. She would inform Dominic what he could do with that delicious rustic bread.

"I'll bring some of the cheese home tomorrow," Dominic said, resuming where he had left off. She could tell he thought the evening had gone far better than anticipated.

"Don't bother."

He looked at her quizzically. "Why not? I think you'll like it."

Her briefcase rested on the floor. She reached down and removed a file that she placed on the table.

"What's this?" her husband said. "Vacation pictures?"

"Open it," she said, not smiling at his feeble joke.

He glanced at the contents. Dominic might have been obtuse but he was not stupid, and almost instantly the situation was clear. Several seconds elapsed before he spoke. She tasted the repeating veal marsala again, wondered where the waiter was with the club soda.

Finally, Dominic cleared his throat, swallowed, and said, "You had me followed?"

"You look at what's in that folder, and the first thing that comes out of your mouth is to ask me if I had you followed? Yes, I had you followed. Obviously. Is there anything else you'd like to say?"

The concentrated aggression his wife displayed neutered him. She watched him attempt to force disparate thoughts to cohere into something he could sell. Shock at having been exposed quickly gave way to irritation over having to deal with it, which yielded to shame about the whole situation. He nervously played with his wineglass.

She waited for him to say something.

Finally, he managed, "What do you want to do?"

She had decided it was imperative that he move out but unexpectedly found his discomfort energizing and wanted to prolong it before getting into logistics. To Christine's surprise, her husband brought his thumb and forefinger to the bridge of his nose, closed his eyes—those *deceitful* eyes—and pursed his lips. Apparently believing himself to be in sufficient control of the maelstrom within, he rested his chin on his fist, opened his eyes, and appeared to examine some breadcrumbs on the white tablecloth. Then he choked back a sob and gazed at the ceiling.

This display of emotion was not what Christine had expected. Like the trial lawyer she had been, she played this scene out in her mind, imagined the various permutations until she had some idea how it would unfold. Hostility and a request for a divorce, perhaps, apology and a plea, maybe, but not this, not tears. Not weeping at Castaldi's over his linguini al vongole. Dominic was still looking at the ceiling—at a light fixture? For an angel? He seemed as breakable as one of the clamshells littering the ceramic bowl in front of him. She had the urge to reach out and take his soft hand.

Dominic glanced guiltily at his wife, whose eyes looked like volcanoes.

"What can I say?" he managed, voice rough with suppressed feeling.

"That's the best you can do?"

He paused and looked away as she awaited his next foray. Pitiably, he said, "I'll do whatever you want." Then: "I love you."

"I love you?" Christine had not expected to hear that. What kind of a gullible dupe did he think she was? Certainly not the kind who would fall for a gambit so transparent.

"I need you to hear that what you've inflicted—" Here her voice gave out. Until now she had been completely in charge. Christine had let him talk about the cheese while she waited like a sniper. But now that the real conversation had begun, it was hard to stick to the dialogue she had so laboriously composed. After a wordless interval during which she willed her intestines to behave, she finally managed to say, "This is the worst day in my entire life." The sadness that started to arise shoved aside the well-cultivated fury, catching her off guard.

. . . *worst day in my entire life.*

That delicate petal floated between the couple, husband not daring to utter a word, wife unsure what to say next.

"You live for twenty years with someone," she said, her voice barely above a whisper, "and you want to believe them."

"That's right."

"And you want to believe in their decency, you know?"

"Yes, I do."

"And just when I need to be able to trust you the most—"

Christine sensed the waiter standing next to her, but when she looked up, she did not see the waiter. What she saw was a bearded toffee-skinned black man in his forties, dressed in a knee-length gray cotton robe buttoned to his neck. At least it appeared to be buttoned to his neck. She couldn't see his neck due to the voluminous nature of the beard that had colonized much of his upper chest. On his head, a white skullcap.

"Christine Lupo?" he asked. The accent was distinctly American. The district attorney, due to her frequent appearances on television, was accustomed to being approached by constituents in public. The man turned to Dominic. "Please forgive the intrusion." His voice was brandy-smooth if his timing was not.

Too flummoxed to respond, and still fighting a welter of feelings, Dominic sat blinking, a frog on a lily pad. But the man did not appear to be dangerous, and Christine secretly welcomed his presence since it temporarily delivered her from continuing to experience the emotional pain that had so recently flared. Since she would appreciate this man's vote in the race for governor, along with that of any other black person he knew who might want to vote for her, she said, "You are—?"

"Imam Ibrahim Muhammad," he said as if he was someone she should know. The name did not ring a bell. "The leader of the mosque the martyr John Eagle attended."

Ah, he *was* someone, more specifically the same someone who had been calling the office nonstop for the past twenty-four hours trying to arrange a meeting with the district attorney, who was not a fan of the word imam. It reminded her of ayatollah, a word she, like many who had lived through the seizure of the American embassy in Teheran, positively loathed. What did imam, in its unutterable foreignness, even mean? Father?

Head Man? And what about his use of the remarkably loaded word "martyr"? That designation could not in this context possibly presage anything encouraging. Muhammad pulled a chair from a vacant table and sat down. Reflexively, Christine looked around for Sean Purcell, her savior in these situations, and remembered he had taken the night off.

"Excuse me, sir," Dominic said, having regained the ability to speak.

"It's all right," his wife said.

"Again, please forgive the intrusion," the imam said. Despite his polite manner, the apology sounded like a threat. He would make them listen.

At this point, the elderly waiter returned with a glass of club soda and the basket of the rustic bread. He looked quizzically at Dominic, presumably the one running things. When Dominic did not say anything, the waiter placed the bread on the table and turned to the imam.

"Will the gentleman be eating?"

"The gentleman will just be here for a minute," Ibrahim Muhammad replied in a slightly bemused tone. The waiter nodded and departed.

The district attorney had recently read an article on the Internet where she learned that an entire one fourth of the Earth's population were adherents of the Muslim faith. To her, this was not welcome news. She was not outwardly prejudiced against Muslims but was highly aware that they were the primary actors in a huge percentage of the conflicts in Africa, Asia, and the Middle East. Further, if these Muslims weren't killing non-Muslims, they were murdering each other at an ever-increasing clip. A massacre in Nigeria one day, a suicide bombing in Iraq the next, all of the violence melted together into a miasma of horror. There were so many of them, and their birth rate was so astronomical that none of the killings would ever make a dent. Not that the District Attorney of Westchester

County thought any killing was a good idea—she didn't. But no government official seemed to know how to deal with this state of affairs, and it made her nervous that the number of Muslims in America was burgeoning, however incrementally.

Until this evening, the DA had been unaware that the shooting victim was Muslim. Her relief at being given a break from the poignant effusions of her adulterous spouse was tempered by the realization that she would now have to get rid of this meddlesome cleric without making a scene. What was it with men? Did they think they could do anything they wanted? Several other diners stole glances in their direction. She took a sip of her club soda.

"I know why you're here," Christine said. "We have channels in our office, and you need to go through them."

"I was not getting satisfaction that way."

"You followed her to the restaurant?" Dominic asked, ever the vigilant spouse.

"And I debated whether or not to go in," the imam replied. "I've been standing outside for an hour and a half. I followed you here from work."

"You were stalking her," Dominic said. "There are laws against that."

Ignoring him, the imam continued, "I nearly interrupted you when you walked into the restaurant, but I had second thoughts and decided to wait for you outside. Then it occurred to me that if I accosted you in the parking lot someone might shoot me." Here he paused, and the tiniest sardonic smile flickered on his lips, "and then another man would have to talk to you on my behalf. I'm sure you can see the problem."

"You should get the hell out." Dominic's intensity surprised both his wife and her visitor. "Maybe I should throw you out."

"I said I'd handle it," the district attorney reminded her husband.

"Your impatience is understandable," the imam said to Dominic. "Once again, I apologize for the untimely intrusion."

Christine was pleased that this man was polite and did not seem to be the type who sent suicide bombers hurtling through barricades.

She asked, "Who are you, exactly?"

"I am the imam at the Lower Westchester Muslim Society. We serve members of the *ummah* who live in the area and build bridges with our neighbors of other faiths in accordance with the Quran and the traditions of the Prophet Muhammad."

"Nice speech," Dominic said. His wife ignored him.

"Tell me, what exactly does 'imam' mean?"

"An imam is a worship leader of Sunni Muslims."

"Proceed," she said, taking another sip of club soda. "You have two minutes."

Ibrahim Muhammad inched his chair closer to the table. Christine noticed he smelled pleasantly of nutmeg and Ivory soap.

"John Eagle was a recent convert to Islam," the imam told her. "He showed up at the mosque one day as a young seeker and requested instruction. I talked to him and recommended some books, and he began to learn how to pray. His life had not gone well. He was lost."

"Is this going anywhere?" Dominic wanted to know. His wife leveled him with a look.

"Inshallah," the imam replied evenly. "God willing. John Eagle was using drugs, and it appeared that he was not mentally stable. I don't know what happened with the officer. I know there were witnesses, and hopefully, those people will tell the truth, you will bring that truth to the grand jury, and they will act by that truth. I am here merely as the representative of a poor man who is unable to advocate for himself. He was without money, and without luck, but he was not without friends. More friends than you probably realize."

More friends? What, exactly, did that mean? Certainly not that the dead man had "friends" in the sense of ones with whom he went bowling but, rather, those with whom he made common cause. Was the imam threatening some mass civil action in the event the situation did not go his way? How many "friends" could some unemployed, mentally unstable victim of police violence have anyway? Other than the imam, who Christine supposed might want to use the current situation to make a name for himself as an activist.

While she considered this, the imam stood up and thanked the Lupos for their time.

"G'bye," Dominic said, not looking at him.

"I wanted you to hear about this man personally," the Iman said. He bowed his head slightly, then departed, gray tunic swishing around his knees.

The district attorney watched as Ibrahim Muhammad navigated through the tables and out the door. In his evident sincerity and high moral purpose, both of which appealed to her sense of fair play, she had infinitely more admiration for this clergyman than she did for her wayward spouse.

"That was weird," Dominic said as if their evening had been going well up to the imam's arrival. He caught his wife's eye and smiled, trying to create a mutual appreciation, a disillusioned but bighearted acceptance of the fruitcakes in this nutty world, the kind of shared experience husbands and wives in long marriages will reflect on early in the morning or before going to sleep, something we'll laugh about in the future, remember the night when the Muslim interrupted our dinner at the Italian restaurant, ha-ha-ha.

"Can you believe that guy's nerve?"

"I want you to move out of the house," Christine said.

Two hours later, her husband relocated to the guest room, the DA sat in bed propped on pillows, unable to sleep, laptop open, in search of distraction from her marital woes. She researched the price of her house on Zillow, since it would surely be a factor in the divorce, purchased a mystery novel from Amazon, then checked tomorrow's headlines. The media reported that Russell Plesko had been placed on desk duty, and the office of the district attorney was continuing their investigation. The situation perplexed Christine, who felt besieged from all sides. What of the imam's request? She understood and believed herself sympathetic to the grievances of the black community. They were valid, and her office needed to address them systematically. And Muslims were certainly entitled to equal protection under the law. However, Plesko, as far as she knew, had not done anything wrong. It was a question of gauging who she wanted standing behind her on the campaign trail, angry activists or first responders. The imam had not helped his case by cornering her in a restaurant. But she loathed that hostile cop who represented Plesko's union.

She wondered who this meddling imam was so she googled him. Originally from Florida, Ibrahim Muhammad's name at birth was Dwayne Sykes. A former U.S. Marine who had done jail time for armed robbery and drug dealing, he had several wives and at least ten children. According to an article in the *Orlando Sentinel*, the U.S. government recruited him to infiltrate radical Muslim organizations but the official relationship terminated when he assaulted his handler. She wondered what the former Dwayne Sykes would have done if Dominic had followed through on his threat to escort him out of the restaurant. The dark part of her, the part that the nuns had made her ashamed of, almost wished she had seen it.

CHAPTER FOURTEEN

The flight to Los Angeles on the private jet that Trey chartered passed with the alacrity of a geological epoch. It felt to Dag like he was checking the time on his phone every five minutes. Church was not happy when his star player called to tell him an urgent family matter would cause him to miss practice. Dag couldn't worry about that now. The team's next game was three days away, and a win would make Church forget today's absence.

Dag looked around the plane. How long was this flight supposed to take? Already, it felt like they'd been flying for twenty-four hours. He rechecked his phone. They'd left New Jersey an hour ago. He and his brother were the only passengers. The pilot, co-pilot, and stewardess, for whom proximity to fame was nothing special, kept to themselves. Trey played games on his laptop while Dag contemplated his phone call with Little Dag.

It had gone like this:

"What's up, little man? Everything okay?"

"Uncle Moochie's visiting Mommy."

Uncle Moochie? Was this what Little Dag had been told to call Moochie Collins, Dag's former teammate when both of them had played for the Milwaukee Bucks?

"What's he doing there?"

"I don't like him."

"Where's Mommy?"

"She's in her room."

It was late morning in Los Angeles. Dag did not want to ask if Moochie had spent the night. There was an unwritten rule in the league that teammates (and once a teammate, always a teammate, the bond everlasting) stayed away from each other's exes. Under no circumstances was this credo to be violated.

"With Moochie?"

"Yeah."

Dag told his son he loved him and would see him soon. Then he told Trey they were going to Los Angeles.

"When?"

"Now."

"What are you gonna tell Church?"

"I got a family emergency," Dag said. There were two things he intended to accomplish in Los Angeles. The incursion of an ex-teammate into his former domain, and his intensely jealous reaction, made him realize that he wanted to make one last-ditch attempt to save his marriage.

He also planned to "bring the ruckus" to Moochie Collins.

For a man of his athletic prowess, professional accomplishment, and celebrity, Dag Maxwell was unusually circumspect. Early in his career, he had released a rap album and, while his rhymes had not risen to the level of art, he had written them himself. Dag had aspirations, a soulful yearning to express what lay within him through means other than slick passing and jump shooting and this urge set him apart from the Darwinian wins and losses world of professional basketball. He had few delusions regarding his musical ability—that he would never be an ace rapper was not surprising—but he found comfort in working his thoughts out in rhyme and recognized the value of having an outlet for his querulous emotions.

He passed the flight trying to corral his feelings into verses on his phone but found it challenging because he was unsure exactly what these feelings were. He thought Brittany was in the past, that the smoking ruins of their relationship were now in the capable hands of lawyers and accountants, and he was primed to reap the rewards of the single life. But his reaction to this new information surprised him almost as much as the information itself.

Dag could not yet see that his last conversation with Jamal intensified his response. Moochie Collins sleeping with his wife—Brittany remained his spouse until the divorce became final—was of a piece with his not being able to swing an endorsement deal with a major carmaker or wring the maximum allowable contract out of Jay Gladstone. It was a sign of disrespect, and he could not abide it. And not just disrespect from Dag's former teammate, who deserved to die, but also from Brittany, who should have known better than to let Moochie Collins soil her family's nest. How could she have done that? Did she not know that Dag still loved her—in a way that was problematic, to be sure, but was nonetheless enduring? As the plane passed over the California desert, Dag, after much internal back-and-forth, concluded that he should have told her this. He hoped it was not too late.

The other part of his conversation with Jamal that contributed to his presence on the chartered jet was the unspoken suggestion that his career was on the downward slope and the end, if not exactly near, was on the horizon. Basketball mortality, once only a vague concept, was beginning to assume unmistakable form.

Through the process of his divorce, Dag twisted himself like a pipe cleaner to arrive at the apparently false conclusion that his love for Brittany was a memory. Now it felt like he could no longer maintain this charade. She was the mother of his children. Eventually, his life would cease to be an endless chain of gyms, restaurants, hotel rooms, and clubs. He would want a home again, with a family. The idea that his mistake had been one of timing tormented him.

Brittany Terry was a cheerleader for the Los Angeles Clippers when she caught the eye of D'Angelo Maxwell at a preseason game. Wary of his intentions, she told him, "I'm no hoochie." She was studying for a business degree at Cal State Northridge and, in her second season as a cheerleader, was wise to the romantic wiles of NBA athletes. Further, the league frowned on players becoming romantically involved with cheerleaders for the simple reason that, legally, these were office romances and could just as easily wind up in marriage or court (unfortunately for Dag, his and Brittany's liaison checked both boxes). But Dag was in love and pursued her with phone calls, gifts, and finally, an invitation to be his date for All-Star Weekend, the annual three-day orgy of celebration the league throws for itself where players of Dag's stature get treated like 17th-century French aristocrats. She capitulated.

Celebrity is an aphrodisiac, and when combined with great wealth it produces otherwise unimaginable results. Women threw themselves at Dag with alarming regularity, cocktail napkins with phone numbers proliferated in his pockets, straight-up propositions in hotel lobbies were an everyday occurrence. But Brittany was different from the usual groupies who crowded his neon life. The daughter of a dentist and a teacher, Brittany had been raised in San Diego, the oldest of three children. An honor student in high school, she planned to get a corporate job after college, then start her own business. Her parents were not thrilled when she brought Dag home and let their daughter know. But Dag charmed them, they relented, and Brittany's life plan shifted. If he were forty when they'd met, he probably never would have cheated.

"You ever see an eclipse?"

Dag looked over at Trey, irritated. "What are you talking about?"

Trey showed Dag his phone. "Article says there's going to be a solar eclipse in a few days. Have you ever seen one?"

"Naw, man. You?"

"I want to," Trey said. Dag was happy to listen to his brother talk about astronomy. Right now, any distraction was welcome. "Moon passes over the sun during the day, and the world gets dark."

"Why you want to see that?" Dag asked. "Can't you just wait 'til nighttime?" He was joking, starting to relax a little.

"Point is, it's nighttime in the daytime," Trey said. "Shows everything don't always have to be the same old same old."

Dag laughed. It was moments like this that he liked having his brother around.

Trey arranged for a rented Porsche to be waiting for them at Van Nuys Airport and just after seven in the evening they were headed south in light traffic on the 405 Freeway, Trey at the wheel. Anyone going nightclubbing would still be home, particularly if it were before her children's bedtime. Trey took the Sunset exit and pointed the Porsche toward Bel Air.

When the Maxwells purchased the luxurious house on St. Cloud Drive with its landscaped grounds and sweeping view of Los Angeles from the towers of downtown all the way to Catalina Island, the idea was that this was where they would raise their family, a place to celebrate birthdays, graduations, and one day, weddings. As the car wended through the densely wooded roads of the posh enclave, Dag felt the sense of plans unfulfilled.

They slowed down and came to a stop in front of a contemporary wood and glass home nestled into the verdant landscape. There were several luxury cars parked in front of the house. Dag hesitated before getting out.

"You want me to come in with you?"

"Don't want you cappin' no one," Dag said.

Trey rolled his eyes. What kind of ghetto fool did his brother take him for?

Dag had never wanted a fire pit. They reminded him of the flaming garbage cans the winos in his neighborhood would gather around in the winter to warm their hands but it was important to Brittany, so he relented. Now, ten men and women (he recognized most of them as Brittany's crew and their boyfriends), surrounded the fire pit on the patio. They held glasses of sangria and were listening to his wife hold forth. Moochie Collins, that disloyal motherfucker, was sitting next to her with his hand on her knee. As for that knee—wrapped in a skintight lemon yellow catsuit, cinched at the waist by a wide calfskin belt. The father of her children would've been far happier if, at that moment, she had been dressed like a Mormon sister-wife.

Dag was barely able to contain his emotions. He stood in the kitchen with Trey, peering out the window looking for a camera crew. He knew his wife was shooting the next season of *Hoop Ladies* and wanted to make sure no one was filming this party. His plan was to chase Moochie off the premises as a prelude to reconciliation with Brittany. He had already disabled the security cameras (it was a matter of flipping a switch on a panel near the front door), so there would be no record of what was about to happen. He assumed his kids were upstairs with their nanny. He would say hello to them when he was done handling his business.

Dag said, "Anyone starts taking pictures with their phone—"

"Ain't gonna have a phone," Trey assured him.

The guests registered a mixture of surprise and alarm when they saw Dag striding toward the fire pit, except for Moochie Collins, who could not hide his considerable panic.

"Why are you here?" Brittany said, trying to keep her voice from shaking. The anger Dag had quelled during the ruminative phase of his trip to Los Angeles had come roaring back. He was not yelling or gesticulating, but the coiled rage he emanated, combined with his size, rendered him terrifying.

Dag ignored Brittany's question. To Moochie, he said: "What the fuck are you doing at my house?"

Trey hovered about ten feet behind Dag. As usual, no one acknowledged his presence. Behind the revelers, the pool glistened in the early evening, the lights of the city a twinkling star field in the distance.

"This isn't your house anymore, D'Angelo," Brittany said.

Moochie rose uneasily from his chair. In his late thirties, he was a light-skinned black man. Six foot two, about a hundred and eighty pounds, a piece of kindling next to Dag.

"What up, D?" Moochie said.

The nervousness of his rival's ersatz smile gave Dag pause. He thought of the two years Moochie was his teammate, how much he had liked him. But Moochie had violated the unwritten laws of the social system where superstars like Dag ruled, and must be made to pay for this unforgivable sin. But how to address the transgression? Certainly not by cursing him out. Dag had just chartered a jet and flown three thousand miles. There was an audience, and it included his wife, whose respect he craved. The predetermined roles of the two men in this drama gave it a nearly Calvinist quality. Everyone present knew Moochie had cuckolded Dag. The circumstances required Dag to act. He had to be resolute, to perform the part, not only of the aggrieved husband but of the basketball star. He had to vanquish Moochie. To trail feebly away, having done nothing other than talk smack, was unacceptable. They would laugh at him. For someone like D'Angelo Maxwell, the only condition more ignominious than defeat was being the object of laughter. Being laughed at was the ultimate affront.

A man raised fatherless and poor, his entire life a twilight struggle to avoid that fate.

Zeus felt the eyes of the mortals. They were waiting. Looking at Moochie now, the man trying not to quake, Dag did not want to lay a beating on him. But he knew he had to.

"What up, Mooch?"

"Have a sangria," Moochie said.

The casual temerity of the suggestion with its We're-all-adults-here implication gave Dag the excuse he required. Without another word, he sprang like an uncaged cheetah and loped around the fire pit toward Moochie.

Brittany screamed for him to stop but Dag was deaf to her agonized shouts. The men in the circle, all of whom were civilians, uneasily rose to their feet but no one had the slightest intention of actually doing anything to protect their fellow party guest. The women, except for Brittany, did not move. Several of them believed Moochie was about to get the whupping he deserved.

Because Dag had blocked access to the house, Moochie sprinted toward the yard, which led to the sight of Dag chasing him around the pool. One of the female guests, a black woman in maroon leggings and a baggy ecru sweater, true to Dag's prediction, aimed her phone at the action and began recording it. She was caught completely by surprise when Trey snatched the device from her hand and flung it in the water where it made a small splash before sinking to the bottom. He told the woman he'd buy her a new one and she cursed him before angrily turning her attention back to what was transpiring on the lawn.

Moochie had circumnavigated the pool and was sprinting back toward the house with Dag in pursuit. At the patio grill, mounted in custom-built brick housing and the place where Dag had cooked hamburgers for his children, Moochie picked up a two-foot-long cooking fork and brandished it at Dag.

"Back off, man," Moochie said, more request than demand. "Let's talk about this like men."

Dag's response to this suggestion was to grab a deck chair and smash it over Moochie's head. This assault sent him sprawling to the flagstone patio. As he scrambled to his feet, Dag set upon him. The universe shrank to this brawl with Moochie Collins. His wife's betrayal, the refusal of Jay Gladstone to meet his demands, his fear and rage at the toll age was taking, all of this found concentrated form in Dag's fists.

The first punch caught Moochie on the chin and sent him reeling although he managed to stay on his feet. He attempted to back away but Dag connected again with another blow, and this one landed Moochie flat on his back.

"All right, Dag, that's enough," he said, rubbing his bruised chin.

Dag was breathing heavily. He looked over and saw his brother standing next to him. Trey indicated that he agreed with Moochie. No more violence tonight. Dag had made his point.

"That's some weak-ass shit, Moochie," Dag said.

"Whatever," Moochie said. He propped himself up on an elbow and spit bloody saliva on to the slate patio.

"You happy now, D'Angelo?" Brittany asked, glaring at her husband. "Is this how you want your kids to behave?" She turned to Trey, who tried to remain impassive in the face of his sister-in-law's contempt. "And you let him act like this? You're useless, Trey. Damn errand boy."

Although being called an errand boy cut him to the quick, Trey did not respond. He knew this was Dag's show.

Moochie had used this lull to get to his feet. He backed away from Dag, moving toward the house.

"Get the fuck outta here, Moochie," Dag said, massaging the back of his sore right hand with the palm of his left.

Brittany said, "Don't you throw my guest out, D'Angelo."

Moochie mumbled something about having to be somewhere

and stole away crossing paths with another one of the guests, a white man in his thirties wearing jeans and a blazer, who had just emerged from the house. He told Brittany the police were on their way. When Moochie heard this, he turned toward Dag.

"I'm not gonna press charges, Dag. Let's keep this between us."

Dag only stared at him. Moochie retreated.

"The police, Dag," Brittany said. "This is what you want?" She thanked the man who had alerted them, then turned her attention back to her husband. "They're going to want to talk to you."

Dag asked Brittany if he could have a word in private. Her girlfriend who had attempted to film the action yelled that she should not go in the house with him, but Dag had never laid a hand on Brittany, and she knew he would not touch her.

They stood in the living room overlooking the yard. He told her that while he had thought the marriage was over, he was wrong and that his feelings for her overwhelmed him. Could she possibly consider reconciling?

"Only person you're thinking about is you."

"That ain't right," Dag said.

"You're always talking about 'my brand this' and 'my brand that' but what you did to Moochie? That was some homeboy bullshit."

"Motherfucker deserved it."

"Look around, Dag. Does this seem like the hood to you?"

Dag knew his former Bel Air home did not resemble the hood. He worked as hard as he did so his surroundings would reflect his self-image. The condescension wounded him. While Brittany saw his obvious emotional distress, he sensed she felt sympathy but not love. It was over between them. She could no longer trust him. She told him that his arrival in her life had diverted her from a well-considered path and she now intended to resume where she had left off.

"On some janky reality show?"

"Call it what you want, D'Angelo, but I've got my own life going on. Because of that 'janky reality show' I'm working on a fashion line, a cosmetics line, and a beauty book. And if you thought you were going to change my mind by beating up Moochie, that shows how little you know me."

"I know who you are," he declared, a forlorn attempt to convey what he thought was his love and regret.

"And I know who *you* are." Her response was unsentimental. "I don't want to be married to you anymore, okay?"

"For real?"

"I'm not feeling it."

In that instant, Dag realized it was over. The woman in front of him was someone to whom he was physically attracted and who, for the rest of his life, would be the mother of his children. He would take care of her as long as she fulfilled that role. But whatever spark had existed between them was extinguished, and he knew it. Moochie had animated a vestigial feeling in Dag, and he had confused shame with love. Why had he come to Los Angeles? Dag wasn't sure other than it was not because he loved Brittany. He was flailing, but since it was a sensation he had not previously experienced, he did not recognize it.

She told him he should fly back to the east coast after he talked to the police, then she returned to her guests. Dag's hand had started to throb. Rooted in what had been his living room, he gazed around. There had been pictures of him and Brittany all over, but none were in evidence, only family photos of her and the kids. He felt a lump in his throat but willed it away. His anger had dissipated, and he went upstairs to visit his children. The two younger ones were asleep, but Little Dag was overjoyed to see his father. When Dag hugged his son, he noted the boy's Portland Trailblazers pajamas—the Blazers were Moochie's most recent team—and realized they must have been a gift from the man sleeping with his wife. This only deepened his sadness. Dag got down on the floor and built Duplo structures with his son until the police arrived.

There were four of them, three men and a woman, and to a person, they were daunted by the presence of D'Angelo Maxwell. Dag welcomed them to the house and told them that some friendly tussling had gotten out of hand and an excitable guest had overreacted, a version of events Trey was happy to corroborate. The police conducted private interviews with Dag, Brittany, Trey, and the guests, including the man who had called them (he reported a donnybrook had occurred and Moochie Collins grievously injured). But since the alleged victim had left the premises and did not appear to be interested in pressing charges, the quartet of cops departed, all of them shaking Dag's hand on the way out.

Dag kissed his sleeping children, said goodbye to Little Dag, who was still awake, and told him he would return as soon as the season ended. Then he and Trey drove to Van Nuys Airport for the flight back to New Jersey.

Stretched out in his seat with a bag of ice on his hand, Dag reflected on what had occurred. Months earlier Brittany made it clear that she was ending their marriage so why did he react with such passion if he already knew it was over? As the plane cruised eastward over the Rocky Mountains, Dag began to understand that the only reason he had flown to California was to avoid looking like a fool.

THE ACE, W.A.C.E. AM
NEW YORK SPORTS TALK RADIO
WITH SAL D'AMICO AND THE SPORTSCHICK

SAL: What possesses a man like Dag Maxwell to charter a private jet, fly to Los Angeles, and kick the crap out of Moochie Collins?

SPORTSCHICK: *Doesn't he know his team's in a dogfight, trying to make the playoffs?*

SAL: *Apparently, it doesn't matter to him.*

SPORTSCHICK: *Yeah, it matters. I mean, come on, he's a professional.*

SAL: *This was unprofessional.*

SPORTSCHICK: *Not to mention what he's done to his brand. He's always talking about his brand. You ever notice that?*

SAL: *Honestly, I don't know how much brand damage he inflicted. I don't need to remind you that Kobe Bryant survived a rape trial.*

SPORTSCHICK: *Then don't remind me.*

SAL: *What I want to know is this: How does he expect ownership to say, 'Hey, you're our guy, you're the face of the franchise,' if he acts like a knucklehead?*

SPORTSCHICK: *Total knucklehead.*

SAL: *But here's the thing—he's not a knucklehead.*

SPORTSCHICK: *Come on, Sal. How is he not a knucklehead?*

SAL: *Guy's never done anything like this in his life. Ever. He's a solid citizen.*

SPORTSCHICK: *Hey, Lee Harvey Oswald never shot anyone before he killed Kennedy.*

SAL: *You're comparing D'Angelo Maxwell to the guy who killed the president?*

SPORTSCHICK: *To make a point, Sal. Say a guy does one dumb thing, but that thing is so freaking stupid that it defines him. Oswald didn't have to shoot anyone else, did he?*

SAL: *Not as far as we know.*

SPORTSCHICK: *One act.*

SAL: *A single act.*

SPORTSCHICK: *And he was defined by that single act.*

SAL: *Your analogy is bananas.*

SPORTSCHICK: What if Dag injured himself?

SAL: What if he can't play?

SPORTSCHICK: Disaster.

SAL: Epic failure. But no one's saying he injured himself. The media's not reporting that and the story's all over the media. No one's reporting he went to the hospital.

SPORTSCHICK: They can keep that stuff under the radar.

SAL: But what if he did? Say he can't play? The team misses out on the playoffs because Dag flew to LA so he could lay a beat-down on Moochie Collins?

SPORTSCHICK: You think Moochie regrets hooking up with Dag's wife?

SAL: You seen Hoop Ladies? She's smokin' hot. She's jalapeno hot. She's hot like magma.

SPORTSCHICK: I get it, Sal. You find her mysteriously attractive. That's not what I'm asking.

SAL: Is he regretting it? Yeah, jeez, would you want to be on the receiving end of a Dag punch? Guy's biceps look like bricks.

SPORTSCHICK: Gladstone and Church Scott, what do they do?

SAL: Suspend him for a couple of games, at the very least.

SPORTSCHICK: And the league?

SAL: You know he's gonna get fined. The commissioner's gonna stick his hand in Dag's wallet and pull out a few hundred grand.

SPORTSCHICK: He can afford it.

SAL: But he's a superstar, so maybe they do nothing.

SPORTSCHICK: Those guys have their own rules.

SAL: Here's my question: Dag wants to be LeBron, but does he have the goods to get there? I say no.

SPORTSCHICK: Then he'd better win a couple of championships.

SAL: Does he stay with the team? Does he take a pay cut and join a contender?

SPORTSCHICK: Let's go to the phones.

SAL: Caller one, you're on the air.

CALLER #1: Yeah, Brad from Livingston. Love the show.

SPORTSCHICK: What do you think about Dag?

CALLER #1: Trade him, he's a bum. Guy's three times the size of Moochie Collins. He's never won anything, he'll never win anything, he's a loser.

SAL: So, Brad, you're a big Dag Maxwell fan?

CALLER #1: Hahaha, yeah.

SPORTSCHICK: Here's the thing, Brad. His value's never been lower. No one knows if he's injured or not. Wrong time to trade him.

CALLER #1: Guy's over the hill.

SAL: What do you do for a living, Brad?

BRAD: I manage a fast food franchise.

SAL: Lotta pressure, right? Lunch, dinner, cars lined up at the drive-thru.

BRAD: I handle it pretty well.

SAL: Let me tell you something, Brad. Dag Maxwell is carrying an entire professional sports franchise.

CALLER #1: For more than twenty million a year.

SAL: Don't take this the wrong way—he's not supervising pimply-faced kids making French fries. Point is, he was brought to New Jersey to be the savior of a business valued at nearly a billion dollars. The franchise was not able to surround him with the best talent, but every night he goes out there in front of eighteen thousand people with all of their expectations and what does he do? He does his job.

CALLER #1: He's lazy.

SAL: He's not lazy, Brad! You don't average nearly nine rebounds a game if you're lazy. So he puts up his twenty-three points and grabs his nine rebounds nightly. The fans are on his back; the press is on his back. You know what that kind of pressure is like, Brad? It's a hell of a lot worse than when the drive-

thru window gets backed up during the dinner rush, and you're running low on ketchup. Do you have any idea what it's like to be a professional athlete in the New York media market? So maybe he's a little frustrated, and maybe he takes that frustration out on Moochie Collins's chin. I don't know, I wasn't there. But when guys like you call and tell me D'Angelo Maxwell is a bum, I'm gonna tell you—you need your head examined.

CALLER #1: It's his job!

SAL: I get that it's his job, but these guys are human beings.

SPORTSCHICK: You're a very sensitive flower today, Sal. Brad, you brought out something new in Sal.

SAL: Hey, I'm not saying they shouldn't trade him. Let's just make an effort to understand.

CALLER #1: I do, Sal. He's still a lazy bum. Gladstone should run him out of town.

SAL: Here's the problem with that, Brad. Gladstone can't run Dag out of town. No one pays to see Jay Gladstone play basketball. They pay to see the Dag Maxwells of the world, okay?

CHAPTER FIFTEEN

T urn that crap off," Jay said to Boris.
They were listening to Sal and the Sportschick on the
car radio and Jay couldn't take it anymore. Boris tuned
the dial to an oldies station.

It was just after nine in the morning as they turned on to the
138th Street Bridge. In a couple of hours, Jay was scheduled to
make a presentation to the Planning Commission on behalf of
the Sapphire, and the last thing he needed was the distraction
D'Angelo Maxwell was providing while the team tried to claw
its way into the playoffs. Boris informed him the story was
blowing up the Internet. Sal and the Sportschick had discussed
nothing else for the past half hour.

Church Scott had called Jay early that morning to notify
him of their star player's problems.

"Praise God, there's no tape," Church said.

"Praise God," Jay repeated. He found his coach's religiosity oddly comforting.

Church told Jay he would speak to Dag as soon as he could
and loop the owner in at the appropriate time. This was the
reason Jay had bestowed the responsibilities of both general
manager and head coach on Church. He knew how to deal
with the modern athlete.

As the car rounded off the bridge and into Harlem, Boris
asked Jay what he intended to do about the D'Angelo Maxwell
situation.

"This is why I pay Church," Jay said.

"You're not going to talk to Dag?"

"Guys like me don't tell guys like Dag what to do."

"You're the owner!"

"Boris, it's 2012. He slugged a guy who was sleeping with his wife. To tell you the truth, I don't blame him."

The building housing the New York City Department of City Planning was a squat, neo-Classical pile in Lower Manhattan, around the corner from City Hall. That morning, the Planning Commission was scheduled to render a decision on the purchase of the city-owned land at 1 Taft Plaza where the Gladstone Company intended to build the Sapphire. Today was the last day testimony, for and against, would be allowed. Rather than attend with a kingly retinue, a display Jay knew would not work in his favor, only Boris accompanied him. When they arrived, he said hello to the four members of the Gladstone team who would be addressing the committee: the president and CEO of the Brooklyn Public Library, an associate of the architect Renzo Piano, a representative from the New York City Economic Development Corporation, and an environmental lawyer retained by the Gladstone Group. After exchanging brief pleasantries, Jay and Boris took seats in the back.

The room was bland and functional. Windowless. A curved desk of blond wood extended along two walls. Behind it sat the ten members of the planning commission, two Latinos, an African-American, and seven whites of varying ethnicity. To their backs were a pair of decorative Corinthian columns in the middle of which were an American flag and the orange, blue, and white flag of New York City. Facing the commission members, an African-American female clerk sat at a table with a microphone. Behind her was a podium. Audience members filled five rows of seats.

Jay glanced at the others in attendance. The people who were not there in support of the project—everyone other than Jay and his band of allies—looked to be a cross-section of middle-class, educated Brooklyn of both sexes, varying in age from twenties to sixties, united in their disdain, he believed, for the free market. Jay knew they regarded him as if he were the rich guy with the top hat and monocle on the Monopoly board.

The chairman, a bow-tied white man of about sixty with graying hair and a hangdog mien, called the room to order. The clerk, who the chair addressed as Madame Secretary, sum-marized what was on the schedule for the day, a litany of prop-erties in Manhattan, Queens, and Brooklyn whose status the Commission would review in this session. Jay had been previ-ously alerted that the discussion of the site he hoped to pur-chase would take up the majority of the meeting. The other business was processed in fifteen minutes, most of which Jay spent pondering his basketball team, how much he was willing to invest in the new arena, and what tax concessions he might be able to wring out of Mayor House, his guest at the recent Celtics game.

When Madame Secretary leaned into her microphone and Jay heard, "the matter of the disposition of city-owned property and acquisition of property concerning 1 Taft Plaza," he perked up. The chairman informed the room that the members of the acquisition team—Jay's allies—were now going to speak, each for an allotted three minutes. The president of the Brooklyn Public Library stepped to the podium.

Patiently, Jay listened to the presentation. An articulate woman in her fifties, with salt and pepper hair that fell to her fitted jacket, she elucidated the dire economic straits of the public library system—the branch currently at 1 Taft Plaza had ten million dollars in immediate maintenance needs—and how the sale of the air rights to the Gladstone Group would bene-fit all of the citizens that use it. When she finished, a represen-tative of the architect Renzo Piano, a man in his thirties, Swiss, with Germanic features Jay tried to not hold against him, discussed the design of the public spaces in and around the proposed building. The woman from the Economic Development Corporation spoke about the potential of public/private partnerships. After the environmental lawyer addressed the impact of the project on the neighborhood (he claimed it would be negligible), it was Jay's turn.

He stepped to the podium, gratified to see smiles of recognition on several faces of the committee members. "My name is Jay Gladstone," he began, without notes. "I'm the co-chairman of the Gladstone Group, the grandson of a plumber, and a lifelong New Yorker." To Jay, who enjoyed speaking to groups under almost any circumstance, this was as easy as floating on his back in a placid lake. He added a hint of trombone to his voice, "Our family business has been around for almost sixty years," and its tenor notes filled the room. "We've developed over twelve thousand apartments across the city in all market segments from affordable housing to middle income to market rate. I'm proud of our history of public/private partnership, and the Sapphire will be the jewel in the crown." He paused to let this reverberate, the idea that the building he proposed would be the culmination of a decades-long Gladstone family effort to make the metropolis gleam for all of its citizens.

"This proposal—it contains a brand-new state-of-the-art library that we are selling back to the city for the grand sum of one dollar—includes one hundred and fourteen units of affordable housing in Sunset Park, which we will build without government subsidies, and the city will own outright. The affordable housing will be divided into two sites. We've closed on one already, and we expect to close on the other by this summer. The residential part of the Sapphire will consist of one hundred and forty-nine condominiums ranging from one to four bedroom apartments. The ground floor will contain two micro-retail spaces of four hundred square feet each that will generate dynamism at street level.

"We want to maintain strict transparency, so there's a website, Gladstonesapphire.com. Finally, we're following the HireNYC plan, and to that end over half the workers on the job will be from Brooklyn, and assured up to three years of union employment. Those are the facts." He paused here as if the facts as stated by Jay Gladstone should be sufficient.

"But there's something else . . . "

Were the committee members leaning forward in their seats or had he imagined that? The room waited for him to continue.

The closer: "I love Brooklyn. My mother was born and raised in Bensonhurst, graduated from New Utrecht High School, class of 1948. I've watched with growing excitement as the borough, neighborhood by vibrant neighborhood, is being returned to its former glory. The Gladstone Group wants to bring the inspiring New York architectural tradition that includes the Woolworth Building, the Chrysler Building, and Rockefeller Center to the great borough of Brooklyn.

"Today, I think of native son Walt Whitman who in his poem *Crossing Brooklyn Ferry* wrote of 'glories strung like beads' and see the Sapphire as a modern glory. I think of the poet Hart Crane who wrote of the Brooklyn Bridge that it would 'lend a myth to God.' These men were dreamers who have inspired me to be more than a builder."

Jay paused to gauge the effect his words were having on the committee. They appeared captivated. He dared not steal a glance at his adversaries. He could establish scholarships, donate liberally to charities, and still these enemies of progress would find him abhorrent.

"I may not share their eloquence, but I share their aspirations. The Sapphire will be in the tradition of the great New York City landmarks and a beacon for tomorrow's dreamers."

Jay knew he was spreading the cream cheese a bit thick on the bagel, employing the beacon-for-dreamers construct to shill for a condominium, however architecturally stunning it might be. He also understood that people responded positively when their better angels were engaged. Should one of the dreamers Jay envisioned want to purchase a condo in the Sapphire, she would need verifiable liquid assets well into seven figures but imparting that information at this time would destroy the beauty of the moment he had just conjured.

While there was no ovation because who applauds a speech, however impressive, in front of the City Planning Commission, he believed he earned one. Jay graciously thanked the committee then blessed the memory of Professor Morris Markowitz, with whom he studied American Lit his sophomore year at Penn, and, rather than sweep out of the room—no one should think he was too grand—returned to his seat.

For the next hour, he listened with an expression that toggled from bemusement to dismay, before finally settling on sanguinity, as a parade of librarians, teachers, community organizers, and ordinary citizens excoriated the proposed building as if it were a portal to the Underworld and Harold Jay Gladstone Beelzebub. The Sapphire was "a blemish," "a monstrosity," and "a symptom of everything that's gone wrong with New York since Reagan was president." Jay—looking right at them, speaker after anguished speaker—was "high handed," "arrogant," and, of course, a "greedy developer." The words "for-profit" were invoked like curses. He sat in his chair and took the abuse. Did they not hear when he mentioned his grandfather the plumber? Why, he wondered, did these people see the world in such binary terms? This was enlightened capitalism working cheek by jowl with the government in a manner to benefit everyone. The tone of the speakers ranged from pique to trembling rage. He wondered if he should have brought a security person with him, some muscle to keep the inflamed public at bay should someone's emotions get out of hand (Boris was no bruiser). It was only a fleeting worry because these weedy utopians pelting him with their words would never pose a physical threat.

The final speaker against the project, a diminutive woman in her sixties, introduced herself as Sonia Trachtenberg. Not much more than five feet tall and with a graying pageboy and large glasses, she wore a denim skirt, white blouse, and a loose-fitting jacket that appeared woven from the wool of a horned animal that shared a postal code with the Dalai Lama. In an accent that was a mixture of Eastern Parkway and eastern Europe, she identified herself as an author who had done research in libraries all over the world and avowed that this one should not be torn down, "no matter what castle in the sky is being fabricated to replace it by the slick flimflam of late stage capitalism."

Jay reflected that, to the untutored eye, he and Sonia Trachtenberg represented the two most common anti-Semitic tropes of the past century, the avaricious moneyman, and the left-wing revolutionary. Jew-haters would have a field day with the pair of us, he thought, two sides of the same shekel. Jay imagined telling the fuming Sonia that they had a great deal in common—starting with their ancient religion but encompassing the love of culture, of literature and libraries, hatred of anti-Semites and Nazis—as the tiny agitator hectored, gesturing with her hands, fingers opening and closing. Her passions continued to rise, and her arms began to semaphore through the air as if she were guiding a 747 into a parking space, all the while imploring the commissioners not to allow this terrible, civilization-shattering transaction to go through. She never glanced at Jay, but he could feel the utter disdain for him and his kind seeping from her pores. He hoped she would grow to enjoy the new library he was going to build.

When the session finally ended after nearly three hours, Jay shook hands with every committee member. Several seemed genuinely glad to meet him and none of them, to Jay's great relief, mentioned D'Angelo Maxwell. Only then did he and Boris leave the chamber. Rather than ride the elevator to the lobby, they walked down five flights. In the event Jay had misread his opponents, he wanted to avoid an unpleasant encounter in a confined area.

It was the kind of morning when office workers take al fresco coffee breaks, savoring the early days of spring. On the sidewalk Jay checked messages on his phone—Nicole wanted him to call her back, Church Scott needed to talk about Dag's new problem, still nothing from Aviva in Israel. He was waiting for Boris to bring the car around when he noticed what he thought was a child move quickly toward his flank. Jay swung his head to the side and realized this was Sonia Trachtenberg, liberated from the relative decorum of the City Planning Commission hearing, her face righteously ablaze.

"You're a criminal, Gladstone," she said, maneuvering directly in front of him. Jay had faced irate citizens for much of his career and was accustomed to these kinds of personal confrontations. Sonia Trachtenberg could not have weighed more than a hundred pounds. "How can you sleep at night?"

"Sometimes I need a martini," he replied, trying to defuse this bespectacled grenade. Jay's cavalier response seemed to further agitate the crusader and her eyes, magnified behind smudged lenses, blackened. She stared at Jay as if trying to decide what kind of disease to wish on him. He smiled at her, but she did not smile back.

"You should rot in Hell," Sonia said in her geographically nonspecific accent, "But you would probably just build condos there."

Jay's look of wry amusement at this witticism froze when the globule of saliva propelled from her angry lips landed squarely on his face. With great restraint, he said, "If your books are as crude as you are, they must be wildly popular."

Sonia Trachtenberg sneered and walked away just as Boris brought the car around. Jay took out a handkerchief and wiped the gout of spit hanging off his smooth cheek.

At the office, he described the meeting and the encounter with Sonia to Bebe who congratulated him on not allowing himself to be provoked. Nicole texted him that she was flying to their house in Aspen for a few days and was presently on her way to the airport. She kept a horse in Colorado and wanted to ride in the mountains "to shake out the cobwebs." He wouldn't mind a few days apart.

Then Jay called Church Scott to talk about Dag. If the team failed to make the playoffs, the Los Angeles escapade would provide an acceptable pretext should they decide to cut him loose.

CHAPTER SIXTEEN

Several hours earlier, in the chemical dawn of northern New Jersey where pink light refracted through a particle haze, the private jet made a bumpy landing. Dag had been dozing fitfully, and the impact jounced him awake. The first thing he noticed was that the over-the-counter painkiller the co-captain fished out of the plane's first-aid kit had worn off and his right hand hurt. It was his shooting hand and a broken bone in that location at this stage of the season was the last thing he needed. He examined the hand as he flexed it. The pain was behind the knuckle of his middle finger. He massaged the tender area with his thumb and flexed the hand again. If he broke it, he would have to play through the discomfort. There was no other choice.

The second thing he noticed was on the screen of his phone: A website that trafficked in the sorrows of celebrity was reporting that there had been an altercation at Brittany Maxwell's home the previous evening. Details were hazy, but witnesses said—

Dag didn't bother to keep reading; he could imagine what witnesses said. It was naïve to think that what he had done would not immediately blast its way into public consciousness where his lack of control, bad decision-making, and a new-found penchant for self-destruction would streak like a comet across the media firmament.

"You see this?" Dag said, showing his phone to Trey.

"Too late to worry about it now," Trey said as the jet taxied to a stop. "How's the hand feel?"

Dag told him he needed to get it looked at immediately.

A person as famous as D'Angelo Maxwell can't just show up at an emergency room for an X-ray so as the Maxwell brothers headed north on the Turnpike, Trey called the team trainer and told him Dag had suffered a minor accident, could he alert the team doctor? Five minutes later the doctor called Dag directly and said he would meet him at his office.

A tall man in his fifties with thinning blond hair, Dr. Harlan Latimer was the leading orthopedist of northern New Jersey. He was waiting in his office dressed in a tracksuit.

"I was on the third mile of a five-mile run when you called," he said.

"Kind of an emergency, Doc," Trey said.

Attempting to be clever, Dr. Latimer said to Dag, "I guess we're not shaking hands today," and offered his elbow, which Dag indulgently bumped with his own.

"I haven't talked to Church yet," Dag said. "Let's keep this on the down low."

Dr. Latimer regarded Dag skeptically. Secrecy was not proper protocol (the organization needed to be apprised of every ding and bump a player suffered) but he said nothing.

Team memorabilia decorated the empty waiting area, and the familiarity of the colors and graphics was a comfort to Dag as he nervously contemplated his future. It was probably nothing, just a scare that would teach him to control his impulses. Maybe it was a blessing. That's what he'd tell the coach. Church loved that word.

"Bone bruise," the doctor said from behind his desk. "There's no break."

Dag stared at the X-rays, mounted on a light box, and thanked the universe.

Trey asked, "Can he play?"

"If it were the non-shooting hand, I'd suggest we put a splint on it."

"I can't wear a splint," Dag said. "Gotta gut it out."

Biggie greeted Dag, stuck a wet snout into his thigh, and waited for his master's attention. Dag ignored the dog. Babatunde and Lourawls were in the kitchen eating breakfast keen to hear what was going on, but Dag went straight upstairs without greeting them. He retreated to his bedroom, drew the shades, and crawled under the covers. Emotionally sapped, he was the sick tired where his limbs tingled with fatigue. But as he lay in bed, instead of falling asleep, he found himself reliving the events of the previous night and imagining what he might have done differently. To start with, he never would have flown to Los Angeles, gone to his old house, confronted Britanny, or assaulted Moochie. In other words: Everything. He imagined the number of times he could have hit the brakes—before climbing on the plane, before stepping out of Brittany's kitchen and into the backyard, before he chased Moochie down. Before he got out of bed yesterday morning.

He pondered what had caused him to do something so out of character, so against his interests. This kind of violence was not going to help in his search for an acceptable contract. And as far as endorsements, what soft drink company would want as their spokesman a player who was in danger of being indicted for felony assault? Moochie had said he was not going to press charges, but it was already clear he could not be trusted. Dag had humiliated him and there was a good chance he would seek redress. At the very least Dag would have to write the man a large check. None of these thoughts were conducive to relaxation, but sheer exhaustion finally lowered him into sleep.

"How's the hand?" Church Scott asked when he entered the room.

Dressed in practice gear of a team sweatshirt and shorts with a layer of compression shorts beneath, kneepads around his ankles, Dag was seated in the small cinderblock office of his coach, just off the gym at the team practice facility in South Orange. Church closed the door and sat behind his metal desk. On the wall, a picture of the University of North Carolina team "sophomore sensation" Church Scott had led to the Final Four of the NCAA tournament before turning pro. There was a family photograph on his desk. Five kids and married to the same woman for twenty-seven years. And he had won an NBA championship. Dag felt rebuked by the man's entire existence. The coach himself, however, appeared nonjudgmental—a great relief. Dag was in no mood for a lecture. He had managed a few hours of sleep earlier, so he was feeling slightly more himself.

"I can play," Dag said.

"Bone bruises in your hand are pretty painful. I had one."

"Don't worry about me, Coach."

Church placidly nodded although he wanted to do to Dag what he surmised Dag had done to Moochie Collins. But the coach/superstar relationship precluded this. Although Church was nominally in charge, everyone in the league knew that superstars called the shots. Dag's actions were going to compromise the coach's job. If the team failed to make the playoffs, both their careers would be damaged.

"Media relations wants to talk to you," Church said. "Media relations" consisted of several people whose job it was to maintain the wall between the players and the press and propagate the illusion that every guy with a league contract was a cipher and thus incapable of antisocial behavior. "I told them we weren't going to make you available to the press for the foreseeable future."

This was a relief. Every sports journalist in the country was going to want a piece of him. Dag's media skills were impeccable, but he had no appetite for being grilled on the subject of what would invariably be described as his "rampage." He planned to apologize to the team before practice for bringing this unwanted attention when all anyone should have been concentrating on was qualifying for the playoffs.

"I appreciate that," Dag said.

"Nobody talks to the media today except me."

Dag heard a knock and then the sound of the door opening. No assistant coach or player would think to enter Church Scott's office without waiting for permission.

"How's the hand, Dag?" Jay Gladstone looked fit and rested, like a man without a worry.

Dag had been hoping to delay this encounter. That the incident had occurred on the heels of their lunch at the Paladin Club did not redound to Dag's benefit. But the look on Jay's face was sympathetic. If he was angry, Dag could not tell. The owner was unreadable.

"Feeling okay," Dag said.

Neither Dag nor Church stood. Both men waited for Jay to speak. Dag wished the coach had told him Gladstone might show up. He didn't want to deal with the owner now. They were facing the Pistons in Detroit in two days, and Jay asked Dag if he expected to play.

"Oh, hell yeah," Dag said with what he hoped was the right measure of don't-worry-about-it. Jay clapped Dag on the shoulder in a friendly way. This gesture gave Dag the opening he needed, and he stood up.

"I'm glad you're here, Jay," Dag said. "I want to apologize to you personally for my conduct." Dag could read the surprise on Jay's face. Superstars were not usually so quick to take responsibility. "I acted a fool, I regret it, and I'm going to make it up to you and the team."

Jay was craning his head to look up at Dag. He blinked a couple of times and said, "I genuinely appreciate that apology, Dag. All I want is for you to succeed."

"We're all trying to win a championship," Church interjected.

"I guarantee we're going to make the playoffs," Dag said.

"Let's hope so," Jay said.

"And after that," Dag said, "Sky's the limit."

"Bang bang, motherfucker," Jay said.

Dag laughed at Jay's invocation of the D'Angelo Maxwell catchphrase. "Bang bang, motherfucker, indeed," he said, and offered his left fist for the owner to bump, which Jay did. That it was Dag's left (non-shooting) hand did not escape Jay's attention.

When Dag excused himself to see the trainer, Jay asked the coach how he thought the player was doing. Church repeated what Dag had told him. There was no point reviewing what had happened, only in finding the best way to navigate the aftermath.

"We all do stupid things," Jay said.

Jay paused, in the hope that Church would bring up the topic they were both avoiding. As the seconds accumulated, he saw the coach glance at a scouting report. Jay was going to have to initiate the conversation.

"What do you think we should do about Dag?"

"Do?"

"Fine him, suspend him. You're the team president, Church. It's your call."

The coach laid the scouting report on his desk. He looked at Jay, waited to see if he would speak. Jay knew that Church was managing him and rather than begrudging it, respected his approach. Usually, people just deferred.

"What Dag was involved in was a non-basketball matter. It happened on his time, away from the team. I don't like it but it's not our business."

Church's stance surprised Jay. The coach preached the Gospel of Accountability and Team First. Dag had ignored it. One of the reasons Jay had hired Church was because the coach believed in discipline. Men like Church Scott were a big reason the whole world, despite always being on the verge of coming apart, continued to function. Was Dag to suffer no consequences for jeopardizing their teetering season?

"So that I understand, your position is to take no action?"

"We're trying to make the playoffs, Jay. I'm not suspending him."

"Don't we have to do something?"

"Yeah, win."

Church uncoiled from his desk. It was time to start practice.

Church stood at center court and blew a whistle signaling practice was about to begin. Players stopped their warm-up routines, stretching, and half speed games of one on one. All of the guys jogged toward him. When they had gathered around, Church told them that their captain had something to say. An assistant coach signaled to Dag, who had been waiting outside the gym because he didn't want to talk to his teammates individually before he addressed them as a group. Now he ambled toward the scrum of players, a piece of protective plastic taped to the back of his shooting hand. They greeted their leader with friendly shouts. To a man, they had read the accounts of what had happened and wanted to show him some love.

Jay stood on the sidelines with Boris. He stared at Dag's hand and wondered if it augured the end to another disappointing season.

Church, the three assistant coaches, and the eleven other team members all waited for the star to tell them what was going on.

"I signed with this franchise to win a championship," Dag began. And then he stopped, uncharacteristically gripped by emotion. There was Drew Hill, the point guard whose slick, no-look passes Dag relished, and Odell Tracy, the lanky center with whom he often played cards on team flights, and Giedrius Kvecevicius who was always inviting him to visit Lithuania in the off-season. He genuinely enjoyed knowing these guys and was touched by their support. "And everything I've done has been with that goal in mind. Yesterday, I talked to my son on the phone. The boy was upset. Hearing my son upset, I got upset. I thought the best way to deal with the situation was to go to Los Angeles. When I got there, I did something I shouldn't have done. I apologized to Coach and Mr. Gladstone, and now I want to apologize to you all."

The players nodded, called out "No need" and "We got your back," and "Fuck Moochie, man," which caused general laughter. Dag was relieved to see his popularity with his teammates had not waned.

Jay looked on in awe at the organism that was a team. He had been around enough of them to know that they were not alike, but this year's group seemed to have genuine affection for one another. One of the marvelous aspects of sports, he reflected, was its capacity to bring participants to psychological states resembling those of childhood.

"We got games to play, games to win," Dag continued, volume rising. "We're gonna make the playoffs, and when we get there, we're gonna make some noise!"

The players clapped and yelled, and their supportive cheers merged with Dag's clarion voice to create a shield that for a brief instant protected them all: from the expectations of sportswriters and fans, from the demands of girlfriends and wives, from the still distant notion that the day would come when they would cease to be members of this charmed circle.

Jay thought a solitary walk around the perimeter of the training facility would lower his blood pressure, so he asked Boris to wait for him in the car. He strongly disliked being put in this situation, but he tempered the displeasure he felt toward Dag because he knew it would cloud his thinking. One of them may have been a superhuman physical specimen, but in the world in which they lived, of bills and spreadsheets, and obligations, it was the man that wielded the capital who moved mountains. Strangely, he admired Dag's boldness. It was the quality that allowed him to rise above the smog-choked streets of Houston, command millions, demand the ball when the game was on the line. When other highly remunerated players quailed and ran for cover, Dag declared he was The Man and took over. Jay rationalized that it was natural for someone like Dag to want to destroy a pissant like Moochie Collins. The team had traded assets to get him (three rotation players and a first round draft pick), but his tenure with the franchise had been disappointing, and the championship he had guaranteed upon signing had not come close to materializing. The fan base was restive. Jay didn't want to suspend Dag; he had wanted Church to do it, at least for a single game. But Church was not going to step into that breach, so if Jay wanted to set the tone for the organization, he would have to act. But the team was struggling to make the playoffs and by suspending Dag wouldn't he be working against the team's interests? And would he then have to rescind his invitation to the Obama dinner? It was a quandary.

An hour later Jay, Boris, and Bebe met Mayor Major House at the Amiri Baraka Junior High School in Newark where they honored twenty Gladstone Scholars. After the beaming students accepted their certificates in front of a small gathering of proud parents and faculty, Bebe gave a short speech in which she pledged that the Gladstone Foundation would provide college scholarships to every one of them who finished high school. There was a photographer from the *Newark Star-Ledger* there, but only because Mayor House insisted.

As Jay was leaving the school, his phone vibrated. A text

from Aviva: *Arriving this afternoon from Israel. Ok if I put a cab from the airport on my AmEx?* For all of the problems in their relationship, Jay controlled the finances, and their arrangement called for his approval of any credit card charge over fifty dollars. Still, he was pleased to hear from her.

It occurred to him: Wasn't she supposed to be home the following week?

He texted back: *I'm coming to pick you up.*

CHAPTER SEVENTEEN

The International Terminal was a flurry of saris, kurtas, salwar kameezes, dashikis, niqabs, djeballahs, jeans, and sweatshirts. A harried Pakistani patriarch herded his exhausted family toward the check-in counters. Two Nigerians reached into trouser pockets for passports and boarding passes that would allow them to go through security and board a flight back to Lagos. Globetrotting Belgian backpackers in tie-dyed T-shirts double-checked luggage to make sure their hemp-positive lifestyles did not cause them to forget they were carrying substances that could get them beheaded in certain third world countries.

"Are you ever going to visit Ukraine?" Jay asked.

"Only if someone kidnaps me," Boris said, chewing a Cinnabon.

Beneath the vaulting ceiling, Jay and Boris stood behind the barrier and watched as a group of women in multihued chadors appeared like an assortment of Fiestaware saltshakers, trailing their luggage behind them. This vibrant gaggle peeled off to reveal Aviva, who was striding out of the tunnel in a sleeveless dress with a sweater tied around her waist. "You didn't have to come," she said. Jay embraced her, and she patted his back with one hand, the other remaining at her side.

Jay inhaled his daughter's scent of rosehips, lemon, and mint. He recalled when she was fourteen and just home from summer camp. That day Aviva learned her parents were getting divorced. She took it exceptionally well. Jay was impressed with her strength, although he did not always appreciate when it manifested as a lack of reluctance to disagree with him.

"I can't pass up an airport reunion," he said, relieved to have her home.

Aviva and Boris greeted each other familiarly.

"Did you solve the problems of the Middle East?" Boris asked. Before Aviva could answer, another voice drew her attention.

"We just got here, baby! The subway took forever!"

A black woman, college-age and breathless from running, threw her arms around Aviva. They embraced, briefly drew back to gaze into each other's eyes, then kissed on the mouth. Holding a cell phone up to record this encounter was a tall young man with blond, shoulder-length hair gathered in a loose ponytail.

Turning to her father, Aviva said, "You remember Imani."

"Of course," Jay said, while he shook her hand and tried to decipher what, exactly, he had just witnessed. He hadn't thought of Imani since briefly meeting her during Aviva's freshman year.

"And my cousin Boris," Aviva said.

Boris, equally puzzled, nodded in the new arrival's direction.

"What up, Boris?" Imani said.

Aviva then hugged the ponytailed man with far more enthusiasm than she had shown her father. Stepping back, she turned to Jay and said, "This guy who's shooting us—he's Axel." The young man shook Jay's hand. "His father was a famous historian."

Axel said, "Yo, Pops. What up?" His voice was deep and full of false bravado. Jay nodded at him and pictured the Bob Marley tattoo he probably had somewhere.

While Aviva introduced Axel to Boris, Imani turned to Jay. "So, you're the owner." There was lightness in her voice, a friendly bounce. But he was not quite sure how to interpret what she said. Was she impressed with his lofty position or had she just offered a subtle critique of his status? She could have said "So, you're Aviva's father," but to Jay, her declaration seemed to imply an agenda.

"Are you a basketball fan?" he asked.

"Other than a ticket out of the hood for a tiny minority, I'm not sure what professional basketball provides, but, hey, go Knicks!"

"Glad we got that settled," Boris said.

Jay grimaced at the mention of the more prominent franchise and informed her that someone else owned the Knicks.

"I know," Imani said.

If Aviva's friend was trying to create a positive impression, she was operating counterintuitively. The daughter offered the father another desultory pat on the back. Axel was wielding his camera phone again, aiming it at Jay.

Imani looked at Boris, sizing him up.

"I'm not sure we did get that settled, actually," Imani said.

Sensing that this person he just met was spoiling for an argument, Boris chose to not pursue the topic.

Aviva said, "I told Mom I was going to stay at her place. Is it all right if Imani and Axel ride back to the city with us? They came all the way to the airport to meet me."

When Jay and his ex-wife divorced, Aviva's mother bought a duplex apartment on Central Park West. Jay said he would be happy to drop them off there. He then requested that Axel stop recording.

"Sure, Pops," Axel said, and put his phone away.

Boris was at the wheel of the Mercedes as they rode into Manhattan, Jay in the passenger seat, and Axel and Imani in the back with Aviva between them. It was late afternoon, and the Van Wyck Expressway was jammed. Jay had hoped that he could debrief his daughter about her Israel trip without a stranger in the immediate vicinity, but the presence of her two friends made this impossible. A bit of small talk revealed that Imani Mayfield was still Aviva's classmate at Tate, concentrating in gender studies, a red flag for the already suspicious senior Gladstone, suggesting as it did the twin bugaboos (to him at least) of radical politics and sexual fluidity. Jay learned that her father was a letter carrier, her mother an elementary school teacher, and she was going to be staying with Aviva at Jay's ex-wife's Upper West Side apartment until the end of their spring vacation. Axel reported that he had dropped out of Tate and was vague about what he did to support himself. "Right now, I'm helping Aviva and Imani with their senior project."

Out of the corner of his eye, Jay discerned movement in the backseat. Aviva appeared to have drawn Imani's hand toward her lap. Were they holding hands? Given that Imani was doing gender studies, he concluded the answer was obvious.

"So, you're back early," Jay said, choosing an oblique approach to the abortive nature of Aviva's trip. He craned his neck to look at her.

"Kind of," she said.

Aviva radiated confidence. As a child, she experienced what her mother coined "threshold anxiety," a reluctance to go into new rooms alone. She refused to climb a staircase by herself. The backyard might as well have been Timbuktu. How everything had changed.

"Thanks for all the emails," Imani said to Aviva. "It's like I was in Palestine with you."

Palestine? The word was a cudgel to Jay. Did she employ it to smite him? Imani obviously knew who Aviva's father was. A simple Internet search would have revealed his Anti-Defamation League Man of the Year Award and consistent support of Israel. But perhaps she only bore the mark of the current American campus zeitgeist—where support for immediate Palestinian nationhood was the litmus test for anyone who did not want to be considered a right-wing troglodyte—and had no idea what his views were. He would give her a pass on that for now. More important, and distressing, Aviva had sent multiple emails to Imani. Jay received none. Who was Imani Mayfield to Aviva anyway? Was this dynamic young woman simply a college comrade of his daughter's, or was Aviva going through some sociologically mandated lesbian phase? Like many people of his acquaintance, he was forward thinking on matters of sexuality, supported gay marriage and LGBT equality, but harbored a deeply held wish to not have a gay child, mostly because Jay suspected that homosexuality would likely make that child's life more challenging. But also, since no one who was openly gay crossed his path until college, gay people to Jay were always somewhat like Bulgarians or Fiji Islanders, perfectly acceptable, but undeniably exotic. He ascribed this vestigial prejudice to his era, chose not to be tortured about it, and contributed annually to Gay Men's Health Crisis. But what was that kiss on the lips back in the terminal? If his daughter *was* gay (which was fine!), her lover was a black woman. While there was nothing wrong with either of those things, to a man born in the Sputnik era, it was—he didn't exactly know what it was. Upsetting? No, that was too strong. Disconcerting? That was close, but not exact either because to admit being disconcerted would be to acknowledge something off the beam about it. Either way, he was going to have to recalibrate his perceptions. Whatever he felt, it was not anything he wanted to say into a microphone. And where did Axel fit into the equation?

"I'm curious to hear about how the trip went," Jay said.

He had planned on waiting until they were alone but had been thrown off by the invocation of the word "Palestine" in the context of his daughter's return from the Middle East.

"It was okay," Aviva said.

"Why are you home early?" He tried to disguise the implied displeasure but was not successful.

"The whole thing is entirely one sided," Aviva said. "Rah-rah Israel, and I wanted to see the other perspective."

"That *is* why they bring you there," Jay pointed out. "It isn't to tell you that things are better in Syria or Yemen."

"It's a great country," she assured him, "but the Palestinians are getting screwed."

"Big-time," Imani chimed.

"Word," Axel said. "They need their own country, like, yesterday."

"We don't have to get into that right now," Jay said, in as pleasant a way as he could manage. Trying to keep the internal tension at bay was only heightening it. He had teed off on people who refused to acknowledge the complexity of the situation between the Israelis and the Palestinians, and as they drove past skeletal remains of the 1964 World's Fair, he was laboring not to let that occur today. "Tell me what happened." Intended to sound casual, Jay worried that his request would be perceived more as a demand.

Imani held Aviva's hand (there was no mistaking it) as if to fortify her friend for the clash with the oppressive forces represented by mondo-Zionist, incontrovertibly *cisgender, heteronormative* Jay.

The lacuna after Jay's appeal for an explanation expanded. It felt like a peach pit had suddenly formed at the base of his neck, and he kneaded it with two fingers.

"Well, the trip is super-controlled," Aviva began. "You're always with the group, whether you're hearing lectures or touring sites, or schlepping up Masada. And the leaders are always telling you how awesome Israel is. You know, 'Israel invented this, Israel built that, Israel high-tech, blah blah blah.' It's a lot to take in."

"What they don't talk about is the Palestinians," Imani informed Jay.

"Really?" Jay said. This Imani person was getting on his nerves. "I didn't realize you were on the trip." He kept his eyes on the road.

"Sorry, you're right," Imani said with a zipping motion across her lips. "This is your daughter's story." She massaged Aviva's shoulder and waited for her to resume.

"Another kid and I traveled to the West Bank," Aviva reported.

Jay's head whipped around. "Did you tell anyone you were going?"

"Of course not. The 'authority figures' wouldn't have let us. Anyway, the Israeli government was planning to destroy this house because a guy who lived there set off a bomb and the—"

"Stop right there," Jay said. "Set off a bomb? It was the house of a terrorist?" He noticed Axel was taking video of him with his phone.

"It's where his family lived," Imani said, information no doubt gleaned from one of the emails Aviva could not be bothered to send her father.

It was an effort for Jay to contain himself. He faced front again. Let the Aryan-looking kid shoot all the footage that he wanted.

"Anyway," Aviva continued, "There's this international student group that was going to coordinate with the villagers to see what they could do to stop it. You know, protest, get the media there, and then, if it came to a head, lie down in front of the bulldozers."

Once again, Jay twisted his body to look at Aviva's face. Axel was still filming.

"Tell me you didn't lie down in front of any bulldozers," Jay implored, mindful of a young American activist that, in similar circumstances, had been crushed to death.

"That would've been the shit," Axel said. "I hope you did."

"No, no, no, we didn't lie down in front of bulldozers," she assured her father. "The army wound up cancelling the operation, I'm not sure why. Anyway, some of us hung out with the little kids there. They have, like, nothing. We brought them pinwheels to play with, they love pinwheels, and we took a bunch of pictures. I posted them on Instagram if you want to see." She held her phone out to her father. Its plastic case was a polka-dot pattern. "Oh, and we spent the night in the West Bank."

"In a Palestinian village?" Jay asked. This jolt blinded him to the phone now suspended in Aviva's hand between the front and back seats.

"In a Bedouin tent," she said. "The Bedouins, by the way, are amazing. And that was kind of it."

Jay nodded, relieved. "What happened?"

"Nothing."

It was hard to know whether to believe her. "Really?"

Axel took the phone from Aviva and began scrolling through the pictures.

"But when I got back to the hotel the next day the group leaders were kind of pissed."

Boris commented, "Just because you snuck into the territories to bait the IDF and spent the night with Bedouins?" like it was nothing.

Only Jay heard the irony and he did not share Boris's sly sense of comedy. This wasn't funny to him.

"Dad, the phone," Aviva said. "Look at the pictures."

She grabbed the phone from Axel and handed it to her father.

"I wish I had been there," Imani said.

"Oh, girl, it was so your scene," Aviva said. "Anyway, I asked if I could talk to our group. The kids are, like, all over the map politically. Some are Peace Now two states and others are prejudiced against Arabs. And that's when the group leader told me to pack my bag because they were sending me home early which kind of sucked because I didn't get to see Tel Aviv and I heard the club scene there is awesome."

"How can the Israelis party with all that suffering going on?" Axel asked.

Jay had no idea where to begin. He didn't want to get into a protracted discussion of Middle Eastern policy. He also was not going to point out that if, as he suspected, Aviva was in a temporarily gay phase and her new Muslim friends found out about it, they might have stoned her to death. Jay scrolled through the pictures taken in the village. The children indeed looked happy with their new pinwheels but it was hard to concentrate on the images. He handed the phone back.

"Cute kids," he remarked, rather than saying what he thought, which was junior Jew-haters.

"I know, right?" Aviva said.

What Jay took away from this entire exchange: It could have been so much worse. Without denying the suffering of the Palestinians, he believed what Aviva had done was rash and irresponsible, although also quite plucky, a quality he admired. Her desire to address the troops, however misguided (in his view), showed embryonic leadership ability. It wasn't as if he could punish her, so he chose to appreciate his daughter's curiosity about the world and the fact that Hamas had not murdered her.

"Oh, I have some news," Jay said, in hopes of relaxing the edgy nature of the conversation. He turned to face the backseat and once again found himself looking into the camera lens of Axel's raised phone. "Excuse me, Alex."

"It's Axel, Pops," he said.

"May I see your phone?"

"Sure," Axel said, handing it over.

Jay slipped it into his jacket pocket. "I'll give it back when we drop you off." Axel knew he had been temporarily outmaneuvered and offered a wry grin. Imani was taken aback but said nothing.

"Dad, give him his phone!"

"I don't want to be taped against my will, all right? Now, that's a reasonable position. I told Axel I'd give it back later, and then he's going to erase whatever he recorded since we've been together."

"Well played, Pops," Axel said.

Paying no attention to Axel, Jay said, "The president of Tate called me and asked if I'd speak at your graduation."

A whoop of joy from Aviva would have been too much to ask for, and Jay did not anticipate that his declaration would elicit one. But he would have liked some positive response. Instead, this information produced nothing at all in the way of emotion. His daughter's face was an empty chalkboard. Imani looked skeptical.

"I hope you didn't say yes," Aviva said.

"I did." Jay tried to hide his disappointment in her disappointment. "Look, it's your day. But let's talk about it at least."

"You should give a speech," Axel said. "They'll love you."

The subtext, served with a ladle, was impossible to miss. Jay wanted to throw this kid out of the car, but that only would have further impaired relations with Aviva, so he ignored the remark.

"No," Aviva said. "That would be too awkward."

"Awkward!" Imani said in an artificially high voice followed by a barely suppressed giggle.

"It's your choice," Aviva concluded.

This declaration was far from the ringing endorsement Jay had desired. In his flattered state after the college president's call, it had not occurred to him that his daughter's mortification might be an issue. As the car inched along, he reproached himself for not considering it.

"Maybe I can draft a speech you like." Aviva did not respond. "I have a dream," he intoned. No one was amused.

The Manhattan skyline loomed, glass towers shimmering. Jay always thrilled to that view. It was possibility and prospect, and in its iconic but ever-changing profile seemed to convey that somehow, the future would always be brighter. In his life, it usually worked that way and today was no different. As Jay contemplated what appeared to be his daughter's moral relativism and budding lesbianism, he discreetly popped an antacid pill and took comfort in knowing that Aviva no longer seemed to suffer from threshold anxiety. He turned to face the three Tate College students in the backseat.

"I hope you're all going to come to our Seder."

CHAPTER EIGHTEEN

On West 139th Street between Adam Clayton Powell Jr. Boulevard to the east and Frederick Douglass Boulevard to the west lay Striver's Row. A landmark block in Harlem, for more than a hundred years it has been a home to African-American notables like Eubie Blake, Bill "Bojangles" Robinson, W.C. Handy, and, more recently, the sports agent Jamal Jones who stood at the second story window in the hallway of the newly renovated brownstone that served as his home and office gazing down at his former client, D'Angelo Maxwell, waiting at the front door below. Across the street, Jamal spotted Trey Maxwell leaning against the McLaren smoking a cigarette.

Dag had called and texted but Jamal, still smarting from being fired, had not responded. News had reached him of Dag's Los Angeles fracas. He thought perhaps his erstwhile friend and client might benefit from experiencing a little of life without Jamal Jones running interference. There were other matters to occupy him and having Dag on his list was no longer essential to the success of his business. Jamal's business was already successful. That morning he had met with a television production company in Midtown to pitch an idea for a show. In half an hour, he was having lunch with a projected NBA lottery pick at Sylvia's Restaurant and expected to sign the kid before the peach cobbler arrived at the table. After that, there were drinks with an agent in town from Atlanta with whom he was thinking of partnering. If the encounter bore fruit the

Jones Group (he named it "Group" when he learned the Gladstones used the same word) would have a second front. Jamal could hear the two junior agents he employed working the phones down the hall. Business was thriving.

"You want me to let him in or not?" The speaker was Donna, Jamal's assistant. An African-American woman in her forties, she wore a patterned knee-length dress and flats. Her head wrapped in a cloth scarf from which several braids snaked. Donna was Jamal's majordomo, taking care of his scheduling, travel, and the day-to-day operations of the Jones Group.

He quickly reviewed any grievances Dag might be nurturing. In light of what the man had inflicted on Moochie Collins, Jamal did not want to forget something he might have done (or that Dag might think he had done) that could be the cause of another violent outburst. Donna narrowed her eyes.

"You're gonna keep Dag standing on the stoop?"

The man hug with which Dag greeted his former agent caught Jamal by surprise. Given how they had parted, he was expecting something a little more formal. They were in Jamal's office, overlooking the street. One of the walls was a gallery of framed photographs, several of which were of Jamal and Dag: at the Super Bowl, on vacation in Mexico, on the court at Sanitary Solutions Arena, all suffused with a bonhomie that reflected their years of friendship. Now Jamal stood in front of his desk and, pointedly, did not offer Dag a seat.

"All right if I sit down?"

"Dag, I got a busy day."

Knowing it was the price he had to pay, Dag remained standing. Jamal wanted to ask about California, about the hand injury, but he was still indignant over being fired. So, he said nothing.

"How are you coming with Chevy?"

"What are you talking about?"

"Chevy trucks, man. You were working on endorsements."

"You forgetting something, Dag?"

"It wasn't Ford, was it? It was Chevy, right?" Dag grinned and waited for Jamal to reciprocate. This would signal that there were no hard feelings. The echo was not forthcoming.

"You fired me."

"Forget that, Jamal. We boys. You got lunch plans?"

"Yeah."

"Cancel 'em. I'm taking you out, my treat."

"Dag—"

"I owe you an apology, man. I'm apologizing to everyone. Already said I was sorry to Church, Gladstone, and the team. Now it's your turn."

"Just checking all the boxes."

If Dag heard the judgment in Jamal's words, he barreled ahead in spite of it.

"I was mad that day at my house, I said some shit I regret, I'm sorry and now let's you and me get back to business."

"Did you apologize to Moochie?"

"Why you worried about Moochie?"

Jamal pondered how it was that guys like Dag rarely understood the ramifications of their actions, how because of their ability to put a ball through a hoop, the ordinary laws of human interaction did not apply.

"Forget Moochie, man. I'm worried about you."

"I appreciate that. I'm gonna write Moochie a check. How much you think I should send him?"

"You're not hearing me, Dag."

"What am I not hearing?"

"You fired my ass."

"I told you, forget that shit."

"You meet with Gladstone to try to negotiate for yourself, you beat up Moochie, injure your hand."

"Ain't gonna miss a single game!"

"That's great, Dag."

Dag seemed surprised at the pushback he was getting from Jamal. He pointed to a picture on the wall. It had been taken the previous summer at the D'Angelo Maxwell Summer Charity Basketball Tournament and showed Dag and Jamal posing with the winning team, a group of gangly teenagers, everyone happy.

"Them kids had a helluva squad. Remember?"

"Yeah, I remember, Dag. I put that tournament together with Trey." Jamal felt he had to namecheck Dag's brother even though he had done most of the work himself. Placating stars was reflexive.

Dag continued to examine the display of framed photographs: Jamal's high school and college teams, Jamal with various sports and entertainment celebrities, Jamal with his wife and two young daughters. All of it spoke to a life independent of D'Angelo Maxwell.

"How do you know I met with Gladstone?"

"The man called because he was worried."

"About what?"

"He was worried you weren't thinking clearly."

However true it might have been, the implication did not please Dag, who was getting more worked up. Jamal kept a Louisville Slugger baseball bat near his desk. It was meant to be decorative but would serve as protection if Dag came at him. "So, he called you?"

"The guy likes you, D'Angelo."

"He'd kick me to the curb like a ten-dollar ho."

Jamal ignored this. They both knew professional sports was transactional and that was the level on which 99% of all decisions were made. When it appeared that Dag was not going to become violent, Jamal relaxed.

"If you want a max contract from a major market team,

maybe you shouldn't have beat up Moochie. That ain't franchise player behavior."

In the course of their friendship, Jamal had never once cas-
tigated Dag. For the player, this represented an unwelcome
new day in their relationship. Jamal cracked his knuckles and
regarded Dag. He enjoyed the shift in their power dynamic
although he took pains not to show it.

"Moochie needed to get schooled," Dag said.

"So now you want me to clean up the big mess you made?"

And like it was the most natural thing in the world, Dag
said: "Yeah."

Jamal put his hands in his pockets. Dag waited.

"You told me I was bush league, Dag. You remember that?
Rinky-dink."

"I did?"

"You don't remember? Maybe you remember this: The last
contract I negotiated for you paid a hundred and twenty million. A hundred. And twenty. Million. That sound rinky-dink
to you?"

"Jamal, from my heart," Dag said, and pounded his chest
with his fist, "I apologize." He looked out the window as if to
draw on the African-American collective capacity for
endurance that had manifested on the sidewalks of this venerable neighborhood. When he turned back to his former agent,
there was an imploring look in his eyes that Jamal had not seen
before. "I need you, man."

Jamal reached up and placed a hand on Dag's shoulder.
Dag smiled ruefully. He genuinely seemed to feel remorse over
his recent actions. For all Dag's superstar affectations, Jamal
believed somewhere inside lived the humble kid he first
encountered at the McDonald's All-Star Camp when they were
in high school.

"I'm gonna think on it, Dag."

Dag stepped back and looked at Jamal as if he were some

bizarre animal species of whose existence he was previously unaware. Agents did not refuse opportunities like this. Jamal's commission on Dag's next contract would be several million dollars. He was going to "*think* on it"?

"What's there to think on?"

"You disrespected me, man."

People did not say no to men like D'Angelo Maxwell, especially anyone in the position to financially benefit from their talents. It contravened the laws of nature and Dag was unsure how to respond. He had apologized already. There was no point in doing that again. This was when they were supposed to clasp hands, embrace, and then go out to the lunch Dag had offered to pay for. Why had Jamal departed from the routine? First Gladstone, then Brittany, now Jamal all were undermining the foundations of his existence. The frustration this engendered and the general sense that something he could not entirely understand had shifted disoriented him.

"That's what you got for me? All the money I made for you?"

"Ain't about the money, Dag. Ain't about the money for you, either."

Dag gestured toward the room, its high ceilings and ornate moldings, all exquisitely restored. "I put you in this townhouse, man. I ain't gonna apologize again."

"You wouldn't let anyone diss you the way you dissed me."

The degree of resolution Jamal exhibited left Dag unmoored. He had a disturbing vision of life without Jamal. How he would manage was not entirely clear.

"What happens if we're not in business together?"

"The lawyers and accountants sort it out."

"That's how you gonna be?"

"I told you I'd think about it."

The ongoing ambiguity was more than Dag could take. He had prostrated himself, begged. The superstar posture had

been dropped, but to no positive end. The existential aloneness his longtime agent's abandonment revealed was terrifying.

"That's fucked up, Jamal."

Jamal watched, unsurprised, as Dag rolled his shoulders
and strode out of the office. He had wanted to provoke him,
to provide the shock that would convey the new reality. He
knew Dag was going to return eventually.

As he passed through the front door and stood on the
stoop, Dag considered going back to Jamal's office and apologizing once more. All that history, their years together held
deep resonance. But he quickly banished the thought. He had
done enough apologizing. If Jamal wanted to throw away what
they had built together, let him. He doubted that would happen. He *hoped* it wouldn't happen. Still, he remained on top of
the brownstone steps. With each passing second, the degree to
which Dag depended on his former advocate came into
sharper focus. He glanced at the windows of Jamal's office.
Should he go back up? No, he told himself; don't do that.
Jamal would realize his error and come crawling back. That
was their essential dynamic. Dag believed he only had to survive the current impasse, and all would be well. He squinted
into the sun.

"Dag Maxwell! What up, G?"

Dag peered down the steps. Rooted there was a trio of
black teenagers. The boys wore identical low-slung baggy
jeans, oversized flannel shirts, and white Jordans accented in
multihued palettes. The one in the middle was average sized,
but his sidekicks were at least six five. The tall kids were twins.
Sideways baseball caps, two Knicks and a Laker. Ballers. It was
the kid in the middle who had spoken.

"What are you doing up here, man?" one of the twins
asked, his voice pitched high with excitement.

"This and that," Dag said, and regally descended the steps.

The boys had abandoned their studied indifference in the presence of this hardwood god.

"We saw you play the Celtics," the non-twin said.

"Should've won that night," Dag replied.

"Can we get a picture with you?" the other twin asked.

Dag had interacted with the public for so long it was part of the fabric of being Dag Maxwell, and he did it like punching a clock. But there was something about these boys, their unbridled joy at spotting him, the pure approbation, no, it was more than that, the worship they radiated as if this were some holy rite and Dag the idol to which they prayed. It was a welcome balm to his spirit on a stressful day. He beckoned Trey over from across the street and told him to take their picture.

The shorter kid produced a phone and handed it over. As the boys gathered around Dag to immortalize the experience, other passersby stopped. An older man dressed in a natty suit, two young mothers pushing strollers, a deliveryman from a laundry service watched and when Dag finished taking pictures with the boys all of them wanted pictures, too. Word filtered down the block in both directions, and a flock of students from Medgar Evers Learning Academy came running over from a nearby playground. They carried cardboard boxes and were accompanied by their Latina science teacher. Dag observed the boxes and wondered what they were for.

Two minutes later there were several dozen people on the sidewalk, young, old, different races, and Dag was autographing pieces of paper, and T-shirts and his smile broadened when he signed a Dag Maxwell jersey with a Sharpie someone handed him. The flock called encouragement, wished him luck in the playoffs (they assumed the team would get there), assured him no one cared about what had happened in California.

Dag was signing an autograph for an older woman who had asked him to make it out to her nephew when he noticed a shadow rolling across the street, covering the cars, the asphalt, the facades of the buildings as if a supernatural being was slowly pulling a shade over the sun. The temperature dipped. The windows of buildings dulled. Without warning the schoolkids placed the cardboard boxes over their heads. Several of the adult bystanders looked toward the sky, but the science teacher warned everyone not to. They waited. Several people whooped. Dag heard someone crying. The street, in half-light for a brief period, was now entirely shrouded.

The moon had slid in front of the sun, and an eerily radiating circular penumbra was the otherworldly result. A solar eclipse. Harlem, Manhattan, New York City: All dark. The crowd, so festive, had quieted. The adults observed the schoolkids, impressed with their seriousness of purpose. Several people shaded their eyes with their hands and glanced fleetingly at the sky. Dag was not sure how to behave in the face of this natural phenomenon. The science teacher suggested he not look directly at the sun. She handed him a pair of goggles. Dag thanked her, slipped them on, and faced the sky.

Almost as impressed with the celestial event she was standing next to as she was with the one occurring in the heavens, Gloria Alvarez took several pictures of Dag with her phone. Haunted by having witnessed the killing of John Eagle, the beauty of this cosmic wonder, in the presence of D'Angelo Maxwell, was a cherished consolation.

Dag shared the goggles with Trey, who held them to his eyes and was instantly transported by what he saw. Trey stared at the sun until his brother asked for them back.

This breathtaking contravention of habitual expectations that held everyone's attention transfixed and unsettled Dag. He believed in signs and warnings. A bird winging into a room brought bad luck. If you accidentally put your clothes on backward, there was money coming. But what was the meaning of a solar eclipse? He had no idea.

CHAPTER NINETEEN

Religion was not a significant factor in Nicole Gladstone's suburban Virginia childhood. Her parents were vaguely Protestant but neither attended church, so other than Christmas, which in the Pflueger home was more about Santa Claus, gifts, and candy canes than anything having to do with the birth of Jesus, there were no markers of the season aside from a liberally tinseled tree. Back in Washington after having pulled the plug on her modeling career, the overt religiosity of many of the politicians she encountered (and her belief that this fervor often seemed motivated more by political expediency than authentic religious feeling) was not appealing, and further rendered any thought she entertained of exploring her nominally Christian roots a nonstarter. When Jay suggested, after they decided to get married, she might want to explore Judaism, or at least take the dreidel out for a test spin, Nicole, always game for new adventures, was willing to investigate the possibility. Following some research, she enrolled in a conversion class taught by a young female rabbi with a halo of curls and a welcoming manner at a Conservative synagogue on the Upper West Side and dutifully attended for several months.

Nicole took pleasure in learning about Jewish history and rituals, but when it became apparent how much actual work was involved—familiarity with not only the Torah, but all of the holidays (What was Shemini Atzeret again?), the *Mishnah*, the *Talmud*, the *Shulchan Aruch*, Maimonides's *Guide for the*

Perplexed, and other texts so numerous her jottings about them filled an entire Moleskine notebook—what seemed an endless list of mysteries all finally blended into one big who-put-the-bop-in-the-bop-shoo-bop and it no longer seemed worth the effort. These arcane requirements never ceased to baffle her. Nicole could not fathom why the Jewish people, a tiny minority of the world's population, did not allow anyone who wanted to share their joys and lamentations to do so without delay. If you declared yourself a Christian, you were a Christian. You accepted Jesus as your savior, and that was the end of it. Anyone wanting a more hardcore experience had the option of being dunked in a baptismal font. No one cared if you knew what St. Paul said to the Ephesians. Methodists, Episcopalians, Baptists, none of them required aspirants to pass a religious exam. Whatever her problems with the theology—most of it seemed beside the point—the Christian attitude struck Nicole as more, well, "Christian." She knew that was simplistic, and perhaps even slightly anti-Semitic, but why did religion have to be so demanding? Wasn't it something that was in your soul? Who cared what she thought about the *Talmud*? It was as if they expected her to earn a Ph.D. in Judaism before she would be allowed to take off her clothes and submerge naked into the welcoming waters of the mikveh bath in order to surface as a recognized member of the tribe.

It's not like she wanted to be a rabbi. Although she found the lighting of Sabbath candles unutterably beautiful, to Nicole the Jews remained inscrutable.

Since Jay was not particularly observant, he lacked the moral authority to press the issue and disappointedly submitted to her announcement that, while she was happy—if he'd like, if he ever wanted, if he insisted—to fast on Tisha B'Av in order to commemorate the destruction of the temple (fat chance), wave a lulav and an etrog around on Sukkot (again, unlikely), light the menorah and exchange gifts during Hanukah (she liked that), and, of course, host the family Seder, she was going to hold off on becoming an actual Jew, particularly if it was going to have no effect on Jay's desire to have another child. If she chose to read a biography of Spinoza, that was her business.

While Nicole was not Jewish, the fact of her marriage rendered her, in real estate terms, Jew-adjacent and as a result, she lived a kind of a dual life. Despite Jay's lack of overt religiosity, and his having never found the time in his packed schedule to visit Israel, he was an ardent Zionist and a staunch defender of the nation (if not every specific policy of whatever government happened to be in power) when friends and acquaintances discussed Middle Eastern politics. Nicole adopted his point of view (At dinner parties, she would declare: "The situation is far more complicated than a lot of well-meaning people in the media seem to think.") and learned to bridle when anyone attacked Israel's right to exist as a Jewish state.

Jay did not reciprocate. Although Nicole harbored a sentimental attachment to seasonal tropes—the carols, the eggnog, the Charlie Brown Christmas Special with its undercurrent of melancholy that transported her back to lonely childhood—he refused to have a Christmas tree in the house ("It reminds me of two thousand years of Christian anti-Semitism," he said) so Hanukah became her domestic marker for the arrival of winter. As for spring, its advent was Passover. This is how a former high school cheerleader from Virginia came to be pushing a cart down the vegetable aisle in the Mt. Kisco Whole Foods on a March afternoon, shopping for the ingredients to make charoset in preparation for her Seder.

It was Nicole's fifth Passover since beginning her life with Jay and the first one where she had stated her intention to supervise the meal. In previous years, they had used caterers who served an elaborate if soulless feast, but this Seder would be prepared in the Gladstone kitchen (by a chef, of course) and have Nicole's artisanal stamp. It was her unstated but firmly held belief that if Jay saw her in this light, as a woman who, however gentile, could nonetheless direct the preparations for this most Jewish of celebrations, the liberation of a people from bondage, perhaps he would unchain her ardent womb.

An hour earlier Nicole was in a Chappaqua cafe eating lunch with her friend Audrey Lindstrom, the thirty-six-year old second wife of an investment banker in his fifties. The two women had met on a committee to plan a gala for the Guggenheim Museum and, upon discovering that they were both former models and second wives of successful businessmen with homes in northern Westchester, established a friendship. Nicole was on her second glass of chardonnay. Audrey wore a fedora and large sunglasses even though they were indoors. Some recent cosmetic injections in her upper cheeks had caused unanticipated swelling.

"I gave one of your necklaces to a friend," Audrey said, picking at a crab salad. "For her birthday? She loved it. Loved it!"

Nicole took a sip of wine. Preoccupied with her ovaries, the asparagus omelet in front of her was untouched. She regarded her slim and preternaturally stunning friend whose skin appeared luminous.

"Which one?"

"With the rubies?"

"That one's nice," Nicole said. Recently, she had been working exclusively with sapphires because of Jay's Brooklyn project of that name, believed it to be good for marital karma. Had he even noticed? She wasn't sure.

"I've been holding out on you," Audrey said, taking a sip of chamomile tea. "I have news." Nicole wrenched her mind from her reproductive system. "I'm pregnant."

Although this was the most brilliant announcement imaginable for Audrey, it was the last thing Nicole wanted to hear. They had talked about having children. Audrey was slightly younger, a fact that always reminded Nicole of her own rapidly advancing age, and with great effort, she feigned joy for her friend.

"That is splendid news," Nicole said. Audrey's husband already had two older children, which made the entire situation even worse since it nearly mirrored her own. Nicole swallowed the last of her wine. It was all she could do to keep from ordering a third glass.

"I had been considering starting a business," Audrey said. You know, like you? But now that the baby's coming, I think I'm going to put it off."

"Makes sense."

"But you find jewelry design fulfilling, don't you?"

"Oh, yes, so fulfilling. I do."

The tears that had formed in Nicole's eyes took her by surprise.

"What's wrong?"

"Nothing, nothing." She produced a tissue from her bag and daubed her cheeks. "I'm thrilled for you."

Nicole sorted through a pile of Granny Smith apples in Whole Foods, pleased that she had repressed the impulse to get drunk. It was bad enough she had cried in front of her friend. Perhaps Audrey interpreted them as "tears of joy." It would mortify Nicole if anyone thought she was jealous or, worse, bitter. She worried that her wine intake was growing at a rate that indicated a prescription for Ativan might be in order. Of course, that was hardly better than medicating herself with wine. It was a puzzle.

The conversation that had taken place with Jay while horseback riding continued to trouble her. She had been turning it over in her mind, examining his words from every angle, and now viewed their spat—was it even a spat? Did it rise to that level?—as indicative of an ungraspable marital fissure. How did Jay see her? She was an accomplished woman, hardly a trophy wife. The work in Washington on the Congressional Ethics Committee attested to that. She was formidable on her own, and were they not partners? Why was he so against having another child? It wasn't as if he would be the one getting up to do the middle-of-the-night feeding, cleaning the spit up from his pajamas. Jay was always saying he wanted to make her happy. Was his refusal a sign of both the emptiness of those words and the lack of seriousness with which he viewed their marriage?

She finished packing the apples into a plastic bag, fastened it with a tie, placed it in her cart, and moved to the beverage aisle.

Nicole had never considered having an affair, but she and Jay hadn't had sex in over a month, and her libido remained vigorous. Something was going on with him. For a man in his fifties, he had a healthy sex drive. Or at least he used to. His recent attempt at making love lacked passion, which is why she resisted. Had that been a mistake? He hardly seemed overly concerned with her rejection of his advances. Could it be that he was the one having an affair? The possibility had not even occurred to her. It was a wild thought. One of her many calculations in marrying Jay was his age and how that would affect his future behavior. Presumably, the need to spread his seed was something for which there was no longer a biological imperative. But if he were feeling dissatisfied in the marriage, if he were no longer finding the emotional sustenance it was meant to provide, then perhaps he was searching for it elsewhere. To Nicole, he never seemed like the cheating type, but a therapist had once told her that "love is giving something we don't have to someone we don't know," from which she concluded anything was possible, and that was the most disturbing realization of all.

She was loading bottles of San Pellegrino water into the cart when she heard an unwelcome voice, at once insinuating and aggressive.

"Nicole!"

A slightly plump middle-aged woman wearing a forest green tracksuit with white piping and tennis shoes was piloting a shopping cart in the opposite direction. Her russet hair naturally fell in tight coils, but the industrial-strength straightening solution her stylist employed gave the tresses a wiry quality. The result was pulled into a short ponytail. Expensive sunglasses perched on her head. Recently, the skin around her light brown eyes had been tightened and despite having abandoned herself to a scalpel belonging to one of the top plastic surgeons in Manhattan the result left her looking as if she were in a perpetual state of surprise. This was Marcy Gladstone, Franklin's wife. It was bad enough that Audrey Lindstrom was pregnant. What malevolent imp had placed this woman in her path? Didn't she live on Long Island?

"Marcy," Nicole trilled.

"Are you sure you have enough matzo?" Marcy said by way of greeting, examining the two boxes of unleavened spelt in Nicole's cart.

"No one eats a lot of matzo," Nicole said. "Too many carbs. What are you doing up here?"

"I was visiting a friend who just put in a new tennis court and I thought I'd get some shopping done before I drove home. What's with the spelt?" she inquired, tapping a fire engine red fingernail on the offending item.

"Jay likes it. It helps with digestion."

"Men and their heartburn," Marcy said, shaking her head. "And their prostates."

This declaration caused Nicole to reflect on Jay's health.

Was he overdue for a checkup? One of the downsides of marrying someone twenty years older was the Prostate Years came earlier.

"I'll bring some regular matzo," Marcy assured her as she began to root around in Nicole's brimming cart.

"What are you doing?"

"Just looking," Marcy said, innocently.

Along with the apples, there were lemons, walnuts, raisins, and cinnamon for the charoset she was going to make, ingredients for kugel, kreplach, borscht, a root vegetable casserole, and an impressive brisket. Marcy eyeballed it. Nicole had no idea what she had done wrong, but apparently, the spelt was not her only offense.

"I also found chopped liver they make from the livers of cage-free chickens," Marcy said. "I'll bring that, too."

"It's not a potluck. You don't have to bring anything."

"Did they have those at your church? Potlucks, I mean?"

"We didn't go to church. My parents weren't religious."

"Right, I forgot. You were nothing." Nicole flared, and Marcy quickly said, "Oh, I'm sorry. That was stupid. I didn't mean it in a negative way."

"I would never take it like that," Nicole lied. Her counterfeit smile failed to find its target, now squinting at the ingredients on a carton of chicken broth with the same discernment she brought to the offending matzo.

It was a deeply held belief of Nicole's that Marcy judged her ability to hew to the holiday traditions and found it wanting. Anyone could prepare a meal, but for the food to have the requisite Jewish soul, her cousin-in-law believed, it required the presence of a Jew in the kitchen. Marcy's attempt to hide her disappointment when Nicole told her she had abandoned her plans to convert was unsuccessful. In Marcy's view, it was bad enough Jay divorced his first wife for reasons she could never comprehend, but he compounded that error by marrying a non-Jew who didn't even know what kind of matzo to buy for Passover. That there would be no Jew supervising the kitchen of the Seder family obligation forced her to attend rankled Marcy almost as much as the concept of her cousin-in-law's intermarriage.

"Am I forgetting something?" Nicole asked.

"No," Marcy said, in a way that conveyed yes. Then, "San Pellegrino?"

"What's wrong?"

"It's not exactly seltzer."

Nicole reflected that if she were to become the Grand Rabbi of the Satmar Hasidim, somehow, she still wouldn't be Jewish enough for Marcy. The first time they had met was at a family brunch. When Nicole had referred to the lox as "smoked salmon" Marcy's laugh devolved into a fit of coughing, which she recovered from to patronizingly explain that no self-respecting Jewish person would ever refer to lox ("It's *lox* for godsakes!") as smoked salmon ("That's like calling a bagel a *roll*!" she pontificated).

"You know, I'm curious why you mentioned prostates," Nicole said, tired of her quasi-relative's self-righteous bullying. "Is Franklin having problems with his?"

Marcy seemed taken aback by the question. She looked around to make sure no one was listening. Several shoppers grazed passively nearby, none paying attention to the Gladstone women.

"What does that have to do with Passover?"

"You brought it up," Nicole reminded her.

Marcy weighed whether to share anything other than her disdain with Nicole.

"He is."

"Can he get an erection?"

If Marcy could have opened her eyes any wider, she would have, but surgery had rendered that impossible. Nicole looked around with feigned concern as if atomic secrets were being discussed. She enjoyed tweaking the prudish Marcy's sense of decorum.

"With or without the little pill?"

"It's not always men's prostates, Marcy. Sometimes you have to spice things up a little."

"Oh?"

"Jay and I made a sex tape."

Somehow Marcy's eyes widened. The thought that two married people, at least one of whom was Jewish, had made a sex tape was like telling her there were eleven commandments.

"No, you didn't."

"It was hot."

"You videoed yourselves?"

"For Purim."

Marcy's mind spun into orbit. Since Purim was the holiday where Jews were encouraged by rabbis to wear costumes of the most outrageous kind, drink wine to the point of intoxication, dance in the street—behaviors Marcy would never in a million years engage in, but still—and pursue all manner of licentiousness short of having sex with other people's spouses, perhaps Nicole was telling the truth.

"You're not serious."

"I was Esther and Jay was Haman."

"Okay, you're kidding, right?" Marcy's eyebrows, which could still move, had nearly reached the sunglasses on her forehead. "Tell me you didn't wear Purim costumes."

"It's not like we're putting it on the Internet. What's the problem?"

"You're married people."

"It's not a sin."

"You had sex in Purim costumes?"

"I can't tell you everything."

"Nicole . . . that's sacrilegious, isn't it?"

"Come on; it's not like people in the Bible didn't have a ton of sex. What do you think all that begat-begat-begat was?"

"They didn't tape themselves."

"Oh, touché, Marcy. You're right about that."

"Tell the truth. Did you make a sex tape?"

Early in their marriage she convinced Jay to make tapes of their lovemaking—the usual gymnastics as well as some light bondage that mostly involved the creative application of her pashmina collection—and in a postcoital haze watch them on her laptop. After they viewed the images (which did not include Purim costumes), the couple laughed with a freedom more satisfying than the actual sex. Jay always made sure she erased them promptly, but Nicole was not going to report any of this to Marcy.

"You two should think about it," Nicole said.

"Making a tape?"

"Ask your rabbi."

"I should ask Rabbi Nachman for permission to make a sex tape with Franklin?" Marcy hooted. "Have you met Franklin?"

"Maybe he'd be into it," Nicole said. "You'd probably feel better about yourself."

"I feel fine about myself."

"Then don't do anything."

Nicole bared her teeth in what a passerby would swear was a smile. To deal with someone like Marcy, it's sometimes necessary to move from a stance of receptivity to one of artfully couched aggression. Having done that, Nicole was now ready to finish the shopping.

"I'll see you at the Seder," she said, and triumphantly thrust her cart down the aisle.

CHAPTER TWENTY

I n the gray dawn light that filtered through the windows of the Crush It health club, a caffeinated Christine Lupo pumped iron in the company of other early risers. She intended to transform her pastry-craving middle-aged body into the kind of smoothly humming machine that could better withstand the rigors of a political campaign. To this end, she rolled out of bed each day at five-thirty, was picked up by Sean Purcell (more than happy to book the additional overtime), and was driven to the gym where she stretched, jogged on a treadmill, and lifted weights for an hour.

As the perspiring district attorney worked out, her uneasy consciousness invariably wandered to the guilt she felt over her divorce, although why she felt guilty mystified her since the whole thing was Dominic's fault. Together they had told the kids, and neither had taken it well. Dominic Jr. stared at the floor and, when his sister's crying jag subsided, asked if he could live with his father. Dominic Sr., to his credit, said that would not be possible. The scene played on an endless loop in her head, and she had to concentrate to think clearly and consistently about her nascent campaign and the duties of her current office.

Through the murk and mist of her professional quandaries (staffing, budgets, trials), the one that kept surfacing and submerging then surfacing again like a mutant swamp goblin was the question of whether or not to convene a grand jury in the shooting of the unarmed civilian John Eagle by Police Officer Russell Plesko.

The shooting had predictably generated a great deal of local media attention, but after an initial press conference (carried by all the local network affiliates), Christine had kept a low profile. How she proceeded would have ramifications for her political career and, while it was important to serve justice, she was intent on handling the situation in a way that would redound to her benefit. But the more she pondered her options, the knottier the problem seemed. To not convene a grand jury would send the message that she was insensitive to the needs of the community. Arrange for one and the police would hate her. Somehow, she believed Obama was responsible for the position she was in.

Rain threatened as the district attorney walked from the parking lot to her office accompanied by her vigilant driver, Sean. She noticed a bus from the County Department of Corrections parked at the side of the building. A daisy chain of shackled prisoners plodded into a side entrance supervised by several armed guards. Christine stopped and watched this motley array of pimps, drug dealers, armed robbers, check kiters, serial shoplifters, deadbeat dads, and sex offenders as they shuffled into the building and imagined Russell Plesko in their ragged midst. The easiest choice would be to bring the case to a grand jury. The DA could control the entire process, and she would never have to see the unlucky officer in one of her courtrooms. But things did not always go as planned. There was a slim possibility, however remote that the grand jury would recommend an indictment and then she would be—

This thought was disrupted when she observed one of the prisoners, a hulking white man in his thirties, glaring at her. She met his rage-filled eyes.

"HEY LUPO, FUUUUCCCKKK YOOOOUUURR AAASSSS!!!"

The man's voice resonated against the building and into the trees. Most prisoners had no idea who the district attorney was, saved their fury for the judges, and rarely expressed it out loud. This criminal was obviously someone who watched local television. A breach of decorum that involved verbal abuse was highly unusual. Visibly provoked by the prisoner's insolence, Sean asked if she would like him to talk to the guards. She motioned for him not to move and waited for the officers to take control. When the procession continued to snake into the building the district attorney lowered her voice an octave and commanded:

"HALT!"

The guards and prisoners ceased moving because they were accustomed to following orders.

Christine marched over to the prisoners, heels sparking off the pavement.

"Guard!" she barked at the one nearest her, a crew-cut young white guy shaped like a fire hydrant. "What's your name?"

"Officer Kimble," he said in a voice suddenly flush with authority. He seemed to know who she was.

"What's the name of the prisoner who shouted that obscenity at me, Kimble?"

Kimble looked up and down the hapless row. Some stared at nothing, submitting meekly to their fate, others eyed the DA with a mixture of fear and contempt.

"Dunno," he admitted. There were fourteen inmates in this human bracelet of unlucky charms. "Could've been any of them."

It was rare that Christine made a move not knowing where it would lead. But now she stood in front of the prisoners unsure what to say. To turn and walk away was not an option. She had chosen to confront the loudmouth who had yelled the insult, and so she approached him. The man gathered over her like a storm. There were several murky tattoos on his neck. He sucked on large teeth. If he was intimidated by the presence of the district attorney his behavior did not reflect it. All eyes were on them.

"The reason you're locked up," she began, "is that you think the laws don't apply to you." Her tone was merciless. "Because of the way you choose to act, you'll be in front of a judge today. I'll find that judge's name. The judge is going to know what you said to me, and he or she will enter it on your record. I'm not going to ask you to apologize because if you had the brains to do that, you probably wouldn't be here today." The prisoner regarded her from his lofty height with what looked to Christine like indifference. She wondered if he would seize this chance to clean up his mess. He did not. "Enjoy your day," she said.

When the DA walked away, she repressed the urge to stick her middle finger over her shoulder and flip off the whole group, including the guards. Sean Purcell increased the length of his strides to keep up with her.

In the office, she pulled up the day's docket on her computer and quickly determined the name of the belligerent prisoner, then dashed off an email to the trial judge reporting what had just occurred. A nerve-jangling telephone conversation with her divorce lawyer took up most of the next hour. There were meetings until lunch, which she ate at her desk while reviewing the various prosecutors' reports on trials currently underway. When she found herself reading the same document for the third time, it occurred to her that the decision regarding the Plesko situation was having a greater effect on her ability to concentrate than she had realized. Why was the decision to convene a grand jury proving such a challenge? Had the bombastic O'Rourke, the head of the police union, intimidated her? That couldn't be possible. She had faced him down, put him in his place, just like she did that obstreperous prisoner earlier in the day. What, then? She told her assistant Kelly to find Lou Pagano.

Ten minutes later he was seated on her office couch, drinking a can of diet soda.

"No grand jury," he said. "What good could come of it?"

"It would be unusual."

"I talked to the witnesses myself, Christine. They all said the same thing. I saw the video the maintenance guy took with his phone. It's a terrible thing that happened, but the cop shot a mentally ill individual who was attacking him. Plesko is clean. He had rotten luck. And I'll tell you something else—he's a nice kid, married with a baby, spotless department record, youth league coach. In this environment, you and I both know what can happen, and if it goes in front of a Bronx jury—"

"Why would we get a Bronx jury in White Plains?" Pagano snorted. He recognized her message. She knew what *Bronx jury* meant.

"You know what I'm talking about."

"So give the cops exactly what they want," she said.

"Police violence is a problem, but this is the wrong defendant," Pagano said. He drained his soda and crumpled the can. "This guy goes to trial, anything can happen, and if he winds up in jail, I'm not gonna sleep well for a while."

Elbows on her desk, Christine made a steeple with her hands and inserted her face. The DA would have more challenging problems than this when she became governor.

"I don't see how we can avoid a grand jury."

Late that afternoon the district attorney looked up from a trial report she was notating to see the jittery Kelly.

"That imam?" Kelly said, "He's back." Her tone was apologetic as if Ibrahim Muhammad's presence was her fault.

"What do you mean, he's back? In the office?"

"No, out front. With some friends."

Christine rose from her chair, crossed to the window, and looked toward the plaza in front of the building. Seventeen stories below, the imam, situated behind a police barricade, led a group of protestors, several of whom held signs she could not make out. A group of police officers observed them from a distance.

"They have a right to be there if that's what they want."

"Should I have Sean bring the car around the back of the building?"

"I'm not scared of them," the DA said.

Against her better judgment, she took a call from her husband, who let her know that he had no intention of taking a beating in the division of their assets. As his agitation intensified and became personal (Him: *Why are you being such a bitch?*"), she resisted the urge to return fire (Her: *I only said you'll regret your behavior."*), but her lack of aggressive pushback only seemed to embolden Dominic Lupo who, by his account, anticipated being subjected to a brand of torment not meted out since the Spanish Inquisition. By the time she hung up on him, the window in which she could accomplish anything having to do with her actual job had slammed shut. She locked her office door and for five minutes sat in her chair and stared at the framed picture of her children that she kept on her desk. Somehow, the district attorney managed not to weep.

Forty-five minutes later, briefcase packed with work, Christine Lupo left the building with Sean at her side and headed across the plaza toward the parking lot. Government employees moved through the twilight in groups of twos and threes toward their cars. All of them were ignoring Imam Ibrahim Muhammad and his band of demonstrators, who stood quietly holding signs that said INDICT PLESKO, JUSTICE FOR JOHN, and ALLAH WILL JUDGE. A mixture of men and women, black and white, some in Muslim garb others in street clothes, stood on the sidewalk at the edge of the plaza and Christine had to walk past them to access the parking lot. Unafraid of the sidewalk foot soldiers or the judgment of their god, she set her shoulders, quickened her step, and nodded to the police officers. They saluted her.

When the protesters recognized the district attorney, the whole scene sprang to life and Ibrahim Muhammad shouted into a bullhorn, "What do we want?" His enthusiastic flock yelled back, "Justice for John!" "When do we want it?" Muhammad loudly asked. The reply: "Now!"

One of the police officers, an imposing black woman, detached from the group of cops and appeared at the DA's side. Her nameplate read "Malone."

"I'm going to walk you to your car if you don't mind, m'am," said Officer Malone.

"I got this, Officer," Sean informed the cop.

Christine told Sean to let the policewoman do her job, and the three of them continued past the chanting protesters, across the street, and into the parking lot where the DA thanked the officer again. Sean held the door open and the DA climbed into the town car.

As Sean backed out of the parking space, turned the wheel, and made for the exit, her mind strayed back to the upsetting conversation with her husband, and it took her a moment to realize that a wedge of activists had broken from the group and swarmed across the street toward her car. Police officers sprinted from the plaza to chase them down.

She watched with increasing concern as Sean calculated whether he had enough time to floor the gas pedal and, with a hard twist of the steering wheel, skirt the protesters and get away before anything could happen or whether he was going to be forced, by the presence of human beings in front of the vehicle, to come to a complete stop. Instead, he did neither, and while two young protesters, a white man and a black woman, threw themselves in front of the car, Sean let the vehicle roll forward. The white man jumped out of the way, but the black woman did not move quickly enough. She lost her footing and the car knocked her to the ground. Sean jammed the brakes as the cops corralled the unruly mob.

The DA jumped out of the car and kneeled by the woman. Several demonstrators surrounded the victim, including Imam Ibrahim Muhammad. Sean stood at his boss's side, alert and prepared to deflect anything incoming.

To Christine's immense relief, the woman did not appear to be badly hurt or hurt at all. Putting the humanitarian concern aside, running over a pedestrian was not the best way to kick off a political campaign. Christine asked the woman if she was all right.

"I think so."

"What's your name?"

"Tamika Crawford."

Christine noticed her left leg had begun to shake. She made an effort to control the timbre of her voice.

"I'm so sorry, Ms. Crawford."

"I'm sorry, ma'am," Sean said, teeth clenched.

Ibrahim Muhammad asked if she wanted an ambulance and Tamika Crawford said no, I didn't hit my head, so let's just get on with it. She climbed to her feet, brushed her jeans off, and trained her gaze on the DA. Christine noticed the woman had unusually long eyelashes.

"You need to serve justice," Tamika said.

"You sure you're okay?" Officer Malone asked the protester, who was examining a scrape on her elbow.

"I think so," she said.

"Then you're under arrest," Malone said, brandishing handcuffs.

This turn came as a surprise to Tamika and she looked at the DA, who understood that an escalation would not be helpful.

"Let's forget it," Christine said to Officer Malone. "Just let her go."

While this was going on several security guards poured out of the building and with their assistance the police detail herded the protesters back across the street.

It occurred to Christine, while the event unfolded, that this would be an extraordinary moment to announce that she was convening a grand jury in the Russell Plesko case. The drama would leap out of news accounts, and cement her reputation as a woman of both compassion and principle. Instead, she wished Tamika Crawford well, expressed her gratitude to the police, and asked Sean to take her to the Parkway Diner. She was meeting with a political consultant and did not want any county officials who frequented the usual watering holes to see her.

When he was in high school and wanted to drink somewhere the management didn't check IDs, Russell Plesko and his friends went to the Fenian in Port Chester. A brackish dive near the train station with a jukebox and cheap drinks, most nights back then it was packed with high school athletes. Russell lettered in three sports, and he and his teammates were regulars. They drank tequila sunrises, ate beer nuts or pickled eggs, then drove back to their family homes careful to go just under the speed limit. He went less regularly now but could usually count on seeing a friendly face. In the early evening on this weeknight, he sat alone at the bar sipping his second beer. A couple of dull-faced commuters nursed restorative cocktails nearby.

The bartender approached him, wiping a glass. A robust woman in her sixties with an unlit cigarette dangling from thin lips, Mrs. Costello was married to the owner. Russell had known her since he was sixteen and he had never called her anything other than Mrs. Costello.

"How are you doing, Russell?" Her voice held a lifetime of Virginia Slims. "You want another beer?"

"No, thanks, Mrs. Costello."

He wasn't in a chatty mood, but Mrs. Costello didn't move. "You know the bar sponsors a Little League team, right?"

"Sure, I know."

"Ralphie Bonfiglia's the coach and his company is transferring him to Boston for a few months."

"Yeah, so?"

"You coach basketball, don't you?"

"That's right."

"Do you want to coach the Little League team until Ralphie comes back?"

The offer flabbergasted Russell. Given the state of limbo he currently occupied, the idea of making plans was something he had not considered.

"Are all the parents on board?"

Russell and Mrs. Costello had avoided any talk about his situation. She had not brought it up, and Russell did not volunteer information.

"Don't worry about the parents. Mr. Costello likes you, he'll talk to anyone who's got a problem."

"And Ralphie's okay with this?"

She told him not to worry about it, everyone would be grateful. Russell had trouble envisioning any return to routine existence, but this gesture showed him he could be accepted back into society despite what he had done. He rubbed his knee, the one that had buckled on him that awful morning. It was still sore.

"All right, then yes."

She nodded and went to check on the customers down the bar.

Russell thought his interview with Lou Pagano of the Westchester County District Attorney's office had gone well.

The encounter had been friendly, and Russell told his story from every possible angle. He liked Pagano who did not seem to have a bad attitude about cops but came away from the meeting not sure how it would work out.

Since the shooting, his days had taken on a strange texture. The White Plains Police Department had placed him on administrative leave and confiscated his firearm. He and his wife fought constantly, and their bickering caused the baby to cry incessantly. Reporters waited for him outside his apartment building. Circumstances led him to the house of his brother, a Yonkers firefighter with a wife and three kids. He had spent the last several nights on a pullout couch in the finished basement. It was not an ideal arrangement. There, he would thrash for hours, unable to sleep. In the morning, he would put on sunglasses and pull a trucker cap low over his eyes before he left for the day. He worked out at a local gym during off hours when he would be less likely to run into anyone he knew. He took his laptop to the library where he read the news in a quiet corner. His friends on the police force called but he parried their invitations to grab lunch or drinks. He prepared himself for the worst. Mrs. Costello's offer of a coaching opportunity was like seeing an angel slide.

That morning he had met with his attorney for the second time, a meeting he had requested. Joan Abelson was a lawyer at Rose, Gardener & Seligman in downtown White Plains. Her manner was as brisk as her wardrobe, which consisted of a tailored gray pantsuit and a white blouse. Blonde hair cut short, two gold studs in her left ear. Russell sat across from her in a sports coat and khakis, cap on his lap. The lawyer sipped a large mug of chai tea. Russell found the scent relaxing.

"How have you been doing?"

"Been better," he said.

He realized that his leg was bouncing and stopped it. He

did not want the lawyer to think he was nervous. She waited for him to talk but Russell was not sure exactly what to say. He knew he needed to ask a question before she told him she had work to do and would call when there was news.

"How long does it usually take before the DA's office says whether it's going to put a grand jury on a case?" He hoped that his edginess was not painfully obvious. At least his voice was forceful.

"As I told you when we met the other day, it varies."

"Is my situation taking longer than usual?"

"If the DA were to make an announcement today, that would fall somewhere into the average length of time. She's not taking too long."

""I've been reading about grand juries."

"And what have you learned?"

"They can be unpredictable," Russell said. He pinched the brim of his cap, now resting on his thigh.

"That's true."

"It's impossible to tell how this is going to play out?"

"Russell, look, as I said, this is a serious case that will have ripples far beyond you and your situation. It would be highly unusual for the district attorney not to convene a grand jury. I can pretty much guarantee it, in fact. But that doesn't mean you have to start worrying yet. If the case goes to trial, you've got a better-than-average chance of beating the charges. Your record is exemplary, you're active in youth sports. It was a bad situation."

"The fucking worst," he said. "Excuse my language."

The attorney nodded supportively. He appreciated that she seemed to be listening to him and was sensitive to his distress. Russell wished he could stop worrying. Joan Abelson certainly seemed untroubled by it. He admired the dispassion lawyers brought to their work. Studying law interested him. If he were allowed to return to his job, perhaps he'd ask to be assigned to the DA's office. The department certainly was not going to put him back on the street anytime soon.

"If the case goes to trial, and I'm not saying it will, we'll get you a sympathetic jury, and I'm going tell them your story."

The door to the bar opened, and Russell heard the men before he saw them. Two black guys. He tensed. They were talking about a school board meeting that had occurred the previous evening. The men, who appeared to be around forty, sat in a booth and ordered drinks. Although people stared at him in public, and some probably judged him harshly, no stranger had spoken to him since the incident. The media had not widely circulated his picture, but he had assumed people would know his identity. That this did not appear to be the case astonished him. Still, Russell was sensitive to the presence of African-Americans, who, he believed, would take a particularly harsh view of what had happened. He glanced at the men and was pleased to see they remained indifferent to his presence.

Russell was not a regular churchgoer but he believed in God, and this put him in a knotty position. In his view, he had not sinned. And yet now a man was dead, and this death was on him. He had caused it. That was horrible but what else could he have done? His life had been in danger. John Eagle could have grabbed his gun. Whether or not he was at fault, the remorse at having taken a life weighed on him. Russell Plesko lived by the words "peace officer." It was the first time he had drawn his weapon on the job.

He took another sip of his beer and peered around the bar. Since he was young, he had wanted to be a cop. He had barely finished college not because he couldn't do the work, but because he wasn't suited for sitting in a classroom. Russell loved being on the force. It allowed him to interact with new people each day and he enjoyed the respect they showed him.

White Plains was a mostly middle-class city, and despite pockets of poverty, it was not a bad place to be in law enforcement. He had planned to work for twenty years then pension out, buy a weekend cabin upstate, spend time in the woods with his family. Now all of it was in jeopardy.

He glanced at the black men. They were still engrossed in conversation. Down the bar, one of the commuters ordered a refill. Russell tossed a couple of bills on the bar, waved to Mrs. Costello, and walked out.

It was early evening and the air had chilled. The sun was low in the sky when he walked into the Fenian. Now traces of purple lingered on the horizon, and he could see the moon rising over downtown Port Chester. Russell had parked around the corner. Turning up the collar of his jacket, he wished he could call Christine Lupo. He needed to know what was going to happen.

It was evident something was wrong when he turned on to the side street where his car was parked. The streetlight lit the windshield of Russell's five-year-old gray Honda Civic unevenly. The illumination reflected in intricate patterns on both lateral extremes, but the middle was bashed clean through and swallowed the glow like a dead star.

Christine regarded her dinner companion across the table at the Parkway Diner. Bruce Lathrop was a husky man with a shaved head and stubbly face, the combination of which lent him a menacing aspect that he undercut with an open, easygoing manner. He wore jeans and a sports coat. The two of them were in a booth, and spoke quietly so as not to be overheard. They were expecting someone else to join them.

As the ambitious politico picked at her salad, the consultant revealed that the initial polling she had commissioned exposed an unfortunate truth: Her name recognition was not as high as either of them had hoped.

"All the drug dealers you lock up, the wife beaters—our research shows that, at least outside of Westchester County, no one cares."

He chewed thoughtfully on a piece of turkey bacon and let this unappetizing reality sink in. Despite the hour, Lathrop had ordered breakfast.

"What about all the times I've been on television?"

"The TV has mostly been local, so some people in the city know you, but upstate, no one." He saw her reaction to this, a barely perceptible downturn of her coral lips, and said, "Hey, you're not paying me to sugarcoat it, right? But look, since you've been in office, you haven't had a genuinely sexy case."

"I was on TV for an entire month when we put away the doctor who killed his wife's boyfriend. CNN did that story on the nightly news."

"Joe Blow in Buffalo? He doesn't care," Lathrop explained. "You can't take it personally."

The district attorney forked a juiceless piece of tomato into her mouth and chewed but did not notice the lack of taste. She took her entire situation personally. The lucrative career in the private sector she had passed up to work twelve hour days for a government salary, dealing with armed criminals, rapists, murderers; her conviction rate was the envy of her colleagues across the country, and yet she remained a nonentity to the public? It was maddening.

"And we convicted the doctor on evidence that was circumstantial," she reminded the bullet-headed operative.

"Which was impressive, don't get me wrong," he said, awarding her the booby prize of his approbation. "But locking up that guy doesn't make people look at you and think"—here he paused for effect, then said in a stentorian tone— "Governor Lupo."

Christine examined the combination of greenery in her bowl as if the configuration in which the chef arranged it contained a code that, when cracked, might offer a solution to this riddle. It ate at her that despite the high level at which she discharged her duties, brought indictments, and put criminals behind bars, she found herself barely better known than some state senator from Poughkeepsie.

Then came the consultant's proposal: "But if there was a case that was the right kind of high-profile—" He didn't need to finish the thought.

"You think I should indict the cop who killed the civilian?"

"Not for political reasons, that's for sure." He tore a piece of wheat toast, dipped it in a pool of egg yolk, placed it in his mouth, chewed and swallowed. "But it would be a publicity bonanza."

"People already say I'm too in love with the cameras."

"You can't be successful in this business if you hang back," he pointed out. "All this racial stuff going on now with the cops, no one's taking them on."

"You know what happens when you antagonize the police?"

"I'm not saying it wouldn't be a gamble, but when you take a hard look at your profile, you might want to think about it."

"Even if I were inclined to do that, this looks like the wrong defendant. My deputy personally interviewed all of the witnesses. He believes the officer was justified in his use of force."

"What's the cop's name, Plesko, right?" The DA confirmed this. She could see the computer in Lathrop's head sort files and bring up a document. "I think that's a Hungarian name, probably Catholic, which falls under the heading of white European. He's not from some ethnic group that's going to rally to his defense."

"You forget the cops," she reminded him. "They're a group. I hosted a delegation of them in my office to discuss this, and I can tell you, they'll be upset."

"They're always upset. And by the way, I'm not advocating either position, just thinking out loud."

"I'm not going to indict that guy to get traction in an election."

Bruce Lathrop held his hands up, palms facing across the booth, stop right there.

"Hey, I would never suggest anything so cynical," he assured her. "Look, you want to be elected governor, you need to win the city. You want to spend your time running around upstate putting the Schenectady-Albany-Troy equation together, be my guest, but that's not how you get elected governor. New York City is a union town. You gotta make inroads down there. On the one hand, if you want to look at this thing through the self-interest prism, you're better off not bringing the case to a grand jury."

"But if I do, then it would look like I had balls."

"Of course," he agreed. "Frankly, I think voters prefer balls to integrity."

"New York is full of liberals who might be pro-union, but they're not particularly pro-police, and it would look like I had more integrity if I did, right? And balls."

"Look at what happened when Reagan fired the air traffic controllers," Lathrop said, wistful at the memory of the routed labor movement. "It was like Washington crossing the Delaware. Balls and integrity in a single package."

"Not that I would ever think that way," the DA said.

"So, you have a conundrum."

"That's your brilliant insight?"

"Hey, don't kill the messenger," he said.

That her frustration had revealed itself further frustrated the DA. It wasn't Bruce Lathrop's fault that she was in this position. Was the harsh tone she had just used misdirected anger she felt toward her husband? It was her suspicion that if she were not going through a divorce at this highly inconvenient time, her thinking around the police shooting would have greater clarity. Her inability to come to a decision was something that she would be happy to lay at her husband's feet if that were not a sign of mental weakness. But it was. She offered her apologies for snapping at Lathrop. Accustomed to far worse from egotistical, narcissistic politicians, he told her not to worry about it.

Outside the window, a black limousine glided into the parking lot and pulled up to the restaurant door. A substantial man in a business suit emerged from the backseat and Christine instantly recognized him. He hustled into the diner and seconds later was hovering over their table. He smiled ingratiatingly at the DA and introduced himself to Lathrop.

"Sorry I'm late," Franklin Gladstone said. The consultant moved over, and the new arrival slid in beside him. He looked at Lathrop's plate. "Who eats breakfast at night? This guy's nuts!" Franklin delivered the words like a punchline, but since they were not funny, he only received forced smiles in response.

The waitress arrived and asked Franklin if he'd like to order something, but he waved her away. The three of them exchanged pleasantries, then Franklin declared the preliminaries over and requested that they discuss the reason he'd driven up to White Plains. Christine admired Franklin's no-nonsense style as it reflected her own. He was someone who "got things done" and was acquainted with a great many potential donors, two qualities she prized. She walked Franklin through her money-raising operation, how much the campaign had already, and what her projected needs were between now and the election. Franklin listened intently, nodding as she enumerated the challenges of putting a donor network together. Having illuminated the financials, the district attorney asked if there were any particular policy issues he wanted to discuss.

"I've already vetted you on policy," he said.

"I need to know you're comfortable," Christine said.

"I can tell you I'm nearly always the smartest person in the room," the hereditary kingpin assured them. "I assess situations quickly based on the data my people put in front of me. I don't like it, I'm out, but if I like it—"

"You're in," Bruce said.

"This guy's a genius," Franklin said.

Christine smiled, pleased by Franklin's enthusiasm. He was a force she could harness. "Do you think you'd like to be a bundler?"

"It would be an honor to encourage my friends to violate campaign finance laws on your behalf." The DA and the consultant stared at Franklin. When he said, "I'm joking!" the pair laughed like it was professional comedy.

The check came, and Christine grabbed it, but while she was digging into her wallet, Franklin picked it up. "It's a thing I like to do," he said. "Indulge me."

In the parking lot, Franklin asked Lathrop if he might have a private word with the district attorney. Deferring to the donor, the consultant shuffled to his Prius.

"My wife and I would like to host a fundraiser for you at our home."

Christine's eyes melted. Franklin Gladstone was the whale she had been praying for. "I would love that," she said, deploying the word *love* strategically with the expectation her new patron would derive warmth from his proximity to its sound.

"Are you free for dinner next week?" Franklin asked. "I have some ideas."

It sounded as if he were asking her on a date. She was not remotely attracted to anything about her new admirer other than the size of his investment portfolio but was nonetheless flattered.

"I think so."

When they shook hands, Christine noticed that Franklin

held hers too long. His was fleshy and slick like an eel. She had been an emotional wreck since viewing the photographic evidence of her husband's perfidy and Franklin's attentions had a palliative effect on her feminine ego. She stood a little taller as she walked to the car, entirely resolved to exploit her new benefactor's remaining hormones.

CHAPTER TWENTY-ONE

When the Biblical Exodus took place and the enslaved Hebrews cast off their chains and lit out from Egypt headed for the land deeded by Yahweh to Abraham as recounted in Genesis 12, crossed the conveniently parted Red Sea which crashed down on the pursuing Egyptians (notoriously non-buoyant), wandered the inhospitable Sinai Desert for forty years—a fractious time during which Moses received the Ten Commandments—then hiked to a mountain summit where, sun-seared eyes feasting on the plains of Canaan and what should have been, if their deity's approbation was any indication, a radiant future, the Chosen People watched their leader expire, at which point, exhausted but unbowed, the ragtag Israelites descended into the beckoning valley and the next phase of their journey through history, the idea that multiple millennia later the descendants of this hardy and disputatious desert tribe, ex-slaves now liberated, would gather in their finery around brisket-laden tables in the New York suburbs to commemorate these unlikely events with song, prayers, and sweet wine would have been inconceivable.

Passover was never Jay's favorite holiday. When Grandpa Jack reached the age where his ego no longer required he host the service, the patriarch announced that, following the Hebrew predilection for primogeniture, the family would now gather for the feast at the home of his eldest son, Bernard (Bingo). At that juncture in the family history, although Bingo was the designated host for the evening, Jay's Uncle Jerry led the service and Jerry's religious devotion, while not full-blown Orthodox, nonetheless significantly exceeded that of his brother. Uncle Jerry was a forbidding presence in the Seders of Jay's youth, presiding at the table in a suit and tie, a model of decorum. His trim physique, in contrast to Bingo's more bulbous one, and his enviable head of well-coiffed, silvery hair, crowned with a yarmulke for the occasion, led Jay and his sister to refer to their uncle as the Jewish Johnny Carson only without the gags, since the prevailing atmosphere during the annual Passover holiday resembled that of a morgue. Jay's cousins exhibited all the liveliness of the daily catch at a fish restaurant until they were tasked with reciting prayers or chanting songs, both of which they would do in passable Hebrew, to the wonder of the children on the other side of the family, for whom the language might as well have been Mandarin.

The absence of anything resembling levity was, for Jay, what defined those dreary celebrations. Uncle Jerry would lead the prayers in a monotone and woe to anyone who did not participate in the hour-long slog with anything other than rapt attention. Bingo, typically a far looser presence, acted as his brother's enforcer. One year Jay and Bebe locked eyes during the Ten Plagues when Uncle Jerry, dipping his fork into a glass of Manischewitz and placing drops of red wine on his white china plate to commemorate each more horrendous curse, hit the word "boils." Jay murmured "zits" to his bored sibling—this passed for wit in a twelve-year-old—and a mutual laughing attack ensued, suppressed at first, hidden behind hands, swallowed in gulps of breath before finally bursting forth into prolonged hysterics that resulted in temporary banishment from the table. Other than his Aunt Estelle's gefilte fish—truly superb with horseradish—it was Jay's only joyful Passover memory.

Jay's mother Helen was a happy participant at those family

gatherings but, at eighty-two and in the early stages of Alzheimer's, she was unable to recall most of them. Still, when he picked her up at her east side condo where she lived with her Jamaican caretaker, Mrs. Braithwaite, her pleasure at the prospect of another Seder pleased her son immensely.

Boris held the back door of the Mercedes as she delicately folded herself in, Mrs. Braithwaite, in a starched dress, beside her.

"Is Uncle Jerry leading the service?" Jay's mother inquired.

"Mom, Uncle Jerry died."

"Really?" she said, her spirit undimmed at this news. "Well, Jerry was very dull." Jay was never sure what she would remember, but her mood usually remained steady. "Will your Aunt Estelle be there?"

Jay chose not to remind his mother that her sister-in-law had been interred next to Uncle Jerry two years earlier, so he only said no.

"She's got somewhere better to be?" Jay's mother asked, reaching into her purse to produce a peppermint candy that she unwrapped and placed in her mouth. "Big shot."

On the ride to Bedford, Jay reflected on the call he had received earlier that day from his ex-wife in which she informed him that their daughter and Imani were sharing a bed. What I'm about to mention isn't gossip, Jude said, but in the interest of co-parenting, I think you should be aware that we might have a gay child. Jay informed her that he already suspected as much and wished his ex-wife a happy Passover. After much cogitation on the subject, he found Aviva's putative homosexuality considerably less distressing than her support for the Palestinians.

He stole glances at his mother in the backseat where she was nibbling Saltines. Before her mind had begun to dissolve, she had been a formidable presence in his life, stern and opinionated. She had expressed pride in Jay but was not shy about letting him know when she disapproved of his behavior, as was the case when he divorced Jude. Nor was she a fan of Nicole although the arrival of her new daughter-in-law coincided with the diminishment of her mental capacity and her negative attitude about the marriage eventually disappeared into the maw of vanished memory. Jay contemplated his mother in sadness at her state, but also because the situation reminded him of the ephemeral quality of everything. A day earlier, his urologist Dr. Tenenbaum had removed a tiny chunk of his prostate because he had noticed something suspicious. He did not want to think about what that procedure might portend.

If you wanted the world to see you in a certain way, there was a limited time in which that could happen. To their congregations at Yom Kippur, the rabbis would intone, "May you be inscribed for another year in the Book of Life." The Book of Life, indeed. Our lives are written in ink, and always hurtling forward, Jay reflected, as they drove north. What has been done cannot be erased. His mother's life, the part of it when a woman known as Helen Gladstone was in charge of her cognitive faculties, had been written. And yet the effect this paragon of rectitude had on her son persisted. Jay's diffidence was his maternal inheritance.

The condition of the modern kitchen in Bedford did not reflect the five hours of preparation the dinner had required because along with the chef Nicole had enlisted to assist her, she had hired two young waitresses, both recent Irish immigrants—they were employed by Jay and Nicole's nearby country club—to serve and clean up. Counters and sinks were clean, covered dishes warming in the oven. The fragrant smell of chicken broth filled the room. As the chef (it was his day off from Babbo) put the finishing touches on the Seder plate, Marcy Gladstone tasted the matzo ball soup simmering in a large pot. Nicole watched her warily, a second glass of chardonnay in her hand. Bebe freshened her spritzer.

"Not bad," Marcy said. "Is the broth from a can?" Nicole nodded. Mouthing the words so the chef wouldn't hear her, Marcy said, "I would have made it for you from scratch. What are you paying him for?"

"My mother used canned broth," Bebe said.

"Who's perfect?" from Marcy.

Nicole topped up her wineglass and imagined herself in a mikveh bath with her cousin-in-law, warm water caressing their naked bodies, united in this millennia-old rite of purification shared by Jewish women, while she held Marcy's head under the water long enough for her to drown.

"Only you," Nicole answered.

The servers set the long table in the sunlit dining room for thirteen. On every plate was a Haggadah. In the living room hors d'oeuvres had been laid out, herring, chopped liver, even gribnitz (fried chicken fat) that Nicole had tracked down at Sammy's Roumanian on the Lower East Side. Everything had been done to reduce the variables and, while the intent of the evening was to honor the holiday and recall the story of the Exodus, Nicole was going to remind Jay—through her actions because she would never be so crass as to lay it out verbally—of her immense skills as a hostess, a wife, and, by implication, a mother. She refilled her wineglass and gazed toward the backyard where Franklin addressed Aviva and Imani, both of whom were drinking vodka and Coke.

"Two black guys are walking past a synagogue during the High Holy Days," Franklin was saying. With one hand, he moved his fingers through the air to simulate walking. His other held a glass of scotch. "And they hear," now Franklin tucked his chin and: "*MMMMMMMMUUUUUUU.*" He repeated the noise in several staccato bursts. Satisfied with his performance, he continued, "One black guy turns to the other and says, 'What's that sound?'"—This question was delivered in the vocal equivalent of blackface—"and the second black guy, he says, 'Dey blowin' de shofar,'" pronouncing it *chauffeur*, with the accent on the initial syllable. "And the first black guy says, 'Dem Jews sho' do know how to treat dey help!'" Franklin's buttery gut shook in delight as he awaited a reaction to his material.

The young women stared at him. Franklin, expecting appreciative laughter, heard crickets.

"I did a little comedy when I was younger," he informed them, in the event they doubted his credentials. "That was Redd Foxx's voice." Still nothing. "You girls have any idea who Redd Foxx is?"

Imani laughed listlessly in a way Franklin wanted to interpret as assent.

Aviva's face remained impassive. Staring at her second cousin, she said, "Where do I even start with that?"

"I'll send you some DVDs," Franklin offered.

"That'd be swell," Imani said.

It dawned on Franklin that a social blunder had been committed and he developed a sudden need to refill his drink. He excused himself, marveling inwardly at the lack of humor in so many young people today and wondering just what was going on with those two.

In the media room, Boris played *Gears of Death* with Ari and Ezra. He did not spend time with the twins outside of family events for two reasons, the first being that they had far more disposable income. This disparity stopped Boris from participating in the bottle service, nightclubbing, Zovirax-ingesting life led by the pair. The other reason: Since they were, to Boris, in their sense of entitlement, incurious intellects, and general obliviousness, a personification of the argument for a one-hundred-percent inheritance tax, he barely tolerated them.

The twins were gaming with Boris because, upon having scrutinized their cousin Aviva's girlfriend and determined that neither of them considered her a potential sex partner (Imani's lesbianism eluded them), they concluded video games were a more valuable use of their time.

Ari and Ezra had discussed violating their father's order to not talk about their bid for the hockey team. The two thought it would increase their status, but fear of Franklin's wrath kept them mute on the subject. Conversely, Boris would have enjoyed lording his involvement with the Sapphire over the twins, but his self-control forbade it.

Ezra deftly maneuvered his controller and destroyed Boris's avatar, which exploded in a cloud of pixilated shrapnel.

To Ari, Ezra said, "Give it up, bro," and they bumped fists.

To Boris, Ari said, "Want to put some money on the next one to make it interesting?"

"It could never be interesting," Boris said.

The empty living room was an oasis and Jay could be found there seated on the sofa with a laptop searching for a relevant, nonreligious text with which to kick off the Seder. After looking through several political speeches, essays, and poems, he chose a passage he found meaningful and went to his upstairs office to print it out. He heard the murmur of voices from the various rooms, a comforting pre-ritual hum, and trusted that this congenial evening would be a respite from his vexations.

The Passover table resembled a glossy magazine layout. The most exquisite white china and linens, the finest silver, and in the middle of it all a Seder plate on which were arrayed the requisite maror, charoset, karpas, shank bone, and roasted hard-boiled egg in a still-life arrangement that Renoir would have been glad to paint had he been able to put his anti-Semitic sentiments aside long enough to complete the task. The tiny bulbs of a crystal chandelier glittered benevolently, light particles knitted into a warm raiment draped across the shoulders and over the heads of those fortunate enough to be present. All of it whispered that if the attendees could not be in Jerusalem on this night, northern Westchester County was the next best place.

Jay presided at one end of the table opposite Nicole. To his left were his mother, Bebe, Franklin, Marcy, and their fifteen-year-old daughter Chloe (wraithlike, saucer eyes, profoundly bored), on his right, Ezra, Ari, Aviva, Imani, and Boris. Mrs. Braithwaite had been invited to dine with the family but elected to eat her dinner in the kitchen.

The Seder began with Jay remarking that while he loved and missed Uncle Jerry, it was his considered view that the evening could benefit from modernization, and to that end, anyone who had a question, or wanted to talk about a topic germane to the themes of the evening should feel free to interpose. To set the tone, he unfolded a piece of paper from his jacket pocket and began to read "I Dream A World" by the African-American poet Langston Hughes. Between the first and second stanzas, Jay glanced at Imani. The poem was intended to be an act of inclusion, but her expression was enigmatic. He finished and cleared his throat. No one said anything. Unsure of what to do, this being a complete departure from every previous Gladstone Seder, the guests waited. Trying to coax conversation, Jay looked from face to face.

"No poetry lovers here?"

Again, nothing.

Resentful of being forced off script, Marcy said, "Interesting choice," followed by Bebe bailing him out by saying, "I liked it," and her affirmation was the end of the discussion.

"Jay," Nicole said, "Why don't you start the Seder?"

"I thought I had," he said, attempting a joviality that barely concealed his displeasure. Had his wife missed the point of what he said about making this a different kind of evening?

"Why don't you light the candles," Jay suggested to his wife.

Nicole stood and lit the candles with a wood matchstick, recited the Hebrew prayer, and glanced obliquely at Marcy to gauge her reaction to the nonkosher nature of the moment. Marcy stared at the cover of her Haggadah and refused to look at the fire-wielding shiksa. Nicole sat back down and took a long pull on her fourth glass of wine. Jay observed what was going on—his wife did not hide her feelings about Franklin's spouse—and prayed neither of them would erupt. A day earlier, Nicole had told him that Marcy had requested via email to light the candles and Nicole hadn't answered. She intended to light the candles herself, and when Jay asked why this mattered since she wasn't Jewish, he was treated to: "Because it's my fucking house."

The first cup of wine, the ceremonial washing of hands, the hiding of the afikomen which Jay placed behind an abstract sculpture in the living room with the poignant knowledge that no one present was still young enough to look for it. He directed each person in succession to read a short portion. Although Jay had made it clear he wanted this Passover to resonate more deeply than those of his youth, no one deviated from the roadmap provided by the Haggadah. The Seder moved briskly along, a direct reaction on Jay's part to the lugubrious, mind-numbing, endless exercises in religiosity presided over by the sonorous Uncle Jerry. Marcy and Franklin read their assignments in Hebrew (then translated the words to English, thereby doubling the time it took to finish, to everyone's dismay), Chloe, as the youngest, listlessly asked the Four Questions, Ari and Ezra read with an excitement that suggested the text was a tax return. Bebe's reading was clean and efficient. Boris delivered his bit with some fervor since he was the only Jew present one generation removed from actual persecution. Aviva and Imani read with brio because they were engaged citizens of a complex and ever-evolving world who believed all wisdom traditions possessed some inherent value, and Nicole committed to her allotted lines with a rogue energy animated by her loathing of Marcy.

The group was going around the table a second time when Ari Gladstone dolefully recited the words, "When we were slaves in the land of Egypt," and Imani answered, half-joking, "What do you mean *we*, white man?"

Not sure what she intended, Ari's brother Ezra said, "Because we were slaves in Egypt."

Imani turned to Jay and politely asked if she might say something out of turn. "Go right ahead," he said, superseding the Uncle Jerry legacy. "The Seder is about freedom."

"You see," Imani said to Ezra, "I've got a problem with that." Marcy stared at her and fretted where this was going. Aviva was interested since it appeared a seminar might be breaking out. Nicole smiled graciously at her young guest, happy that the interruption seemed to annoy Marcy.

"You've got a problem with freedom?" Ezra said, more a statement than a question.

"No, because that would be ironic," Imani said, "Wouldn't it? Being African-American and all." She waited while the puzzlement on his face retreated and the usual self-satisfied expression returned. "The problem I have is with the whole idea of Jews and slavery."

"What problem is that?" Marcy asked.

"It's the idea—" Imani paused. "How do I put this?"

Unable to contain her irritation, Marcy interrupted, "We were *slaves* in Egypt, Imani." Her tone brooked no contradiction.

Feeling expansive, Imani said, "My point isn't the historical record." The vodka and Cokes had loosened her up considerably. "Although, frankly, who knows if any of this is true, right?"

"Oh, it's true," Franklin assured her, earning several marital points in the process. He enjoyed displaying his commitment to the faith in front of his religiously observant wife.

"Lots of people don't think Jesus was real," Imani pointed out. "It's just that in the American narrative, my people, black people, *own* slavery, you know? We were brought here in chains, the middle passage, the plantation, right? Slavery is *our* thing. You all have the Holocaust and, yeah, it's horrible, maybe the worst tragedy ever, you probably win that one—not that it's a contest—but what I'm asking, I guess, is why do the Jews need slavery?"

"You're quite the little provocateur, aren't you?" Jay said.

"I'm just saying," Imani replied.

"Well, Jay," Nicole drawled, "You wanted a discussion." Her pointed words hung in the air. It felt as if some baleful force had sucked all of the oxygen out of the house. Silence lay like a giant upon the table, awaiting the slightest stimulation to awaken and wreak havoc. The only sound was Chloe's exhalation of breath caused by her despair that this marathon of devotion would never end.

Bebe looked sympathetically at Jay, a general whose elegant strategy had suddenly gone awry. Franklin gripped Marcy's perspiring hand. Boris watched Ari and Ezra and hoped one of them would say something appalling. He was not going to engage with Imani in this situation but would be happy to see her pummel either one of the twins.

Marcy was the first to break the polar hush. "First of all, Imani, bringing the Holocaust, the greatest tragedy to ever befall humankind, into this conversation is not appropriate or acceptable. And second, no offense, but the Jews were slaves before the blacks."

Imani asked, "So the Jews own slavery, too?"

"*Too?*" Franklin said. "What is *that* supposed to mean?"

"You need slavery *and* the Holocaust?" Imani said. "I mean, pick *one.*"

This request appeared too daunting for Marcy, who rolled her head back and focused on the chandelier while she marshaled her disorderly thoughts. The friendly confines of the discussion group she attended at Temple Rodef Shalom in a leafy section of Great Neck did not prepare her for live fire. Franklin placed a steadying hand on his wife's arm.

"Imani," Jay said, attempting to smooth the turbulent waters, "it isn't that the Jews need slavery, per se, but it's a vital part of the story of the birth of Israel as a nation."

Franklin removed his hand from his wife's shoulder and now held both of his palms out as if trying to stop the flow of traffic. "Wait, wait, wait," he said, seizing the role of interlocutor. "I'd like this young lady to clarify her last remark."

"She means Jews own a lot of stuff," Aviva said, feeling more oppressed by her bourgeois origins than usual.

"Oprah owns tons of stuff," Ari pointed out.

"Last we heard, she was still black," Ezra alerted the table. "Not Jewish."

"Check your privilege, Casper," Imani said to Ezra, or perhaps it was Ari. To her, they were interchangeable.

"What's that supposed to mean?" Ari asked, echoing his father.

"You've had all kinds of advantages," Aviva said, "so maybe you shouldn't have an opinion on this?"

"I can't have an opinion," Ari said as if he didn't particularly care either way.

"Why isn't he entitled to an opinion, Aviva?" Marcy asked.

"She called you Casper," Ezra said to Ari, stifling a laugh.

"All right, all right," Jay interrupted. "Everyone's entitled to an opinion because we're in America. And this kind of exchange is good because if you think about the Jews spending forty years in the desert, there was probably a lot of arguing, right?"

This attempt at levity elicited some nervous titters. Even Marcy forced a nod of acknowledgment that led Jay to believe the evening could now be retrieved from the ditch into which it had lurched.

"Jews love to argue," Franklin said. Then, to his wife, "Right, babe?" She covered her surgically enhanced eyes with her hand and did not answer.

Jay resumed, "Perhaps we can all think about slavery as a horror that both Jews and blacks endured, and that shared affliction is something that can bring the two peoples together because when you think about it, there's a lot of common ground."

General nodding.

"You know, Imani," Marcy said, "matzo is called the bread of affliction."

"That's what black folks should call cornbread," Imani replied.

Aviva's eyes blazed as she looked at Imani. Her girl was winning this Seder.

Jay hesitated, waiting to see if anyone was going to pursue that thread. To his relief, no one did. Control restored, he said, "Ezra, I think you were reading."

But before Ezra could resume, the newcomer, trying to avert further misunderstanding, attempted to clarify her position. "I didn't mean to imply anything about what Jews physically own," Imani said, as the older adults (not including Helen, absently chewing on a piece of matzo) inwardly moaned, eager to navigate out of this conversational cul-de-sac. "I was trying to establish a connection between the narrative of the Jews as it relates to the story of black people."

"What is she talking about?" Marcy asked Franklin, who shrugged.

"*This* is what I'm talking about," Imani said. "For you all, America is the Promised Land, but black people, we're still in Egypt, you dig?" Ever since taking African-American Feminism as a Tate freshman, she spiced her conversation with bebop lingo. Satisfied that her last remark had hit its target, and gaining strength from the unwavering attention trained on her, Imani forged ahead. "Look at America. You see all kinds of institutions that are structured to keep black people down, whether it's access to housing, or jobs, or quality public education."

"There are interlocking systems of oppression," Aviva chimed in.

"The establishment fixed the game," Imani continued. "It's the same situation with the Palestinians. They're still in Egypt, too."

"Here we go," Franklin said.

"They're in Palestine," Ezra said.

"You mean the Territories," Franklin corrected. "There is no Palestine."

"Anyone knows that who reads the newspaper," Marcy dripped. Whether her condescension was directed at her son, who only looked at the sports section, or Imani was unclear.

"The reason there's no official Palestinian state," Imani said, "is because the Jews—"

"Are you an anti-Semite?" Marcy inquired.

"No!"

"You mean the Israelis," Aviva offered, sotto voce.

"Sorry, you're right, baby," Imani said. "Because the Israelis refuse to give back the land they stole."

"The land they *stole*?" Franklin roared. "You mean the land God gave to the Jewish people in the story we're trying to tell here tonight if you would quit interrupting." Imani appeared startled at the anger she had unleashed, but Franklin took no notice. Everyone stared at him. His voice grew louder as he declaimed, "Since Biblical times Israel has been Jewish land and anyone else who thinks they can claim it, I'm telling you, it's a false claim! A false claim! They're outta their cottonpickin' minds! That land is ours!"

At the head of the table, Jay's mother leaned toward her son and wondered, "Why is Uncle Jerry yelling at the cleaning woman?"

"She's a guest," Jay whispered. "She's not the cleaning woman. And that's Jerry's son, Franklin."

Satisfied with this explanation, Helen sank back into her seat oblivious that the last exchange between her nephew and Imani had once again decimated the atmosphere. Even Chloe had stopped texting and was swiveling her raccoon eyes between her father and Aviva's defiant friend.

"*Cottonpickin'*?" Imani said, more amused than outraged.

Aviva and Imani shared a glance familiar to anyone who has inflicted their family upon a romantic partner for the first time. See? The glance said. I told you. They're bananas. But our coupledom will be forged in these flames and made stronger.

"A figure of speech," Franklin clarified. His fulmination had aggravated his digestion, and he massaged his upper intestine.

"Kind of racist," Aviva pronounced. Then, to the group: "Everyone needs to take a cleansing breath."

"I think we've had enough discussion," Jay said. "We're not going to solve the problems of the Middle East tonight, so let's move along."

"Thou shalt not steal," Imani said, unable to contain herself. "That's in the Bible."

While Aviva suggested to her girlfriend that she had said enough, for now, Marcy rose from her seat like a hot air balloon unleashed from its tether, pointed at Imani and said, "You're an anti-Semite." Turning to the head of the table, she continued, "Jay, what kind of cockamamie Seder are you running?"

With a flick of an angry wrist, she threw her white linen napkin on her bone china plate and, torso pitched forward, stalked away.

This display was more than Nicole could take.

"Sit down, you condescending cow," the aggrieved hostess said, "and stop judging everyone!"

The command arrested Marcy in her tracks. She whirled around and fixed her persecutor with a gaze to level a pyramid. "Excuse me?" she said, her voice pinched by the constriction of her throat into a higher register.

"You're not going to ruin Passover," the hostess snarled.

Franklin turned to Jay and muttered, "You better control your wife."

As much as it pained Jay to do anything Franklin suggested, his cousin and business partner had a valid point, so he called across the white tablecloth to his inebriated spouse, "Nicole, perhaps it would be helpful if we all just dialed it down a notch."

Everyone's heads rotated from Jay to Nicole, to Marcy, whose slight forward angle now seemed to suggest that she might leap at her opponent. Even the apathetic Chloe was riveted by the show. The twins stared at their flustered mother, who was agitatedly working one of her palms with the fingertips of the same hand.

Aviva monitored her father, wondering if he could assert himself as the leader of this squabbling band of (mostly) Jews and deliver everyone safely to the coconut macaroons that marked the end of the meal.

Imani eyed Aviva and questioned her attraction to this guilt-ridden member of the ruling class. Bebe reached across the oblivious Helen and gave her brother's arm a supportive squeeze. Stricken at the turn the evening had taken, Jay's eyes darted between his livid wife and the reeling Marcy. Right now, he wished the Jews had never thrown off their chains and left Egypt in the first place.

Nicole's blood felt like fire. The small of her back moistened. Despite the winey haze that enshrouded her, she remembered her intense desire to have Jay's baby and her level of inebriation was not so acute that she didn't realize burning the house down with the righteous anger she felt toward Marcy would fail to advance her cause. With this fresh and timely awareness, the internal tumblers that had become so misaligned locked into place and she faced her guests, all of whom were staring at her, stunned at what had occurred, and said with great conviction, "That was unforgivably rude, and I apologize to all of you." To her target, she implored, "Would you please come back to the table, Marcy? I especially apologize to you."

While the distressed Marcy thought this over, Nicole turned to Imani. "And would you mind not talking about the Middle East for the rest of the night?"

"Of course," Imani said, chastened by the hurricane of repressed emotions her rhetoric had unleashed. "My bad." Aviva rubbed her girlfriend's back, in hopes of conveying that she did not bear all of the responsibility for the direction the evening had taken. Several anxious seconds passed during which Marcy displayed no more movement than a recently discovered Pleistocene mastodon that had spent the last ten thousand years in a block of ice.

"Mom, come back to the table," Ari said.

"No more Middle East," Bebe said. "Let's talk about Obama."

"He's no friend of the Jews," Franklin said.

"I voted for him," Marcy informed the room, then returned to her chair and sat down as if nothing had happened. She didn't look at Nicole. "But I'm disappointed."

"I believe Ari was reading," Jay reminded everyone.

"Back to the fairy tale," Imani said.

"What?" Marcy nearly screamed, her serenity vanishing in an instant.

Jay put his hand up, indicating that he would take care of it. He turned to Imani.

"What did you say?"

"The exodus story is a fairy tale. It's bull, and the Jews use it to justify their oppression of the—"

"Okay, that's enough," Jay snapped. His volume louder than anyone present had ever heard at a Seder. "That is quite enough!"

"Jay—" Nicole ventured.

"No!" Jay said to his wife. "I need to say this." Then, to Imani, "It's people like you who are delegitimizing the Jewish state. You're a direct threat to Israel, which is the only democracy in the Middle East."

Although Imani was startled by her host's tone, she remained poised. "Me? I don't think so."

"You need to leave. You're no longer welcome here. Get out."

"Jay—" Nicole said, meekly.

"I'll take care of this!" he shouted.

Aviva indicated to Imani that she should remain calm. Imani's lips did not move, but her eyes implored What did I do?

Aviva said, "Dad, what are you doing?"

Enraged, Jay glared at his daughter, who raised her Haggadah like a shield. "If you want, you can go with her!"

Aviva opened her mouth, but nothing emerged. Imani rose and left the room.

"I can't believe you did that," Aviva said, and followed her girlfriend. The whole table watched them go. Then everyone looked at Jay. Several mortifying seconds elapsed.

Finally, he said, "I think Ari was reading."

Like the other guests, Ari was surprised by Jay's outburst, but he nevertheless turned his attention to the heretofore noncontroversial part about the Jews being slaves in Egypt, finished the passage, and to everyone's relief the Seder limped forward. Jay forged ahead to the part where dinner is served, and platters of food were brought to the table and passed around. The matzo ball soup, kreplach, gefilte fish, brisket, and kugel were all first rate, but Jay could hardly taste any of it. Only the nuclear intensity of the freshly ground horseradish could penetrate the torpor that had descended upon him.

Aviva and Imani ignored each other.

Facing the woods with their backs to the house and separated by twenty feet of dirt road, they waited, slightly drunk. It was a cloudy night, the moon barely visible through the twisting branches. The scent of pine and decomposing leaves filled the air. Aviva had called a cab, and after five minutes of watching the trees, those were the only words either had spoken.

It was a mystery why her girlfriend had chosen the Gladstone family Seder as the place to declare slavery an exclusive cultural inheritance that did not include Jews. Aviva would not have gone to a dinner with Imani's family and instigated a discussion of anything having to do with black people other than to say she admired them. Her thoughts were more complicated than that. Lately, she wondered if she fetishized blackness and her attraction to Imani was a manifestation of some colonialist orientation—not the lesbian part, although she did not entirely identify as a lesbian, rather as polyamorous (to her a more palatable category)—and this possibility only compounded her sense of white privilege. Just to think about it was draining. If you had a problem with people of color you were racist, but if you liked them too much you were—what? Was admiring communities of color another manifestation of white privilege? They were not asking for her admiration. Further, many members of those communities would be offended by her use of the word "they" since it conveyed otherness (except when used as a pronoun by the newly voluble trans population). All of it made her head hurt.

Aviva did not believe she was fetishizing anyone. She was drawn to Imani, the person. Not at this particular juncture, admittedly, but for the most part, she loved her. As for tonight? Imani's performance at the Seder was enormously uncool. How could she let that slide?

"Your father is the problem," Imani said.

It was a relief to have the impasse broken.

"He can be difficult."

"He's a Zionist thug."

The phrase jabbed. Aviva had hoped for a quick reconciliation and was taken aback by the aggressive words. Jay Gladstone, a thug? Her father was—she did not know how to characterize him at this point, but a thug? The term only revealed a paucity of imagination.

"Maybe if you had said you were sorry, it wouldn't have gotten out of hand."

"You think *I* should have apologized?"

"It wasn't an academic conference."

"Oh, word to the 'nice Jewish girl.'"

"We should stop this conversation because it's already too fucking offensive."

"We're supposed to stop because *you're* offended?"

"Don't apologize if your pride won't let you."

"My pride?"

"You don't think I know what an a-hole my father can be?"

"I bet you know *that*."

"But he's okay."

"For a plutocrat."

Money again? Aviva's college friends had teased her about this since freshman year when Axel had seen an article about Jay on the Internet and asked if she was related to "*that* Jay

Gladstone." Aviva thought about responding to Imani, but the idea of defending her father's net worth was enervating. She couldn't remove the stigma of her family's wealth. To keep the fight from accelerating Aviva walked across the road.

"Where are you going?" Imani asked.

Aviva disregarded her and peered into the trees. She stood there for a full minute. The glow of the house did not extend to where they were standing, and the woods were gloomy and endless. Finally, she turned around, walked toward Imani. She stopped in the middle of the dirt road, lowered herself to the ground. Then she lay flat on her back, arms perpendicular to her body. How much vodka had she poured in that Coke?

"What're you doing?"

"Why don't you crucify me?"

"What?"

"Since there's no way I can change the essence of who I am," Aviva said to the sky.

"You're just gonna lie there in the road?"

"If you don't like who I am, the question becomes to be or not to be."

"Get the fuck up!"

"There's no point. I'm white; I'm a Jewish girl who's at least a semi-Zionist. I come from the Gladstone family. It's the trifecta of everything you hate." She was speaking in a monotone. "I should just expire."

"I don't hate Jews because that would be racist."

"Jews aren't a race."

"Aviva, get up out of the road! Nothing is going to run you over out here. What's a trifecta, anyway?"

"It's from horse racing." Aviva looked up at the moon. She felt silly lying in the middle of the road (and for having used a horse-related term). From her prone position, she checked the time on her phone. "How long have we been waiting?"

"This isn't funny."

A pair of headlights sliced through the trees. Imani glanced around nervously. The car headed toward them.

"Aviva, get up."

"I'm sleepy," Aviva said and closed her eyes.

"Get up, girl."

"Lie down with me."

Unable to take it any longer, Imani walked to where Aviva lay and pulled her inert girlfriend to the side of the road by her armpits. The heels of Aviva's boots dragged along the dirt road.

Imani said, "I'm sorry, I'm sorry, I'm sorry."

Aviva started to laugh. Then Imani began laughing. Aviva wasn't sure whether that had been an actual apology, but it was enough to ameliorate the hurt feelings. Clambering to her feet, she quickly kissed Imani on the mouth.

Their argument was unresolved, but Aviva could no longer bear to perpetuate it.

Following the main course, after the third ceremonial cup of wine (but before the macaroons, rugelach, and coffee), it was time to place the traditional glass of Manischewitz on the front steps of the house. Every year, Bingo used to say: Elijah never comes, he's not coming, why bother? And everyone would laugh. Jay poured the glass, stood and, rather than delegating the task, availed himself of the opportunity to leave the table.

The first thing he did was peek in the guest room, then out the front door. He wanted to know if Aviva and Imani were still on the premises so he could cauterize the wound. Jay assumed they had made their way to the train station. He stepped out on the back porch and inhaled the crisp air. The clouds had parted, and several constellations were visible. From the roof of his office building, he had observed the recent eclipse and had vowed to increase his knowledge of astronomy. Placing the wineglass down, he surveyed the lawn and the stable silhouetted against the sky with its striations of indigo and violet, a wafer moon illuminating the woods and meadow. However much the temporal world might pitch and heave he felt secure with his back to the house as he stood between his querulous relatives and the flickering stars. He thought about his dead father, his diminished mother, his troublesome daughter. Whatever Aviva was going through, Jay was confident she would one day come to understand how a family could at once be a font of almost insurmountable exasperation but also of pride and the deepest security.

He pulled out a phone and texted her:

I feel terrible about what happened tonight. Please call me so we can talk.

Jay had wrenched the Seder back from the brink of a plague-like disaster. If he could make peace with his daughter and her sexuality ("Let the shift be temporary, please God."), it would be a challenge to embrace her current girlfriend. Although Nicole had tried her hardest to make the evening a success before the arrival of the guests, her outburst at Marcy, however warranted, had embarrassed him.

Jay had received a report from an auditor tasked with taking a closer look at Franklin's books and had been dismayed by what he read. And he had to fly to South Africa the following day because the ambitious Gladstone project over there had reached a critical point and his presence was required. This trip was going to cause him to miss the Obama dinner at the Waldorf. He was counting on face time with the president to enhance his chances of an ambassadorship.

All of this weighed on Jay when he returned to the table where, to his relief, hostilities had not again broken out. He cajoled the assembled guests to sing *"Dayenu,"* which they did in several keys simultaneously, and the Gladstone family Seder concluded—*Next year in Jerusalem!*—with some bruised feelings but without further incident.

After dinner, Franklin approached the host and whispered in his ear, "You should never have divorced Jude." Jay was offended but not surprised and before he could respond Franklin beckoned to Ari and Ezra, and the three of them lumbered off.

Nicole was in the kitchen drinking coffee and commiserating with Bebe when Jay approached and asked if she was all right. She assured him that she had never been better and that this was the last time she was going to host a goddamn Seder since no one seemed to appreciate all the work that had gone into it, and instead the evening had turned into a burlesque of what it was meant to celebrate. Since it would have been unwise for Jay to underline her part in the meltdown, he chose to elide it. Instead, he told her how much he and everyone else appreciated what she had done, thanked her again for her efforts, and said they could talk about what was going to happen next year when the time came.

Jay found Franklin savoring a postprandial smoke in the backyard with Ari and Ezra. They greeted Jay, and Franklin offered him an impressive looking cigar.

"It's Cuban," he said. "The best."

Jay politely declined and asked the twins if they would mind giving their father and him some privacy. Franklin indicated they should scram.

"Let's go, Casper," Ezra said to Ari, and the two of them dissolved into giggles as they wandered back to the house.

Jay peered into the darkness, uncertain how to begin. The stables were behind Franklin and what Jay wanted to do was go down there, check on the horses, and not have this conversation. He wanted to mention Franklin's crack about Jude but realized that would only serve to muddy the waters of what he had come outside to say. His cousin, who seemed to enjoy Jay's discomfort, regarded him askance and waited. The surrounding woods pressed toward them.

"Sorry about Nicole," Jay began. "She's under a lot of stress."

"It happens," Franklin allowed. He took a puff of his cigar and blew a smoke ring as if to show how unperturbed he was. "Could you believe that little *shvartze* in there?"

Shvartze, Yiddish, literally translates as "black," but there's a stink to it. A dated, lower-class word used by uneducated Jews. Raised in Sands Point, Franklin should have known better. Whatever Jay thought of Imani's behavior, that term was repugnant to him. He had heard Franklin use it before and it always made him squirm. But this was not the time to lecture his cousin about the pernicious effects of casual racism—it wasn't as if the man possessed the psychological tools to change—so he let it go.

"She's a kid," Jay said.

"An animal," Franklin said. "Which reminds me. You know who Christine Lupo is?" Jay said he was familiar with her but was unclear on the connection between the Westchester County District Attorney and Imani. "Christine believes in traditional values, not the left-wing bullshit Aviva's friend subjected us to." Jay let that go. "She's running for governor and Marcy and I are going to host a fundraiser for her." This information surprised Jay since Franklin, for all of his opinions, had never involved himself directly in politics. "I know you're a liberal and all, but I think you'd like her. She's a lovely lady, and you and Nicole should come."

Jay let that go, too. "I never received those reports I asked for," he said.

Franklin did not immediately respond to this shift in the conversation. Instead, he took another puff of his cigar and exhaled the smoke in an unruly swirl, rather than the more relaxed ring. He looked at Jay appraisingly as if sizing up his current appetite for conflict.

"We had a delicious meal, and now I'm enjoying my Havana," Franklin said. "You sure you don't want to leave this for another time?"

"Would you rather I tell you in an email?"

"Tell me what?"

Now it was Jay's turn to relish his cousin's discomfort. He had always envied the relationship between his father and his Uncle Jerry, two men of strong will whose dialectical qualities complemented each other and led to the creation of a stronger whole from which the entire family continued to benefit. Jay and Franklin were meant to honor that fraternal tradition.

"Bebe and I have commissioned a formal audit of the family's operations in Asia."

It had taken Jay several days to prepare himself to impart this information because he was expecting pushback but Franklin didn't blink.

"I could have you audited, too."

"You're welcome to do an audit if you think I'm hiding anything." Franklin nodded as if he was considering the possibility. "We didn't want to go down this road, but you're not giving us any choice. It isn't that we don't trust you, so please don't think that. It could be a mistake by the accounting department, or who knows what. We're discharging our fiduciary duty."

Another drag of his fat cigar, another exhalation of smoke. Franklin forced a noise out of his gullet meant as a disparaging laugh.

"You think you're King Pharaoh," Franklin said, "coming in here swinging your staff around, smiting the Jews."

"Would that make you Moses?"

"Of all the bulrushes in the world, you had to walk into this one," Franklin said conflating *Exodus* and *Casablanca* in the voice of Humphrey Bogart.

Jay nearly laughed but refused to let Franklin believe he had disarmed him, although the Bogart impression was considerably better than many of the others he did.

"No, I don't believe I'm like King Pharaoh at all." He awaited Franklin's response, which arrived in the form of a question.

"What do you guess our fathers would say?"

"They'd be disappointed," Jay said. "Highly disappointed. But those two didn't keep secrets from each other."

"Someone's keeping secrets?" Franklin asked, the implication laughable. "Why do you even mention your sister? Don't pretend this isn't all you." He tapped the ash off the end of his cigar.

"I just don't want you to be surprised, Franklin. I'm glad you were here tonight. I didn't want to have this conversation in the office because it's personal."

Jay waited to see if his cousin would respond. Instead, Franklin jammed the cigar in his mouth and looked toward the woods. Jay had done all he could do. He gave Franklin the opportunity to behave honorably. For a full minute, they stood on the lawn, wordless as two ghosts. Marcy appeared at the door and beckoned to Franklin. The drive back to Long Island would take more than an hour and she was ready to leave. As Franklin trudged toward the house, Jay waved agreeably to Marcy and thanked her for coming.

CHAPTER TWENTY-TWO

Nicole was sitting up in bed pretending to read the Spinoza biography when Jay emerged from the bathroom in a Penn T-shirt and pajama bottoms. Her hair was loose, and her face scrubbed clean of makeup. The stress of the evening was gone—several cups of coffee had fought the chardonnay to a draw—and now, in a chemise with the covers pulled to her waist, she exuded tranquil radiance. When Jay slipped in beside her, Nicole put the book down and turned off the bedside lamp. She caressed the inside of his wrist with the tips of her fingers.

"I'm ovulating."

From the corner of his eye, Jay could see her lopsided smile. It was a look that in its earlier iteration had placed him in her thrall. But the events of the evening had so taxed his nervous system that he would have preferred to sleep alone and only chose not to because he believed it would have exasperated Nicole.

She said, "We can make a porno."

"On Passover?" He laughed.

"You don't want to show our son how we created him?"

"That's perverse."

"Come on, Jay. Where's your sense of humor?"

Nicole rolled on her side and faced him, head propped on her palm. She did not appear fatigued in the least. It was as if the outburst at dinner had exorcised an entire gang of demons and left her in a state of alert relaxation. She reached for a bottle of lotion on her night table and squirted a dab on her palm.

"I'm spent," he said as she slid her hand beneath the sheets and began to stroke his retreating penis.

"Could I have been a better Jew this evening?" Her hand was a metronome.

"I'm flying to South Africa tomorrow night," he said. "I'll miss the Obama dinner."

He expected the announcement of his projected absence would cause Nicole to conclude her exertions but whatever disappointment she may have felt was not reflected in any cessation of her hand motion. Up and down his shaft she labored, from the root to the tip, flicking the glans with her thumbnail and stroking his balls, her enthusiasm undiminished by the ongoing lack of tumescence.

"I'll represent the family," Nicole said.

Why wasn't Jay responding? She kissed his neck, redoubled her efforts. His condition remained invertebrate. After a couple of minutes, she took a break, still holding his uncooperative penis in her hand, but no longer moving.

"Is something wrong?"

"I told you," Jay said. "I'm wiped out."

Undeterred, Nicole released him. She opened a drawer in her nightstand, removed a blue pill, and handed it to him. He asked her what it was.

"It's medicine for erectile dysfunction."

Placing the pill on his nightstand, he said, "I don't have erectile dysfunction," despite current evidence to the contrary. The implication offended him since it called to mind both their age difference and his perceived inability to attend to his wife's needs, neither of which, in Jay's mind, were rooted in a physical cause. "Where'd you get it?"

"My internist had samples lying around. I told him we weren't having regular sex."

"Our issue isn't biological."

She was not sure how to respond to his declaration. They

had reached that point in sex play where the initiator's plan had somehow gone awry and now either both partners would tacitly agree to ignore whatever discomfort was afoot and start fucking, or one would determine that the other had crossed a line thereby destroying what remained of "the mood." She was baffled by what seemed to be happening. Hadn't she just produced the Seder to end all Seders? Yes, Marcy and Imani had conspired to destroy it, but Nicole had done all Jay could have reasonably expected. Transformed her home into a temple of culinary Jewishness, provided everything from the finest gefilte fish (her mother-in-law's recipe, no less) to the best macaroons (as identified by the food critic of the *New York Times*), and put up with his irritating relatives. Now he was off to South Africa, another business trip, and he had not even told her how long he would be away. She thought of her own family, her barely extant relations with them. The men she had slept with cycled through her consciousness, and her complicity in those loveless liaisons. Her condition now, though materially superior, left her bereft and longing for not simply a rebirth but an actual baby. The modeling career, the time with the House Ethics Committee, what had it amounted to? She began to tremble. Had she engineered this reaction as a means of manipulating her husband or was this bodily vibration legitimate? No, no, she concluded, it was legitimate, thereby permissible, and she did not attempt to bring it under control.

"Are you all right?"

He caressed her arm, and she tried to relax.

"I'm still a little upset about tonight."

"Thanks again for everything you did," Jay said. "I know you put yourself out and I appreciate it."

She took this as her opening and informed him, "I want a nursery in the house, I want to get up at 2:00 in the morning for a year, and I want my tits to sag from breastfeeding." His answer, which she expected, was to say nothing. "I know we've talked this thing into the ground, but I've been thinking about it, you know, and it's nonnegotiable for me at this point." In hopes of weakening his resolve, she had imbued the previous sentence with hints of softness, understanding, and a not-to-be-trifled with love, the one thing she had to give.

"I don't want to upset you," he said, "and I certainly don't want to fight, particularly after what happened tonight. But that isn't going to happen. I don't want another child. The end."

"What if I were to have one with someone else?"

"What?"

"I get someone else to impregnate me, I raise the baby, you don't have to do anything, and if the unthinkable happens and we split up, I have a baby that you bear no responsibility for. And saggy tits."

"Nicole, that's a bad idea."

"What about artificial insemination?"

"You're missing the point which is that I've been a father. I've raised a kid, it did not go particularly well if tonight was any indication, and I'm not doing it again."

"She's grown. No one looked for the afikomen this evening."

"We can wait for a grandchild."

"Hah! You think Aviva and Imani are going to be parents?"

Jay still was not convinced his daughter was gay, nor was he pondering how her life would progress past college. The idea of Imani Mayfield as his future daughter-in-law was beyond comprehension.

"I'm choosing not to think about it."

"Meet your grandson, Louis Farrakhan Gladstone."

Despite himself, Jay laughed. "Listen to me, Nickie." The childhood nickname only brought out when he needed to communicate something meant to reach the deepest layer of her core. Jay sensed she was girding herself. He gently caressed her arm, gazed directly into her eyes, and said: "No more kids."

She absorbed this declaration and did not reply. Instead, she turned away and climbed out of bed. From a chair, she retrieved a robe and threw it on, fists shooting through the sleeves like a fighter's. She grabbed the Spinoza biography and shoved it under her arm.

"Where are you going?"

"I'm sleeping in the pool house," slamming the door behind her.

What Jay felt more than frustration or anger was sweet relief. He was not worried. A version of this exchange had occurred several times and invariably Nicole, upon reflection (and the recognition of the reality that a signed agreement existed stating she accepted there would be no children in the marriage), softened her stance and allowed peace to reign.

Jay took a sleeping pill and dozed off wondering why his wife was reading about Spinoza of all people, an iconoclast who challenged man's relationship to God, who questioned the very nature of God. Wasn't he the Jew other Jews wanted to be rid of? Jay had wrestled with Spinoza in college when he wrote a paper on 16th century Amsterdam that paired the philosopher with the painter Vermeer with whom he overlapped. Jay had told Nicole about it when he saw she was reading the book. Something about Spinoza's story did not ring true to him. However outrageously an individual carried on in the realm of family, business, or theology, the Jews were not supposed to excommunicate. With his exquisitely rendered, orderly canvasses that spoke to a rational, mercantile world, the artist had been a far greater source of pleasure than the philosopher.

When Jay awoke the following morning, Nicole had not returned. He showered, dressed, ate breakfast, and still no sign of her. Since her Range Rover was in the garage, he assumed she was horseback riding. It was their custom to leave a note signed with several xs and os if one of them left the house on anything other than a short errand. On that morning, Jay's pen remained in his pocket. He would not see her before leaving for Africa.

CHAPTER TWENTY-THREE

T he degradation of our increasingly delicate planet caused by the merciless extraction of fossil fuel led the eco-aware Jay a decade earlier to renounce the use of private jets in any but the most unusual circumstances, so late that evening, after drinks with Church Scott during which they resolved the D'Angelo Maxwell contract situation (there would be no max deal, although they would raise their initial offer, and no deal at all if the team failed to qualify for the playoffs), and an early dinner with Bebe at the Paladin Club, he boarded a commercial flight to Johannesburg, South Africa. Following the complimentary glass of champagne served in the first-class cabin Jay's seat morphed into a bed surrounded by a curved fiberglass shell that made him feel like he was lying in a large egg.

For a couple of hours, he read *A History of the Weimar Republic* and listened to German language lessons. He would send President Obama a note apologizing for missing the dinner at the Waldorf and include a copy of the book as a gift. As Jay covered himself with a quilt and tried to find a comfortable position, his thoughts turned, as they often did, to his father. During the 1970s, at the height of the apartheid regime, the two had often argued about South Africa. Although Bingo believed all races and creeds were equal, he saw nothing wrong with speculating in the Krugerrand, an activity his son found abhorrent. Jay made no effort to hide his strong feelings but although Bingo celebrated Nelson Mandela's release from

Robben Island with the rest of the world and applauded the collapse of the regime that soon followed, the decisions the elder Gladstone made regarding his financial dealings lacked the moral dimension Jay vowed his own would not. When the events of the previous evening—the Seder, the wife, the daughter, her friend—intruded upon his thoughts, as they had throughout the day, he smiled to himself and thought about what Bingo Gladstone would have made of Imani Mayfield, and then tried to crowbar those unwelcome reminders of last night back to a less accessible place.

But as Jay continued to search for a position in which sleep might visit, pesky thoughts of Aviva sailed over the ramparts of his consciousness like arrows. His text from the night before had gone unreturned. Until now he had congratulated himself on his imperturbability in the face of his daughter's new identity. He had done a little reading about the "gender fluidity" of her generation and, since he viewed himself as a paragon of tolerance, felt slightly hypocritical at even having acknowledged, if only to himself, that he was not comfortable with her sexuality. If she persisted in traveling that road he would learn to live with it. More problematic for him was her complete lack of interest in the family business. This attitude did not look to be changing anytime soon, which made his thoughts turn, as they invariably did, toward the unhappy Nicole, from whom he had not heard all day. She had failed to respond to the multiple conciliatory messages he had left. "Hey, it's me," he said, trying to maintain an even tone. "Just wanted to say goodbye and I love you, and to quote the Beatles, 'We can work it out.'" He regretted the Beatles quote immediately—too corny—but hoped she would appreciate the sentiment.

He was no longer quite so certain why he had insisted on the execution of a prenup forbidding children as a condition of their marriage. At the time, five years previous, it had seemed like the way to go. Although Jay loved Aviva, he did not romanticize the idea of children and the thought of another infant, who would not develop into an interesting conversational partner for at least a decade and a half, had little appeal. That was a given. But legacy was something he allowed himself to think about occasionally, and it was one of the ways he framed his relationship with his father, who remained the most influential person in Jay's life. He doubted Aviva would say that about her father and this troubled him. There were so many ways Bingo resonated in Jay, from his posture, to the steely nature of his resolve to the sanguinity of his worldview. Bingo passed away soon after Jay had married Nicole, but he let his son know how much he liked his second wife. Bingo's approval meant a great deal, and he found himself considering this as the plane soared through the night.

Perhaps the behavior of his wife, the drinking, the outbursts, was related to thwarted maternal desire. Of course, those patterns were never traceable to one thing, but this particular situation was not having a positive effect on her state of mind. Nicole had the skills to be a mother, certainly. She was kind and loving, and although her relations with her own family were not the best, she made an effort with the various Gladstones. Certainly, the connection Nicole had with Bingo was real. His father told Jay that he admired the manner in which she had claimed her place in the world ("She's got a lot of moxie," Bingo said) and that was one of the qualities that made her attractive to Jay. The more he considered the question of a child and his stubbornness around the subject, the more he regretted his behavior.

While he thought about Nicole, he felt an unwelcome twinge in his lower abdomen. What was that? The oysters he had consumed earlier at the Paladin Club were the of highest quality so they couldn't be the cause. Jay was not the kind of man who ascribed every unfamiliar sensation to disease, but his mind just then dropped three inches from abdomen to prostate. Was he feeling something there, too, or was that his imagination? What sinister florescence might be occurring in that highly vulnerable neighborhood? A friend in the real estate business had only last year received a cancer diagnosis, been told what he had was treatable, and died three weeks later. A lawyer he worked with, a veritable Yo-Yo Ma of the tax code was cooking a ragu in his Martha's Vineyard kitchen the previous summer and dropped dead from an embolism.

Death encroached.

The notion that who knew how long any of us would live was not one Jay often dwelled on but now he found himself thinking about it. Perhaps he would revisit the idea of having a child with Nicole. It was his calculation that her desire to have a baby was far greater than his desire to avoid one. If he were not going to get another divorce, a new Gladstone would only make his life easier. He could name a son (a son!) after his father. In the Jewish tradition, one was only required to use the first letter in the naming of the baby, so the options were many: Benjamin, Barrett, Barack. Barack Gladstone! Named in blessed memory of Bernard of the Bronx. It would be worth calling the baby Barack just to tweak his cousin Franklin.

What was that abdominal pain he was feeling? It was there for a few seconds, and then it was gone. He shifted his weight, and the pain returned, or did it? Determined not to have the night derailed by minor discomfort, he sat up, reached beneath the seat for his bag, and rooted out the painkillers he congratulated himself for having remembered to pack. He swallowed one, chased it with water, and again reclined on the egg bed where he continued to think about Nicole and her desire to expand their family. He vowed to revisit the situation when he returned from the trip.

In South Africa, Jay met with the minister of trade and industry, the local engineering team, and the president, who had been following the Gladstone project with eager interest. Jay visited the site of the proposed town, thirty kilometers from Durban, along with a delegation of government ministers and representatives of the local media. When he gazed over the land, he thought of his father's proudest achievement, Gladstone Green, affordable housing built in the Queens of the 1960s, and a smile danced on his lips as he felt Bingo's spirit rise within his breast.

He followed the news at home and was thrilled that his team beat the Charlotte Hornets, disappointed they lost to the Chicago Bulls, noting that Dag had scored twenty-five points in the loss, but sat out the win because his knee had flared up.

Jay initiated a rapprochement with Nicole—she finally picked up the phone when he called—and was optimistic about the improvement of relations upon his return, particularly given that he had decided he was going to broach the subject of the hoped-for pregnancy. The only blight on Jay's time in Africa was the sensation in the area where his urologist had extracted tissue samples. As he worked his way through the increasingly ineffective painkillers, he feared a return visit to the doctor would occur sooner than planned.

Jay's trip had been so efficient that he was able to cut it short. The journey from Africa back to New York would have been wholly uneventful were it not for the ratcheting up of the pain he was experiencing. The long westward flight passed in fractured sleep, a haze of movies he couldn't remember, and whiskeys he shouldn't have consumed. The stewardess offered champagne before landing, and he drank several glasses. When Boris met him late in the evening at Kennedy Airport, Jay was not in the mood to talk about his trip, or anything else, and slid exhaustedly into the backseat of the Mercedes for the drive to Bedford. It was after eleven and he fell asleep as they drove over the Whitestone Bridge.

Jay awoke as Boris guided the Mercedes to a stop in the

driveway. He did not feel well when he climbed out of the car and steadied himself for the walk up the steps to the front door. When Boris departed, Jay lumbered upstairs, carrying a diamond pendant purchased in Johannesburg with which to surprise Nicole (he had not informed her of this change in travel plans). Because there were lights on he assumed she was home, but as he moved from room to room calling her name there was no response.

Sometimes when Nicole could not sleep, she would visit the stables and commune with the horses. That evening the property was wreathed in mist and when Jay looked toward the stables from a second-floor window all he could discern was a great swath of darkness. But a soft blush of interior illumination lit the pool house situated down a small incline from the main residence. With the diamond in his pocket, he made his way unsteadily downstairs, his hand on the smooth stained oak banister. How much liquor had he consumed on the plane? He couldn't recall as he stopped in the kitchen to pour a glass of water that he drained in one continuous gulp before tilting in the direction of the backyard.

The dewy grass was already lush from the spring rains and slick under the feet of his leather-soled loafers. The cicadas had arrived, and their symphonic hum seemed louder and more insistent than usual. The chilly night air customarily would have invigorated Jay but because of something unholy going on between what he had eaten, the whiskey he had imbibed, and the painkillers, it only added to his queasiness. Perhaps after he greeted Nicole, he would ask her to drive him to Northern Westchester Hospital. He comforted himself with the nostrum that a course of antibiotics would take care of whatever it was.

Nicole had transformed the pool house into a guest cottage and jewelry studio. The door opened into an art-filled space with a small kitchen to one side and across from that a workbench with neatly arranged materials and tools. Beyond was the bed-room.

The glow Jay discerned was coming from the pool house bedroom where the door was slightly ajar. He padded over a Turkish rug that belonged on a museum wall—the couple had recently purchased it on a whim in Istanbul—so as not to wake Nicole in the event she had fallen asleep while reading in bed. Had she finished the Spinoza biography yet? As he reached for the diamond pendant, he thought about their wedding day, and about how being apart for a week threw her best qualities into sharper relief. These memories cut through the physical pain that clawed him. It would be good to see his wife.

Gently, Jay pushed the door open and in the dimly lit room beheld Nicole on the bed astride a man, bucking wildly up and down in a rhythmic trance of ecstasy punctuated with sounds her husband had never before heard her produce. The physi-cal force generated by this image felt to Jay as if it would send him reeling back but the weakness of his body kept him rooted in place, and he stared in mute bewilderment. The musk of sex filled his nostrils. His lower jaw moved down and up, once, twice; but whether it was a nervous twitch or an attempt to speak was impossible to tell.

Before Jay could form words, the male figure in the bed said, "Oh, shit," in a subterranean timbre and that was when Jay realized the man penetrating his wife was D'Angelo Maxwell.

Nicole whirled around and shrieked. She rolled off the nine-time All-Star, grabbed the floral duvet, and reflexively covered her breasts. Dag did not move.

Jay inclined his head two degrees left and with as much savoir-faire as he could manage, given the situation, plaintively asked:

"Why does everyone in this family need to have sex with black people?"

Later, he never denied uttering those words.

CHAPTER TWENTY-FOUR

I t should be noted that Jay's question was posed in genuine wonderment as if he wanted to know how iron was extracted from mountains and transformed into skyscrapers or how feathers were related to the concept of flight. It was empirical, an attempt to expand limited knowledge. Bafflement and incandescent rage were threaded into his question, too, but indeed, at that ghastly moment, the undeniable nadir of his entire life (until then), he needed to *know*. Because that was how he could create a delay, a habitable nothingness in which he could dwell, and not have to address what was in front of him and its more global ramifications.

"This never shoulda happened," Dag said.

Boxers slipped on; trousers pulled up; the player buttoned his shirt with its starched upturned collar. When Dag rose to his immense height and threw his jacket over his shoulders, Jay realized he was wearing a tuxedo. Nicole's dress, one of her closet full of slinky designer numbers, was draped on a chair. Jay remembered: the Waldorf-Astoria event for President Obama.

The errant wife huddled in bed, watching her addled husband, who had not followed up his initial query with a statement, another question, an accusation, or any sound at all. Nicole seemed to be of the mind that this was a propitious time to say nothing. Condition red, she idled and waited to see what Jay might do.

"Did you get to meet the president?"

"Y-yes," she managed.

Dag ignored the question, assumed it was not for him.

The membrane of insouciance Jay attempted to maintain was straining against the weight of the immense psychological force unleashed by his discovery, and the emotional battering blended with his ongoing physical discomfort to nearly undo him. His stomach seemed to have plummeted several inches, crowding his pubis, his bowels felt as if they were sliding down, and what was going on with his prostate?

"Sorry about this," Dag mumbled. "No excuse." Striding to the door, he loomed like an ocean liner. The mixture of sweat and body spray wafting off him was overpowering. Jay glanced in his direction as if the man were something repulsive that had become affixed to a shoe, but the difference in their dimensions allayed whatever mad notion the owner might have for a nanosecond entertained about wreaking physical revenge on the player. Jay would never strike anyone, much less a man of D'Angelo Maxwell's intimidating dimensions, but he wanted to say something that would make an impression, anything really, other than the lame question he had posed in a misguided attempt at suavity. If this was the extent of his verbal capacity, better to have already left the scene.

Unfortunately, Dag beat him to it and Jay turned to watch the player's retreating form pass through the workroom and out the door.

Nicole murmured, "I'm so sorry, Jay."

He wheeled to face her and considered unleashing a stream of invective whose heat would bleach the equine-themed wallpaper behind the bed.

"Oh, god, I made a terrible decision," his wife simpered. Her voice was a simulacrum of kindness and repentance braided with fear of what she had wrought. "Will you talk to me?"

The Nicole Era was over, but there was unfinished business

with the man who had just left the room. The last words of D'Angelo Maxwell to Jay Gladstone when they parted in front of the Paladin Club: *We're good men*, he said. *We do what's right.*

Jay heard Nicole's plangent voice calling his name like a ringing bell, once, twice, three times, as he slanted across the Turkish rug and out the door. Adrenaline kicked his system into dangerously high gear. Animated by an overwhelming desire to confront Dag and discuss how the athlete squared his professed morality with such dubious behavior, Jay squinted into the darkness searching for his quarry. In the distance, a tuxedoed silhouette could be seen making for the driveway. Jay called out, but Dag did not turn around. He just wanted to talk, about what he was not sure. Dag had already apologized. Did he require more deferential words? Or perhaps on some unfathomable level, he desired a physical confrontation that would both salvage his manhood and end in his annihilation.

The player was no longer in Jay's field of vision. Intent on forcing the issue, and having, he believed, retrieved sufficient control of his faculties Jay staggered uphill struggling for traction on the slippery grass and nearly falling twice. He glanced toward the porch but saw no one. He did not suspect that, after what had happened, Dag would let himself in the house, yet somehow, he had dematerialized. Where was Dag's car? Jay's eyes went to the street and—there! Dag was jogging down the road.

Jay yanked the door of the Mercedes open and fell into the driver's seat. For the briefest moment, he wondered whether he was clearheaded enough to drive. Boris always left the key under the seat and Jay was relieved to find that at least one person in his orbit could be relied upon not to betray him. He rammed the key into the ignition, shifted into reverse, and hit the gas sending the sedan shooting backward. He cut the wheel hard, crushed the brake, then shifted into drive and again stomped his foot on the gas pedal. The wheels screamed as the car shot forward.

He raced out of the driveway, nearly losing control, and swerved on to the country lane. There were no streetlights and Jay cursed as he peered through the darkness. The car gained speed, bumped over the uneven surface, and accelerated as Jay swiveled his head like a prison floodlight, one way then the other. Less than a hundred yards ahead Dag appeared on the side of the road looking incongruously dapper. His back was to the car as he loped unevenly along, the tiny light of his cell phone screen visible. Had he summoned his entourage?

The same interaction of painkillers and whiskey that led Jay to believe it was a good idea to leap into his car to confront the younger, more virile, and incomparably stronger man, steered him to the wild notion that he should accelerate toward Dag and stop just short of striking him. It would terrorize his adversary, and terror is what Jay needed to inflict in order to quash the feelings of impotence and shame which had temporarily deranged him. As the Mercedes continued to gather speed, Jay lifted his foot off the gas, intending to jam it down on the brake with great force. But the adverse chemical conditions caused the irrational driver to mistake the accelerator for the brake so when he thrust his foot down, instead of skidding to a dramatic halt, the car shot forward and caught the long-legged athlete just above the knees. The collision sent him sailing through the night sky higher than a basketball hoop before he crashed to the road taking most of the impact of the landing on his left shoulder and his head. The Mercedes smashed into a tree and the force that crushed the grille and collapsed the hood snapped Jay's head back, then forward into the steering wheel. He blacked out.

When Jay emerged from the car, he wasn't sure how long he had been there. His face and shirt were drenched in blood, knees banged up, chest bruised. What had happened? Moments earlier, he had been in his house and now he was standing unsteadily on the side of the road and the car was wrecked. What had he done?

A bolt of dread shot through Jay when he saw Dag lying on the ground, limbs arranged in an unnatural configuration. This was followed by another jolt when he realized Dag was unconscious. He kneeled down to take Dag's pulse, and the large hand flopped out of the tuxedo sleeve. Jay thought he felt life, and then it was gone. He couldn't tell what was real and what his short-circuiting brain madly imagined. Dag's head was twisted at an odd angle, blood trickling from his mouth. Jay placed his fingers on one of Dag's neck tattoos. Was he already dead? Had he been killed instantly?

Jay was lightheaded. Every cell in his body vibrated, his entire organism spinning out of control. He struggled to his feet. Blood spilled from his nose. Jay took his shirt off and held it to his face. Stripped to the waist, he shivered. The Mercedes headlight that had not shattered cast a ghostly light in the woods where the trunks of pine trees stood straight as jury members waiting for the judge to enter the courtroom. Whether D'Angelo Maxwell was dead or had suffered severe injuries but clung to life, or—and dear God, let it be this, anything else is unacceptable!—the damage was minor, and he would make a full recovery, the disastrous situation in which Jay Gladstone found himself was going to be exceedingly difficult to explain.

PART II

"In the struggle between you and the world,
bet on the world."
—FRANZ KAFKA

CHAPTER TWENTY-FIVE

The year the Watergate Committee put the screws to Nixon, Jay sailed through his freshman year at the University of Pennsylvania. He spent the summer working in the family business, commuting from Scarsdale to Manhattan each day with Bingo in a Cadillac Eldorado. His father allowed Jay to listen to rock music on the radio for half the ride, but when they rolled past Yankee Stadium, he twirled the dial to the news station and the two of them savored the increasingly dire travails of the president, or, as Bingo referred to him: "That anti-Semitic sonofabitch."

A Roosevelt Democrat, Bingo liked to discuss politics at the dinner table, and between bites of roast chicken or Salisbury steak he would quiz Jay and Bebe on their knowledge. Which president passed the Civil Rights Act? Who is Robert McNamara? What is the Jackson-Vanik Amendment? The last question held particular resonance for Bingo because he had a personal stake in it. The Jackson-Vanik Amendment was intended to force countries with nonmarket economies (Communist) to ease immigration of minority groups (Jews) in return for favorable trade status.

Although Bingo was a secular man, the fate of his coreligionists was never far from his mind. One night at dinner he told his family about the spring of 1937, his senior year in high school. He and his brother Jerry were walking along the Grand Concourse arguing about whether the Yankees would win the World Series that season, and if Joe DiMaggio could beat out

Luke Appling of the Chicago White Sox for the batting title, when they noticed everyone around them craning their necks, staring at the sky. The two boys looked up to see the Hindenburg blimp looming imperially over their Bronx neighborhood. In those days, it was still rare to spot a plane, and the Nazi zeppelin was the most impressive aircraft they had ever seen. Immense and silvery with a giant swastika emblazoned on its tail, the Hindenburg seemed to have emerged directly from Hitler's fevered psyche. To his family, Bingo said: I thought those Nazi bastards were coming to kill me.

The summer of Nixon's agony was uneventful for Jay. He did errands for his father and Uncle Jerry, picked up lunch, delivered gifts to city officials. Occasionally he was allowed to attend meetings, but never when his father and uncle discussed anything important. The company offices were in the East Fifties and during his lunch breaks he would sit on a bench in Central Park, eat a sandwich from home, and read a paperback. His cousin Franklin spent the summer working on a kibbutz in Israel and Jay often thought he should have joined him there. He considered transferring from Penn to Berkeley. California intrigued him, and in those burning years it looked like New York had no future.

When the following summer arrived, Bingo prevailed on Jay to give the real estate business another shot. I'm going to show you how it works, he said, the guts of it. Reluctantly, Jay agreed. The Jackson-Vanik Amendment had passed, and the result was to open the spigot and allow the flow of captive Jews out of the Soviet Union. Bingo was a member of several organizations dedicated to resettling the ones who landed in America and he gave a number of them jobs. In early June of 1975, he called his son into his office. Sitting in a chair was a floor safe named Marat Reznikov.

His father said, "Say hello to our cousin."

The man got up from his seat and smiled at Jay, revealing a

gold incisor. He wore a tight suit with a black shirt and no tie. His face was pockmarked. He had thick lips and a one-inch vertical scar on his left cheek. His eyes were dark caves. He was five foot nine but looked like he could stop the F train with his elbow. When they shook hands, Jay noticed Cyrillic letters tattooed on his fingers. Jay knew no one with tattoos. To see them on someone's fingers was unimaginable. Bingo informed his son that Marat had been a successful business-man in Odessa, a port city on the Black Sea, and would be employed by the Gladstones as a rent collector.

"Hello, cousin." Marat's voice had the texture of a bear's paw.

Jay nodded mutely.

"You're going to work together," Bingo said.

"Your father's grandfather and mine—brothers," Marat said to Jay, who knew how important the idea of family was to his father. Marat grabbed Jay's bicep and pointed at Bingo. "Your father *khoroshiy chelovek*, good man." The consonants of his accent banged and clicked.

"You'll get to use a company car," Bingo told his son by way of inducement.

Jay did not have to be sold. He liked the idea of getting out of the office and into the field. This cousin seemed to be what his father referred to as "a character," someone who willfully differed from the prevailing norms. At thirty-two, Marat was twelve years older than Jay. He had served in the Soviet Army, earned a degree in mathematics, and used his expertise to immerse himself in the black market where he supplied the apparatchiks with whatever sex, drugs, and rock 'n' roll they required. Bingo knew about the mathematics degree and the military service but was not privy to the spicier corners of his cousin's resume. For Bingo, the man's identity as a Jew was the only salient fact. As for Marat, a Jew in name only who did not keep kosher, did not *daven*, and did not know the Ten

Commandments except to violate them, his religious status was just another hustle he was happy to use to escape the bleak Ukraine for the crumbling disco inferno of 1970s New York.

In those years, the Gladstones owned over a thousand rental units in the Bronx stretched over the largely black and Latino neighborhoods of Mott Haven, Hunts Point, and East Tremont. Most of the tenants paid their rent on time, and the Gladstone brothers did not look to cause problems. If the rent was two weeks late, a letter was sent requesting payment. A month in arrears and another letter would arrive reminding the renter of his obligation. Six weeks of nonpayment resulted in a visit from a representative of the landlords, and it was this function that Marat Reznikov was hired to perform.

The Bronx that summer was no longer the borough of Bingo Gladstone. Burned husks of buildings, abandoned cars stripped to their axles, streets furrowed with potholes, medians overgrown and littered with trash, junkies on the nod, and the whole rotting body festooned with explosions of graffiti, bursts of life shouting that the venerable borough would not die gently. From the subway platform on the Jerome Avenue line, say, or the Concourse line, or the Pelham line, you watched trains surge in, every car decorated with spray-painted designs, the mobile oeuvre of taggers with names like TAKI183, Batz 4, Mitch 77. And the dogs! Heinz 57s, Rottweilers, and Dobermans, beasts on thick chains that could barely control their hellish aggression, all barking in maniacal communication. And the *pop pop pop* of gunfire that would occur without warning. All of this was news to Jay, whose personal experience of the city's northern borough was confined to Yankee Stadium and the Bronx Zoo.

The company car that Bingo provided turned out to be a 1972 brown Ford Pinto with a balky transmission that Jay nicknamed Lucille, after B.B. King's guitar. Because Marat did not have a driver's license, Jay piloted the Pinto around the potholes and down the battered streets with his cousin in the passenger seat chain-smoking Lucky Strikes, whose packaging, appropriately, featured a target. Although Marat lived in the Kingsbridge neighborhood, he had only resided in the borough for two months and was unfamiliar with the geography, so the two of them relied on a grubby map provided by a clerk in the office. Jay picked up Marat in front of his apartment every morning at eight, and the two of them made their humid rounds. The air conditioning in the dinged-up car was a rumor, and Jay's clothes stuck to his skin. In the urban swelter, they toiled until four with a break for lunch. They tried to finish their rounds before people returned from work, because that reduced the chance of confrontations. The Bronx stank of uncollected garbage, but it was the scent of imminent violence that had Jay on edge all day—he wore Adidas to make running easier—while his cousin, cigarette glued to his lip and a blasé expression on his scarred face, was unconcerned.

Marat Reznikov was like no Jew Jay had ever met. His English was sparse, but he wanted to learn so he consistently engaged Jay in conversation. He talked about his years in the Soviet Army and the scams he ran after he was discharged. In Odessa, gangs controlled the rackets and Marat survived by a combination of guile and intimidation. Once, he beat a man who owed him money, then put a leash around his victim's neck and made him walk down the street naked on all fours, like a dog. To Jay it seemed depraved, but Marat told the story like it was funny.

They parked Lucille in front of whatever Gladstone building they entered. It didn't matter if the parking space was illegal, in those years Bronx cops didn't write a lot of parking tickets. Then, they opened the front door with a master key and headed for the deadbeat apartments, starting on the highest floor and working their way down. The halls were dark and uninviting, and often smelled of urine. The glass of shattered lightbulbs crunched beneath their feet. Marat would pound on a door, Jay standing behind him. Less than half the time someone answered. Every apartment had more locks than Rikers Island, and the tenants would unbolt them—*click click click click click*, slide the chain—and open the door. Whatever the size, shape, and age of their bodies, their eyes were a blend of anger and defeat. Marat used his limited English to explain the situation, and the tenant would either pay up or Jay would hand over a legal notice informing them of the grim fate that lay ahead should they fail to honor the terms of their lease. The first few times they did this, Jay had to take deep breaths to still his rampaging heart. But Marat, despite his imperfect command of the language, seemed to frighten most of the people they encountered. When Jay realized this, he became less tense.

The first week passed without incident.

That weekend Jay played tennis with a high school friend at his parents' country club. Afterwards, they had drinks in the bar overlooking a golf course that resembled an English landscape painting. The friend was about to leave for a summer program at the Sorbonne and planned to travel on a Eurail pass for August. Sipping his second Heineken, the sense of distance between the foundation of his family's income and the life it provided came into sharper focus. He wanted to discuss it with his friend but lacked the vocabulary. Instead, he talked about this wild Ukrainian his father was making him work with and when he repeated the story about the naked man on the leash the two of them hooted with laughter, although Jay was still not entirely sure why it was amusing.

The following Monday, in a building with a broken elevator in East Tremont, a Puerto Rican tenant—a dissipated man in his forties gripping a quart bottle of Colt malt liquor, Guzman, three months back rent owed—shoved Marat and slammed the door in his face. Already out of sorts from climbing five flights,

Marat was livid. He pounded his fist on the door and shouted curses in Russian. Thumped it with his foot. A Latina woman in curlers cuddling a crying baby stuck her head out of another apartment and told him to shut the fuck up. Marat cursed her. He thrashed the door for five minutes, but Guzman remained inside. Jay taped an eviction notice to the door and with great difficulty convinced his fulminating cousin to leave.

An hour later they were on foot in Mott Haven. It was late morning, and the temperature was already in the nineties. They had just purchased sodas at a bodega and were crossing East 139th Street, headed back to the Pinto. Marat was asking Jay if he knew anything about how bond trading worked when a gypsy cab bumped him. Marat yelled something at the driver, who blasted his horn and screamed *Get your ass outta the street*. Marat whipped his can of soda against the windshield of the cab, and the driver threw the door open. A pasty-faced white man in a Mets hat, waving a crowbar. His eyes were cracks as he lumbered toward Marat. Jay had never been this close to real violence, and the sight pinned him like a butterfly to where he stood. The man raised the crowbar to swing at Marat, but before he could bring it down on the Russian's head, he froze. A smiling Marat was pointing a gun in his face. In the sunshine of the Bronx morning, his gold incisor glinted. The passenger in the cab, a black woman wearing a summer dress and a wide-brimmed straw hat, climbed out of the door and scuttled in the opposite direction.

The frightened cabbie moved away from Marat as if by centrifugal force and Jay thought that was the end of it, so he was alarmed when Marat brought the butt of his gun down on the man's head and sent him crashing to the pavement. The fear turned to revulsion when Marat pistol-whipped him once more and then kicked him in the stomach. Jay grabbed Marat, who spun on him, hand raised, ready to strike again. He relaxed when he saw it was Jay.

"I need another soda," Marat said.

Jay suggested they get it somewhere else and as the two of them walked quickly to the Pinto, he kept his eyes focused straight ahead. Only in the car did he glance back and see the man struggling to his feet. To Jay's great relief, Marat had not killed him. He believed something criminal had occurred—the guy provoked Marat, certainly, but then Marat viciously assaulted him—and was ambivalent about leaving the scene. On the other hand, he did not want to be in the middle of anything that involved the police.

Marat lit a cigarette and reminded Jay to start the car.

Since it was nearly lunchtime, they drove to a diner near the Hunts Point market. There were jukeboxes on all the tables, and someone was playing "Love Will Keep Us Together" by the Captain and Tennille. Jay ate a cheeseburger and studied Marat as he devoured a liverwurst sandwich. Marat enjoyed his lunch as if it were another day at the office. The violence did not seem to have registered. Jay marveled at this, did not know how it was possible. He wondered if Marat had ever killed anyone. It wasn't a question you asked. Marat flirted with the Puerto Rican waitress and smoked another Lucky. He explained to his younger cousin that you could never, under any circumstances, let someone think they could fuck with you. Jay thought Marat was slightly unhinged, but what truly frightened him was how unemotional he was, both when he beat the driver and when he provided the philosophical underpinning of his behavior.

They split the check, got iced coffees to go. That afternoon, Marat held forth and told stories about Odessa. But the metallic aftertaste of the morning's viciousness remained with Jay. The previous winter Jay had gotten into a shoving match in a fraternity league basketball game at Penn, and the tension had remained with him for hours. Violence was preverbal, stupid. He abhorred it. That night Jay thought about telling Bingo what he had witnessed, it was on the tip of his tongue, but decided against sharing the information. Marat was good at his job and the percentage of tenants behind in their rent payments was declining. Bingo liked him. If he learned about this incident, it might jeopardize Marat's employment, and Jay did not want to be the cause of that. He did tell his father that the elevator in Mr. Guzman's building needed to be fixed.

The next day, and the one after that, Jay dreaded a repeat performance. He worried that someone would rile Marat and that his cousin would respond criminally. But it did not happen. Marat was able to convey the kind of individual he was without saying anything, and people acted accordingly. Big, scary looking men, white, black, Latino, treated him civilly. They might not do what he suggested, as far as paying the rent on time, but no one challenged him. It was uncanny.

The following week they were in Highbridge, a neighborhood peppered with a mix of blacks, Dominicans, and Irish. It was the end of the day, and they had one more unit to visit. A young couple lived there, Irish, rent two months overdue. Only the wife was home, a rail-thin woman with thick red hair and a bruise under her right eye. She explained to Marat that they didn't have the money but would have it next time—Can you give us a break?

Jay saw Marat think about it. The woman leaned on the door frame. She asked them if they wanted something cold to drink. Marat told Jay to go downstairs and wait for him in the Pinto. In the Bronx, victims sat in parked cars, but he wasn't going to contradict his cousin. Marat came down twenty minutes later and handed Jay a beer. Jay did not ask what happened.

And so, the sweltering summer of 1975 passed. Marat's English improved under Jay's tutelage, and Jay absorbed some of Marat's swagger. His fear of the streets had not entirely abated, but he was far more comfortable in the dashiki precincts of the Bronx than any kid from Scarsdale had a right to be. After work, they hit the bars on Fordham Road and drank Schaeffer on tap. Marat became a Yankee fan (his favorite player was the ornery Thurman Munson), and they even attended a couple of games together. The night they watched the Yankees beat Cleveland, flames of a tenement fire licked the sky beyond center field. On Fridays, Marat brought Jay to the Turkish baths on 10th Street where they *shvitzed* while being thrashed with oak branches wielded like maces by burly Russians. It was there that Jay noticed a gold Star of David nestled in Marat's voluminous chest hair. When he remarked on it, Marat said, "Is good to be Jew in New York." Was that true? Marat owed his immigration status to being a Jew, and his job. For this irrepressible refugee, Jews were his gang.

It was late August, and the following week Jay was scheduled to go back to college for his junior year. The city was in the middle of another heat wave, and the mixture of tropical humidity and the heightened aroma of the streets intensified everything. Marat told Jay he wanted to buy him a steak dinner as a gesture of appreciation for being his guide to New York City. Jay didn't think he had been anyone's guide, but Marat was sentimental and feeling expansive toward his princely relative. Jay had plans, so Marat had instead treated him to valedictory lunch at a steakhouse on Gun Hill Road near Woodlawn Cemetery.

"You are *khoroshiy chelovek, boychik*," Marat said. "When you finish university, you work for me."

Jay laughed. He said: "As a rent collector?"

"Laugh now," Marat said.

They each had a few beers and were pleasantly buzzed when they rolled out of the restaurant and into the Pinto. The first building they would visit after lunch, Marat said, was Mr. Guzman's. On the short ride to Mott Haven Marat sang along to the songs on the radio, his rutted voice alternately caressing and assaulting the unsuspecting melodies. To Jay's relief, his father had taken care of the broken elevator. As they rode to the top floor, Marat joked about what he was going to do to Guzman, the beating he would deliver. Jay assumed he was kidding. He believed Marat was only returning to the apartment to check it off the list so they could begin formal eviction proceedings. The last time they had been there a week earlier the tenant had not opened the door. But when they arrived at the fifth floor, rather than going to Guzman's apartment, Marat headed for the roof. Before disappearing into the stairwell, he told Jay to wait in front of Guzman's door. Slightly drunk, Jay obeyed.

It was around three thirty. He had a date that night with a girl who lived in Morningside Heights. They were going to a reggae concert at the Wollman Skating Rink in Central Park. Jay was thinking about the approaching evening when he heard a shout from inside the apartment and then what sounded like glass breaking and something heavy hitting a wall. When the door opened from the inside, Jay saw Marat holding a dazed-looking Guzman, who was bleeding from his mouth. Jay immediately noticed the gun in his cousin's hand. Without a word, Marat pushed past Jay and made for the stairwell, dragging the tenant. Guzman suddenly realized the severity of his predicament and began to resist actively. "Help me," Marat ordered. Without realizing what he was doing, Jay was beside Guzman and, with his cousin, hustled him up the stairwell.

There was no one on the roof. Jay looked around to the other buildings, where the roofs were similarly unoccupied. He could hear the sound of traffic and the distant rumble of the IRT. Salsa blared from an open window. Guzman shook Jay off and swung at Marat. He missed.

Jay was scared of what his cousin might do. "Let's just

report the nonpayment and get out of here, okay?" Marat was not interested. He pointed his gun at Guzman who swayed backward before regaining his footing. Looked over his shoulder. The adjacent tenement was about ten feet away. There was a pigeon coop over there, and Jay could hear the birds. Guzman glanced in that direction once more. Jay thought he might try to leap between the rooftops.

"Why you not just pay?" Marat asked, as if he was going to be reasonable for Jay's benefit.

"Porque eres un puto Judio codiciosos," Guzman said.

"You hear what he call me?" Marat asked. Jay knew the meaning of *Judio*. And *puto*. To Guzman, Marat said, "Do I call you Puerto Rican piece of shit?" *Piece of shit* was a phrase he had recently learned and now used whenever possible.

"Joder tu madre," Guzman said.

Marat charged at Guzman, who, trying to avoid being caught, found himself close to the edge of the roof. A flock of sparrows rose from the adjacent rooftop as if to get a better look. Jay had an impulse to call for help but had no idea to whom. Guzman reached into his pocket and pulled a knife. He carved the air in front of Marat.

Marat said: "I have gun, you fucking idiot." He pronounced it "eee-dyote." "Put down knife."

Guzman stared at Marat dully. His pickled brain slowly adjusted. Realizing his error, he gently laid the knife down. Had he heard a note of mercy in Marat's voice? If so, he was mistaken. Marat grabbed Guzman, spun him around, and shoved him off the roof. Then he looked at Jay and shrugged. He put two fingers to a cut on his cheek and licked the blood off.

Jay walked gingerly to the edge of the roof and peered down. Guzman was splayed in the alley between the two buildings. The sight of the body, and the height from which he observed it, dizzied him. Before losing his balance, Jay stepped away from the precipice. He turned and walked past

Marat, ran down the stairs, and got into the Pinto. When Marat joined him moments later, he was nonchalant. Jay couldn't look at him.

"Why did you do that?"

"Teach him to not fuck with Jew," Marat explained. He stuck a cigarette in his mouth and lit it, drawing the smoke into his lungs. Jay slumped behind the wheel, but from the corner of his eye he sensed his cousin staring at him. He slowly faced Marat. Marat touched the tip of his finger to the edge of his eye socket, then pointed at Jay's eye. He gently shook his head side to side. "You no see." The semblance of a smile Marat offered combined reassurance and threat in a way that was entirely new to Jay. He felt sick. "Understand?" Jay could barely nod. All of his muscles were rigid. Marat told Jay to start the engine and drive.

Jay canceled his date for that night. He told his mother he wasn't feeling well and spent the evening in his room. When his father arrived home, he said nothing. He barely slept, panicked that the police were going to knock on his door in the middle of the night and drag him to some precinct in the Bronx, then to court the next morning and charge him as an accessory. But the police did not come that day, or the day after, or the day after that. For a week, he bought all three daily newspapers but never saw anything. Jay did not yet understand that the fate of people like Guzman was of no interest to the tabloids, or to anyone else.

The knowledge of what he had witnessed gnawed at his gut. From the time that he brushed his teeth in the morning, and the memory of what had occurred sucker punched him, through his commute to the city, and all through the workday, it was present. When he returned home at night and, most intensely, when he lay in bed, Jay was tempted to reveal what he had seen. He would never have gone to the police but, again and again, he thought about telling his father. What made him bear the secret? On the most animal level, he was scared of what Marat would do. The man was a killer. Marat's casual manner in the aftermath of the incident led Jay to surmise that Guzman was not his first victim. Would this Odessan gangster dare to take revenge if Jay reported what he had observed? He did not want to find out. But it was more than fear of Marat that made Jay hold his tongue. Even as a young man he had intuitively understood that if he told Bingo, he would pass the terrible burden along, hand it off, leave it to someone else. Bingo was Marat's employer, his American sponsor—his blood relative. Jay would not put his father in the position of having to decide whether to inform the police.

Jay went back to college as if what he had seen on that rooftop in the Bronx had never occurred. He enrolled in his courses, participated in the life of his fraternity. He studied, worked out, partied. Occasionally, he would have distressing dreams, and more than once he awoke convinced he had killed someone. Along the border of sleep and wakefulness, he suffered ineffable torment and faced a hollowness so profound it seemed to negate his essential self. The feeling would persist for several hours, even days, and propel him back to that summer. He never told his father about what had happened, nor either of his wives. The melodrama of Marat killing Guzman in front of him was absurd, but overriding the absurdity of the crime was the absurdity of Jay's having been there. This suburban boy, this twig: Eyewitness to a killing. He never wanted to believe the world worked like this. Yet now he knew, incontrovertibly, it did. Over the next several decades of his inexorable rise, there was always the thought lurking in the back of his mind that somehow, as the constellations shifted in the sky, as the planets revolved in their paths, a celestial alignment would arrive whose geometry would announce Jay Gladstone's karmic payback.

Chapter Twenty-Six

Blood sluiced from Jay's nose as he called 911 on his cell phone and kneeled by the unconscious Dag. He apologized, told him he had never meant to cause harm. He implored him to hang on, dear God, and wake up, please, please, wake up because the ramifications of not waking up were too horrifying to imagine. By the time the beams of the ambulance lights juddered along the dirt road, Dag had briefly returned to consciousness. Jay knew this because Dag had looked directly into his eyes. He couldn't interpret what the player was attempting to convey, and it didn't matter to Jay whether it was hatred (understandable), or apology (less likely, but not out of the question), or something in between. The only thing that mattered was that he had not killed the man.

A police car arrived on the scene just as the EMTs were finishing their work. The officer told Jay he would see him at the hospital to take a statement. Jay was relieved to hear this since it would give him time to decide what to say. The ambulance ride along the dark roads was nerve-racking. He crouched next to the gurney on which Dag lay, neck stabilized, oxygen mask obscuring his features, and attempted to will the big man back to consciousness. Eyes riveted to Dag's inanimate, deeply familiar face, a face known to millions, a face Jay had seen fully embody exaltation and despair, he implored Dag not to die. With one hand, Jay held a towel to his own nose, which still had not stopped bleeding. With the other, he braced himself as the ambulance screamed down the twisty rural roads.

At least Dag was breathing.

Recognizing the limits of his own will, Jay tried talking to him: "Dag, can you hear me? Dag? Wake up, buddy." (*Buddy?* Where had that come from?) But there was no response.

Across the gurney was a young Latino EMT who introduced himself as Luis. The driver was a burly white man with a small cross dangling from his ear, who immediately recognized Dag when they arrived at the scene. Luis had hooked Dag up to a monitor and was watching the lines on the screen. His jaw worked a wad of gum. Satisfied that everything appeared to be in order, he became curious.

"What happened, Mr. Gladstone?"

"I don't know."

He looked at the face of the EMT to gauge his reaction to the nonresponse. Jay was going to have to formulate a plausible version of events at some point, but now was not the time. The ambulance careened through a red light at an empty intersection. Luis seemed to be gauging whether or not to continue the conversation. Jay began to think about whom he would call when they reached the hospital.

"You got an NBA All-Star lying in the street, and you don't know what happened?"

"That's what I said."

"You got a lawyer?"

"Excuse me?"

The impertinence! Who was this kid to speak with Jay Gladstone as if they had gone to school together? Jay had enough of his wits about him not to reveal anything. As concerned as he was with Dag's condition, he was aware of his tenuous legal position, and anything he said to Luis would be of interest to a judge. What to tell that cop? Right before Jay tilted his head back to let the blood from his nose flow in another direction, he saw a sign that read Welcome to Mt. Kisco.

"Hey, no offense, Mr. Gladstone," Luis said. "Sometimes I joke around 'cause of all the tension. I apologize."

Jay was not listening. The taste of blood in his mouth, he wondered whether Dag would have had sex with his wife had more money been offered in the contract negotiation. Was Dag paying him back? Yes, he was! What else could it have been? Wait! Had they been having an affair or merely charmed each other at the Obama dinner? Had they been overtly flirting? Was an entire table of Obama donors convinced D'Angelo Maxwell was sleeping with Jay Gladstone's wife?

Despite the confusion, the feelings of helplessness and rage that ebbed and flowed, what Jay felt most was remorse. He wanted to rewind time and tell Boris to take him to the apartment in New York rather than to Bedford.

And what of Nicole, with whom he had intended to grow old? Who he had decided, eventually and after much deliberation, would be a wonderful mother to his second—as yet imaginary—child. Now his marriage had burst into a million radioactive pieces.

The siren's wail in the empty night seemed to mimic the dissonant drone in his head and served to distract from the pain of his physical injuries, but it did nothing to hide the psychic wounds which continued to suppurate.

The ambulance zoomed into the ER bay. Someone flung the rear doors open, and Dag was whisked into the building. Jay trailed the stretcher like an afterthought and presented himself to the on-duty nurse at the reception desk. Dag was already in the ER.

The arrival of a gravely injured person always sets off a flurry in a hospital, and when the person is a celebrity, the volume kicks up several notches. On-duty personnel summoned sleeping doctors from their beds and relegated Jay to the waiting room. Several times he tried to find out what was happening with Dag but was rebuffed.

Over the next forty-five minutes, during which Jay observed two doctors blow swiftly through the metal doors to the restricted area where Dag lay, he could only wait. He woke Bebe with a phone call and relayed a concise version of what had happened, leaving out the part about wanting to scare Dag, along with the detail about Dag and Nicole. He intended to keep that appalling, inflammatory, deeply embarrassing information private.

"Do you want me to drive up there?"

"I don't think that's necessary," Jay said.

Asking Bebe to drive up would be to admit that he needed his sister and to acknowledge that degree of vulnerability was out of character. To arrange the best care for Dag once he passed triage stage, Jay phoned a prominent surgeon he knew. The call went directly to voice mail and Jay left a message. During this time, he received two texts from Nicole, neither of which he read. When his phone vibrated and he saw that she was calling, he did not answer.

After what seemed like a week but was less than an hour, a stocky male nurse with a blond crew cut finally appeared to do an intake interview. An X-ray of Jay's nose revealed a small fracture.

Jay perched on an examination table in one of the small side rooms in the warren that was the ER of Northern Westchester Hospital as Dr. Sunil Viswanathan, a bespectacled young resident, set the break. He had changed into a flimsy hospital gown. His bloody shirt was rolled up in a plastic bag on a nearby chair. Dr. Viswanathan was solicitous but formal and addressed Jay as Mr. Gladstone while he attempted to manipulate the bone back to where it belonged. As the doctor pushed it gently into place, Jay winced at the pressure.

"You're lucky you didn't do more damage," Dr. Viswanathan said.

"Yes, I'm incredibly lucky," Jay said, unconvinced. The gauze packed in his nose made his voice sound strange to him. Although the pain radiated dully in every direction, he was barely aware of it, being utterly preoccupied by what had occurred. He had been in the ER for an hour and a half, and the last he had heard about Dag was that he was still alive. He hoped that remained true.

"Would you mind finding out how D'Angelo Maxwell is doing?"

"The hospital does not give out information to non-family members," Dr. Viswanathan said. "As I've already explained to you twice."

"These are unique circumstances," Jay said.

"How so?" the doctor inquired, as he continued to fuss with the nose.

Jay was getting impatient. In his estimation, the manner in which circumstances were unique was proportional to the degree in which he was involved in them. The function of most people with whom he came in contact was to do his bidding, and given that he was unfailingly polite, Jay felt justified in his attitude. Dr. Viswanathan did not seem to understand this concept. Still, he rarely played the do-you-know-who-I-am card because it was almost never necessary. Jay asked the doctor if he was a sports fan.

"I like the Yankees."

"D'Angelo Maxwell is a professional basketball player."

"I know who he is."

"Dag's a colleague, and I need to call some people who are close to him and let them know what's going on."

"The hospital is taking care of it."

"How does the hospital do that?" Jay's posed the question with more vinegar than he intended. Not being able to direct the way the evening was unfolding increased his agitation. Along with concern for what had happened to Dag, he envisioned a public relations debacle. His first instinct was to control the flow of information, and the doctor was impeding this plan.

"Just let everyone do their jobs, Mr. Gladstone."

"I'd like to do mine," Jay said.

"Your job right now is to sit here and let me deal with your broken nose. Now hold on, this might hurt a little." He tweaked the bone to its final place, and Jay felt a pain shoot into his skull so excruciating that his sockets seemed to swallow his eyes. After a few seconds, the ache began to subside into something more manageable, and his eyelids fluttered open.

The doctor placed a piece of plastic over Jay's nose and bandaged it to his face. "Tomorrow you're going to look like you went fifteen rounds with Mike Tyson," Dr. Viswanathan said, scribbling on a pad. "Are you allergic to any medications?" Jay was not. "This is for the pain." He tore the page from his pad and handed it to Jay, who pocketed it.

"Doctor, I wonder if there's something else I could talk to you about."

"What's on your mind?"

"I had a diagnostic procedure on my prostate recently."

"Would you like me to take a look?"

"No, no, no! But I think an infection might have developed. I was taking painkillers and—" He described the symptoms. Dr. Viswanathan prescribed a course of antibiotics and suggested Jay call his urologist if it didn't resolve in a few days.

"Doc, is it okay if I have a word with the patient?"

Jay looked up and saw the police officer from the scene of the accident standing in the doorway. In his hand was a device the size of an electric razor. Dr. Viswanathan asked Jay if he was ready to talk to the authorities and received an affirmative answer.

"Take care, Mr. Gladstone," Dr. Viswanathan said. He shook Jay's hand and was gone. With that, Jay felt the thin scrim of civilization evaporate. He was now facing the elements.

The cop was in his forties and looked like he spent a lot of time at the gym. He ambled into the room and introduced himself as Officer Wysocki. With his cropped blond hair and strong jaw, Jay thought he resembled the kind of guy they recruited back in Vitebsk when a mob was needed to terrorize Jews.

"I probably shouldn't let you know this, but I'm a fan of your team."

That was welcome news. Perhaps this was going to go more easily than Jay had anticipated.

"I'll make sure you get tickets to a game."

"We're not supposed to accept gifts."

"Then forget what I said."

"But for that, maybe I can make an exception."

Jay was not in a mood to banter. He needed to start gathering facts and begin to assert command over the situation. "Have you heard anything about Dag?"

"He's in an operating room, that's all I know."

Jay wished he had some idea of exactly what was transpiring, the condition, the prognosis, anything at all. The cop's laconic demeanor did not seem to fit the situation. Jay wanted to get this over with.

"What can I do for you?"

"You can start by telling me what happened."

Now he would have to declare his definitive version of events. Whatever story he decided to tell was the one he would be stuck with since an investigator was going to pounce on any inconsistencies. If he dissembled in any way, he was setting a trap for himself because once a discrepancy was discovered, everything he said would be called into question. Yet, could he be sure he was capable of giving a cogent version of events? What *had* happened? He knew his brain had not been functioning properly at the time. He could say *that* since he believed it to be true. But how was he supposed to convey what was going on with him neurologically to this cop? Had he blacked out? He couldn't remember.

"Mr. Gladstone?"

"I want to consult with my attorney before I make a statement."

"You understand you haven't been charged with a crime?"

"I didn't commit a crime."

"Great. Then I'm going to need you to blow into this thing," the cop said, displaying the gizmo. It was a Breathalyzer. "We need to check your blood alcohol concentration."

"I'm not legally obligated to blow into that, am I?"

Officer Wysocki had heard this question many times before and had a standard answer that he proceeded to supply: "While you are not legally obligated to take the test, refusal to do so will result in loss of your driver's license for a period of one year."

That got Jay's attention, although, with Boris at his disposal, he didn't need to do a lot of driving. Still, Jay Gladstone was not the kind of man who had his license suspended. How much liquor had he consumed, anyway? Two drinks, three at the most—but the pills! Those pain pills must have interacted with the alcohol. He wasn't going to mention the pain pills to Officer Wysocki.

"Mr. Gladstone, if I arrest you, I can make you take the test because you'll be legally obligated. Do you want me to book you?"

Jay thought about this. He did not want to be arrested. But who knew what the Breathalyzer would reveal.

"Why would you arrest me?"

"For starters, you were in a one-car accident that resulted in a near fatality. I could take you in on suspicion of reckless endangerment." The cop waited to see whether this would loosen Jay's tongue. It did not. "Look, Mr. Gladstone, this is gonna be all over the news. So, you might ask yourself: Do I want the accounts to show I refused to take a breath test?"

"I certainly do not."

"Then please blow into the Breathalyzer."

Wysocki handed the device to Jay, who looked it over. On the front was a digital display and a mouthpiece protruded from one side. Jay clamped his lips around the mouthpiece. After five seconds passed and he had still not blown into it, he removed the Breathalyzer from his mouth and handed it back to Wysocki, who failed to hide his exasperation.

"I want to talk to my lawyer."

"Call him."

Jay pulled out his phone and asked for privacy. Wysocki stepped out of the room.

The Gladstone Group commanded a platoon of lawyers but when there was anything sensitive or personal, Jay sought the counsel of Herman Doomer, Esq. He had been Bingo's attorney and had known Jay for his entire adult life. Doomer picked up on the fourth ring, having been awakened from a deep sleep.

"I'm so sorry to bother you, Herman."

"What is it, Jay?" he asked, foggy. "Are you all right?"

Jay quickly apprised him of the situation. The lawyer advised him not to take the test and said he would meet him in court the next morning for the arraignment. The words "court" and "arraignment" jolted Jay.

"Court?"

"Yes, well, they'll arrest you, and you'll be taken to jail. They'll hold you overnight and bring you to court in the morning where they'll arraign you."

"You can't get me out of jail tonight?"

"That would take the intervention of a judge and judges don't enjoy being woken up in the middle of the night."

After thinking this over, Jay decided not to press the issue. He could handle a night in jail if he had to. Anyway, the important thing was Dag's condition. He needed to arrange the finest medical care as quickly as possible. Locking him up would foreclose that prospect.

"What if I take the test?"

"Do you think you might have been intoxicated, Jay? Please say no."

"I just got back from Africa," Jay explained. "I was taking painkillers, and I had a few drinks on the plane."

"You don't want to take that test."

Sliding the phone back into his pocket, Jay summoned Wysocki and informed him of his decision.

"Does your wife know where you are?"

"Don't worry about my wife," Jay said with more pepper than necessary.

"Someone should bring you a clean shirt."

When Jay did not answer, the cop ordered him to place his hands in front of him since he was now under arrest.

"I've got a broken nose," Jay pointed out. "I want to spend the night in the hospital."

Jay demanded to see the doctor, and Dr. Viswanathan dutifully reappeared. He explained to Jay that his injuries were not severe enough to avoid having to do what any citizen would be compelled to do. Jay considered arguing, but recognized he was not going to win and submitted to the doctor's decree. When Viswanathan departed, the cop again asked Jay to present his wrists. He submitted to this indignity and walked out of the examination room toward the parking lot wearing pants and an open-backed hospital gown that concealed the bracelets.

When they exited the ER and entered the reception area, Jay purposely did not make eye contact with the clerk on duty. He noticed a young black man pacing in front of two other young black men seated in chairs. The pacer spotted Jay and quickly approached. He looked vaguely familiar. Jay wondered if this guy realized he was handcuffed.

"Mr. Gladstone, I'm Trey Maxwell, Dag's brother."

"Yes, yes. I'm glad you're here."

"How's he doing? They won't tell us anything."

"I wish I knew," Jay said. "They won't tell me anything either."

Rather than continuing to lead Jay through the reception area, Officer Wysocki allowed the discussion to proceed.

"What happened tonight?" Trey asked. The other two young men had joined them, one short and sturdy, the other the size of a refrigerator. Jay saw the cop taking their measure. He remembered that Dag's brother got cut when he had tried out for the team.

"There was a car accident. They brought us here. That's all I know."

Trey was visibly upset. "He gonna be okay?"

"I hope so," Jay said, unable to come up with something more specific.

Wysocki informed Jay it was time to go and led him away. Before they took two steps, the electric doors slid open, and Bebe appeared. Despite his compromised condition and his mortification at the circumstances, Jay was immensely relieved to see her. An ally, a friendly face, Bebe cut a chic figure in the pitiless light of the hospital waiting area.

"You didn't have to come," he said.

"I wasn't doing anything."

"Could I have a word with my sister?" Jay asked.

Dazzled by Bebe, Wysocki acceded to this request and moved away.

She asked if Jay was all right and whether anything had changed since they last spoke, other than the fact that he was now wearing handcuffs. He updated Bebe, and when she learned he was being taken to jail she cast a disbelieving glance toward Officer Wysocki, now standing at the nurses' station keeping a wary eye on them.

"I need you to be my advocate here," Jay said. "Find out what's going on." His sister assured him she would.

Seconds later, Officer Wysocki approached. Bebe embraced her brother, and then the cop led Jay away.

A news van pulled into the hospital parking lot. To Jay's horror, a shaggy-haired young man with a beer gut was running toward him, a video camera affixed to his shoulder. Tottering on high heels in his wake was a young Asian woman with a microphone.

"Mr. Gladstone—Mayumi Miyata, Lynx News. Could I talk to you?"

Jay turned to the cop. "Would you get me out of here, please."

"Do you know D'Angelo Maxwell's condition?" she asked. Jay did not answer.

She tried again. "What happened to your face?"

Jay remained tight-lipped as Wysocki opened the rear door of the cruiser, placed his hand on Jay's head, and guided him into the backseat. The cop closed the door and got behind the wheel.

"Are you under arrest?" the woman shouted. "Why have you been arrested?"

Wysocki backed up and cranked the steering wheel, nearly taking out the reporter and her cameraman in the process. As they sped off another news van careened into the parking lot.

In his most reasonable manner, Jay inquired whether absolutely anything could be done to avoid spending the night in jail.

"I'd like to help you out because you're a nice guy and all," Wysocki said, "but the same sun shines on the rich and the poor."

To lecture the cop on the naïvete of that statement would have required more energy than Jay possessed. Instead, he miserably attended to the dryness of his mouth, the degree to which his muscles ached, the dull throb of the broken bone in his nose. Even through his clothes, the seat felt slick. What parade of lowlifes had the police crammed back here?

"You want me to call your wife and ask her to bring you some clean clothes?"

"No, thank you."

It was the rump end of the night when they entered the Bedford police station, Wysocki's palm pressed against Jay's lower back. Several officers were in the bullpen drinking coffee and they stared in disbelief as one of the town's most prominent citizens was frog-marched into their territory.

The antiseptic hallway held three cells. A young white man in work pants and a plaid shirt was curled up asleep in the first one. Wysocki unlocked the third cell and gestured for Jay to enter. He was grateful to be separated from the other inmate by an entire cell. The spartan unit held a metal bed with no mattress or blanket. Wysocki removed the handcuffs and asked whether Jay would like something to eat. He declined. The reverberant clang of the cell door intensified the clamor in his head. Jay did not turn to watch as the cop walked away. He sat down on the bunk and placed his head in his hands. This position caused the blood to rush to his nose, exacerbating the aching sensation. He straightened his back and leaned against the wall, which alleviated some of the pain. His thoughts turned to Nicole and Dag and whether Dag was still alive.

Jay Gladstone pondered the condition of his soul.

There is a gulf between those who can commit violent acts and those who cannot. Jay always believed himself to dwell on one side of the chasm, and his place on that side, he believed, was permanent. As a child, he was horrified when the family dog was struck by a car and killed. The one time he sat ringside at a prizefight, he was repulsed. Jay had never struck anyone in anger. He shied away from any violence, and the deepest part of him believed he had not meant to hit Dag with the car. But was that true? Was there not a sliver of something foul, unconscionable, hidden but leeringly present, a tinge of murderous intent inside of him that not only wanted revenge but also was prepared to act on that most savage impulse and take it to its awful conclusion? Did violence lurk in him only waiting for an impetus to be delivered so it could spring to life? Was the only difference between Jay and Marat Reznikov the circumstances into which they had been born?

Time seemed to move backward, then forward again, then stop. Jay's mind reeled from questions about his deepest nature, to what he had gotten wrong about his marriage, to his week in South Africa, to the fortunes of his team, to whether Dag was going to survive. And how was Jay going to survive what had happened to Dag? Although scalded by guilt, the level he endured minute-to-minute rose and fell in contrary proportion to how often his thoughts turned to what Nicole had done.

In this manner, nose packed tight with gauze, disquiet spiking inversely to his diminishing energy, Jay passed the hollow night in the clutches of jet lag—remember, he had arrived home from Africa hours earlier—and intense physical discomfort, able to breathe only through his mouth, battling despair that reached inside him to separate tendon from bone.

CHAPTER TWENTY-SEVEN

D ag had nearly canceled. To spend several hours at a political dinner in the company of Jay Gladstone held no appeal but he was keen to meet President Obama and believed if the evening went well perhaps Church would forgive him for the Moochie Collins incident. The coach acted like he had absolved him but Dag knew it was a façade. A champion like Church Scott could not abide knucklehead behavior. Dag knew how the man thought and, despite their unequal status—in the hierarchy of professional basketball certain stars outranked the coach—Dag still craved Church's respect.

Babatunde had taken his tuxedo to be cleaned and as Dag stood in front of the full-length mirror in his bedroom, he shot his cuffs and admired the reflection. His physique showed clothes beyond the imagining of those who designed them. Broad shoulders tapered into a trim waist and endless legs. His size sixteen feet, ensconced in patent leather slippers the size of Alaskan salmon, made a well-proportioned base. His mood was already better because practice had gone well. Dag's shooting stroke looked smooth and, although his hand was sore, the degree to which he favored it was not readily evident. If the team scrapped its way into the playoffs, he would be at full strength. Dag posed hips rotated, an over-the-shoulder gaze. He smiled at his own vanity.

When the Maxwell brothers sailed over the George Washington Bridge in the McClaren, Trey at the wheel, Mobb

Deep blasting from the speakers, Dag felt the familiar swelling in his breast as he watched the curtain rise on the lights of the Manhattan skyline. He turned up the music so its strength would better reflect his own. As Trey downshifted on to the exit ramp, Dag vowed to charm Gladstone into a larger contract, play out the deal, and then ascend the golden escalator to the elite corporate realms embodied by the glittering metropolis that unfolded before him.

Dag got out of the car at the hotel and told Trey he'd phone him when it was time to go home.

"Tell Obama I say what up," Trey said.

"Most definitely," Dag said, adjusting a cuff link.

"And don't cause problems."

Dag told his brother not to worry. "I got this," he said.

Because the president was going to attend, security was unusually heavy. A perimeter had been set up around the Waldorf Astoria but Dag was not asked for ID. Rather, several guards welcomed him as he walked past. Wherever Dag went, there were stares because of his size but when people recognized him, commotions of varying intensity invariably ensued. Even in places like the Waldorf Astoria. After he passed through the second screening area just outside the lobby he was approached by three Asian businessmen that had seen him play an exhibition game in China the previous year. Dag signed a few autographs, allowed himself to be photographed by a white family from Georgia who arrayed themselves around him like a blanket, signed more autographs, then proceeded up the ornate staircase that led to the second-floor ballroom.

Five hundred fashionably turned out people filled the space, a mixtape of races, if not incomes. Chandeliers the size of pianos lit flocked wallpaper, gold molding, white linens. Celebrities (Missy Elliott, Samuel L. Jackson, George Clooney) and politicians (Bill de Blasio, Kirsten Gillibrand) happy to bask in the president's reflected light. A female volunteer, young, eager, and black, utterly tickled to be in close proximity to D'Angelo Maxwell, escorted him to his table near the dais where Church Scott, his wife Sharon, a stunningly beautiful white woman to whom he'd been married twenty-five years, Nicole Gladstone, and three other white couples he did not recognize were engaged in conversation. Dag and Church were the only African-Americans at the table. Everyone was drinking wine. The people he didn't know greeted him enthusiastically. They all looked as if they had been born at the Waldorf, comfortable and shining. Dag barely acknowledged them. He was not thrilled there were strangers at the table. Where was Jay?

The owner's wife gestured to the empty seat next to her and indicated he should sit there. Dag had planned on showcasing D'Angelo Maxwell, Inc., for her husband this evening, to atone for his screwup and to demonstrate to Jay that he still had enough juice to be the face of a professional sports franchise, a brand name that deserved to be compensated at the highest rate. But Jay had stood him up without so much as a phone call. He thought about walking out. He did not relish an evening of small talk but was prescient enough to realize that a hasty exit would only compound his problems. If he had to spend the evening talking to Nicole, he would. Tonight, she was dressed in a mid-length, rust-colored silk wraparound dress with a plunging V-neck.

Dag lowered his frame into the chair. As soon as he did, Nicole placed her hand on his shoulder. Dag turned and saw large hazel eyes beaming in his direction. They had never been this close before so he had never noticed the flecks of gold in her irises. A tiny flake of makeup balanced on a long lash. He had the strange urge to brush it away. Before this evening, they had only exchanged a few words over the course of several encounters at team events. She leaned toward him. Her smell was intoxicating, fresh, and delicately floral. When she spoke, he felt her warm breath on his neck.

"My husband sends his apologies," she said. "He's in Africa."

Dag shook his head. "Sorry to hear that," he said.

"Don't act so disappointed."

He realized that she thought he was playing.

"I *am* a little disappointed," Dag said.

"Well, at least the president hasn't cancelled."

It would have been preferable to Dag if the president *had* been the one to not show. Gladstone was the man with whom he needed to mend fences. He loved Obama, but right now Jay was a larger presence in his life.

A waiter appeared and filled Dag's wine glass with red. Dag took a sip as Nicole drained what was left of hers and asked for a refill. He was glad for the red wine. It would not be easy to drink quickly. He saw Nicole eyeing his injured hand. He hoped she wasn't going to ask him about it.

"Does your hand hurt?"

"It's a little sore," he said.

"What you did was chivalrous."

"You ought to tell your husband so he doesn't suspend me."

"I would if I were speaking to him."

She smiled and he couldn't tell if she was flirting. Whatever she was doing, it was making him uncomfortable. He was attracted to her but why go there? When a waiter spoke to Nicole, Dag turned toward the coach's wife and asked whether she had met Obama.

Sharon Scott liked to talk to him and he indulged her. She informed him she had met the president on a previous occasion and was smitten; did Dag know him? He told her that they had never met. Church leaned across his wife and confided to Dag that the second biggest reason he wanted to win another NBA championship was that it would improve his chances of getting an invitation to play golf with Obama.

"We need to get you on the links, D'Angelo," Church said.

"So you can kick my ass?" Dag said. Church and the women laughed. "I like to dominate."

"You'd be a heck of a golfer," Church said.

"I'm a golf widow in the summer," Sharon informed the table.

Dag turned to Nicole. "You play golf?"

"I ride horses," she said.

"I don't like horses," Dag said.

"Because you can't dominate them," Nicole said.

"Exactly," Dag said.

"You ever try polo?" Church asked Nicole.

"Not yet," she said. "But I'm always up for a new experience."

"Sort of like golf on a horse," Dag observed.

"Two things you can't do," Nicole said.

Church lifted an eyebrow. Sharon said, "Oh ho!" amused by Nicole's impudence.

Dag was taken aback by the remark. He did not traffic in self-deprecation and to have someone else lampoon his flaws, no matter how jocular the intent (or how irrelevant the flaws), was slightly disorienting. But she smiled when she said it, and lightly touched his bicep. When she removed her hand, she brushed his arm with the backs of her fingers. If she was trying to placate him, it worked.

"I bet I could learn both," he said.

"I bet you could, too," Nicole said.

"You'd probably be better at golf than polo," Church said.

"If you ever want a riding lesson," Nicole said, "I've been around horses since I was a girl, so let me know."

Dinner was served and just as Dag was eating his dessert, Senator Schumer stopped by the table to say hello. Dag proudly introduced the politician to his tablemates. It pleased him to be on familiar terms with a U.S. senator and to see the reaction of his companions. The politician joked once again with Dag about joining the Knicks and Dag, who had consumed a couple of glasses of wine, played along this time, far more at ease than he had been during their first encounter at Jay's club.

"I'm reporting you to the league," Dag said and the senator cackled in delight.

Church's wife had been looking at George Clooney all night and was thrilled when the movie star introduced the president. Church said, "My wife wants a free pass for Clooney," and everyone laughed. Obama charmed for fifteen minutes and his remarks about the economic recovery, the Middle East, and his Republican opponents had the audience singing from the hymnal. Nicole and Dag were both enthralled and he had to resist the urge to reach for her hand. Several million dollars were raised. Before coffee was served, a Secret Service agent approached Dag and reported that the president had asked to meet him.

As Dag got out of his seat, Nicole said, "I'm coming, too."

"I'm sorry, ma'am," the agent said.

"If my husband is going to meet the president," Nicole said, indicating Dag, "Then I'm his plus one."

Church and Sharon were trying to suppress their amusement.

The agent spoke into a microphone on his lapel. He registered the response he received in his earpiece. To Nicole, he said, "All right, let's go."

Nicole had met Obama previously and the president, Dag, and she shared a laugh about how she pretended to be Mrs. Maxwell. Obama wished Dag luck in making the playoffs. Nicole said she hoped she would get a chance to see him again on Martha's Vineyard this summer. Obama thanked them for coming and turned his attention to Halle Berry.

Back at their seats Dag marveled at Nicole's buoyancy as she described the encounter to their tablemates. The evening was far more convivial than he had anticipated. Nicole was older than he (how old was she, anyway?), but no less magnetic for it. Had she been single, he would have made it a point to take her out.

When the evening ended, they left the ballroom together. She grazed the area above his elbow with her shoulder and he felt a frisson. As they passed from the ballroom to the foyer, she sleepily murmured: "Would you like me to teach you to ride a horse?"

They had both consumed several glasses of wine so Dag wasn't sure he had heard correctly. He glanced down and saw the diamond lights of the chandeliers flickering in her eyes. The expression on her face was enigmatic. Women hit on Dag with planetary regularity but this was an entirely singular experience. He waited for her to laugh or punch him in the arm. She did neither. Instead, Nicole's lips curled into an enticing smile, equal parts innocence and lubricity. It acted in concert with the wine and made him more receptive to her proposition than he might have otherwise been. Dag called Trey and told him he would be playing an away game tonight and did not need a ride home.

CHAPTER TWENTY-EIGHT

W hen Jay flew from the guest house, Nicole slithered into the dress she had earlier peeled off. Then she sat down and waited for her husband to return. Although the sex with Dag had been a letdown—he was too drunk to produce an erection, and when one finally arrived he was done three seconds later (the wild bucking Jay witnessed was her attempt to remedy this)—she enjoyed his company, his tenderness, and his humor. But she had no illusions about pursuing any relationship with him. A little too much wine had led to rash behavior, and there was no doubt it would not happen again. She intended to express further contrition, ongoing contrition, endless contrition if need be, and dedicate herself to the salvation of their teetering marriage. As she waited, the feats of self-abnegation she imagined grew in intensity. Whatever prostrations Jay required, she would perform.

But as the minutes crept by with no sign of him her thoughts turned in another less charitable direction. Why had she gone to bed with Dag in the first place? It wasn't because her marriage was going swimmingly. The last time she had seen Jay was when she stalked out of their bedroom the night before he left for Africa. Their fragile ceasefire had been negotiated over brief phone calls and emails, and had not been certified by physical proximity much less consummated with armistice sex. It didn't exactly justify her behavior, but it was not as if Jay was blameless. Self-erasure was not her style. The longer Jay failed to return, the less inclined she was to throw herself at his mercy. Where were Jay and Dag? Had they patched things up and gone out for a drink? Unlikely, but why had her husband not reappeared? If he didn't want to save the marriage, why should she?

With her heels dangling from two fingers over her shoulder, Nicole sashayed barefoot up the hill toward the house. How much time had passed since Jay ran off into the night? In the distance, she heard a siren wail. Probably some old duffer with a stroke, she thought. The wet grass was slippery beneath the soles of her feet. The certitude with which she held to the notion of non-surrender had already begun to abate, and she was back to the idea of begging. Her thoughts were thrown into further disarray by her inability to suppress the desire to have more sex with Dag (when he wasn't drunk), although she understood that that was a foolish idea and tried to put it out of her mind.

Warily, she entered the house through the back door and called Jay's name. When he did not respond, she went from the living room, to the den, to the library with its shelves of bound leather volumes, the media room, the dining room that had so recently seen the Gladstone Seder, then the kitchen she had designed to her exact specifications.

Nicole climbed the stairs, still calling, "Jay, Jaaaaaayyy—" She tried to keep the plaintive tone at bay, but it was difficult. The emptiness of the house was starting to feel creepy. She understood if he was not answering because he was angry. He had every right. She could only imagine her reaction if the situation had been reversed and she had walked in on him having sex with her friend Audrey Lindstrom. She would have been shattered. Thinking of lovely, lithe Audrey, whose husband doted on her, recalled Audrey's pregnancy (Who cared about being lithe when you could be pregnant?), and her despondency deepened. It wasn't as if Nicole had led a life devoid of mistakes, but she had not risen to her current position by making bad decisions. She was appalled by her behavior.

The bedroom was empty, and the master bath, and the other bedrooms, and Jay's home office, walls lined with photographs of the two of them taken on holidays in Aspen, Nantucket, on the yacht they had chartered in the Greek islands. Where had he gone? She pulled her phone from her purse and called him. It went directly to voice mail, and she left a simple message, asking him to call her. Then she texted:

I love you so much.

After she pressed send it occurred to her that perhaps that sentiment was insufficient, so she googled forgiveness. A moment later, she texted:

"Sweet mercy is nobility's true badge." William Shakespeare.

But that didn't quite convey what she was feeling either and was more than a little self-serving. Back to Google. What she found was too long to text, so she furiously typed an email:

Jay, my love, Stephen Hawking wrote, "My advice to other disabled people would be, concentrate on things your disability doesn't prevent you doing well and don't regret the things it interferes with. Don't be disabled in spirit as well as physically." I am spiritually crippled, but if you're willing to help me, I can heal.

As soon as she hit send, she knew that it was too mawkish, but under the circumstances, it seemed justified.

Nicole wanted to take a shower and scrub the evening off her skin, but when she shed her gown and stood in her sheer bra and panties, her first reaction was to throw on a pair of jeans and a blouse. In the event Jay returned, she didn't want to be naked. After waiting another ten minutes, she checked her phone and saw that Jay had not responded to her attempts at communication. She packed an overnight bag, pulled her Range Rover out of the garage, tuned the radio to the country station, and drove into the city. She never listened to country music when Jay was in the car. Perhaps because it hinted too strongly at her Virginia roots, the rural aroma of pastures and stables. Nicole rode English style now, but that's not the way she had learned. As a girl, she rode like a cowboy, high in the stirrups on a big western saddle.

Had she reined herself in too much to be Mrs. Jay Gladstone?

CHAPTER TWENTY-NINE

A round the time Jay dropped behind the wheel of the Mercedes and tore out of his Bedford driveway, Christine Lupo lay in bed reading the third in a series of popular mystery novels about a Dublin coroner. He had an estranged wife, a heroin-addicted son, and a drinking problem sparked by the first two circumstances. He loved Guinness stout and Roquefort cheese, and suffered from gout and mild depression. Still, he nabbed the criminals in the first two books and Christine expected the third to resolve with some clarity and hope. As far as she was concerned, for all of his hardships, the coroner's professional life was far easier than hers.

Dressed in a flannel nightgown, she fingered the small gold cross hanging from a thin chain around her neck. It was pleasant to be alone. The implosion of her marriage was troubling from a logistical perspective, but she was relieved to be done with Dominic Lupo. The discovery of infidelity will make a person question everything they believe to be true and for Christine—who craved certainty—that was unbearable. She noticed the time on the digital clock on the nightstand. Closing the book, she got out of bed and padded across the upstairs hallway to check on her kids, who slept in adjacent bedrooms. Lucia was already asleep, and Dominic Jr. was in bed listening to music on headphones. He had his father's thin face and dark hair and wore a black T-shirt that said *Thank God I'm An Atheist* in bold white lettering. She was not amused. For the oldest child of a Republican gubernatorial candidate to be seen wearing it would cause problems upstate and on Long Island.

"Where did you get that T-shirt?"

He took off the headphones in a way that conveyed to his mother he was not pleased with being interrupted. She repeated the question.

"The Internet."

"Don't wear it outside the house," she ordered.

"Why?"

"Because I'm telling you."

"Yeah, whatever."

"Don't whatever me, Dom. I mean it."

Under his breath, he said, "Fascist," still loud enough for his mother to hear.

"What did you say?"

Emboldened: "I said you're a fascist."

"What do you know about fascists?"

"They're against freedom."

"Anything else?"

"That's all I know."

"Obviously, because you got a 'C' in history." She hadn't meant to insult him like that but, just like his father, this kid could get under her skin. He was upset about the divorce. She needed to give him a break, but it was hard given how he was looking at her. Like she was his enemy.

"Can you just leave me out of your life? I didn't ask you to run for office, and I'll wear this fuckin' T-shirt if I want, and I'll get you one for your birthday."

Her charitable impulse vaporized. That kind of impudence would not be tolerated, but given that Dominic Jr. had already expressed a preference for living with his father she didn't want to make the situation worse. What she said: "Ha ha."

Believing he had bested his mother, the boy shifted his

attention to the Katy Perry poster taped to the wall opposite his bed.

Christine, who was constitutionally unable to let her son off the hook, ordered him to remove the T-shirt and hand it to her. He resisted but when she said "Dominic, if you don't want to be grounded, take off that goddamn T-shirt and hand it over," it was clear that resistance was futile. He peeled the T-shirt off and hurled it in her direction. She picked it up off the floor.

"It cost twenty-five bucks!"

"You should spend your money more wisely."

Ordinarily, she would have asked if he had completed his homework but her son had been accepted at two colleges that week, so she just said goodnight. He grunted at her and slipped the headphones back on. Christine worried that the boy blamed the failure of the marriage on her, and since she and her husband had mutually agreed to withhold the circumstances from their children, she decided that there was no option but to endure the current situation and hope for its resolution at some indeterminate future date.

Back in her bedroom, she considered reading another chapter of the novel. She enjoyed books like this because they presented evil and then punished it, unlike her job where compromise was usually the order of the day. Criminals in her world were found not guilty at trial, others plea bargained their sentences down and barely paid the price for their crimes. If a mystery novel was ambivalent on the subject of right and wrong, if it trafficked in the belief that the police and the criminals had something in common, if it was in any way morally ambivalent, she wanted to throw it across the room. To have a story tied up in a bow was a great comfort.

Just after four, Christine's cell phone vibrated. The phone buzzed for nearly thirty seconds before the DA woke up and grabbed it. Her deputy, Lou Pagano, apologized for awakening her. He had received a call from the night shift felony ADA informing him police arrested Jay Gladstone in Bedford, arraignment at the County Courthouse in a few hours. Since the defendant was a public figure, whose presence in the courtroom was guaranteed to generate considerable attention, did she have any special instructions? Christine was only a casual sports fan— she knew what a contemporary New York politician needed to know for small talk (Yankees in playoffs, Jets struggling, Knicks hopeful)—and was aware of Jay Gladstone more from his role as a real estate magnate than as a team owner. But even in a sleep-addled state, it did not escape her that the police shooting incident had occurred at Gladstone Village. As the most consequential citizen to ever enter her domain, his would be the most high-profile prosecution since a private school headmistress murdered a prominent doctor back in the early 1980s, a case that had fascinated a gawping nation and spawned several quickie books and a made-for-television movie.

She sat up in bed. "What's he being charged with?"

Pagano recited the facts as best he knew them at that point. Christine was already energized by the prospect of having someone as prominent as Jay Gladstone in one of her courtrooms, but when Pagano informed her that the injured party was the NBA All-Star D'Angelo Maxwell, she nearly gasped. Only vaguely aware of him as an individual, the phrase "All-Star" illuminated his celebrity status as if with klieg lights.

D'Angelo Maxwell's race did not escape Christine's attention either.

Jangling like a tambourine, she was unable to get back to sleep. Her driver would not pick her up for several hours. How would she fill the time? She grabbed a notepad and jotted down a few thoughts, but found it difficult to focus. She needed to be lucid to get anything useful done. But what an opening this was! No one would ever misjudge her if she were able to put someone like Jay Gladstone behind bars. Not that insufferable head of the police union, or that foul-mouthed criminal who had cursed her in public, and certainly not a political opponent. She wanted to go to the office immediately, but that was impossible. She glanced around the bedroom and saw her son's T-shirt. She had tossed it on a chair earlier intending to dispose of it in the morning. Now she grabbed it and headed downstairs.

Dominic Sr. liked to barbecue during the summer months. He cooked the usual sausages and peppers, burgers and chicken, the occasional ribeye steaks. Last year he had purchased a new gas grill, and it sat forlornly on the patio, unused since the previous autumn. Christine was about to change that. She had thrown a jacket over her nightgown. The night was a sea of stars. No lights were on at the neighbors' houses. She lifted the metal cover and placed the T-shirt on the grill.

While the DA was doing this, she pondered her options. The universe was serving her Jay Gladstone on a platter. Only the severity of the charges against him remained to be determined. Were they sufficiently grave, it might grant her maneuverability in the John Eagle case. Because the victim was black, the Gladstone indictment would give her cover for not convening a grand jury in the cop shooting. It was the most elegant juridical jiujitsu imaginable. She knew what happened when a famous person was on trial. It was the legal equivalent of a jet engine, sucking up all other cases in its wake.

Briefly, her mind alighted on the morality of this idea. She certainly didn't want D'Angelo Maxwell to die. Grievous bodily harm would serve her purposes, too. She didn't want that either; recognized it would be ghoulish to wish for anything remotely close. But she couldn't help it if Jay Gladstone ran a famous athlete over with his car. It was a nasty situation. If she could wrest a single positive consequence from something so awful, was that inherently wrong? Did she possess the capacity to engineer something so audacious? If she had the nerve, it would be a masterstroke.

Christine baptized the T-shirt with lighter fluid, struck a match, and ignited it. The flames curled up and illuminated her face, already flushed with anticipation and possibility. The T-shirt burned easily, the fibers blackening like a marshmallow. In the morning, she would show her son the ashes.

THE ACE, W.A.C.E. AM
NEW YORK SPORTS TALK RADIO
WITH SAL D'AMICO AND THE SPORTSCHICK

SAL: The story right now, Sportschick, and all anyone is talking about is D'Angelo Maxwell and Prince Jay Gladstone.
SPORTSCHICK: All we know is there was a car accident up in Westchester County and Jay Gladstone got arrested.
SAL: An ambulance took both of them to the hospital. It's all over the Internet. A terrible accident, we have no idea why Gladstone was arrested, and we hope both of them are okay. Our thoughts and prayers are with the families.
SPORTSCHICK: Jay Gladstone is a stand-up guy. I interviewed him last year, and he's a real gentleman.
SAL: Old school.
SPORTSCHICK: I like Dag, too. Treats the media with respect.
SAL: Very bright guy. Very personable. Both of them major figures in the world of sports, one in the hospital, the other one in serious legal trouble.
SPORTSCHICK: We wish the two of them a speedy recovery.
SAL: Definitely. Fellas, get well soon! And let's also mention what this means for the team. The timing of this from a basketball standpoint could not have been worse. The ball club is currently only one game out of the playoffs, and now their best player is in intensive care. If they make the playoffs, will he be back in time?
SPORTSCHICK: We don't even know if he's gonna play again.

SAL: *You're right. Forget the playoffs. Hey, we're not even thinking playoffs. We still don't know the extent of his injuries. We just hope he's okay. So, what went down last night?*

SPORTSCHICK: *Let's be clear to the listeners that we don't have any special knowledge here on the ACE. We're speculating.*

SAL: *So, speculate.*

SPORTSCHICK: *First of all, who was driving? Do we even know?*

SAL: *Let's back up. The accident happened in Bedford, which is where Jay Gladstone lives. What was Dag Maxwell doing in Bedford?*

SPORTSCHICK: *Visiting?*

SAL: *You think they socialize?*

SPORTSCHICK: *Why not?*

SAL: *Lemme tell you why not. Jay Gladstone does not socialize with his players. Very few owners do that.*

SPORTSCHICK: *All right, who do you think was driving?*

SAL: *I'm gonna say Dag was driving. It's a one-car accident on a country road. Dag wraps the car around a tree.*

SPORTSCHICK: *No chance Gladstone was driving?*

SAL: *Are you—what? No! It's a one-car accident! Jay Gladstone is the most controlled, level headed, passion-free guy in New York sports today and any caller who wants to tell me his team is in New Jersey—put a cork in it. I know. It's still New York sports, okay? Gladstone's in his fifties, the man is not a drag racer. The man does not crash his car unless he's under the influence and no one's seen a blood alcohol report.*

SPORTSCHICK: *So it was Dag?*

SAL: *Most definitely.*

SPORTSCHICK: *Definitely?*

SAL: *Likely.*

SPORTSCHICK: *Wanna know what I think?*

SAL: *Lemme guess, you disagree?*

SPORTSCHICK: I think Gladstone was driving. Dag in the passenger seat. He was up there visiting.

SAL: What, playing pinochle?

SPORTSCHICK: Pinochle? Sal, what are we, in 1962?

SAL: Everyone knows you're younger than me. Don't rub it in.

SPORTSCHICK: Maybe they're playing video games.

SAL: They don't socialize! You got a young black guy and an old white guy. What are they gonna talk about?

SPORTSCHICK: Money!

SAL: Get outta here!

SPORTSCHICK: Wouldja lemme finish?

SAL: I'm not stopping you.

SPORTSCHICK: Gladstone is driving—the wife is home, right?

SAL: The wife!

SPORTSCHICK: Gladstone's at the wheel of the car and they're going somewhere.

SAL: Where are they going in the middle of the night? You think Gladstone is taking Dag to the train?

SPORTSCHICK: Maybe a strip club.

SAL: In northern Westchester? You ever been there? All they have is trees.

SPORTSCHICK: Okay, I don't know where they were going. I'm just saying, why would Dag be driving Gladstone somewhere? Gladstone's the one who lives there.

SAL: Maybe the wife was driving.

SPORTSCHICK: The wife wasn't in the car.

SAL: Hear me out. The wife is driving, she wrecks the car, and one of the guys takes the fall.

SPORTSCHICK: You see that in a movie?

SAL: What if I did?

SPORTSCHICK: Takes the fall for what, Sal? If she was driving, and that's a pretty big if—

SAL: Hey, we're in the realm of speculation.

SPORTSCHICK: *If she was driving and she cracks the car up, no fatalities, why is anyone taking the fall? So her insurance rates don't go up?*

SAL: *I don't know. But I'm telling you, there's a story here that's gonna come out. Should we take a call?*

SPORTSCHICK: *Maybe someone can explain it.*

SAL: *Tommy from Queens, you're on the Ace, W.A.C.E.*

TOMMY: *How you guys doing?*

SPORTSCHICK: *What do you think happened, Tommy?*

TOMMY: *Personally, I think Dag wanted to get paid.*

SAL: *It's business, Tommy. He shouldn't get paid?*

TOMMY: *The team didn't want to back up the money truck, Dag gets pissed off, Gladstone runs him over.*

SAL: *You're saying it was on purpose?*

TOMMY: *People do things you never thought they could do.*

SPORTSCHICK: *Instead of trading him, the owner runs over the player?*

TOMMY: *It's a theory. Let's face it, Dag hasn't lived up to expectations, he's asking for the moon, Gladstone gets mad, and bing-bang-boom!*

SAL: *He takes a shot at his number one asset with his car?*

TOMMY: *I'm not saying it was rational. Guy gets angry; he does a stupid thing. Wouldn't be the first time. I'll tell you this: If that's what happened, Gladstone's gonna get away with it.*

SAL: *Why?*

TOMMY: *Because he's rich.*

SPORTSCHICK: *Guy's got a point, Sal.*

SAL: *First of all, no way Gladstone was driving the car. What sports owner—football, baseball, hockey, or basketball—is going to run over his number one asset with a car? Especially a by-the-book guy like Jay Gladstone. Tommy, don't take this the wrong way, your theory is bonkers. Let's take another call.*

CHAPTER THIRTY

In Franklin and Marcy Gladstone's Long Island kitchen, the coffee was brewing, and the television on the white marble countertop was tuned to the morning news. An African-American female correspondent was reporting on an event President Obama had attended at the Waldorf the previous evening. Dressed in a terrycloth robe, Franklin Gladstone stood in front of the open refrigerator, a look of consternation stamped on his face. He was holding a nearly empty carton of orange juice and watching the TV out of one eye. For much of the night, sleep had eluded him.

He called out, "Carmen, where are you?"

There was no sign of the live-in housekeeper. This situation did not improve his already dyspeptic mood. It exasperated Franklin to hear yet another news report about Obama, whose re-election he fervently opposed, and the orange juice situation further irritated him. Three times he had awakened the previous night, twice to urinate, and one time because who knows why? He had a lot on his mind. It could have been his daughter who was failing trigonometry; it could have been business, what did it matter? He had not slept well since the night of the Seder when Jay told him he wanted to audit the books of the Asian operation.

"Carmen!" Louder. "I told you not to let the orange juice run out!"

Where was that woman? Usually, she was bustling around the kitchen at this time of day preparing his breakfast, half a grapefruit cut twelve ways for easy scooping of the chunks, and a slice of wheat toast, dry. Grapefruit and wheat toast? It was torture. To Marcy, he kvetched: The terrorists at Guantanamo eat better! Franklin used to love to consume marbled steaks, French cheeses, rich desserts. But since his cardiologist told him might drop dead if he didn't lower his cholesterol, he had grown to dread meals. Poured the ounce of juice that remained into a glass, drank it down, and threw the carton in the garbage can under the sink. Cursed under his breath and served himself some coffee with nonfat milk. Did he have to manage the maid, too? He would tell Marcy to talk to Carmen.

As he emptied the third packet of artificial sweetener into his cup, he heard the anchorman say the name Jay Gladstone and Franklin wearily turned his head toward the television. Out of orange juice, no sign of the maid, and again Jay was getting more attention he didn't deserve. If this was the kind of day it was going to be, he might as well go back to bed.

"Can I get a tattoo?" His daughter Chloe had come down sleepy-eyed for breakfast. The short skirt she wore barely concealed her pudendum, and a midriff strained to establish contact with the spandex waistband. "A little one?"

"Shush," he said, intent on the television.

She shrugged and opened the refrigerator.

Although hearing his more prominent cousin's name in the media unfailingly triggered negative emotions, he could never stop listening or reading, or in any way tune out Jay's superior achievements for long. But today was different. Something terrible had happened. There had been an accident. A basketball player in critical condition. Jay injured. And there were legal problems of some kind. Had he heard the word "arraignment"? Arraignment for what? What had his cousin done?

"It's Carmen's day off," Marcy said. While Franklin was staring at the television, his wife had entered the kitchen dressed in canary yellow workout clothes for her indoor tennis game.

"Shush." he said.

Marcy did not like being told to pipe down. "What?"

"Quiet!"

"Why are we out of orange juice?" Chloe asked.

Having failed to get her husband's attention, Marcy tried once more: "Franklin, what?"

"Is everybody deaf?" Chloe again, head to the side, weight on one leg.

Ignoring his daughter, Franklin pointed at the screen, and Marcy followed his gaze. Seeing her parents mesmerized, Chloe joined them. For the next minute, they watched as the most wild-eyed version of the previous night's events was breathlessly recounted: "Horrific accident," "airlifted," "clinging to life."

"Did Jay kill someone?" Chloe asked. This possibility seemed to penetrate her usual languor and excite a level of interest she rarely displayed. "Fuck."

Marcy, who forbade her daughter from using profanity, was too distracted to notice.

"No one's dead yet," Franklin said.

"Should you call him?" Marcy asked. When Franklin did not immediately reach for a phone, she asked what he was waiting for. Franklin had not bothered to tell her about the Asian situation or Jay's suspicions. He had no desire to talk to his cousin right now, but explaining exactly why this was so to his wife was a prospect even less appetizing. He snatched the phone off the cradle on the kitchen counter and punched in Jay's number. To his relief, Jay did not answer.

"It's Franklin," he said, attempting to convey sympathy to the voice mail. "We heard what happened and we're very worried." Hanging up, he glanced at Marcy to see how his performance had played. Although Franklin typically blustered through most situations, he cared a great deal about how his wife viewed him. He wanted to be perceived as a man of honor and feared her reaction should his mischief come to light.

"Better him than you," she said. "But it sounds awful. Here, gimme." Marcy took the phone and began dialing Nicole's number ("Never mind I'm not crazy about her, she's family"), but after she pressed the area code, it became apparent that she couldn't remember it.

"Chloe, my phone's on the night table. Be a doll and get it."

The girl rolled her eyes and slinked off.

"What was D'Angelo Maxwell doing in Bedford?" Franklin asked.

"When did Jay get back from Africa?" Marcy answered.

The two of them ruminated over these questions for several seconds.

Chloe returned, handed Marcy her phone. She called Nicole, who did not pick up. Marcy left a brief message concluding with, "Call us if there's anything we can do."

"Where was she when all this was going on?" Franklin asked.

"What do you think, we're in a book club together? I haven't talked to her since that fakakta Seder."

"I had no idea Jay hung out with the players at his house."

"God forbid he invites us," Marcy said.

"You want to hang out with a bunch of overgrown schvartzes, be my guest."

"I don't like that word."

"All of a sudden you're so politically correct?"

"Well, whatever was going on," Marcy said, "I'm sure Nicole knows *all* about it."

That statement, with its disreputable implications, caught Franklin's attention.

"What are you saying?"

"I'm not saying anything."

"Is somebody going to make egg whites?" Chloe asked, again peering into the refrigerator.

Marcy kissed Franklin goodbye, asked her daughter if that was what she planned to wear to school (Chloe: "Your outfit is totally ghetto, and I'm the one getting busted?"), reminded her to use sunscreen (Marcy: "You'll thank me when all your friends have melanoma"), and headed out to her tennis game.

Chloe presented a carton of eggs to Franklin.

"Dad?"

He had forgotten his daughter was in the room. "What?"

"Can you make my scrambled egg whites?"

While Chloe sat at the kitchen table and finished her home-work, Franklin stood at the stove separating the yolks from the whites and thought about Jay. Franklin had not covered his tracks as well as he thought and Jay's recent trip to South Africa had provided a reprieve during which he intended to devise a new plan. He had spent much of the past week hud-dled with a forensic accountant and a lawyer trying to deter-mine if there was a way to reverse engineer the books that would not result in leaving him vulnerable to being charged with committing massive fraud. Unfortunately, there was not. The lawyer had given Franklin the disquieting news that his best course of action right now was to shield his twin sons from legal culpability in the event Jay were to file charges. Last night's events had the potential to change the equation. He still had no idea of the extent of his cousin's injuries, or the depth of his legal troubles. Whatever they were, the man was teeter-ing on his plinth. Whether he would topple and shatter remained to be seen.

CHAPTER THIRTY-ONE

The early morning sun peeked over the rooftops of Long Island City and painted sparkling daubs of orange and gold on the swiftly flowing East River as the helicopter carrying D'Angelo Maxwell swept over the 59th Street Bridge south to the NYU Medical Center. Along with head trauma Dag had suffered internal injuries that included a bruised kidney, and several fractured ribs, one of which had punctured a lung. A team of orderlies was waiting when the pilot landed on the riverside helipad, and as the blades whirred overhead, they rushed the helicopter, removed Dag, and hustled him directly into the hospital, on to an elevator, and to an operating room where a surgical team was ready to take over.

When the gurney bearing the unconscious athlete entered the operating theater, a tall man with dark brown skin and an erect, almost military bearing was pulling on surgical gloves. He was the head surgeon, Dr. Theo Bannister (Cornell University basketball, All-Ivy 1980-81). Assisting Dr. Bannister were another brain surgeon and a surgical resident. A nurse had, on Dr. Bannister's request, placed Handel's *Music for the Royal Fireworks* in the CD player. Dr. Bannister stepped to the table, and the resident placed a drill in his hand. Like many surgeons, Bannister enjoyed music in the operating room and made his choices based on where they were in the course of whatever procedure he was performing. Once he completed the drilling and the more delicate work commenced, he would request Brahms.

When a sympathetic nurse at Northern Westchester Hospital informed a distraught Trey Maxwell that they were going to fly his brother to the city and there was no additional room in the helicopter, he, Babatunde, and Lourawls climbed into their Escalade and drove to Manhattan where they arrived just before dawn. Too upset to eat, Trey and Lourawls had been camped in the airless visitors' lounge texting friends and relatives and waiting for someone to provide information about Dag. Babatunde sat nearby, thumbing through a Bible someone had left behind.

In front of the hospital on First Avenue, a media Woodstock was camped on the sidewalk. Reporters from NBC, ABC, CBS, CNN, FOX, Univision, Lynx, and TMZ, along with all of the local New York stations, scrambled for information. The foreign television contingent included crews from England, France, Germany, Japan, Israel, and Italy. There were radio reporters and newspaper reporters, bloggers, and fans. Everyone looking for someone who knew something, and no one talking.

The series of procedures the surgical team performed took five hours. Once completed, the patient, swathed in bandages, lay unconscious in the intensive care unit hooked up to a breathing apparatus, monitors, tubes for intravenous feeding and hydration, and a catheter, attended by a team of nurses.

In the visitors' lounge, Trey, Lourawls, and Babatunde were watching a live CNN report about Dag when a commanding black man in surgical scrubs approached and asked Trey if he was D'Angelo Maxwell's brother. Trey jumped to his feet and introduced himself. Babatunde and Lourawls huddled nearby.

"I'm Dr. Bannister," the man said. His voice was like water. "I just operated on Mr. Maxwell."

"How's my boy doing?" Lourawls asked. When Trey admonished him to shut up and let the doctor talk, he apologized and fell silent.

"Your brother sustained several serious injuries and is still in a coma," Dr. Bannister began. "The good news is the swelling in his brain is going down."

"A coma?" The word battered Trey.

"A medically induced coma," the doctor said. "It will help speed the healing."

"Can I see him?"

"Not for a while. He's in the ICU, and his body is very susceptible to infection right now."

Trey felt his throat tighten. His chest thudded. Dr. Bannister's forthrightness did little to comfort him.

"My brother's in a coma," he managed, "and I can't see him?"

"Someone will keep you posted and assuming his condition improves—"

Trey interrupted, "What do you mean 'assuming?'"

"Mr. Maxwell, your brother, as I was saying, is not out of danger. We're hopeful that he'll recover but with injuries that involve significant head trauma—right now the prognosis is uncertain." Here he paused, weighing his words. "I don't want to alarm you, but D'Angelo is not out of danger."

What did that mean? He might die?

Trey took a step back from the doctor. Lourawls looked toward the ceiling and dragged his palms over the stubble on his cheeks. Babatunde closed his eyes and prayed.

Trey asked, "But he's gonna live?"

"We hope so."

"You don't know?"

"Your brother is getting the best care in the world, Mr. Maxwell."

Trey chose to be reassured by this. He regarded Bannister and for the first time registered the doctor's height. Their eyes were on the same level.

"You play ball?" Trey asked.

"In college," Bannister said. "I'm a big fan of your brother's. We're going to do all we can to get him back on his feet."

"Word," Trey said and offered his fist, which the doctor bumped. Seeing this unexpected aspect of the interaction, Babatunde and Lourawls both offered their fists and received reassuring dap from Dr. Bannister.

"Let's assume he's gonna be okay," Trey said. "He gonna be himself?"

"Head injuries are unpredictable," Dr. Bannister said.

Babatunde ground his teeth, muttered, "Please, Lord," to no one in particular. Lourawls wrapped his arm around Trey's shoulder, said, "Dag's gonna be all right."

Trey knew this to be true because the theme of his sibling's life was Triumph, and what was this but another challenge. He rubbed his neck and thought about the cross tattooed there. It made him feel like a hypocrite since he was not much of a Christian what with all the weed, and the drinking, and the fornicating, not to mention his complete inability to find Jesus relatable. What was the point of praying to a dead white man? But at moments like this, when his soul was in torment, Dag's brother longed for faith. He needed God to intervene.

CHAPTER THIRTY-TWO

The desire to know whether Dag had survived consumed Jay, but no one would tell him anything. He still did not have his phone, so he had not heard from Bebe. It was impossible to know how much trouble awaited him. He wore a red polo shirt with *Bedford Police Golf Outing 2011* stitched across the breast in yellow thread. Given to him by a sympathetic cop, the size was XXL. It hung on him like a tent.

"Sorry, Mr. Gladstone," Officer Hartzell said, "but I gotta put the cuffs on."

Jay had just arrived at the county courthouse, and Hartzell was the New York State court officer escorting him to the holding cell adjacent to the courtroom. He was overweight and sported a comb-over.

"Are you worried I'm going to escape?"

"Regulations."

He handcuffed Jay and led him down a cinderblock hallway to a bank of elevators. They rode up several floors then disembarked. They walked down another hallway before Hartzell opened a door and beckoned Jay inside. He entered a chamber that contained a holding cell in which several prisoners waited patiently on benches under the vigilant eyes of another guard, a sour-looking black man with freckles twice as dark as the rest of his skin. The second guard signed the paper on Hartzell's clipboard and handed it back. Jay took a seat on a bench in the cell, grateful that his fellow prisoners had chosen to ignore his arrival.

"Mr. Gladstone," the new guard said. His manner was friendly. Jay looked at his nametag: Caldwell. "How about you get me some tickets to a game?"

"I'll see what I can do," Jay said. He wanted nothing more than to be allowed to go home and take a shower. Horror at what he had witnessed and what he had done enervated him, and his entire body was sore. He realized with some amazement that the recent course of antibiotics seemed to be working because whatever had been going on in his prostate area no longer seemed dire. Now, if his doctor would only tell him he didn't have cancer.

Ten minutes later another court officer appeared and called, "Gladstone!"

When he entered the courtroom, Jay had the unwelcome sense of stepping on to a stage. As a first-rate speaker who usually welcomed the chance to regale an audience, the shame that overcame him was nearly crippling. At least he was no longer wearing handcuffs. The court officer gestured to an enclosed area to the side of the courtroom that held several chairs and indicated Jay should sit down. Averting his eyes from the gallery, he complied. Judge Daryl Rice, a black man in his sixties with wire-rimmed half-glasses and a full head of white hair, was arranging a trial date for a young woman wearing tight jeans and a fake fur jacket, a female public defender on her flank.

The isolation of the pen beneath the high ceiling of the courtroom reinforced the feeling of inconsequentiality he had been experiencing in the last several hours. Other than jury duty years earlier, Jay had never been in a courtroom, but the bench, counsel tables, empty jury box, and jammed gallery—he knew it was jammed after finally stealing a glance—were familiar from countless movies and television shows. That he found himself a participant in this environment, rather than a spectator peering at it on a plasma screen, lent the morning a surreal cast.

He recognized several beat reporters who covered the team, along with members of the non-sports media. Surrounding the reporters and correspondents was the herd, drawn like ancient Romans by the timeless drama of a prominent citizen brought low. It was sickening.

The woman with fake fur and her attorney stepped away from the bench as Jay heard the bailiff call his name. From somewhere behind him, an angular, older gentleman appeared. A fringe of salt and pepper hair surrounded his bald dome, eyes the pale blue of Russian winter. The bespoke gray suit he wore hung on a tall frame. A patterned tie bisected a white Brooks Brothers shirt. Black oxfords, polished. In a sepulchral voice that held decades of secrets, Herman Doomer inquired how he was faring. "Never better," Jay said, the mild sarcasm meant to show that he had not broken down. The attorney assured his client this bit of "housekeeping" would not take long, and he would have him out of here shortly. Jay was greatly relieved by Doomer's presence. The wise counsel he prudently offered had guided Gladstone family interests for years, and this morning the low-key certitude of his manner conveyed the unspoken assurance that he would be Jay's Virgil.

"Do you have any idea how D'Angelo is doing?" Jay asked.

"I've only heard what the media is reporting."

"Which is what?"

"They're saying he's in critical condition, but no details."

Doomer guided Jay to the bench where Judge Rice presided. There he introduced himself with little fanfare. The judge nodded and turned to Jay.

"Mr. Gladstone," Judge Rice said. "This is a surprise."

"I can assure you," Jay said, "No one is more surprised than I am."

The red shirt with the yellow stitching that spelled out *Bedford Police Golf Outing 2011* in cursive would have made him feel underdressed on a weekday morning in most circumstances, but standing in a courtroom he might as well have been naked. Doomer stood at Jay's right. There was now another man in front of the judge.

He said, "Louis Pagano, Your Honor, representing the State of New York."

"This must be a significant case if Ms. Lupo sent you to the courtroom for the arraignment, Mr. Pagano." Was the judge bantering with Pagano? Jay was not encouraged by the familiarity between them. "What are the charges?"

"We'd like to introduce initial charges today, Your Honor, and hold off on the others pending the outcome of the victim's treatment."

The *victim*? Jay had not thought of Dag in that context until now—a misfortune had befallen him for which he (Dag) bore some responsibility. The two were colleagues. "Victim" seemed too impersonal, although that was what he was. Jay was the perpetrator. That simple realization set off sparks.

"What are the initial charges?" the judge asked.

"We've got driving while intoxicated, felony assault, reckless endangerment in the first degree—" Pagano stopped as if he had still more to say.

Hearing the litany intoned by the deputy DA one after the other only added to Jay's already brimming distress. The judge asked if those were the extent of the charges. Again, Pagano hesitated. Was he finished? Whether the man was trying to collect his thoughts or pausing for effect, Jay did not know.

"For now," Pagano said.

The difference between the first and second degree in the universe of reckless endangerment was lost on Jay, although he sensed the one they intended to charge him with was worse. Doomer asked permission to approach the bench, and the judge beckoned both counsels forward.

"Thank you, Your Honor. As I'm sure Mr.—" Herman

Doomer looked at the opposing counsel. "Forgive me, sir, I can't recall your name."

"Pagano," the deputy said, failing to hide his pique.

"So it is." Doomer offered a courtly nod before turning his attention back to Judge Rice with a conspicuous display of forbearance. "As I'm sure my esteemed colleague Mr. Pagano understands, in the State of New York, the charge of reckless endangerment in the first degree demands that the prosecution prove depraved indifference to human life. *Depraved* indifference, Your Honor. My client, Harold Jay Gladstone, I hardly need to say, is a business leader of great distinction, a celebrated professional sports team owner, a husband, a father, and the kind of citizen any polis"—yes, he said *polis*—"would be lucky to call its own."

Under other circumstances, Jay might have taken quiet satisfaction in hearing this recitation, but he only wanted the arraignment to be over.

"We all know he's an exemplary citizen, Mr. Doomer," the judge said. "Please come to the point."

Doomer took the interruption in stride and did not react, something Jay appreciated. He did not want his attorney to alienate the judge.

"Of course, Jay Gladstone has no prior criminal record. So, to associate the word 'depraved' with an individual of my client's stature is nonsensical. Last night, what occurred was a car accident in which Mr. Gladstone suffered a serious injury. It was not felony assault much less reckless endangerment in the first degree, or the second degree, or any degree at all. Further, there are no breathalyzer results, so the DUI is not provable. Mr. Gladstone will willingly surrender his driver's license for one year as New York State law demands. Your Honor, I hereby move that the court dismiss all charges."

The judge grinned at Doomer, one professional to another. The spiel he had just delivered on his client's behalf was a corker.

"Denied."

Pagano tried to suppress a rogue smile.

"Mr. Pagano," the judge said, "I assume, given the seriousness of the charges, the district attorney's office intends to convene a grand jury."

"We do, Your Honor."

"All right, then. We'll reconvene when the grand jury
weighs in. In the matter of bail, what does the State request?"

Without hesitation, Pagano said, "The State requests bail
be set at one million dollars."

A close observer would have noticed Herman Doomer's
right eyebrow ascend slightly before returning to its usual place
on his creased forehead. As for Jay, the figure seemed unduly
high, the high that augured further and more challenging difficulties.

"Your Honor," Doomer said evenly, "Mr. Gladstone is not a
flight risk, which appears to be what counsel is suggesting.
Further, although my client is an individual of means and could
raise the amount of money counsel has requested without undue
hardship, we submit that a bail figure of that size is prejudicial to
the potential jury pool in the event that this case ever goes to trial,
since it implies a level of gravity which the charges do not merit."

The judge looked at the prosecutor.

"We disagree," Pagano said. "Just because a citizen of the
defendant's stature is in court doesn't mean he gets treated differently than anyone else."

"Mr. Pagano—" the judge said.

The deputy DA held his hand up, indicating a desire to
speak. "Your Honor, may I?" Judge Rice nodded. "As you
know, someone convicted of reckless endangerment in the first
degree faces a prison sentence of up to seven years, and the
state submits that anyone facing that kind of prison time is a
potential flight risk.

The judge asked Pagano if he was finished and the deputy

district attorney said he was. Jay watched as the judge made a note on his pad. He used a fountain pen, and from this Jay extrapolated that the court might be sympathetic to him.

"Bail is set at one million dollars and the defendant is ordered to immediately surrender his passport."

Jay turned to Doomer who, with a subtle downward motion of his hand, indicated that he should not react. He asked Jay where his passport was.

"It's with my wallet and belt."

A Court Officer was dispatched to retrieve the item, and it was returned to Jay who handed it to the lawyer who passed it to the judge. Doomer leaned toward Jay and whispered that he had arranged for the two of them to wait in an empty office while the bail logistics were being worked out. Along with another court officer, he led his client out of the courtroom where they were met by a pair of bruisers, white and black, clad in dark suits. Jay did not recognize them. When Jay looked questioningly at Doomer, the lawyer explained that he had taken the precaution of hiring private security guards for the day. As reporters approached, the bodyguards politely but firmly requested the media keep their distance.

The court officer led the party down a hallway to an empty office and closed the door behind them, one guard remaining inside. The other was dispatched to procure for Jay a more appropriate shirt so he could finally get rid of the one gifted to him by the Bedford Police Department.

The room, painted sea green, held a desk and several chairs. The walls were bare. It was the first space in the county courthouse Jay had occupied that had a window. He looked down to the sidewalk below and saw several television trucks parked at the curb. Jay contacted his banker. A vending machine candy bar appeared. While they waited, Doomer called the hospital to get an update on Dag's condition. When the results were not immediate, Jay asked for the phone.

"This is Jay Gladstone," he said, with the casual assurance of someone who merely needed to invoke that name to make doors fly open, "and I'd like to speak to whoever runs the hospital." The person on the other end informed Jay that she would have to take a message. "Tell them to return my call," was the best he could do. Fighting the urge to yell, and sensing whatever other demands he might make would remain unmet, he handed the phone back to Doomer. It pained Jay for the lawyer to see his impotence.

"We should be able to beat this, right?"

"Ted Kennedy walked away from Chappaquiddick," Doomer said. "There were no charges, and someone died. You haven't killed anyone."

The history lesson comforted Jay, as did thoughts of Ted Kennedy's subsequent distinguished legislative career. Americans mourned when he passed from the scene. All of this allowed Jay to believe everything was going to work out.

When Jay appeared in front of the courthouse, the media surrounded him. Beyond them in the distance was the familiar sight of Boris standing sentinel next to the kind of black SUV seen in motorcades transporting world leaders. The members of the press were loud and insistent, full of brass and the class resentment that arises when a specimen like Jay Gladstone finds himself in front of a courthouse after just having been arraigned. Doomer put his hand on Jay's arm, indicating he should remain in place. He wanted nothing more than to sprint to the car, but Jay was not paying the attorney in order to ignore his advice.

The reporters shouted:

"What happened last night, Jay?"

"Jay, Jay, over here!"

"Was someone else in the car beside you and Dag?"

"Mr. Gladstone!"

"Is your nose broken?"

"Hey, Prince Jay!"

"Where were you and Dag going when the accident occurred?"

"Will you take a plea deal?"

"Jay, Jay, Jay, look this way!"

The shutters of cameras rapidly clicked, video cameras shot footage that would be played and replayed on the evening news, reporters continued to call out questions that sounded like commands, and, perhaps most jarring to Jay, ordinary citizens held up cell phone cameras to record the circus, until Herman Doomer indicated he intended to speak and their collective attention shifted to his unruffled presence.

"My client will not be making a statement this morning," he said. The horde erupted again, and Doomer waited for the questions to subside. "What we can say at this time is that our primary focus is on the health of D'Angelo Maxwell, and we wish him a speedy recovery as I'm sure all of you do as well. He's not only a terrific basketball player but he's also a leader engaged in projects with Mr. Gladstone for the betterment of the community"—Jay was not aware of any projects the two of them were doing together but marveled at Doomer's ability to shade the truth in service of his client—"and we all want to see him engaged in that work again and back on the court helping the team win an NBA title. As for Mr. Gladstone's legal situation, we will fight to have these charges dismissed, and if the case winds up going to trial, which I don't think is going to happen, we will prevail. Thank you, that's all for today."

The questions rained down once more, but now Doomer propelled Jay toward the car.

Christine Lupo stood at her office window and observed the Gladstone motorcade. It was a challenge to hide from her colleagues the glee she felt at the opportunity fate had delivered.

To show anything other than pure professionalism would have been improper, not to say morbid. She had already reviewed the police reports, the court papers, and the memo Pagano generated outlining potential case strategy. Watching the SUV carrying Jay Gladstone retreat toward the Bronx River Parkway was a satisfying conclusion to the overture.

She turned to face the large man on the couch. In a gray suit, one leg folded over the other, squinting at the screen of his smart phone, Harry Van Pelt was the bureau chief of the Local Criminal Courts and Grand Juries Division. He was the man tasked with prosecuting the tens of thousands of criminal cases originating in the city, town, and village courts of Westchester County. Van Pelt was, nominally, going to decide the charges Jay Gladstone would ultimately face and in what court they would try him. Seated in a chair, Lou Pagano consumed yogurt from a small container with a plastic spoon and watched his boss.

"So?" she said. On days like this one, when Christine was in warrior queen mode, she liked to, rather than ask a question, offer a prompt to see what would come out of the mouths of her foot soldiers.

"Going to be hard for them to make the playoffs with Dag out," Pagano offered.

"Christ, Lou, the guy's in the hospital," Van Pelt said. "Too soon."

"Do we know his condition?" the DA asked.

"The Internet's all over the place," Van Pelt said, rechecking his phone. He was on a prominent sports website where there were already several stories reporting and parsing the Maxwell/Gladstone saga. "He'll make a full recovery; he's near death—bottom line is no one knows jack. No way to say what Gladstone's indictment might be at this point. Second-degree reckless endangerment—"

"We said we were filing first degree this morning," Pagano interrupted.

"Yeah, I know," Van Pelt said. "But we don't know if the grand jury's gonna support that. So you got second-degree reckless endangerment potentially all the way up to who knows. I'm not saying this is gonna happen, I hope to Christ it doesn't, but Dag croaks and you got manslaughter."

"Maybe murder," Pagano said.

"Murder?" Christine echoed. "Why murder?"

"We don't know the circumstances yet, do we?" Pagano said, spooning a bite of yogurt into his mouth.

The DA perched on the edge of the desk. "We have no idea what his condition is?"

"The doctor hasn't made a statement," Van Pelt said. "We know he's got a head injury."

"Poor guy could be a cucumber," Pagano said.

Christine's desk phone buzzed. Stuart Berger, a town judge in Bedford, was on line two. A barely perceptible smile crossed the DA's lips, one that a conductor might flash when the violins arrive on cue. She picked up the receiver.

"Hello, Stuart," she crooned like he was a long-lost relative. "I heard it was a pretty wild night up there." She listened as the judge explained the value of showing that justice was local and to his request that the Gladstone prosecution take place in his Town of Bedford courtroom. The district attorney nodded. "Yes, yes, of course," she said. "Justice is most definitely local, Stuart. But, listen, here's the thing: There's going to be a certain amount of attention focused on this trial and, of course, there are going to be security concerns that I'm not sure you're equipped to handle up there, which is no reflection on your operation. So, I will take your request under advisement, and my office will let you know when we decide how this is going to play out, all right?" Placing the phone back on the cradle, she said, "That little twerp thought *he* was going to try this case?"

Pagano and Van Pelt shook their heads in wonder. Didn't

Judge Stuart Berger watch television? The State of New York v. Harold Jay Gladstone was going to be District Attorney Lupo's show.

When the meeting ended, Christine called Press Relations. She wanted to alert the media that in the matter of Jay Gladstone, a grand jury would be impaneled and its verdict scrupulously adhered to. Then she placed another call, this one to Franklin Gladstone. He sounded happy to hear from her. The DA quickly ascertained that Franklin was aware of what had befallen his relative.

"I'm calling to let you know that your cousin's case is under my purview. I can't tell you what's going to happen, of course, but I hope it won't change the relationship that you and I have established."

Franklin thanked her for calling and told her there was no need to worry about that. It would not change anything. Christine signed off, relieved. Then she picked the iPod up from her desk where it lay next to Pagano's report on this morning's proceedings, quickly made her selection, and placed it on the dock. The DA sat in her chair and leaned back. Eyes closed, fingers entwined on her lap, she savored the opening notes of the Bayreuth Festival Orchestra's version of *Der Ring des Nibelungen*, luxuriating on a cloud of Wagnerian bliss and imagining her picture adorning the homepage of the *New York Times*.

In the courthouse media area a few hours later, Christine stood in front of the television crews and print hacks. There were around sixty people in the room. Flanked by an American flag, the flag of the State of New York, and her deputy Lou Pagano, the district attorney stared at the bank of cameras.

"When I am asked to adjudicate a matter as important as this one," she began, "the responsibility weighs on me heavily.

Since the shooting of John Eagle occurred, I have thought of little else. He was a hardworking man who wrestled with mental illness, and he deserves, both in life and in death, our attention. No one will deny that his killing was a tragedy. That the state failed him on some level, there can be no doubt. Police Officer Russell Plesko was responding to a routine call when he showed up at the scene. He attempted to talk with Mr. Eagle, and unfortunately, the situation escalated. From having reviewed extensive interviews with witnesses, I will tell you that the officer followed correct police procedure. One of the factors that made this decision so difficult was that Mr. Eagle was unarmed. In trying to balance both of these lives, one now tragically lost, I have strived for fairness and impartiality. It has not been easy. On the matter of the shooting of John Eagle, I have decided not to convene a grand jury. There will be no charges filed, and my office now considers the matter closed."

A barrage of questions followed, and for twenty-five minutes Christine answered them. Reporters asked why she didn't trust the grand jury process. They asked if her office was in the tank for the Police Department. They asked if she thought there would be a political benefit to her decision or a backlash. The DA answered all of them in a forthright, measured tone, said, of course, she trusted the process, supported both the police and the public, and weren't they essentially the same thing: people. A reporter from a local cable news channel asked her about Jay Gladstone.

"Jay Gladstone," she said, "will be treated like any other citizen."

CHAPTER THIRTY-THREE

After Jay fled the courthouse, he went to his Manhattan apartment on East End Avenue. Increasingly frantic about Dag's condition, the phone calls he made during the drive left him unable to ascertain what it was. The doctors were silent, and nothing had leaked. Why did no one make a statement? Tell the world Dag is sitting up in bed, talking, eating—something! Of course, no statement meant that he, most likely, was not dead and that was cause for celebration.

The uniformed doorman saluted him with a touch of the cap and the usual, "Mr. Gladstone, sir." In the discreet manner of those who serve the ultra-wealthy, the man did not acknowledge Jay's battered appearance. At the elevator bank, Jay pressed the button and glanced over his shoulder to check if someone was approaching from behind. He wanted to avoid any interactions. Since it was the middle of the day, most of the tenants—they included a former Secretary of the Treasury, several CEOs, and a Saudi prince—were at offices where they pulled the invisible strings that moved the world, and Jay hoped that when the elevator arrived, it would be empty. An interminable fifteen seconds later the door opened, and a well-dressed older woman emerged. Mrs. Wessel, 16B, the wife of a Wall Street gorilla. Jay offered what he hoped was a smile tight enough to forestall any inquiries about what had occurred last night. She looked up at him with heavily made-up eyes.

"Are you doing all right?"

"Yes, thank you, Mrs. Wessel."

"Were you wearing a seat belt?"

"I was," he lied.

Jay got on the elevator and pressed 20. The encounter with Mrs. Wessel had jangled his already frayed nerves. Which details had made it into the news reports? He could only imagine, along with the degree to which the entire metropolitan area was chattering about it. At least she hadn't asked about Dag.

The Gladstone apartment was the only one on the floor. The elevator opened on to a vestibule decorated with two Currier and Ives prints, an antique side table where the mail appeared, and a copper stand from which several furled umbrellas protruded. Jay stepped off and absently picked up the pile of mail that had accumulated since his last visit. About to insert his key into the lock, he thought: What if Nicole is here? They had not connected since the incident and Jay had no idea where she was. He had not responded to her texts and right now, he realized, she could be waiting for him on the other side of the door. He hesitated while he considered this possibility but his intense desire for a hot shower overrode any discomfort at the idea of confronting her and he warily entered the apartment.

Closing the door quietly behind him, Jay peered around and braced himself for an encounter. Furnished in contemporary style with king-of-the-world views to the south, east, north, and west, the dwelling reflected Jay and Nicole's taste and, for all of its refinement, looked like actual human beings lived there. On a table in the entry area was a framed photograph of Jay, Nicole, and an unsmiling Aviva at her high school graduation. In front of him the spacious living room where an Anselm Kiefer canvas took up most of a wall. Across from the painting, custom-built bookshelves crammed with hardcovers that looked as if they had been read. To the right was the formal dining room with its Gustav Klimt portrait of a Viennese socialite, and seating for twelve, and beyond that the kitchen area. To his left a den/screening room and a hallway that led to the bedrooms. In all directions, an expanse of unobtrusive rugs.

Jay listened for the sound of the television, a running tap, the click of heels against parquet. He called her name as neutrally as he could, considering the welter of strong emotions he was experiencing, and waited. He wondered how he would react when he heard her voice. When there was no response, he repeated her name. Again, nothing. Satisfied he was alone, Jay entered the master bedroom. He half-expected to see his wife waiting for him demurely in a chair, legs crossed, nonchalantly perusing a magazine, but there was no sign of her. The bed was immaculate.

Jay's phone rang. It was Boris, who informed him that Dag was alive and now being treated at NYU Medical Center. Jay sat in a chair and gazed toward Central Park. It was sunny, and there were high clouds in the western distance. He gave a loud sob and placed his head in his hands. Jay remained in that position for several minutes.

When he regained control of his emotions, Jay shed his clothes. He stood in the steam-shower, careful to keep the bandage covering his nose dry, and let the scalding water course over his tired body and open his pores until it washed the last vestige of jail from his mottled skin. Although the three-ring circus in his head had prevented any rest, nerves rendered him wide-awake, and as he toweled off, he tried to formulate a plan for the remainder of the day. There were messages from Bebe, Franklin, Church Scott, Mayor Major House, his ex-wife Jude, and a litany of business associates including Renzo Piano, calling from Italy (the story, unfortunately, was international), all of whom expressed concern for his health. Several conveyed sympathies for the legal predicament he was in, although no one seemed to understand quite what it was.

Naked, Jay examined his face in the bathroom mirror. He gently peeled the bandage off his nose. It was not a bad break and, although there was some swelling and it was tender to the touch, the fear that he would look like a proboscis monkey had not come to pass. The bruises under his eyes resembled small mussel shells. It would be possible to appear in public without a bag over his head. He would need sunglasses, though. Where had he left them? He glanced down at his nakedness. For a man in his fifties, he didn't look terrible. Jay sucked in his modest paunch then let it out. He shaved and dressed. Crisp, pin-striped suit, red patterned tie.

Earlier, Jay informed Boris that he wanted him to familiarize himself with the family's Asia holdings—he did not say why—and since this might require that Boris travel there, Jay would be breaking in another driver. This had been duly arranged.

Before leaving the apartment, Jay went to the kitchen where he filled a glass with filtered water and swallowed an Oxycontin left over from the previous winter when he had tweaked his knee skiing in France. Sunglasses on, he pulled a Yankee cap low over his forehead. Thus disguised, he took the elevator to the lobby.

In the passenger seat of the SUV, Jay stared through the tinted window as Second Avenue blurred past his bloodshot eyes. The driver was a skinny young man from the mailroom who was the son of one of Bebe's friends, and he had the presence of mind to not ask questions. The black bodyguard Doomer had produced at the courthouse, Dequan Corbett, kept vigil from the backseat. Jay observed the pedestrians striding purposefully along the sidewalks singly and in pairs, deliverymen, business people, students, all in their worlds, and he wondered how many of them were aware of his plight. He believed that most people who had heard about the story viewed it through the prism of a famous athlete's hard luck, and that the general public would perceive him, Jay Gladstone, as a supporting player.

Jay had brought Dag to the team hoping to link their names through a championship trophy, the unassailable seal of NBA greatness and the longed-for apotheosis of both of their sporting lives. He could not give into negative thoughts now, much less despair. Despair was for people who did not have enough to do. Jay Gladstone had plenty to do. Plenty! To leap back into his life he had to believe a full recovery was possible for Dag. Yes, it was! Medical science had reached inconceivable heights. Dag was still alive, and because he had survived such a horrific accident, it was evident to Jay he was not going to die. Yes, he had suffered a traumatic brain injury, but the best brain surgeons in the world could be summoned. Just a few years earlier a madman had shot a member of Congress in the head, and she had survived the bullet! A bullet! People said it was a miracle, but that was science. If that brave member of the House of Representatives had recovered, so would Dag. He had to! The idea that Jay could one day be in the situation where he had caused the death of another human being, much less one as prominent as D'Angelo Maxwell, was too unbearable even to contemplate. He had to exile that thought from his consciousness. If his father had bequeathed a single quality to him, it was optimism. He thought of Bingo's birth date, March 4th, a direct order.

But then Nicole invaded his thoughts and, as the car sailed across 42nd Street, his stomach twisted. Although he knew their marriage was beginning to fray, it hadn't occurred to him that it could come undone quite so impressively. But had it? Had he not already decided to revisit the question of a child? He had intended to let her know about his change of attitude as he entered the pool house in Bedford less than twenty-four hours earlier. By any objective standard—if it were not for one unfortunate detail—the Gladstone marriage had not disintegrated; rather, it was experiencing some turbulence. But that detail, oh that detail. And how to deal with that detail? There were representations of the wronged husband in the arts from the time of the ancients, and they were nearly always farcical figures, older men with randy young wives who sought the company of more virile partners, in other words, exactly what had happened. Jay could not abide the role into which Nicole's behavior cast him. But he was a modern man with a high degree of psychological acuity. Could he not see past his emotional response and reach a decision based on careful cogitation? Jay might look his wife in the eye, acknowledge the betrayal, the underlying tensions that had caused it, perhaps even take ownership of his part in what had occurred, and agree to move forward. Or he could let her know he wanted to dissolve the marriage as quickly as the State of New York allowed. Either way, he would have time to formulate a plan before confronting her.

A throng of about a hundred loitered on the sidewalk in front of the hospital. Gawkers with camera phones, media members, and a Senegalese vendor selling T-shirts with Dag's smiling visage all jostled for space. Church Scott had caused an uproar fifteen minutes earlier when he got out of a cab and entered without answering questions. Several of Dag's teammates were already there.

The SUV rolled up and Dequan jumped out to open the door for Jay. The sunglasses and Yankee cap threw no one off the scent, and the mob immediately converged, microphones, cell phones, cameras pointed like guns.

WHAT HAPPENED LAST NIGHT, JAY? WHAT DO YOU KNOW ABOUT DAG'S CONDITION? HOW SERIOUS IS IT? WERE YOU AND DAG AT THE OBAMA DINNER? WHAT HAPPENED TO YOU? WILL THE

CHARGES BE DISMISSED? CAN THE TEAM MAKE THE PLAYOFFS NOW?

Dequan cleared a path into the hospital. To the volley of questions, Jay held his hands up, said, "Nice to see everyone. I hope you're all having a terrific day," to which Mayumi Miyata, who had driven down from Northern Westchester Hospital with her Lynx News crew, called out, "It'd be a better day if you answered a couple of questions." Jay said, "You get around, don't you?" before entering the revolving door and disappearing into the hospital lobby. Several reporters attempted to follow, but hospital security stopped them.

Three young black men huddled outside the room. Jay recognized one of them as Dag's brother, who he had just seen at the hospital last night. He assumed the other two were part of the player's retinue. Neither looked at Jay, unlike Dag's brother, who stared down at him from his imposing height. Jay nodded at the brother, who blankly returned the greeting.

Jay was visibly upset by what confronted him in the room. Pulleys in casts suspended the long legs above the surface of the bed. The head wrapped in bandages, face obscured by an oxygen mask. Wires ran from the torso to monitors where bright green lines and numbers quantified the misery. A bag containing an inch of urine hung to the side. Afternoon light poured into the room and conferred an almost religious aspect on the broken body. The abstract nature that the situation had assumed for Jay instantly coalesced back into a reality whose sheer awfulness throttled him. He had a vague awareness of enormous figures looming over the bed, but could not look away from what he had wrought.

"Don't worry, Jay. God only makes happy endings," a tired-looking Church Scott said from a chair in a corner. "If it's not happy, it's not the end."

The coach rose, and they exchanged comforting pats on the shoulder. Jay looked back toward the bed, and the behemoths

370 · SETH GREENLAND

revealed themselves to be spindly Odell Tracy and the Lithuanian, Giedrius Kvecevicius. Between them Drew Hill, the point guard. The players respectfully acknowledged Jay and did not mention his physical appearance.

"Thanks for coming," Jay said as if this were an event he was hosting. The words felt wrong as soon as they emerged from his mouth.

"Praise the Lord, D'Angelo survived," Church said.

"Praise the Lord," Jay echoed. He did not as a rule say *Praise the Lord* but this was Church Scott's room, and right now Jay was happy to cede power.

"Truth," Drew Hill said. Giedrius and Odell nodded their assent.

The coach placed a soothing hand on Jay's back and said, "We all know this must be incredibly hard for you."

Hard for *him*? The statement amazed Jay. As the author of this disaster, he had anticipated, at best, a neutral response to his presence. The owner had incapacitated the team's flamboyant cornerstone in ambiguous circumstances. No one would expect the coach to show sympathy for anyone but the injured party. After the quick calculation that occurred when he realized the coach was present, Jay anticipated matter-of-factness employed to disguise, at the very least, suspicion. But Church was a champion, a motivator, an athletic icon, and he had offered understanding.

"It's terrible, just terrible," Jay said. Then, because sometimes even the most composed individuals keep talking when they should not, "but a lot worse for Dag." The players murmured agreement and looked at their coach. What were they thinking? Jay could only hope they would follow their leader and extend him the benefit of the doubt.

Church had spoken with the surgeon and filled Jay in. The situation had not changed: Medically induced coma, uncertain prognosis, watch and wait. While Church was reporting what he knew, Jay's eyes roved from the coach to the injured player and back. The universe had shrunk to the three of them. Then his perception narrowed to just Church, a deeply sympathetic individual whose ministerial qualities shone in situations like this one, and Dag, a flawed man whose misery at this moment far exceeded anything he deserved. Jay's attention pivoted from one to the other, then—

"Hello, Jay," Nicole said.

Was this an aural hallucination? He wheeled around and— alarm and dismay mingled with a brief resurgence of vulnerability, a spasm of—what *the hell*? What was his wife doing here? Had she been in the bathroom? Wherever she had materialized from, her sudden and startling arrival was an unwelcome intrusion. In her absence, she was less a person than an idea. Wife distorted into Betrayer. Nicole's presence obliterated the atmosphere of benevolent healing created by Church Scott, and forced Jay once again to confront the ur-story that had led them all to gather in this hospital room, not the accident but what had preceded it, and the memory of the previous evening burst the thin membrane that held it at bay, momentarily flooding his consciousness.

But success in the business world at Jay's level does not come to the fragile, and in the startling arrival of Nicole, he was able to draw on deep reserves of mettle.

With calibrated sarcasm, he said, "Nice to see you."

"You, too."

Sleep had been a stranger to Nicole as well. Makeup, lightly applied, barely covered the dark circles under her eyes. Although she was putting up a strong front, the nervous tension was evident in the tautness of her jaw.

"How are you feeling?"

She seemed genuinely concerned. Jay noticed her voice was scratchy. Was she getting a cold? And why, why, why had she come to the hospital?

"Terrific," he said, still searching for his bearings.

Did anyone else in the room have any idea what had happened last night? Might Church have figured it out? Why did the coach think Nicole was here? One of the monarch's favored warriors was wounded, and the queen wanted to pay her respects? Or did the coach discern a motivation more disconcerting? When not in a vegetative state, Dag exuded an ineffable grace that, combined with his athletic prowess and charm, made women all over the world want to inhale his pheromones. Church might have connected that to Nicole's presence. Would he speculate that the two of them not only had sex the night of the Obama dinner, but were currently engaged in an ongoing violation of marital vows? And Jay didn't know? Or, worse, Jay *knew*. Is that what Church thought? That Jay was aware of their behavior and countenanced it? What did the players think the owner's wife was doing at Dag's bedside? They *must* be aware of what had happened and if they did not know exactly, certainly they had some idea. But *did* they know? Could they even suspect? Dag's behavior was so reckless as to be almost incomprehensible. From time immemorial, locker rooms were torn apart by one player dallying with the wife or girlfriend of another, but that kind of conduct, while reprehensible, was a hazard of the modern workplace. What had occurred here was beyond the pale. It was like visiting the White House and having sex with the First Lady. What kind of person would even think of it? Could these young men remotely apprehend the events of last night? Jay glanced at the players positioned at Dag's bedside with bowed heads. He looked at Church Scott. Who knew what any of them were imagining?

"I'm glad you're all right," Nicole said. Jay could barely tolerate being in the same room with her. What was she implying? I'm glad *you're* all right after you nearly killed this man for doing what you had no interest in doing. Is that what she meant? Or was she genuinely concerned? She placed a tentative hand on his arm but he tensed at her touch and she removed it. The sizeable diamond she wore on her ring finger in tandem with her gold wedding band glinted impressively even in the dull light of the hospital room. He wondered if she had taken her jewelry off last night before—but his thoughts were interrupted by the voice of Church Scott.

"Let's pray."

Although Jay's belief in a Supreme Being wavered, he was aware of studies about the efficacy of prayer in situations like this one and, while beseeching the Supreme Being might not have occurred to him had he been alone, he was happy to try. A further benefit of prayer was that he would be spared having to make small talk around Nicole for a while longer and so could collect the febrile thoughts ricocheting around his skull.

"Please join hands," Church said, grasping Jay's right hand in his left.

Join hands? Jay had not anticipated this. It would be impossible to avoid physical contact with Nicole without making it clear that that was what he was doing. From across the bed, Odell Tracy gave his big left hand to Giedrius Kvecevicius then reached his right across Dag toward Nicole. With her left hand, she took Odell's right and extended her right hand to Jay. There it was, hovering in the air between them. Waist high. Manicured and ringed, her fingers extending outward. Waiting for his. There was no way he could not take it. Jay moved his hand toward hers but rather than grasp it naturally as he ordinarily would have done, instead he took her fingers lightly in his, taking care not to intertwine them. It was as if he held a brittle autumn leaf, or a fragment of papyrus that might disintegrate on contact. From her response—she mirrored the airiness of his touch—Nicole seemed to understand, and was not going to pretend the circumstances between them were unchanged.

"Dear Lord," Church intoned. "Our brother Dag needs you today. He needs your love. He needs your tender mercy, and he needs it right now. His body is damaged, but the man is a fighter, Lord, he's had to fight for everything he's ever received, and with your help, Dag's going to fight through this, too, and he's going to win, Lord! With your love, he's going to heal. We know the body is a temporary home for our eternal soul, Lord, and for our soul to dwell for eternity in the Kingdom of Heaven we all have to vacate the premises. However painful it is to leave this Earth, in our hearts we *understand*. But we beseech you to hear our prayers today, Lord. Hear our prayers. Our brother D'Angelo Maxwell is not ready to leave his earthly incarnation. He's not prepared to vacate the premises. We know you want him, Lord, and you'll get him one day. But please, Lord, not today. Not today or tomorrow or the next day. He's a young man, Lord. He's a young man who tries to live right. His teammates love him, and his coaches love him. Jay and Nicole, they love him, too." Turning his attention from the Lord to the supine figure on the bed, he said. "I love you, Dag."

Taking Church Scott's cue, Drew Hill said, "We love you, Dag."

Giedrius cleared his throat. "I love you, man," he said, his Lithuanian accent conveying a Baltic awareness of inevitable misfortune.

"I love you, bruh," Odell mumbled, tears sliding down his cheeks. The giant rubbed them away with the heel of his massive hand.

The outpouring from the coach and the three players deeply touched Jay, who found himself toggling between paroxysms of guilt about Dag, sympathy for the players and coach, and the desire to murder his wife.

"We love you, Dag," Nicole whispered as if the situation had knocked the breath from her chest. *We* love you. At least,

Jay thought, she did not have the temerity to say *I* love you to
D'Angelo Maxwell in front of her husband. It was then he realized everyone in the room was looking at him. They were waiting. Why hadn't Church resumed speaking? Wasn't the coach
leading this service? Then Jay realized. He was supposed to
express his love.

Jay again bowed his head as if redoubling his efforts at
prayer and gazed at the floor. The squares of oatmeal-colored
linoleum gleamed. Somehow the person who had last mopped
it had missed a scuff mark. Was it from a shoe? Or had the
wheels on one of the machines jammed when an orderly was
sliding it into place and left a trace of rubber? A tone was coming from one of the devices Dag was hooked up to. *Beedink,
beedink, beedink.* It emerged at a steady rhythm, and from the
bee to the *dink* there was a climb of several notes on the scale.
It was almost musical. Had it been making that sound the
entire time? Or had it just begun? No one was doing anything
about it, so it had probably been making intermittent noise
since Jay had arrived. Bile dripped, acid drizzling his stomach
lining. When had he last eaten? Was it on the plane from
Africa? He took in Dag's damaged body, felt the kind eyes of
Church. Across the bed, the players formed an imposing wall.
He saw Nicole with her head down. Everyone waited. Several
more seconds passed.

"All right," Church said, delivering Jay from having to
speak. "Some prayers are silent."

Odell said, "Amen," looked at Jay, and winked in approval.
The enormous center believed he had been praying. In his way,
he *was* praying. More than anything, Jay wanted Dag to
recover. But to profess love? That was going too far.

CHAPTER THIRTY-FOUR

The lounge down the hall from Dag's room was unoccupied save for an Indian woman wearing a yellow sari dozing in a chair. A television mounted in the corner showed a news program. At a window overlooking the East River, Jay and Nicole faced each other.

"I came to the hospital because I thought you might be here," Nicole said.

"So you could confront me in public?"

"This is not public."

"A hospital room with four team employees there?"

"I haven't slept," she said.

"I spent the night in jail. Let's not play who had it worse."

"Oh, no. Poor thing."

"I don't recommend it."

"Are you okay?"

"I survived."

"How's your nose?"

"It's broken," Jay informed her.

"I'm sorry. Does it hurt?"

"They gave me painkillers."

"I'm going to tell you one thing," Nicole said, "and you have to believe me."

"After I hear what it is, I'll decide."

"It was one time."

"Was it?"

"Yes! God, of course!"

"Really?"

"One!"

"Does it matter now? D'Angelo's down the hall and—"

"Do you think he's going to—"

"Die?" Jay asked. "I don't know."

"Fuck."

"I won't be able to live with myself," he said. "I'll tell you that."

"I'm ashamed," Nicole declared. "Utterly ashamed. It's my fault."

"Fault isn't the issue now," Jay said.

"I think I might have a drinking problem."

"That's your excuse? Too much chardonnay?"

"No, no, no, of course not. No. There's no excuse," Nicole said. "It was unforgivable. I can be as abject as you want me to be. I will do whatever you want."

"I hope you'll get past it."

"I hope *you'll* get past it."

"Well, I have a mental picture nothing can erase, so I don't know that I'll be able to get past it and, honestly, it's not even the worst mental picture that got burned into my brain last night."

"I will apologize to my dying day."

"No one should have to do that."

"But I will," Nicole said.

"I'm not certain we'll be in touch at that point."

"I love being married to you."

"Funny way to show it."

"Everyone's marriage has problems," she pointed out. "We've both been married before. Mistakes get made. I don't know if you've ever cheated on me. I wouldn't ask."

"I haven't."

"I love you," Nicole assured him. "I didn't do what I did because I don't love you."

"You did it because you have a drinking problem."

"Don't twist my words."

Jay regretted his role in this exchange. He did not want to reduce the cataclysmic nature of their situation to the back and forth of a squabble. He glanced at the Indian woman. She was still sleeping.

"You know, Nicole, a hospital lounge is probably not the place to have this conversation. I have a lot to deal with today, like Dag's medical care. He needs an advocate."

"And it's going to be you? I love that."

Someone was waiting to talk to them. Jay looked over and saw a tall, athletic-looking doctor. "Mr. Gladstone, I'm Dr. Bannister. I performed the surgery on Mr. Maxwell."

Jay shook the doctor's hand and said, "This is my wife." How strange the word "wife" felt to him.

"Nicole Gladstone," she said.

"Well, I'm glad I have both of you, then," Dr. Bannister said, turning his attention back to Jay. "I heard you got a little banged up last night, too."

"I'll be fine," Jay said. "Don't worry about me."

Dr. Bannister did not press the matter. They listened as he walked them through what had occurred in the operating room, and Dag's uncertain prognosis.

"Mr. Gladstone," the doctor intoned, "I don't have to tell a man like you what's happened to medical costs over the last couple of decades," and then began a fundraising appeal for the hospital. Jay and Nicole could have a room named after them, a wing perhaps, or if they liked, because a couple of their means could certainly afford it, a pavilion.

"Imagine that, Mrs. Gladstone," the doctor said. "The Nicole and Jay Gladstone Pavilion."

"It has a nice ring to it," Nicole said.

Jay looked at her. What did she think she was doing?

The doctor said, "For a donation of a hundred million we could make it happen."

"Only a hundred million?" Jay hoped the mild irony in his tone was apparent.

"And your company could build it," the doctor reminded him.

The notion of their names linked for eternity, carved into the marble façade of a major hospital was repellent, but the doctor, having no idea, pushed on and inquired whether they would not like to stand in front of a group of dignitaries at the groundbreaking of the Nicole and Harold Jay Gladstone Pavilion.

"That's an arresting image," Jay allowed.

"Great families like yours are the backbone of New York."

"The Gladstones have always been about family," Jay said, glancing at Nicole, whose attention was focused on the doctor.

"Some generous, family-minded donors choose to honor their parents this way," the doctor helpfully pointed out. "The Bernard and Helen Gladstone Family Pavilion. How does that sound?"

Dr. Bannister had done his research.

"Your father would have loved that," Nicole said.

"I understand he was a great New Yorker, Mr. Gladstone."

"He was," Nicole said, "a titan."

"I'm sorry I was never able to meet him."

Jay wished the doctor would vanish, but he listened politely and nodded. It was torture for him to hear Nicole talk about Bingo. Perhaps he would tell her he wanted a divorce now. Did he want a divorce? He still did not know. But he needed to get Bannister out of here so requested that the doctor call his sister Bebe, who handled solicitations of this scope at the Gladstone Family Foundation.

"Bebe is terrific, the best," Nicole said, working overtime to curry favor with her husband, who ignored this remark.

Attempting to bring the conversation to a close, Jay said, "You're doing great work, and I commend you for that."

"With your help, Mr. and Mrs. Gladstone, we can scale new heights," Bannister replied, taking the hint. Jay asked for the doctor's private cell phone number so he could call him directly to check on the patient's condition and Bannister instantly provided it.

"Save D'Angelo," Jay said.

"Please," Nicole implored.

Dr. Bannister assured the couple he would do his best and departed.

Nicole said, "I don't want a divorce, Jay," as if they had not been interrupted.

"Did you just try to give away a hundred million dollars?" Fatigued and besieged already, the doctor's request, and Nicole's response to it, further overloaded his system.

"All I said was that having a hospital named after the family was an idea that your father would have liked. I'll write the doctor a note and tell him I misspoke if you want."

"Forget it."

Jay felt enervated by the conversation with the doctor and Nicole's ongoing presence was not helping. He craved solitude. To be alone on his horse, in the woods, riding along a quiet path. Nicole was quicksilver, mystification, and needs.

"I don't want to split up," she said.

"I haven't mentioned that."

"You just implied—"

"A lot of crap has happened. I'm processing it. There's a legal situation and—" He didn't want to get into it.

"What is it?"

"I feel like a lobster in a pot and, frankly, I don't want to deal with your mishegas right now."

"That's fair," she said. "I'm sorry for my behavior. I know you're tired of hearing it."

"Not as tired as I am of thinking about it."

"Can I ask you a question?"

"Apparently, you can do whatever."

Here she paused, as if trying to determine whether or not this was something she genuinely wanted to know. Jay waited. Her makeup barely concealed her pallor. She looked spent. He expected her to say never mind, or forget it.

"Did you run him over on purpose?"

"Of course not!"

"It would be understandable on some lizard brain level."

"I told you—" Jay's attention had wandered to the television over Nicole's shoulder. His face darkened. "Oh, for godsakes."

The reporter Mayumi Miyata was standing in front of the hospital. Footage of Dag nailing a three-point shot appeared on the screen followed by a still photograph of Jay in a business suit and a hard hat. The report cut to a shot of the Gladstones' Bedford home, then to the site of the accident (Jay's car no longer there), then to Northern Westchester Hospital. Even absent the sound, Jay could see they were hitting the highlights of the story. Mercifully, there was no footage of the pool house and nothing of Nicole. At least those details had not leaked. An African-American anchorwoman addressed the camera. As far as Jay could tell, she was not excoriating him. When a commercial for a life insurance company that featured two septuagenarians holding hands on a beach appeared, he turned his attention back to Nicole.

"I'm going to be in the apartment for at least the next few days," he said. "I'm not ready to go back to the house."

"I'm staying at the Pierre until we decide what we're doing. I hope you can forgive me."

There would be no commitment. When Nicole left he turned toward the window and stared at the Queens shore until he was certain his wife was gone. He texted his driver and requested they rendezvous at a side door to escape the attention of the media. A slow circuit of the hospital floor decreased the likelihood he would encounter his wife at the elevator bank. He reflected on his conversation with Dr. Bannister. Perhaps he would build the Gladstone Pavilion and name it after his parents. How had they managed to stay married for so long? As he reached the elevators one of the doors opened, and he saw the player agent Jamal Jones emerge with a striking black woman he recognized as Dag's wife. Jay froze and waited while they proceeded down the corridor. It did not escape him that Jay Gladstone, this paragon of authority and success, a man admired and feted, was concealing himself from an agent and a reality TV star, skulking like a criminal.

CHAPTER THIRTY-FIVE

Tightly packed storm clouds gathered over the borough of Queens. A high-pressure front had blown in from Canada causing the barometer to drop, and what started as an early spring day had turned blustery and cold. Winds whipped along the avenues. Scraps of newspaper caroused with discarded parking tickets and plastic bags on the sidewalks. The shiny black limousine stood out like a leopard in a herd of donkeys as it bumped along Astoria Boulevard surrounded by city buses, cabs, and delivery trucks. Nestled in the backseat, Franklin gazed out the window at the kebab shops, unisex salons, liquor stores, Greek diners, and discount furniture emporiums that comprised the neighborhood, relieved he did not have to live in a place like this. If high Manhattan rents kept those who lived here in the outer boroughs, then that was an added benefit to a landlord like Franklin, since Queens played a significant role in the Gladstone real estate portfolio.

The driver was a middle-aged Egyptian whose name Franklin could never remember. Ahmed, Ahmoud? It didn't matter. He called him "Acky." Why should someone like that expect to live in Manhattan? A person should live where he could pay his bills on time each month. Franklin couldn't understand it when he would read articles that reported Manhattan was now "unaffordable." Unaffordable to whom? It was only unaffordable if you couldn't afford it. Plenty of wealthy Americans could, along with Europeans, Chinese, and

Arabs. And many of the foreigners did not even live in the city. For most of the year, their apartments were empty. They were the best tenants, even the Arabs. To Franklin Gladstone, the ideal building was one where every unit was rented or sold, and no one lived in any of them. In Franklin's perfect world, tumbleweeds rolled down the deserted hallways of luxury buildings. The proletarians scuttling along the Astoria sidewalks—old-timers, immigrants, hipsters—they belonged here. Queens existed for the Mets and the U.S. Open tennis tournament; as far as Franklin was concerned, there was no other reason to be driving down this street. But the man he was meeting refused to come to the office.

The previous week Franklin and Christine Lupo had dined at a dimly lit restaurant in the east Sixties. Although he would not dream of cheating on Marcy, it felt, at least from his perspective, a lot like a date. He sat across from the glamorous public servant and gazed into her dusky eyes so intently he could see a reflection of flickering candlelight. The button-front blouse she wore was open at the neckline where a diamond pendant glinted. There was a whisper of cleavage, but Franklin forced himself to keep his eyes on deck. For twenty minutes, they discussed various plans to raise campaign funds, but by the time they had finished their cocktails—vodka, rocks for him, dirty martini for the DA—and were decimating the first bottle of wine, she alluded to her personal life. That afternoon she had spoken with her divorce lawyer and learned her husband planned to sue for alimony.

"The scumbag," Franklin said.

"Tell me about it," she concurred. "The guy cheats on me, and now I'm supposed to write checks to him?"

Seeing the door open a crack, Franklin wasted no time dashing through. He asked what happened and she told him how she had hired a private investigator. Not only were there incriminating photographs, but the PI was also a denizen of the cyber world and the guy Christine hired retained someone who hacked into her husband's various devices and produced the texts, emails, and receipts that enabled her to reconstruct the entire sordid mess.

Franklin had subsequently called the DA and asked for the name of the man who could tease secrets from computers and smart phones. "My marriage is fine," he hastened to add. "It's business." Franklin contacted the PI, and this man passed along the name Arun Prakash. Franklin reached out to Prakash and, upon learning the computer specialist would not come to the Gladstone offices, agreed to meet at his Queens apartment. He had considered bringing Ari and Ezra along since this would be a valuable lesson, but thought better of it. The twins did not know what plausible deniability meant. Better to keep it that way.

Ten minutes later the limousine parked in front of a tan brick apartment building in Jackson Heights. Franklin told "Acky" to wait for him in front and scrambled out of the backseat. A cold drizzle was falling. As he turned up the collar of his topcoat, a Korean woman pushing a cart filled with shopping bags eyed the limousine and stared at Franklin. He ignored her and strutted into the building. In the vestibule, he located the name "Prakash"—below "Odigwe" and above "Rabindranath"—and pressed the buzzer.

"Yeah?" said a wary voice emanating from the intercom. Franklin identified himself, and the door clicked open. The deserted lobby was in need of a facelift. The kind of place a crime might be committed. Franklin glanced around nervously while he waited for the elevator and wondered if he should have asked "Acky" to accompany him. The elevator arrived, and an older white woman who smelled of talcum powder got out, a holdover from when a different group of immigrants populated this neighborhood. Grim-faced, she pushed past Franklin, ignoring his presence. Franklin got in and pressed the scuffed button. The elevator chugged to the fourth floor. He got out, and the smell of spicy cooking immediately hit him. It was a cuisine he did not recognize and this added to his general discomfort. He knocked on the dented metal door of apartment 4H.

Arun Prakash was about thirty. Dark skin and a luxuriant head of jet-black hair. Rangy and athletic, he wore jeans and a gray hoodie over a white T-shirt. Blue and gold sneakers on his feet. He did not resemble the gnomish geek Franklin had expected.

"Mr. Gladstone?" His accent was American.

"Guilty."

Arun stepped aside and gestured toward the apartment. "Sweet coat."

"Cashmere, from Barney's."

"Yeah, I got the same one. Mine's at the dry cleaner."

Whether this was meant honestly or not, Franklin didn't react. "Where are you from?" he asked, as Arun closed the door behind him.

"New Jersey."

Franklin acted as if this was interesting. He had yet to digest that the Indian immigration had begun four decades earlier and Arun's generation was born here. While contemplating how someone who looked to him like a worker manning a call center in Bangalore could somehow have been born just across the Hudson River, Franklin took in the apartment with the practiced eye of a lifelong real estate man. The unit was a one bedroom that looked out at the apartment building directly behind it. A fixed wheel bicycle leaned against the wall in the otherwise barren entryway. The living room was sparsely furnished and anchored by a table constructed from a piece of wood the size of a door resting on construction horses, its surface littered with several laptops, two of which were running, one displaying a chart, the other a soccer game. There was a large screen television with an imitation leather lounge chair directly in front of it and several expensive gaming consoles Franklin recognized from the collections of his sons. On the walls were framed posters of obscure martial arts movies, the titles rendered in bold Hindi letters. Several houseplants were displayed, none of them reflecting an owner with horticultural aptitude. "High All the Time" by 50 Cent insinuated at low volume from one of the computers.

"What about your parents? Where are they from?"

"Tamil Nadu," Arun said. "You know where that is?"

"Should I?"

"If you don't want to be ignorant." Arun paused, as if to gauge Franklin's reaction to his effrontery. Franklin said nothing, not because he was offended but because he did not give a shit what someone like this thought of his geographical expertise. "It's in southern India." Arun took a swig from the quart bottle of Mountain Dew he was holding. "What do you want to talk about?"

"How come you wouldn't come to my office?"

"I don't like to attract attention. So."

"Yeah, yeah," Franklin said, not wanting to be hurried. "But you let a complete stranger come to your apartment."

"I checked you out, dude. While we were talking on the phone. I'm not worried unless you're here to evict me and I'm pretty sure this is one of the buildings you don't own."

Franklin was flattered by Arun's acknowledgment of his status, something to which he was unusually susceptible.

"Yeah, but I could have been someone pretending to be me."

The host regarded his visitor like he was a slow child. "Caller ID?"

"I'm just fooling around."

"You're hilarious," Arun said, drily.

Franklin glanced toward the bedroom door where a beaded curtain hung. "Anybody in there?"

"No."

"Mind if I look?"

"Shouldn't I be the one who's paranoid, Mr. Gladstone? You're the one in my crib."

"Why would you be paranoid?"

Arun let his eyes drift to the ceiling.

"Check the bedroom."

Franklin parted the beaded curtain and peeked in. An unmade bed, clothes strewn on the floor, a bureau with a half-opened drawer. He listened intently, but the only sound was the murmur of the song playing in the other room. Satisfied they were alone, he took off his coat, folded it over the back of a chair, then plopped himself on the living room couch ready to gab.

Arun spun his desk chair around and sat. "Talk to me."

Franklin put his hands behind his head and leaned back to give the impression that nerves did not consume him. What was about to occur represented the crossing of an invisible boundary and while he liked to believe he had the stones required for this kind of warfare, in quiet moments of self-reflection—because of the pain they engendered, these were exceedingly rare—it was not clear he was so endowed. His stomach gurgled, and he wondered if it was audible. Arun patiently waited, feet together, knees parted, hands on his thighs. He looked Franklin directly in the eyes.

"Okay, okay," Franklin inauspiciously began. Why did this kid make him nervous? "There's someone I'm—ahhh—" (*You schmuck*, he razzed himself, *Enough with the hesitating, get to the goddamn point*). "There's a person I'm in business with, and I need to get some information."

"A person?"

"Yes." Still wavering.

"Are you going to tell me who that person is?"

An indiscernible sound trickled out of Franklin's mouth.

"I didn't hear you."

"A relative."

"Which one?"

"Jay Gladstone," Franklin blurted.

Arun nodded, impressed. People knew that name. Jay's membership in the family reflected well on all of the relatives, but once again, his less well-known cousin suffered this as belittlement. He suppressed the urge to inquire whether Arun was familiar with the name Franklin Gladstone before their interaction.

"Okay, what about Jay Gladstone?"

"I, umm—"

Could he go through with this? Franklin was tempted just to get up, throw his coat on, and leave without another word. But he remained rooted to the couch.

"You want me to mess with him?"

Franklin did not want to "mess" with Jay. He would have preferred just going about his business. For all of his pugnacity, he did not consider himself underhanded and regarded his current circumstances with ambivalence. But Jay had cornered him. There was no choice.

"I don't know if I'd put it that way," Franklin said.

"But you want me to hack him which, to be clear, is not something that I have agreed to do."

"That's right."

"Please take out your phone and let me see you turn it off."

Franklin complied with the request.

"Now, I'm going to ask you to remove your shirt."

Franklin reacted as if he were being asked to perform calisthenics. "What?"

"Take your shirt off," Arun said. "I need to know you're not wired up."

"What are you talking about?"

"With a microphone. It's protocol. If you don't want to do it, there's the door."

Arun leaned back in the chair and crossed his arms. He was not going to do anything until his visitor granted the request. Franklin had not counted on this. He had no intention of disrobing. Arun waited.

Mustering all his available hauteur, Franklin said, "You do know who I am, right?"

"I don't give a fuck if you're the Queen of England."

No one had spoken to Franklin this way in decades. Was Arun going to make him remove his clothes? He wished he could have asked the office IT person to help, but that was not an option.

"You've gotta be kidding."

"I'm busy, so if you don't want to strip down, I get it, but then you should leave 'cause I got stuff to do for paying clients."

"You're really going to make me do this?"

"I already said you could go."

Reluctantly, Franklin heaved off the couch. He removed his suit jacket and placed it next to where he had been sitting. He loosened his tie then unbuttoned his shirt, revealing a white T-shirt beneath it.

"Okay?" This striptease was all he was going to do.

"You've seen this in the movies, right? Where one guy makes another guy prove he's not wearing a wire."

"Sure."

"Then you know this is the part where you're supposed to take the shirt all the way off and lose the T-shirt, too." Franklin looked at him, incredulous. At least his sons were not here to witness this indignity. "Sorry, man. Gotta do it."

Franklin reluctantly displayed himself to Arun, naked from the waist up. Pale and flabby, upper body carpeted with hair, breasts nearly female.

"Satisfied?"

Not wanting to meet Arun's impassive gaze, he looked

toward the window. The rain rushed down the panes like it was late to a meeting.

"You should work out more," Arun observed. Franklin chose not to respond. If this is what it took to get what he wanted, it was a fair price. "Turn around."

As Franklin pirouetted, the image of a dancing bear popped into his head, further discomfiting him. He completed the circle and said, "Okay?" not bothering to hide his annoyance.

"You're clean."

Shaking his head at the humiliation he had been made to endure, Franklin quickly put himself back together. Rather than knotting his tie again, he rolled it up and stuffed it in his jacket pocket. He lowered himself back on to the couch and hoped the preliminaries were over.

"We had to do that?"

"Look, Mr. Gladstone, according to the laws of New York State some of the services I perform are a little sketchy, so I take precautions."

"Didn't you do work for the DA up in Westchester?"

"I don't know anything about that."

Franklin had not expected this degree of caginess on the part of someone being offered a temporary spot on the Gladstone payroll, even if it was off the books. Why wasn't this Arun Prakash person just glad to have the opportunity? Franklin felt the need to reassert his primacy.

"Before we get started, why don't you tell me some of the things you've done?"

Arun exhaled. Franklin was trying his patience. "Look, I could say I've penetrated the servers of major corporations, or looked at nude pictures in the private Instagram accounts of half the actresses in Hollywood, or I could claim I hacked the Defense Department for shits and giggles, but I would never admit to any of it. Maybe I did all that; maybe I didn't.

Hacking isn't a business where a guy has a website. It's trust-based."

Franklin thought about this. It occurred to him again that he could just get up and go. The rain had gathered in intensity, and the storm increased his sense of isolation. If he did nothing, Jay would eventually discover everything. Franklin had to take advantage of whatever avenues were available. He knew this was a long shot and the path he was contemplating was not a righteous one. Jay led a life above reproach. Whatever he had done to D'Angelo Maxwell, Franklin suspected his cousin would ultimately swat it away. He told himself to leave. This plan was reckless and foolish. What was he doing in the apartment of some Tamil hacker in Queens?

Even without his topcoat on, the room felt hot. The rain had turned to hail and struck the windows like buckshot. But what was Franklin supposed to do, let the Maxwell situation play out in Jay's favor (as he feared it invariably would), and then wait for the walls to close in, squeezing him until his nemesis invoked the Gladstone family contract that all of them signed upon entry into the business? The one that formally legislated upright behavior? He would be out on the sidewalk. The prospect was a loss of face he could not bear. He would never have been in this position if he had resisted the temptation to pilfer the accounts. Yes, he needed more than a hundred million to execute the purchase of the hockey franchise, but had he tried to obtain bank financing, he likely could have cobbled it together. Why, then, had he done it? To demonstrate that Franklin Gladstone was free-range, his own man, beholden to no one. Particularly his cousins. And he intended to pay it back. If only Jay hadn't threatened him, he wouldn't be in this degrading situation.

"Okay, I get it," Franklin said. "Let's do this."

"Now, your cousin, he's a public figure."

"How does that figure in?"

"The price goes, like, way up."

"Don't worry about that."

"Do you mind if I ask what you're looking for?"

"His correspondence. Emails, texts, everything. Where he's been on the Internet, who he's communicating with. The whole cyber footprint." Franklin was pleased with his use of the phrase "cyber footprint," recently encountered in a business journal, and believed it suggested computer literacy. Having already turned him into a dancing bear, Arun was starting to make Franklin feel unintelligent.

"Typically, those kinds of businesses have pretty tight security packages in place."

"I'm going to give you the passwords," Franklin said. "Where do you look?"

"More places than you can name."

That sounded impressive. For a moment, Franklin considered asking Arun for additional details but he stopped himself. If in his sweaty desolation he chose to unleash a malevolent force, it was probably best not to think too much about what was being done on his behalf.

CHAPTER THIRTY-SIX

An African-American man behind the wheel of an expensive car must hew to the speed limit or raise the risk of being pulled over for "driving while black." It does not matter how accomplished or famous or educated the black man is, the cognitive dissonance this sight causes across a swath of American law enforcement has created a phenomenon with which virtually all black males are familiar. For this reason, Lourawls maintained a steady sixty miles per hour on the Palisades Parkway behind the wheel of the Escalade. It was early evening. He and Babatunde had been at the hospital all day and were drained. They were going home to shower and get some rest before returning for the night shift. The ride uptown and over the bridge was devoid of their typical to and fro. They usually listened to hip-hop in the car, but this evening felt distinctly unmusical.

Running through both of their minds was the future and what it might look like without Dag in the picture. The pair shared an optimistic outlook, so neither wanted to mention it, but they were not comforted by the doctor's palaver. Coma was a dangerous word. When they were all still living in Houston, a high school friend took a bullet in the head. He was in a coma for two weeks and then expired. If Dag somehow miraculously defied the odds and recovered, what were the chances he would play again? A guy with the chronic physical problems likely to result from this kind of trauma required a staff of nurses, not sidekicks. Where did that leave them? They were both around Dag's age. Too old for life on the perimeter of someone else's life.

Lourawls said, "They got hunting season for deer."

Babatunde's head swung from right to left. "You see a deer?"

"Naw, man."

"Then what are you talking about?"

"Don't need a hunting season for black men."

Babatunde slumped in the seat. "I'm too tired to talk about this shit now."

"Always open season on the black man."

"Come on, Lou. Just drive, okay?"

"They're not gonna put that cop up in Westchester on trial," Lourawls said.

"If you say so."

"I'm not predicting, man. Already happened. You gotta keep up with the news."

"I follow sports," Babatunde reminded him.

"The cracker motherfucker capped that kid down in Florida, Trayvon? Same thing. He's gonna walk."

"That happen already?"

"No, that's a prediction," Lourawls said. "But I'll bet you."

"I ain't betting you."

"You know I'm right."

"I told you," Babatunde said. "I'm too tired to talk about this shit now."

"Same DA in Westchester who didn't indict that cop? She's in charge of Dag's situation."

Babatunde said, "You feeling McDonald's?"

"I ain't hungry. And I'll tell you something else."

"I know you will."

"Jay Gladstone," Lourawls said.

"What about him?"

"If he committed a crime, if there was some lawbreaking he did?"

"It was a car accident," Babatunde said.

"That's all they're saying so far," Lourawls said, "but you don't know. If there was a crime."

"Say there was."

"You think that white DA lady is gonna indict Gladstone? He'll never spend a day incarcerated."

"They locked the man up already," Babatunde remarked.

"All right, one night. But that's it. No more jail for him."

"Gladstone seems like an okay dude."

"He cut Trey from the damn team," Lourawls reminded him.

"Church Scott cut Trey. He's the coach."

"He runs everything past Gladstone."

"How do you know that?"

"He works for him, Babs."

"I got no problem with Gladstone."

"The man is white," Lourawls said.

"So?"

"So, you think he's gonna be himself around you? Liberal white people be all friendly around black people. But when they're by themselves."

"What?"

"Watch out," Lourawls said.

"You sure you not hungry?" Babatunde asked.

"How'm I supposed to eat, man?" Lourawls shook his head from side to side as if he could not understand how Babatunde could be so obtuse. "You always reading that civil war stuff, slavery stuff, the underground railroad and shit."

"So?"

"That's how white people still look at us."

Babatunde declared: "The president is a black man."

"Don't let that deceive you."

Lourawls took the exit for Alpine. They were on a commercial strip and then on a road lined with tall trees and big homes.

"How many black people do you think live in these houses?" Lourawls asked.

"Chris Rock lives around here."

"Besides Chris Rock."

"I don't know," Babatunde said "A few."

"The black population is pretty much you, me, Trey, and Dag, and if Dag ain't here—"

"Why wouldn't Dag be here?"

"I don't know, man. Weird shit happens. If Dag ain't here, you think these people want us around?"

"I haven't thought about it."

"Dag is famous, and he's rich. His color is money."

"The man is black, Lourawls!"

"And green."

"What's your point?"

A flashing light appeared in the rearview mirror. Babatunde and Lourawls exchanged a resigned glance. It had been nearly two months since they had been pulled over for no reason. The cop must be new. Lourawls guided the car to the shoulder, put it in neutral, rolled down the window. Both men made sure their hands were visible. Then they waited for the routine to begin.

A young police officer appeared at the window on the driver's side. He couldn't have been twenty-five years old. Lourawls handed him his license and registration.

"You can put those away, sir," the cop said. "How's Dag?" Lourawls and Babatunde looked at each other, confused. "This is his car, isn't it?"

"He's in a coma, man," Babatunde said.

The cop chewed his cheek, unhappy to get confirmation of what he had seen on the Internet. "Everyone at the station is praying for him."

They mumbled thanks, and the cop told them to have a peaceful night. Lourawls put the car in gear, stepped on the gas, and drove slowly away. For a few seconds, neither of them spoke. Then, as if nothing had happened, Lourawls said:

"You best be thinking about your future."

"I got Trey's back," Babatunde said.

"I got Trey's back, too. But Trey goes hard in the paint. He can look after himself."

"You burying Dag?"

"No, I ain't burying Dag," Lourawls said. "I'm praying he's all right, like those motherfuckin' cops. Full recovery."

"Boy gonna bounce back."

Lourawls guided the Escalade through the gates. The automatic lights were on, illuminating the trees and casting nervous shadows on the lawn. They got out of the car and trudged to the front door, each wondering how long they would continue to live in this house on this street.

CHAPTER THIRTY-SEVEN

After the hospital visit Jay considered going to the office, but the sight of Dag's prostrate, unconscious, intubated body wired to all of those beeping devices combined with the unexpected Nicole encounter to create an effect so disconcerting that he beat a tactical retreat to the apartment. His primary goal for the day: To ensure Dag would receive the best care available. From having served on hospital boards, Jay's list of contacts was formidable. He determined that two of the finest brain trauma specialists were in Geneva and Toronto. After ample donations were promised to their institutions, both agreed to fly in for consultations the following day. Private jets were dispatched to collect them.

It was late afternoon when Jay called his club and asked them to send over an order of Dover sole. While he waited for the food to arrive, he poured himself a glass of scotch and returned phone calls. Given that the last exchange with Franklin, at Passover, had been inauspicious, he hesitated before calling him back but decided it would better serve his purpose to not act like anything between them was amiss. Franklin expressed sympathy, asked if there was anything he could do to help, and did not mention the potential audit Jay had alluded to when they last spoke. He next called Bebe, who wanted to visit him at the apartment and bring soup. Jay declined the offer and said he would see her in the office the next day. Mayor House was thrilled to hear from him, asked how he was doing and whether the media reports about Dag's condition were accurate. After Jay briefed the politician, he suggested the deal on the new arena be expedited and requested that the city's lawyers review the contract so they could get it signed. The team had a home game against the Miami Heat Saturday night, and Jay invited the mayor to join him there.

Although everyone he spoke to expressed sympathy at his predicament, talking on the phone further exhausted him. He knew if he went to bed now he would pass out for several hours, wake up, and not be able to get back to sleep. The food still hadn't arrived. He needed to eat. He considered turning on the television but did not want to watch the news and knew he wouldn't be able to concentrate on anything else. He lay down on the sofa in the living room and thought about whether he should work what had happened to him into the Tate commencement address. "Taking responsibility," "overcoming adversity," "doing for others"—these were universal themes.

Ten minutes later his phone rang. It was Aviva.

"Mom asked me to check in and see how you're doing."

The two had not spoken since she and Imani fled the Seder table. Despite the distance in her voice, he was relieved to get the call. Aviva planned to be in the city tomorrow and asked if they could meet for lunch. When Jay suggested the Paladin Club, she countered with a Vietnamese restaurant on Ninth Avenue where "no one knows the Gladstones."

They agreed to meet there.

Jay ate dinner, took a sleeping pill, and thought about what lay ahead. His relationship with the team he owned would be affected, but other than that he clung to the wild hope that his business life would proceed without too many obstacles. In the moments when he was not consumed with Dag's condition, thoughts about his own fate crept in (the man, after all, was not a saint). The political appointment he had been gunning for was in jeopardy. Could the ambassadorship to Germany or Austria (and, frankly, at this point, he'd be willing to accept a posting anywhere without a war going on) be awarded to someone involved in this kind of nastiness? There must be some precedent. But what did it matter? None of this held the same meaning that it did a week earlier. Jay would gladly have traded any future opportunity for Dag's full return to health.

Why had he gotten in the car that night? How could he have done something so deranged?

He comforted himself: People made mistakes, terrible things occurred.

He reassured himself: Dag would recover, rehabilitate his injuries and, with the help of another marquee free agent signing, lead the team to a title.

He encouraged himself: In two years, he would return from a diplomatic posting—perhaps a remote Pacific Island nation—to attend the championship round.

Yet he could not fall asleep. Because he worried he might be kidding himself.

Like many of his brethren, Jay took pride in visible Jewish achievement. One of the first ballplayers his father told him about was Hank Greenberg, the Detroit Tigers slugger from the 1940s. He reveled in the Bob Dylans and Norman Mailers of the world, the Golda Meirs and Felix Frankfurters. But the binary of these superstars were the villains: the gangsters, the notorious insider traders, the Bernard Madoffs. Bernie Madoff! The *gonif* to end all *gonifs*! That gift to anti-Semites! (Jay personally knew people he had capsized.) He thought of his cousin Marat Reznikov, whom he had watched commit murder in the Bronx.

At summer camp, Jay and his bunkmates would lie awake at night and make lists of The Greatest Jews of All Time, and that is what he did now. He began with the Bible, and after he ticked off Abraham, Moses, Kings David and Solomon, Sarah,

Rachel, and Leah, he remembered Jesus was a Jew, and his disciples. From there his mind leaped to Maimonides and Gustav Mahler, the poet Heinrich Heine (anyone who converted because of societal pressure still counted as a member of the tribe for Jay's purposes), then alighted on Benjamin Disraeli, before winging off to Sigmund Freud, the Gershwins, and Anne Frank. Back and forth he ranged over Jewish history, through artists and athletes, public servants and philanthropists, totting up numbers until his laurel circle swelled to a hundred. This was the group of super achievers he aspired to join. Tormented by the thought that he was sinking into the underworld and somehow his image would come to be linked with the tiny handful of high-profile Jews who had horrified the world, Jay strove to keep hopelessness at bay.

He considered whether it was a Jewish instinct to think in these terms. Did Baptists keep a tally of their fellow adherents, the ones that best represented the faith or the miscreants that brought shame upon it? Did Hindus or Buddhists? Was the position of the Jews in the universe so precarious that they had to prove their worth to themselves with recitations like this one? Was life a perpetual trial and this tendency the presenting of evidence to the world that was once ready to believe Jews used the blood of Christian children to make matzo? And what was making his mind work this way? Matzo and the blood of Christian children? That was demented! This was America in 2012. Jay was assimilated, married (at least for now) to a non-Jew, had never even traveled to Israel. He had other, more personal things to worry about than the public image of his co-religionists. While Jay was thinking about this, Baruch Spinoza peeked out from behind a curtain in his unconscious. Had he remembered to put him on his list? Spinoza made him think of Nicole because before Jay's entire life began to fall apart, she had been plowing through a biography of the Dutch philosopher. His thoughts quickly slipped from his wife's reading habits to her physical presence, the smoothness of her skin as he ran his hand along the curve of her hip, the faint lemon scent of her shampoo, the memory of her pungent taste on his fingers, and to his surprise an entirely unwelcome erotic longing consumed him. What does it mean to want to have sex with someone who just reached down your throat and ripped your insides out? Jay did not want to think about it. Since they were married, he had imagined it was she who would watch him die. He had envisioned decades of companionship.

Was the physicist Niels Bohr Jewish? Jay added him to the record.

And so, he rattled through the night.

He woke up, not even sure he had slept. Showered, ate a bowl of bran, donned his office armor of suit and tie, and walked to work. The surgeons were due to fly in from Switzerland and Canada today, and this prospect raised his spirits. It was a chilly, bright morning and the air further invigorated him. The dead-eyed faces of pedestrians came to life when they recognized Jay Gladstone. Several asked how he was doing. The driver of a delivery truck called out, "Hang in there, brother!" and Jay waved to him in gratitude. At the office, after having accepted the felicitations of the support staff, and explained that, no, he was not hurt badly and they all should say a prayer for Dag, he called the hospital to check on the patient's condition.

It remained unchanged.

Because this was the day he had planned to return from Africa, there was nothing on his schedule. He presented himself to Bebe, and his intact condition allayed her immediate concern. She closed the door to the office and turned to her brother.

"What happened in Bedford?"

He could reveal everything to his sister now, unburden

himself and risk the loss of her esteem. Or he could be discreet and hope the details would remain cloudy. He realized he still did not know the story he was going to tell to the world, his version of events. Herman Doomer had not even asked what had transpired.

"I'm not sure," he began.

"What do you mean you're not sure?"

"Dag was on the road. I was going to give him a ride—"

"What was he doing on the road?"

"His car—" Jay remembered that he had not seen Dag's car and immediately reversed himself before he was deep into a lie. And why was he going to lie? This was his sister, the person to whom he was closest in the world. "Bebe, you know what? I'm not exactly sure what happened. I was jet-lagged, I'd had a few drinks, I was taking painkillers."

"Were you driving drunk?"

"No. At least I don't think so. I don't know. Look, this is all extremely upsetting, and the worst of it is what I did to Dag. We'll have lots of time to talk about this going forward, but right now, I don't appreciate the third degree. I could just use your support."

"You have it, Jay. But I want you to be straight with me."

"I will."

"Where was Nicole?"

"At the house."

"She was there when this happened?"

"Bebe, what did I just say? Nicole was at the house, Dag is in the hospital. There's nothing else to tell you at this point."

"At this point?"

"What are you doing?"

"I'm trying to help you but I can't if you won't tell me what's going on."

Jay stiffened his back. He was going to need to draw on resources he was not sure he had. Hers was friendly questioning.

Unlike his sister, the world would not come toward him from a position of love.

"Please. Don't ask me any more questions right now."

"I understand," she said. "Just remember, I'm someone who wants to help you."

To change the subject, Bebe informed him that their family foundation was doing a Gladstone Scholar Awards presentation in Newark that afternoon and suggested he make an appearance. Jay demurred and told her he needed to take it easy for a few days.

"Seeing that Dag receives the best care in the world has to be my priority."

"You're a mensch," she said. No matter how his world shook, Bebe's sense of familial devotion was immutable and eternal.

Next, he stuck his head in his cousin's office. Franklin was on the phone and covered the mouthpiece when he warmly greeted Jay.

In the voice of John Wayne, he said, "You don't look too bad, pilgrim." Franklin wanted to be filled in, and Jay obliged, providing a brief and sanitized version. Now was not the optimum time to press the Asian matter.

He spent the rest of the morning drafting a letter to the chairman of the New York City Planning Commission regarding their consideration of the Sapphire project.

Jay always liked to arrive at a restaurant early since he believed it lent him a proprietary air and at five minutes to one he was seated against the wall at a back table reading the *New York Times* on his phone. The Vietnamese eatery was simple, bare tables and framed travel posters. A young couple sat near the front, the only other patrons. In addition to the news of the accident and his arraignment on criminal charges, a columnist in the sports section ruminated at length on the fate of the team without Dag. With a little luck and the passage of time, Jay believed, the public would move on to the next garish spectacle.

He was reading an article about Christine Lupo, who was about to announce whether she was running for governor, when he heard a familiar voice saying, "Thank God you're all right!" and looked up to see his ex-wife, Jude Feldman Gladstone, standing next to their daughter Aviva.

"Jude, hello!" he exclaimed, quickly rising from his chair. "What are you doing here?"

"I invited her," Aviva said. His daughter made no move to hug him or in any way show affection. Jay stepped around the table and folded her into a clumsy embrace.

Now in her early fifties, Jude's dark hair was a mane of styled ringlets. Fashionable pumps, black leggings, and a loose maroon sweater. A quartz crystal pendant, three inches long, hung from her neck, a purple stone the size of a walnut on her forefinger. Since when did Jude wear such bold jewelry? She looked better than she had in years. Whatever she was doing with the lavish divorce settlement, it agreed with her. Rather than initiate physical contact, she inspected him and said, "I am so relieved." He thanked her and indicated that they should sit.

"So," he said to his ex-wife, unable to think of anything else. "You look beautiful."

"I'm glad you're alive," she said.

"How was jail?" his daughter asked, taking a seat next to her mother.

Jay wondered if that was a taunt. "You can imagine," he said.

Aviva wore her early spring uniform of Chucks, jeans, and a pea coat. Jude asked how Dag was doing and Jay gave the report.

"Must be pretty awkward for you," Aviva said.

She leaned back in her chair, creating maximum distance between them. Jay tried not to be bothered by this. As an enlightened parent, he was responsible for maintaining a safe environment in which his daughter was able to express whatever it was she needed to communicate.

"That would be putting it mildly," he said. To make this seem like an average family lunch, Jay opened the menu and observed, "I don't think I've ever eaten in a Vietnamese restaurant before."

"They aren't fancy enough," Aviva said.

"No, but I don't associate Vietnam with their cuisine," Jay said.

"Just the imperialist war," Aviva said.

"Which your father marched against," Jude informed her.

"I was fourteen," Jay said.

"Yay for you," Aviva said to Jay, who was making every effort to not respond to his daughter's provocations. "Champion of the oppressed."

"I didn't want to get drafted," he said, examining the menu.

The waitress approached. When they had all ordered, Jude placed her elbows on the table, fingers intertwined. The purple ring was genuinely impressive.

She said, "You're probably wondering why I'm here."

"That's fair," Jay said. "I am."

"I didn't feel safe when we were together the last time," Aviva said.

Her remark puzzled Jay. "What does that mean?"

"I would have brought Imani today, but I know how much you hate her."

"I don't hate Imani. I'm not a hater. I'm not sure she's the best person for you, but that's another conversation."

"You don't know her," Aviva said.

"We're getting off track here," Jude said to her daughter. Then, to Jay: "She has something to talk to you about."

"I don't want you to yell at me," Aviva told her father.

408 - SETH GREENLAND

Jay leaned forward and tried to disarm her with a gentle smile. "I'm such a yeller?"

"You were yelling like a banshee at the Seder."

Jay tried to laugh it off. "First of all, I would hardly say that's an accurate description."

"Aviva told me what happened," Jude said.

"Did she tell you I was provoked?" he asked, no longer smiling. "Did she tell you how obnoxious her friend was?"

Aviva turned to her mother. "See? He's attacking."

Jude held up her hands in a gesture of peace. "I'm not sure that qualifies as an attack. My therapist offered to do a session with the three of us. Maybe that's the best way to handle this."

"I'm not going to talk to your therapist," Jay said.

"I just wanted to put it out there," Jude said.

Jay tried to plead his case. "Her friend Imani was needlessly provocative. She offended everyone there, Franklin, Marcy, the twins—everyone."

"She didn't offend me," Aviva said.

"Well, I don't know what it would take to offend you," Jay said. "Maybe you'd be offended if someone said something bad about Muslims."

"Imani supports a free Palestine. What's the big whoop? So do I."

"It was a Seder," Jay said. "Not a conference."

To Aviva, this was deeply unfair. "Franklin and Marcy can make all their right-wing speeches about the Middle East and Imani isn't allowed to have an opinion?"

Jay asked his ex-wife if she had met their daughter's girlfriend.

"I have, and I think she's kind of cool."

"Everyone's entitled to their opinion," Jay said. "Imani is obviously an intelligent young woman."

"You're always telling us Passover is about freedom," Aviva said. "Every year you give that speech, don't you?"

Jay sat back in his chair, pressed his fingers to his temples, and let his eyelids drop. Yes, he did give that speech because he was trying to inject life into an ancient ceremony. Now his efforts were being thrown in his face. Was the restaurant unusually warm? He could feel his body temperature rising. There was a bitter taste in his mouth, discomfort in his gut. He had taken a painkiller when he woke up, but its effects were starting to dissipate. When he opened his eyes, they were staring at him. Jude asked if he was all right.

"Never better," he said. "Look, I'm not here to relitigate Passover. I'm sorry I lost my cool, and I apologize to you for that."

"You should apologize to Imani, too," Aviva said.

"I'll write her a note."

The waitress brought the food out. Jay looked at the bowl of pho, but his appetite was gone. He requested a ginger ale. Perhaps the carbonation would help pacify his churning stomach. He watched Aviva deftly maneuver her chopsticks around the noodles and lift them to her mouth.

"As I was telling you," Jude said, "Our daughter has something she would like to discuss."

Aviva held up a finger to indicate she would tell him when she was finished chewing. Jay remembered teaching her to use chopsticks as a ten-year-old at a Chinese restaurant on the Upper West Side after a matinee of *The Music Man*.

"You can't speak at my commencement," she said.

"You mean you don't want me to."

"That's right."

"This is your daughter," Jude said.

"I know that. Ordinarily, I would just say 'fine.' I'd call the president of the college and bow out. But I'm in an unusual position."

"So am I. I'm graduating."

"I'm proud of you," Jay said.

"I only do it once."

"I am well aware of that, believe me. But my image is taking a beating right now."

"You're worried about your image?" Jude asked.

"I am, and I make no apologies."

"Of course not," Aviva said. "Why would Harold Jay Gladstone ever apologize for anything?"

Jay chose to ignore the dig. He didn't want to steamroll his daughter. In a measured tone, he said, "I'm a public figure, and my ability to do business is affected by how I'm perceived. I got hauled into court yesterday morning after spending the night in jail. You can't possibly have any idea what that was like, either of you." He paused to see if his daughter would come at him again, but she held fire. "I'm being accused of a crime that was entirely unintentional. The media is flaying me. To have the chance to make a speech, which the press will cover—"

"You can't talk about your situation at Aviva's graduation."

"Would you let me finish, please?"

"Fine. Finish." Jude said.

Distant, long-forgotten arguments with Jude burbled up. He would not allow himself to reenact the dynamic that contributed to their schism. The steaming pho reminded him of an outdoor hot tub at a ski resort in the Rockies twenty years earlier where they had frolicked after a day on the slopes, twinned futures assured. The distant scene was nearly unimaginable to him. Then Nicole and Dag detonated in his consciousness, a perversely timed depth charge. As far as he knew, Jude had never betrayed him. He felt a new generosity toward her.

"Of course, I'm not going to discuss my situation. But if I give a talk that resonates with the values of the graduates it might get into the ether, then maybe the potential jury pool has a better opinion of me. If there's no plea bargain, and I have to go to trial, that's going to make me appear more sympathetic." He looked toward Jude to see how this was going over. The expression on her face gave nothing away. Since his remarriage, he had often thought that his daughter and ex-wife presented a united front against him that, regardless of what he did—emotionally, financially, it did not matter—was indivisible. "Don't worry, Aviva. You'll be proud of me."

This claim was too much for her. "Are you joking?"

Jay looked into his daughter's livid eyes and thought of Sonia Trachtenberg, the woman who spat in his face after the Planning Commission hearing. Aviva reminded him of that little ball of self-righteous anger. Jay would never understand how she turned out like this after having been showered with so much love. He assured her he wasn't joking.

"Do you not get that you're going to embarrass me if you do that?"

"I understand that you don't want me to do it," Jay said. "But I'm trying to have a rational discussion."

"Please put yourself in my position, okay? How do you think I'm going to feel if my father, the master builder, gets up in front of my classmates and uses their graduation to rehabilitate his image?"

"I know I'm asking a lot."

"I get that you're in an uncomfortable position."

"It's more than uncomfortable," he said.

"You're not faultless or anything," Aviva continued, "but you're more or less an ethical person."

"Thank you," he said. "I appreciate that."

"So why can't you understand what I'm telling you? I only graduate one time." Aviva pushed herself away from the table and crossed her arms. Jay tried to make eye contact, but she would not look at him. Why wouldn't Jude help mollify her?

"I do understand, Aviva," Jay said. "I do."

"You need to listen to your daughter," Jude said.

Quietly, he said, "Perhaps I haven't made myself clear."

"You can't put your own needs first," Jude said.

"Would you for godsakes let me finish?" That came out less quietly. Aviva stared at her lap. "I know it's an outlandish request. I get that, yes. But I don't know what else to do."

"Why don't you hold a press conference?" Jude asked.

"I don't want to take questions."

"Then just make a statement," his ex-wife said.

"They want to bury me," he said. "My lawyer's trying to get the charges dismissed but I need to move forward assuming that's not going to happen. There's a genuine possibility I could go to prison. Do you want that?"

Now Aviva looked directly at him. "Of course not," she said.

"No one wants that, Jay."

"They could pack me off to one of those upstate hellholes near the Canadian border where I'd be serving time with rapists and murderers. I'm not the kind of person who would thrive in that environment."

"It sucks to be in your situation," Aviva said. "I feel so sorry for you. If I had accidentally run someone over with my car, I can't even—"

"I'm glad you understand," Jay said.

"But for you to get up in front of my graduating class to serve your own needs—"

"Your needs can't be the priority here, Jay," Jude said to her ex-husband.

Jay nodded in an attempt to convey the depth with which their concerns resonated. He was affected by the ache his daughter expressed and was loath to be the cause. But it was essential to him that the complexity of his predicament be acknowledged.

"I believe myself to be a good person," he said.

"I basically said that," Aviva reminded him.

"And you are, too," he assured her.

"Something the two of you agree on," Jude said, attempting to lighten the mood.

"I have flaws," Jay continued, "Lots of them. But if I can speak at Tate, and convey who I am, perhaps then I'll be understood if not forgiven. I'd like to give it a shot. Please."

"If you do that," Aviva said, "they can send me my degree."

His daughter's obstinacy was unacceptable. She showed bottomless sympathy for the downtrodden, but there appeared little of it left for her father. It was incomprehensible to him that, given what he was facing, she could not connect with the agony in front of her.

"For someone who has benefitted as clearly as you have from our family's position, your lack of loyalty baffles me," Jay said. Aviva turned away. Was she reacting to his perceived obtuseness, or disagreeing with the ungenerous assessment of her fealty? Jay could not tell and, moreover, did not care. He fought to keep the tremor out of his voice. "My father, who came from the streets, who broke his ass working for us, knew a little bit about how tough life on this planet could be. He taught me that family was the most important thing on Earth, the only thing you could depend on when the world was chewing you up. Your family, Aviva. Those words were sacred to him, and they are to me." Jay awaited a response, but none was forthcoming. "I'm sorry. I don't know what else to tell you."

"I'm sorry, too," Aviva said. "Everybody's sorry."

Jay looked at Jude, who was rubbing her daughter's back. He had the urge to perform the same act of comfort but sensed it would not be welcome.

"I remember when you put half of the city's homeless population in winter coats for your bat mitzvah project," Jay said. "I admire you for that. But it kills me that you're more interested in helping a bunch of homeless people you don't know than your father."

"You still think you're going to speak at my graduation," Aviva said.

The sympathy he felt for his daughter mingled with the incipient terror his invocation of prison time had awakened. Jay's world was spinning. Aviva had ceased to be his daughter and was now a force he needed to subdue to reassert the ability to control his fate.

"Your Aunt Bebe is visiting Newark today to give awards to the Gladstone Scholars. You should go with her. You'll see kids who haven't had any of the advantages that you've had. We help them."

"With money," Aviva said.

"Yes, with money. We give these kids scholarships. What's wrong with that?"

Aviva stared at her cuticles.

Jay resumed, "I'm trying not to be unreasonable. Right now, I'm scared. I don't like admitting it. You know the situation. But I'll tell you what. Even though the president of the college personally asked me to speak at the commencement, I'm willing to turn down the honor. If you think about it, if you're willing to put yourself in my position and imagine how badly things could go from a legal perspective, and you still don't want me to do it, then I won't."

"I don't believe you."

"Why?"

"You said my friends were welcome at the Seder. Well, look what happened."

"Aviva, I told you I would reconsider, and I mean it."

"Whatever."

Fear overwhelmed him. He gripped the edge of the table and rose from his chair. He reflexively threw down some bills and walked out. Jude called after him, but he did not turn around. On the sidewalk, Jay tried to remember if he had paid for the lunch. He did not want to stick his daughter and ex-wife with the check, but he certainly wasn't going back into the restaurant. To reach for his wallet was reflexive behavior for a Gladstone father. Hailing a cab Jay thought of Bingo, all of the restaurant tabs he had picked up, the grabbing of the check as if his father wanted to host the world, and the sense of isolation that came over him was lunar.

The media herd was gone, and Jay entered the hospital unnoticed. There he met with the doctors he had flown in from Switzerland and Canada. Both had extensive experience treating the kind of brain trauma Dag had suffered. They examined the patient, reviewed the charts and X-rays. They consulted with Dr. Bannister and informed Jay that they concurred with the treatment. They would remain available in both diagnostic and advisory capacities and would fly in again if necessary.

Aviva was in a window seat on the evening train to Schuylkill. After the altercation with her father, Jude, to Aviva's displeasure, assumed a neutral position.

"Your father has every right to be upset," she said. "He's in a terrible situation."

Aviva recognized that she loved her father in some undefinable way that probably had to do with biology. And when the heat of their encounter abated, and a vision of him in prison took shape—the disgrace, confinement, and loneliness, all over a period of years—it was impossible not to feel a degree of sympathetic dread. And yet. She experienced their disagreements as wounds and, on a deeper level, as a denial of her essence, something rooted in Aviva's psyche, a permanent side effect of being Jay Gladstone'a daughter.

But just because Aviva was born into prosperity and comfort did not mean she had to be a prisoner of her class. She had recently devoured a film about Che Guevara in her Revolutionary Motifs in World Cinema course. He was the son of a well-to-do family who took up arms, led a revolution, and wound up on a million dorm room walls. She wondered what Che would have done if Jay had been his father. Che would not have let his parent speak at a ceremony where he wasn't wanted, of that she was certain. Aviva thought about Jay's offer to withdraw but still refused to believe he would do it. She was not going to beg him. If he failed to arrive at the correct decision on his own, she would blow off the ceremony. What was a graduation anyway? Nothing more than a costume party that only served to codify the separation of an educated elite from the rest of society. If her father wanted to spoil it, that was his business.

She reached into her backpack and removed the copy of *The Wretched of the Earth* that Axel had given her, opened it to where she had left off, and began to read. Ten minutes later she put it down. In her view, Fanon's thesis could be boiled down to the world was unfair. Aviva already knew that.

CHAPTER THIRTY-EIGHT

The blowback from Christine Lupo's decision to not convene a grand jury when the white Officer Russell Plesko killed the African-American John Eagle was substantial. Eloquent displeasure expressed by religious lead ers, vitriolic emails to her office, censorious editorials. Al Sharpton had, in tandem with Imam Ibrahim Muhammad, led a demonstration attended by several hundred people where he called for the DA's resignation. Her colleague, Vere Olmstead, with whom she had recently shared a furtive cigarette, gave her the stink eye every time they crossed paths. Most unfortunately, the governor of New York publically questioned her decision. He was a Democrat, but that did not soften the blow. The subtext of all of this was that Christine Lupo was at best racially insensitive, at worst, straight-up racist. Now she could reverse the perception that had begun to crystallize and demonstrate that the law treats all citizens equally. She would be doing a great deal of this demonstrating on television. Jay Gladstone was going to be a national story. No, strike national; this story was going to erupt worldwide.

The secretary signaled Russell Plesko. He rose from his seat in the waiting area of the DA's office and followed her down the hallway. He was back in uniform. It was his lunch hour and he had hustled over for an appointment he had requested. As soon as Christine Lupo revealed her decision, the White Plains Police Department had informed him he was no longer on administrative leave and placed him on desk duty. He had other ideas. The secretary stopped in front of an office and gestured for Russell to enter.

Lou Pagano stood up from behind his desk and stuck out his hand. Russell pumped it.

"Congratulations," Pagano said. Russell was nervous and waited to see if Pagano would say anything else. He didn't. But the deputy DA indicated he should sit down.

When they were both seated, Russell said, "I wanted to say thanks in person for shutting down the grand jury."

"Hey," Pagano said, with a sharpness that caught Russell by surprise. "No one shut anything down. The facts were the facts. I talked to everyone who was there. I made my recommendation and the DA made her decision."

"Right, right," Russell said. "I didn't mean to imply anything."

"Okay. So. Officer Plesko." Russell waited. He had the distinct impression Pagano was sizing him up. "Are you talking to a counselor?"

"I met with a psychologist. The department mandates it."

"I know it's mandated. I'm not implying you're screwy. You had a traumatic experience is all I'm saying."

"I'm handling it okay."

"How's it going out in the world? Any problems?"

"It's not too bad. Someone smashed my windshield."

"Were you in the car at the time?"

"No."

"Then it could've been worse. You're back at work."

"I am."

"How's it going?"

"That's what I want to talk to you about."

After lunch, Pagano walked into the office kitchen for his usual black coffee, two sugars. Christine Lupo was rinsing her cup in the sink. Pagano told her he wanted to discuss Russell Plesko. She did not appear happy to hear this.

"Aren't we done with that guy?"

"He wanted to see me. They've got him stuck at headquarters pushing paper around."

"That's standard after what he was involved in."

"Yeah, well, the guy wants to be reassigned," Pagano informed her.

Lupo dried her cup with a towel and placed it in the cabinet. She had no idea where Pagano was going with this and little interest. She had hoped not to hear the name Russell Plesko for a while.

"Shouldn't he talk to his supervisor?"

"He'd like to be detailed to our office," Pagano said. "He's interested in becoming a lawyer. For what it's worth, my opinion—he's all right."

She thought about what her political consultant had said at the Parkway Diner: Voters have more respect for balls than integrity. The DA had to admire Plesko's balls. The most controversial police officer on the force and he had the nerve for an ask like this? It was impressive. Hiring Russell Plesko—an unlucky cop who deserved a break—could only solidify her support with the police. But to bring him into her world would be to embrace him and that might further enrage the black community. Wait a minute, though. She was about to throw the black community Jay Gladstone, and that was going to improve her standing significantly. With Gladstone in a courtroom, no one would care who worked in her office.

"You want to help him out," the DA said, "go ahead."

CHAPTER THIRTY-NINE

For two days, Trey had been at the hospital without a break. Lourawls and Babatunde returned to the mansion in New Jersey at night, but Trey slept in a chair in Dag's room. He had not changed his clothes and was self-conscious about it when he met the pair of eminent doctors Gladstone had produced. He was exhausted and his back ached. He was scared his brother was going to die and didn't know what he would do if that happened. Dag was his anchor. He had never had a real job. Being Dag's brother was Trey's job, and it was more than a job, it was a purpose, the warp and woof of his life, the boundary that defined his existence. As much as Trey thought about the future—not a great deal, admittedly—it involved his sibling. Dag World was multi-tiered, and as long as Dag was alive, there would always be a place for Trey. If Dag were not alive, that was going to be a problem. As the coma persisted (Didn't matter if it was "medically induced." It was still a damn coma.) fear crept into Trey's consciousness, spreading out, making itself at home. He was not religious, but he prayed. From the chair across from Dag's bed, he prayed to whatever deity might be tuned in. He prayed for healing. He prayed for healthy brain function. He prayed for Dag to miraculously recover and lead his team to victory in the playoffs. He knew the last request was unlikely to be granted, but he also believed miracles could occur. He prayed for a miracle.

Trey had kicked a pack-a-day habit a few years earlier, but

in times of stress he would reach for a cigarette, and after Dag's first day in the hospital he had bought a pack at a nearby bodega. It was around dinnertime, but he wasn't hungry. Lourawls and Babatunde had gone out to eat. Their positive chatter had begun to grate. There had been no improvement and listening to those two was getting on his nerves. Trey was intent on remaining upbeat, but he knew the situation could go either way.

His friends would be back in an hour. It was hard to stare at Dag all day, prostrate in bed, hooked up to all of those machines, and try to remain hopeful when what he wanted to do was cry. The room was stuffy and he needed a break, so he rode the elevator down to the lobby. In the twilight, Trey stood on First Avenue smoking a cigarette. The media had vanished. Pedestrians streamed by, no one paying attention. Cars and taxis crawled uptown in the molasses of rush hour. The temperature was in the forties, and Trey hunched his shoulders as he inhaled, letting the smoke expand inside him. He wished he had worn his coat.

A black man approached. The stranger, who had a beard and wore a white skullcap, introduced himself and told Trey how upset he was about what had happened to his brother, how much Dag's accomplishments meant to him and the entire community, what an important figure he was. He told Trey how it was their responsibility—his, Trey's, and that of the community—to hold Jay Gladstone's feet to the fire and see that justice was done. Trey agreed with all of this. The man informed Trey that he ran an organization and had contacts in the media. The man asked, "Who's going to speak for D'Angelo? Who will give him his voice? Will it be you, my brother?" Trey wished he could provide a voice for Dag, but extemporaneous speaking in front of television cameras was not one of his talents.

From the river of pedestrians emerged Lourawls and

Babatunde, who handed Trey a tuna sandwich they had purchased for him at a nearby Korean market.

"Fellas, say hello to—sorry, what'd you say your name was?"

"Imam Ibrahim Muhammad."

The imam's inviting smile shone in the gloom.

Chapter Forty

I t would have been so much better if the situation with your daughter didn't play out in the public sphere," Herman Doomer said. "People misinterpret."

"And now every schmuck in New York has a camera."

They were in the attorney's Midtown office, the lawyer in a wing chair, Jay across from him on the sofa. Between them on the coffee table rested the day's edition of the *New York Post*. On the front page, above a picture of Jay, Aviva, and Jude at the Vietnamese restaurant, the headline screamed: *GLAD-STONE FAMILY FEUD*. Someone in the restaurant had a phone with a camera. The accompanying article was short on details since neither of the principals spoke to the reporter who wrote it, but there was speculation that a family argument had boiled over and father and daughter were estranged.

"Why is it so important to you to give that commencement address?"

Jay had been asking himself that question. His conversation with Aviva gnawed at him and, given all the angst the possibility stirred up, he was beginning to doubt whether it was worth it. To what degree could a speech to a bunch of liberal arts kids penetrate the zeitgeist if the speaker wasn't someone like Steve Jobs? Jay had planned to talk about the role of the builder in society and how the graduates were "the builders of their own lives," but given his self-inflicted wound this no longer seemed wise.

"I've been having second thoughts about it."

"For the time being, I don't think any public appearances are prudent. Perhaps you should consider the idea of managed seclusion."

"Like Einstein in New Jersey?"

"That's exile."

"What's the difference?"

"You wouldn't have to disappear, exactly, but choose your spots carefully."

"I'm not going away, Herman. That's not going to happen."

Doomer pointed to the copy of the *Post*. "This complicates my task." He was spread out in the chair, spidery limbs barely filling his gray suit. He pressed his palms together and touched the tips of his fingers to his thin lips as he contemplated his client.

"I'm sorry, Herman. I don't know what's going on with her."

"You two should probably stay away from each other for the time being."

"That won't be a problem."

"All of it is prejudicial to a jury. You want the jurors to like you. They can't think you have a pattern of conflict."

Doomer picked up the copy of the *Post* and waved it at Jay. "You need help with this stuff. I want you to think about hiring Robert Tackman. He specializes in crisis communications. Do you know him?"

"Why would I?"

"No reason. Robert's a behind-the-scenes operator. He's the fellow British Petroleum calls when one of their tankers spills oil in some pristine body of water, and the whole world wants to burn down their headquarters. The Republican Party hired him when Iran-Contra happened. He worked with Michael Jackson who, let me remind you, never served a single day in jail."

"I don't like the idea of bringing in someone I don't know."

"You need a strategy, Jay."

"There won't be any more problems. Let's just deal with what's in front of us. I don't want to work with a P.R. team to rehabilitate my image."

"You don't want to take my advice, don't take it. Now, what do you want to do about Nicole?"

Jay had spared Doomer the details of what occurred in the pool house, only hinting that the marriage was not thriving. The lawyer listened with his usual equanimity, and upon receipt of the information merely nodded. He had been married to the same woman for fifty-two years and whatever opinions he had in this area he kept to himself.

Jay asked, "How enforceable is the prenup?"

"I reviewed it this morning, and it's airtight. But look, you should think about whether you want to be going through a divorce if the criminal case goes to trial. Either one is highly stressful. And there's the matter of the Sapphire, isn't there? We haven't even touched on that. The Planning Commission haven't given their approval yet, have they?"

"We're optimistic."

"Well, until they do, I would advise you to keep your name out of the headlines to the degree that you can, and after your accident, and the incident with Aviva, you're not off to a flying start."

CHAPTER FORTY-ONE

Three days had passed since Nicole left the house and set up camp on the tenth floor of the Pierre Hotel. Her suite overlooked Central Park, but she was too distracted to enjoy the view. The flowers she'd ordered to cheer herself up had started to wilt. Since encountering her husband at the hospital she had kept a low profile, only venturing out to have lunch with the newly pregnant Audrey, who she had not seen since before that dreadful Seder. She couldn't bring herself to tell her friend what had happened and so had to listen as the loquacious former model filled the time describing the nursery she was designing and ruminating on where the child would be enrolled in preschool. It was all Nicole could do to keep from breaking into wracking sobs.

Although Jay's situation was international news, Nicole had not heard from either her parents or siblings. Dressed in leggings and a cashmere V-neck, she swanned around the suite swilling copious amounts of champagne (in a vain attempt to make circumstances slightly less appalling she had switched from the usual chardonnay), and picked at a succession of egg-white omelets from room service while trying to tame her extravagant emotions. She composed a series of self-excoriating emails to Jay but did not send them and continually refreshed her browser for news of Dag's condition. If only meditation were possible, she thought, but just the idea of attempting to tame her whirling mind was risible. On the morning of the second day, she parked on a sofa cushion she had arranged on the floor of her living room to give it a try, but after thirty seconds felt too upset to continue. Desperate to find some peace, she practiced walking across the suite with the Spinoza biography balanced on her head. This feat was achieved on the third try, and she celebrated by weeping so uncontrollably it took four Advil to get rid of the headache that ensued.

In the aftermath, she tried to read the book, which she was only able to do in fits and starts. Despite the painfully slow pace, Nicole was able to assemble scraps of Spinoza's life and found that she connected to the Dutch philosopher. Contemplating her potential exile from the bosom of the Jews, she reflected on the excommunication endured by Spinoza. Yes, he may have been a brilliant thinker who fomented an intellectual revolution in seventeenth-century Europe, and she only a model turned congressional aide turned tycoon's repentant wife, but the unmooring suffered by Spinoza at the hands of his brethren felt unnervingly familiar to her. She was cut off from her family of origin and her suburban Virginia background. Two careers had not left her with a surfeit of people who qualified as friends. Spinoza's parents named him Baruch, but as a result of all he had undergone he came to be known as Benedict, a moniker of popes. Baruch Spinoza, Jew of Amsterdam, had become someone new. She had been Nicole Pflueger, then McGrory, and Gladstone. To be Nicole Gladstone, wife of Jay Gladstone, had felt like the realization of an essential, irreducible self. That was where the similarity ended, where she conveniently stopped thinking about what happened to Spinoza and turned her focus inward. No metaphysician, Nicole's fate was inextricably tied to that of her marriage. She could rebuild her life if she had to, of course. People did.

It occurred to her to reach out to D'Angelo's wife, but she had no idea how to frame the conversation so quickly abandoned the notion. Visiting the hospital again seemed like the right thing to do, but she did not want to risk calling attention to herself. Every idea only seemed to generate more negativity, and the overall effect compounded her lassitude.

She hoped that Jay would decide to remain in the marriage, but was subject to paroxysms of self-loathing for putting her fate in his hands. In her befuddled state, she allowed herself to believe that Jay might agree to renegotiate the prenup. Every time she ran through what to ask for in the divorce—he could keep the house in Aspen, but she wanted the one in East Hampton, he could hang on to the New York apartment, but she wanted the Bedford place with its stables, paddock, and riding trails—she chastised herself for negative ideation. Adultery on so impressive a scale was a shocking thing, but her remorse had not gone unexpressed. Nicole was far more than a standard-issue trophy wife, trotted out like a royal consort to smile and wave. Educated and accomplished, she was still young (ish), gorgeous, and charming, in all ways an enviable mate for someone like Jay. If he chose not to reveal what had happened, she certainly was not going to. As for D'Angelo, it was not clear he would even survive his injuries. Or how compromised he would be if he did. If he lived, and was sentient, and decided to divulge the events of that evening, all Jay and Nicole had to do was deny everything. Given that he had suffered brain damage, who would believe him? Any information D'Angelo Maxwell might offer—assuming he roused from the coma—would be unreliable. She recognized how cold and calculated this was and added it to the list of things over which she was berating herself. But feelings for Dag—in her view they had forged a genuine connection—were beside the point. If she had anything to say about it, the events of that night in Bedford would forever remain between Mr. and Mrs. Jay Gladstone.

One afternoon Nicole read an item on a website about Jay

and Aviva. Although distressed at this news, and the way it had burst into public view, she resisted the impulse to call him and commiserate. She did, however, send a text:

So sorry to see that stuff with you and Aviva in the media!
Thinking about you and hope you're okay!

Jay did not text back. She consoled herself with the thought that he had more than enough on his mind, but a darker interpretation was unavoidable. More champagne. She hadn't showered in several days. A peek in the bathroom mirror revealed a dog's breakfast. She was too depressed to care. Her svelte frame had begun to wither. Would her appetite return? The trees in Central Park were performing their annual sun salutations, but Nicole did not notice. How long could she remain hidden in the Pierre?

On Friday morning, hungover, ignoring a room service omelet, and trying to read the complimentary *New York Times* for the first time since the accident, she received a text from Jay:

Please meet me at my office.

This invitation—and the crapulous Nicole chose to read it as an invitation rather than an order—sent her into a tizzy. She quickly made an appointment to have her hair blown out. She peeled off her clothes and showered. Her pores sang as the steaming water coursed over her naked body. Her face was puffy from all the weeping but years spent strutting the runway had gifted her with a professional knowledge of powder and paint. She applied her makeup as if the brush belonged to Vermeer, who was on her mind because of his countryman Spinoza. The two were almost exact contemporaries. Delicately shading her eyes, she wondered if the painter and the philosopher were acquainted. Jay had just recently told her about a paper he had written in college linking them. How she missed talking to him. He once asked her who she would invite to a fantasy dinner party. She had so loved the question. What a fine thing it would be to have Spinoza and Vermeer to dinner. If she and Jay lived in Amsterdam four centuries ago, she would have put that together. If they remained married, she vowed to use her position to arrange dinners like that in the future. When Jay received the anticipated ambassadorship, she would establish the couple in whatever European capital President Obama saw fit to post them. They would be magnets for the international glitterati, their embassy a nexus of American glory. She would devote the rest of her life to the perfection of their marriage.

On the cab ride to the Gladstone offices, Nicole took out her phone and ordered a biography of Jacqueline Kennedy Onassis from Amazon. That legendary dervish of the social whirl would be her new role model. But despite the enthusiasm to reclaim her life and direct it to new heights, all the while Nicole recognized the element of wishful thinking she was engaged in. The fact remained, it was highly likely Jay would divorce her. In his position, she suspected that is what she would do. Yet she did not feel hopeless because she was not going into the situation unarmed. If a divorce was what Jay wanted, Nicole had certain information to impart that might get him to reconsider. Her pulse quickened as the cab turned on to Park Avenue.

When a life-changing event occurs, say, a dire health diagnosis, or the death of a close relative or the dissolution of one's marriage, the physical world can take on a different aspect. To Nicole's relief, the lobby of the Gladstone building, with its immaculately waxed floors, gleaming gold elevator doors, and uniformed attendants who nodded in deferential recognition, was as reassuringly mundane as a favorite childhood meal.

In the elevator, she breathed deeply to steady her nerves. The young female receptionist offered a friendly welcome and instantly waved her toward the inner sanctum. On the walls of the hallway leading to the executive offices were brilliantly

colored paintings of Gladstone buildings Bingo commissioned
from a famous artist known for his portraits of sports figures.
Although she found the work a little kitschy, Nicole always
enjoyed seeing it. Franklin's twin sons looked up from an
architectural blueprint they were reviewing and greeted her as
she passed. Bebe appeared from around a corner with a cell
phone to her ear. She mouthed, "How are you?" Nicole gave a
little wave and dearly hoped Jay had not revealed anything to
his sister.

It was the previous autumn when Nicole last visited the
office, and she had not seen the Renzo Piano model of the
Sapphire, so when Jay rose from behind his desk but did not
move toward her, she tried to defuse the awkwardness of the
moment by effusively admiring the design.

"It's just stunning," she said.

"We're hoping the Planning Commission approves it in the
next week or two," he said. There was an undeniable stiffness
to his manner. She knew it was unrealistic to expect that their
initial post-Bedford interaction would be anything other than
prickly. "I spoke at the hearing before I went to Africa."

"I'm sure you'll get to build it."

All the nervousness had been for naught, she reflected.
Whatever the upshot, Jay did not seem angry or guarded. He
thanked her for coming, rounded the desk, and indicated she
should take a seat on the couch against the wall. She sat, but
he remained standing.

"Should we order a drink?" she said.

He laughed and offered her coffee, which she declined. The
first time Nicole visited Jay at his office confirmed her impression of him as a modern King Herod. The design and furnish-
ing reflected an amalgamation of authority and taste and when
she thought of her husband it was often in this majestic setting.
Today Jay seemed less robust than usual. Although the bruises
under his eyes had begun to heal, he still looked tired and

drawn. She thought about asking after Aviva but realized that could set a negative tone and chose to let Jay take the lead.

Then he sat next to her on the couch. Nicole had expected him to take a seat in one of the guest chairs opposite, but here he was, nearby. She tried to tamp down the optimism his proximity engendered.

"How've you been?" he asked.

"Terrible," she said. Rather than embellish the story with a description of her forlorn, self-loathing, and semi-inebriated interlude at the Pierre, she allowed that one word to sit there and gather force. She thought about apologizing again, but knew there was nothing to be gained. He already knew how she felt. Then something remarkable occurred. Jay took her hand in his. She had not touched his flesh since they were standing at Dag's bedside in the hospital. His hand was warm. She unspooled her fingers into his palm, and he caressed them. Her heart fluttered.

"How is D'Angelo?" she asked. "All I know is what I see on the Internet."

Jay told her he had gone back to the hospital that morning, about the team of doctors he assembled, how they confirmed the uncertainty of the initial prognosis; they were all just waiting to see how the patient responded. She listened attentively.

"The doctors are cautiously optimistic," he said.

"Thank God."

For several moments, neither of them spoke. Nicole would wait. She didn't want to fill the stillness with chatter.

"I've been doing a lot of reflecting," Jay began. *I have, too*, she wanted to say but did not. "I've examined this from every angle, tried to take my ego out of it, and considered everything we've experienced together, all the things we've shared." He stopped. She bit her upper lip. "And I think we should get a divorce."

Like a guillotine, the cut was quick and final.

Removing her hand from his, she said, "All right." Nicole had already decided not to argue if this was the outcome of their meeting. To push back would be unbecoming and she wanted to maintain decorum insofar as it was possible. To her relief, she did not have a visible physical reaction.

She said: "I understand."

It felt as if her chest had collapsed.

"I'm going to have the prenuptial agreement voided."

Nicole was dumbstruck. The contract was already generous and after what she had done, Jay was going to offer her more in the settlement? Beatific gratitude coursed through her. It was a relief to know that he valued their years together as much as she did.

"Thank you." It seemed like the best response.

His eyes betrayed a flicker of amusement. "I'm going to write you a check for two million dollars."

She wasn't sure she understood. "And then what?"

"And then that's it. Herman Doomer is going to send you papers to sign, and the records will be sealed. If you contest it, you'll get nothing."

This turnabout confounded Nicole. Reeling from his declaration that the marriage was over, she absorbed the deathblow of his intent to void their agreement. It felt like an assault.

"Two million dollars? Jay, that's preposterous," she said as if he was offering her a loaf of bread and a glass of water. "What am I supposed to do with two million dollars?"

"Under the circumstances, it's generous."

Searing heat moved through her body, veins burning. She felt lightheaded. Nausea stirred in her stomach. Everything began to implode.

"You can't do that," she managed to whisper.

"Read the agreement," Jay said. "There's a moral turpitude clause."

Nicole rummaged through her memory bank and tripped over a vague recollection of the detail Jay was recalling. The lawyer who reviewed the contract on her behalf had advised getting the offending paragraph excised, but she assumed there would never be a need to invoke it and blithely signed the document.

Jay rose from the couch—he can't be near me, she thought—and sat on the edge of his desk. For a full minute, neither of them uttered a word. When she recovered from the news he had delivered, her calculations were not about contrition because that was now a failed strategy.

"There's something you should know about, darling."

Darling? It was more of an incision than an endearment. Whatever she planned to sling in his direction, Jay was ready. Affecting boredom, he said, "You and Dag were carrying on for months."

"No, we weren't," she said. "I never lied to you."

He sighed. "What is it you'd like to tell me?"

"I made a tape that night," she said. "Dag never knew. We were drunk, and it was stupid, but now I think maybe it wasn't so stupid."

"Nicole, this is so beneath you."

"Your voice is on it."

"My voice?"

"And you said something you might not want out there."

He stared in disbelief then turned his head away from her until it rested at an oblique angle. She could see him scouring his brain, trying to recollect details of the scene. Wondering what he had said. Did he think she was bluffing? Did he remember the sex videos they made early in their marriage? The one she had mentioned to Marcy. This memory made Nicole recall the Seder and the way Jay had erupted at Imani. Would there be an explosion in the office? He had never interacted with her in that way, but the situation between them had only now degenerated to this point. Who knew what he might do? She wondered if perhaps it would have been wiser to conduct this business over the phone. Going toe to toe with Jay Gladstone was not easy for people far harder-edged than she. For all his congeniality, everyone knew Jay could play rough. The fierceness of the glare he fixed her with was unsettling.

"I have no idea what you're talking about. Even if it's true, if you're threatening me and your threat involves you releasing some sordid tape, then I don't know what to tell you. You'll look a lot worse than I will."

"Actually," she said, getting up from the couch, "I'm not sure that's accurate. Now listen, I want you to rethink what you said. Let's not go nuclear. You'll honor the prenup, and I won't release the tape."

"Be glad I'm not going to say what I think of you right now."

"I'm not going to put it out there, Jay." She pulled on her coat. "You just need to do the honorable thing. It's Friday, so you have until Monday at the end of the day."

Before leaving the office, she walked over to the model of the Sapphire. The building represented the world from which she was being cast out, and in her bitterness, it seemed like a relic of a lost civilization, a monument to vanity and arrogance. She turned to her husband and said, "I only want what's fair for the both of us."

He did not reply.

When she exited his office, every repressed emotion began to bubble to the surface. Nicole fumed past the paintings of Gladstone buildings, and the friendly receptionist. How dare he attempt to undercut their legally binding agreement? Yes, her behavior had been reprehensible—she acknowledged there was no excuse—but they were civilized people, and his idea of sentencing her to penury was simply not going to fly.

Jay would learn that soon enough. Two million dollars in New York? A cruel jape. A spiteful insult! Any co-op she would be willing to live in required liquidity of at least three times the purchase price. A two bedroom on Fifth with park views would be a pipe dream, a one bedroom at an acceptable address out of reach. Did he expect her to live in some horrid nondescript high-rise rental on Second Avenue? What did he think she was going to do once she blew through the pittance he offered? Resume her Washington career as a subcommittee worker bee? Take up modeling again? Forty was hurtling toward her like a meteor! Nicole's jaw stiffened as she prepared for battle. Her ability to not debase herself in Jay's office with some shameful display of emotion was the quality of which she was most proud. As she rode the elevator to the lobby for what was certainly the last time, she congratulated herself on an admirable performance.

Ten minutes later her fury had not cooled, and she was in Central Park near the carousel. Having no particular place to go, she sat on a bench. Nearby, young mothers and nannies kept vigil while children rode the brightly painted wooden horses. The smells of the thawing earth and the reawakening trees, the sounds of the carousel and shouts of the children, and the sun's rays, which had become exceedingly warm, were nearly overwhelming. Purchasing bottled water from a vendor, she returned to the bench and sipped it. To calm herself, she closed her eyes and performed visualization exercises. Swimming in turquoise waters off the white sand beach in St. Kitts, riding her horse on a trail near the house she and Jay owned in Aspen. And so on.

After she had been there for a few minutes, her mind began to unclutter. And it was then Nicole was seized by a thought: She did not want to get divorced. When she and Jay were married, she truly had meant it to last until one of them died. Why had she so readily agreed to his pronouncement? He was under unimaginable stress. It was nearly impossible to conceive what it was like for a man like Jay to face such punishing charges. She needed to be patient and let time pass. Perhaps he would begin to realize the benefits of their union. Marriages survived infidelity. After a spasm of self-laceration, it occurred to her to visit the hospital to see Dag. Given what had passed between them, that would be the humane thing to do. But Nicole had no idea whether she would be observed and didn't want to risk doing anything to undermine her new plan. She was going to win her husband back.

CHAPTER FORTY-TWO

A lthough he was glad to be rid of his wife, her departure left him morose. One of the benefits of marriage was to have someone at your side when life became difficult, but when those difficulties were caused by the person meant to assuage them, it threw the entire calculation into chaos. He would never have run Dag over if Nicole had not brought him to their home. Jay dealt with problems by isolating them from each other, prioritizing their severity, and attacking the most challenging one first. He had to euthanize the reeling Gladstone marriage, and now that was done. Doomer would handle the district attorney's office. He called Dr. Bannister's private number to check on Dag. The doctor informed Jay that the patient's condition remained critical and he would contact him if anything changed. Had he been in touch with the medical team Jay had brought in? Yes, yes, they're in the loop.

Jay and Bebe agreed to file a lawsuit against Franklin and ask for an injunction barring their cousin from participating in the day-to-day operations of the business. Jay suggested a plan for dealing with the aftermath of this move, a restructuring that would elevate Bebe to Franklin's position, and she readily acceded. Boris would serve as her deputy, a position that would place him above Franklin's sons. When Jay returned, he called Boris into his office and demanded to know whether there was any word from the Planning Commission. There was not. Jay asked Boris to remain in the office and indicated he should sit on the couch so recently occupied by Nicole. Had Boris seen Franklin today?

"About an hour ago. He was headed out."

"Do you know where?"

"He doesn't share his schedule with me."

"I've held off on telling you this." Jay felt like a skydiver about to leap from a plane. Boris regarded him expectantly. "I'm going to try and have Franklin removed from his position in the organization."

Boris was aghast and when he asked the reason why, Jay quickly led him through what had occurred.

"Can you do that?"

"It's in the company bylaws."

"What about Ari and Ezra?"

"They'll report to Bebe." Jay leaned back in his desk chair, contented with his plan. Boris couldn't believe it. "When it happens, you and Bebe are going to fly to Asia and meet with all the executives over there." Jay was not certain that Boris had absorbed all of this. His cousin was staring at the wall, rhythmically drumming his fingers on the couch cushion. "Say something."

He stopped drumming and looked Jay directly in the eye. "Are you sure?"

"You've been shadowing me nearly ten years. You're ready, and you're going to be reporting to my sister. I didn't make you the head of the company."

"She's down with this?"

"Happy to have the help. You'll have to spend a lot of time in Asia, which isn't something she wants to do."

"When's it going to happen?"

"Monday." The look of amazement and gratitude on Boris's face lifted Jay's spirits. It pleased him to reward someone for their honest work. "Enjoy the weekend."

CHAPTER FORTY-THREE

T he team had won their only game in Dag's absence, beating the Portland Trailblazers, and were now on the cusp of qualifying for the eighth and final seed in the playoffs. The Miami Heat were currently the best team in the league, and they were visiting Sanitary Solutions Arena on Saturday night. If the home team won, they were in. Jay envisioned ecstatic fans, the manna of playoff revenues, and a significant bump in the valuation of the team. Whatever was going on in his personal life, he intended to be in his courtside seats.

Managed seclusion didn't mean vanishing.

Jay and Boris drove to Bedford that evening. He wanted company on the ride to and from the arena the next night so he invited Boris to stay at the house for the weekend. Jay sold it by saying they could talk about the complexities of running the Asian operation but the fact was he did not want to be alone. Boris made himself at home in a guest room overlooking the paddock while Jay ordered dinner from a local restaurant. Boris could not understand why someone as wealthy as his cousin had so few servants—there was a maid who did not live on the premises, and a groom who cared for the stables— but the one time he asked about it Jay explained that he simply didn't like people who were not family members lurking around.

The next morning, Jay saddled Mingus up and cantered out of the barn toward a trail. The animal snorted, pleased to be free of his stall. There was no snow on the ground and the morning sun caressed the grass. Old-growth trees revealed their spring line of buds. Crocuses and daffodils had started to appear. Jay turned his face toward the azure sky. A westerly wind chased strands of cirrus clouds. As he followed the trail into the woods, his problems seemed far away. Jay rode for an hour, and his mind ranged lightly over recent events. He thought about the speech he would deliver at the Tate College commencement in May. Aviva would come around. It was in her interest to have a father not viewed as a criminal. She could not have been happy that their family argument had become public. Perhaps he would use the platform to announce the endowment of a scholarship fund at the college for students committed to careers in social justice. By the time Jay returned to the house his mood had improved considerably.

Boris was standing in the kitchen drinking coffee and staring at his phone.

"You're not going to like this," Boris said, handing Jay the device.

Jay handed it back. "I don't have my reading glasses."

"It's personal. You're sure you want me to—"

"Read the damn thing, Boris."

Boris took a deep breath and read, "Dag and Gladstones In Racist Sex Romp."

Jay grabbed the phone from his cousin's hand. He left the room and went upstairs. On the nightstand, next to his copy of *Weimar Culture: The Outsider as Insider*, was a pair of reading glasses. He put them on and looked at Boris's phone. From the brief article, he determined the tape to which Nicole alluded had been distributed to several media outlets late last night. And there it was, the pull quote, the quote the person who edited this slag heap of a website believed most conveyed the tenor of the piece:

Why does everyone in this family want to have sex with black people?

When he got over the initial kick in the teeth, he noticed that the site had linked to the actual tape. He pressed play. And there, like a recurring nightmare rising from the murky depths of his consciousness, was his naked wife in the half-lit pool house pumping like a piston. One, two, three seconds elapsed, her orgasmic groans emanating from the tiny cell phone speaker with surprising clarity. At the peak of her ride, she turned and looked over her shoulder. Jay heard her bleat of distress when she saw him. Then the sound of what was unmistakably his voice: "Why does everyone in this family want to have sex with black people?" The feigned nonchalance, the slight slur of his words, the way *sex* sounded almost like *shex*. It was horrifying.

Sunshine saturated the room in mustard light. Outside the windows, birds laughed. It was not yet eight o'clock. The landline on the bedside table began to ring. Jay checked the caller ID: Herman Doomer. He composed himself and picked up the phone. Perfunctory greetings, then the lawyer said:

"This will cause difficulties in your case."

Doomer was rusticating at his weekend house in South Salem, and they arranged to meet there. Over the next hour, there were texts from several reporters that went unanswered. He considered contacting Nicole but what would that accomplish? She must be reveling in her hollow triumph. He wondered how many more times she could betray him.

With the scent of the stable still on his clothes, Jay showered and changed into clean jeans and a chamois shirt. Boris refrained from asking about what was going on when Jay said he would drive himself to Doomer's house.

The northern Westchester roads were winding and wooded, large homes set far back on lawns framed by towering trees.

The overall effect was one of timelessness. The feeling of remove it provided was a quality that Jay cherished. Only the other cars that passed him in the opposite direction hinted at the year.

The phrase *Racist Sex Romp* kept recurring. What had he said or done that was racist? How was it possible for anyone to believe him to be a bigot? His liberal credentials were impeccable. He thought about asking Church Scott to make a statement on his behalf but realized that, since he was an employee, it would not have the optical purity the situation required. He needed black friends to speak up. The problem: He did not have any. Growing up in Scarsdale, the only black people of whom he was conscious (other than Claudie, the maid) were the athletes, authors, and musicians he venerated. In his current life, he knew plenty of black people but had no close friends who were African-American.

As the road rose and fell through the tree-stippled hills, Jay kept thinking about Nicole and how she could have done something so utterly self-destructive. She was an intelligent woman, and although Jay had blustered during their last meeting, he expected a negotiation to evolve. Instead, she had not only violated all bounds of decorum but destroyed whatever leverage she possessed. What incomprehensible strategy was this? No longer able to contain the impulse, he called her from the car. Nicole picked up immediately.

Before he could utter a word of condemnation, she said, "I have no idea how that got out there." This denial brought him up short. "Jay, I swear." Nicole sounded shaken. Could she possibly be telling the truth? It seemed unlikely.

"You said you would wait until Monday."

"I promise you; I have no fucking idea how this happened."

"You had nothing to do with it?"

"Someone must have hacked my phone."

"Who would have wanted to do that?"

"How am I supposed to know? I'm not a public person. I don't have enemies."

"I have enemies who would want to destroy me?"

"The tape is of me, Jay! Me!"

"YOU THREATENED TO RELEASE IT!" He was shouting now. The trees on either side of the road were a blur. His foot was heavy on the gas pedal, the car going over sixty on the country road.

"I never would have done that." Her voice was tremulous, threaded with pain. "I don't want a divorce, Jay. I know how this sounds right now, but I want to reconcile. I haven't given up. Why would I release that tape?"

Jay took a corner and felt the centrifugal force of the Mercedes loaner pull him hard to his right. Only then did he realize the vehicle was nearly out of control. He pressed the brake and slowed down.

"I don't believe you."

"Look in the mirror, Jay. Don't blame me for this."

He hung up, uncertain whether Nicole was dissembling or this was just part of some larger more sinister plan to undo him. She had left his office in a rage—her unruffled demeanor did not fool him—and he knew she wanted to advocate for her interests, but his wife was not one to wage total war. She was more strategic in her thinking. Yet who else could have been responsible? From the plaintive notes she just now sounded, he again considered the possibility of her innocence. Nicole was not that good an actress. But it was impossible to know. His phone rang. He geared himself up to deal with Nicole once more, but it was his sister Bebe. He hesitated before answering but realized he would have to talk to her eventually.

"I assume you heard about the tape," he said.

"How are you holding up?"

"It was bad. Now it's worse."

"Is there anything I can do?"

"Not unless you can wave a wand and make it all go away."

Jay thanked his sister for checking in with him and said he would speak with her soon. He concentrated on maintaining the speed limit, gripped the steering wheel tightly, and thought about what he would say to Doomer.

The Doomers lived in a country contemporary up a long driveway on a bluff of land overlooking a lake. Jay parked his car in the circular driveway and rang the doorbell. Doomer answered wearing khakis and a fleece. As Jay followed him into the open-plan house, he could not recall ever having seen him in anything other than a business suit. The matriarchal Mrs. Doomer waved hello from the kitchen and went back to her crossword puzzle. In a knee-length skirt and down vest, glasses on the end of her nose, she was a model of constancy and rectitude. Was she aware of the perverse circus Jay's life had become? Did she believe his racial attitudes were suspect? As a lifelong Democrat, she would have taken a dim view of anything illiberal, so he was unsure how to interpret her aloofness.

Through the floor-to-ceiling windows of the sunny living room a lone canoeist could be seen paddling in the distance. Several pieces of modern art hung on the walls. Family photographs arranged on tables. A man who appeared to be in his mid-sixties was leafing through an art book. Slightly overweight, gray hair cut short, he wore a maroon cardigan over a white shirt with a paisley ascot, dark pants, and oxblood cordovan shoes. He closed the book and looked Jay over.

"Jay, meet Robert Tackman," Doomer said.

"Bobby," Tackman said, extending his hand, which Jay shook. "I should probably tell you, old boy—I'm a Knicks season ticket holder."

Jay could only manage a wan smile. Ordinarily, he would have offered his standard riposte of "My condolences," but he was not in a jocular mood. And what was with the "old boy"?

The Tackman accent was indeterminate, a mid-Atlantic mélange typical in movies of the 1940s.

"Where are you from?" Jay asked.

"Originally? Rhode Island."

The tea and crumpets attitude affected by Tackman reminded Jay of the time his uncle Jerry came up with the name "Windsor Village."

"I invited Bobby here today," Doomer said, "because we're going to hire him."

Jay looked from his lawyer to Tackman, unsure how to react. In his world, he was the one who did all critical hiring. Doomer's assuming this function was a breach of protocol but these were uncharted waters. "All right," he finally managed.

The men faced each other on two leather sofas arranged perpendicularly on a thick rug, Jay and Doomer next to each other, Tackman alone on his. A fire crackled in the stone fireplace.

Tackman asked, "Is that your voice on the tape?"

"Unfortunately."

"Then we're not going to bother with a denial?" Before Jay could answer, Tackman continued, "Because voice recognition software is still dodgy."

"I think we should skip the denial phase," Jay said. He proceeded to outline his dealings with Nicole leading up to their recent phone call. Doomer asked Jay who he thought leaked the tape to the media.

"I have absolutely no idea," Jay said.

Doomer liked Jay's wife and, to him, something about the situation did not compute. It was not as if there was a history of erratic behavior. "*Could* it have been Nicole?"

"She swears it wasn't her and told me she doesn't want a divorce, so I don't know. Someone who intends to ruin the two of us, perhaps. Nowadays, personal destruction is a sport."

"It could be some pimply teenager living in his parents'

basement," Tackman said. "But at this point how it got out there doesn't particularly matter."

Doomer leaned back and crossed an ankle over his knee. He picked a piece of lint off his sleeve and rolled it between his fingers.

"Here's the problem," the lawyer said. "It gives the prosecution a motive."

Although this was obvious, the dissemination of the tape had so derailed Jay that he had not given any thought to the legal ramifications. He felt his weight sinking into the soft leather.

"What do we do?" His voice was lifeless.

"Just because they have a motive doesn't mean they'll convict you," Doomer said. "They can only present it as a theory. The prosecution still has to convince a jury."

Jay shifted uneasily. An awful word: *Prosecution*. He was going to be hearing it a lot. He wished he had never divorced Jude. None of this would be happening if he had followed his father's path and stayed in one long marriage.

"I'm going to survive this, Herman."

"For heaven's sake, you're a model citizen. Accidents happen. We'll convince them, don't worry. And I think we should hold off on trying to lower the boom on your cousin. At least until this latest thing blows over." Jay reluctantly agreed. "Robert?"

Tackman leaned forward and focused on his new client. "First thing," he began.

"I'll keep out of trouble, don't worry."

"I know you will. It's not that. I don't think you should go out in public without a bodyguard." This advice did not sit well with Jay, who looked askance at his new adviser. "Not permanently, of course, but for the time being. Herman tells me you pride yourself on having the common touch, but there are a lot of unbalanced people out there."

After some back and forth, Jay acceded to this request.

Tackman asked, "When do you next expect to be at a public event?"

"I'm going to the game tonight."

"Really?" The news surprised Tackman. "You're a brave man, Jay. So soon?"

"I'm not going to hide."

"All right, that's admirable. Kooky, but admirable."

Jay did not appreciate Tackman's familiarity.

"I'm a public man."

"Where do you sit?"

"Courtside."

"Not tonight," Tackman informed him. "You have a skybox? Obviously, you do, you're the owner. Tonight, that's where you're going to sit, above the crowd." Jay agreed to do that. "Have you talked to any press today?" Jay reported that he had not spoken with anyone other than his sister, his wife, and Boris. Tackman was pleased. "Media strategy is vital. I know you have a lot of relationships with reporters and you get positive coverage in the press, but right now you're not going to talk to anyone, no radio, newspapers, or websites. I want to give someone a television exclusive. Either Diane Sawyer or Anderson Cooper."

Jay glanced at Doomer, who indicated that he thought this was a superb idea.

"You get a chance to introduce your character to the world," Tackman said.

"My character?"

"The likable chap who caught his wife cheating and deserves everyone's sympathy."

"Oh, god," Jay said. Each time he was reminded of the particulars was like absorbing another kill shot. "I can't talk about that on television. You expect me to discuss the tape with Anderson Cooper?"

"Or Diane Sawyer, yes," Tackman said. "It'll help you, I promise."

"Let me understand this," Jay said. "I'm supposed to go in front of an audience on national television and convince the world my racial attitudes pass muster?"

Tackman looked at Doomer like a dog unsure of his master's intent. Did the worldly Jay Gladstone not understand his role?

"I agree with what Bobby is suggesting," Doomer said.

Jay gazed beyond Tackman toward the backyard where a deer was peacefully feeding on the leaves of a bush. Jay noticed the fragile limbs, muscles twitching barely perceptibly as she chewed, ever alert to peril.

"All right," he said.

Tackman wanted to be familiar with Jay the man and Jay did his best to oblige the request. They talked for the next hour. Despite the friendliness he affected, Jay was not the kind of person who revealed himself to strangers but Doomer's endorsement of Tackman eased his mind on this account, and the consultant seemed to like him personally, a factor that always weighed heavily with Jay.

"If the television interview goes well," Tackman said, "and I'm sure it will, you're going to visit the Abyssinian Baptist Church in Harlem." This idea alarmed Jay. It was one thing to stare down a television camera in an antiseptic studio. A sea of disapproving black faces in a Harlem church was a different matter. Tackman was sensitive to his reluctance. "One thing at a time, I know. But the reverend is a friend."

"Let's not get carried away, Bobby," Doomer said on his client's behalf. Tackman agreed that a church visit would only be used to build on a positive television appearance.

Fatigue began to overtake Jay. He had not slept well and wanted to rest before going to the game. Although he valued Doomer's counsel and was beginning to accept Tackman's presence, the two men had exceeded their client's capacity for taking advice. As he had so many times in his life as an executive, Jay adjourned the meeting. Tackman said he would write a memo outlining the plan. They would meet for lunch on Monday. When Doomer retrieved Jay's coat from the closet by the front door, Mrs. Doomer asked if he would like to stay for the meal she had prepared. Pleased to be invited, he could not imagine that this lifelong liberal did not know what he had done and the invitation indicated that she did not consider him a pariah. Perhaps there was hope. But he had no appetite so politely declined.

When Jay returned to his house, Boris was in the kitchen.

"I drove back to my place and got something for you."

"What is it?"

With a nod, Boris gestured to the countertop. Next to a bowl of fruit was a Smith and Wesson handgun. Jay started to laugh.

"What am I supposed to do with that?"

"Hopefully, nothing."

"Get it out of here."

"No."

"Boris—"

"Just keep it in the house. You're here alone sometimes. Can't hurt to have it."

Although it was painful to admit, Jay knew his cousin was correct. Who knew from what direction harm might come? No one could predict anything. Jay put the gun in an upstairs safe behind a picture of him and Nicole at the Parthenon in Athens. Something else would have to go there. He did not want to be reminded of Aristotle when reaching for his gun. Nor did he want to be reminded of Nicole.

CHAPTER FORTY-FOUR

On the ride to the game, Jay sat in the back and scrolled through his phone as Boris drove with Dequan next to him in the passenger seat. Coverage had expanded exponentially, and the story was now the lead item on every sports, news, and entertainment website he visited. Whatever the demographic, the gist was identical. From the Wall Street Journal (Team Owner Caught Up In Scandal) to ESPN.com (Gladstone a Racist?) to TMZ (Blue Stones: Owner Watches Wife Have Sex With Star), all of it was ghastly. Boris kept a first-aid kit in the car and Jay popped antacid pills for the entire ride. Stupefied and infuriated, Jay nonetheless knew enough to take the long view. For the first time, he was happy that Herman Doomer had insisted on a public relations consultant. Scandals erupted with clocklike regularity, their intensity amplified by the hothouse of the Internet; and soon enough they were replaced by other scandals in an ever-shifting pattern of outrage. Now was his turn to bear the coruscating effect, and as the lights of Sanitary Solutions Arena blazed in the distance just east of the New Jersey Turnpike he heard Bingo's voice telling him there was nothing to do but "march forth."

The game was sold out and the organization planned to give free T-shirts with Dag's picture on them to every fan in attendance. Jay's phone had been blowing up all day, and there were so many texts that he stopped reading them. Now he could talk to the sportswriters, greet the fans, and show he wasn't cowering in a cave. Yes, Tackman had wanted him to keep a low profile at the game, but Jay knew he could draw on the energy of the high rollers in the expensive seats before repairing to his skybox.

The ritual Jay followed before each home game consisted of a visit with Church Scott in the coach's office adjacent to the locker room where they would discuss team business, then the customary scotch and a pregame nosh with whomever his guests were that night in the Executive Club on the loge level, and few minutes before tip-off the group would head to the owner's seats, Jay glad-handing season ticket holders along the way. But tonight, the usual routine allowed for too many variables. To permit the contact Jay typically enjoyed before a game seemed unwise.

The first indication that this would not be an ordinary night was the scene in front of the arena. It was an hour before game time when the SUV swung into the parking lot. The first detail Jay noticed was that next to the usual line of fans streaming into the building was a multiracial cluster of protesters chanting and waving placards: *SELL THE TEAM, JAY, NEW OWNER WANTED: BIGOTS NEED NOT APPLY*, and (oddly) *ZIONISM IS RACISM*. Demonstrators brandished large posters of Dag wearing the team uniform, his body lithe and unbroken. Jay repressed the urge to tell Boris to make a U-turn and take him to Canada.

The leader of the protests was Imam Ibrahim Muhammad, who stood on a crate and held a bullhorn to his mouth as he chanted, *Hey, hey, ho, ho, Jay Gladstone has to go*, a call echoed volubly by the protestors, who shook their signs and pumped their fists. There was someone who looked familiar standing next to him. Trey Maxwell. What was he doing with that troublemaker? Television crews recorded the action; fans filmed it on their phones. Jay considered getting out right there and talking to the crowd, confronting that rabble-rousing imam in full view of the media and directly making his case, but that felt excessively risky, not to say physically dangerous. Tackman had advised against unmediated personal contact with the public.

He had another idea.

Boris let Jay and his bodyguard out at the players' entrance. Jay was not comfortable with the proximity to the players and staff that a locker room visit would entail, so he arranged for Church Scott to meet him in the security office. Boris had alerted the staff that the boss would be attending the game and additional precautions had been taken. In a cinderblock room, deep in the bowels of the arena, the black chief of security waited. A chesty ex-Marine named Bo McCants, he was matter-of-fact by nature, so Jay did not read into the flatness of his greeting. Skipping any pleasantries, he briefed Jay on the arrangement for the game. McCants reported that he had mustered an additional thirty men, ten of whom were to be stationed directly behind the owner's seats, the rest to be deployed around the court. Jay informed McCants he would be seated in a skybox once the game started and the security chief assured him the necessary adjustments would be made. If McCants was judging him, Jay could not tell; the security chief had bloodlessly imparted the information. Jay had the disconcerting sensation that he should apologize. But for what?

As McCants finished his briefing, Church Scott swept in. He seemed harried and did not offer his usual handshake. The affability with which he glazed every off-court encounter was absent. Again, Jay felt like apologizing. Was every encounter with a black person going to make him feel this way? They discussed Dag's condition (unchanged) and the night's opponent before Jay dropped the following bombshell:

"I'm going to say a few words from center court before the game."

He knew Tackman would have ordered him not to but the P.R. maven surely was unaware of the deep connection Jay had with the team's fans.

"You sure?"

"Just a few remarks," he said, ignoring the surprise on Church Scott's face. "In light of recent events, I'd like to show the flag, talk about D'Angelo"—not *Dag*, the entire name more respectful—"let the fans know there's a steady hand on the tiller."

Church's brow furrowed. During his years as a point guard in the league, a cerebral style of play was his signature. With a safecracker's patience, he probed a defense until he uncovered a weakness and would rarely execute an ill-considered move. Church asked Jay if he was entirely certain he wanted to get in front of eighteen thousand people tonight.

"There's a lot of residual goodwill toward me in this building."

"Well, the fans are one thing," the coach said. "But listen, I have to tell you something." Jay readied himself to absorb whatever blow was in the offing. "We've got a situation brewing in the locker room."

"What kind of situation?"

"The players are talking about boycotting the game."

The news flabbergasted Jay. His relationship with the roster had always been terrific, from the stars to the scrubs on the end of the bench. He was never less than polite, encouraging, and concerned when it came to the players. Boycotting the game would be bad for the league and a disaster for Jay. It felt personal. Dequan was standing several feet away with his back to them, his frame filling the doorway. Jay wondered if he was listening to the conversation.

"Why would they do that?"

"The guys all heard those words," the coach said. He was tactful enough not to say: *And saw the tape*. "They didn't like it."

This response seemed like an overreaction. The players knew him. Perhaps not well, but he believed they sensed the man he was. "Should I talk to them?"

"Nooooooo," Church said. The feeble laugh that issued from his lips revealed discomfort with that notion. "I think I moved them off the idea for one night." The relief Jay felt caused oxygen to rush from his lungs. "You want to make a speech to the folks out there tonight, hey, you're the boss. I'm just a dumb ex-ballplayer. Maybe you know something I don't."

Jay had idolized men like Church Scott since boyhood. He still retained a fan's respect for the greatest of them and the coach was championship caliber. Jay was not above being flattered by Church's assessment and this reinvigorated him.

"I want you to introduce me," Jay said.

"I can't do that," Church said.

"Yes, you can. Everyone respects you."

"I'll lose the locker room."

It had never occurred to Jay that the coach would turn down a request like this. Theirs was a collegial relationship, one of mutual respect. Church routinely sought Jay's counsel in business matters and reciprocated by tutoring Jay in the intricacies of elite basketball. He considered Church a friend.

"You need to set an example for them," Jay said. *Them.* Players, coaches, fans who might sit in judgment. "You're the leader."

"I'm a black man, Jay," he said, unnecessarily. "Most of the guys on the team are, too. They're wondering what's in your heart right now."

"You can tell them what's in my heart."

"I can't tell them because I don't know."

Church's words were hurtful and Jay was unsure how to respond. They had worked together for five years and if

Church Scott could say something like that, to his face no less, what was the wider world going to think? Was what he had done so bad? The man had walked in on his wife in flagrante and in his understandable disorientation he had asked a question. It was not as if he had used an epithet. Was he to be drawn and quartered for a single ambiguous sentence?

Jay whispered: "I'm telling you what's in my heart, Church. You know me."

He couldn't say I'm not a racist to a black man. That meant it was already too late.

Church nodded. "Okay," he said. "All right." What he did not say was I *believe you*. He patted Jay on the shoulder and told him, "I'm praying on this," and then was gone with an encouraging clap on the back from Dequan as he left. Was the bodyguard endorsing the coach's position? Did the back clap portend some further palace revolt? Jay could not be bothered with that right now. Wherever Dequan's sympathy lay, there was enough security in the arena tonight.

He pondered his encounter with Church.

Praying on this?

In his most dire hour, he requested a simple favor, a small gesture of friendship, and Church denied it. Stabbed in the back by his most trusted basketball lieutenant, Jay's first inclination was to fire him immediately and order the lead assistant to take over, but his business success did not derive from acting impulsively, and he instantly recognized the kind of reactive, negative thinking he abhorred. He would wait until the end of the season before relieving Church Scott of his duties.

Boris had been biding his time nearby and now approached.

"Are you sure you want put yourself in front of eighteen thousand people?"

"Goddammit, Boris," Jay growled. "Don't second guess

me." From Boris's alarmed expression, he knew he needed to get his emotions under control. Jay glanced toward Dequan and McCants, and was pleased to see both of them peering at a bank of security monitors, neither paying attention to him. He didn't want anyone to think he was agitated. He asked Boris to please notify the appropriate people that he intended to say a few words after the national anthem.

Rather than go out before the game, Jay thought it best to remain in the tunnel that led to the court until right before the announcer introduced him. The fans focused on the players doing their warm-ups, whomever the team had arranged to warble the night's version of "The Star-Spangled Banner," and their phones.

With Dequan next to him surveying the arena—however much sympathy the bodyguard may have harbored for Church Scott, at least he had not abandoned his post—Jay watched from the shadows as "We Takin' Over" by DJ Khaled blared while a co-ed group of bouncy team employees buzzed around the court wielding bazookas that blasted tightly rolled T-shirts emblazoned with Dag's face into the outstretched hands of the jacked-up fans. The squads finished their pregame stretching and shooting and lined up along opposite foul lines facing one another for the national anthem. A Navy color guard marched out bearing the flag. And then—

The home team stripped off their warm-up jackets and were revealed to be wearing black T-shirts over their regulation league-approved jerseys. The sight of the T-shirts, their symbolism unmistakable, elicited whoops of approval from several fans and a smattering of applause. This display on the part of the players was a violation of league rules and a direct rebuke to Jay, who was dismayed when he saw it. Did Church know this was going to happen and choose not to warn him? At least they're out there and prepared to play the game, he told himself. The boycott bullet dodged.

An obscure female R&B singer belted the national anthem. As she sang, "Land of the freeeeeeeeee," extending the note in the glass-shattering manner those tapped to sing this song will often do, and the fans began to cheer and applaud in anticipation of its end, Jay felt a tap on his shoulder. He looked over and saw the nervously smiling face of Major House, who greeted him in a voice several decibels too loud. They had arranged to meet in the skybox. Why was he in the tunnel right before Jay was going out on the court?

"I bought a pair of tickets for the game," the Mayor said. "It's better that way right now."

"Why?" He instantly knew why.

"I don't have a problem with you, Jay. You know that. But Newark's a black city."

"Newark was a black city when you were my guest last time."

"I can't be sitting next to you at a game right now."

"Now is when I could use you."

"Hey, you know I'm your friend," he said and clapped Jay on the back. "We'll talk on the phone Monday. I'll even come to the office if you want. But not tonight."

Mayor House lingered as if he wanted to make sure that Jay was all right with being abandoned like this by a putative ally just before tip-off, because who would understand the consideration of practical matters if not Jay Gladstone.

"*Et tu*, Major?" Jay said.

"*Et tu*? Come on, man, I'm up for re-election in the fall."

Jay wondered if the mayor had conferred with Church Scott. They were friendly, and he would not have been surprised to hear the two of them had coordinated their response. A voice on the P.A. system crackled, and in his rapidly spinning mind, Jay heard every third word: *Tonight. Team. Special.* Before Jay could ask the mayor if he was colluding with the coach, the public-address announcer intoned, "Please welcome

Jay Gladstone," and he squared his shoulders and propelled himself past the politician—*Why am I doing this? Don't do this. Let's do this!*—out of the shadows, and on to the blindingly bright basketball court.

The powerful lights bounced off the polished hardwood and into Jay's retinas. Multiple levels of yellow, orange, green, and blue seats extending several hundred feet up blurred into one pulsating organism that gave forth scattered boos, several catcalls he could not make out, and some anemic cheering. None of it was encouraging. The brilliant illumination created a bell jar effect and what lay outside the lighted area was not readily discernible.

Like something from a dream, Jay absorbed thousands of smiling D'Angelo Maxwells observing him from the T-shirts sported by every fan. Although the picture appeared hallucinatory, it was not a trick of perception. There were over eighteen thousand images of Dag's face, and an ocean of Dag's eyes locked in on him.

The teams had repaired to their benches to await the buzzer that would summon the starters to the court for the opening tip. The color guard had retreated. The bazooka-wielding T-shirt crew kneeled under one of the baskets. At the center of the court, a team lackey handed a cordless microphone to Jay. The sounds died down, and Jay gazed up to the nosebleed seats. He had a brief and comforting memory of the Knicks-Bullets playoff game he had seen from that vantage point as a teenager nearly forty years earlier.

In a steady voice, he began, "Thank you all for coming tonight."

From near the rafters, someone yelled, "WHERE'S YOUR WIFE?"

Scattered laughter. The outburst could have been worse, and Jay was relieved to hear someone else shout, "LET HIM TALK, ASSHOLE!" followed by more laughs. Should he have listened to Tackman's advice? Not tonight. Jay knew what he was doing, had addressed unpredictable groups before. Were his knees trembling? He steadied himself. While he waited for the murmur to die down, he glanced over to the bench and saw Church in his seat, elbows on knees, looking at the floor. His gaze shifted to the Miami bench where every player was staring at him, waiting to see what he would say. Were they staring or scowling? It was hard to tell.

"As you all know," Jay continued, his voice steady as it resonated to the upper deck, "D'Angelo Maxwell is in the hospital so I'd like to begin with a moment of silent prayer for him." As Jay said this, he again looked over at Church Scott, who was shaking his head, in either disdain or admiration. Which was it? It didn't matter. Jay congratulated himself on the courage of the move. It had come to him spontaneously, and he had acted on it in front of the crowd, all of whom must know what had occurred between Dag and Nicole. No one could miss the magnanimity of the gesture. Certainly, Bobby Tackman would approve.

As the arena quieted, Jay waited, every receptor quivering, the warmth of the lights on his face, the pungent smell of sweat on the court, the lingering taste of the antacid tablets, the otherworldly stillness. He would have prayed if he had not been considering what to say next. Jay remembered his appearance in front of the Planning Commission. He did not compose a word of it beforehand and had delivered a first-rate soliloquy. He knew how to wing it.

After what seemed like a respectable amount of time had passed (five seconds), he resumed, "I wanted to talk to you tonight so that I could apologize. The accident was a dreadful thing, but I want to say here in public in front of the team's fans that it was an *accident*. An accident for which I take full responsibility." That was the key point to hit, he knew. Americans want to hear that whoever caused a scandal took "responsibility" for it. They dispensed a public lashing and then everyone could "move on." Jay knew the Stations of the Contrition Cross, had seen them traversed by countless others that the shame machine trained its sights on. He would not say anything about moving on tonight, though. The contract was implied.

"And by taking responsibility . . . "

An object landed on the court near Jay's feet. From high up, a fan had hurled a tightly rolled T-shirt. It skimmed past him. The arena remained strangely hushed. Not sure what to do but wanting to convey amiability, Jay leaned down, picked up the T-shirt and tossed it back in the stands.

"Someone else might want this," he said.

A fan shouted from the upper deck, "Racist!" the harsh intonation screaming like a missile before detonating on the floor. Jay tensed. Another T-shirt hit the court, then three more. Two sailed over his head, tossed from behind him. He could not throw them all back.

"I like your passion," Jay said, a projectile striking his leg. "But it's not true. So by taking responsibility—"

Boos began to roll in from the upper decks, boos gathering force in the lower bowl, boos coming from behind him and from either side, rising in volume and combining with wild voices emerging from hundreds of throats, all swelling into a crescendo of contempt. Fans rose in their seats yelling, gesticulating, and Dag Maxwell T-shirts began to rain down on the court from all directions, filling the noisy air like snowballs, some arcing gracefully toward their target, others shooting at Jay with laser-like precision. What collective insanity had broken loose? He wasn't a bad actor—he was good!—and this was atonement of the first order! He apologized! He took responsibility!

As one T-shirt struck him in the back and another glanced off his shoulder, Jay reflexively held his hand up to protect his recently broken nose. A phalanx of security charged in his direction.

"ANY FAN CAUGHT THROWING AN OBJECT ON THE COURT WILL BE EJECTED. PLEASE DO NOT THROW OBJECTS. YOU WILL BE EJECTED IMMEDI-ATELY."

But the T-shirts continued to land on the court near Jay along with drink cups, team hats, and anything else that could be hurled through the air. Bellows of indignation, howling imprecations, curses of all kinds unleashed. Distorted faces and cruel laughter added to the sensory overload. Security men waded in, trying to stop fans from contributing to the chaos.

Dequan sprinted toward him. A T-shirt struck the body-guard in the face, and he tripped over a guard who had fallen while chasing a fan. Dequan picked himself up and, pushing other members of the security detail out of the way, found Jay. Several guards chased other fans that had dashed on to the court wielding T-shirts, arms cocked, attempting to get a bet-ter shot at the petrified owner. On the sidelines, players and coaches stood frozen and watched the action unfold like a video game.

Cutting through the roar of the unhinged mob, an authori-tative voice: "THIS IS THE MAYOR OF NEWARK." There was a brief lull in the mayhem, mischief-makers calibrating their reaction to this attempted assertion of control. "ALL FANS RETURN TO YOUR SEATS IMMEDIATELY." But just as quickly, the noise level climbed, bedlam resumed, and although the mayor continued to assert his authority—"YOU ARE BRINGING SHAME ON THE CITY OF NEWARK! RETURN TO YOUR SEATS!"—the fans ignored him.

Dequan threw an arm around Jay and, shoving people out of their path, guided him toward the tunnel. When they were twenty feet from the entrance Jay felt a blow to his head as if someone had punched him. He wheeled and saw that one of the T-shirt bazooka marksmen had scored a direct hit with the weapon. Several security men wrestled him to the floor as he hooted in celebration. Dequan hustled Jay into the mouth of the tunnel. Through the din, he heard the agitated voice of his erstwhile ally continue to implore, "THIS IS THE MAYOR OF NEWARK, RETURN TO YOUR DAMN SEATS!"

Relieved the T-shirt had not further damaged his already broken nose but undone by the riot his presence caused, he waited with Boris in the security office until Bo McCants determined it was safe to leave the building. Jay was shaking, short of breath. It took several minutes for his pulse to slow, and he thought he might be having a coronary. Huddled in the claustrophobic room, he tried to get his bearings. Blood roared in his ears. There was the strange sensation of thinking he might begin to cry. It seemed as if the entire building had lost its collective mind. Where was the residual goodwill he had anticipated? Where was the collective memory of his generosity? Bo McCants stood at the door peering up and down the corridor. What was he waiting for? Finally—how long had they been stuck there?—he indicated that the time had come to move out.

A close formation of security guards surrounded Jay and escorted him toward the exit. They emerged from the building, and he was relieved to see only a smattering of people outside. The outdoor protest had ended, and in the brisk evening air, the scene appeared like any other game night. As a safety precaution, an additional detail of security men piled into a van and tailed the SUV as it ferried Jay into the city.

When Bo McCants's squad finally restored order at Sanitary Solutions Arena, over a hundred fans were ejected from the building. Police made twenty-seven arrests for disorderly conduct and public drunkenness. Jay was watching the local feed of the game with Boris on the large screen television in his apartment and, in what felt like an afterthought, saw the home team beat the Miami Heat 107-105, thereby qualifying for the NBA playoffs. Boris offered his congratulations, but Jay was not in a festive mood.

In the postgame wrap-up, rather than simply celebrate the twin accomplishments of knocking off a formidable foe and making it to the postseason, the announcers chose to discuss the melee that had occurred earlier.

The white play-by-play man, a career New York broadcaster named Al Klinger, declared, "The fans' behavior tonight was outrageous. Jay Gladstone's a decent guy."

Pro basketball games are usually broadcast by duos: The play-by-play announcer who describes the action as it's occurring and the "color" man who provides insights and analysis. The color man is often a former player and often, although not always, African-American, rendering the term "color man" unfortunate. Al Klinger's partner was Kenny Jamison, a former Chicago Bull. He was black. To Klinger's remark, Kenny Jamison responded, "You're so sure he's a decent guy?"

Jay sat wrapped in a bathrobe, a bowl of low-fat mint chip ice cream on his lap, and watched this unfold.

"I think he's a decent guy," the white announcer said. "You don't?" Jay could see Al suddenly wondering whether he should have asked his broadcast partner this particular question.

The pause that ensued while Kenny Jamison thought about what he might say was agonizing. Kenny Jamison was an employee of the home team. Kenny Jamison, technically speaking, worked for Jay Gladstone.

"You want my honest opinion?"

Kenny Jamison's employer, sitting in front of the television high in the Manhattan sky, paused the spoonful of ice cream that was halfway to his mouth, unsure how much he wanted to know the man's honest opinion.

Kenny Jamison: "I think it's complicated."

Complicated? String theory was complicated! Deciphering ancient runes was complicated! Jay Gladstone had uttered a few words that could have been interpreted by well-meaning people multiple ways and then publicly apologized! What was complicated about that?

Jay turned off the television. He did not want to hear that the quality of his character was "complicated." If he could fire Church Scott when the playoffs were over, could he fire Kenny Jamison, too? Of course not. He couldn't just get rid of everyone, make them take loyalty oaths, swear fealty to him.

"How is it possible that I have no black friends?"

"What about Church?"

"That backstabber?"

"He's in an impossible position."

"Don't defend him, Boris." Jay's tone did not invite a response.

Boris leaned back on the sofa, stretched his arms over his head. Jay put the ice cream down. It had lost its taste.

"Someone needs to start a business," Boris said. "Black friends for white liberals. Reduces black unemployment, erases white guilt. All credit cards accepted."

There was no laughter from Jay.

The men did not talk for the next several minutes, just remained together, each brooding about how dire the situation had become. Boris asked if Jay would be all right alone in the apartment. Upon receiving an affirmative response, he departed.

In bed, Jay wondered about the effects of the night's events. It was hard to believe only hours earlier he had stood at the center of a basketball court and been subjected to the jeers of the mob, many of whom could not confine their abuse to the verbal realm and had either hurled objects or tried to attack him physically. It was bizarre. Jay had from his earliest years fantasized what it was like to be on the court with the full attention of the crowd. But in his fantasy, he was much younger and wearing a basketball uniform, and the crowd he envisioned was an adoring one cheering his achievements. Reversal of the image from worship to denigration disrupted the circuitry. He knew there would be a backlash from what had happened with Dag, but he had not expected this. The model citizen who had led a sober life as an executive, civic leader, and—until recently—family man was now the target of free-ranging scorn that seemed to have come unstuck from its original cause and taken on a life of its own. But perhaps something positive might come from it, he reflected. Being the victim of public shaming on such a scale might create sympathy and reverse the trend that seemed to be taking hold. Or, would what had occurred only reinforce his role as a villain, validate the feelings of those inclined to be cruel, and permit them to give their disgust free rein?

And when would Dag emerge from the coma? Were that to happen, Jay could at least temporarily decrease the rate and frequency of his self-flagellation.

CHAPTER FORTY-FIVE

Late Saturday evening while Jay was watching the post-game broadcast with Boris, Imani Mayfield sat down at her dorm room desk, opened her laptop, and began to type. As a scholar and, in her view, a fair-minded woman, she took great pains to find the right tone. She wanted to condemn, but not destroy. Jay Gladstone's daughter was one of her closest friends. Should she mention that? No, it was irrelevant. But there would be no ad hominem attack. It took several drafts, and in the end, she was satisfied. The next morning everyone affiliated with Tate College, including the trustees (one of whom was Jay Gladstone), woke up to find the following email waiting for them:

From: Imani Mayfield, Tate College, '12
To: All members of the Tate College community
This email contains upsetting material so if you have been a victim of racism consider this a trigger warning.

I am writing to you as a student at Tate College and a progressive woman of color. Tate College has a long history of tolerance. It is a nexus of competing ideas and an incubator of challenging thought. But even at a place like Tate, some ideas are so unacceptable that their expression must be banned. As you may already know, Jay Gladstone has been invited to address the class of 2012 at our graduation in May. As a student, this was not a decision I approved of, but I believe in the free exchange of ideas, and despite his controversial record as a New York City landlord,

I did not raise my voice in protest. Now circumstances have changed, and today I respectfully call on all members of the college community, students, faculty, and staff, to join me in demanding the immediate withdrawal of this invitation.

Some of you may not be aware of the recent events that have led me to take this step: Gladstone was heard on a tape making a racially charged comment. If you haven't heard about the incident and want to read about it yourself to provide some context you can find stories on the Internet here: www.nytimes.com, here: www.espn.com, or here: www.gawker.com, and on lots of other sites. Here is what he said:

"Why does everyone in this family want to have sex with black people?"

I'm sorry to have to drop that in the middle of your computer screen, or your smartphone, or whatever device you're reading this on but that's how it is. With or without context, the comment is deeply hurtful and racist. If you don't know, Gladstone's wife was having sexual relations with one of his black male employees, and he caught them. I'm a human being. I feel for Jay Gladstone. But that does not diminish the harmfulness of what he said. While I wish my eyes could unsee his words, my eyes cannot unsee them. I will, however, offer an interpretation because this is the basis for my demand to withdraw the invitation to speak at graduation. Jay Gladstone's objectification of the black body has a long, ugly, and dangerous history in America. Since our ancestors arrived on these shores in chains, white folk, to put it mildly, have had a complex relationship with people of color. Make no mistake: Black bodies built this nation. Black bodies are worshipped in this nation. Black bodies are feared in this nation. Black bodies are rendered abstract, decoupled from their personhood, and sexualized. Jay Gladstone, through his hateful words, invokes the antebellum magnolias-in-the-moonlight slave-owning landscape of Mandingo, *a depraved world of delicate white folk whose respectability and decorum are vanquished by untamed black sexuality and the people of color who pay for that depravity with their lives. That original sin from which this nation is still recovering grew out of the white supremacist vision of men like Thomas Jefferson and Andrew Jackson, and Jay Gladstone is their heir. As a personification of white male privilege, he declares himself unfit to be a speaker on this campus.*

Please join me in calling the office of President Chapin at (845) 456-7395 or contacting him at Pres.Chapin@Tatecollege.edu and letting the man know that people like Jay Gladstone are not welcome at a place like Tate. The college must rescind the invitation to speak.

One love, Imani Mayfield

Jay blearily perused the email with his morning coffee, stomach migrating incrementally downward as he read. By the time he reached the end, he was wide-awake. Then he reread it. He was wounded and outraged. Although Imani's words were upsetting, they were to be expected considering the source. She had a score to settle with Jay. Her characterization of him was wildly off base, but enemies had caricatured him before, and as a landlord he was accustomed to being vilified. *No one ever compared me to Thomas Jefferson,* he reflected. *If my mother weren't senile, she'd be thrilled.* He expected this entreaty to ignite a prairie fire at the college that would burn until it consumed him. Had Aviva signed off on her friend's email? Had she co-written the thing? It had certainly been a bold stroke. Not only would the opportunity to speak there probably be denied as a result of what Imani had done, but his very presence at his daughter's graduation would also now be unwelcome. This situation horrified him. As sour as it was between them, Aviva was his only child, and he intended to watch her graduate from college.

It occurred to Jay that in the wake of her friend's missive Aviva might call or send him an email using Imani's to buttress her case. But he did not hear from her. After last night's events, the shift in his circumstances was unmistakable. He could endow a new science or humanities center, underwrite chairs in every department; none of it mattered now. Aviva's friend had checkmated him.

CHAPTER FORTY-SIX

The banks of the Hudson around Schuylkill are densely forested. Although the well-heeled have, since the 19th century, erected palaces along the swiftly flowing river, great swaths of the land remain undeveloped. Hickory, hemlock, and black birch soar over the primeval landscape, much of which continues to be unchanged from the time of the Algonquin. Over two centuries earlier, these woods were filled with British soldiers under the command of General Cornwallis attempting to rout the ragtag revolutionary troops led by the upstart George Washington. America was born, and the crack of martial gunfire was now heard only in the context of video games. More recently, for circumscribed periods each year, licensed sportsmen draped in orange reflective gear tracked through the area hoisting rifles and obliterating deer. But it was not hunting season, and as the sun winked above the treetops melting the frost that had formed overnight on the fallen branches and old leaves that carpeted the ground, four soldiers swarmed through the woods cradling weapons.

Aviva, Imani, and Noah were participating in an acting exercise devised by Axel that he had dubbed "full environmental immersion" and it consisted of the performer enacting the part he or she was playing in the actual context where the action depicted on stage occurred or, failing that, in the closest manageable approximation. In theory, this would allow the performer to draw on sense memories—the peaty smell of the woods, the crack of a twig snapping underfoot—acquired in the course of the exercise and use them to create a deeper, more evocative portrayal. Axel modeled this particular one on the military training devised by Field Marshall Cinque to prepare his followers in the Symbionese Liberation Army for taking over television studios, or power plants, or kidnapping heiresses. Their sneakers didn't make a sound as they stole through the woods.

They had gone out early to avoid running into anyone. Axel drove them in his truck and parked in front of an unoccupied summer home on a dirt road off the two-lane highway that ran parallel to the river about a mile from the east bank. After a brief safety lecture, he distributed the guns and they hiked into the woods.

Axel had attended a gun show and purchased two .22 caliber handguns and a pair of military rifles. Aviva and Imani cradled the rifles and the young men each gripped a pistol. Axel was comfortable with a weapon and handled it like he would any tool. But the others were not as relaxed at first and arranged themselves in poses inspired by films and television shows, taking care not to point the barrels at one another. Axel reprimanded them and reminded everyone that art and politics were serious business, and if anyone wanted to goof around, they could go home.

"This isn't like that bullshit in the West Bank," he said to Aviva. "This shit is real."

"How was that bullshit?" Noah said. "The IDF could've fucked her up."

"Yeah, but did they? No, they did not." Axel said. "They didn't even bother to show up. You guys had no firearms, there was no confrontation. It was all a big nothing."

"At least we were there," Aviva said as they continued to make their way along the path.

Axel just snorted.

To the east, a roiling bank of indigo clouds appeared over

the hills. The sun vanished and cast the toy soldiers in shadow. In the darkening woods, Axel ran them through a series of drills, dashing, crouching, maneuvering on their stomachs, drawing their weapons, aiming, pretending to fire. When Aviva stumbled and fell, he asked if she was all right. He showed Imani how to take her gun apart and put it back together. But when Noah questioned why they were doing a particular thing, Axel ordered him to shut up. Since what they were engaged in was essentially a form of play, Noah accepted his lesser role but expected Axel to not act like a dick. When their legs got tangled as they ran through a clearing, Axel shoved Noah, who went sprawling and cursed his friend.

"You could get us killed," Axel said.

"Dude, it's a game," Noah replied as he got up and brushed leaves off his clothes. A stray leaf stuck to his head and Imani plucked it off.

Aviva believed she had acquired all the sense memories necessary for her performance after five minutes but did not want to complain and be labeled a lightweight. It felt silly to be running around the woods waving guns as if they were Sandinistas or members of FARC. Only Axel seemed to be taking it seriously.

When they had been training for nearly an hour, Noah asked why Axel had loaded the guns if he didn't want anyone to shoot.

"Because people need to feel what it's like to hold power in their hands."

"I want to shoot," Aviva said.

Axel said: "So shoot."

Noah looked at Axel in surprise and asked why he was going to allow Aviva to fire her gun while he (Noah) was not permitted.

"Because Patty sprays her weapon, fool."

Axel had always dictated the terms of their friendship. He

led a wilder life, read more, agonized more. He was on his own in the world while Noah would graduate from college in a little over a month free to pursue his destiny with a manageable level of student debt. Because of this disparity, Noah didn't mind being patronized by him when they were alone, but it was unacceptable in the presence of Aviva and Imani.

"What the fuck are you doing?" Axel said.

Noah was pointing the pistol at him.

"Just seeing what power feels like."

"Put the gun down, fool." Noah kept pointing it at him. He narrowed an eye. Was he aiming? "I said put the motherfucking gun down. Lay it on the ground and step away from it." Noah did neither. Aviva watched them, unable to believe what she was seeing. These guys had been friends since freshman year. What damage was programmed into their DNA that made the threat of violence the wordless language of their gender?

"Drop the gun, Jewboy," Imani said. She was leveling her rifle at Noah's half black, half-Jewish dreadhead.

It started to drizzle.

Aviva stared at them in mute disbelief. She had never heard her friend use that word in conversation. Axel told Imani not to worry; he would handle this. She did not obey.

"Lower your weapon," Axel told her. He was oddly relaxed.

Imani looked at him as if he had asked her to whistle. "What? Why?"

"Just stand down, girl. I got this."

The intensity of the rain increased. To Aviva's relief, Imani tentatively lowered the barrel of the rifle. The situation was getting too weird. Axel addressed Noah: "How do you like the way power feels?"

"I like it, white boy," Noah said. "Let me see you drop your weapon."

"Why do you want me to do that?"

Noah said: "Drop the motherfucker."

When Axel's pistol landed on the moist forest floor, it barely made a sound. Aviva saw Imani catch Axel's eye with a look that asked if he wanted her to aim her gun at Noah again, but with a faint shake of his head, he indicated no. Rain angled down their faces.

Noah ordered Axel to step away from the gun. "And Imani, don't point that fucking thing at me."

Axel backed away from the gun on the ground. Aviva rushed forward and grabbed it.

Axel asked her: "Are you with him?"

"You're both acting like idiots," Aviva said. "Quit fucking around, Noah."

Ignoring Aviva, Noah said to Axel: "You're not a revolutionary, dude. You just play. What have you ever done? That story you tell about liberating the pig farm? Couldn't find it anywhere on the Internet. How do you explain that? An army of liberated pigs wandering the hills of Oregon and no mention anywhere? You're full of shit."

Aviva looked from one boy to the other, guns dangling at her side. Axel glanced toward the guns and then looked at Noah. Ten feet separated them. Then, he slowly walked toward the barrel of Noah's weapon.

"Shoot me," Axel said. "See what it feels like."

Noah had been holding the pistol perpendicular to the ground. Now he shifted his arm, and the angle changed to forty-five degrees.

Aviva could see his hand was trembling. Axel was five feet away.

She said: "Put the gun down, Noah."

He ignored her. Axel took another step. Aviva could not comprehend what she was seeing: Two blood-engorged rams butting heads in some parody of natural selection.

"I'm warning you, man," Noah said, but when Axel grabbed the gun from his hand, he did not resist. He seemed relieved and smiled stupidly. He said, "I was just playing," and gave a nervous laugh. But distress seized his features when Axel in one lightning motion pressed the barrel against Noah's temple.

A current of terror shot through Aviva, paralyzing her.

"Axel, what the fuck," Imani screamed.

"Never give up your weapon," Axel hissed. Noah closed his eyes, quaking.

Axel pulled the trigger and—nothing.

For a moment, no one said anything. Axel stepped away.

"You m-m-motherfucker," Noah stammered. The air had flown from his narrow body.

Aviva shoved Axel hard. "You're such an asshole!"

Axel did not respond to her admonishment. Instead, he jammed the pistol into his belt and said, "You think I'd give any of you clowns a loaded weapon?" Then he threw his head back and uncorked a whoop of laughter that rose to the treetops where it frightened the starlings roosting in the branches.

It was still raining when they marched out of the woods. Axel kept apologizing. Noah didn't want to hear it at first, but Axel called him an outlaw and a bad motherfucker, said he could shoot all he wanted, and they could even go to a gun range across the river that afternoon.

The bass and drum of thunder grumbled, and lightning strobe-lit the landscape.

"Follow me," Noah said and ran across the street toward a white Colonial with green shutters. Aviva and Imani looked at each other and trailed him, Axel in the rear. Noah appeared to have recovered from what happened earlier. Behind the house, a set of concrete steps led to the back door. Noah climbed the steps. The door had nine rectangular windowpanes. Aviva thought he was going to punch one of them out to let them in.

"Noah, don't," she said.

"Don't what?" There was a key under the doormat. "Do you want to stand out here and get soaked?"

Aviva considered his question. It was breaking and entering.

He inserted the key in the door, turned the knob, and stepped inside.

"This place is the shit," Imani said from the dining room.

"Who lives here?" Aviva asked. Having overcome her trepidation, she was looking around the kitchen.

"Some white-collar criminal," Noah said.

Aviva looked alarmed. "So, he could show up any minute?"

"He's only here in the summer," Noah assured her. "I did a little sleuthing. He works mostly in London."

Rain pelted the windows. Noah found a glass, filled it with water from the tap, and drank. He lit a joint while Axel rummaged through the cabinets. Noah offered Aviva the joint, but she declined. Axel took a hit.

Overhead Aviva could hear the faint sound of Imani's footsteps. They had stopped sleeping together. Aviva had told her she had been shouldering a lot of conflicting emotions and wanted to handle it alone. Imani had accepted this, said she had never really believed Aviva was gay and asked if Aviva was breaking up with her so she could fuck Axel. At the time Aviva wasn't sure if that was true, but after what had happened with the guns, she did not want to be Axel's lover.

Now she watched him searching for the sell-by date on a can of peaches. He had grown wilder from when they first met. She still found him charismatic, but now his behavior evoked the kind of guy who, just to be provocative, might hold a gun to a woman's head while he was inside her. His fearlessness appealed, but the less assertive Noah was more like someone she could see herself with as an adult. That was the thing: None of them seemed like adults, not Imani, or

Noah, or Axel. Aviva didn't seem like one to herself, and she was about to graduate from college. What she felt more than anything was puzzlement. Upset by the situation with her father, uncertain in her sexuality, and now the passive participant in a crime. It was disorienting to be standing in a house she had broken into. It was wrong, she knew, but the lawlessness excited her.

Axel opened the can of peaches. Imani entered the kitchen waving her phone and asked if any of them had seen the email she had blasted to everyone with a Tate College account. No one had checked his or her in-box that morning. Imani took a hit from the joint Noah offered. Then she read:

"I am writing to you as a student at Tate College and a progressive woman of color—"

Imani savored the text, relishing her performance, emphasizing words like *toxic*, and *depraved*, and *magnolias*. No one looked at Aviva, who tried to hide the shame lacerating her. The reading seemed to go on for a long time.

When Imani finished, Noah said, "That's brilliant."

"The writing's impressive," was Axel's comment.

Imani informed them that she had done a great deal of reading on the subject.

"How come you didn't show it to me before you sent it?" Aviva wanted to know.

Imani said, "I knew you might have a problem with it."

Aviva thought about defending her father. She had not spoken up on his behalf to anyone since the scandal occurred. What had he done, really, other than say a few words in a challenging situation that had become a Rorschach blot for whoever heard them? But people chose what team they were on, and she knew hers. Or at least she thought she did. These were her people, restless, empathic, champions of the downtrodden. But they didn't know her father as she did. It was one thing for her to criticize him, but it was entirely different when the world seemed bent on destroying the man. Jay Gladstone may have been an oblivious plutocrat, but he was hardly a personification of racist evil. He supported her endeavors, donated enormous sums to the right causes. Yet the terrible condition of the world was the result of the people that were in charge, and he was one of them.

It was difficult for her to choose whom to betray.

"My father might be a lot of things," Aviva said, "but he's not a racist."

"Why did he say that shit?" Noah asked.

"He was in a wonky situation and blurted out some words," Aviva said. "It sounds bad but now the whole world is on his ass, and it's not fair."

"The man's a stone racist," Imani said.

"Whether or not he's racist," Noah said, "he supports an economic system that continues to benefit from the exploitation of people of color, so yeah."

"He is not racist," Aviva repeated. To Imani: "You were in his house, and you sincerely believe my father is racist?"

"Hey, I get that he can't help it. He's a creature of the system."

"That is such bullshit," Aviva said. "He's a human being."

"You forget that he threw me out."

"Not because you're black."

"Why then?"

"Because you were rude."

"Well, you can take the girl out of Westchester," Imani said.

The women faced off. The degree of anger between them was new. Axel had been drinking peach juice from the can. He burped. "Hey, don't forget you two are on the same side. The empire wants us to destroy each other."

Aviva and Imani took Axel's interjection as an excuse to stand down.

"I defended you," Aviva said.

"Whatever," Imani said. Then: "Okay, I may have been a little rude."

Conflict temporarily defused.

Noah was looking at his phone. "There's a blast from the college president. Your dad's out. He's not speaking at commencement. It says he voluntarily withdrew."

The effects of the abuse her friends heaped on her father compromised the relief Aviva felt at this news. That he had not been sufficiently moved by his own daughter's request, yet had capitulated as a result of Imani's efforts was beyond Aviva's capacity to understand.

"I'm almost sorry the situation got resolved," Noah said. "It would've been fun to protest."

"Could've occupied the president's office," Imani said.

"Kidnapped him," Noah said.

"The college president?" Axel asked.

"Why not?" Noah said. "It'd be an epic prank, like something from the sixties."

"The American left is dead," Axel said, beating a favorite drum.

"You can still do it," Imani said. A deft ironist, her tone was indeterminate.

Noah said, "We can grab him at his house, get him over here, and keep him prisoner for just, like, a day. If we wore balaclavas, he'd never know it was us, and he'd be blindfolded anyway."

"Okay, that's stupid," Imani said, clarifying her position.

"You sound like you've thought about this," Aviva said.

"All we need is duct tape, rope, and a blanket," Noah said.

Was he serious? Aviva had no idea.

Axel slapped his palm on the counter. "You know who we should kidnap? Aviva's dad."

"That's even more stupid," Aviva said.

"No, listen," Axel said. "When the SLA kidnapped Patty

Hearst they got her father to donate, like, millions of dollars' worth of food to poor people in the Bay Area. What if we did that?"

"What, like, fake kidnap Aviva?" Noah said.

Aviva nearly shouted: "No one is fake kidnapping me!" They were all looking at her, and she experienced the creeping sensation that these friends, all of whom were from another social world, might suddenly determine she was a class enemy and turn on her. "How high are you guys?"

"Kushed out," Noah said, laughing.

"You could always fake kidnap me," Imani said. "For ransom, you might get a corn dog."

Aviva did not appreciate the stab at humor.

"No, no, no," Noah said. "We kidnap Aviva's dad, we hold him here, we make one of those hostage videos and get him to denounce racism."

Aviva said, "That's so beyond dumb, I don't even—"

"Why?" Imani asked.

"Well, first of all," Aviva said, "it's a major crime. Let's start with that. Then he's supposed to write a check and end world hunger?"

"Dude is a billionaire," Axel pointed out. On his tongue, it sounded like "child molester."

"He could do it," Noah said.

Aviva thought about her father's multiple homes, the enormity of the wealth he controlled, and she considered the toxicity of their last encounter. But kidnapping? Audacious, definitely, and exceedingly simpleminded.

"You guys should do it," she said. "I'll visit you in jail."

Noah began to giggle from the weed. He shook, doubled over as he envisioned the hilarity of this group of pranksters in jail. They waited for him to finish.

"Please do," he said with a long sigh as he regained control of his thin body.

"We can't do it without you," Axel said to Aviva. When she asked why they needed her help, he said: "Because he'll never press charges if you're part of it."

Aviva thought about her father and how he had mucked up her life by leaving her mother, by being unnecessarily wealthy, and—in her view—wanting her to be something other than what she was. Now, as a result of his increasingly baroque public difficulties, the problem had only intensified. She resented him for never being able to accept his imperfect, oversensitive, yearning daughter. That fate had bound them together was cruel. She was exhausted from being tarred with the Gladstone brush. Could she never escape this imposed identity? Children separated from parents, it was the natural order; and yet was there ever a real escape from the DNA bequeathed in the form of physical characteristics, psychological traits, all of the visible and invisible qualities that bind families? She was dying to break away, but the mystifying love Aviva felt for her father made the situation intractable.

"I'm not kidnapping my father."

"What about a bomb?" Axel said. They looked at him skeptically. Somehow, this seemed on a different order of magnitude from kidnapping. "You know, like the Weathermen."

Noah asked, "Who do you want to bomb?"

Axel reacted like it was a dim-witted question. "Well, we could destroy President Chapin's house for inviting Aviva's dad in the first place, or we could bomb Aviva's dad's house."

"Which one?" Imani asked.

Axel and Noah laughed. Aviva did not.

"You want to blow up my father?"

Axel said of course not, there was no way he wanted to blow anyone up, but some property destruction would make a statement. Aviva asked what that might be. His response: "Against racism."

"How would anyone know that?"

"We take a name like the People's Army Against Racism, call the media from one of those phones drug dealers use, and we're the reincarnation of Baader-Meinhof."

Noah asked, "Do you know how to build a bomb?"

"We liberated that pig farm in Oregon with bombs."

"The one I couldn't find any mention of on the Internet."

"You don't believe me?"

Aviva's eyes darted back and forth. She hoped they wouldn't point guns at each other again.

Noah said, "Axel, I'm only saying that if it happened—"

"If it happened, what? There are things the government suppresses, Noah. Information they don't want you to know."

All the testosterone had become tiresome. But there was something about exploding a bomb that was a declaration, as long as no one got hurt. Aviva thought about the house in Bedford, where she had lived full-time until her parents' divorce. The basketball court that her father built for her despite her indifference to the game. The horses she had no interest in riding. Walking to the swimming pool, her uneven gait serving as a reminder with each step she took that she did not conform to his idea of perfection. To blow a hole in all of it would be—would be what? She caught herself. A bomb? It was ludicrous. Playacting. Posturing. Aviva listened as her friends continued their gabbing, confident the dialogue would exhaust itself.

They talked about explosives, the variety, their relative ease of assembly, whether people would be sympathetic to their cause if they blew something up, had bombs ever been an efficient way to blah blah blah. Aviva pretended to be excited by the idea of direct action but had no intention of following through. After listening to the conversation, Imani tempered her eagerness. Noah implied he didn't believe the others were up to it anyway so what were they even talking about, but Axel's desire for a dramatic gesture seemed to grow.

The downpour had stopped. In the western sky, sunlight spilled from a fissure in the clouds. When they left the house after an hour, the one thing they agreed on was that if racism was going to be defeated, something must be done.

CHAPTER FORTY-SEVEN

L ate Sunday afternoon, Jay received a phone call from the commissioner of the league. A man both affable and indomitable, he had ruled his fiefdom smoothly for several decades, navigating a middle path between the owners and players that led both groups to feel he was secretly in the pocket of the other. He was sickened by what happened at Sanitary Solutions Arena the previous evening and expressed his desire for those who created the disturbance to be prosecuted and banned from further attendance at games. The commissioner asked: Are you doing okay, Jay? The commissioner remarked: No one should have to endure this. The commissioner wondered: Would you mind coming to the league offices first thing on Monday morning to talk about damage control?

At last, Jay thought, someone not just piling on but looking for ways to ameliorate the situation. He went to bed that night despondent over what he had done to Dag, disappointed that he had not heard from Aviva in the wake of his withdrawal from the commencement, but secure in his alliance with the man who governed professional basketball.

Because the disturbance at the Miami game occurred too late in the day to make the Sunday morning papers, the Monday editions made up for it with extensive accounts of the mayhem. *GLADSTONE BOMBARDMENT!* shrieked the *New York Post* above a picture of Jay beneath a barrage of flying T-shirts. The *New York Times* reported: *Fans Express Rage*

Toward Owner Prior to Victory. A columnist for the *Daily News* opined: While what Gladstone said was undeniably racist, it would behoove the fans to express themselves in a more civilized way.

Undeniably racist? Jay nearly choked when he read that. His family foundation handed out Gladstone Scholarships to black kids like candy and now his "racism" was undeniable? Today he was having lunch with Bobby Tackman at his club. He hoped Tackman had some idea how to unwind the narrative that had taken hold.

It was with this in mind that Jay rode the elevator to the League offices. He had informed Dequan he did not need a bodyguard today. In the elevator with him were a man and a woman, both in business dress. Neither acknowledged his presence. Jay was the first to get off, and when the door closed behind him, he imagined the two strangers were bonding over their ride with New York's latest public enemy and saying disparaging things about him. The receptionist, a young black woman he recognized from a recent visit, offered a terse greeting. He suspected she was sitting in judgment.

She alerted the commissioner's office to Jay's arrival. Jay waited for the woman to wave him back, but she told him to take a seat. "They'll let me know when they're ready for you." The head of the league was going to keep him waiting. That had never happened. He sank into a couch and pulled out his phone to see if there was any news from the Planning Commission about the Sapphire. His chief operating officer had told him they expected to get the approval to break ground in the fall, but there was still no word. The elevator doors opened, and two league attorneys emerged. Trim and athletic, they glanced at Jay but said nothing. The receptionist buzzed them in. Jay continued to wait. A minute later the elevator door opened again, and a middle-aged black man emerged. Jay recognized him as a veteran referee, someone he had watched call many games from his courtside seats. The man walked to the receptionist's desk, gave his name, and sat down in the waiting area across from Jay where he picked up a magazine and began to leaf through it. Jay waited to see whether the ref would express sympathy about what had happened to him at Sanitary Solutions Arena, or even deign to greet him. When he did neither, Jay said, "How are you?" The man looked up from the magazine and grunted a greeting but said nothing. Their respective places on the social food chain would have ordinarily demanded obeisance on the part of the game official toward the owner, but recent events had jumbled that equation. The receptionist called the referee's name and said he could go back. Ten more minutes crawled by before she told Jay they were ready for him.

"Sorry we made you wait," the commissioner said.

They were in the conference room seated at a large oval table surrounded by twelve chairs. Jay sat on one side of the table, the commissioner across from him flanked by the deputy commissioner, a bald white man in his forties, and the chief counsel, a white woman with a brunette bob, also in her forties. Though they were both highly competent professionals, Jay considered them cogs in the league machine. The commissioner had held his position for nearly a quarter of a century. An avuncular man, he had a tanned face with prominent features and an impressive head of graying hair. He looked well-rested. With a forefinger, he pushed his gold-framed glasses back on the bridge of his nose.

"Saturday night was regrettable." His voice a purr.

"Terrifying," Jay said.

"It must have been. How are you feeling?"

"I've been better." He hoped the smidgen of pathos in his voice would engender compassion that he could use to his advantage. The deputy commissioner and the chief counsel made sympathetic noises. Jay ignored them. He noticed that the chief counsel had a manila folder in front of her.

The Commissioner: "What about D'Angelo?"

"I have the best doctors in the world monitoring his condition."

Jay hoped that the commissioner had a plan to extract him from the thicket in which he found himself. The two had always enjoyed good relations, chatted at league meetings, had played several rounds of golf together at league-sponsored charity events. Jay even invited the commissioner to go horseback riding with him—"Jews ride horses?" the commissioner (who was Jewish) had asked with mock surprise—and although he had not yet taken Jay up on his offer, the leader of the NBA had made it clear that it was only a matter of time before they saddled up together. So, the two men were friendly, if not exactly friends. Jay had heard that the commissioner's parents spoke Yiddish at home, and since the entire world seemed to be in the process of retreating to the ethnic categories from which they issued, he was not above trying to connect on a tribal level.

"Honestly, this whole *megilla* feels like a lot of *tsuris* for *bupkis*."

From the blank stares of the lieutenants and the Commissioner's phlegmatic expression, Jay realized he had overreached. He wanted to pluck the ill-timed Yiddish out of the air and cram it back down his throat. All of a sudden, he was channeling a Catskills *tummler*? From what hidden closet had Jay pulled the Jew-face?

"Let me cut right to the chase," the commissioner said. "I talked with Church Scott last night, and he told me about the potential for a player boycott."

"The players are young men," Jay said. "They're emotional."

"The playoffs start this weekend," the commissioner reminded him.

"I know," Jay said. "We qualified." A smile creased his face. The lieutenants offered congratulations. He nodded in acknowledgment.

"Church informed me that if you don't sell the team, the players aren't going to suit up."

Before Jay could respond, the general counsel said, "Here's how it would work: You put the team in a temporary trust—"

Jay interrupted her: "Whoa, whoa, whoa. I'm not selling the team."

"Just a minute," the commissioner said. "Hear us out. Ultimately, it's your decision, of course."

Jay thought about getting up and leaving but realized a display of petulance would accomplish nothing. He needed the league on his side. He angled his head at the general counsel to indicate she should continue.

"Once the team is in a trust, the league will take over the day-to-day operations. It's what we did with the New Orleans franchise, so there's already a precedent for this."

"Then I sell the team to the highest bidder?"

"We already have someone in mind," the commissioner said. "He's Russian, and I think we can get you one point five billion, maybe a little more. You paid eight hundred million a few years ago, so you'd make half a billion dollars. That's a lot of rubles." The commissioner laughed, as did his accomplices. All of them looked at Jay as if he should pick up the cue and laugh with them. Ruble was a funny word in this context and at least worth a chuckle, wasn't it?

"I'm never going to agree to that," Jay said. "You can't force me to sell. I'll tie you up in court for years."

The commissioner did not immediately respond. The others didn't dare speak. To Jay, this was a kangaroo court and he was not going to submit. He waited.

The commissioner assumed an expression of strained patience. "The playoffs are the most important part of our season," he pointed out. "Your league partners need your team on the court. We have a television deal that I intend to honor."

"I know all about the television deal," Jay said. "I helped negotiate it."

"Then you know we have to play the games," the deputy commissioner said.

Jay looked at him askance: "You're allowed to talk?" Jay meant it jocularly, but the edge in his voice made it read like the insult it was.

"Occasionally," the deputy said, glancing at his boss who did not react.

"I'm going to talk to Church, and then I'll talk to the players," Jay said. "I'll take care of it. My team is going to be on the court this weekend."

"I hope you're right," the commissioner said. "But Jay, don't take it the wrong way because it's not personal, but if we don't resolve this by the end of the week, the league is prepared to go to federal court to get an injunction forcing you to at least temporarily surrender control of the franchise."

The general counsel opened her folder, removed a document, and slid it across the table. "This is a brief outline of what we have in mind," she said. "You should let your attorney take a look at it."

Jay ignored the document. "I always had great respect for you," he said to the commissioner. "Because you had the spine to stand up to the players and the owners. But the mob starts braying, and you're prepared to sell me down the river?"

The commissioner and his team stared at him. No one said anything. The deputy commissioner ended the standoff when he said:

"You realize that selling someone down the river refers to slavery, right?"

Jay exhaled in exasperation. Would his torments never cease?

"It hadn't occurred to me."

The deputy said, "I would advise you not to use that image if you're going to be doing interviews."

Jay wanted to smack him.

The general counsel raised her hand to her mouth to hide that she was smiling. Jay noticed her reaction. "Yes, this is hilarious," he said. "A man's life is being destroyed."

Her grin vanished.

Jay pushed away from the table and got out of his chair. He wanted to calibrate his words with the greatest precision:

"This is a travesty. You are dictatorially adjudicating this matter without the due process that I'm entitled to, and I'm not going to let you do it."

As he stalked out of the room, the commissioner implored, "Try to understand our position," but Jay was no longer listening.

The Fifth Avenue sidewalk panorama looked like it did every weekday morning: men and women in business attire hustling to offices, tourists examining guidebooks and craning their necks, people charging in all directions. Yet to Jay, it seemed different because his relationship to all of it had changed. He wore a baseball cap and sunglasses, and no one paid attention to him. Telling Dequan his bodyguard services were not required today looked like the right idea. That would've attracted *more* notice. From the sidewalk, Jay called Church Scott. His call went to voice mail, and he left a message saying he intended to come to the team's practice facility today to talk with the players. If he could speak to them directly, he knew they would see reason. They were young athletes. From what he knew, most of them were not political. He would appeal to them on a human level, talk about his philanthropy, his lifelong love of basketball. They would see reason.

He pulled the brim of his cap lower and began walking to the Paladin Club for his lunch with Bobby Tackman.

Five minutes later his phone vibrated. Church Scott was returning his call. The players were in open rebellion, Church reported. There were ten black men and two white men on the active roster, and every one of them was in agreement. The players had made it clear that as long as Jay Gladstone owned the team, they would refuse to take the court. Jay tried to hide his incredulity. They were professionals. They had contracts. How could these young men be so completely unreasonable? When Jay asked if it would be helpful for him to address the team, Church said, "No, no, no, that would only inflame the situation. If they hear you're coming to practice, they'll all get in their cars and go home."

"They won't even listen?"

"Not now," Church said.

Jay asked when he thought that might change. Church told him not to hold his breath.

The city howled in his ears. He hung up and quickened his pace.

Jay was early to his lunch appointment, and while he waited for the crisis specialist to appear, he found an obscure corner of the club in which to sit and phoned Herman Doomer. When he reported what had occurred at the league offices Doomer was not surprised. "We're living a different climate today," the lawyer said. "People are unforgiving." In no mood for a philosophical disquisition, Jay asked what kind of legal challenge they could mount. "If the league files an injunction against you, we can challenge it, but it's a steep climb. The judge will weigh the interests of all the other owners against yours, and it's hard to see how we can get a favorable ruling given the imminence of the playoffs." Jay cursed under his breath. "That might be the least bad piece of news I'm going to give you on this phone call," Doomer said.

"What are you talking about?"

"I heard from Christine Lupo's office today. They're going to charge you with a hate crime."

What the lawyer told him was incomprehensible.

"A hate crime? Herman, it was an accident."

"Those words cast the whole business in a racial light, unfortunately. Maybe we can get them to drop it eventually, but it's going to be part of a larger negotiation."

"This has no basis in reality. It's illogical!"

"Not from their point of view. The more the DA's office piles on, the thinking goes, the greater chance that we'll negotiate to avoid a trial."

"I am not negotiating."

Doomer agreed that they should try and resolve the situation with the league and preserve Jay's ownership position. The attorney asked if he wanted to proceed with the attempt to temporarily remove Franklin from the business but Jay balked at taking that step. There were too many other things to address this week. Dealing with Franklin could wait.

CHAPTER FORTY-EIGHT

J ay had not been to his club since the accident. He absently picked at his poached salmon as he withstood the gale force of Bobby Tackman's storm: "What did you think would happen when you stepped out on that court in front of all those people after you ran over their hero with your car? Why did you hire me if you're going to go off half-baked and do whatever you want? I nearly called you that night and resigned. The clients I'm able to benefit are the ones who listen."

Tackman had not touched his tuna melt.

After the meeting at the league office, Jay's insides were in an uproar. He had said hello to the club manager upon his arrival, and Jean-Pierre looked at him strangely, as if he wanted to say something but could not quite bring himself to do it. None of the other diners had called out to him as he made his way to the table—Jay believed they wanted to give him privacy. Now, this onslaught from the garrulous consultant was intensifying his already foul mood. Wasn't it his job to be the dispassionate one? As Tackman continued to enumerate the ways the misadventure at the arena had made his job infinitely more challenging, Jay fought the urge to sack him on the spot. But he had dug a China-sized hole and the man's services were required for him to climb out of it, so instead he listened and stewed.

Tackman had concluded that Anderson Cooper offered the best platform from which to embark on what he referred to as "your apology tour." He was friendly with the popular television host and thought Cooper's ability to apprehend events in a nuanced manner would render him at least somewhat sensitive to Jay's plight.

"What if he asks me about the accident?"

"I spoke with your lawyer about this. It's his opinion that you insist what happened was entirely unintentional, and that on the advice of counsel you cannot say anything else. But you want the interviewer to ask the question. You can emphasize that it was an accident, one which you deeply regret, and will haunt you until—choose your time frame."

"Forever."

"Forever works. And once you've got that out of the way, what you want to do is apologize to everyone, to Dag and Dag's family, the basketball community, the black community, and this is the most important apology of all: To everyone I have hurt."

"To everyone I have hurt?"

"Do you have a problem with that? It's essential."

For someone whose guiding principle was simply to be a moral actor, the idea of apologizing to "everyone I have hurt" was unspeakable. In a religious studies class, Jay had learned about the Jains, a group in India whose members swept the path in front of them with a broom as they walked so as not to harm any form of life with their feet. While Jay knew he was no Jain, the idea that he had hurt people on a scale this apology would imply was an assault on his core identity. Yet there it was. His version of accepting responsibility had resulted in a barrage of projectiles aimed in his direction. He had no choice but to trust Tackman, who, taking a break from his peroration, was finally forking a bite of the tuna melt into his mouth.

"You have to understand, Jay, we're living in a different time." Tackman took a sip of his tomato juice and grew thoughtful. "No one cares about the tragedies of kings. Those days are gone. Now, it's all about who's the most aggrieved, who can whine the loudest. Heaven forbid someone like you has a complaint. It's not allowed. No one is interested in your story anymore. It's the Time of the Victim, and you are in no shape or form a victim. You know what else you're not? A protagonist. You, old chum, are the villain in this tale. Our job is to make you the protagonist."

Jay knew this, but to hear it spoken aloud was unnerving.

"You go on CNN Wednesday, the first playoff game is Sunday, right? If the interview goes well, I think you'll get a reprieve from the league. Maybe you don't have to sell the team."

The idea that going on television with Anderson Cooper might lead to a "reprieve"—and whatever form it took had to be better than what was happening now—lightened the crushing weight Jay felt. He surveyed the bustling dining room. Well-dressed men and women having lunch, they talked, they gestured, their voices rising in a pleasing din. Jean-Pierre greeted the diners. A waiter circulated with a dessert cart. An ordinary day, one in which Jay would have table-hopped. There was a network head having lunch with the president of a prominent advertising agency. And wasn't that the woman who ran the Rockefeller Foundation? He would say hello on the way out, shake some hands, pat a few backs. Surely these people, his people, knew what had happened to him at Sanitary Solutions Arena. Surely, they would want to offer their sympathy.

Jay was only able to finish half his lunch. He signaled for the waiter to remove his plate.

"I've withdrawn from speaking at the Tate College commencement."

Tackman finished chewing what was in his mouth, took a drink of water. "Giving a speech at a liberal arts college was a terrible idea. Frankly, I don't know what you were thinking."

While they drank coffee, Tackman mentioned that he was

still working on arranging an invitation for Jay to speak at the Abyssinian Baptist Church in Harlem. The minister was open to the idea, but apparently several of the deacons were opposed. In the meantime, Jay should keep a low profile and not do anything in public that might draw attention.

Managed seclusion. This time Jay would listen.

"If you do well with Anderson, maybe you won't have to do anything else."

That did not sound likely. Penance involved more than getting your passport back into polite society stamped during a television appearance with Anderson Cooper. But he appreciated any words of encouragement. He signed the bill and walked Tackman out of the dining room, intending to return and greet several acquaintances. But while he stood with his guest at the coat check stand, Jean-Pierre pulled him aside. Jay expected some buck-up-we're-all-behind-you words from the club's manager and jauntily waved to the departing Tackman.

"Several members have spoken to me, Mr. Gladstone," Jean-Pierre began. "Please understand this is not my personal opinion." The club manager paused. This task was causing him considerable discomfort. The pause got a little longer.

"What is it?"

"They believe that perhaps it is best for you to not come to the club now."

Jay's mind raced as he tried to figure out who could be behind this. As far as he knew, he had no enemies at the club. Members of several other real estate families belonged, but they were friendly rivals. It battered his already wounded psyche to learn that hidden antagonists now threatened the one place he considered a refuge from what had befallen him. He had been a member for over thirty years.

"Who said this?"

"I can't say. You understand."

"No, Jean-Pierre, I don't understand at all." Jay tried to keep his voice from rising. A man Jay knew walked toward the dining room without acknowledging him. "I'm being blackballed?"

"Not blackballed, Mr. Gladstone. But we have African-American members."

"That's who's complaining? I'll talk to them."

"No, please," Jean-Pierre said. "The African-American members are not complaining. The people who have brought this to my attention are white. Please understand my position. A club is a friendly place. The executive committee is meeting to discuss it tonight."

Jay thanked Jean-Pierre for notifying him and said he would think about whether to stay away but knew he only said that to save face. When this whole tornado subsided, he would return and quietly find out who was conspiring against him. He chose to forgo the dining room handshakes and schmoozing and walk to the office. Perhaps there would be news on the fate of the Sapphire.

As Jay walked east he began to experience an oddly claustrophobic sensation. There were too many people on the sidewalks. The sky he glimpsed between buildings looked like bars of cobalt. The temperature had dropped, and the wind had picked up. Wearing the baseball cap and sunglasses, Jay nestled into his coat as he walked to the office and tried to shake off the feeling. He had appeared on the local news several times talking to field correspondents and had been on Charlie Rose with two other real estate magnates to discuss urban development. He keenly anticipated the chance to make his case later in the week.

When he rounded the corner, and began walking south on Park Avenue, he saw the demonstrators in front of the building. Imam Ibrahim Muhammad was leading a group of about forty of them chanting: *Hey, hey, ho, ho, we'll be here till Gladstone goes!*

They were a mixture of black, white, and Latino, men and

women, mostly young. Several bored-looking police officers stood to the side and watched. Sawhorses had been placed on the sidewalk to circumscribe the movements of the group, who paraded in a circle with the imam in the center shouting into a bullhorn. Reflexively, Jay retraced his steps around the corner and paused at the side of the building where he would be out of sight.

It was an ordinary day on Park Avenue. Workers tended the flowerbeds in the median in front of the building. Well-dressed pedestrians ambled along the sidewalks. Jay was not sure he should try to run the hostile gauntlet without Dequan at his side. He already knew the speed with which people's condemnation could manifest in physical violence. He heard Tackman's voice telling him to keep a low profile and not do anything public. Was this public, the space in front of an office building his family owned? Unfortunately, he concluded, it was. As people passed him on the sidewalk, he faced the building and looked at his phone, so it wouldn't appear to anyone who glanced in his direction that he was just standing there.

The crackle of the bullhorn, the shouts of the pack, bored into his skull. His hand reflexively traveled to his nose. These people could attack and get him on the ground before the police restored order. Who knew what harm they could do? He needed to reach his office if for no other reason than to be in an environment with people who were on his side.

The protestors maintained their rhythmic chant. Pedestrians walked past the hubbub, most of them barely glancing at it, another obstacle to be navigated in the course of a city day. Jay realized he could not remain where he was. He either had to force his way into the building or gain access through a service entrance. He could not bear the thought of sneaking into a property his family owned, but neither could he see barreling through the demonstrators to get to the lobby.

Cautiously, Jay stepped around the corner to reassess the

scene. As the imam led the chant, he thrust his fist into the air. To Jay, it felt like each thrust was punching him. Boom! To the body! Boom! To the chops! His nose still delicate, Jay had no appetite for confrontation. Once again, he thought about what had occurred at the arena, turned around, and began walking north on Park Avenue.

"Gladstone!" a voice shouted. Someone had spotted him. Another: "That's him!"

Jay glanced over his shoulder to see several of the demonstrators had broken from the circle and were running in his direction chased by a collection of slow-footed cops. Jay broke into what he hoped would be a run, but it had been years, and he instantly felt his left hamstring scream in protest. In seconds, they caught up. Several demonstrators encircled him, shouting insults. They were black, and white, and both genders, and although none of them laid a hand on him, their anger was blistering. Jay turned this way and that but they had blocked his egress. Sweat broke out on his forehead.

He shouted: "What do you people want?"

A white man wearing a knit Rastafarian hat said, "You people?"

"Racist motherfucker," from a black woman in oversized sunglasses.

The cops shoved the demonstrators away from Jay. A Latino officer whose name tag read Ortiz asked Jay if he was all right. Jay nodded and requested an escort into the building.

Officer Ortiz rode up in the elevator with Jay to make sure he got to the office safely.

"Is that protest lawful?" Jay asked.

"Some judge gave them a permit," Ortiz said. *On a Monday morning?* That judge, Jay reflected, must want to destroy me.

Jay's effort to reach Mayor Bloomberg resulted in an exchange with a deputy. "The permit," he carped, "was probably issued by some rogue judge, and I want it revoked."

The deputy assured him he would look into it. This did not satisfy Jay who insisted that his friend "Mike" call him back as soon as possible and to punctuate his displeasure slammed the phone into the cradle. He then retreated to the couch and assumed the prone position Bebe found him in a few minutes later.

"Maybe you shouldn't come into work for a few days," Bebe suggested.

"I should let this goddamn imam chase me away?"

"That's not what I'm saying."

To be pursued by a mob up Park Avenue and have to be once again rescued had taken a baleful toll. He glanced at the model of the Sapphire, its exquisite geometry a reliable source of serenity. Today it seemed nothing more than a meaningless agglomeration of cardboard, wood, and paste. There had still been no word from the Planning Commission, further curdling his mood. But he didn't want Bebe to see him in this condition, so he roused himself, sat up, and briefed her on his meeting with the commissioner and the upcoming television interview. He predicted they would shortly receive the approval for the Sapphire. He asked about their mother, who he had not seen since the Seder. Jay's relationship with his sister comforted him and helped to render the chaos manageable. When it was just the two of them alone, high in their steel tower, the world was more logical, pliant, and forgiving. Still, what she said next surprised him:

"I'm going to that fundraiser Franklin is hosting for Christine Lupo tonight."

"He invited me, too, but it might be problematic if I went," Jay said, which made his sister laugh.

"I'm going so I can size up your adversary."

"Can you believe that conniving worm is holding an event for her in his home?"

"In fairness, he was cultivating her before."

"Don't defend him.

"I'm going to see if I can get her to drop the indictment."

Now it was Jay's turn to laugh. Bebe promised to share her impressions of Christine Lupo the next day.

Alone at his desk, Jay turned on his computer. A casual perusal of the Internet was all Jay needed to understand the degree to which he had damaged himself. Only right-wing sites defended him. There he was a "victim," a "hero," a "sacrificial lamb." He ventured into one comments section and was treated to the usual invective, which he read out of sheer perversity but quickly fled when it seemed as if the level of vitriol that bleached the screen would cause his eyes to melt. Hundreds of ordinary citizens had somehow accessed his private email, and although a few people offered words of support, waves of animosity drowned out their voices. The cumulative effect left him physically weakened. Jay returned to the sofa where he curled up on his side, drew his knees up, and waited for the pounding in his head to subside.

Mayor Bloomberg did not return Jay's phone call but several hours later the protesters dispersed and Jay, accompanied once again by security guards, was able to leave the building without incident. A car service brought him to his apartment, and again there was a crowd carrying signs in front. Jay slumped in his seat. Rather than get out, Jay told the driver to cruise slowly past. These people were not there to protest his attitudes or his right to exist. The Service Employees International Union was on strike.

Jay was on the ropes and Gus Breeze, the union leader whose corruption he had threatened to expose, had decided to take advantage of the opportunity and pummel him. Breeze was daring Jay to call him out.

He told the driver to take him to Bedford.

CHAPTER FORTY-NINE

The weekend had been taxing for Nicole. She spent most of it holed up in the hotel suite frantically trying to figure out who had hacked her. She still had no idea. Her friend Audrey called on Saturday to commiserate and invite her to Nantucket, but Nicole declined. She felt safer in the city. As far as Nicole's vague plan to somehow repair her marriage, the release of the tape rendered the degree of difficulty nearly insurmountable. Not only was it humiliating for all the obvious reasons, but she had inadvertently added another layer of stress to Jay's life, and knew her chances of getting him to reverse his decision existed in inverse proportion to his anxiety. She surmised it was still DEFCON 4 in her husband's head. She wanted to talk with him but not enough time had passed. Yesterday afternoon she contacted Bebe. To Nicole's relief, Bebe did not sound angry on the phone, nor was her affect in any way chilly. Jay's sister made sympathetic noises and when Nicole asked if her sister-in-law would join her for a drink after work the next day Bebe was game.

They met at the Oak Room in the Plaza Hotel. Nicole was in a corner, nibbling mixed nuts, nursing a glass of chardonnay. Bebe sat down and ordered a vodka martini. Nicole thanked her profusely for coming, a crumpled a cocktail napkin in her hand. Nerves. When Bebe asked how she was doing Nicole looked down, shook her head, and moaned. She put the napkin on the table and with and proceeded to smooth it out. It was around six, and the bar was starting to fill up with after-work pleasure seekers and several tables of tourists. The waiter placed Bebe's drink in front of her, glanced at Nicole—did he recognize her? She hoped not— and departed. Bebe took a sip and gazed into Nicole's watery eyes.

"What possessed you to make a tape?"

"I was drunk; it was idiotic. I was mad at your brother."

"You were going to show it to him?"

"No. I don't know. I wish I could unwind everything." She told Bebe about their fight before he left for Africa, her desire to have a child, his unwillingness, and her resentment. "I keep telling myself I'm going to call my therapist who I haven't talked to in five years, but I don't want him to judge me."

"He's a therapist. They're not allowed to judge you." One of the many reasons social success accrued to Nicole was because she exuded a potent mixture of refinement and aplomb that captivated men and women alike. She operated in a matrix of hints and signals. Her default mode was one of sur- passing subtlety, but with the decision to take Dag to bed she had precluded that approach and the luxury of indirection was no longer hers. Too much was slipping away too quickly.

"Who do you think put that tape out there?"

"You're asking me?" Bebe said. "How would I know? I have no idea."

Nicole was at a loss. "I might as well ask the waiter."

Bebe studied the martini.

"How can I help?"

"Talk to Jay," Nicole suggested.

"And say what?"

"I love him, I'm horrified by my behavior, and I'll do any- thing to get him back."

"I'm not sure he's going to be receptive to that message right now, but when I talk to him next I'll try to figure out what he's thinking, and if it's appropriate, I'll say something. All right?"

Nicole effusively expressed her gratitude. Bebe told her she had to get going. Franklin had invited her to a fundraiser for Christine Lupo, and because she enjoyed harassing her cousin, and wanted to take the measure of the woman who was prosecuting her brother, she could not resist.

"Wait a minute," Nicole said. "Franklin is hosting her in his home? Why would he do that?"

"To be fair, I think he arranged this before Jay's—" Bebe searched for the right word—"setback happened."

"Franklin should have canceled the event," Nicole said.

"Franklin," Bebe said, "should have done a lot of things."

When the waiter brought the check, Nicole took it and placed a credit card on the table. She began to say something, hesitated, then asked, "Do you think Franklin would mind if I came with you?"

"Probably."

A look of concern clouded Nicole's worn face. Continually recalibrating her social position was exhausting and, given its downward trajectory, destabilizing.

"You really think he'd have a problem?"

"Yes," Bebe said. "Which is why you're going to be my date."

The Statue of Liberty set against the velvet jewel box lining of New York Harbor at night never failed to move Christine. She stood at the window of a Tribeca penthouse in a guest bedroom having gone there to take a phone call from her daughter, who had a question about homework. Christine remembered when her parents brought her downtown as a small child, how they pointed to Ellis Island, the portal through which her grandparents passed on their journey from Italy to the Bronx. She remembered standing on the docks for the bicentennial celebrations, July 4th, 1976, captivated by the sight of the tall ships sailing upriver as bouquets of fireworks burst overhead, tendrils of light illuminating the New York and New Jersey shorelines. Recalled bringing her children down here to see the display on a more recent July 4th, and how she had told Dominic Jr. and Lucia they were all part of a chain and that one day they would bring their children to watch the celebration in the harbor. Her relationship with Dominic Jr. had deteriorated since he discovered what she had done to his T-shirt, but he would get over it. Mothers and sons found each other in the end.

Perhaps she would stage a photo op for her campaign on Liberty Island, one mighty, torch-wielding woman in the shadow of another. A link with history, an image for tomorrow. Her immigrant grandparents could not in their wildest imaginings have conceived that their granddaughter might rise from Arthur Avenue to become the Governor of New York.

The idea of charging Jay Gladstone with a hate crime was Lou Pagano's, but this didn't matter because, as District Attorney of Westchester County, she would get the credit. It was a bold move that would demonstrate her credentials as a crusader against racism and generate support in the black community (plummeting since the nonindictment of Russell Plesko) while doing nothing to antagonize law enforcement. It was an elegant legal maneuver that was sure to pay political dividends. But the decision to add the charge to the indictment had not been arrived at easily. Pagano called her at home on Sunday and was surprised she had not immediately agreed but instead had asked for time to think about it. To charge Jay Gladstone with a hate crime was to raise the stakes considerably. The bar for proof was high, but it could serve as a useful bargaining chip, should he decide to accept a deal. More important, it would send a signal to voters that she was sensitive enough in matters of race to bring the weightiest charges against one of New York's ruling elite.

Again, she called Franklin Gladstone. Now that they were about to augment the original indictment with a charge that would immeasurably compound its severity, she felt the need to at least mention it as a courtesy so her patron would not be caught off guard when he heard about it. Franklin told her not to worry and expressed his admiration for her integrity.

To Christine's pleasure, the hate crime charges had led the local news that evening. She noted with no little satisfaction that Imam Ibrahim Muhammad had called a well-attended press conference during which he commented that while the Westchester County District Attorney's office should have brought charges against the officer who killed John Eagle, the new ones against Jay Gladstone were "a positive step in her relations with African-Americans."

All of this was going through her mind as she tore herself away from the view to greet the guests at the fundraiser Franklin and Marcy Gladstone were hosting for her gubernatorial candidacy. From the other room came the restless sound of money.

Despite the retention of a prominent interior design team, Franklin and Marcy had expensively decorated their penthouse loft in no particular style. The gathering of more than a hundred that filled the living room and spilled out on to the deck was a glittering portrait of achievement. A smattering of media people gathered in a corner listening to Roger Ailes hold forth. Across the room, Rupert Murdoch chatted with the actor Jon Voight. Near the free bar manned by a white-jacketed waiter, Ezra Gladstone and his twin brother Ari sipped artisanal beer and engaged the daughter of a casino mogul with whom they were exploring a co-venture. Dr. Bannister and his wife chatted with Michael Steele, who had recently become the first black man to chair the Republican National Committee. It was a coup to have attracted such prominent African-Americans.

A hedge fund manager approached with his wife and asked

about Wall Street regulation. Several others immediately were drawn to her orbit, and so Christine Lupo began to work the room.

Standing in front of a framed pair of boxing trunks worn by the heavyweight fighter Sonny Liston, Franklin was talking to a bond trader from whom he planned to extract a six-figure contribution when he noticed a woman scanning the crowd. It was his cousin Bebe, chatting to another woman who had her back to him. He immediately realized that Bebe's companion was Jay's wife. He had invited his cousin as a courtesy never imagining she would attend. That she had brought Nicole was an overt provocation. Why had Nicole come? Franklin immediately crossed the room to greet the women.

"I didn't expect to see you two," he said, approximating friendliness.

Bebe said, "You invited me, didn't you?" She was drinking club soda. "Nicole wanted to come. Who was I to say no? I like your loft."

Franklin nodded at Nicole, who smiled uncomfortably and said something about how it was important to listen to all political points of view.

Franklin to Bebe: "Haven't you been here before?"

"Remind me," she said. "When would that have been?"

Franklin's parrying skills were minimal, but his arrogance rendered them unnecessary. Rather than offering a wisecrack, he said, "Well, I'm glad you're here tonight. I think Christine's going to make a hell of a governor."

Bebe raised her well-tended eyebrows. "She seems like a strong-minded woman. I'd like to meet her." Franklin looked stricken, which only heightened Bebe's determination. Turning to her sister-in-law, she suggested the two of them immediately say hello to the candidate.

"She's getting ready to speak," Franklin said.

"If you don't introduce us," Bebe said, "I will. Come on, Nicole. I want to talk to her."

Nicole excused herself and went to refill her wineglass as Franklin grumpily accompanied his cousin across the room. From her position near the bar, she watched Franklin introduce Bebe to Christine Lupo. The politician was pretty and relaxed, two qualities Nicole felt herself to be decidedly lacking at present. Men beset Nicole whenever she stood alone at a party; they would babble and flirt, gauge their chances with the unobtainable. But tonight, many of the guests had probably watched her have sex with D'Angelo Maxwell, so she had no idea what to expect. The amateur porn shattered the illusion of her inviolability. A spasm of self-doubt seized her. Why had she come? Did she really want to face the woman who was trying to send her husband to prison? Was it only because she could not endure once again returning to her hotel suite alone?

A familiar-looking man in a business suit approached. Mannequin handsome, with graying hair and a friendly expression, he seemed to know her. Who was he?

"Nicole?"

"Yes, hello, you are—?"

"Fred Panzer, Lynx News."

That was it! She didn't know him, just recognized his face from television. Immediately, she wanted to retract the warmth of her greeting.

He said, "I'm a little surprised to see you here."

"You don't know me so why would you expect one thing over another?"

Panzer shrugged. "No reason." She looked over his shoulder for someone else to talk to. "Have you thought about doing an interview?"

"About what?" She knew what but wanted to make the creature say it. The wine in her glass was disappearing again.

"Recent events. Get your version out there, gain control of the story."

"I think you want to contact my husband."

"He won't talk to us."

"Because he's a very intelligent man," Nicole said.

"Jay Gladstone would be the get of the decade today. He's O.J. in reverse."

"What does that mean?"

"Famous white guy who killed an African-American. The trial's going to be a circus."

"My husband didn't kill anyone."

"Dag's still in that coma, isn't he?"

Nicole briefly thought about tossing her drink in Panzer's face but preferred to consume the dregs of the glass. Now another problem presented itself. Marcy was slicing through the guests like a Coast Guard cutter, headed in her direction. What could that woman possibly want? Marcy might ask her what she was doing here or, worse, suggest she leave. Without saying goodbye to Panzer, Nicole tottered off to find a bathroom. There was one adjacent to the kitchen where the busy wait staff were working. She felt their eyes on her as she passed through.

When it came to audacity in another woman, Christine Lupo was of two minds: Since it was the quality she cultivated that allowed her to achieve her eminent position, she admired those who possessed it. But when it was employed by another woman to challenge her, she found it distinctly less appealing. Men she squished like they were bugs. They didn't scare her the way women did. This Gladstone lady had fixed her with a dark-eyed gaze and, as Franklin gaped like a trout, was saying, "To not at least convene a grand jury seems like a remarkably tone-deaf response to what happened. How can black people have any confidence in the government if they don't get their day in court?"

"I'm sorry, tell me your name again."

"Beatrice," Bebe said. The nickname was for people she liked.

"Well, Beatrice, to answer your question, I don't think about what works for me on a personal level because that would be a betrayal of the contract I have with the citizens of this state. You're a New Yorker?"

"Born and bred."

"Well, I will never betray you. I weighed the facts and made the best decision for the citizens of Westchester County."

"You're dying to be governor," Bebe said. "Aren't you?"

"I will be governor." Then Christine Lupo winked at her interlocutor. "With the help of people like you."

Wanting to end the conversation, Franklin said, "I think it's time for the DA to speak."

As the host led the guest of honor to safety in another part of the room, Bebe watched them. While she was not going to mention her brother's case, she had intended to test the politician. The DA was a formidable adversary, self-possessed and unyielding. Words bounced off her armor. Jay needed to prepare for war.

Where was Nicole? Bebe peered around the room, searching for her. Had she gotten flustered and left? That would be understandable.

Marcy approached and demanded to know whether she was enjoying herself.

"Immensely," Bebe said.

"How's Jay doing?" Marcy asked, with barely concealed relish.

"Under the circumstances, he's all right."

"What he did? It's a *shanda*!" Bebe looked at her quizzically. "D'Angelo, the tape—" Her voice trailed off as if she could barely bring herself to enumerate his transgressions. "Why did you bring her?"

"You wouldn't understand."

"Hmmpf," Marcy said, a noise intended to convey that to respond would be beneath her. But curiosity won out: "Try me."

Before Bebe could answer, Franklin tapped a spoon on a glass and called the room to order. Without bothering to excuse herself, Marcy flew to his side and when everyone had turned their attention to the host and hostess, Franklin introduced Christine Lupo as the next governor of New York. After the polite applause died down the district attorney spieled with great conviction about lower taxes, more police, and eliminating regulations that limit what businesses can do. Attentively, the wallets listened. "And for everyone in this room who works on Wall Street, I want you to know that a Lupo administration will be in your pocket." Far from humorless, the district attorney knew how to land a well-timed joke. After the briefest pause during which the marks realized the verbal slip was intentional, a wave of laughter rippled through the room. She shouted: "I mean on your side!" and the levity rose.

In the wings, hands clasped at his waist, Franklin beamed. Christine Lupo was his politician and who could identify her ceiling? The DA had everyone reaching for their checkbooks.

Nicole spent five minutes locked in the bathroom, several of them staring at her reflection in the mirror. How could she have let herself sink to such depths? The dalliance with D'Angelo was bad enough, her role in his current predicament unbearable, but an emotional collapse in its wake? That was inexcusable. Malingering for days in a luxury hotel suite swilling champagne like some dissipated royal was not how she had reached her enviable station in life, and neither was hiding out in Franklin's bathroom. Why did she not stand her ground with Marcy? She couldn't let that virago intimidate her. Why should she care what Marcy thought? Marcy was a rigid, conformist nonentity, mother of three spoiled children, all of whom would be living in a cardboard box under a bridge were they not born Gladstones, a woman whose entire existence involved doing the bidding of her overbearing husband. Marcy was nothing.

Nicole reapplied her lipstick and touched up her eye makeup. She wanted to have a word with that Lupo woman.

When Nicole emerged from the kitchen, her target was addressing the packed room. She pushed between two tall bankers to get a better view. There was Franklin, staring at the guest of honor adoringly with Marcy next to him, thrilled to have famous people in their home. There were Ezra and Ari, those charter members of the lucky sperm club. The Lynx reporter lurked near Bebe.

The guests were rapt. Nicole could not understand it. Yes, the politician was a compelling woman who seemed in control of her life in a way that shone a light on Nicole's precipitous fall. But Christine Lupo struck her as decidedly second-rate, an ambitious hack whose road company charisma stood in sharp contrast to that of President Obama, the only politician Nicole had truly loved. Why had she not done more than just say hello to him at the Waldorf dinner? She had been too distracted by Dag. She remembered his speech in Chicago the night he was elected. The poetry of his words had brought her to tears. Christine Lupo droned; the moneyed mollusks opened. Who were these pasty-faced white people? And who were these black people? What were they doing in the enemy camp? Could none of them discern the falsity at her core? The clones of these men and women packed Washington to the rotting gills. Nicole knew them, worked with them, slept with them, and now their avatar, an empty suit with padded shoulders, intended to use the power of her office to ruin Jay's life.

"A few minutes ago, I was looking out the window at the Statue of Liberty, and I thought of my grandmother who was born in Calabria, Italy, and took a boat to Ellis Island where—"

From the back of the room, Nicole said, "You're a fake," loud enough to be heard. Several pairs of eyes swung in her direction. The attention only emboldened her. Christine Lupo stopped in the middle of a sentence and looked in her direction.

"Excuse me," she said.

A woman shushed Nicole, but she paid her no mind. "You're a big fake and shame on you for using Jay Gladstone to advance your political career!"

Several people made hissing noises to indicate their displeasure. Who is that woman, someone said. Oh, for heaven's sake, said another, it's Jay Gladstone's wife. Is she drunk? Jon Voight and Roger Ailes were gaping at her. As Nicole continued to interrupt the DA, the *quiet downs* and *shushes* increased in volume. The Lynx reporter filmed with his cell phone.

Franklin moved in her direction.

Nicole was undeterred. Louder: "You need a well-off white man on the docket so you can prove you have no racial bias, but you didn't have the guts to lock up the cop who killed that black guy."

The two bankers flanking Nicole moved away from her so Franklin, his face tainted with rage, had a clear shot. He seized her arm, pushed his face close—the tip of his nose pressed against her hair, she shuddered in revulsion—and whispered, "Everyone's sorry your phone got hacked, but you should leave right now."

"Franklin, it's okay," Christine Lupo said. He looked at her questioningly but did not release his grip. "Let the lady speak."

Under his breath, he hissed, "Goddammit."

Nicole wrenched her arm away and said to Franklin, "You're a putz."

How much had she imbibed? There were the two glasses of wine at the Oak Bar, two at the loft—wait, no, one and a half at the loft. She wasn't *that* drunk. A little food might help. Perhaps she'd grab a canapé on her way out. Nicole cleared her throat and focused on the district attorney: "The people here tonight, who have a lot more in common with my husband than they do with that poor black man who got killed by a policeman, they're all nodding in agreement because by crucifying Jay you absolve them of their sins."

She waited now, pleased with her insight, the freedom with which she expressed it, and wondering if Christine Lupo would respond. Would the Christian reference disturb Marcy? She had more: "Who made you Pontius Pilate?" The smile on Nicole's face after delivering the last barb was disreputable and rakishly appealing, the kind one uncharitably recalls when sobriety reasserts itself. Nicole deployed it like a ninja.

"It's nice to meet you, Mrs. Gladstone," Christine Lupo said from the front of the room. Her manner was noncombative. "You look better in person than you do on the Internet."

There was a brief pause while the refined attendees contemplated whether it was permissible to display their delight at this insult, concluded that Nicole deserved it, and burst into sustained laughter followed by applause. Nicole felt hot, blinding shame that rose from her feet to her calves, her hips, belly, up through her back, flaming her neck and thickening her tongue. The entire room was mocking her. Why had she not left ten minutes earlier? Why had she come at all?

Christine Lupo concluded with, "I can't comment on a pending case."

Bebe was at her side. They were in the elevator. The air in the street refreshed her.

"That was impressive," Bebe said.

"I don't care what those assholes think of me."

Bebe asked if she was all right and Nicole told her she was, and that calling out Christine Lupo was liberating. Heckling was not Bebe's style, but she was impressed with Nicole's commitment, rash though it might have seemed. Her brother was already in bad shape. It was hard to see how his wife's outburst could make it worse.

They chatted about the presidential election during the cab ride uptown.

Nicole hoped Bebe would tell Jay exactly what his wife had done, although she wasn't going to ask her. If Jay's sister performed that modest task, the wretched humiliation Nicole experienced in Franklin's penthouse would be worth it.

What was it Franklin had told her? *Everyone's sorry your phone got hacked.* How did he know someone hacked her? None of the accounts she read had mentioned that detail. No one knew that that horrid clip had come from her phone. What else would have provided it? No one used video cameras anymore. Franklin had assumed—that was all. But the more she thought about it, the less sense her conjecture made. Franklin wasn't clever enough to guess something like that. When she returned to the hotel Nicole sent the following text to her husband:

Franklin hacked my phone. He's the leaker.

CHAPTER FIFTY

It was a serene Christine Lupo that gazed across the East River at the Queens skyline from the backseat of her town car as Russell Plesko drove north on the FDR. Pagano's request had gone through, and the cop had been assigned to the DA's office where he filled in on an as-needed basis. The evening had been an unmitigated triumph. Christine's ability to charm a roomful of New York City honchos had her thrumming with confidence. They didn't just respond to the message—they loved her. Her policies, humor, and improvisatory ability combined to showcase considerable political skills and all of it resonated with the donor base. Even that slatternly wife of Jay Gladstone was a gift. The interruption had allowed the district attorney to display poise, forbearance, and quick-wittedness. The woman had opened fire with both barrels and Christine had crushed her without sacrificing likeability. What a nasty person that pipe-cleaner skinny, entitled, rich bitch seemed to be. Christine thought of the Bronx nuns who taught her at Our Lady of Perpetual Sorrow. They would have loved the poke she delivered. What kind of depraved world was this where people leaked sex tapes on the Internet? She wondered if the woman had done it herself. This suspicion made her think of Dominic Lupo and the personal dishonor she had suffered as a result of his behavior. At least the evidence of his sexual incontinence wasn't smeared all over the Internet.

Poor Jay Gladstone. She immediately froze the sympathy she felt and examined it. The declaration became a question:

Poor Jay Gladstone? Yes, yes, he was a man made of blood and sinew and a beating heart. Christine Lupo understood what it was like to have a spouse who was a curse. Her quarry was an estimable man—It's what made him such valuable prey—brought down by a poor choice in mates. Certainly, his predicament was thornier than that, the car had not run over D'Angelo Maxwell by itself, but none of the auto-da-fé he was enduring would have occurred had his wife honored her marital vows. As for the fiasco that had taken place in the basketball arena, the man had paid for his sins in the currency of shame.

These thoughts created a disturbance in her well-ordered moral universe. Before this evening, Jay Gladstone was only a prominent citizen charged with crimes, an abstraction. But seeing his wife tonight—flushed face, firing squad eyes—listening to her aria of abuse, had brought Jay into sharper focus, and the picture that formed was of a human being who was suffering. And suffering caused by a cheating spouse was something about which Christine was not without sympathy.

Then what of mercy? Well, mercy was not exactly hers to dispense, was it? That was more God's bailiwick. Why was she even thinking these thoughts? Sin and mercy were not helpful when considering a defendant in a pending criminal case. Sin and mercy were ideas, and she needed to stick to facts. If the luxury of a Jesuitical debate were permitted, she would never prosecute anyone. Many of the accused that came under her purview had partners who betrayed them. Humanizing a defendant was against the rules.

As the car sailed over the Third Avenue Bridge and north on the Major Deegan Expressway, Christine realized that something about Jay had been peeled back by his wife's presence and it kept niggling at her because it felt familiar. She and Jay were public people with families in the process of fracturing. Until recently, they both had been paragons, the kind of citizens others were encouraged to emulate. The vehicular assault charges he faced? Had she not done something similar in the parking lot at work? Sean Purcell had bumped a demonstrator with her official vehicle. Knocked the woman down. A black woman, no less. It wasn't on the cataclysmic scale of what Jay had done but to pretend there was no parallel would be disingenuous. Had that been racially motivated? Of course not! Moreover, Christine knew it was an accident. By a stroke of luck, no one had reported that incident. Who knows what cynics might have made of it? What if what Jay had done was an accident? What if his lawyer's claims were accurate? Was she persecuting him? Reasonable people might disagree on whether there was a political tinge to the initial indictment and the subsequent hate crime charge but Jay Gladstone would get his day in court. That was the beauty of the system. She needed to stop seeing moral equivalence where there was none. Ultimately, all that united them was philandering spouses. It was impossible to have anything in common with someone so wealthy. Still, her cerebral push and pull would not cease

They were riding east on the Cross-Westchester Expressway.

"Russell, what do you think about Jay Gladstone? Do you think he's guilty?"

Plesko did not answer right away. Christine waited. She didn't want to influence him so did not offer a further prompt.

"Permission to speak frankly?"

"Granted," she said.

"He did it, that's pretty obvious. But did he mean to do it?"

"That's what I'm asking."

"People wanted to hang me," Plesko said. "Like they could all read my mind. But no one can do that. I don't care who they are. If Gladstone says it was an accident, I believe him."

"Even after what he witnessed? He accidentally ran over the man he caught with his wife?"

Plesko adjusted the rearview mirror so he could see his passenger. "Does he seem like a violent guy to you?"

"I indicted him."

"Hey, look, you gave me a break, and I'll always be grateful for it."

"Tell me what you think," the DA said.

"I guess you can't let everyone off."

With all the certainty at her disposal, she declared: "Jay Gladstone has had enough breaks."

By the time she climbed out of the car in her driveway Christine had convinced herself it was true.

Her mind returned to Jay as she lay in bed. Their fathers were both men of the Bronx, first-generation Americans who served in World War II, raised families in New York, pillars of their respective communities. Bingo Gladstone was a version of Mario Lupo with a lot more money. Like something caught between her teeth, the similarities continued to nag her. To her growing consternation, all of it added to this nascent kinship with Jay that she found harder and harder to dismiss.

Twenty minutes later, when she could not fall asleep, Christine went to the kitchen to make a cup of herbal tea. As she waited for the water to boil, she booted up her laptop. Jay had an extensive online presence. Christine skimmed sports pages and business sites, noted his philanthropic activities and the awards he had received. There was a group photograph with Archbishop Desmond Tutu celebrating Universal Children's Day that she had previously missed. It was not the profile of a criminal.

When the kettle whistled, she brewed the tea, spooned honey into the cup, and returned to the computer. On a real estate site, she typed in Jay's Bedford address, which for reasons Christine did not want to think about she knew by memory. Up came a single photograph and a description. The image of the palatial house on a hundred and twenty acres, with pool house, barn, paddock, and bridle paths did not produce resentment or envy or in any way stick in the DA's craw. Jay Gladstone had Sultan of Brunei money, but he employed thousands of people and paid untold millions of taxes into the public treasury. In her view, this was how America was meant to work.

Since the separation from her husband, Christine occasionally found herself missing, not Dominic Lupo exactly, but the companionship he had provided. Case in point: The night of the incinerated T-shirt on the backyard grill. Had Dominic been there, she would have asked him to play the heavy. Something in her had loosened. It was energizing.

She finished the tea, rinsed the cup, and put it in the dishwasher. Went upstairs, but instead of getting into bed, she slipped on a pair of jeans and a sweater. Checked on her sleeping children and went downstairs. Closing the back door quietly behind her, she climbed into her black Lexus sedan, slipped *La Boheme* into the CD player, and backed out of the garage.

CHAPTER FIFTY-ONE

J ust after eight the same evening, Bobby Tackman arrived at
Jay's Bedford estate to conduct a simulated interview in
preparation for the real one. The communications expert
reviewed a list of fifty likely questions and made sure his client
had responses to each of them. The theme of the evening was
Apology. Keep apologizing, he advised. Then apologize some
more, and you will be redeemed because America loves a
redemption story.

When Tackman left, Jay called Herman Doomer. A team of
attorneys was preparing to wage war with the league, but the
lawyer warned him that when facing a player boycott, their
influence was limited. "You have to knock this interview out of
the park," Doomer said. Jay asked what was going on with the
Planning Commission regarding the Sapphire situation.
Doomer had made inquiries, but as far as he knew, no new
information was available. Jay had hoped to hear from Aviva
since he had withdrawn from participating in the commencement, but she had not returned his calls. With all of this on his
mind, he shambled to bed.

It was a surprise to find the house situated on a dirt road
bounded by low walls built from stones. This evocation of the
rural past left Christine strangely moved. She, too, yearned for
a time before the current fractiousness, when America had a
common purpose. What were Jay's political preferences? Her
Internet scavenging revealed he had made contributions to

Democrats and Republicans. What he believed in, she recognized, was the efficacy of the system.

She parked on the road in front of the property, turned off the headlights but left the engine idling. The night was cloudless, pricked with stars, and a half moon impassively shone. Although the house was dark, several security lights painted the grounds in pale yellow. A single light illuminated an upstairs window. Probably on a timer, she thought. From a fawning profile on Forbes.com, she knew Jay owned horses and wondered if whoever looked after them lived on the premises. Lowering the car window, she inhaled the pleasing earthy scent. An owl broadcast its presence. A breeze disturbed the branches. Homes like this one often had security cameras, but none were visible.

She placed her hand on the steering wheel and saw her bare ring finger, moonlit. For ten minutes, she observed the house. No cars passed. Christine had never done anything remotely like this. The burning of her son's T-shirt, she knew, was indicative of the heightened emotional state she was in, but this amounted to stalking. As long as it did not become a habit, she believed her behavior on this night was justifiable. How else to get a feel for her adversary if not by entering his world? She wanted to know what it was like to be this man, to live in storybook surroundings with a gorgeous young wife and a geyser that spouted money. She imagined him riding a horse along the edge of a luminous meadow, wind at his back, savoring yet another victory. And then he was not alone. There she was, Christine Lupo, the girl from Arthur Avenue, astride a golden palomino. The two of them, together in the gloaming, the broad land spread out intoxicatingly before them, like a Technicolor movie. She could almost hear the brass and strings swell on the soundtrack. Christine had never ridden a horse. Once, as a girl, her father had put her on a pony at a church fair in Yonkers. What was she doing on an imaginary horse next to Jay Gladstone riding into a Hollywood sunset? Smirking at the silliness of it, she repressed the vision. Jay Gladstone and Christine Lupo together in a sylvan fantasy, on horses, no less. It was ridiculous.

Jay was drifting off when Nicole's text arrived. Was Franklin the mastermind? Nicole certainly thought so. It was impossible to know if she was drunk and raving, or if it was true. He turned off his phone, but could not get back to sleep. For half an hour, he lay in bed listening to the night and trying to slow his rampaging mind. Was Franklin capable of treachery on this level? It was not beyond the realm of possibility. But could he have acted so aggressively? Jay did not realize he possessed that degree of malevolence. Perhaps he had underestimated him. As reprehensible as it was, Jay had to give his cousin credit. The sheer chutzpah of the gesture was impressive.

The road in front of the house rarely saw nocturnal traffic and Jay listened as a car engine hummed in the distance increasing in volume as it rolled past and then died away. Several minutes later he heard another car. It got louder as it drew nearer but then the sound did not recede. A lone vehicle in the middle of the night was not a welcome sound. Someone had parked in front of the property. He lay there for a few seconds, but when he did not hear the car go away, he climbed out of bed, crossed the hall, and entered a guest bedroom in the front of the house where a timer light was on.

Sitting in the car, Christine was in a reverie. Dominic was gone, she had a career-making case on her hands, and with adroit handling, there was no reason she could not spin it into political gold. Thomas Dewey was a New York prosecutor, and he had nearly become president. No one knew how far she could go. Then the light in Jay Gladstone's upstairs window went out.

Jay immediately saw the car at the end of his driveway. It was not there because of a flat tire. Whoever it was, they were there for him. In a way, he had wanted this. It was why he was reluctant to be saddled with personal security even after the rampage at the arena. He went to the safe, opened the combination lock. Removed the gun, felt the heft of the weapon in his hand. Checked the clip. Fifteen rounds. Boris had shown him how to shoot.

He walked downstairs and sat in a chair facing the front door with the weapon on his lap. He thought about prison versus death and concluded death might be preferable. He wished he could have resolved the situation with Aviva. His will was in order. The floor was cool against the soles of his bare feet. He wondered who would say Kaddish for him.

After sitting there for ten minutes, his nerve failed him, and he called the police. The cop on duty the night of the accident arrived at the house. Officer Wysocki. He acted like he was pleased to see Jay and asked how he was doing. He told Jay there were no other cars on the road.

When Wysocki left, Jay drove into the city.

CHAPTER FIFTY-TWO

The next morning, he did not make the mistake of arriving at the office alone. Behind a flying wedge of corn-fed security, he made it through the demonstrators without incident. He had coffee. He met with Bebe and Boris and briefed them on his preparations with Tackman. The Sapphire matter was taking suspiciously long to resolve and Bebe told him she was going to reach out to someone she knew in the city bureaucracy to find out what was going on. Jay told Boris to prepare to fly to Hong Kong the following week to familiarize himself with the Asian branch of the business and brief Bebe when he returned. When the confab was over, Bebe stayed behind and reported what Nicole had done at Franklin's house the previous evening. They were in the sitting area of Jay's office. He tilted his head back and closed his eyes.

"She was battling for you."

"That's not the way to do it," he said, rubbing his temples.

"Nicole wants to save the marriage."

Jay opened his eyes and regarded his sister. "Would you stay married to someone like that?"

"You remember the secretary who worked for Dad in the late seventies?"

"Miss Sloves?" Bebe nodded. She had a throaty laugh and always acted pleased to see him when he visited the office as a gangly teenager. "What about her?" Bebe's knowing look spilled the old secret. "You can't be serious." She slowly nodded.

Layers of certainty, conviction, and belief began to dissolve.

Jay found himself searching for words to express inchoate thoughts. His father, who had coached him in youth basketball, who had passed him the Torah at his bar mitzvah, had been prowling around Manhattan unpeeling his secretary? It was inconceivable. "How do you know?"

"Mom told me years ago. She almost left him, but she didn't."

The news caused a tectonic shift in Jay's perception. The ground swayed. Foundations adjusted, recalibrated. For his entire life, he had modeled himself on his father, held him up as a shining example of how to be a man in the world, prostrated at the feet of his exemplary life when all the time, in this most basic measurement of goodness, Bingo was an imposter, a failure. But as much of a punch to the solar plexus that this represented, in some indeterminate way that he could only begin to discern, it was a relief.

When Bebe left the office, Jay lay on the sofa and thought about his father and how he had behaved in the wake of this dalliance. He reviewed family dinners, Sundays watching football, skiing and sailing vacations, business meetings, shows, charity events they'd attended, endless conversations shared about topics distant and local, and there was nothing he could remember that hinted at Bingo carrying on with his secretary. So, did Jay have to reexamine his perception of his father, adjust his place in the pantheon? Did he have to demote him?

It was with all of this still reverberating that Franklin appeared. Jay did not want to deal with his cousin, who was standing at the foot of the sofa looking down at him over his gelatinous belly.

"Your wife caused quite a scene last night," Franklin said, satisfaction mixed with the outrage he was impelled to convey.

"I heard. As you know, I can't control her."

"Someone needs to. She's an embarrassment."

His cousin's presence further agitated Jay, who rose from

the sofa and lumbered to his desk where he flopped into the chair. He thought about the text he had received last night from Nicole: *Franklin hacked my phone. He's the leaker.* What had led her to that conclusion? Could it possibly be true? It was certainly of a piece with Franklin's surreptitious financial maneuvers.

"What did you want to talk about?"

"You've got a lot on your plate," Franklin said. "For your own well-being, I think maybe you shouldn't come to work until things cool down."

Here was the Franklin he knew, blunt, artless. Bebe had said nearly the exact words, but her intent was far different.

"Did you hear what happened to me on Saturday night?"

"It was all over the sports page."

"But you didn't call or text to see if I was all right?"

Franklin ignored the question. "Fans, Christ, they're fuckin' fickle! You okay?"

"Yes," Jay said. "Thanks for your concern."

Never before had he felt vulnerable to Franklin. The dynamics of their relationship had been set years earlier and had remained static. Jay believed that Franklin had come to accept the structure of the company and was satisfied with his role. For his cousin to use the current situation to try and maneuver him out of the way seemed entirely out of character. But that appeared to be what was going on. He second-guessed telling Doomer to delay bringing legal action.

"What do you know about that tape?"

Franklin regarded him uncertainly. "What do you mean?"

"Was I not clear? Do you know anything about how that tape got out there?"

"Only what I read," Franklin said.

"You're sure?"

"What are you asking me? It's awful. It's a crock of politically correct bullshit what's happening to you. I'll tell you something, Jay, I never liked Nicole. She was beneath you. Between you and me, if I had walked in on Marcy *schtupping* some guy, I would've killed them both."

"Yes, I'm sure that's what you would have done." Jay had not checked with the hospital since yesterday. He made a mental note to do that when he finished with his cousin.

"Crime of passion," Franklin said. "People understand." He made a brisk motion with his hand as if to wave away culpability.

"About the tape?"

"I sympathize, believe me. I do."

"Did you leak it?"

Jay saw Franklin's slack body stiffen, the planes of his face become rigid.

"What? No! Me? Wha—?" Franklin shook his head vigorously. "No, no, no. Why would you say that?"

"You know nothing about it?"

"Jay, come on! Are you fucking kidding me?"

"I'm going to tell you one thing, and then we're done." Jay paused to let the weight of what he was about to impart sink in. It appeared Franklin might say something but his only response came from his shoulders, driven upward by the tension he was unable to conceal. "If I find out you had anything to do with the leaking of that tape, I will cut your legs off. Between that and what else you've been up to, I'll have you so tied up in court you'll be afraid to leave your house without calling your lawyer to see if it's allowed."

"I had nothing to do with it."

"I don't believe you."

"Why not?"

"Because I know what's going on in Asia," Jay said.

"What are you talking about?"

"Let's not get into that now. Did you or did you not hack my wife's phone and leak that tape?"

"Did I hack her phone? I can barely work a fucking blender."

"I don't believe you."

"Hand to God, Jay." Like a Boy Scout taking an oath, he held his hand up.

"Hand to God? Now I know you're bullshitting."

"You don't trust me? Go fuck yourself."

"Go fuck *my*self?"

"You got what you deserved," Franklin said. "You're an arrogant schmuck, and you always were."

He left the office, barreling through the door and slamming it behind him. The room was silent as a cave. Absent Franklin's sulfurous presence, it felt strangely empty. Jay still had no idea if Nicole's accusation was valid, or if she had been drunk texting. He had assumed it was the latter. After having confronted Franklin, he was unimpressed with his denial. There was a risk in trying to ascertain guilt. If Franklin was culpable, the ramifications for the future of the business were profound. But a rupture in their relationship was inevitable anyway. It was going to happen as soon as Jay informed Franklin of the lawsuit he intended to file.

An unfamiliar sensation overcame him, and his heart began to tom-tom. He cursed to himself. Was this a heart attack? Unbelievable. Franklin will have finished the job. He remembered that a coronary event was often accompanied by pain radiating down the arm. Was it the left or the right? He didn't feel pain in either one. He willed himself to relax and took several deep breaths, letting the air run slowly out of his nose, which he was able to do since the swelling had decreased. A minute later his heart rate ceased its campaign of terror.

When Jay reached Dr. Bannister, the surgeon informed him there had been some hopeful signs since they had last spoken. Something about brain waves that Jay did not have the bandwidth to absorb but had encouraged the doctor. He called Doomer and inquired about the situation with the league. Doomer reported that the commissioner was intransigent. The league was insisting that he sell the team. In desperation, Jay pulled up the list of NBA owners on his computer. He knew them all from league meetings and considered himself friends with several of them. Of the twenty-eight calls his secretary placed, she managed to reach five of the owners. Jay jumped on the phone with each. He wheedled and inveigled. He recounted his history and reminded them of his sterling reputation. They listened dutifully. But of these five men, all of whom expressed sorrow at his predicament and conveyed their sincere sympathies, none would speak on his behalf in public. Too sensitive, was the consensus.

Bastards, Jay thought.

CHAPTER FIFTY-THREE

L ate that afternoon, the television crew arrived at the apartment to set up. Bobby Tackman paced and offered silken words of encouragement as Jay sat in a chair with a bib over his shirt having makeup applied by a quiet young woman with a nose ring and a tattoo of a peace sign on her forearm. She treated him professionally, which he took to be a positive sign.

Jay was in the kitchen nursing a glass of whiskey when Anderson Cooper arrived and said hello before conferring with the producer, a fussy man in a snug suit who seemed barely out of his teens. Jay freshened his drink and as the whiskey slid into his bloodstream he began to feel its effects. Nervousness receded. It occurred to Jay that in many ways he had been preparing for this his entire life. Always he had chosen to rein in his personality, content to let the light shine on Bingo. This self-abnegation had begun when he was young and continued until his father's passing. But now circumstances required Jay to step on stage, and he was ready.

Tackman continued his magpie chatter, but Jay was no longer listening. He visualized himself conversing sagely with Anderson Cooper about the scars of American history, the travails of black people, and "the deep well of empathy I've drawn from my whole life." He pictured the easygoing host nodding sympathetically. He imagined viewers across America, around the globe, and all of them coming to see the untarnished quality of his soul. Church Scott (that traitor!) didn't know what was in his heart? Jay would show the world. He took another sip of whiskey.

"Ten minutes," a production assistant said.

Jay slipped on his suit jacket. Tackman looked him over. The consultant did not like the picture.

"You need to lose the suit. Put a sweater on."

"I always wear a suit in public."

"Millions of people are going to watch this and you're going to remind them of their boss. A sweater makes you more relatable."

In his bedroom Jay selected a gray cashmere number with a V-neck. As he pulled it over his head, the soft material masking his face, he felt dizzy so he sat on the bed. To steady himself he took several deep breaths. His balance returned and he felt a surge of energy. He wanted to talk, get a few things off his chest.

In the living room, Jay sat in a director's chair next to Anderson Cooper, who was checking notes on a clipboard. A sound technician pinned a microphone to him. The television lights were warm, but he was not uncomfortable. Behind one of the two cameras, Tackman stood next to the producer and gave a thumbs-up. A voice said, "Rolling," and Anderson Cooper introduced Harold Jay Gladstone as a real estate executive and NBA franchise owner to the millions of viewers who would be watching the interview later that evening.

"Please call me Jay," he said.

"All right," Anderson Cooper said. Then: "Are you a racist?"

Man, Jay thought, right out of the gate. But he was ready.

"I am not a racist. I made a terrible mistake and I'm here to apologize to all the people I've hurt. I don't know how I could say such disrespectful words. I'm so sorry."

"Who, specifically, do you want to apologize to?"

Jay was ready:

"There are so many people, starting with D'Angelo

Maxwell." Here Jay paused. Acknowledging this first seemed like the wisest course. He wanted the first apology to resonate like a bell. "I feel terrible about what happened to him. I wish I could undo it. When he recovers I will do everything in my power to make it up to him. He's doing better, you know. I talked to the doctor this morning, and he's improving." Again, Jay paused. He wanted to allow any helpful information time to register. "And I hurt my wife, Nicole. She didn't need this. I blew up her life."

"You seem remarkably forgiving about her behavior. What about what she did? She had relations with a player and you caught them."

Anderson Cooper was not pulling punches. Jay pressed on.

"Yes, I did. I did. But this isn't about her."

He congratulated himself on the magnanimity he displayed. So far, he was hewing to the Tackman plan. This was easier than expected.

"Did you know you were being recorded?"

"Of course not. I did a terrible thing and I want to explain. I'm not sure how to say this because for a man in my position, well, everything can be misinterpreted."

Anderson Cooper wanted some elaboration, but Jay just looked at him. He was having trouble accessing this part of what he had reviewed with Tackman. All he could remember was the apologizing he was supposed to do, and he had already done that. His mind went back to the previous night and the car that stopped in front of his house. By the time the police officer arrived at the house, it was gone. Now he wasn't even sure a car had been there at all. The sweater was making him hot. What did Anderson Cooper want him to say?

"I think you better ask me another question."

"You said 'Why is everyone in this family having sex with black people.' What did that mean?"

"That's the question you're going to ask now?" Jay was trying to be light, amusing. Cooper was stone-faced. "Don't you want to work up to it?"

"It would help if you answered it. What did that mean?"

"What did that mean? It meant what I said."

"Everyone in this family?" Jay did not respond. "Would you elaborate?"

Jay paused for a long time. The television lights were getting hotter. His lower back was swampy. He could feel Tackman's eyes willing him to take control. To steady himself, Jay locked into Anderson Cooper's unwavering gaze. "I have a daughter who I love very much. She's an intelligent young person who is in a phase of life where she is experimenting. Her girlfriend is a black woman, which is fine. Nothing wrong with that. So, there's my daughter and my wife. The word 'everyone' was hyperbole, something perhaps you can understand, under the circumstances."

Anderson Cooper wanted more but Jay decided that he had said enough on the subject. He leaned back and waited for the next question. But before it arrived, Jay wanted to make another point:

"My daughter's friend happens to be very anti-Israel and she expressed that opinion at our Seder where she was a guest. So, I admit, I may have had some residual bad feeling. But, look, I'm not saying that excuses anything."

"What do the political opinions of your daughter's girlfriend have to do with what occurred?"

"We had a rainbow Passover this year, black people, white people, a thing of beauty. The next day I flew to South Africa where I'm doing a major project. When I arrived home, I said a few unfortunate words that, believe me, I'll regret for the rest of my life. That's not how I talk. You can ask anyone who knows me. I don't talk about people. I talk about ideas. May I tell you what I'm doing in South Africa?"

"Let's stay on this subject for now. Who do you think released the tape?"

"I can't say on television, but I believe I know the person's identity and he's someone who for his own personal reasons does not wish me well."

Although Jay was tempted to go into more detail, he chose not to.

"When you first heard the tape, did you remember making that statement?"

"I've said all I have to say about those words."

"All right, let's talk about you."

"I'm responsible. I have twenty-nine partners in the league. They're an incredible group of men. I want to apologize to my partners and the commissioner. This mess lands on his desk and I caused it and I'm sorry. Stupid words. Foolish. A man gets upset, says things he shouldn't say. I was jealous."

Revisiting the experience was making Jay increasingly uneasy. His mouth was dry. He wanted a glass of water.

"The league wants you out."

"The media wants me out."

"And the league. I've had sources tell me—"

"Look, I put the league in a difficult position. My partners there are understandably angry. I have a lot of respect for the commissioner and he's frustrated. But let me ask you—is what I did so terrible that it merits banishment? Is it fair that I should lose a business that I've been devoted to, that I love, because of a few words that are being misinterpreted? No one who knows me will tell you I'm a racist. *No one.* My family has been in the real estate business for generations. Years ago, not every landlord would rent to black people. There are prominent real estate families in New York City—I'm thinking of one in particular—that would not rent to minorities. That was never the Gladstone way. Back in the 1930s, when my father was on his high school prom committee, he refused to hold the event at a hotel where they were going to make the black kids use the service entrance."

"What does that have to do with—"

"I'm telling you. I'm not saying Bingo Gladstone was Abraham Lincoln, but what I am saying is that I was raised in a liberal tradition, my parents taught me that God created everyone equal, and that's how I've always lived my life."

"Church Scott, the coach of your team, was quoted as saying, 'I don't know what's in his heart, but I'm praying for him.' What would you say to Church Scott?"

"Church Scott's reaction to this—" Jay considered his words. "I'm disappointed. That's my only comment. He's a friend and I wish him well. Do you know he's the highest paid coach in the league?"

"You say that like he mugged you."

"He *mugged me*? He didn't mug me," Jay said. "Don't put words in my mouth."

"Are you saying that because you're his employer, he should suspend judgment?"

"In this situation, I think he should get the players to stop this silly talk about a boycott, suit up, and go win some playoff games."

"When Mayor House of Newark was asked to weigh in on your situation, he had no comment. What would you say to Mayor House?"

"Mayor House is a fine man who's a little confused right now."

"Confused how?"

Jay knew he was standing on the edge of a cliff. He took a step back.

"I'm not going there. Let me just say that our family foundation has given away millions of dollars in scholarships, we've funded nutrition programs. Half the charitable organizations in Harlem, Bed-Stuy, and Newark have the name Gladstone on the wall because we want to help. But there's someone else who's leading the attack on me, this Imam Ibrahim Muhammad fellow, who happens to be a Muslim."

"What does that have to do with the situation?"

"I want to tread lightly here because it's a sensitive area. Some Muslims, not all of them, have issues with Jews. Some of them take extreme points of view. Some of them, quite frankly, are worse than Rumanians, who during the Holocaust were worse than the Nazis."

"Some of them. Is that code for—"

"No, no, no! It's not code for anything. This particular imam has been leading demonstrations against me in front of the arena where the team plays, violent demonstrations in front of my offices, spreading the most scurrilous lies. It's pretty obvious that my personal situation is being used to advance several agendas that have nothing to do with me. But I occupy a certain position in society so people feel like they can say whatever they want. And you know what? That's fine. The Constitution guarantees that right. Everyone just needs to be a little less sensitive, but people are extremely sensitive, they're so sensitive it's like no one has skin anymore, only nerve endings. So once again, I want to be clear, I apologize to everyone."

"You have said that your words have been misinterpreted, misunderstood—"

"I have."

"I want to give you a platform now to say whatever you want to our audience."

"Thank you." Jay turned directly to the camera. He paused, and then said, "Please look inside and ask yourselves whether you have ever done, or said, or even *thought* something that would embarrass you if it were made public. I would like to say to anyone who hasn't, you're a better person than I am."

"What happened that night in Bedford?"

Jay was prepared for this. What further light could he shine on the question that would not doom his chances of exoneration? That he had been cuckolded by Dag and in a spectacularly misguided attempt to—to what, exactly? To discuss what had occurred? To arrive at some kind of rapprochement? He still did not know. Now the door was open and his restless intellect pressed him to articulate all the subtle gradations of intent that had led to the catastrophe and then dive into the waves of remorse that subsequently rolled in and gambol like a seal. But instead, he said:

"It was an accident."

Anderson Cooper let the moment linger. Considering the circumstances, Jay was relatively pleased with how the interview had gone, and would not be lured into a rhetorical trap to be destroyed by his own words.

"That's the extent of your comment on the subject?"

"On the advice of my attorney, that's all I can say about it."

Anderson Cooper recognized the immovable object in front of him and pivoted.

"Will you sell the team?"

"When Hell freezes over."

CHAPTER FIFTY-FOUR

Jay believed the insight and distress he had displayed would go a long way toward rehabilitating his image. He believed he had come across as folksy, honest, and repentant. He believed he was on his way back to the sunny uplands of acceptance and admiration. When the interview ended, the panicked look on Bobby Tackman's face told him otherwise. Tackman took Jay aside and ordered him to not say another word to the host. He watched as the consultant buttonholed Anderson Cooper, who was being congratulated by his now ecstatic producer, a man who knew broadcast gold when he saw it, and begged him to not run the interview, a request that was summarily rejected. The television crew wrapped their gear and vanished.

Jay was in the kitchen sipping a glass of water when Tackman barged in. He made it clear that the opportunity had been outstandingly botched. Jay listened as the consultant enumerated his sins:

"You can't apologize and then disparage your daughter's black girlfriend, why did you express any opinion at all about Church Scott or the mayor of Newark? How would you feel if some well-meaning black man spouted off about Jews? And don't get me started on what you said about the Muslims. I'm not even sure you and I can work together anymore."

Tackman ordered him to not engage in further direct contact with the media until they could formulate a new plan.

As Jay absorbed this litany of transgressions, the apartment, which seemed to have cooled with the extinguishing of the television lights and disappearance of the crew, felt like it was heating up again. A mule was trying to kick its way out of his skull. He was about to respond to Tackman when he noticed the vision in his left eye had become occluded and the entire room lost definition, straight planes bending, becoming curvilinear, vibrating, melting, the floor rising and the entire space beginning to disintegrate. Tackman had stopped talking and was looking at him strangely. Jay lost his balance and crumpled, his head striking the floor. Indistinct voices rose and fell. There was so much to do and undo, and yet as consciousness slipped away, what he felt, oddly, was release.

An ambulance brought Jay to Mt. Sinai Hospital where doctors determined that he had not had a coronary or a stroke. He had fainted, the resident who examined him concluded. Probably from stress. He ordered Jay to remain in the hospital under observation for the night. A nurse inserted a needle into his arm for hydration.

Jay had been born at Mt. Sinai. Although his parents lived in Queens at the time, his mother had insisted on it because she wanted her son to be able to say he had been born on Fifth Avenue. When thoughts of his death inevitably arose, he marveled at the symmetry. Staring at the ceiling Jay felt the weakness and frustration that had become his constant companions, but, more than anything, there was the growing sense that he had slipped on some cosmic banana peel and was now in a continuous state of imbalance. From Dag to Nicole to Aviva, the ability to make things conform to the way he wanted them to be had deserted him.

Although Dag had shown slight improvement, the doctors had hinted that a full recovery might not be possible, something that would forever haunt Jay. Additionally, although it paled in comparison to how he felt about the havoc he had wreaked, he feared losing his NBA franchise and not receiving permission from the city to begin construction on the Sapphire, because those endeavors represented a significant part of his future. But what overrode all of this, casting a shadow the size of the world itself, was death. It wasn't so much that he dreaded the prospect of nonexistence, although he had a healthy terror of that. What concerned him was that he would die now, with his reputation not just deteriorating but seemingly in free fall. How long was he going to live if stress landed him in a hospital bed? Long enough to salvage his reputation and avoid the ignominy of dying in disgrace?

It was not difficult to locate Dag's room and because he was wearing a hospital gown, the night nurses assumed Jay was just padding along the crypt-quiet halls on a late walk. When he peeked in and saw Dag was alone, he entered and sat in the chair next to the bed.

Dag's long, lean frame lay still. His chest rose and fell. Clear fluid ran from an IV drip into the soft flesh of his wrist. An oxygen mask covered his features. His eyes were closed. Someone had arranged for a shave, and his cheeks were smooth. Jay glanced at the squiggly green lines of the monitors.

Leaning his head back, he said to the ceiling, "I don't do this often, but please God, save this man. Please, please Yahweh, Jesus, Allah, whoever is listening." Humble and emotionally naked, he felt like he was performing a sacred duty. "Little help here, okay? I'm begging."

Tentatively, he reached his hand out and laid it on Dag's bicep. It was warm. There was a hitch in Dag's breathing which caused Jay to start, and he removed his hand and watched Dag's face for signs of distress. When steady breathing resumed, Jay gently returned his hand to the big man's arm.

He leaned toward Dag's ear and whispered, "I have no idea if you can hear me, probably not. But, listen. I'm so deeply sorry for this. With my hand on a Bible, I will tell you I didn't mean for it to happen. I was angry, and because you humiliated me, I wanted to scare you. I admit that. I wanted to put the fear into you in a way you would never forget, and then I did the most unimaginable thing I've ever done. I will regret my behavior as long as I'm alive, Dag. I will pray for your recovery each day, and when you recover, I hope you can forgive me."

Dag's eyes opened. Jay was dumbfounded, tried to talk, but his tongue would not obey.

"I'm going to be all right," Dag said.

Jay was crying, tears streaking his face. The mixture of relief, shock, and gratitude paralyzed him. Again, he tried to talk but his tongue expanded to fill his mouth and words would not come.

"How are you feeling?"

Whose voice was that? He still could not get words out.

Swimming to consciousness, he saw Doomer and Tackman at the foot of the bed. Next to them was his sister Bebe. He had been dreaming. It was morning. Through the fog, he realized the tears were real and he wiped them away with the back of his hand. He hoped his visitors didn't notice. It was Bebe who had spoken. Her voice was soft and solicitous. Once more she asked how he was feeling.

CHAPTER FIFTY-FIVE

A nurse arrived to administer another round of intravenous hydration. The hospital would discharge him as soon as she checked his vital signs. The only thing the attending physician prescribed was blood pressure medication and a few days of rest.

Jay tried to concentrate as Tackman related the extent of the damage. This took several minutes. True to Tackman's postgame analysis, the Anderson Cooper interview did not serve the purpose Jay had hoped. The reaction, on television and the Internet, was predictably merciless. "Self-indulgent," "non-apology apology," and "insensitive" were leitmotifs, as were "slanderous," "anti-Muslim," and, of course, "racist." Jay was a whipping boy, caricatured, lampooned, dismissed, and the consensus was that his time was over, what he represented was an abomination to right-thinking people, and the acceptable repentance, according to public opinion, was to self-immolate in the middle of Marcus Garvey Boulevard. Tackman concluded by saying, "The only surprise was that no Rumanians complained."

"There's still time," Jay said. The rattle of his laugh had the gallows in it. Everything had gone so transcendently wrong it had begun to seem perversely funny.

"I spoke with the commissioner this morning," Doomer reported. "He wants to know if you've reconsidered. The team is still refusing to play."

"I'm not selling," Jay said.

"You're certainly within your rights to maintain that position," the lawyer said. "However, we've been notified that if you don't sell the team, he's going to ban you for life. They can go to court and force a sale. They can get a judge to issue an injunction removing you from day-to-day management of the team by asserting that the rights of the other owners now supersede yours. We can challenge it, but they'll win."

"This is America," Jay reminded them. "The government can't seize your property because you said something stupid."

Tackman suggested they explain the interview by saying Jay was "pre-stroke."

"I stand by every word," Jay said.

The consultant looked at the lawyer, imploring him to intercede.

"Jay, I think Bobby is right. You can help yourself by embracing the stroke."

"I didn't have a stroke."

"*Pre*-stroke," Doomer said.

"It makes you a victim," Tackman pointed out. "The equation changes. We can suggest the entire episode, going back to the car accident, was a result of physical deterioration."

"There could be significant ramifications for your legal defense," Doomer said. "It's a persuasive mitigating circumstance."

Bebe had heard enough. "My brother didn't get to be who he is by bending to the prevailing winds," she said. "As long as he's in possession of his faculties, I think we can all depend on him to make a sound decision." Bebe held Jay's hand. Their eye contact excluded Doomer and Tackman, who knew not to intrude. "Jay, you need to wait until you're out of the hospital and you've gotten some rest. Don't make any decisions today."

He appreciated his sister's advice and neither Doomer nor Tackman contradicted it. They arranged a conference call for the next day to discuss subsequent steps. Boris arrived and, after a few minutes, the others departed. While they waited for a doctor to sign the discharge papers, Jay complained: He had believed in the legal system his entire life, and now it was gearing up to steamroll him.

But he had another idea.

CHAPTER FIFTY-SIX

On a summer day about a month after Jay graduated from college, his mother invited him to accompany her on a roots trip to her old haunts. They visited her modest home on a quiet street in Bensonhurst. Several members of the Italian-American family that lived there were home and when Helen explained that she had grown up in the house, she and Jay were invited in to look around. The rooms were neat and small and Jay remembered thinking that it could not be possible that his mother, who explored multiple continents, hosted sophisticated dinner parties, and lovingly smoothed the jagged edges of her coarser husband, could possibly have grown up in such mundane circumstances. To be able to witness the distance she had traveled was to be reminded of his own astonishing luck. After lunch at Nathan's in Coney Island they went to Brooklyn College where Helen had graduated, although did not attend the ceremony because she had to work that day and so never collected her diploma. Miraculously, it remained on file decades later:

Helen Shirley Goldstein, BA
Brooklyn College, 1952

Jay was aware that his mother existed in a whorl of parents, siblings, aunts, uncles, and cousins before she married her husband and eventually became Helen Gladstone of Scarsdale, but his mental image of her earlier identity remained unformed.

This tangible evidence, first her house, and then the degree, and the pride that filled her as she held it in her unwrinkled hands, enabled him to complete a vibrant picture. She seemed younger than he had ever seen her that afternoon, and so vivid. Now he was glad she could not understand what was happening to him because it would utterly violate the sense of propriety she had worked so hard to cultivate.

A wedge of purpling clouds roiled over Sheepshead Bay and by the time Jay and Boris arrived in Brighton Beach the sky was sloppy with rain. Boris slid the SUV into a parking space down the street from the Rasputin nightclub and he and Jay jogged along the sidewalk through the deluge. They breathed the salt air and heard the rough surf batter the deserted beach a few hundred yards away. Boris pounded three times on the door. A pierogi-shaped woman with six inches of teased black hair waddled past them holding an umbrella and smoking a cigarette. She was walking a small dog with the muzzle of a lion. When the dog sniffed Jay's leg the woman said something to it in guttural Russian and jerked the animal's chain without stopping. A moment later the door opened revealing a huge man in a tracksuit. Unkempt brown hair and a mustache the size of a pickle. He, too, was smoking a cigarette. In a borscht-flavored accent he asked what they wanted. Boris told him whom they were there to see. The man ordered them to wait and closed the door. The rain intensified. After all Jay had accomplished, after reaching the dizzying heights he had, socially and in business, he was standing on a rain-splattered sidewalk in front of a nightclub in Brighton Beach. He almost laughed at the wildly improbable nature of the situation but was interrupted by the return of the bearish man, who waved them inside.

The words were being sung in Russian but the big, sultry voice was unmistakably that of a black woman, or a white woman who was trying to sound black. The unseen chanteuse was belting the disco anthem "I Will Survive" in the language of the Moscow trials. The place smelled like a mixture of sea breeze, disinfectant, and stale cigarettes. Jay had to adjust his eyes to the shadowy darkness. The nightclub was a large, multi-tiered space ringed with tables surrounding a dance floor. On a small stage, the singer, a statuesque black woman with a huge Afro, belted the Russian lyrics as if she had been raised on the banks of the Dnieper. A laptop that stored her backing tracks rested next to her on a high stool.

The mustache motioned for Jay and Boris to wait. He approached a table where two men in suits sat listening to the performance. When the song ended, the men conferred. In English, the singer asked if they wanted her to sing another song and one of the men replied that she should audition for one of those talent shows on television, but meanwhile, they would like her to perform in the club starting this weekend. The diva thanked them, gathered her gear, and hustled off the stage. One of the men rose from the table and escorted her out a side door. The mustache beckoned Jay and Boris to the table.

It had been years since Jay had seen Marat, from whom he kept a wary distance. He did occasional favors for him, like arranging apartments for associates in Gladstone buildings, but their contact was minimal. Marat rose from his chair, smiled, and embraced Jay and Boris in succession.

Only his height was unchanged. When Jay thought of Marat, it was as he looked in the 1970s, with a barrel chest, more hair, and a coiled aspect. In his late sixties now, his hair had thinned and grayed. The Cyrillic letters tattooed on his ringed fingers had faded. His chest had shrunk, and his girth expanded. Most surprising to Jay, he smiled when he asked if they had enjoyed the singer. They assured him that her talents were exemplary.

"During sixties, in Soviet Union, all kinds of Africans

showed up to attend school," he said. "She reminds me of those days."

Marat indicated they should join him at the table. He inquired whether they would like a drink and, without waiting for an answer, called into the darkness for a bottle of vodka. He asked after Boris's mother, and Boris told him that she was well. Marat sent his greetings.

"Is my son causing you problems?" Marat asked with mock concern. Boris looked away, embarrassed by the teasing. Jay assured him he was not. He had trouble imagining what it must be like for Boris to have Marat Reznikov as a father.

A beefy woman with bleached blonde hair appeared with the vodka, deposited it on the table, and toddled away. Marat poured three glasses and lit a Lucky Strike.

"I'm trying to quit," he said, taking a deep drag and blowing an impressive cloud. "You see how well it's going."

Boris asked if he could have a cigarette. His father lit one and handed it to him. It was a surprisingly intimate gesture. Jay had never seen Boris smoke.

Marat stared at Jay. "You look like shit."

"It's been a difficult time."

"I always tried to keep my name out of the papers." Marat waved the smoke away. "The more people know your name, the more people want to take you down. Why you go on television? I watched that interview. You dug your own grave with your mouth." Jay did not respond. Being addressed like this in front of Boris was painful. "What kind of idiot goes on television?" Marat still pronounced it "eee-dyote." His accent still redolent of the Odessa docks.

"My advisors suggested it."

"Your *advisors*?" He spat the word like a bloody tooth. Now it sounded jarring in Jay's ears. Marat called out for appetizers. The same waitress arrived in seconds with a plate of herring and crackers. Marat slapped her backside as she departed.

Jay thought back to the summer when he met his Ukrainian cousin for the first time. To a college student from a world far removed from the first-generation Bronx and Brooklyn experience of his parents, this immigrant seemed like a wild beast. His surface was composed, but underneath something simmered that could erupt without warning, like the steamy day when the two of them crossed a potholed street in the Mott Haven section of the Bronx, and the gypsy cab lightly struck Marat. Jay never forgot the sick feeling that overcame him as he watched his cousin pistol-whip the driver.

His mouth full of herring, Marat said, "You drove all the way to Brooklyn to see me on this beautiful day. What's on your mind?"

Jay wrenched his thoughts back from the Bronx. He outlined his situation with the league, related that the playoffs started soon, and told Marat that a judge was going to rule on the matter shortly.

"What can I do?"

"You still know a lot of people in the sports book in Las Vegas?"

"One or two."

"And that league referee who went to prison for gambling."

"Not personally, no."

"There are rumors, Marat, we discuss them at the owners' meetings."

"Always there are rumors."

"Any hint of fixing in a sport can make people think it's like professional wrestling. It would kill the league."

"Rumors are like oxygen, Jay." Marat glanced around the dim room, over one shoulder, then the other, to illustrate his point. "Everywhere."

"I'm not asking you to confirm or deny."

The expression that had been so welcoming hardened,

replaced by a feral wariness that appeared at home in Marat's weathered features.

"Boris, give us a minute," Jay said. He did not want his protégé to witness his further abasement. Boris took his glass of vodka and retreated.

Jay leaned over the table, lowered his voice: "I only want to be able to communicate to the commissioner that facts might come to light that could cause trouble for the league exponentially worse than what my situation is causing so he'll have to back off and figure out a way to line up behind me."

Jay hadn't intended to drink the vodka, but now he took a sip.

"That's your plan?"

"I don't have a lot of options."

"If they push back then on top of all the other trouble, they'll get you for extortion. Not only will they get you, they get me, and then I'm going back to prison. But, Jay, I'm not going back to prison." Marat had done time upstate for running a gasoline racket.

"I can't go to prison."

Marat took another drag of his cigarette and released a plume of smoke.

"Take your medicine. I did five years. You are big boy, you can do it."

The club was starting to feel like the middle of the night on a deserted subway platform in the 1970s, the atmosphere rank with bad possibilities. Jay started to perspire. His clothes were already moist from the downpour and now he wanted to take a shower.

"Listen to me, Marat."

"I'm listening."

"When you asked me to forget what I saw—"

Marat interrupted, "I'm not going to tell you I'm grateful because I don't know what you're talking about." He drained the vodka in one gulp and poured another.

Jay knew his cousin would admit nothing out loud but it didn't matter. It was a decision that went against his grain at the time and in the ensuing years he had carried like a virus.

"That's all you're going to say?"

"You are bigger man than your father, and Bingo was great man. Is handicap to be born with money because hard to learn how shit works. But you learned."

Marat, philosopher.

Marat, dispenser of favors.

Marat, lands' end court for petitioners with no hope.

Jay knew exactly how shit worked, which was why he was here in the Rasputin nightclub swilling vodka with his grizzled cousin. He reflected on his father, wondered if he would have traveled to Brooklyn to sit down with Marat and attempted to pull invisible levers that would shift the planes on which everything was built. He concluded that that is just what Bingo would have done. But Jay didn't know if he had Bingo's nerve. Perhaps the easiest thing would be to arrange a deal with Marat and then not live up to his half of the bargain. Marat would turn him into a pavement stain and that would be the end of it.

"I could lose everything."

"What everything? Don't be dramatic. You're a fucking billionaire." Marat picked a piece of tobacco from between his teeth and flicked it off his finger with a callused thumb. "I tell you what. Say I make a couple of phone calls." Jay straightened his back. This negotiation is why he was in Brooklyn. "What can you do for me?"

"Whatever you want."

"I didn't say I would do it."

"Marat, just ask."

"I love basketball."

"I do, too."

"Remember when Russian men's team stole 1972 Olympics from the Americans?"

"Who can forget?"

Marat smiled as if he were the one who had arranged that farce himself. He drained his glass and called for coffee. The same waitress arrived with the same speed and placed two espressos in front of them. Jay inhaled the pleasant smell. Its familiarity comforted him, but he did not touch his cup. Marat downed the shot in one gulp.

"I hear your team is worth more than billion dollars."

"So I'm told."

"Give me half."

"Cash?"

"Ownership."

His cousin was throwing him a lifeline, but it was one that would strangle him. A partnership with Marat would be like sharing a confined space with a sleeping lion. Eventually, the cat would awaken.

"That's not possible."

"I should risk my ass for a box of chocolates?"

Jay insisted such a transaction would be remarkably difficult to engineer. There are few businesses as public as professional sports. Owners have to vote, Marat was a convicted felon. There were ways to disguise ownership, Marat said. His name was on only a fraction of the enterprises he controlled.

"Those are illegitimate businesses."

At first, Marat seemed insulted. At this point, Jay did not care.

"Not all of them, boychik. Not all of them." Marat named a well-known Manhattan restaurant operated by a famous chef and informed Jay that he owned a controlling share. When Marat saw the look of surprise on Jay's face, he said, "See, even a guy as smart as you, you don't know everything."

"I don't think it can work."

"Don't tell me it can't work if what you want to say is you don't have the balls to pull it off."

Jay said he would think about Marat's offer and call him. Marat told him not to use the phone. He should come back and shake on the agreement in person.

"If you don't want to do it, I understand. Big decisions are not easy. When time comes, if things are bad, perhaps then I help you."

"How?"

"You say you can't go to prison."

"I won't do that."

"Then maybe you want to disappear."

It was still raining when they drove back to Manhattan. Jay did not mention the particulars of his discussion with Marat, only that he had agreed to consider helping him. Boris listened and nodded. Who knew what he was thinking about his father, their relationship, and the different roads their lives had taken.

Was it worth it to make Marat a silent partner? If it could help Jay avoid prison, perhaps it was. One of the reasons he had hired Boris out of college was because Marat had asked, but also, he viewed it as a means to keep Boris out of his father's orbit. As corny as it was, Jay wanted to be the kind of example for his young cousin that his father had been for him, someone to admire, to emulate. In going to Brighton Beach, he had utterly betrayed that idea. In the Gates of Heaven Cemetery, Bingo Gladstone lay not far from where Babe Ruth was buried. Today Jay was glad of it. As they drove over the Brooklyn Bridge and slid beneath the cloud-shrouded towers of Manhattan, the wash of shame he experienced was tempered by the distant hope that his gambit might work.

CHAPTER FIFTY-SEVEN

Dag's coma lasted ten days. After a week, when Dr. Bannister and his team attempted to bring him out of it, the patient was unresponsive. The wounds were beginning to heal, but his slightly enhanced brain function proved a false dawn. The prognosis went from hopeful to guarded. The international medical team Jay had assembled could not say if he would emerge from a "persistent vegetative state." Jamal Jones had not been back after the first week and Brittany Maxwell had returned to California to look after her children. But Dag's brother Trey, Lourawls, and Babatunde were a constant presence, as was Imam Ibrahim Muhammad. When his friends took a break, Trey remained at his brother's side with the imam.

Muhammad told Trey his own story: The crimes, prison time, and conversion. They discussed the fragility of existence and the innate need of humans to submit to something greater than themselves. The cross on Trey's neck was inked when he was trying to make Church Scott's team and he derived limited comfort from the art when he was cut loose. He told the imam that he wished it had been something more than a decoration. Now that his life had once again derailed he found himself compelled by the spiritual succor his new friend offered. The words of Ibrahim Muhammad were seductive and welcoming and offered sensible solutions to seemingly intractable problems.

At Dag's bedside Trey perused the pamphlets the imam gave him with heightened interest. What he knew about Islam mostly came from television: Jihad, Kareem Abdul-Jabbar, seventy-two virgins, a grab bag that did not cohere into anything he could comprehend. Because white people controlled the media, he viewed much of what it purveyed as inherently suspect. He wanted solace in a time of need, not to strap on a suicide vest and blow himself up. He was impressed that the Prophet was a warrior who vanquished his adversaries and had multiple wives (the Prophet actually reminded him of several guys he knew growing up in Houston). The idea of being part of a vast community of believers that stretched around the world held deep appeal. The no drugs or alcohol business might be a problem, but following *every* rule wasn't the point, was it? Besides, if he had to quit, he could.

He considered the Five Pillars of Islam: Al-Shahadah (Testimony), Al-Salah (Prayer), Al-Siyam (Fasting), Al-Zakat (Almsgiving), and Al-Hajj (Pilgrimage). All of them seemed not only doable but an effective program for gaining control of a sybaritic existence defined by running errands for his brother, whom he loved, but wasn't it time to think about his own life? Trey Maxwell needed to create some sacred space for himself. He needed to stand up and be his own man, gain inner strength, purify, and if one point six billion Muslims could be trusted, Islam was the answer, the word, the "for real" thing.

Dag's room was on the tenth floor, overlooking the heliport adjacent to the East River. Each day the helicopters would come and go, arriving and departing in an endless cycle. One came in and another took off, climbing above the river and banking into the distance. There was something mystical about the helicopters to Trey, something he could not quite put into words. But he felt it. Then, it hit him: The helicopters lifting off reminded him of the Prophet Muhammad ascending from Al Aqsa astride his winged steed to begin his heavenly journey. His mind never used to work like that. He felt something good was happening.

When the imam arrived at the hospital the following day, Trey asked how he could become a Muslim. The imam praised him and said he knew Trey would find happiness, tranquility, and inner peace. His friends took the news in stride, which is to say they asked him if he was going to wear white robes and sell bean pies up on 125th Street. When Trey said, "Ain't funny," and they saw he was serious, that temporarily ended the comedy.

On Wednesday afternoon of the second week Dag was in the hospital Trey, Lourawls, and Babatunde were playing poker (Trey's conversion did not include a prohibition against a friendly card game in Dag's room). Exuding the false cheer of hospital rooms where the possibility of upsetting news flickers like a lightning storm on the horizon, Lourawls gloated as he raked in a twenty-three-dollar pot. Babatunde cursed and told Lourawls he had no talent for the game, it was just luck. Trey ordered the winner to shut up and deal the next hand. As Lourawls began to distribute the cards, Dr. Bannister entered with a group of residents and asked if they would mind stepping out. This was routine, Bannister saw Dag each day, and the entourage left the room. The banter continued in the hallway while they waited for the doctor to finish the examination.

Bannister emerged from the room accompanied by the residents, the graveyard in his eyes. He said, "It looks like your brother might have sepsis." Trey had no idea what sepsis was and asked if it was dangerous. "It's a systemic inflammatory response and, yes, it's dangerous. His organs are failing."

Trey asked if they could do anything to reverse what was happening and Bannister informed him they were doing all they could.

Trey spent the night at the hospital, grabbing snatches of sleep in the chair next to his brother's bed. Teams of doctors attended Dag, changing IVs, hooking him up to different machines. As the night wore on Trey stared at the blinking lights. He talked to Allah and with every cell in his body he supplicated, begged, and prayed. Dawn arrived and, bleary-eyed, Trey watched as helicopters rose up like flying horses and arced over the river through the early morning light soaring above the pallid sun toward Arabia.

D'Angelo Maxwell died that afternoon.

PART III

"And the days keep worryin' me,
There's a hellhound on my trail."
—ROBERT JOHNSON

CHAPTER FIFTY-EIGHT

Jay was in a conference room with several lawyers at Doomer's firm. They were planning to file an injunction against the league when one of the attorneys looked up from his phone like a night watchman who has just discovered an empty vault. When Jay heard the news, he went numb. He slumped in his chair. The lawyers all looked away, as if an electromagnetic shield had materialized around their client that deflected their glances. After Jay's silence became prolonged they decided to adjourn for a few minutes so he could collect himself.

Jay had the urge to go somewhere but did not want to be seen in public so he repaired to Herman Doomer's office. As he reeled through the workplace, he felt the stares of the support staff falling on him like blows. Rooted to a chair, he could not look at Doomer, who had emerged from behind his desk and joined Jay in the sitting area. He told Jay there was a bottle in his desk if wanted a drink. In a monotone, Jay declined the offer.

In his nearly six decades on earth, Jay had never felt so isolated from humanity. Now I've killed someone, he thought. Of all the Commandments, I have violated the most sacred one. His mouth tasted like ashes. He felt as if the sky itself had fractured and collapsed on him.

For a man like Jay Gladstone, who prided himself on his essential decency, this was an unbearable burden. Whatever acts of contrition, or self-abasement, or restitution he performed, the stain was indelible. He would pay the moral wages of that night for as long as he lived. The ghost of the life he took would be with him always and its presence a prison from which he could never escape. An image from Tolstoy visited, from an essay he had read as a young man: In a bottomless pit, he dangled from a delicate branch cantilevered over the nothingness, tongue extended toward a drop of honey that, like hope, had miraculously appeared. But his fingers lost their grip, and he tumbled into the abyss.

"What happens now?"

"We wait to hear from the DA's office," Doomer said.

Jay obtained Brittany Maxwell's number and called to offer condolences. She did not pick up the phone so he left a message requesting she reach out to him if there was anything he could do. He could not weep for D'Angelo Maxwell and he could not weep for himself. The days since the accident had bled him. The only sensation he felt was the hollowness that seemed to be expanding inside him, pushing against his ribs, splitting him open and revealing not lungs, liver, and twisted intestines but only emptiness. If Jay Gladstone was a killer, then the self that Jay thought he knew no longer existed.

CHAPTER FIFTY-NINE

Christine Lupo was in her White Plains office working on a speech to be delivered at a Girl Scouts of America banquet that evening when Lou Pagano gusted in. He had been negotiating a plea bargain with the lawyer of a man who had committed wire fraud when his phone vibrated with a notification. He told the attorney he'd be right back and nearly ran down the hall to his boss's office. The DA and her deputy were blitzed by the news. They had planned to prosecute Jay Gladstone for vehicular assault. Neither had expected the victim to die, and this would only ratchet up the already intense scrutiny on the case. Pagano asked how she intended to proceed, expecting a quick answer. To his surprise, the DA said she wanted to think about it.

He said: "What's to think about?"

She said: "Jay Gladstone is a human being and I want to take my time with this decision. We're not going to throw him to the wolves."

Pagano mumbled unhappily and retreated.

Christine considered her options. To bring murder charges would cause the biggest splash but that would involve proving intent to kill. The hate crime designation was already a reach. She was surprised the whole racial angle of the case had blown up the way it had and shocked by the vilification Jay Gladstone was experiencing. She would not have predicted the public could turn on someone so viciously, but attitudes evolved, certainties became notions, firmly held opinions became I don't know. In the social circles the DA traveled, ten years earlier gay marriage was anathema. Last summer she attended a colleague's gay wedding. As a politician, it was her task to apprehend the mood of the public, but in the case of Jay Gladstone she had not been prescient. Accounts of the violence that had occurred at Sanitary Solutions Arena astounded her. Voters yowled for red meat. To raise the charge to murder would only add to the clamor.

Participating in marriage counseling with a licensed psychologist had heightened Christine's self-awareness and recently she had begun to explore why, on a personal level, she chose to prosecute certain cases. How did her own psychology insinuate itself into her decision-making? As she pondered The State of New York v. Jay Gladstone, she wondered whether the antipathy she felt toward the defendant, powerful, heterosexual, white, was in some way a residue of the negative feelings she had toward Dominic Lupo. Like her husband, Gladstone was smooth, successful, and unconstrained. The urge to destroy him nearly overwhelmed her. But she recognized that perhaps this impulse had something to do with what was going on in her personal life and, further, that it made her less than impartial. This was troubling. As a public servant, she took great pride in the intellectual rigor she brought to bear on her office. She was raised in an overheated, emotional household. Married a man—she realized too late—with the disposition of an opera singer. What had attracted her to the law in the first place was the constraint it placed on passion. It was imperative to Christine's sense of self that she not let her decision be influenced by the manner in which her marriage ran aground.

That evening Bebe came to see Jay at his apartment. He had gone there directly from Doomer's office and had not touched food, or had anything other than water to drink. It was around nine and they were seated on a sofa in the living room. A box of macaroons Bebe had brought from the Carnegie Deli lay unopened on the coffee table. She had been there for several hours and they had barely spoken. Jay's mind flitted from what he had done to Dag's family to his own uncertain future to his father and how much he would have liked to hear from him now. Because Jay was not a member of a synagogue, there was no rabbi to talk to, no one who could ease his burden with pertinent servings of spiritual wisdom. What did the prophets say about those who accidentally killed someone? He would have to investigate that when his ability to concentrate returned. Perhaps he would find some comfort in scripture, although he doubted it.

Bebe asked him if she could do anything.

"There's nothing to do," he said. His voice was hoarse, pensive. "We had the best doctors, and it didn't matter."

Bebe would not allow her brother to succumb to self-pity. She reminded him of their father's maxim: "March forth, Jay. Be a moving target. Don't let this define you."

"But it does, don't you see?"

"You're not the ogre they're making you out to be. It was a terrible mistake, but you're an honorable man."

"Am I?" There was no hope in the question.

As the night wore on, he asked variations of: What can I do to atone? How does a person get past this? Will anyone ever forgive me?

The following day, Jay walked to Central Synagogue on Lexington Avenue. Absent any pressing reason to go to the office, he found himself drawn to the historic temple. He had attended weddings and bar mitzvahs there but had not been inside for several years. The ornate and exquisitely maintained Moorish Revival sanctuary was spacious and light. On the side walls, twelve two-story stained-glass windows. At the front of the room, the ark. Several people sat in pews carved from walnut and ash, deep in private meditation. No one looked up when Jay entered. He found a seat near the back and settled in, gazing straight ahead. The interior of the landmark synagogue had a timeless quality. Jay felt as if he might have slipped into the skin of an ancestor a hundred years earlier in Prague, or Warsaw, or Budapest. Although he had never particularly enjoyed attending religious services, being in a contemplative setting had a soothing effect. A wave of fatigue engulfed him and he briefly closed his eyes.

On the back of the pew in front of him was a rack that contained several prayer books. He opened one and leafed through it. After a few moments, he found what he was looking for. On the right side of the book was the Hebrew, and on the left side the English transliteration.

Quietly, Jay began to recite Kaddish for Dag.

CHAPTER SIXTY

Trey Maxwell was inconsolable. But his sadness at his brother's passing was shot through with fury so raw it surged through his veins and took over his body. He sobbed and he trembled. The inside of his head felt like the fall of Fallujah, a forest of outstretched arms reaching to a smoke-blackened sky, shrieks, grinding engines. Trey's mind burst with fevered images of childhood pickup games, Dag's college recruitment, draft night (when he became an NBA lottery pick), the time Dag bailed Trey out of jail after he had mouthed off to a cop at a traffic stop in Houston and how the two of them had gone out for beers on the way home and laughed about it. They were pure brothers, straight down the line, none of this *half*, or *step*, or any other category that might have weakened the connection that had come to define Trey's existence. He was Trey Maxwell, for sure, a straight-up baller in his own right, a friend and a son, but when boiled down to his essence Trey was D'Angelo Maxwell's little brother. Imam Ibrahim Muhammad had said Dag was the mighty oak tree in whose cool shade Trey stood. The younger sibling failed to appreciate it at the time, perhaps because he recognized how true it was and did not like being reminded. But when he thought about it now, he suddenly felt as if the years had been torn away and he was flung back through time to when he was small and vulnerable, and Dag hovered in the air like a funky genie. All that was over now. Aloneness overwhelmed him, and vulnerability fueled his rage. When Lourawls put a well-meaning arm around his friend's shoulder Trey reflexively swiped it off and tried to push him away. Trey quickly apologized. Berated himself for his reaction. Then he hugged Lourawls and held on to him for a long time as Babatunde rubbed his back and tried to comfort him.

Trey had never been called upon to arrange a funeral before but he took it upon himself to organize Dag's. Church Scott offered to help but Trey insisted on there being no involvement from his brother's team while Jay Gladstone owned it. Imam Ibrahim Muhammad's proposal to preside over the service at the largest mosque in New York was briefly considered but, given that Dag was not a Muslim, Trey did not believe that to be appropriate. Instead, it was to be held at the Cathedral of St. John the Divine.

In the three days before the funeral, Trey wandered the house in New Jersey. Lourawls and Babatunde stayed out of his way. In every room, he felt his brother's presence. The food Dag liked to eat was in the refrigerator. His trophies and plaques lined a wall. During the intervals between the endless logistical phone calls, Trey did not have the concentration to watch television or play video games and his new spiritual calling meant that he could not smoke weed. The only place he was able to focus his attention was on the religious tracts the imam had given him. He sat in the backyard and became familiar with the idea that there is no God but God, Muhammad is his messenger, and his word is revealed in the Quran. The imam had given Trey a copy and he tried to read it but gave up after ten minutes. For the time being he decided to stick with the pamphlets. If he had questions he could go on the Internet. Unlike the Jihadi vision peddled by the western media clearly intended—according to his new teacher—to fuel the bottomless appetite for American wars in Muslim nations, Islam, as far as he could tell, was peaceful, tolerant, and inspiring. It was the quickest route to a fair and just world. In one of the pamphlets, this passage caught his eye: "The Quran says, 'We sent aforetime our messengers with clear Signs and sent down with them the Book and the Balance that men may stand forth in Justice' (Quran 57:25)."

That sounded right.

He brooded over the death of his brother and became obsessed with the idea of justice and whether it would be done. The court system was notoriously unpredictable. Trey believed justice was rarely impartial, especially when it came to people of color. A promising middleweight fighter named Hurricane Carter served eighteen years for murder, the Central Park Five did serious time for a gang rape. None of them were guilty. Then, there was that white bitch everyone believed killed her three-year old daughter who went free. The American jury system was a crapshoot.

Bingo Gladstone used to say he never attended the funeral of someone who was not a saint and so it was with D'Angelo Maxwell.

The service was held on a Friday morning and over one thousand people packed the cathedral. Speakers were set up on the sidewalks so the overflow crowd could hear the service. The three young men who encountered Jay at the Celtics game, and Dag on Striver's Row in Harlem, cut their classes at Riverdale Country Day and stood across Amsterdam Avenue near the schoolteacher Gloria Alvarez. She had called in sick and was clutching the goggles Dag had worn during the eclipse like a holy relic. Church Scott and the entire roster were there. Every NBA All-Star whose team was playing on the east coast that day flew in, along with several coaches. In the front row, Brittany Maxwell and her three children, escorted by Jamal Jones. Mayor House of Newark sat with Mayor Bloomberg of New York. Alicia Keys sang "Amazing Grace" and the commissioner of the NBA gave a eulogy in which he declared

D'Angelo Maxwell to be a "mensch." Church Scott and several of Dag's teammates shared memories. Imam Ibrahim Muhammad chose not to say anything during the service, preferring to sit in the congregation and comfort Trey. On the sidewalk afterward, he addressed the media and extolled Dag as a great humanitarian who deserved a statue in front of the new arena.

Nicole thought about going but decided against it. As much as she would have liked to pay her respects to Dag, her attendance would cause a massive distraction. She had not been feeling well for the past few days and was not sure whether to ascribe it to nervous tension or something physical. Whatever it was, she chose to hole up in the Pierre that morning.

Jay wanted to attend the service. He knew there would be many who would not welcome him yet he held that it was the moral thing to do. Bobby Tackman insisted he stay away, believing his presence might incite something similar to the riot that had broken out at Sanitary Solutions and to make sure his client obeyed watched the Internet live-stream of the service with him from the relative safety of Jay's apartment.

CHAPTER SIXTY-ONE

Church Scott informed his players that he had received assurances from the league office that the team would be sold and so a boycott of the first playoff game was avoided. Jay instructed Tackman to issue a press release saying he intended to fight it in court but this had no effect one way or another on the team. The media treated the announcement as the pathetic raving of a deluded white man who refused to acknowledge he had lost more than a legal skirmish. According to the Internet, Jay was: "out of touch," "schizo," "a loser." On Sunday afternoon, he watched from his apartment as his team (and they were his team until a court ruled otherwise) were routed by the Chicago Bulls 113-91 in Chicago.

After Dag's death, Jay became a prisoner in his apartment, only going out for evening walks on side streets. He did not visit the synagogue again. Meals were sent up, but barely touched. Boris and Bebe visited but he did not want to talk so they played poker and gin rummy. He wondered if he would hear from Aviva but she did not call. Neither did he hear from his cousin Marat, nor from the commissioner, which meant the wily Ukrainian had decided not to stick his neck out. What a fool's errand that had been. Jay added having beseeched Marat to the increasingly long list of behaviors he lambasted himself over. Franklin and Marcy sent a cellophane-wrapped gift basket from Zabar's with a note that said: *Your luck has to improve!* Jay interpreted this as a taunt.

The nights were endless. He took sleeping pills but would wake hours before dawn and thrash from side to side oscillating between uneasy dreams and fraught wakefulness, seized by a torpor that bordered on nullity.

One night Jay thought about suicide. He had read that if you jump from a great height you lose consciousness before splattering on the sidewalk. Was the building tall enough? He could take pills and chase them with liquor, hang himself in the bathroom, slit his wrists. Then everyone would talk about how Jay Gladstone had allowed himself to be driven to suicide. No one wanted that in his obituary. Like King Kong clinging to the Empire State Building, he swatted at these thoughts as if they were dive-bombing airplanes and one after another batted them away. Jay could never take his own life because it would represent an admission of defeat foreign to his constitution, a weakness of character he was congenitally unable to admit he suffered. Whatever happened, he would persevere because, like Martin Luther King, Jay believed that the arc of the universe bent toward justice. He thought about how Dr. King had inspired him as a young man, how brave the civil rights leader had been in the face of adversity, the famous Letter From Birmingham Jail—Jail! That wrenched his mind back to the possibility of prison, and what awaited him there, and so the night staggered on.

Before dawn he climbed out of bed and stared down at the empty streets. The alienation from the city he had undergone as a result of the trials visited upon him was intolerable, an exile he did not know if he could endure. But the Gladstones were survivors. This lesson was imparted by Bingo from the time Jay was a child and it was in his bones. Because of this, Jay believed he was unbreakable.

March forth.

On Monday morning Herman Doomer called.

"They're going to charge you with murder."

CHAPTER SIXTY-TWO

This information would have sent him reeling a week earlier but Jay had steeled himself, and he recovered quickly. He asked what it meant on a practical level.

"It's a negotiating tactic," Doomer said. He informed Jay that he had arranged for the two of them to meet with the district attorney in person that afternoon.

Jay put on a suit and tie and examined himself in the mirror. Other than the dark circles under his eyes, he looked surprisingly unbowed. The misery diet had already caused five pounds to disappear, and the contours of his face were less curved. Although the whites of his eyes were still striated with red, the facial swelling had gone down. He threw his head back, thrust his chin out. He was accustomed to charming public officials to get what he wanted.

Doomer arrived in a Volvo sedan and Jay got into the passenger seat. As they cruised uptown, Doomer informed him that the DA had wanted to revoke bail (based on his foreign holdings, they deemed Jay a flight risk), but the lawyer, citing openness to a plea deal, had successfully argued against that. Doomer had been bargaining with the DA's office all morning and gotten them to agree to a reduction in charges if Jay would accept a plea.

"Do you think I should?"

"Juries are unpredictable."

They barely talked for the remainder of the ride to White Plains. The Bronx River Parkway was greening, the maples, elms, and oaks of his childhood. Jay had barely been out of his apartment and savored the glorious day as if nature provided it for his delectation.

When they arrived at the courthouse, Jay was relieved to see no one was staking it out, and he was able to walk into the building unmolested. They passed through the metal detector, signed in, rode the elevator up. A secretary brought them back to the offices of the district attorney.

Jay and Doomer sat across the table in the conference room discussing the team's chances in the playoffs after the shellacking in Chicago when Christine Lupo arrived followed by Lou Pagano. Introductions were brief. No one shook hands. Lupo and Pagano sat across from Jay and Doomer. The DA thanked them for coming. She seemed like a reasonable woman. A little cold, but that was to be expected.

"I gather you know my cousin Franklin," was Jay's opener.

"I do," she said. "He's an entertaining guy."

"Get him to do his impression of Sydney Greenstreet for you."

"I will." There was a pause, then: "Mr. Doomer," done with the preliminaries, "my office wants to sound out your client on the possibility of a plea deal."

"My client is open to that," the lawyer said. "What do you have in mind?"

Jay held his breath. He had worked it out. A seven-year sentence meant getting out in half the time. He could do that.

Lupo said: "We're willing to drop the murder charge," Jay looked at Doomer, who did not break eye contact with the district attorney, "if your client agrees to a twenty-year sentence."

Twenty years? Jay could not believe what he had heard. Two decades? He would be nearly eighty when he was released! Even if a judge reduced the sentence for good behavior, it would be at least a decade, and that was assuming he survived confinement. His state of mind must have been apparent because he felt Doomer's palm rest on his forearm.

"Twenty years seems excessive for what my client has consistently maintained was an accident."

"We're confident we can get a jury to convict," Pagano said. "With these charges, he's looking at a life sentence."

Jay stared at the public officials. He was usually able to handle people like this with the Gladstone bluff and bluster. But he had nothing to bargain with, no threats to make.

"Twenty years?" He could barely get the words out.

"Let's look at this objectively," Doomer said to the DA. "My client has a record of philanthropy, leadership, and general civic virtue that is unimpeachable. We won't be the only ones taking a risk if this goes to trial."

Having berated himself so extensively, Jay occasionally lost sight of his accomplishments. He was cheered by his lawyer's words.

The DA informed them that this was a chance her office was willing to take.

"We have a motive," Lou Pagano said. "No one disputes the basic facts that Mr. Gladstone, in a jealous rage, struck the victim with a deadly weapon."

Doomer rumbled, "Prosecutorial overreach."

"We believe we can win this case," Lupo said, her voice flecked with steel.

Jay gazed out the window. Cirrus clouds floated over White Plains. A small plane buzzed north over the Bronx River, nature and the city going about their business. Patterns too byzantine to be decoded shifting and resolving, subsuming individuals into the larger matrix, human agency an illusion. Jay turned toward the DA.

"If I accept the offer, how long would I have to serve?"

She said: "With time off for good behavior, probably about twelve years."

A dozen years in some vile penitentiary surrounded by rapists and murderers? They would regard him like a mouth-watering veal shank, his pelt a trophy. Jay heard Doomer ask when they needed an answer.

"By the end of the week," Christine Lupo said. "Mr. Gladstone will surrender to the authorities on that day at a location to be determined and begin serving his sentence immediately. In the meantime, my office will announce the murder charges."

"Given the possibility of a plea bargain," Doomer said, "is that necessary?"

Christine Lupo considered this. "Mr. Gladstone is being charged with murder, so it is my responsibility to enter it into the public record."

"My client has significant business holdings," Doomer said. "He'll need several months to make custodial arrangements before he begins serving his sentence, assuming we don't go to trial."

Christine Lupo said, "If he chooses not to go to trial, your client has until a week from Friday to get his affairs in order."

On the ride back to Manhattan, the sky pressed down, and the trees leaned in. As the car skirted Scarsdale, a flock of starlings formed a shroud. The self-assurance Jay had managed to feign earlier had evaporated and been replaced by nausea. His skin felt clammy. It was clear that the DA relished the idea of a trial. The publicity would be career making, and to her, the possibility that she might lose was worth the gamble. But the risk of a trial for Jay was exponentially greater. In the current climate, he was simply too unsympathetic a defendant. No jury was going to acquit. They would make him an example. Too many years were people repressed, their aspirations ignored, their hopes derailed. The new world would devour the old, and its dawn demanded human sacrifice. The conclusion of the national spectacle called for society to throw Jay Gladstone into the volcano.

He could flee, but was taking flight a realistic option? Where could he go? Anyplace he was willing to live had an extradition treaty with the United States and would render his time there nerve-wracking and brief.

Tokyo: *Tick-tock*.

Barcelona: *Tick-tock*.

London: *Tick-tock. Boom*.

He laughed mirthlessly to himself upon the realization that he was reviewing a list of vacation destinations. Flight was not a holiday. He could change his identity, but he wasn't exactly anonymous, so how long would that ruse last? And the heir of an international real estate fortune reduced to pretending to be someone else did not sound like a noble path. So that left where? Cuba where the Castro brothers would have to agree to his presence? South America where he would have to go into hiding like an ex-Nazi in Argentina? The options were all unacceptable.

When Christine Lupo announced the murder charges, Internet comment threads filled with dark assessments of Jay's situation, the majority of them disagreeing with his own. He would never be convicted. He would somehow buy off the jury. The trial would be a sham because no one like Jay Gladstone ever serves time for anything. The idea that Jay would escape punishment gained purchase. He could only hope the predictions of his enemies might prove accurate.

CHAPTER SIXTY-THREE

The days since his brother's funeral were brutal for Trey. Dag's business managers were organizing his estate, and they informed Trey that the house was going on the market. He, Lourawls, and Babatunde were given a month to find somewhere else to live. Dag's wife was due to receive half of what he owned and most of what remained would go to his children. Trey received a small annuity. It was enough to live on, but not in the style to which he had become accustomed as his brother's right hand. Without Dag, the gravitational pull that kept the planets in orbit vanished. Lourawls went back to Houston to work for his cousin's construction business. Babatunde planned to move to Los Angeles and resume his career as a personal trainer. A cop in South Carolina had killed a black man during a traffic stop and Imam Ibrahim Muhammad, who had been such a regular presence at the hospital and in the days leading up to the funeral, traveled there to offer his assistance.

Trey was alone. In the morning, he put on gym clothes and worked out for hours at a time. He drank water and ate cereal. He took Biggie for walks in the neighborhood. Tried to pray the requisite five times a day but that turned out to be harder than he had imagined. He forgot his prayer rug, or neglected to set the timer meant to remind him to face Mecca. He visited a mosque in Jersey City a few times and was welcomed there but realized he preferred the fellowship of a team to that of a religious institution, and with Dag's passing that was what he found himself missing. And he was angry about it. He had planned to spend his life at Dag's side and now that this had been denied him his bitterness began to metastasize. When Biggie lingered to sniff something under a bush, Trey yanked his chain so hard the dog yelped. On Palisades Parkway, when another driver cut him off, Trey floored the gas pedal and nearly rammed the other car before he stopped himself.

The day Babatunde left for California, Trey went to a fast food burger joint for lunch. The teenager behind the counter messed up his order, and Trey exploded. He threw the food at the quaking kid and was about to hit him with the tray when he realized what he was doing and apologized. Trey left the restaurant without his food, sat in his car, and cried. There in the parking lot, he became concerned with his mental stability. He thought about seeing a doctor but what would a doctor do but prescribe some drug and his new religion forbade that.

Later, he put on boxing gloves to work out with a speed bag but after five strenuous minutes realized he did not want to be pounding a speed bag. He wanted to be hitting a human being, and the human being he wanted to be hitting was a rich-ass motherfucker named Jay Gladstone. The man who had killed his brother hung around training camp the year Trey tried to make the team. He acted friendly to some of the players but never said a word to Trey. Because of this, Trey saw the owner's hand in his fate. Ever since being cut right before the first regular season game, he had loathed him.

Jay Gladstone's current predicament was a boon to Trey. He hoped the courts would do their job and send him away forever but realized that was unlikely. Men like Gladstone never got what they deserved. Trey could not depend on the court system to avenge Dag. He would have to do it himself. But how could he possibly justify this behavior? He searched for answers in the Quran Ibrahim Muhammad had given him and discovered that Muslims, like Jews, adhered to the Old Testament dictum of "an eye for an eye." That was all the validation he needed.

CHAPTER SIXTY-FOUR

Although Aviva was no longer sharing a bed with Imani, their theater project kept them in proximity, and this did not improve Aviva's mood, especially when her former girlfriend began to flirt with Axel. In their discussions of the radical milieu, his opinions became more strident. Assassinations engaged in by political extremists were a favorite topic, and Axel wondered why those tactics almost never made their way to America. Aviva listened as he expounded on his fascination with the bombing campaigns the American left engaged in during the latter half of the twentieth century, notably the Mad Bomber who terrorized New York City in the late sixties and the Weathermen cell that accidentally blew up a townhouse in Greenwich Village.

It turned out that making a bomb was remarkably easy. Axel found a target he pressed on the others: The statue of the Pilgrim Father in Central Park. On the east side of the park between 72nd and 73rd Streets at the base of Pilgrim Hill, the musket-toting bronze figure represented both the northern European rape of the land and the ongoing subjection of non-white peoples and so was a textbook symbol. Because all they were going to blow up was a statue, he tried to sell the idea that the whole operation would be a lark. It didn't involve acquiring anything as exotic as Semtex or C4; the ingredients were readily available in local stores.

Axel asked each of the group to visit a different retail location to obtain nails, gunpowder, electrical wire, a timing device, and a pressure cooker. Mindful of the Weathermen who blew themselves up, they became sticklers for safety. Axel determined that before their action it was necessary to do a test and so the woods near the school were designated Alamogordo. But upon further reflection, the group collectively decided an explosion in the woods might still attract unwanted attention. He suggested they purchase a kayak from a local sporting goods store, pack the device into it, and launch it on the river. The current would sweep the craft downriver, and the detonation would take place at a safe distance. If they did it in the middle of the night, the chances of anyone observing them, or of an innocent person getting hurt, were minimal. Aviva, Noah, and Imani believed the action in the woods would be the extent of their pyrotechnics. No one thought Axel would blow up a statue in Central Park.

At midnight, Axel and Noah picked up Aviva and Imani. They parked on a dark road near the river. Axel led the way with a small flashlight. Aviva carried the inflatable kayak, Noah and Imani the nonexplosive ingredients. Axel was in charge of the gunpowder. Darkness had swallowed most of the moon, but the inky sky was devoid of clouds, and ghostly light illuminated their path. The only sounds were their footfalls. In a clearing near the riverbank, Axel assembled the bomb while the other three took turns blowing air into the kayak.

Noah's cheeks popped out like a squirrel's as he emptied his lungs into the mouthpiece. After exhausting his capacity and passing the kayak to Imani, he said to Aviva, "What do you think your father would say if he could see you right now?"

Why were they so obsessed with her father? Was it a means of marginalizing her, of their letting it be known she would never truly be one of them?

"I don't know, Noah. What do you think?"

"I think he'd shit himself," Noah said.

"Because we're testing a bomb?" Aviva asked.

"Because you're in the woods with two black people," Imani said, her laughter mingling with Noah's.

Axel told them to stop joking around and finish the job. Five minutes later, they had inflated the craft. Shivering against the chill, they placed the kayak in the river, Noah holding on to the stern to keep it from floating away in the swift current. Axel set the timer and nestled the pressure cooker in the well. He gave the signal, and Noah released his grip. The kayak immediately began to float south, picking up speed. Aviva noticed the satisfied grin on Axel's face. Noah was bouncing on the balls of his feet. Imani had her hands on her hips and wore a questioning expression as if she were having second thoughts. Aviva watched the kayak's progress, pleased that they had the foresight to do a test run. She remembered that her father had always taught her to be thorough when performing a task. When the kayak was no more than a hundred yards away, its movement ceased.

"Shit," Axel said. "It must have caught on a log or something."

The explosion was sudden and concussive. The fireball that enveloped the kayak rose twenty feet above the water and illuminated the river in a vivid glow. And then Aviva heard Noah scream and curse. Axel shone his flashlight on Noah. Blood streaked his neck. Cut with a piece of flying shrapnel. Imani looked like she might faint.

"Fuck fuck fuck," Noah shouted.

"Hold still," Aviva ordered.

She looked at the wound and was able to determine it was not deep. "You're going to be okay," she said, trying to convince herself that her friend could avoid a hospital visit.

"Fuck," Noah said, bloody fingers pressed to the side of his head.

The next morning Aviva got a text from Imani during her gender studies seminar. Could they meet up later?

In the cafeteria, students were eating seitan burgers, chatting about the merits of different weed strains, contemplating Indonesian poetry on the screens of their e-readers. Obscure indie rock trickled from hidden speakers. Aviva looked around the room. Nearly to a person, these students supported radical change, yet how many of them were prepared to do anything about it? She spotted Imani, waiting for her at a table. Aviva sat across from her.

"I'm out," Imani said. She looked like she hadn't slept.

"Why?"

"For starters, Noah nearly got killed."

"He's fine."

"What are we going to accomplish by blowing up a statue of some pilgrim dude?"

"It sends an anti-racist message." When Imani laughed, she said, "What?"

"Would you listen to yourself?"

"It's just a statue," Aviva said. "No one gets hurt."

"What if they catch us?"

"In the middle of the night?"

Imani shook her head, took a sip of coffee. Aviva waited. The idea that she was the one advocating for direct action against America's history of racism and not Imani made her uneasy.

Imani said, "The revolution came and went, and we missed it."

"But it's such an ideal symbol of white dominion."

"You gotta work out your daddy issues some other way."

That blow hit her hard. Aviva felt herself starting to answer, but she didn't want to fight with Imani. Outside the window, a white kid dressed entirely in hemp threw a Frisbee to a Labradoodle with a red bandana tied around his neck.

"That's what you think this is?"

"Hey, we all got our shit," Imani said.

Aviva fought the impulse to get up and leave. As she shifted in her chair and looked away from Imani a rush of blood coursed through her ears and the sounds of students' voices, music playing, the scraping of chairs, grew muffled. She floated out of the room like a Chagall fiddler, over the campus and east toward her childhood home and recalled an adolescent afternoon when her father tried for what turned out to be the last time to coax her on to the 20' x 20' asphalt basketball court he had built for her. There was the transparent fiberglass backboard, and her father held a new ball.

"Won't you even try?" he said.

"I hate this game."

The look on his face that day made her realize for the first time that she had the ability to inflict pain on the colossus in whose rumbling steps she walked.

She heard Imani say: "I got into grad school last week."

"Grad school?" Aviva was shocked. "You didn't even tell me you applied."

"Well, I did."

"What are you going to study?"

"Education." Then, in her "street" voice—the ghetto intonation nearly always used ironically, but not this time—Imani explained: "Black girl don't have the opportunities white girl got. You wanna blow up some bronze Pilgrim, go ahead. But we graduate in a month, and then shit gets real."

"When did you become so cynical?"

"My people don't have the luxury of purity," Imani said.

That afternoon Noah texted Aviva and Axel that he was out, too. Nearly having been decapitated the previous night convinced him that the armed wing of the antiracism crusade would have to make do without him.

Aviva had a paper due the next day for her critical theory

class but could not concentrate. The confidence with which she held her political beliefs remained steady, but her ideas about how to enact them were no longer so certain. If Imani and Noah, both of whom were African-American, were not going to participate in Axel's plan, then what was she doing? Would it not be patronizing to take it upon herself to make a point in such dramatic fashion when two of the people that the action was intended to benefit wanted no part in it? What Imani said distressed her. Aviva's advantages allowed her to play at changing the world. Imani had to enroll in graduate school to improve her chances of getting a job. What job would Aviva ever have to get? She could renounce her birthright and pretend to be a proletarian warrior for social justice, but there would always be a net ready to catch her should she fall. Although she might experiment with her identity, there was no changing the root of who she was.

Aviva turned her computer off, pulled on a jacket, and in late afternoon light walked to the weathered two-story house with the view of the Catskill Mountains that Axel shared with Noah and several other Tate students. Two guys were smoking weed and playing a video game in the living room. When she asked where Axel was, they pointed to the kitchen. She found him straining lentils over the sink. He gave her a rueful smile. *Comadre.*

"I'm done," she said.

Axel stopped what he was doing. His smile vanished.

"With what?"

"Everything. It's stupid."

"Because those two pussies bailed, you're out? That is bull-shit, Aviva."

"We're doing a play, Axel. We're not revolutionaries."

"Come on! We can go down to the city tonight. It'll be fucking awesome."

"Forget it. Not happening."

"For real?" He inclined his head and stared at her. She met his gaze. From the other room came the sound of the video game. Automatic weapons, screaming tires, hip-hop.

"You shouldn't do it either, Axel. It's a terrible idea."

Aviva observed him processing her words, how his expression shaded from disbelief to resentment. She thought about freshman year, the times they had slept together.

"You might wanna cover up, Aviva, your origins are showing."

Ordinarily, this insult would have offended her, but after the explosion in the woods and the sight of her friend's blood, Aviva was less sensitive to personal attacks.

"That's all you've got?" she said.

"What else is there?"

"The revolution's in your head," she said.

"Oh, snap," was his comeback.

"Noah could've been hurt way worse."

"A flesh wound," Axel said, as he turned his attention to the lentils, emptying them from the colander into a pot. His back was to her.

"I've been listening to you since I was a freshman, Axel. You said read Fanon, so I read Fanon, and Edward Said, and the postcolonial African novelists."

"You're welcome."

"I learned a lot, so thanks, I guess. But I'm playing Patty Hearst in a play; I'm not turning into her."

"For sure, you're not." He lit a match and turned on the gas.

"You can keep fooling around with guns and bombs and whatever other delusional shit you're into, but I have a paper due tomorrow, and I'm gonna finish it now."

He turned around to face her.

"You're such a lightweight, Aviva."

"And you're a poser."

"That's what you think?"

"You were born in the wrong era. What you really ought to build is a time machine. That way you can fight the fascists in Spain, or join up with the Castro brothers in the mountains of Cuba or sign on with Patrice Lumumba in the Congo, but until you figure out how to slip through a hole in the time-space continuum, you're stuck in 2012 with the rest of us."

The contempt on his face did not move her. Aviva left the kitchen. She walked past the gamers getting high in the living room without acknowledging them, and out the front door. The struggle would endure but on her terms. What would the destruction of a statue accomplish? The whole idea was juvenile.

CHAPTER SIXTY-FIVE

When his team was swept 4-0 in the playoffs, the world blamed Jay. If the owner had not caused such a calamity, the hive mind declared on websites and their vitriolic comment threads, on television shows and in barroom conversations, surely the result would have been different. Jay ignored the opprobrium and rarely even turned his computer on anymore.

After the murder charge was made public, the City Planning Commission postponed their ruling on the Sapphire project until Jay resolved his legal situation. He expected this and accepted it philosophically. A line of potential buyers had materialized, all of them making generous offers, and league sources were crowing about how quickly they had excised the outdated and unacceptable attitudes that Harold Jay Gladstone represented.

After consultations with Bebe and Doomer, and much reflection, Jay had come to believe what Marat had told him: He could do prison. He would read books; learn a foreign language. He had agreed to surrender on the following Friday morning. The arrangement called for him to arrive at the Westchester County Courthouse to be formally sentenced and from there be taken into custody to begin serving his time at a prison three hundred and twenty-eight miles north of Manhattan. He spent most of the week in the city, tidying up business affairs. In the evenings, he returned to Bedford.

Doomer had informed Jay that he could initiate legal

proceedings against Franklin from prison. He continued to meet with the lawyers who were helping him contest the sale of the team. He vowed the Sapphire would be built and planned to petition the Planning Commission. He visited his mother, explaining that he had to go away on an extended business trip but would try to call her whenever he could. Helen Gladstone believed in rectitude. Jay was thankful his mother could not understand what was going on.

He continued to exercise and watch his diet, but the ordeal had taken a toll. The ongoing stress of his situation caused his blood pressure to rise. More gray hair appeared, and he fought against a further thickening of his middle. He did not have the stamina he once did. Two flights of stairs left him short of breath. Mirrors revealed his father's visage staring back. With prison rushing at him, time seemed to accelerate.

He thought about Nicole and reflected on his part in the dissolution of their relationship. She may have been responsible for her actions, but Jay recognized that it was his stubbornness that pushed the marriage over the edge. That he had not been more open to having another child filled him with regret. It pained him to realize that he had viewed Nicole's desire as a distraction from plans for another skyscraper, or the pursuit of a sports championship, or an ambassadorial post, and now that all of these things receded before him, forever out of reach, he could not escape the mortifying thought that the abundance of his life before the trials that befell him had somehow not been sufficient.

Although Jay agonized over the people in whose misfortunes his behavior played a role, he did not consider himself guilty of anything other than hubris. But something about his way of passing through the world had robbed him of his family and his freedom, and he could not shake the idea that everything might have been different if he had only listened to the people that he loved.

Each morning no later than 7:30, Jay drank his coffee then sauntered down to the barn. He stepped into the shadows and savored the gamy perfume of hay and manure. He saddled Mingus, mounted, and rode the trails around his house. Sunlight filtered through the tall trees as the horse's hooves clopped over the carpet of pine needles. Jay found himself vacillating between the sense of profound contentment engendered by the pastoral surroundings and sheer terror in anticipation of what lay ahead. Swaying in the saddle, he took comfort in the notion that he would not be the first person of distinction to be removed from society against his will. Napoleon sprung to mind, and Gandhi, and of course Nelson Mandela. Although Napoleon came to a sticky end when he fled Elba, Gandhi and Nelson Mandela achieved their greatest victories upon release. In no way did Jay consider himself equal to these men—he understood the comparison to be both grandiose and vaguely comical—but this benighted tradition of jailing figures who deserved better was a consolation during the gloomy hours. On the mornings when he moved Mingus from a trot to a canter to a gallop, the lives of those heroes suffused him with a vivifying brightness.

Jay spent the night prior to his surrender writing emails, attending to as many loose ends as he could reasonably manage. Bebe met him for dinner in a nearby town, and when she asked if he wanted her to stay with him at the house so he would not be alone on his final night of freedom, he declined.

"I'm not going to have complete solitude again for years," he told her. "I want to savor it."

Before he went to bed that night, he turned on all the lights in the house and walked through every room, spending a couple of minutes in each one, imprinting the geometry and the textures in his brain so he could call on them in his imprisonment. He no longer felt sorry for himself. People had survived worse.

Lou Pagano from the district attorney's office had insisted on escorting Jay to the courthouse, and he was due to arrive at nine o'clock the next morning. Jay set his alarm to be sure he rose early for the last ride on his horse.

Russell Plesko could not believe his fortune. He had quickly shifted from the life of a patrolman to being a part of the district attorney's team. While he may have only been a low-level grunt, working with the lawyers fired his ambitions. After an encouraging talk with Lou Pagano, now considered a mentor, Russell planned to finish his undergraduate degree and then take the law boards. Several of the local universities offered night courses, and if he applied himself, he would get his degree in four years. He and his wife reconciled, and he had moved back into his Port Chester home.

The alarm went off as usual at six thirty. Crystal rolled over and stroked his hair, half awake. She had been up for the usual middle of the night feeding, and Russell wanted to let her rest. He hit the snooze button, promising to only sleep another few minutes, but before drifting off, he heard his daughter fussing in the other room.

As he hoisted the baby from the crib and placed her on the adjacent changing table, he thought about the coming weekend. Because the family lived in a one bedroom apartment, they had transformed the living room into a nursery, and Russell was determined that his kid was going to have a room of her own. Russell and Crystal had been looking for a larger apartment for the last three months. He hoped they would find a new place tomorrow. Now he changed the diaper and put his daughter back in the crib while he quickly prepared a bottle of pre-pumped breast milk. Crystal was religious about breast milk. His daughter took the bottle hungrily, and Russell returned to the bedroom to get dressed.

Although he was now working for the district attorney's

office, he still wore his police uniform every day. It pleased him that his new co-workers seemed to like cops. He showered and shaved and before going into the closet listened to see if his daughter was making noise.

All quiet on the Plesko front.

One of the advantages of his new posting was that he was no longer required to wear the patrolman's belt, although he still carried a gun. He pulled on his uniform, slid his holster on to his belt, and leaned over to kiss his wife. Crystal was one of those women who could clean the apartment on a ninety-degree day in August and somehow still smell like a window box filled with geraniums. Russell loved that about her.

"The baby has a bottle," he said.

His wife murmured her thanks and went back to sleep. Russell went into the living room, picked his daughter up from the crib, kissed her neck, and inhaled the milk and talcum powder baby smell. He laid the girl back down and touched the mobile that hung over the crib so its movement would draw her attention.

Lou Pagano had asked Russell to meet him at the county courthouse an hour before they usually appeared at the office. The two of them were going to pick up Jay Gladstone and convey him to court where he would officially enter the prison system. Russell already knew how lucky he had been to avoid prosecution, but today he felt exceptionally fortunate. Jay Gladstone's situation could have been his own. He was a free man and next week he would begin his duties as the interim coach of the Fenian's Little League team. When Russell saw Pagano waiting for him in the parking lot drinking takeout coffee, he fought the urge to hug him.

It was dawn when he slid the barn door open. Jay had risen early to go on a longer ramble than usual. The sun made a feeble attempt to assert itself, but the slate sky let nothing through. He didn't care if he got caught in the rain. He hoped it *would* rain so he could store as many sense memories as possible. He greeted Mingus and scratched the animal behind the ears while he fed him a carrot. He ran his fingers through the horse's thick mane and pressed his face against the muzzle, inhaling the animal's musky odor. He opened the gate, led the horse to the trough, mucked the stall, shoveling the manure into a bucket and dumping the contents into a composter behind the barn. This activity was usually the duty of the groom, but today Jay wanted to perform every task himself. Only then did he throw the saddle over the horse's back, affix the straps, and mount.

On his ride, he reflected on how he had arrived at this point. The failure of two marriages, the alienation from his daughter, who, as he saw it, rejected him for no logical reason. Then there were Franklin's machinations, the vanished opportunity to gift the city he loved with one of the world's great buildings, the imminent loss of his team. All of it continued to fester, and he concluded that this burgeoning litany of trouble had one thing in common with the countless blessings life had visited upon him. They had happened for no reason at all. He considered the expression: "If I knew then." But if he knew then, what? Would he have handled those situations differently? He would have led the same life, made nearly all the same choices. The complete randomness of the whole business came as a revelation. It was bewildering.

Jay was half a mile from the house. He had been riding for over an hour, and it was getting near the time his police escort was due to arrive. As far as he was concerned, they could wait. It would be his last act of self-assertion for a while. Much of the ride had been spent managing his rising nervousness. He noticed his breathing was shallow and he had to consistently remind himself to take gulps of the piney air and let his breath out slowly. Birds chittered. A chipmunk fled. It was a timeless rural landscape and yet he felt his anxiety begin to spike. He chided himself, frustrated at his inability to master his nerve, and took another deep breath. He stretched his arms to his sides and over his head, shook the tension from his hands. If any government agents were at his home when he emerged from the woods, he wanted them to see just how in command he was.

Jay slid back in the saddle as he rode down a declivity and when the grade evened he headed for a dogleg in the trail that would deliver him back to the barn. He was feeling good again but did not want to canter as he usually did at this point in the ride. Today there was no rush to get back to the house. He had focused his attention on a red-tailed hawk that was gliding over the treetops, so he heard the man before he saw him.

"Yo, Gladstone."

Just off the trail not more than fifteen feet ahead stood a tall black man dressed in athletic gear. He looked vaguely familiar—but from where? Then, Jay realized: This was Dag's brother, the one they had cut in training camp. What was his name again? And for what purpose was he in these woods? That was when Jay noticed the handgun dangling at his side. The man raised the gun and pointed the barrel at him.

"Jay Gladstone," he pronounced.

"What are you doing?"

"Don't you worry."

"Jay Gladstone—" The voice was resonant and filled the woods. "In the name of Allah—"

Allah? What was this imbecile talking about? The man's face showed the purest contempt, and he was walking toward Jay, who stared down at him from the height of the saddle, momentarily transfixed. He's not going to. No.

"Bang bang, motherfucker."

"It was an *accident*!"

The bullet tore into Jay's thigh, rending his flesh. Mingus

started at the gunshot. As the man squeezed the trigger again, the stallion reared up and whinnied, hooves wildly punching the air. Pain burning through his leg, Jay gripped the reins and prepared for the impact of another gunshot, but there was only the agitation of the horse and the indecipherable muttering of the would-be assassin who was again trying to shoot him. The gun had jammed.

When the horse's front hooves hit the trail, Dag's brother was examining the weapon, trying to make it work. Jay dug his heels in and sped past the assailant, who tried to grab his leg and rip him out of the saddle. Jay galloped down the trail toward the barn, ten, twenty, thirty yards. He heard another gunshot and a bullet whizzed past. He bent over the animal's mane and once more spurred him with the heels of his boots, one of which was filling with blood.

The government-issued brown sedan pulled into the Gladstones' Bedford driveway. Lou Pagano climbed out of the passenger seat, Officer Russell Plesko from behind the wheel. Today was the summit of Pagano's career. It wasn't every day someone in the DA's office got to haul in a catch this size. Pagano couldn't wait to tell his wife about it, his colleagues at the office, the guys with whom he fished in Pelham Bay on weekends. Although Gladstone's lawyer had negotiated a media blackout, Pagano had tipped off a photographer so there would be at least one picture of him and Gladstone in every paper and on every news website in the country.

He took in the house, its scale, the Gilded Age atmosphere. Why was anyone in America permitted to have this kind of money, Pagano wondered. He was no Bolshevik but that degree of wealth—something from a parallel universe—disgusted him and, on a level so deep he refused to acknowledge it, made him feel insignificant. But Lou Pagano was not insignificant, far from it. An esteemed member of the New York State Bar, a dedicated public servant. And today, as a representative of the people, he was going to haul the great Jay Gladstone to prison.

"You hear that?" Plesko asked.

"What?"

"Sounded like gunfire."

"Probably some rich prick, fooling around with a deer rifle," Pagano said.

"You don't think Gladstone killed himself in the backyard or something?"

"Too much self-regard."

Pagano lifted his chin to indicate that Plesko should move toward the house. He wanted to stand right where he was and watch as Gladstone opened the door and took it all in, the uniformed officer, the official vehicle, the deputy district attorney on his lawn like a stone-cold avenger. Gladstone would have to walk as a supplicant toward Lou Pagano.

Plesko climbed the steps and stopped. At the front door was a gym bag. Had Gladstone left it there and gone for a walk? Was he watching them? Spidery legs skittered up Pagano's spine. Maybe they'd call Gladstone on the phone and tell him to come out.

"Hey, Russell," he yelled.

The cop was holding the bag when he turned around.

"Yeah?"

There was an ear-shattering roar and then a blazing mixture of sulfur, charcoal, and potassium nitrate enveloped Plesko in a luminous cloud that blasted a hole in the front of the house. The force of the explosion knocked Pagano to the ground where for several seconds he lay disoriented and terrified. The acrid smell of gunpowder was overpowering. Torn strips of soot, oil, and ash drifted through the air. His ears rang, and all he could hear was what sounded like a rushing river. He couldn't see anything. He realized his eyes were filled with blood and he wiped it off with the forearm of his suit coat. Tried to get his bearings. Twenty feet away lay a tree branch that he realized was a human arm. Pagano examined himself to confirm that it did not belong to him. He unsteadily clambered to his feet. After making sure everything was intact, his first instinct was to check the perimeter to make sure the explosion did not portend more havoc. He wheeled toward the road and saw nothing. He turned around nearly losing his footing in the process and took in the destruction. Plesko was gone, and the part of the house where the front door used to be was on fire. In the ethereal quiet Pagano heard a percussive sound, a rhythm beating as if from deep in the earth. Then Gladstone appeared over the crest of the hill astride a horse. High in the saddle, silhouetted against low gray clouds, he resembled a Cossack galloping through the wispy smoke of a battlefield. There was a dark blotch on his leg.

It was impossible for Jay to know what had happened. After the second gunshot, he had managed to get the horse, crazed with fear, to gallop. They had burst from the woods and were charging toward the house when an explosion rocked the property. At first, he thought perhaps it was the boiler or a gas leak, but when he rounded the corner and absorbed the carnage, he realized it was far worse. Lou Pagano was stumbling around, grievously injured. A car he did not recognize was damaged. His home was on fire. Jay had to decide on the fly. Unlike the time he faced down D'Angelo Maxwell when the temporary opacity of his mind had inhibited his thinking, on this day everything was clear.

Pagano gestured toward him, raised his arms. The man was trying to talk. His jaw jittered, but no words emerged. He looked like the ghastly dummy of an evil ventriloquist. Jay's natural instinct to help rose up, but he recognized that it was impossible. Whatever had caused this nightmarish vision, the world would blame him. An already intractable legal situation would only get worse. He dug the heel of his good leg into the horse and kept riding.

Jay Gladstone was not the kind of man who went out for a carton of milk and did not return. He was dependable and trustworthy, a man of substance, a man whose absence was unimaginable. Yet he vanished.

THE ACE, W.A.C.E. AM
NEW YORK SPORTS TALK RADIO
WITH SAL D'AMICO AND THE SPORTSCHICK
Sal: He's guilty. No doubt in my mind. Guilty, guilty, guilty.
Sportschick: How do you know? You don't know anything.
Sal: My gut tells me, okay? The guy is due to surrender then he changes his mind.
Sportschick: And he blows up a cop?
Sal: He's no better than a terrorist.
Sportschick: Jay Gladstone would never have done this.
Sal: I'm not saying he did it himself.
Sportschick: Who helped?
Sal: Maybe the Mob, maybe the Mossad. What do I know? He's headed to jail, a bomb goes off, and who benefits? Gladstone! Come on! Guy's probably on a tropical island wiggling his toes in the sand.
Sportschick: So, your theory is this guy who was an upstanding citizen his whole life—
Sal: A slumlord.
Sportschick: Jay Gladstone is not a slumlord.
Sal: Anyone who owns buildings in the Bronx is a slumlord.
Sportschick: All of a sudden, he becomes a terrorist?
Sal: Who else had a motive? Gladstone knew he was going

down and wanted to take someone with him. Simple as that. Let's go to a caller. Daryl from Staten Island, you're on the ACE.

Caller #1: What's up guys, longtime listener, first-time caller. Here's my theory.

Sal: Let's hear it.

Caller #1: Al-Qaeda.

Sportschick: Al-Qaeda killed that cop?

Caller #1: Yeah, but their target was Jay Gladstone. Look, he was racist, anti-Muslim, and he was going to be out of their reach so when they had a chance—KABOOM! The cop got in the way.

Sal: I don't think so. Mikey from Tenafly, you're on the ACE.

Caller #2: It was his wife.

Sportschick: Nicole made a bomb?

Caller #2: No, listen. She wanted to help him get away. Has anyone seen her since this went down? They're back together.

Sal: That's not what happened, Mikey. Gladstone built that bomb or hired someone to build it for him, which is more likely. He set it to go off when the cops arrived. In my book that makes the guy a serial killer. He needs to be hunted down, brought to justice, tried, and, if convicted, spend the rest of his life stamping license plates.

Sportschick: You're maligning him, Sal, just like every other mook in America. What is it about the destruction of prominent people that we love so much? Why do we revel in it?

Sal: Who's reveling? I'm not reveling! Guy's a vicious killer, a lowlife, and you're defending him? What's wrong with you? Let's go to another caller.

Sportchick: Don't go to another caller, not yet. Look in the mirror, Sal. We're jackals, okay? Jumping a wounded animal and tearing into it with our teeth for what, entertainment? We're selling advertising time on the back of a tragedy and, honestly, I'm disgusted. Are you not in the least disgusted?

Sal: If I were disgusted by horrible human behavior would I be doing sports talk radio? I talk about horrible human behavior

602 · SETH GREENLAND

because it reminds me I don't act like that. We need the Jay Gladstones of the world, the terrible human beings, because they let us feel good about ourselves. As far as his behavior goes, I'm entertained by it, and the fans will tell us if they're not entertained, and when they're not entertained, we'll stop doing it.

Sportschick: And when are they going to stop being entertained by the misery of other people?

Sal: That would be, let's see—never? All right. Let's take a call. Phil from Floral Park is on the line.

EPILOGUE

By his disappearance, Jay Gladstone no longer had legal standing to pursue a lawsuit against his cousin Franklin, so his sister Bebe became the chief plaintiff and she prepared for a protracted conflict. After vowing to fight until all avenues were exhausted, Franklin quickly settled the case. He paid back the funds he had "borrowed" from the company, and agreed to cover all of Bebe's legal fees. They divided the kingdom into two separate and discrete entities with no ownership overlap. The agreement prohibited Franklin from using the name Gladstone to designate any of his future endeavors.

The transition from second in command to being the CEO of the Gladstone Group was effortless for Bebe. With Boris as her deputy, she managed the business with steady competence that instilled confidence in every employee worried about the harmful consequences of Jay's absence. Every day she hoped for news from her brother and, although she understood that it would be risky for him to contact her, she longed to at least receive word that he was alive.

A year went by, then another. She did not hear from him.

It was early morning in Amagansett on the eastern end of Long Island, and Bebe had just finished a call with Boris, who was in Abu Dhabi supervising their first project in the Middle East. There had been a problem with the delivery of Chinese steel, and to resolve the situation an industrialist from Beijing had to be looped into the conversation. In turquoise linen shorts and a white T-shirt, Bebe stood on the deck of her sprawling home and gazed over undulating dunes flecked with patches of straw grass beyond which the Atlantic Ocean boomed. An arrow formation of Canadian geese bisected the low-slung sun, beating north to Newfoundland for the summer. Shielding her eyes, she watched as their wings etched the cerulean dome of sky.

Aviva stepped into the morning and inhaled the salty air. She wore a sleek one-piece bathing suit and a floppy straw hat. A tube of sunscreen in one hand, a mug of tea in the other, and a beach bag slung over her shoulder. Bebe informed her that they were going to spend the day on a friend's yacht and sail to Fishers Island off the coast of Connecticut.

"I can't remember the last time I was on a boat," Aviva said.

"Just do what the captain tells you."

Aviva mock-saluted her aunt, who mock-saluted back. "Can we talk about how patriarchal the whole 'captain' thing is?"

With a sly half-smile, Bebe said, "The captain is a woman, so your assumption was a little sexist."

For a moment Aviva looked embarrassed at having been exposed as an adherent of the status quo, but then she grinned, as if in surrender. Bebe appreciated the easy rapport they had, a recent development. They had not been close when Aviva was growing up. Whether it was because of the divorce or because Aviva was just not drawn to her, she was never certain. Whatever the cause, Bebe was grateful for the shift. Since Aviva moved to Brooklyn after college, Bebe tried to see her semi-regularly for lunch or a movie but the two women were both busy with work and travel, and it was not always easy to find the time. She was pleased that Aviva agreed to spend the weekend at the beach house.

Bebe gestured to a pair of Adirondack chairs on the deck and asked Aviva to sit down; there was a matter she wanted to discuss. Settling in, Aviva regarded her aunt guardedly, wondering if this barefoot morning had become more formal.

"Am I in trouble?"

Bebe laughed. "No, nothing like that." She paused a moment, sea breeze rippling her hair, trying to decide where to begin. "I've got so much going on—the project in Abu Dhabi, and now it looks like we might be doing something in Bahrain, and I haven't been able to pay proper attention to our family foundation, which was incredibly important to my brother. So." Aviva inclined her head, which Bebe took to be an encouraging sign of interest. "What's been going on with your work?"

"I'm producing a documentary with a couple of partners." Aviva's voice ascended slightly at the conclusion of the sentence as if she couldn't quite believe it herself and was asking her aunt whether it was true. The information did not surprise Bebe. Aviva's family money brought her into contact with a world of people, some genuinely talented, others less so, all of whom were exhilarated by the possibilities it offered. "The project came together a month ago, and I'm going to Germany next week so we can start shooting. It's about the refugee crisis." Bebe was amused by this and Aviva noticed. "What?"

"Your grandfather hated Germans," Bebe said. "*Hated* them."

"It's a new world," Aviva said. "Now they're the good guys."

"Anyway, the foundation was never much more than your father and me, but there's a significant endowment, and I'd like for you to get involved."

Aviva's face glowed. "Do you remember who you're talking to? I'm barely an adult."

Bebe ignored this. "I need to know if you want to step up because if things work out, you'll eventually be running it."

Although flattered by her aunt's suggestion, Aviva didn't answer right away. Instead, she squirted sunscreen on to her palm and began to apply it to her legs. "You're not going to believe who left a message on my phone," she said. "A producer for Christine Lupo's TV show."

"You're not serious."

"For the third time."

"That woman wouldn't dare call me," Bebe declared, recalling their encounter at Franklin's penthouse. It was no surprise to Bebe that after Christine Lupo got crushed in the gubernatorial election, she was hired to host a cable news show with a particular emphasis on crime.

"Like I'm going to go on TV and talk about my father," Aviva said.

Bebe marveled at the solidarity her niece exhibited. Jay used to talk about how little he thought family meant to his daughter.

Finished with her legs, Aviva squeezed sunscreen on to her arms. "You know, he once asked me to go with you to give scholarships to kids."

"Why didn't you come?"

"I was mad at him," Aviva said, a shadow passing over her face at the unpleasant memory. "If he knew you were asking me to participate in the foundation—"

"He would love it," Bebe said.

"Hah!"

While Bebe sensed that Aviva had grown to understand her father's complexity, and this resulted in what appeared to be a greater degree of compassion for his suffering, she could tell that a residue of deep ambivalence remained.

"Promise me you'll think about it," Bebe said.

Aviva rose from the chair and handed her aunt the sunscreen. "Would you please do my back?"

Bebe began to rub the lotion over Aviva's smooth shoulders. The smell was pleasant, and they did not talk as she massaged in a circular motion. Aviva was twenty-four now and had matured more quickly than her aunt had expected, given the stories Jay had told when his daughter was growing up. Perhaps it was the seriousness of what befell her father, or maybe it would have happened anyway, but Aviva was different from the angry child she had been.

"So, are you interested?"

"We should talk about it," Aviva said, sitting back in the Adirondack chair. She removed her hat and began to brush her hair. In the salty air, it required extra attention.

Bebe felt gratified as she began to apply sunscreen. Her muscles were still taut. Her complexion remained youthful. There were endless new obligations and yet Bebe was not so harried that she couldn't spend a tranquil day on the Long Island Sound with her niece and some friends. She had not expected to find herself in this position but inhabited the role as if it had always been hers. Bebe had recently taken on a more public profile—giving speeches, hosting charitable events—and found that people responded positively. Profoundly affected by Jay's situation and the treatment he received from those in lofty positions, she was thinking about getting into politics.

The baby's eager cries could barely be heard over the banging of the steel hammer Nicole employed to fabricate the silver and onyx bracelet she was crafting at the living room workbench in her Manhattan apartment. Orders had been pouring into her jewelry business, and she was keen to show this piece to a department store buyer with whom she was meeting later that week. But nap time was over, and there were other priorities. The boy smiled when he saw his mother and bounced on the balls of his feet waiting to be picked up from the crib. He was eighteen months old with coppery skin, and his black hair corkscrewed in all directions. Already big for his age.

Afternoon light streamed through the curtains and

brightened the assortment of toys on the floor. Stepping over them to get to a fresh diaper, Nicole placed her son on the changing table, smeared ointment on what remained of a minor rash, wafted some powder over his wriggling body, and fastened the adhesives.

With her hair in a ponytail and a touch of makeup, Nicole pushed the stroller out of the postwar building and on to East 87th Street. She headed west across Third Avenue toward Central Park where she was going to meet her friend Audrey. The toy truck that the baby held was a gift from his uncle Trey, who sent it from Europe where he was playing with a professional basketball team in the Spanish league.

In the time since Jay disappeared Nicole had found an apartment, given birth, and filed for divorce. Her marital status was currently in limbo since there was no way to reach the other party. Speculation abounded. There were accounts of him in Caracas, and Buenos Aires, and various cities in Africa, but no one could say for sure where he was living. On a day as magnificent as this, she did her best to not worry about it.

For several months Nicole couldn't walk down the street without some paparazzi shoving a camera in her face. Interest in her travails withered when shiny new scandals flowered, ones that had nothing to do with Nicole or her notorious husband, but bloomed again when she became visibly pregnant. The usual innuendo and conjecture saturated the media, and she was offered large sums of money to tell her story but declined to capitalize on the scandal. There were no magazine profiles with which she cooperated, or television talk show appearances, or interactive Internet engagements.

Nicole and Audrey usually met at the Alice in Wonderland statue. She was early today and sat on a bench facing Central Park West. Caretakers of multiple nationalities surrounded her and the excited shouts of their charges rang in the air. She pulled out a bag of goldfish crackers and gave a handful to her son, who shoved them into his mouth and ran toward the Lewis Carroll characters. As she watched the boy try to figure out how to navigate the stepladder of bronze mushrooms that would deliver him to the Mad Hatter, she thought about how little it took, finally, to achieve some facsimile of contentment.

"Nicole, did you see this?"

There was Audrey pushing her daughter in a stroller. She waved a copy of the *New York Post* with the headline:

Feds Nab Gladstone Bomber

Nicole took the newspaper from her friend and glanced at the first paragraph of the article. The FBI had caught up with Axel Testa in New Mexico. Nicole was relieved that the government was going to punish this domestic terrorist although she was still troubled by her role in what had transpired. She marveled at how a single rash act could lead to an unforeseeable cascade of misfortune.

Audrey wiped her daughter's face and lifted her from the stroller. The girl shouted when she saw Nicole's son and toddled off to join him. While Audrey watched the kids, Nicole devoured the article, eyes widening as she scanned the page, transported through time to the bejeweled existence that had so swiftly and irreversibly slipped from her grasp. There were pictures of her and Jay, and the grand estate where they had lived. Seeing all of it rendered in the grainy black and white of a New York tabloid, crowned with lurid headlines, was to be reminded how much she treasured her new life. She shuddered and returned the newspaper to Audrey.

The boy and girl were chasing each other around the statue as Nicole leaned back to let the dappled rays of the afternoon sun play on her winter-pale skin. It would be good to get some color in her cheeks. She was going to a gallery opening that night with a divorced sculptor. This was their third date.

A few years later, on a winter night in New York, two men met for dinner.

"I was shocked when I heard that Jay had surfaced in Israel," Robert Tackman said, cutting into the last of the breaded lobster tail on his plate and dipping the meat in drawn butter before forking it into his mouth. "How did he manage to get there?"

Herman Doomer chewed pensively on his rare filet mignon and swallowed. He lifted his wineglass and sipped the cabernet he always ordered, wondering exactly how much to disclose. "Jay Gladstone is nothing if not resourceful."

The dining room of Doomer's club was a burnished old shoe of a space where gold-jacketed waiters bustled between the tables and the menu had not changed since the Kennedy administration. Because it was unusual for a Doomer client to require the services of a Robert Tackman, they had not spoken for some time. The dinner was purely social.

Tackman said, "I never understood why he fled in the first place."

"The district attorney believed he might have had a role in the bombing. Despite our considerable efforts, Jay was not beloved. No one was going to give him the benefit of the doubt."

Tackman considered this, tried to remember the degree of opprobrium heaped on his former patron. "Why did he agree to return home?"

"Being a fugitive is undignified," Doomer said. "After taking stock of his circumstances—he was exhausted and beaten down from the ordeal, you see—he chose to face his legal difficulties. Jay Gladstone loves his country."

"Brave man."

"The charges were renegotiated, and he pled to lesser offenses."

Tackman arranged his utensils parallel on the Wedgwood

plate to indicate to the waiter that he had finished. "Where is he serving his sentence?"

"Auburn Correctional Facility," Doomer said. "It's a maximum-security prison in the Finger Lakes region."

A graying eyebrow lifted. "Maximum security?"

"He pled guilty to a violent crime."

"Poor bastard." Tackman shook his head in sympathy. "Have you gone to see him?"

"I haven't been able to get up there," Doomer said. "It's a five-hour drive."

"Life intrudes."

"And I haven't heard from him."

With his tongue, Tackman dislodged a piece of lobster that had become stuck between his teeth. He took a drink of water. "Hard to believe he's making a lot of friends."

"The prison population is predominantly African-American, and I've heard they consider Jay to be a celebrity sportsman who didn't deserve what happened to him."

Alert to the paradox, Tackman said, "Welcome to America."

"The prisoners understood the nature of his crime, and they absolved it."

Doomer sipped the remains of his wine and wiped his lips with the linen napkin. A busboy materialized to remove the plates.

"Where are you getting your information?"

"Someone is writing a book about him," Doomer reported. "A journalist. She came to the office and interviewed me last week. I imagine she'll want to speak with you."

Tackman would be happy to cooperate. "How's our friend holding up?"

"Well, apparently. He's adapted to prison life and become quite self-reliant. I hear he reads a great deal, teaches a weekly class in basic job skills—and this is extraordinary—he serves as the commissioner of the prison basketball league."

Tackman guffawed. "Oh, that's perfect!"

Doomer didn't laugh. "Poetic justice, I suppose."

A waiter appeared to ask if the gentlemen would like anything else. The chocolate soufflé was available; it would take twenty minutes to prepare. They briefly discussed sharing a slice of cheesecake, but the lawyer had recently learned that his blood sugar was elevated and the P.R. man was trying to lose ten pounds. Tackman requested an espresso, Doomer a snifter of brandy.

After the waiter departed, the two men briefly returned to the tribulations of Jay Gladstone, and when the topic was exhausted, they began to gossip about someone else.

Acknowledgments

I'd like to thank Susan Kaiser Greenland, as always, my first and best reader. I want to thank my agents Henry Dunow and Sylvie Rabineau for their friendship and advice. I'm grateful to my friends who read this novel in its various stages and offered valuable suggestions: Bruce Bauman, Barry Blaustein, Cliff Chenfeld, John Coles, Larry David, Drew Greenland, Panio Gianopoulos, Sam Harper, Albert Litewka, Tom Lutz, and Diana Wagman. Thanks to Francis Carroll for filling in the blanks with regard to the legal system. Thanks to my editor Kent Carroll and the team at Europa Editions. I appreciate the time and consideration everyone gave me and salute them all.

Seth Greenland is the author of five novels. The last two, *The Angry Buddhist* (2011) and *I Regret Everything* (2015), were published by Europa Editions. Greenland is also a playwright and screenwriter, and has worked as a producer for HBO. Born in New York City, he currently lives and works in Los Angeles.